MW01193649

PRAISE FOR *SILENT WARRIORS*

... Something for every reader

"It would be impossible for one book to adequately tell the individual stories of the nearly 16,000 submariners who battled in the Pacific theater during World War II. Collectively, they served on 263 submarines and made 1,472 war patrols while taking that fight *to* the Japanese. They paid a high price: 52 lost boats and 3,482 dead submariners. *Silent Warriors* effectively uses the fictional exploits of one such submariner—Jake Lawlor—to encapsulate their angst, bravery, commitment, and dedication.

Over . . . 44 months, Jake introduces us to fascinating characters—both real and fictional—and chronicles their heroic actions.

Silent Warriors has something for every reader . . . daring deeds to quicken the pulse of the adventurous . . . battle and campaign details aplenty. Submariners and 'Old Salts' can be transported back by the tactical and technical depictions. Even romantics will find a love story that surfaces among the chaos of submarine warfare and endures in the changed world that emerges from the carnage that was World War II."

—JOE DOYLE, a career submariner, 13 years enlisted, 14 years an officer. Duty stations included six submarines and a variety of submarine support shore assignments in Atlantic and Pacific theaters. Retired from the Navy in 1993.

* * * * *

Characters that make the story come alive

"Author Gene Masters delivers an action-packed, artful, and well-paced tale of WWII submarine warfare. As a Navy veteran, I found *Silent Warriors* to be a rich and detailed look at the fictional *USS Orca*, its crew, and its mission. The

author skillfully uses his first hand naval experience to craft a suspenseful and thoroughly fascinating 'reading' voyage.
 A bonus is the rich rendering of characters that make the story come alive. I wish the epilogue were longer . . . *but* I can't wait for the sequel."

—BOB WALKER, Lt., USN, *USS Annapolis (AGMR-1)*, former CEO Promotion Mechanics, Inc., a Division of Ogilvy & Mather Advertising, NYC

* * * * *

A compelling Story

"*Silent Warriors* is the thrilling account of submarine warfare in the Pacific from 1942 to 1945. The title of Gene Masters' first novel refers primarily to the men who manned the boats, but also alludes to the boats themselves.

Masters tells a compelling story about the wartime experience of submariners and their families, but does so in the context of a detailed and fascinating description of submarine technology and function. Jacob Lawlor, a U.S. Naval Academy graduate and commander of the submarine *Orca*, leads his men through eleven war patrols, challenged by both the limits of their own humanity and the submarine technology available to them.

All who enjoy historical fiction will find *Silent Warriors* a satisfying and rewarding read."

—ANTHONY J. INTINTOLI, Lt. Col, USAFR, Ret.

SILENT WARRIORS
Submarine Warfare in the Pacific

A Novel

by

Gene Masters

Published in the United States of America by
Escarpment Press, Hendersonville, NC 28739

www.escarpmentpress.weebly.com
Hendersonville, NC

Submarine silhouette © Alexandr Makedonskly/Shutterstock
Cover Artwork ©MIRO3D - Can Stock Photo Inc.

Dedication

For Ruth

SILENT WARRIORS

Submarine Warfare in the Pacific

A Novel

by

Gene Masters

Preface

This novel, a work of historical fiction, is mostly about diesel-electric submarines. More specifically, it is about a particular fictitious diesel electric boat named *USS Orca* (yes, submarines are "boats" and not "ships.")

It is also a novel about the War in the Pacific, waged by the United States against the Empire of Japan, from December 7, 1941, though September 28, 1945. As such, the story occasionally deviates from the role of the submarine force in prosecuting the war.

Just hours after the Japanese attack on Pearl Harbor, the Chief of Naval Operations, Admiral Harold Rainsford Stark, unleashed unrestricted submarine and air warfare against the Empire of Japan. (It was never clear that Stark had the authority to issue such an order, which, was, nonetheless, never countermanded.) Thus began an all-out, no-holds-barred campaign by the U.S. Submarine Force against all Japanese maritime assets.

Shortly after the United States declared war on Japan in response to Pearl Harbor, Japan's Tripartite Treaty allies, Germany and Italy, declared war on the United States. Suddenly the United States found itself in a two-theater war. President Franklin Roosevelt placed America's first priority on the defeat of Nazi Germany, and elected to wage a more-or-less holding war in the Pacific. In the Pacific, Japanese forces rampaged unchecked across China, Hong Kong, the Philippines, Southeast Asia, the Netherlands East Indies, New Britain, New Guinea, Singapore, Burma, Guam, and even the western Aleutians.

In the beginning, the only force opposing the Japanese onslaught in the Pacific was the U.S. Submarine Service. The Pacific submarine force at the beginning of the conflict numbered just fifty-one boats, and a dozen of these were the older-type S-boats. More alarming still, these boats went to war equipped with defective and unreliable torpedoes. Even as the force was slowly supplemented with new construction or "fleet-type" boats, the problem of defective torpedoes lasted through 1943.

Nonetheless, in the course of the war, U.S. Submarines sank 214 warships, totaling just under 600,000 tons, and 1,178 merchant vessels, totaling over 5,000,000 tons. This accounted for almost half of the number of Japanese vessels, and 55 percent of gross tonnage, sunk during the war. And all of this was accomplished by just 1.6% of the total of all naval personnel. In addition, the boats conducted clandestine surveillance, rescued fliers, laid mines, stood picket duty, and landed and extracted commandos.

By the end of the war, Japan had been brought to her knees, starved of the material required to wage war, and bereft of fuel, raw materials, weapons, ammunition, and foodstuffs. Relentless unrestricted submarine warfare was in no small way responsible for that state of affairs.

Also by the end of the war, 52 of 288 submarines in service were lost, along with 3,484 lives, or 11.6 percent of all those volunteers who served in submarines.

The story of the U.S. submarine in the Pacific is the story told here, the story of Jacob Julius Lawlor, USN, 1933 graduate of the U.S. Naval Academy. At the beginning of hostilities, Lawlor is serving as Executive Officer in *S-49*, stationed at the U.S. Naval Base in Cavite, in the Philippines.

The fate of *S-49* is borrowed from an actual incident in the war, as are many of the submarine incidents narrated throughout the book.

Jake Lawlor moves on to the command of the newly commissioned *USS Orca*, and the story proceeds from there.

Most of the characters are, of course, fictional. But, whenever possible, and wherever it helps to tell the story, real people are depicted. In all cases, where such depictions are used, every effort was made to stay true to the character and demeanor of the actual person. Where words have been put into their mouths, the attempt was made to make them the words they very well might have said under the circumstances described.

Some liberties have been taken in deploying *Orca* and the way the boats were actually deployed. In order to develop the story's characters, *Orca* stayed in port between patrols far longer than was the actual practice. Unless going into overhaul or for extended maintenance, typical turnaround period between patrols was about two weeks. Further, Jake Lawlor serves as *Orca*'s commanding officer through eleven war patrols, whereas boat commanders were typically relieved after three, or at most four patrols.

In writing this story, I have also drawn from my experiences and memories serving aboard *USS Angler (SS 240)* in the early 1960s. Long before I served aboard her, *Angler* made seven war patrols.

Any errors and miscalculations in the book are entirely mine. My thanks to my friend and shipmate the late Tom Burke for his editing, advice, and encouragement.

Gene Masters
Knoxville, Tennessee
2018

Chapter 1

USS S-49: 9 December 1941 to 19 January 1942

A billion pinpricks of light lit up the dome of the moonless night sky. The waters of the Makassar Strait stretched out before the boat like a gently swelling sheet of pure onyx, the only visible disturbances in the water the boat's bow wake and the phosphorescent gray foam of its following trail.

For the first time in recent memory, both power trains were working, and the submarine was making maximum speed on the surface—just over fourteen knots—so when she struck the reef, she struck hard.

Nobody knew exactly what had happened when the boat suddenly shuddered, stopping dead in her tracks with that awful crunching, tearing sound of metal rending against unyielding rock. Lieutenant Junior Grade (Lt. j.g.) Stetson had the deck and enough presence of mind to sound the collision alarm immediately. Automatically, the watch section and men ripped from their bunks in panic buttoned up the boat, isolating each compartment from the next throughout the boat. All watertight doors between the compartments were secured, as were all bulkhead flapper valves between compartments, effectively shutting down all ventilation in the boat. Only the closed-cell ventilation in the battery remained active.

It was immediately reported to the control room that the door between the torpedo room and the battery compartment was sprung, probably from the force of the grounding, and could not be secured. The crewmen forward reacted quickly to the sudden flooding of the torpedo compartment, forming a damage control (DC) team under the direction of Chief Torpedoman Floyd Sweat, and going to work immediately to staunch the flow of seawater with whatever was at hand. The rip in the pressure hull was not only huge, it was also almost inaccessible because of the large upright impulse air tank right in the way, and because of the tight spaces between the torpedo tubes. The DC team stuffed the hole as best they could with mattresses held in place by whatever was available — a length of pipe, a crowbar, anything. And while the flow of seawater into the boat was significantly slowed, it could not be staunched. Seawater continued to flow into the torpedo room.

The pressure hull let out an unnerving, grating shriek with each gentle swell of the surrounding sea, as her pierced plating ground itself against the razor-sharp coral of the reef. With each swell, the boat shifted, and the gash in the grounded hull opened just a little wider, just a little longer, and more seawater gushed into the *USS S-49*. The upward angle of the boat allowed seawater to enter the battery compartment through the sprung doorway, and the 120-cell Exide battery was slowly flooding, releasing chlorine gas into the living spaces. The gas would eventually drive the crew out of the boat and onto her deck, heaving in time with two-foot swells.

Lieutenant Harry Loveless, commanding officer of *S-49*, thought at first that the boat might have struck a submerged wreck, but the chart showed hundreds of feet of water beneath *S-49*'s hull. Further, the Admiralty charts for this part of the Makassar Strait showed no underwater obstruction within a hundred miles, and while submerged reefs this far from any shoreline were not unheard of, they were hardly common. Yet here it was. It was painfully obvious that *S-49* had struck an uncharted reef, had struck hard, and was now held fast by it. For the second time on this, the boat's first war patrol, her Captain ordered life preservers issued to all personnel.

All efforts to back off the reef using the ship's propulsion failed. All the backing succeeded in doing was enlarging the hole in the pressure hull, and disturbing the damage control patch, such as it was.

Loveless ordered the radioman, 27-year-old, second-class petty officer Hal Wentworth, to send an urgent encrypted message to Pacific Submarine Command, or COMSUBPAC, giving *S-49*'s position, and describing the boat's predicament:

1901421812Z. AT 1901421740Z, STRUCK UNCHARTED REEF MAKASSAR STRAIT 04.57.17S, 18.33.04E. BOAT HELD FAST, ATTEMPTING TO FREE. NO PERSONNEL INJURED. SITUATION CRITICAL. LOVELESS.

Twelve hours of useless struggling later, Loveless realized the situation was completely hopeless. All crew not actively engaged in damage control were already on deck, and seawater had completely compromised the battery. The battery compartment and the torpedo room were inundated with chlorine gas. Loveless ordered all hands still below to secure any belowdecks activity and to lay topside. Last out, just before Loveless himself, was Wentworth, whom Loveless had just ordered to send a Mayday in the clear. Then they both scrambled out of the boat through the bridge access trunk, securing the bridge hatch behind them. All the hatches were shut, thus trapping as much air inside the boat as possible, but that only delayed the inevitable. *S-49* was sinking. Eventually, the only thing holding her on the surface would be the reef, but when the boat got heavy enough, or the sea violent enough, even the reef would have to let her go. Hopefully, she would stay on the surface long enough for the thirty-six officers and men on deck to be safely evacuated. If the Mayday had been ever received. And if whoever received it was friendly.

Lieutenant Jake Lawlor, U.S. Naval Academy, '33, served as Executive Officer aboard the *USS S-49*, which was home-ported in Cavite, Luzon, U.S. Commonwealth of the Philippines. Now he sweltered on her deck, witnessing her death throes, and his biggest disappointment was that the old girl had barely begun to bloody the nose of the enemy. And now she was dying, not

3

because of any enemy action, but because of an unmarked reef on an outdated chart.

Jake was not a tall man; at five feet, nine inches, he wasn't exactly short, but he was certainly *not*, he felt, tall enough to impress anyone with his height. That is, of course, until you saw that Jake was powerfully built, with a barrel chest, and muscular arms and legs.

Jacob Julius Lawlor was born in Des Moines, Iowa, on May 8, 1911, the youngest child of five children born to Ezekiel and Sally Lawlor, and the only boy. Jake was more or less a surprise; Sally Lawlor thought surely she was past having children. Her last daughter had been produced a full five years earlier.

And Zeke Lawlor was delighted to at last have a son. Zeke was a talented machinist, who managed to work steadily, even through the Great Depression that gripped the country through the 1930s. The Lawlors were hardly wealthy by any measure, but they lived simply, there was always enough to eat, and Zeke and Sally were loving parents. The Lawlors were also devout Presbyterians, and the entire family attended services every Sunday.

Why, despite being raised in a house full of them, Jake became painfully shy around all other females was a complete mystery to his parents and his sisters. Although far less withdrawn when dealing with other boys, he was still socially awkward overall, and compensated with his studies, and especially with sports. He excelled at both. He was an A-plus student, a creditable guard in basketball, and eventually the starting halfback for the West High School Dragons. As his peers grew more and more interested in, and confident around, the opposite sex, Jake shared their interest but never matched their confidence. He was simply insufficiently courageous, for example, to ask a girl out to his high school senior prom, so he just stayed home.

Jake had wanted to go on to college, but there was no way his parents could afford it. An education at the Naval Academy or at West Point, however, was free. Jake wrote an appeal to his

Congressman seeking an appointment to one of the academies. He was overjoyed when he received an appointment, applied to, and was accepted at Annapolis. He had never seen an ocean, could barely swim, but he was going to join the Navy!

His Academy classmates were surprised that despite his physique and boyish good looks, Jake wasn't cutting large swaths through the field of young women that visited the Academy regularly. But their classmate seemed oblivious to the admiring stares from the ladies.

After graduation, and his commissioning as ensign, USN, Jake was assigned duty aboard the destroyer *USS Adrian Long* out of Norfolk, Virginia. It was on the *Long* that Ensign Lawlor volunteered for, and was assigned to Officer's Submarine School, in Groton, Connecticut. The *USS S-12*, one of the six "Sugar-Boats" home ported in Pearl Harbor, Hawaii, was Jake's first boat right out of Sub School. It was during his year in *S-12* that he qualified in submarines and pinned on his gold dolphins. There then followed two years aboard the *USS Blem*, one of the sixteen newer fleet type *Sargo*-class boats also operating out of Pearl. In *Blem* he served first as Engineering Officer, and then as Navigator. Jake then received his assignment as XO aboard *S-49*.

And now, almost two years later, his boat was stuck on a reef in the middle of nowhere. Serving as XO on *S-49* had put him in line for command of a boat of his own, but now, with *S-49* running aground and most likely lost, chances looked bleak that Jake would ever get a command, certainly not in submarines. The Navy was, if nothing else, unforgiving of a major screw-up—such as losing a boat to what appears to be simply lousy seamanship. He was sure he could also kiss goodbye that next half-stripe, and possibly even his career in the Navy. What Jake did not fully realize was that the peacetime Navy was not the same service as the wartime Navy.

S-49's Captain, Lt. Harry Loveless, USNA '31, was a tall, gaunt, man, with a serious-looking face, one that was a perfect clue to his nervous disposition and an almost complete lack of a sense of humor. Jake's association with his skipper was one of mutual respect, and Loveless frequently consulted with his "XO" before deciding on a particular course of action. Jake and the crew of *S-49* regarded Harry Loveless as an extremely competent submarine commander, a person who was also very cautious, and who would never subject his boat to unnecessary risk. And so, nobody in the crew, including Jake, would ever question any order Loveless gave, and every man aboard *S-49* had confidence in his ability to lead them into battle.

When Loveless received *S-49's* orders in port in Cavite, on December 9, 1941, to *"put to sea at the earliest and to proceed to the East China Sea shipping lanes off Okinawa, there to seek out and destroy all shipping flying the flag of the Empire of Japan, or that of any of its allies,"* he regarded them with both exultation and trepidation. He was eager to defend his country's wounded honor. But *S-49* was an old boat; her keel had been laid in 1919 and she had been in commission since the '20s. Keeping her ancient Busch-Sulzer diesels running was a continuous challenge, and the seals on both propulsion shafts had a tendency to leak on the surface — never mind when she was submerged.

But orders are orders, and Loveless immediately dispatched *S-49's* Chief of the Boat, or "COB," Chief Boatswain's Mate Wendell Buckner, to the two sub tenders *USS Holland* and *USS Canopus,* and to the base shore facilities. There, "Bucky" was to scrounge whatever extra niceties he could beg, barter, or steal (this function usually described as the ability to "cumshaw"). Other crewmen and officers saw to expediting repairs. Both the starboard engine and all the seals — as always — badly needed attention. Crew, base, and *Canopus* personnel labored around the clock. Submarine-qualified, Torpedo man Chief — TMC (SS) — Floyd Sweat and his team set about loading *S-49's* full complement of fourteen, Mark-10 torpedoes and all the ammunition the boat could carry for her 4-inch, 50-caliber forward deck gun, and her little 20mm Oerlikon gun, which could be set in a mount aft of the bridge.

The Japanese invasion of the Philippines and Guam began on December 10, 1941, the day after *S-49* received her orders. Two nights later, as the boat was still being readied for sea, Japanese planes bombed and strafed Cavite, mortally crippling the submarine *USS Sealion*. There were also reported troop landings elsewhere in Luzon and Mindanao. For *S-49*, and the other twenty-six boats capable of leaving Subase Cavite, it was time to get out of Dodge.

Five days after receiving orders, on Saturday, December 14th, with two men short of her total complement of thirty eight, a full load of water, fuel, torpedoes (twelve forward and two aft), and a full magazine of shells for her guns, *S-49* set out for her patrol area. The boat had barely passed muster on her trim and test dives in the waters just outside of Manila Bay only the previous day.

In transit to the patrol zone, and after clearing the Philippines, the crew settled into the boat's at-sea routine. Watches were in three sections of twelve men each, four hours on and eight hours off, with only the Captain not standing watches. And life aboard a boat at sea, moreover, was not exactly comfortable. Space was at a premium, filled with equipment and material of every sort, and living spaces appeared to be an afterthought for the boat's designers. Sleeping racks for crew forward were wedged between torpedoes.

Water was in limited supply, and the boat's distiller unit, which made fresh water from seawater, was there mainly for providing distilled water for the batteries. Only then were the crew's needs for drinking water and cooking met. There was a little water for shaving and brushing teeth, but none for bathing (excepting for the cooks), and certainly *none* for washing clothes. After two days at sea, bodies were ripe — never mind by the end of a patrol. Luckily, the stench of diesel fuel and stale cigarette smoke permeated the boat at all times, and helped cover up the stink of unwashed bodies.

Arriving on station a week later, *S-49* began her first — and last — war patrol. There were two Japanese airfields on Okinawa, so any close approach to the island on the surface was dangerous at night—*and* suicide during daylight. But for *S-49*, remaining submerged for any length of time was a challenge. The ship fitters at Cavite had done their best to repack and tighten down her propulsion shaft seals in the limited time they were allotted, and they had held during her test dive back off Manila Bay. But, at her 200-foot maximum operating depth, the seals once again began to ship copious amounts of water. Loveless was therefore not inclined to spend much time going deep.

At periscope depth, the seals were fairly tight—the ship fitters had been able to accomplish at least that much. At periscope depth, however, in these waters, and in most sea conditions, the boat was very detectable from the air as a slowly moving dark shadow, 266 feet long. So Loveless, on Jake's advice, compromised by cruising during daylight at 90 feet. There the boat's drain pump could mostly stay even with the incoming seawater, and she *had* to be less visible from the air. He would routinely surface the boat after dark each night, well out of sight of land, and run the diesels to charge the battery. Only when the "can" (battery) was fully charged, would Loveless venture his boat near land.

The Japanese on Okinawa were apparently unconcerned about any Allied attack. As far as Jake could tell, they had made no attempt to hide themselves from seaward, and while the principal port of Naha was hardly as brightly lit as a major port in the States, it was still very easy to distinguish its location over the horizon as a gentle glow in the night sky. Furthermore, no attempt whatever had been made to extinguish lighted navigational aids.

S-49 was into her third week on patrol. The crew had spent Christmas Day submerged. New Year's Day came and went, practically unnoticed, just another uncomfortable day on patrol.

Mechanical and electrical problems quickly began to plague the boat. Lubrication failures became common, particularly on the starboard drive train. The "Sugar-Boats" had no air conditioning, and humidity levels inside the boat while submerged were unbearable. Despite cork insulation, the pressure hull bulkheads were constantly dripping with condensation. Worse than the crew's discomfort, the humidity was causing frequent electrical shorts, and blown fuses.

Naha was a fairly busy port, but thus far any tempting target presented no firing solution. Ships were always too far away, or traveling either too fast or on the wrong course for Loveless to maneuver *S-49* into firing position. Invariably, had the potential target passed just a half-hour — or even a few minutes — earlier, or just a thousand yards closer, the boat would have been in perfect position to take a shot.

The Mark-10 torpedo was the only torpedo currently in the Navy's arsenal that *S-49* was able to fire, since her tubes were too short to accommodate the newer Mark-14s. The Mark-10 was gyroscopically controlled, but unlike the Mark-14, it could only travel in straight line. So Loveless and his firing team, headed up by his XO Jake Lawlor as Assistant Approach Officer, had to attain a firing solution, and then maneuver *S-49*, actually aiming the boat so that its course coincided with the torpedo track required for the weapon to intercept the target.

S-49 had no radar. Radar equipment, newly perfected by the British, was an installed innovation on the new fleet boats, and some air defense SD radar sets had been back-fitted onto other, older boats, those that had actually been given names instead of numbers. But, at this point in the war, none of the enemy ships had radar either; in fact, right up to the end of the war, only Imperial Japanese Navy (IJN) capital ships and some escort vessels were ever radar-equipped.

Unlike most of the boats in her class, *S-49* was equipped with passive sonar. Her JK hydrophone provided good underwater listening capability. But the boat had no active sonar capability, that is, she could not project and receive returning sound signals (ping) to locate targets. Her sonar operator could, with the boat submerged, say if he heard another ship out there, and provide its general direction. But without an active sonar capability, he could not give any accurate estimate of bearing or range. However, even that small amount of crude sonar gave *S-49* an edge, since IJN ships also had little sonar capability at that point in the war. IJN ships were equipped with excellent passive sound gear, but the sound operators were poorly trained, and most of their commanders oblivious to its utility. (Active sonar capability came to the IJN later in the war, but, again, commanders of escort ships so equipped were never well versed in its capability or usefulness.)

On a submerged approach, it was up to the periscope operator—at general quarters, always Loveless himself acting as Approach Officer—to provide a range to the target. This was done on later boats using a stadimeter, a device built into the periscope. Unfortunately, *S-49's* periscope had no such device, and Loveless could only estimate the range based on his experience. The Approach Officer would also estimate the target's angle-on-the-bow (AOB), which was the angle between the target's bow and, left or right, to the line of sight.

Using his estimates, the fire control team, headed up by Jake with the assistance of the boat's navigator, Lt. j.g. Joseph Stetson, and his quartermaster used relative bearing worksheets (known as maneuvering boards), a position chart, and a hand-held, slide-rule-like device known as an "Is-Was," to compute target course and speed. The solution was checked and rechecked each time Loveless made an observation. Jake acted as liaison between the Captain in the conning tower and the fire control team in the control room. When Stetson had some confidence in his solution, and Lawlor had evaluated the team's efforts and confirmed Stetson's confidence, then, and only then, would Loveless bring the boat onto final firing course. One last observation, a quick 360-degree look-around to insure there were no surprises from any other surface contacts, one last quick check of the firing solution, and a torpedo was launched at the target. Given the operational range of the torpedo, the ideal firing position was from between 750 and 1,500 yards from the target. The shorter the distance, the less time the target would have to maneuver away from the torpedo.

Surface attacks were simpler, if only because *S-49* was far more maneuverable on the surface. Bearing to the target was determined from the bridge, using a pelorus, an optical device with a bezel-mounted aiming telescope. It could be swiveled around and brought onto the target, giving the target's relative bearing. Without radar or active sonar, range estimates were still judgment calls, as were angles-on-the-bow, and this information was conveyed to the fire control team below decks in the control room. Otherwise the procedure was the same, with the fire control team providing a calculated course for the boat so that the torpedo would be on track to hit the target.

On January 4, 1942, *S-49* was cruising on the surface with her battery fully charged. According to a fleet wide report intercepted that evening, Japan had captured Manila two days earlier. But on this particular night, outside the Port of Naha, Okinawa, *S-49* was presented with a sitting duck. Loveless could hardly believe his good fortune. A fully-loaded Japanese cargo ship, about 5,000 tons displacement, was moored near the breakwater, apparently awaiting transit to the port loading docks the next morning. Oblivious to any danger, she had her anchor lights lit and clearly visible. Loveless had only to line the boat up with the target, and, making bare steerageway, launch a torpedo straight ahead from 1,500 yards — actually a long torpedo run. But Loveless was leery of venturing too close to shore, and a 1,500-yard run was within the torpedo's "advertised capability."

The night was overcast, and while the moon had been full only two nights earlier, now it shed little light. Loveless sounded "general quarters, surface action torpedo," and brought the boat around to head 009 degrees, the target's compass bearing. He cautioned the four lookouts, each on his perch alongside the masthead: "Forget what I'm doing. Keep a sharp eye out. Make sure we don't get any unexpected company."

11

"Aye, aye, Sir," the lookouts answered in unison, and they continued to scan the horizon with their binoculars for any contacts, either on the sea or in the air.

Loveless passed the word to the forward torpedo room to prepare tubes one and two for firing. He only needed one "fish," but it never hurt to have a second ace up your sleeve. The water was relatively shallow here, and he was unsure of the cargo ship's actual draft, so he ordered the torpedoes set for shallow running—six instead of the usual twelve feet. He checked his heading; it was still at 009, and the boat was pointed straight at the unmoving target. All the Mark-10 torpedo would be required to do to hit the target was go straight ahead and stay on course. Loveless passed the word to the engine room, "All stop." Then, "Fire one." The boat lurched, and the torpedo was on its way, trailing a wake of fine bubbles behind it.

With the torpedo traveling at 46 knots or about 77 feet per second, Loveless worked out in his head that it would take just under a minute for it to travel the 1,500 yards to the target. Exactly fifty-eight seconds later, Loveless first saw the splash and the flash as the torpedo struck the target just aft of amidships. Just over a second later, he heard the explosion.

It was 0057 hours, January 5th.

The target ship began to sink quickly and spectacularly. Her cargo was obviously something incendiary, and, ablaze, the doomed ship quickly lit up the harbor. Instead of immediately clearing the area, Loveless stayed to watch the terror that *S-49* had wrought.

He had thought only of sinking a ship, and had not allowed himself to consider that human lives were lost in the process. Now he watched, sickened, as men, some aflame, jumped over the side of their ship and into the sea. And yet, despite the horror of what he had done, he knew he would do it again, to other ships and to other men, given the chance. As he watched, the clouds above slowly parted unnoticed, and a barely waning full moon lit up the night.

If Loveless was slow to react and clear the area, the Japanese were quick enough in their response to the violent explosion and a ship aflame in the harbor. It was fortunate for Loveless that the forward starboard lookout had followed orders and stayed sharp. When he reported "Surface contact! Just forward of the starboard beam!" Loveless looked away from the burning hulk and could just spot the surface contact. Like a ghost on the horizon, it was coming on fast out of Naha port, just about 5,000 yards away.

Loveless, guessing that the contact bearing down on them was either a Japanese motor patrol boat or, worse, a destroyer, quickly ordered a course to clear the harbor and make maximum surface knots. "All ahead full! Left full rudder!" he shouted. "Come about to course two-six-five!"

Loveless maneuvered the boat to put the contact dead astern, in position to possibly fire the boat's after torpedo tube at his new tormentor, now clearly a destroyer, silhouetted against the burning, sinking, cargo ship. And she was coming on *very* fast.

Almost immediately, Lovelace's boat was in trouble. Before he could order the boat's single, after tube to be prepared for firing, the engine room reported lubrication oil failure on the starboard engine. Loveless had no choice but to immediately switch tactics and crash dive the boat. Then, and *only* when the boat was settled out on depth, could he attempt, with the target dead astern, to fire a torpedo at the pursuing destroyer from the after tube.

Because of constant practice, the orders came by rote, quickly given and quickly executed. "Clear the bridge!" shouted Lovelace. The lookouts scrambled from their perches and disappeared fast down the bridge access hatch. Sounding the claxon and yelling "Dive! Dive!" Loveless followed them down, securing the hatch behind him. "All hands forward! Take her to one hundred feet! Prepare to fire from the stern tube!"

Men at "GQ" (General Quarters), fleeing an enemy bent on their destruction, reacted even more quickly, their training kicking in, performing automatically. Anyone without a critical GQ post scrambled forward to the torpedo room to put as much weight as possible in the bow.

The moment the claxon sounded the diving alarm, the engines were shut down, the engine intake manifold was closed, and propulsion was manually switched over to battery power. In the interim, there was no power to the screws, and only the boat's forward momentum propelled the dive. The starboard engine's oil lubrication problem could be ignored for the moment. All ballast tank vents were opened, allowing the ballast tanks, always open to sea at the tank bottom, to flood with seawater, making the boat heavy, giving it negative buoyancy. The planesmen put both the bow and stern diving planes on full dive. With propulsion now on battery power, the boat's twin screws drove S-49 under.

The Engineer Officer, Lt. j.g. Bill Burke, was GQ diving officer, and, in the control room, called off the boat's depth to the keel. The COB was at the indicator panel showing the position of all deck hatches and ballast tank valves. The panel indicated that all ballast tank, vent valves were open, and all hatches were shut, all in the correct position for the dive. The ship's crew had practiced this continually, and the boat was below the surface in just over a minute. Jake, at Loveless' direction, relieved Burke as diving officer and sent him aft to see to the problems with the starboard drive train.

Now, the problem was how quickly the rarely used after torpedo tube could be made ready to fire. The after torpedo tube was almost an afterthought on the few S-boats equipped with them. S-49's was installed on her last refit at Mare Island Naval Shipyard, Vallejo, California, three years earlier. The tube was fitted in the aftermost compartment, known as the "Stoker's Mess," and was located on the starboard side, astern of the motor control switchboard. One torpedo was kept loaded in the tube, and a second torpedo was stored on the port side of the compartment.

To fire the after tube, Loveless had to maneuver the boat to insure that the target was dead astern. But as quick as the boat might have been in accomplishing this, the destroyer was quicker.

14

Before the boat could line up and fire its after tube, the destroyer rolled a depth charge on the spot where *S-49* had last been seen, which exploded off the port quarter as the boat passed 100 feet.

Jake had known simulated depth charging in fleet exercises, grenades dropped overboard by the hunters on the surface to simulate the real thing. But nothing could have prepared him for this. Seconds passed, and another explosion sounded. It seemed to be inside the boat itself, which lurched violently, first away from and then toward each explosion, as if doing some jerky, violent dance. Jake was knocked off his feet and slammed into the chart table. He grabbed for anything to steady himself, finally finding some piping, grasping and holding on, waiting for another explosion to be the last thing he would ever hear. He could not know that none of the depth charges was near enough to deal a mortal blow. What damage they *did* do, however, was bad enough.

Immediately, the bow planesman reported, "Lost power to the bow planes. Bow planes not responding!"

Getting to his feet, Jake ordered, "Shift to hand control of the bow planes," and the bow planesman began switching over to the cumbersome hand control.

Bucky Buckner then reported, "The gyrocompass is out. Its lights are out, and it sounds like it's winding down."

Then, fuses blew on the starboard lighting circuit, and first-class motorman Greg Dansforth, in the motor room, reported broken lights.

"What's the sounding here, Joe?" Loveless asked Stetson, on the chart plot.

"Two hundred ten feet, Captain," he replied.

"Good," Loveless said, "Make your depth one hundred fifty feet."

"One hundred fifty feet, aye, Sir," Jake acknowledged, ordering the planesmen to "Make your depth one-five-zero. Five degrees down bubble." The planesmen manipulated the diving planes until the bubble in the level indicator showed that the boat was on a five-degree down angle. As the boat approached the ordered depth, they eased off on the planes, bringing the bubble back to zero degrees.

"At one hundred fifty feet, Captain," Jake announced.

"Very well." Loveless acknowledged. But he worried about the increased depth's affect on his leaky boat.

By the time the boat reached 150 feet, the gyrocompass somehow began working again on its own.

At least something is going our way, thought Jake.

Loveless slowed to one-third speed, and began a slow turn to starboard, a conscious effort to keep the destroyer astern. But the boat's depth control and trim were shaky.

Then, Bill Burke reported from the motor room that the starboard motor bearing had begun to smoke, and that Dansforth was applying oil to the bearing by hand, with a squirt can. Burke also reported that the shaft seals were now leaking very badly, and the boat was taking on "a lot" of water, that the bilge was quickly filling, and the water was just four inches below the deck plates. Jake couldn't hold the boat at 150 feet, and the boat began going ever deeper. He knew the drain pump was already running, and began pumping the trim tanks to sea. Soon, the depth gauge read 170 feet.

"I can't hold depth at this speed, Captain," Jake reported. "And the trim tanks are almost dry."

"Very well," Loveless said. "All ahead two-thirds." With the increased speed, Jake was able to bring the boat back to 150 feet.

Sonar reported the destroyer's screws slowing, as it continued the hunt. It dropped another depth charge, but was well astern and to port. Jake, now far less terrified, shook off the admittedly muted explosion with a defiant grimace.

About forty-five minutes into the dive, the boat began to lose depth control entirely, and it *really* began to sink. Jake helplessly watched as the depth gauge indicated greater and greater keel depth. Apprised of the situation, Loveless again asked Stetson for the sounding shown on the chart for their current position. "Two hundred fifty feet, Sir," was the answer.

At 230 feet, in desperation, with Loveless in agreement, Jake ordered, "Bucky, put a bubble in number two main ballast tank." The COB first shut the tank vent, and then released a small amount of compressed air into the tank. The boat, now lighter, steadied somewhat on depth, but still refused to rise.

Five minutes later, *S-49* started to sink again.

"Captain," Jake called out to Loveless at the conn, "permission to put another bubble in number two main ballast."

Loveless nodded, "Do it."

Jake nodded to Bucky: "Put another bubble in number two ballast tank." The COB hit the tank with a second short blast of compressed air. The air expanded inside the tank, pushing additional water out of it. Finally, the boat, now much lighter, began to rise, first imperceptibly, and then quickly—then, *too* quickly. As the boat rose, the compressed air inside the tank expanded against the reduced sea pressure, pushing still more water out of the tank, making the boat all the more buoyant. To avoid broaching, Jake ordered, "Cycle the vent on number two ballast tank."

Now, bubbles of air vented at the top of the tank were released to the surface, indicating the boat's exact position to an astute hunter on the surface. And while the destroyer above continued to hunt, it apparently had not been close enough, or its lookouts astute enough, to spot the telltale bubbles.

Finally, with the ballast tank alternatively vented and re-flooded in stages, Jake was able to eventually settle the boat out at 95 feet. But water kept entering the boat faster than it could be pumped out, and the boat once more began to sink.

Sonar reported the sound of the destroyer's screws alternately fading and getting louder—and the boat kept going deeper and deeper, depth soon approaching 150 feet. As a precaution, Loveless ordered life jackets and escape lungs issued to everyone. However, sonar continued to report hearing, however faintly, the screws of the hunter above.

By 0515, January 5th, thanks to the feverish efforts of Bill Burke's electricians and machinist mates, control over all the boat's systems was reestablished. Sonar reported, finally, that the destroyer's screws were no longer audible. The trim was still out of whack, and the lubrication system was still out. Loveless increased speed to ahead full, and the boat slowly eased to periscope depth. He did a 360-degree sweep with the search periscope, and saw that *S-49* was alone in the sea.

Loveless surfaced the boat, and, ordering a battery charge on the port engine, cleared the area as quickly as possible. The lookouts were cautioned once again to keep a sharp eye out for contacts of any kind. There were, thankfully, none for the rest of the day, and by nightfall, the lubrication system was repaired. There was no telling, however, how well the starboard motor would function, her main bearing having been operated for hours being lubricated only by Greg Dansforth's steady hand with the squirt can.

At last, the starboard power train was fired up, and appeared to be operating normally. By dawn, even though the lubrication system was still working, the starboard motor bearing started smoking again, although not nearly as badly as before. With the battery charge secured, the boat submerged for the day.

That afternoon, the entire starboard motor lubrication system failed again.

On surfacing that night, Loveless reported his condition to SUBPAC. Hours later, in the wee hours of January 6th, orders were received, indicating that, since Cavite was now under Japanese control, *S-49* was to proceed instead to the Dutch submarine base in Surabaya, Netherlands East Indies, for repairs. Now all Loveless had to do was figure out how to get his crippled boat to Surabaya, almost 3,000 miles away—through enemy-controlled open water.

Joe Stetson plotted, and Loveless approved, a route passing east of the Philippines and then proceeding southwest, entering the Celebes Sea, on through the Makassar Strait, and then more or less southward to Surabaya. *S-49* carried excellent charts for the

Philippines and surrounding waters, and very good charts for Okinawa. But the charts she carried for the Celebes Sea, the Makassar Strait, and NEI waters were older British Admiralty charts. Loveless was worried about their accuracy — but not *overly* so. He was more concerned about the condition of his boat.

It was an interesting passage, skirting around the Philippines. Japanese activity was everywhere, and was especially intense around Luzon. What shipping they saw was too far out of position to even contemplate an attack, which would have been foolhardy in any case, considering the boat's mechanical problems. Aircraft activity was especially heavy. They apparently went unnoticed, though, as long as they stayed submerged during daylight hours. Each day, however, presented another engineering challenge. The starboard drive train continued to malfunction, and the leakage around the shaft seals grew worse daily.

Enemy activity diminished somewhat as the boat cleared the Philippines. The crew continued repairs to the starboard motor, but they were unable to keep it running for more than a few hours at a time. With only the port drive train functioning reliably, the boat was averaging a mere six knots, or 144 nautical miles a day.

It took ten days, but on the morning of January 16th, *S-49* reached the Celebes Sea. Submerging, she set a course for the Makassar Strait. Mechanical problems continued to plague the boat. At noon, fire broke out in the starboard main motor auxiliary circulating pump, but it was quickly extinguished. Again, the apparent cause was a lube oil circulation failure. Still, the engine gang managed to get the starboard power train running again, and when the boat surfaced at dusk it began making good time. At dawn *S-49* submerged again after a good night's run.

When the boat surfaced after dark, the following day, they were entering the Makassar Strait. Both drive trains came on line flawlessly and the boat began averaging just over 14 knots. Loveless remarked to Lawlor that they had just experienced their first 24 hours straight since departing their patrol zone "without a major mechanical failure."

At 0540 local time, *S-49* struck the reef.

After a sweltering day on deck with their boat sinking beneath them, a Dutch motor patrol boat out of Makassar, NEI, evacuated the crew. *USS S-49* was then scuttled, and sank quickly behind them, finally freeing herself from the reef.

Chapter 2

USS Orca: *29 January 1942 to 11 January 1943*

LCDR Jacob Lawlor stood on the bridge of his first command, the *USS Orca*, a *Gato*-class fleet submarine. The boat had made its way south, down the four miles along the Thames River from the U.S. Naval Submarine Base New London, Groton, Connecticut to the waters of Long Island Sound. *Orca* was en route to its patrol station in the Pacific, thousands of miles away from its birthplace at the Electric Boat Company, which was just downriver from the subase.

Jake's XO, Lt. Clement Dwyer, had the conn. Clem was a tall, wiry, redheaded Irishman from Milwaukee who had spent time on both a Sugar boat and one of the newer fleet boats. Both Jake and Clem were barely shielded from the driving wind by *Orca*'s bridge coaming. The boat had gone from keel to commissioning in just under twelve months, a record for the yard, which would eventually turn out a submarine a month before the war ended in an Allied victory. But on that frigid, blustery day, Monday, December 7, 1942, exactly one year after Pearl Harbor, the outcome of the war with Germany, Italy, and Japan was by no means certain. And *Orca* was sailing into the thick of it.

Jake was selected to take command of the new boat not long after the Naval Board of Inquiry into the loss of *USS S-49* had decided that neither he, nor the ill-fated boat's skipper, Lt. Harry Loveless, had been at fault in the loss of the ship.

While the enemy was busy capturing and securing the port of Rabaul on New Britain in New Guinea, a Naval Board of Inquiry into the loss of *S-49* had been convened on January 29, 1942, in Brisbane, Australia.

The Board had conducted its business with surprising alacrity (for the Navy) and determined on February 16, 1942, that "...*the reef struck by USS S-49 on January 18, 1942, had indeed been missing from the British Admiralty charts in official use by the U.S. Navy for the Makassar Strait, and that the reef being submerged in its entirety, and as there was no cause for a competent mariner to have expected the reef's existence . . .*"

The Board also found no fault in any of the subsequent actions of the boat's commander, Lt. Harry Loveless, or any of the boat's other officers and crew. The Board actually decided instead to award S-49 a battle star for her performance against the enemy, sinking one enemy cargo vessel, and for the safe evacuation of the crew from the stricken boat without loss of life.

Just eleven days after the Board reached its decision, Allied navies suffered a decisive defeat at the hands of the Imperial Japanese Navy in the Battle of the Java Sea; the war was going badly for the Allies.

Harry Loveless was promoted to Lieutenant Commander and assigned to SUBSOWESPAC staff in Fremantle, Australia. There he would eventually serve as aide to COMSUBSOWESPAC, the Commander, Submarines, Southwest Pacific, Captain Charles Lockwood. Harry would also eventually accompany Lockwood to Submarines, Pacific, in Pearl Harbor, where, as COMSUBPAC, Rear Admiral Lockwood would become famous as "Uncle Charlie" throughout the fleet (but never to his face).

At the same time, Lt. Jacob Lawlor received orders to report aboard *USS Narwhal* in Pearl Harbor for a Prospective Commanding Officer (PCO) patrol. *Narwhal* was scheduled to leave Pearl on her first war patrol in early February.

Jake Lawlor reported aboard the *USS Narwhal,* Lt. Cmdr. Charles W. "Weary" Wilson, USNR, commanding, for his PCO patrol on January 28, 1942. Fifty-two days earlier, on Dec. 7, 1941, the naval base and U.S. Army Air Force facility at Pearl had been attacked by Japanese carrier-borne airplanes and miniature submarines.

In arriving at Pearl, Jake was awestruck by the extent of the devastation still visible. Intermittent blooms of fuel oil could still be seen rising from some of the wrecks along Battleship Alley, and the last of the destroyed airplanes was still being cleared. Once-mighty capital ships remained sunk or capsized, and fuel oil was still being pumped out from the submerged hulk of *Arizona.* There were no visible floating bodies, but at least a thousand souls were still inside the blasted remains left behind by the invaders.

Narwhal was one of five submarines in port, all undergoing overhaul, when the Japanese attacked. Within minutes of the first enemy bombs dropping on Ford Island, *Narwhal's* gunners were in action. They claimed two Japanese torpedo planes. Among the failures of the Japanese raid was leaving the submarine base relatively unscathed. Another was missing the carrier fleet altogether (all the carriers were at sea that Sunday). These omissions eventually proved to be costly mistakes for the invaders.

Jake was present on the bridge when *Narwhal* departed Pearl Harbor on her first war patrol on February 2, 1942. She spent two days on a reconnaissance of Wake Island, 2,450 miles later. She still had to traverse another 2,500 miles before entering waters familiar to Jake from *S-49's* war patrol, the East China Sea, in the vicinity of the Ryukyu Islands.

On February 28th, while on station in the East China Sea southwest of the Ryukyus, *Narwhal's* lookouts spotted two heavily laden merchant ships accompanied by a destroyer escort. Wilson positioned his boat with an end-around run on the surface and then submerged for a shot at the larger vessel, a 6,500-ton freighter. Unlike practically all submarine commanders, who preferred to personally man the periscope throughout an entire attack, Wilson preferred to let his XO, Lt. Jerry Murphy, run the periscope while he coordinated the attack based on his evaluation of the XO's observations, the chart plot, and passive sonar reports.

With Jake observing, when Wilson was satisfied with his team's firing solution, he brought *Narwhal* about to firing course and waited until the target had closed to 700 yards. He then fired two Mark-10 torpedoes at the freighter. One of the torpedoes hit its mark, exploding on contact, and, according to Murphy's periscope observations (confirmed by Jake), inflicted heavy damage.

Reacting quickly, the escort came on hard and fast, following down the torpedo wakes. The destroyer rolled off a depth charge in the place where the wakes converged, followed by two more along what the destroyer's captain assumed was his prey's escape route. But Wilson had taken the boat deep at full speed on the destroyer's approach, and then, with the boat rigged for silent running, began to creep slowly away, continually changing course, steering to keep the depth charge explosions further and further astern. He ultimately took the boat, shaken, but not mortally damaged, to safety.

Six days later, still in the East China Sea, another, smaller, unescorted freighter of about 1,200 tons was sighted. Attacking on the surface, Wilson sank her with a single torpedo. The remainder of the patrol was uneventful, and *Narwhal* returned to Pearl Harbor on March 28th.

The war in the Pacific was still not going well for the Allies during the first few months of 1942. The Japanese had taken control of the Philippines, Indochina, Thailand, Singapore, the Netherlands East Indies, Wake Island, the Gilbert Islands, and Guam. The Dutch, occupied by Nazi Germany, could do little to defend their East Indies colonies; Japan easily seized Borneo (refineries) and Sumatra (oil fields). These victories promised to make the Japanese self-sufficient in the fuel required for domestic use and for the formidable requirements of their war machine. In addition, Japan now had sources for coal, bauxite, rubber, copra, nickel, timber, and quinine, as well as needed foodstuffs such as sugar, rice, tea, and coffee.

During *Narwhal's* first war patrol, Jake learned a great deal from her captain, Weary Wilson. He was always cool-headed and calm, even in a combat situation, and his crew seemed to adopt his demeanor, obviously confident of his leadership ability. Wilson kept firing solutions as simple as possible, and Jake admired the way he and his XO Murphy worked as a team, with Murphy on the periscope and Wilson in overall charge of the fire control team. Jake saw the wisdom in this approach, and determined to use it himself when he assumed command of a boat.

For his part, Wilson had been observing Jake, asking questions, evaluating his responses, and learning his capabilities. Jake was overjoyed when he later learned that Wilson had wholeheartedly recommended him for command. Wilson's final wry words to Jake as he departed *Narwhal* for his 4,900-mile journey to Connecticut were, "Remember, Jake, there are just two kinds of ships: submarines and targets."

Jake Lawlor reported to the U.S. Naval Submarine Base New London, Groton, Connecticut, three weeks later to assume his new command: *USS Orca,* still under construction at the Electric Boat Company (EB).

Orca was a *Gato*-class submarine, and American submarine design had been frozen with the *Gato*-class configuration. The design was updated in 1943 with the *USS Balao* and subsequent *Balao*-class boats, and after that, in 1944, with the *Tench*-class. Those boats were built with thicker, stronger pressure hulls and could dive deeper, but the configuration remained essentially the same. All told, 77 *Gato*-class boats were built by various shipyards during the war.

At the time, *Gato* was the finest submarine ever built, light years ahead of even the remarkably effective German U-boats that were raising hell with Allied shipping in the Atlantic. At 1,400 tons displacement, and 312 feet long, *Gato* packed a formidable punch. She carried ten torpedo tubes, six forward and four aft; space for twenty-one torpedoes; a four-inch, fifty-caliber deck gun; and two-anti-aircraft guns—one forty millimeter and one twenty millimeter.

Gato's propulsion was provided by four, sixteen-cylinder General Motors diesels directly powering motor generators, which, in turn, provided power to four, high-speed General Electric DC motors, two per shaft. The diesel's generators could provide electric power to the propulsion motors directly, or provide power to charge the batteries. With the diesels off line, the batteries provided power directly to the propulsion motors. In another configuration, the diesels could charge the batteries while the batteries provided power to the motors—a "propulsion charge."

A manually operated bank of large levers—switches, actually—in the maneuvering room selected each particular power configuration. Two, 126-cell, Sargo lead-acid batteries were located belowdecks in separate compartments. The forward battery was directly aft of the forward torpedo room, and the after battery was just aft of the control room.

Gato-class boats had two periscopes, a nine-and-a-half-inch search scope, and a seven-and-a-half-inch attack scope. Both scopes were improvements over previous models, which were practically useless for attacks at night, unless there was a full moon and no overcast. The scopes on *Gato* had much improved optics, and the scopes were equipped with a stadimeter for more accurate range determination. They were tapered at the top to minimize their wakes and the possibility of visual detection.

Orca was only slightly different compared to *Gato*, and even more advanced. Unlike the German boats, and practically all of the Imperial Japanese Navy at the time, *Gato*-class boats had both sonar and radar capability.

Chief Boatswain's Mate Wendell Buckner had been Harry Loveless's Chief of the Boat (COB) on *S-49*. When it became clear that Harry Loveless would not (at least not immediately—and perhaps never) be given another boat to command, Jake had specifically requested "Bucky" Buckner's assignment to *Orca*. For his part, Bucky had respected and admired *S-49's* former XO, and was happy to serve under him as *Orca's* first COB. The fact that Bucky made Groton his home only sweetened the deal.

Bucky's orders to *Orca* were such that he reached the shipyard two weeks ahead of Jake. As on *S-49*, Bucky would be the highest ranking enlisted man aboard, and, truth be told, second most-powerful man aboard after Jake himself. Even on the most effective boats, where the XO and the COB functioned pretty much as a team, the XO usually wisely deferred to the COB, especially where the discipline of the crew was at issue. When Jake reported aboard his new command, he was delighted to find that his COB had already been on the job, and had personally inspected every piece of equipment installed to date.

Bucky had joined the Navy at 16, with his parent's permission. They had, in fact, been happy to sign, because Bucky had proven himself a difficult son.

Raised in south Chicago, the fifth child born into a German immigrant family of eight children, Wendell Dieter Buckner never quite took to the precepts of the rest of his family's Lutheran tradition. Bucky preferred carousing with his neighborhood friends to attending school.

Boot camp at Naval Station Great Lakes in North Chicago proved almost enjoyable for Bucky. Bucky's drill instructor quickly singled him out as an intelligent and natural leader. To his surprise, he enjoyed being given even the little responsibility he had as platoon guidon. He particularly enjoyed having his platoon mates looking to him as an example and for advice. He graduated from boot camp with high marks. His first duty station was a heavy cruiser out of Norfolk, where he discovered that Boatswain's Mates ran the Navy, and from that point on, made being the foulest-mouthed, hardest-steaming, and most squared-away Boatswain's Mate in the Navy his life's work.

In mid-April, 1942, sixteen U.S. Army Air Force B-25B Mitchell Medium Bombers were launched without fighter escort from the deck of the USS Hornet *in the Western Pacific. Led by Lieutenant Colonel James Doolittle, the bombers conducted an air raid on the Japanese capital, Tokyo, and other locations on the principal Japanese Island of Honshu. The raid did little actual damage, but provided a significant boost to U.S. morale.*

Jake was commuting between his room in the Bachelor Officer's Quarters (BOQ) on the base and EB when his promotion to lieutenant commander came through. The notice from BUPERS, the Naval Bureau of Personnel, was on his desk when he arrived at the shipyard in late April, just six months before *Orca* was commissioned.

It was a promotion much deserved. Jake's service record had been impressive: he had graduated third in his class at the Academy, and first in his sub school class. Jake had been rated "superior" or "outstanding" in all of his fitness reports, and had been specifically recommended for command at the earliest by both his last skipper Harry Loveless and his squadron commander. Finally, while the old *R* and *S* boats were commanded by lieutenants, the staff at BUPERS would see to it that none of these new "fleet" boats would be entrusted to anyone of lower rank than a lieutenant commander.

A week later, Jake's new XO reported for duty.

Lieutenant Clement Xavier Dwyer was a heavy-set, tall, and fun-loving Irish Catholic. Clem was in the Naval Reserve Officer Training Corps, or NROTC, at Northwestern University, the site of one of the few of these university-based, officer-training units established at that time. At Northwestern, he had earned both a degree in Mechanical Engineering, and, upon graduation, a commission as an ensign in the U.S. Naval Reserve. Clem's achievements at Northwestern had not been that remarkable — he finished somewhere in the middle of his 1936 class, excelling in his naval science and engineering courses. He just got by in math and his other required courses. Strangely enough, he aced his non-engineering courses, excelling in English and Economics.

His first active duty assignment was to a WWI-vintage destroyer. His first commanding officer decided that Ensign Dwyer would make an ideal submarine officer, and talked him into applying for sub school.

Clem was a natural for submarine warfare. He could envision and calculate a firing solution in his head. The Mark III torpedo data computer, or TDC, installed aboard *Orca*, might have been a tad more accurate than Clem, but was by no means faster. Aboard *Seal*, he had qualified for his gold dolphins in record time.

The gold dolphin breast pin, dolphins flanking the bow and conning tower of a submarine, its bow planes extended on full dive, was awarded to qualified submarine officers. Qualifying for dolphins involved at least a year of rigorous study and testing.

There was a similar qualification program for enlisted submariners, and a dolphin arm patch, in blue for white uniforms, and in white for blue uniforms, was worn on the right forearm by submarine-qualified enlisted men. It was not until after the war that the patches were replaced by silver dolphin breast pins.

In *Seal*, Dwyer eventually served as weapons officer, navigator, and finally as engineer officer, before being assigned to *Orca*.

After Clem's arrival, assigned officers and enlisted began to report aboard on a daily basis. All were submarine volunteers (the submarine service accepted only volunteers, but not all volunteers were accepted) and only a handful had actual submarine experience outside of basics from officer's or enlisted sub school. Now, they were learning *Orca* from the ground up, crawling over her bones, learning her systems, memorizing her pipe runs and her cable ways. By the time underway trials began, *Orca* had her full complement of seven officers and sixty-eight enlisted aboard.

Orca's complement of officers shook out as follows: Lieutenant Commander Jacob Lawlor, USN, Commanding; Lieutenant Clement Dwyer, USNR; Executive Officer; Lieutenant Harold Chapman, USN; Engineer Officer Lieutenant Louis Carillo, USN, Navigator; Lieutenant JG Early Sender, USN, Weapons Officer; Lieutenant JG Joe Bob Clanton, USNR, Communications Officer; Ensign William Salton, USN, Assistant Engineering Officer

And the Chief Petty Officers were: BMC (SS) Wendell Buckner, COB; TMC (SS) Clyde Walakurski; MMC (SS) William Clements; RMC (SS) Francis O'Grady; EMC (SS) Robert Lione.

Among the officers, only Lt. j.g. Joe Bob Clanton, and Ensign William Salton had not yet qualified in submarines, and besides Jake, they were also the only bachelors. In *Orca*, as aboard most boats, the XO was in charge of officer qualification; enlisted qualification came under the COB's responsibilities.

Clem and Bucky Buckner soon developed an unusual, close relationship, built on mutual respect and a genuine friendship. Louise Buckner and Miriam Dwyer, introduced to each other by their respective husbands, also became fast friends. For the two women their friendship proved to be mutually beneficial as they came to rely on one another for emotional support over the long periods when their husbands were away.

Clem Dwyer reported for duty just as the Battle of the Coral Sea raged off the southeastern Solomon Islands.

For the Japanese, with their occupation of Tulagi, and in the number of ships lost, which included the carrier USS Lexington, *The Battle of the Coral Sea proved to be a tactical victory. But it also proved to be a*

strategic victory for the Allied fleets, in that the Japanese were denied the occupation of Port Moresby in New Guinea, and two Japanese carriers were so badly damaged that they could not participate in the later battle of Midway. Had they been able to participate, they well might have provided a decisive edge to the Japanese.

A month later, between the 4th and the 7th of June, 1942, the battle of Midway proved to be the beginning of the end for Japanese Naval forces in the Pacific. Japan lost four carriers in the battle, one heavy cruiser, and two hundred and forty-eight aircraft. The U.S. lost one carrier, the USS Yorktown, *a destroyer, and about one hundred and fifty aircraft.*

USS Nautilus *played a significant (if inadvertent) role in the battle.* Nautilus *was one of sixteen boats scouting for the Japanese fleet off Midway when its skipper, Lt. Cmdr. Bill Brockman, raised his periscope on the morning of June 4th in the middle of the Japanese fleet. "Ships all over the place," he later reported. He fired at a battleship and missed before being driven deep by a destroyer. He returned to fire three more fish at the carrier* Kaga. *Two torpedoes missed, but the third struck the ship and failed to explode. Again attacked by a destroyer,* Nautilus *dived and fled the scene. The destroyer meanwhile continued to drop depth charges on the* Nautilus' *last location. When it finally gave up and decided to return to the Japanese carrier task force, it was spotted by a Dauntless dive-bomber squadron from the* USS Enterprise, *led by Cmdr. Wade McClusky, which was searching for the Japanese fleet. Seeing the destroyer in a hurry "to go someplace," McClusky, on a hunch, followed it to the carrier* Hiryu, *which was soon turned into a burning wreck.*

The Japanese Navy never recovered from their losses at Midway because they could never match the American ability to absorb, rebuild, and to recruit and train new pilots.

Chapter 3

Jake, feeling awkward in civilian clothes (mufti), knocked on Clem Dwyer's door. He had brought a bottle of California red wine to go with dinner (French wine being unavailable—what pre-war French vintage was for sale was exorbitantly expensive). Clem answered the door, dressed casually in civvies, although his trousers were recycled work khakis. "Hey, Skipper," he said, "Come on in, Miriam's been dying to meet you!"

Miriam greeted Jake at the entrance to an unexpectedly big kitchen. "Captain Lawlor, how nice to finally meet you! Clement talks about you so much I feel I've known you for years!"

Miriam Dwyer was tiny and very Irish: slim and certainly not much over five feet tall, reddish brown curls, green eyes, freckles, and a knockout smile. She was radiant even in an apron, a plain white blouse, and grey slacks.

"It's Jake, please, and everything Clem's told you is a lie—I'm not really that much of a slave driver!"

She laughed, a big laugh from such a little person, "He never said you were," she said. "I'm the one who said that."

And Jake knew that he and Miriam were going to get along just fine.

Orca passed her sea trials easily, and was commissioned on an unusually sweltering day for a New England Autumn, in October 1942. After moving to a berth at the sub base, the boat was allowed a shakedown cruise to test all the boat's systems, and for training to begin in earnest. Jake drove the crew mercilessly, taking the boat into Long Island Sound, and exercising the crew continually. They dived and surfaced the boat; practiced torpedo attacks, both on the surface and submerged against other boats;

exercised the deck gun on towed surface targets; fired the anti-aircraft guns at towed airborne targets; ran emergency drills of all kinds; fired practice torpedoes; and then did it all over and over again.

By December, SUBLANT—Submarines, Atlantic, to which *Orca* had been assigned for training—deemed her ready for duty. Jake was not so sure. Like all earlier submarine designs, *Orca* was, basically, a surface vessel capable of submerging. Her ability to submerge, however, was her edge over all surface vessels.

Archimedes had discovered the principles of buoyancy about 2,200 years earlier in ancient Greece. A floating object floats because it is lighter than the water it displaces. If an object is heavier than the water it displaces, it sinks. If an object weighs the same as the water it displaces (neutral buoyancy) it will float just beneath the surface. A submarine uses these principles to manipulate her environment.

All fleet submarines have a number of buoyancy tanks, tanks arranged along their pressure hulls like saddles on a horse. The bottom of these tanks are open to the sea, and when closed on top and filled with air, they are like a child's water wings, and the boat, lighter than the water it displaces, floats on the surface. If the tanks are vented, by opening a valve on the top of each tank, water enters the tanks from the bottom, the boat gets heavy—heavier than the water it displaces—and it submerges. To surface, the tank vents are closed, and the tanks are filled with compressed air. The boat, now once again lighter than the water it displaces, rises to the surface and floats.

The ability to submerge gives the submarine a whole other dimension in which to work. It provides a place from which to attack unseen with its torpedoes; a place from which to lay mines unseen; a place from which to observe without being observed; and a place to which to run and hide when necessary. The ability to submerge gives the submarine the ability to survive and to fight again.

And that's precisely why being able to dive quickly, was so critical. Jake was deeply concerned that it still took just under a minute to dive the boat, this despite the boat's added features that speeded up the process: a bow buoyancy tank, and a negative tank. "Negative" was a hardened tank (one of several inside the pressure hull able to withstand sea pressure) just forward of amidships. Negative tank was flooded on the sounding of the diving alarm, giving the ship immediate negative buoyancy. When the boat was well into the dive, "negative" was "blown to the mark," that is, a predetermined mark on the tank's capacity gauge, where the boat could most easily be settled out on diving trim in an effort to attain neutral buoyancy.

Jake was sure *Orca* could be dived in under forty seconds, and was determined to drill the crew until it happened. He was also unhappy with the speed of the crew in manning the boat's guns. It took them too long to prepare the guns to fire, and the flow of ammunition from the magazines to the deck really needed improvement. But, again, that was nothing that more practice would not improve.

Despite all the drilling, the crew never complained. They understood (and if they didn't at first, they did after the COB drummed it into their heads) that their survival as a crew depended on being able to outfight the enemy—*and* that their ability to fight depended on their functioning as a perfect team. Even the lowest-ranking seaman aboard came to understand that his performance was every bit as critical to *Orca's* survival as the highest-ranking officer or petty officer. Like it or not, they *really were* all in this together, and everyone aboard was dependent on everyone else, regardless of rating or rank. And this was probably the primary reason that the Submarine Service was, after all, such an elite service.

German submarine activity along the east coast of the United States, in 1942 and 1943 especially, was a well-established danger, as many merchant ships, particularly coastal oilers, became painfully and fatally aware. Now *Orca*, in company with *USS Seasprite* (Lt. Cmdr. Chester Adams, USN, commanding), a boat built and newly commissioned at Quincy, Massachusetts, by Bethlehem Shipbuilding Corporation, ran the gauntlet down the east coast to the Panama Canal.

The two boats made the transit entirely on the surface under the watchful eye of a destroyer escort, the *USS Harold Wilkes*, the convoy averaging sixteen knots, and following a random-pattern zigzag course. Lieutenant Commander Jonathan Orly, USN, CO of the *Wilkes*, was Senior Officer Present Afloat, or SOPA, and as such he was in command of the little convoy. Each submarine had its short-range SD air search radar activated and its deck watch on full alert.

The two boats and their escort traveled the 2,280 miles from their rendezvous point off New London to the Canal entrance in just seven days. Through the Canal, and on their way to Pearl Harbor, both boats came under the command of Submarines, Pacific. Now they had only to cross the 5,000 miles to Hawaii to get to their new homeport.

The transit to Hawaii was not without danger, but while Japanese submarine attack was not an impossibility, it was highly unlikely, and the Navy provided no escort for this part of their journey. Both boats nonetheless maintained their vigilance, air search radars and watch standers on full alert.

Once she was aboard the base at Pearl, on December 30, *Orca* was allowed one week of Individual Ship's Exercises, or ISE, before proceeding on her first war patrol. But first there was New Year's Eve to celebrate, and they would celebrate it in Honolulu.

Orca had been turned over to a relief crew, and her regular crew had been assigned rooms at the Royal Hawaiian Hotel, the "Pink Palace of the Pacific," at 2259 Kalakaua, Honolulu (the Navy had taken over the hotel for the duration of the war for the exclusive rest and recreation of their submariners, no tourists allowed).

Jake remained on base at the BOQ, operating on the premise that it was unseemly for a ship's captain to carouse with his crew, a premise not universally shared by most submarine commanders. Clem Dwyer certainly felt no such restraint, nor did Bucky Buckner or any of the other officers and chiefs.

The stiff, formal, relationships between a naval vessel's captain and his officers and crew, and between officers and enlisted men in the surface fleet, did not hold in the submarine force. All officers, save the captain, were still addressed as "Mister" by the enlisted crew. In turn, officers usually addressed enlisted crewmen using their surnames, although addressing enlisted men using their nicknames was common. *Orca's* COB, for example, was "Bucky" to everyone. Similarly, all officers (again, save the captain) were on a first name basis with each other. A boat's commander was always addressed as "Captain" or "Skipper" by everyone. The only exception to this rule extended to the XO, when, in private, the XO might address the skipper by his first name, and then only with the tacit approval of the commander. Such approval was usually not formally extended, but something that came to be understood between the two individuals, as between friends.

But the relaxed relationship between officers and enlisted men went only so far, even in submarines. Segregation between officers and enlisted men was too far steeped in naval tradition to be discarded entirely. While all meals were prepared in the general mess, submarine officers still took their meals in the wardroom, apart from the enlisted men, and their meals were served by an enlisted man, a steward's mate. The two steward's mates aboard were almost always Filipino, but were also sometimes black. They bunked in the forward torpedo room, and while friendly with the rest of the crew, almost always kept to themselves. The WWII Navy was still a segregated Navy, and at least self-imposed segregation was the norm even in the submarine force. Segregated or not, stewards were still part of the boat's duty roster, and still had GQ stations, usually in the forward torpedo room.

Officers' quarters were in the forward battery compartment. Most enlisted men's quarters were in the after battery compartment, which also housed the crew's mess and the enlisted men's toilet (or head) and showers. There was an additional enlisted men's head in the after torpedo room. The remainder of the enlisted men bunked in the forward and after torpedo rooms. The officers' head and shower were in the forward torpedo room.

In submarines, while chief petty officers were still enlisted men, their bunkroom (the "Goat Locker") was in the forward battery, just forward of the control room, and decidedly in "officers' country." On capital ships, officers' country was inviolate, and an enlisted man had to ask permission to enter or even pass through it. On a boat, however, the passage through the forward battery compartment was the only means for reaching the forward torpedo room (and, for some, their bunk), and to limit free passage by enlisted men through that compartment would have been silly.

For submariners, only in port were there any uniform requirements, and these were usually set by the port commander. Aboard the boat itself, such in-port regulations were somewhat loosely enforced, and were almost entirely ignored at sea, where shorts and sandals were the norm for everyone, captain included. The longer the boat was away from port, the more relaxed the crew's attention to its appearance became, and, of course, the more aromatic became their bodies and their clothing.

Shower facilities used fresh water, and fresh water was at a premium at sea. Officers and men were allowed a "Navy shower" every three days. (A Navy shower required quickly wetting down, soaping up with the water off, and then quickly rinsing. The ongoing joke in the fleet was that a good Navy shower was one where the deck never got wet.) Aboard submarines, only the cooks were permitted daily showers. Only in port, whenever fresh water was supplied from alongside, did the onboard showers see any regular use.

Tobacco use, particularly cigarettes, was endemic throughout the fleet. The "Smoking Lamp" was generally lit in ships at sea and on naval bases, except in the berthing quarters in the hours between taps and reveille, at general quarters, or during activities or in areas where an open flame might be hazardous. The gun deck in fleet submarines, just aft of the bridge, was called the "Cigarette Deck" because small groups of off-duty crewmen were sometimes allowed there to enjoy a smoke and friendly conversation in the open air. Smoking was a habit that Jake Lawlor never developed, but he, along with the other nonsmokers in the fleet, was in the minority.

Also endemic was "salty" language. Vulgarity and profanity were the *lingua franca* of the military, and sailors were their acknowledged masters. A sailor particularly well versed in the art could break up a multi-syllabic English word and insert vulgarities between the syllables. Aboard *Orca*, it was common knowledge that the skipper did not use or approve of such language, and the crew instinctively watched their mouths when they knew Jake was within hearing distance. Not that Jake had ever expressed his predilections one way or the other; it had simply become a silent understanding among *Orca's* officers and crew.

Liberty in Honolulu was the first occasion that any of the crew could actually meet any of their counterparts on *Seasprite*, and from the first liberty, the two crews bonded and set about some serious partying—on New Year's Eve. Some of the revelers left the hotel in small groups to seek other diversion in the city itself, but most stayed at the hotel, making full use of the facilities, the cheap booze, and whatever female company wandered in.

Clem and Bucky stayed at the hotel, and confined their reveling to consuming copious amounts of an excellent single malt. They awoke to the New Year, 1943, in their shared hotel room with monumental hangovers.   The partying and the drinking continued, however, and when it became time to report back to the boat for morning muster, January 4th, most of the crew were nursing unbelievable headaches and looking rather the worse for wear.

In February 1943, now Rear Admiral "Uncle Charlie" Lockwood became COMSUBPAC.

Orca's last shakedown before her first war patrol began on that January 4th. The shakedown was a concentrated repetition of the boat's last six weeks in New London, this time in company with *USS Grampus*, with each boat practicing firing runs on each other in between conducting individual ship's drills. The first day at sea was a performance disaster, with most of the crew still recovering from their hard liberty, but by week's end Jake was elated when his crew managed to dive the boat in just thirty-eight seconds.

Orca departed Pearl on her first war patrol at 0930 on Monday, January 11, 1943. There was no fanfare, and no bands were playing, but the Squadron Commander and three members of his staff did see her off. What followed was a 4,500-mile trek to the Bismarck Sea, with orders "to interdict and destroy the shipping of the Empire of Japan and her allies, with priority given to ships of the Imperial Japanese Navy operating north of New Guinea and the Japanese base at Rabaul."

Aboard was a less-than-full complement of torpedoes, twenty-one, instead of twenty-four, due to a shortage of torpedoes throughout the fleet. The newer Mark-14 torpedoes were especially scarce and on this trip, and *Orca* carried only eleven. The remaining ten were the older Mark-10 model. *Orca's* torpedo tubes could fire either model, but only the Mark-14s could import firing data from the TDC and come to a specific course, regardless of the course of the boat. The older, shorter, Mark-10s could be fired from the TDC, but could only go straight ahead.

Jake had ordered tubes one through four, forward-loaded with Mark-14s, five and six with Mark-10s. The racks forward held four more Mark-14s and four more Mark-10s.

Aft, tubes seven, eight, and nine were loaded with Mark-14s, and ten with a Mark-10. The racks aft held the remaining three, Mark 10s. Rack space for three more torpedoes aft remained empty.

The mix of torpedoes was not all bad. The word around the fleet was that all models of torpedoes in the fleet had problems, but that the Mark-14s were particularly plagued. Commanders of several of the boats had reported duds (torpedoes that failed to explode), others that exploded prematurely, and all failed to run at set depth. There were at least a dozen, well-documented instances where torpedoes fired on target had missed, failed to explode on contact (they had actually been heard striking the target), or exploded prematurely. The complaining commanders claimed that the Mark-14s were running *deeper* than pre-set depth (a fault also shared by the Mark-10s), and that the new magnetic-influence firing mechanism, and possibly even the contact exploder were defective.

Even worse, the Mark-14 torpedoes were found to sometime run "circular," that is, they failed to straighten out on their pre-set course, and instead ran in a large circle, returning to the firing vessel. Regardless of solid evidence to the contrary, and relying upon its own inconclusive firing tests (with torpedoes fired from a barge and not an actual submarine), the Bureau of Ordnance stood by their design and refused to make any changes. On the advice of the more-experience skippers at Pearl, Jake made sure that all tubes were loaded with a mix of the torpedo types.

Chapter 4

Orca: *First Patrol – 23 January 1943 to 9 February 1943*

While still en route to their patrol station, on January 23rd, Clem walked into the tiny wardroom, where Jake was enjoying a few minutes break. He was alone, every other officer on board either on duty or in their racks. *Orca* was passing through a patch of very heavy seas, and about half of the crew was, to some degree at least, seasick. Their number included Lt. Carillo, Lt j.g. Sender, and Ensign Salton. And the word was that Chief O'Grady was standing his watches alongside a barf bucket.

"This will interest you, Jake, message sent from Ty Jacobs in *Sargo*, bitching to SUBPAC that the Mark Fourteens are crap. Says he was dead certain he placed his fish on target, and every one of 'em was a dud."

"Jacobs did that? Sent it to the Admiral?"

"Yes indeedy!"

Jake chuckled. "Must have really been pissed, though you really can't blame him. To take on SUBPAC like that, that takes some *cojones*. But he's a pretty senior skipper, full commander, so he'll probably get away with it."

"Just about every skipper in the sub fleet says the torpedoes are junk. Why in blazes isn't the Admiral doing anything?"

"Politics, Clem, ring-knocker stuff. USN brass versus USN brass. Maybe SUBPAC isn't willing to cross BUORD. Makes me kinda glad they didn't have enough Mark Fourteens to give us a full load. I've seen a Mark Ten blow a hole in a cargo ship. I know *they* work."

"Yeah, if you set them shallow enough."

Fifteen days after leaving Pearl, on January 27th, *Orca* arrived at the sea routes north of New Guinea in the Bismarck Sea, and the Japanese stronghold at Rabaul. None of the time in transit had been wasted. Jake continued to hold emergency drills, at least one daily, keeping the crew razor sharp.

The previous August, in what passed for the dead of winter in that part of the world, the U.S. Marines had stormed Tulagi, Gavutu, and Tanambogo in the Solomons, driving the Japs off those strongholds in preparation for the closely following assault on nearby Guadalcanal. The Tulagi campaign cost 115 Marines their lives in contrast to 783 of the enemy. The butcher's bill for Guadalcanal was far greater, with 7,100 Marine dead and 31,000 Japanese.

After their losses in the Solomons, the Japanese were intent on maintaining their foothold in New Guinea, and their stronghold at Rabaul. A continuous string of supply ships and troop transports, heavily escorted, filled the shipping routes between the Japanese base at Rabaul, other holdings in the area, and the home islands. These sea routes were now Orca's *hunting grounds.*

The first weeks passed without incident. *Orca* remained submerged, usually at periscope depth, in daylight, at slow speed, searching with her directional JP hydrophone (her passive, listen-only, sonar system) and the search periscope for targets. The SD, the vaguely directional short-range air search radar, could only be used when the boat was surfaced.

The QC/JK sonar transducer was mounted under *Orca's* bow. *Orca* was among the first boats in the submarine fleet equipped with this system. The QC was active sonar, useful for detecting submerged submarines, and providing an accurate range and bearing to any contact, but it could provide no information as to the target's depth. Its pinging could also be heard through the hull of any target sub or by a sound listening device on a surface vessel, revealing *Orca's* presence.

The passive, JK sonar transducer reception was masked by whatever noise the boat was making. It was the only passive sonar, however, available to the surfaced submarine. The JP hydrophone was another new device; again *Orca* was among the first submarines so equipped. The T-shaped JP hydrophone was mounted on deck, just aft of the bow. The passive JP hydrophone could be trained on its target, and was capable of providing accurate target bearings, but was obviously useful only when the boat was submerged.

Orca would only surface after dark to charge batteries, and then only after doing a 360-degree sweep with the search periscope to look for contacts. Her six-mile-range, non-directional, SD radar was also used on the surface to detect, and avoid, enemy aircraft. Jake, old school, had standing orders that on the surface, the radar was only a supplement to the Mark One eyeball, and that he expected his lookouts to stay sharp. He reminded them every time he was on the bridge that the lives of everyone aboard depended on them.

In the early hours on Tuesday, February 9th, *Orca* drew blood for the first time.

There was a quarter moon low on the horizon, the sea was calm, and the weather was clear. At 0032, while *Orca* was cruising southwest of Labur Bay, off Latangai Island, the port lookout reported what he thought were ship's masts hull down on the horizon to the southwest, probably heading out from Rabaul. *Orca's* position put them between the moon and the contacts, so Jake ordered a course and speed to do an end-around, getting the targets between *Orca* and the moon, and giving *Orca* a good shot at getting into a favorable firing position. By 0257, Jake felt he had *Orca* in just the right spot. If the target continued on course, in just about an hour, they would pass within 700 yards of the boat and, with a 90-degree-left angle-on-the-bow, she'd be illuminated quite nicely by the rising moon.

At 0312, Clem was on the search periscope and spotted not one, but the wispy shapes of three targets, but he could not identify them. They were headed due north, in line, making an estimated twelve knots. The lookouts spotted three ghostly hulls on the horizon at 0317. Jake, on the bridge with Early Sender as Officer of the Deck on his regular morning watch, wasn't too worried about being spotted. *Orca* sat low, and they were on the dark side of the horizon. *Orca* was making bare steerageway, and the boat had drifted away from the targets' estimated track. The projected closest point of approach (CPA) was now 1,800 yards. Jake had maneuvered the boat to point at the targets, and *Orca* was heading 170 degrees true.

Jake sounded, "Battle stations, surface," and relieved Early as OOD. Early went below to his battle station in the conning tower on the TDC. Clem reported up through the hatch that he was on station in the conning tower, and manning the periscope. Seconds later, Bucky called up through the 1MC that all battle stations, surface, were manned. On the bridge with Jake were now QM2 "Squid" Phillips on the Pelorus, and the four lookouts, LaGrange, Rubidot, Catinella and Rogers. Seaman Robert Olds was on the sound-powered phones and was immediately below, in the conning tower. Olds functioned as "talker" for both the bridge and the conning tower, and was in contact with other talkers stationed in compartments throughout the boat.

Clem called up from the conning tower. "Captain, contacts changed course to three-five-zero, still in line, still making about twelve knots."

"Very well. We should still be in pretty good firing position." Jake searched the horizon with his binoculars. "Lookouts, you see anything?"

Seaman John Catinella, the forward port quarter lookout, reported, "There's something out there, Captain, about ten degrees off the port bow. Just shadows, but there's something there.

Each of the other lookouts reported "Nothing in my quarter, Captain."

"Okay, Catinella, don't forget to sweep the horizon regularly, too. And watch for planes. You, too, Hal. Stay sharp. Can you see 'em yet, Squid?"

Jake peered through his binoculars. Nothing. Phillips was hunched over the dummy Pelorus, aimed in the direction of the contacts. The dummy Pelorus allowed Phillips to read the position of the target in degrees relative to the fore and aft axis of the boat. "Not yet, Captain . . . no, wait . . . I can just about make out a ship — nope, lost it."

Jake shouted down the hatch to Clem, "What bearing have you got, Clem?'

"One-six-eight to the lead ship. Looks like an escort, a destroyer"

"Have radar staying sharp, and looking for any aircraft. I don't want any surprises."

"Yessir, Captain," Clem replied, and relayed the message to Chief O'Grady on the radar.

Jake did the simple math in his head. The boat was on course 070, the contact was at 168. That meant that the contacts were two degrees to port, or at 358 degrees on the dummy Pelorus. "Okay, Squid, put the Pelorus on three-five-eight and see what you have."

"Aye, aye, Captain."

Phillips looked up from the Pelorus, and using a dimmed, red-lensed flashlight to read the numbers, aimed its scope on 358, and bent down again to peer through it. It took a few seconds for his eyes to readjust to the dark, and, finally: "Got 'em! Can't say what as yet, though."

"Okay, keep on 'em." Jake could see the shadows now, through his binoculars.

"Yessir."

Minutes passed. Clem sounded out from the conning tower, "Lead contact definitely a destroyer, possibly *Fubuki*-class. Second ship is much larger, a cargo ship of some sort. Can't see the third contact yet."

"Very well," Jake answered. He could see them himself, now. At least two ships: the first in line, low on the horizon; the second, behind it, much higher, much larger. "Clem, what's our CPA with the lead ship if we stay put?"

"One thousand yards, Captain."

"One thousand yards, aye. Clem. I want a course to aim the boat and get a zero-angle shot at the lead escort amidships from about seven-five-zero yards. I plan to fire a Mark-Ten at him. Then, right quick, I want to fire a Mark-Fourteen, two-torpedo spread at the cargo ship, and then another Mark-Fourteen at whatever's behind her. Set all the torpedoes to run at five feet deep. Got that?"

Clem understood that Jake was confident he could hit the lead ship with a single shot, but was doubling up on the second because of lack of confidence in the Mark-14s and the firing solution. He had even less confidence in the firing solution for the third ship, but was still willing to "waste" another Mark-14 on the chance of hitting her.

"Yessir, aiming course to hit the lead ship from seven-five-zero yards, along with solutions for the second and third targets in line."

"Correct."

Thirty seconds later, Clem shouted up, "Captain, recommend course zero-eight-nine, speed three. Second target torpedo course zero-nine-two, third target zero-nine-five. I have the third target on the scope now, Captain. It's another destroyer. And the first escort is definitely a *Mutsuki*-class. Looks like that cargo ship has some really important cargo, aboard. I'm thinkin' troop transport, Captain."

"Very well. That sounds about right, if there are two escorts. In that case, Clem, I'm gonna want a firing solution to put a Mark-Ten in that second escort. We'll fire at the first one with a Mark-Ten, the transport with two Mark-Fourteens right afterward, and then come around right to aim the boat at the second escort and hit her with another Mark-Ten. Please tell me we have Mark-Tens in tubes five and six like I ordered."

"Yessir, Captain, that sounds right, but I'll check."

Thirty seconds later. "Wally [Chief Walakurski] reports from the forward torpedo room, Captain, tubes five and six forward are loaded with Mark-Tens as is number ten aft. All other tubes are loaded with Mark-Fourteens, just like you ordered, and all are set to run shallow per your standing order."

"Thank you, Clem, and my apologies to Wally for ever doubting him. And don't forget that firing solution on the second escort."

Clem understood that he wanted the boat's next course on the second Mark-10's torpedo track for a zero-angle shot. "Yessir," he replied.

Now there was nothing to do but wait.

"I'd be willing to bet that maru is a troop transport, Captain, right configuration, and big, I'm guessing about sixty-five hundred tons. The bad news is that the second escort is another *Mutsuki*."

Jake mulled over Clem's report. He could see the three ships clearly in his binoculars, now, silhouetted against the quarter moon. Steaming more or less north, in line, about a thousand yards apart. *Orca* was making bare steerageway, now, Jake keeping the bow pointed on the lead *Mutsuki*, giving as small a visual target to his prey as possible.

Clem again. "Recommend coming left to zero-eight-eight, Captain. We're coming up on showtime!'

"Come left to zero-eight-eight. Open the outer doors forward. Ready torpedoes in tubes one, two, five, and six."

The Helmsman, Quartermaster Striker—QMSN—Henry Coons, "Coming left to course zero-eight-eight."

And, seconds later, from Clem, "Forward torpedo room reports forward outer doors open, and torpedoes ready in one and two, and in five and six."

Then. "Steering zero-eight-eight."

"On target for first contact, Captain, torpedo run seven-five-zero yards, TDC has solution for second target, zero-nine-three, torpedoes spread two degrees left and right, torpedo run seven-eight-zero."

"Very well. Fire five."

The boat pulsed as compressed air forced water from the torpedo impulse tank to enter the tube, pushing the torpedo out of the flooded tube in a slug of seawater. A lever in the tube tripped the propulsion start; the torpedo would arm itself once it had cleared *Orca* by three hundred yards. Again, before a bubble of compressed air could escape the tube and give away the firing boat's location, the poppet valve on the tube opened up, venting the air back into the boat, and again flooding the tube with sea water. Once the tube was filled with water, the valve closed.

Once again, just like clockwork.

"Fire tubes one and two."

Two more pulses, the process repeating on tubes one and two. This time, the gyroscopes in the Mark-14 torpedoes set to gyro angles fed to them from the torpedo data computer in the control room.

Clem again. "Sonar reports three torpedoes running hot, straight, and normal. Recommend coming right to zero-nine-six. Third target torpedo run eight-one-zero yards"

"Come right to zero-nine-six."

"Coming right to zero-nine-six." Then, after what seemed to Jake to take forever, "Steering course zero-nine-six."

Almost simultaneously with the helmsman's report, there was an enormous explosion to port as the lead *Mutsuki* went up in a column of fire and water. Not allowing himself to be distracted, Jake shouted, "Fire six!" The satisfying lurch from forward told him his order had been heard and executed. "Shut outer doors forward."

The second *Mutsuki*, seeing her sister ship practically disappear, turned sharply left toward her tormentor's torpedo wakes and kicked her screws up to full speed, just in time to see

Orca's torpedo pass close aboard down her starboard side. Almost lost in the ensuing commotion was the "Outer torpedo doors forward shut, Captain," as Jake ordered

"Right full rudder, full speed ahead!"

Jake barely heard the helmsman's response "Rudder right full, Sir!" when he glanced down at the pelorus and quickly estimated a course to put the *Mutsuki* dead astern.

"Steer course two-six-zero."

"Coming to course two-six-zero, Sir." The boat was slow in the turn, even with the four diesels straining.

"Open the outer doors aft! Make tube ten ready! Clear the bridge!"

The lookouts and Phillips scrambled below as Jake peered aft, eyeing the pursuing destroyer, placing it in his mind's eye dead astern. He aligned the Pelorus scope to aim at the destroyer. He couldn't actually visually aim the scope, the periscope shears obscured the view, so his best guess would have to be good enough. Reading the relative bearing, he instinctively did the math in his head and refined his order to the helmsman. "Make your course two-six-three."

"After torpedo room reports outer doors open, tube ten ready," shouted Clem from the conning tower. Knowing exactly what Jake was planning, he also reported, "Range to second *Mutsuki*, seven-zero-zero yards and closing"

"Steering course two-six-three, Captain"

Jake confirmed that the destroyer was now dead astern, and ordered, "Fire ten!"

This time no firing pulse was felt as *Orca* surged forward at full throttle. Jake prayed that the torpedo would have the 300 yards travel required to arm itself before reaching its target. At a torpedo speed of forty knots, Jake knew that it would take just over thirteen seconds to cover that distance. He forced himself to count slowly to thirteen. Nothing. The destroyer was still bearing down on *Orca*, devouring the distance between them, and Jake was certain *Orca* was now doomed. Four seconds later, as the

Mutsuki's bow disappeared with a horrendous blast, the destroyer literally drove herself beneath the sea.

Either both of the Mark-14s missed, or both failed to go off, because the transport was still very much afloat, and now beating its way south back toward Rabaul at what was probably its flank speed of thirteen knots. Jake pictured its radio operator shouting for help from anything at sea or in the air that might save her. As Phillips, LaGrange, Rubidot, Catinella, and Rogers repopulated the bridge, he ordered a course to intercept with the boat still making maximum turns. He also ordered the now empty tubes reloaded with Mark-10s. This would be no easy task.

Reloading tubes at sea was an arduous process at the best of times, and in the best of conditions. It was normally done with the boat submerged and on a predictably even keel. But even with a calm sea, a boat running on the surface at full speed was not exactly a stable platform. The torpedomen forward had to deal with the bow bouncing up and down, and the torpedomen aft had to deal with a gyrating, heaving stern.

First, the flooded tubes had to be drained into the bilges, then the inner doors opened (the inner and outer doors were interlocked with brass rods so that they could not be both opened at the same time), and then the torpedoes manhandled into the tubes with block and tackle and chain hoists. Making matters worse, tubes five and six forward were below the deck plates. Chief Walakurski begged Clem to ask the Captain if he could please load the Mark-10s into tubes one and two because then they would be ready faster, and permission was quickly given.

Tubes one and two were reported loaded with Mark-10s and ready to go just as *Orca* was closing on the transport. Less than an hour had passed since its escorts were scrubbed, and the transport had fled in panic. It was very close to daybreak, and the scene was bathed in an eerie light. Clem was on the periscope, using maximum magnification, near enough now to transcribe the

Japanese characters from the ship's stern, when an amazing thing happened.

The transport stopped, heaved to, and began to put its boats over the side. Jake stopped *Orca* as well, staying well away from the transport. "Search with the active sonar, single ping," Jake ordered. "Let's make sure there are no enemy subs hiding out."

"Aye, aye, Sir," the response came up from the conning tower.

Soon enough, the ping of the active sonar could be heard on the bridge. Later, again from below, the transport. "One contact, Captain, bearing two-four-nine, range eight-five-zero yards."

"Very well," Jake responded.

With Jake's permission, Clem came up to the bridge, leaving Louis Carillo to man the scope. Everyone on the bridge watched as, in apparent good order, the ship was being abandoned. Clem passed the word down for the radar operator to stay alert, especially for aircraft, noting that dead in the water on the surface, they were sitting ducks.

"How many troops do you reckon are aboard her, Captain?" Philips asked.

"Don't know, Squid. Ship that size could hold upwards of five thousand men, not to mention about forty to crew her. Doesn't seem like there's enough room in those boats for near that many."

"No, not hardly," Clem agreed. "And it's getting light. We can't stick around here forever. They surely must have put out a Mayday. Catinella, Rogers, don't you be looking at anything but the horizon."

The two lookouts, caught napping, sheepishly returned their binoculars to the horizon.

Then something else strange happened. Men in uniform suddenly appeared on deck and began firing down into the troops in the boats. "What the hell is that about?" Clem wondered aloud.

"My guess," Jake offered, "Is that those are Jap officers unhappy with the idea of their troops abandoning the ship.

Troops should be willing to gladly die for the Emperor, I guess, regardless of the circumstances."

A man in civilian clothes was then seen being thrown overboard from the ship's bridge. "And that might be the ship's Master, being rewarded for surrendering his ship."

The forward torpedo room sent word up that number two tube had now also been reloaded with a Mark-10.

"What do we do now, Captain? Wait 'til the ship's abandoned? Man the deck guns and get the troops in the water?" Clem asked.

"I don't see as we have much of a choice. But we can't just murder those poor bastards in the water in cold blood — at least *I* can't. On the other hand, it will be broad daylight in a matter of minutes, and we can't just wait around for the ship to empty out and then some Jap plane attacks us."

"That ship has gun turrets mounted aft, Captain," Carillo called up from the conning tower. "Looks like they're manning them."

Jake scanned the ship with his binoculars. Carillo was right. A minute later a shell sailed overhead, landing in the water well clear of the boat. Soon others followed, every one missing them by a wide margin.

"Those Nips can't shoot very well," Phillips volunteered.

"Those are anti-aircraft guns, Squid," Jake replied. "They probably just can't depress them low enough to hit us."

Suddenly, there were pinging sounds, bullets randomly hitting the metal around them. "Small arms fire!"

The men firing at them were probably too far away for any accuracy, but Jake was not about to take any unnecessary chances. "Guess that settles the dilemma — there'll be no waiting around now!" He yelled up to the lookouts, perched on their respective platforms on the periscope shears, "Lookouts, get down from there quick! Get below, now!"

The four lookouts scrambled down from their stations and disappeared down the hatch without a word.

"You too, Squid, Clem, get below!"

"Yessir, Captain." And Phillips cleared the deck; he was eager to get below. Clem, less so.

"You sure you want me below, Captain?"

"Go below, Clem, I need you on the scope. Let me know when we've closed to seven hundred yards. And keep radar on the alert for aircraft!"

Dwyer scrambled down the hatch, returning to the conning tower, just as Jake ordered, "Open the outer doors on tubes three and four. Let's see if the Mark-Fourteens work this time. All ahead slow."

Old habits die hard, and Jake ordered the boat brought around, aiming it directly at the transport, just as he would have done with *S-49*. The men firing small arms at *Orca* were improving their aim as the boat closed, and Jake heard and felt a round whiz close by. *Well, at least now they have less to aim at.*

"Doors open on three and four." And then, "Seven-zero-zero yards to the target, Captain," Clem shouted up from the conning tower.

The boats that were in the water were now frantically pulling away from the transport, the men still being fired on from the deck of the transport, while others were still firing at *Orca*. The port deck gun continued futilely lobbing shells overhead. Not willing to take foolish chances, Jake ducked below the deck coaming, taking advantage of what little cover it provided.

"All Stop. Fire tubes three and four."

The now familiar pulse forward as the two Mark-14 torpedoes swam to their target. The wakes were clearly visible in the dawn light. The men in the boats pointed to the wakes, and the firing from the transport's deck stopped as the men above stared at their approaching doom. Except it wasn't. Two more duds, as sonar reported that the fish audibly struck the ship but failed to detonate.

"Crap, Captain, you seen that?" Clem, on the periscope, exclaimed from the conning tower in amazement.

"Open outer door on tubes one and two," was Jake's only response. "I'm gonna send two fish into that bastard one way or another and make sure it never sails again!"

"Outer doors on tubes one and two open."

"Fire one."

The pulse.

"One away."

Jake noted that the wake placed the torpedo on the target just forward of amidships. The boat was still making bare steerageway. "Right full rudder."

"Rudder is right full"

Jake stood up long enough to confirm *Orca's* swing to the right. He sighted down the pelorus until the boat was aimed at the after quarter of the transport. He yelled, "Fire two!" just as the first torpedo struck forward. This time, the first torpedo was no dud. Neither was the second torpedo.

Orca was now down eight torpedoes, four Mark-14s, all of which had failed to detonate, and four Mark-10s, which had accounted for all three kills. There were seven Mark-14s left aboard, and six Mark-10s. Three Mark-10s were loaded in tubes forward, tube numbers four, five and six. Chief Walakurski had consulted with Clem, arguing that the shorter Mark-10 torpedoes would be easier to load into the lower tubes at sea than Mark-14s, and Jake had agreed. Tubes one, two, and three forward had been reloaded with Mark-14s. That left one Mark-14 and one Mark-10 on the racks forward.

Aft there were still three tubes loaded with Mark-14s, tubes seven, eight and nine. Tube ten had been reloaded with a Mark-10. That left two Mark-10s on the racks aft.

* * * * *

Jake, Clem, Bucky Buckner, Weapons Officer Early Sender, Wally Walakurski, and two torpedomen, TM1 (SS) Clive "Arny" Arnold, and TM2 (SS) Austin Rhodes, sat in the wardroom and discussed the problems with the Mark-14 fish.

"Damn things just aren't reliable," Bucky observed. "Might just as well spit at the targets."

Early let his Chief do all the talking. They had discussed this very thing, and he knew his Chief had some real insights into the Mark-14 and its problems.

"They've had problems ever since we've actually had to use them," Walakurski volunteered. "First they were diving deep and then running too deep. Okay, we can fix that by setting them to run shallow and then they run at the right depth. But those magnetic detonators don't work. Either they fire off the fish too early or they don't go off at all. And the contact detonator ain't much better. Then there's the torpedo's wanting to do a circular run and come back and hit the boat firing it—now ain't that just wonderful?"

"Any idea what causes that, Wally?" Jake asked.

"The circular run?"

"Yes."

"Well, I have my own personal theory on that. It seems to happen only when the course fed to the torpedo requires a large circular correction. My take would be that then the steering mechanism jams, and the fish just continues around in a circle."

"Okay," Jake asked, "and can we stop that, and if so, how?"

"I think I can speak to that," Clem volunteered. "We can probably avoid the problem altogether by not requiring the torpedo to make large course corrections, to aim the boat itself at the target as much as possible. In other words, to fire the fish as much as possible like you normally do Mark-Tens."

"Makes sense," Jake volunteered, and, addressing Arnold and Rhodes, "What do you guys think?"

"Well," Arnold answered, "seems to me if you don't run the mechanism into its stops, it's gotta be less likely to jam." Walakurski and Rhodes nodded in agreement.

"Okay," Jake countered, "then what about the detonators?"

"Let's open up a fish and check," suggested Clem. "I've got a couple ideas, and I think these guys," nodding toward Arnold and Rhodes, "Probably got some of their own."

"Okay. Do it," ordered Jake. "And get back to us as fast as you can. Early and Bucky, this is the most important thing we have on our plate right now. See to it that it gets done

"Aye, aye, Sir!" the COB responded.

Chapter 5

Orca: *First Patrol — 17 February 1943 to 11 March 1943*

A week passed after the events of February 9th. On Wednesday, February 17th, *Orca* was surprised on the surface at night by a Japanese patrol plane. There had been a full moon only four nights earlier, and on this brightly moonlit night the weather was clear and balmy. The port lookout, on the ball, spotted the plane and reported it to the Officer of the Deck. "Plane, Sir, off the port quarter, just above the horizon!"

The OD, Early Sender, turned around and confirmed the sighting. Without hesitation, he cleared the bridge and dived the boat, settling her out at 100 feet. Submerged, *Orca* cleared the area. She surfaced two hours later, resumed the battery charge, and dived again at dawn. Jake wanted to know why the SD radar hadn't detected the plane.

"It was apparently on the fritz, Captain," Bill Salton pleaded, "and there's no way to know if it's not working unless it misses a contact. The electrician trained to maintain it, Gibbons, found a dead vacuum tube and replaced it, and it seems to be fixed — you know, picking up contacts again. But I don't know how you'd ever know it was broken until it actually misses a contact like it did last night."

Jake realized that the SD may well have been down when they were at dead stop on the surface the night they nailed the transport. With no lookouts on the bridge, *Orca* could have easily been surprised from the air.

"Okay, Bill," Jake said, dismissing the penitent ensign and resolving to never again depend solely on a machine if he could help it. Radar, he had always contended, would never replace an alert lookout, and this incident only reinforced his convictions.

Almost daily since their meeting in the wardroom, Jake, Clem, and Bucky had pestered Early and Walakurski for a solution to the Mark-14's detonator problems. Wally would never be hard to find aboard the boat, in any case. Whenever he was off watch, you could always count on his continual presence in the forward torpedo room, the guts of the Mark-14 in the starboard torpedo rack exposed, while he, Arny Arnold, and Austin Rhodes, with Early Sender looking over their shoulders, consulted the engineering drawings in the torpedo manuals. After a few days, Wally became testy, and Jake and Clem let up on him, but Bucky never did. Nor did Jake nor Clem let up on Early.

Jake was in his cabin. It wasn't very big, just a tiny room catty-corner from the wardroom, built into the starboard contour of the pressure hull, just large enough for a bunk, a small desk, an actual closet, and a stainless steel lavatory that drained when it was folded back onto the bulkhead. *But* it was the Captain's alone, shared with nobody else. The XO, after all, shared his cabin with up to three bunkmates—more if they "hot bunked," that is, when two men shared a bunk, one sleeping in it while the other was awake.

Jake heard a knock on the bulkhead outside his doorway, and Chief Walakurski peered his rumpled face in, the COB and Early Sender right behind him.

"I think we can do it, Captain," Walakurski beamed. "I think we can disable the magnetic detonator, and make the contact pistol more reliable." He cradled a large manual in the crook of his right arm.

"Wait. Let me get the XO in on this," Jake replied.

They found Dwyer in the wardroom reading the day's dispatches, and Jake, Early, and the two Chiefs joined him. Walakurski then explained in detail, using diagrams and drawings in the manual, exactly what he and his crew planned to do to bypass the magnetic detonator, and improve the contact pistol's reliability. He gave most of the credit for the fix to TM2 Austin Rhodes, the one person who had been the quietist during their meeting two weeks earlier.

"Well, what do you think, Clem, you're the mechanical genius," Jake baited his XO.

"I don't know about that, Captain, but from where I sit it looks like Rhodes deserves a medal. Hell, all *three* of the torpedo guys do." Walakurski beamed, but if Bucky was pleased, you would never have known it. The COB was like that.

"Okay then, Wally, go to it," Jake said, "and start with the Fourteens in the tubes first."

"Aye, aye, Captain."

On February 24th, Early Sender had reported that all seven of the Mark-14s still aboard had been modified.

On Sunday, February 26th, the boat was submerged in the Bismarck Sea, close to the sea lanes about 125 miles northwest of Rabaul, with Dyaul Island due east. The day was overcast, with visibility about fifteen miles, the sea calm, with only the occasional chop. Sonar reported fast screws approaching from the northeast. The boat was at periscope depth, and the search scope revealed no contacts. Assuming sonar had correctly fixed the direction of the contact, Clem put *Orca* on a course to intercept, and notified Jake. It was about noon when the contact's masts were seen poking over the horizon in the search periscope, and Clem called Jake to the conning tower.

Slowly the ship hove into view. It was clearly a Japanese cruiser, a big one, AOB, or angle-on-the-bow, 15 left.

"We have an enemy heavy cruiser, Captain, range approximately ten thousand yards, angle-on-the-bow fifteen left," Clem reported.

"Pass the word, set battle stations, submerged," commanded Jake.

GQ was sounded throughout the boat. Early Sender manned the TDC. Hal Chapman took his post as the diving officer. Bucky Buckner manned the hydraulic manifold. Lou Carillo was at the chart table in the control room, and Bill Salton was below in Sonar. Jake stayed in the conning tower by Squid Phillips at the plotting table.

Using the manual that illustrated the silhouettes of all the known Japanese Imperial Navy capital ships, the target was identified as a *Takao* class heavy cruiser. With Clem on the attack scope reporting AOBs, bearings, and using the known masthead height of a *Takao* class cruiser, Clem could provide fairly accurate ranges to the target. At the chart table in the control room, Jake was able to evaluate the progress of the attack and coordinate it. Carillo calculated the target's course at 116, speed 28 knots.

With a target making twenty-eight knots and closing fast, things happen quickly. Few minutes would pass between first sighting and a firing opportunity. Just before Jake was ready to take the shot, the target zigged toward. What had been an AOB 40 left at 2,000 yards was now AOB 15 left at 1,600 yards. Clem had been careful not to keep the scope exposed for more than the seven seconds it took to make an observation, but the watch on the cruiser may well have spotted the scope and turned toward it, with the intention of ramming.

Jake had positioned the boat to fire at the cruiser from the bow tubes as it passed, but now, with the boat almost broadside to the target, the greatest chance of a hit was to come right and bring the stern tubes to bear. "Right full rudder, all ahead full," he ordered, bringing the boat into the new firing position.

The new target information was just as quickly fed into the TDC. The boat was about twenty degrees short of being stern to the target, when Jake stopped the turn and slowed back to one-third speed. "Open outer doors aft," he ordered.

Clem had already raised the scope. "Target angle-on-the-bow forty left, range one thousand yards and closing."

Seaman Olds on the sound-powered phones reported, "All outer torpedo doors aft open, Captain."

"I have a firing solution, Captain," Early Sender volunteered from the TDC.

"Get the scope up, Clem," Jake ordered. "Early, I want to stop this guy dead if we can—a spread of three fish, three degrees left, center, and three degrees right—I'm taking no chances."

"Got it, Captain, three left, center, three right."

"Fire seven."

"Seven away."

"Fire eight."

"Eight away."

"Fire nine,"

"Nine away."

"Sonar reports three fish in the water, Captain, running hot, straight, and normal."

"What do you see, Clem?"

"The *Takao* is still coming, Captain, angle-on-the-bow about five-zero left, range seven hundred yards. Wait! He must have spotted the torpedo wakes. He's turning right, and his angle-on-the-bow is opening. It's six-zero left and opening fast to the right . . . we got a hit!"

A second later, the sound of the explosion reached the ship.

"I think I see the wake of another fish passing in front of the bow — that's a miss."

Thirty more seconds passed.

"No sign of the third fish, must have missed or been a dud," offered Clem. "The *Takao* is slowed, but it's still moving. It looks like he's clearing out. I think he's had enough."

With the damaged cruiser leaving the scene, Jake attempted to bring *Orca* about to bring the bow tubes to bear, but the cruiser was still able to make about twenty knots, and was too far away for the shot by the time the boat was in firing position. "Well," Jake reasoned, "maybe he got away, but he'll never forget the day we met!"

Three more torpedoes had been expended, but at least *Orca* had a damaged cruiser to show for them. Jake wondered aloud to Clem if he should have been more conservative with the number of torpedoes he had fired at the individual targets. He ran through the litany of the number of fish he had expended relative to the number of targets they had actually hit.

"You can't argue with success, Jake," Clem answered. "And we'd have been toast if only a single shot had been fired and that single shot had missed, or, even pathetically worse, had been a dud."

There were now four Mark-14s left aboard, and still six Mark-10s. Three Mark-10s were in tubes forward, tubes number four, five and six. Tubes one, two, and three forward still held Mark-14s. One Mark-14 remained on the racks forward.

All the Mark-14s originally aft had been in the tubes, and all were expended. Tubes seven and eight were reloaded with Mark-10s. Tube nine was left empty. Tube ten held a Mark-10. There were no spare torpedoes on the racks aft.

Orca was now forty-one days out of Pearl, and had been on station for twenty-six days. There were ten torpedoes left, and fuel and provisions left for at least another month.

That evening, at dusk, *Orca* had just surfaced and was charging her batteries. Joe Bob Clanton decoded a dispatch from SUBPAC marked "Urgent" that he brought immediately to Jake. The message ordered *Orca* and *USS Seasprite* to proceed at speed to a spot some two hundred miles south-southwest of *Orca's* current position, in the Bismarck Sea, north of New Britain Island, to intercept a Japanese convoy leaving Rabaul and en route to reinforce Japanese bases in New Guinea. The convoy was reported to consist of eight troop transports under escort of as many destroyers and under air cover. Japanese submarines were also reported to be in the area.

Other Allied forces attacking the convoy would consist of land-based aircraft and PT boats. All Allied forces had been cautioned that *Orca* and *Seasprite* would be operating in the area and that no attacks would be made on submarines not positively identified as enemy.

"And you know how much that *last* particular directive is worth," was Clem's comment on reading the dispatch. "We had damn well better watch our asses, because nobody will be doing it for us." Jake nodded in solemn agreement. "And I wonder how SUBPAC can be so precise," Clem continued. "I mean, how do they know there will be exactly *eight* transports and *eight* destroyers? Why not *six*, or *nine*? How in blazes do they know?"

"Beats me," Jake admitted. "Maybe they have observers ashore, or something, who knows? The important thing is that they found out somehow, and now we're going to stop 'em."

What neither man could have known was that Navy code breakers had broken the Japanese Naval code, and decrypted the dispatch from IJN command that had set the convoy in motion.

Orca went onto a propulsion charge. This meant that she ran her diesels (all four main propulsion and the auxiliary) flat out, with the generators working to charge her batteries, while she headed to her assigned destination with propulsion under battery power, proceeding at ten knots. That way she would arrive a hundred and twenty miles closer to her station as soon as possible, *but* with her batteries fully charged, or very nearly so.

At dawn, *Orca* submerged, continued the transit at five knots, and arrived at her destination on the early afternoon of March 2nd. After a sweep with the search periscope revealed no visible contacts, *Orca's* sonar operator, however, reported multiple contacts extending from bearing 278 through 290, ranging from 11,000 to 17,000 yards.

Clem notified Jake of the sonar contacts and maneuvered the boat to close with them on course 280.

When he could see ships' masts on the horizon, he shouted down the hatch into the control room, "Pass the word, Captain to the conn."

Jake arrived in the conn, and went to the search scope to see for himself. There were now multiple ships' masts in sight. "Crap," he said, "that is a mess! But I have no doubt that that's the convoy we're looking for. Keep on 'em, Clem, and let us know when and *if* you sort 'em out. "

"Roger that, Skipper," Clem replied, returning to the scope.

"Okay. It's broad daylight, so we stay submerged, and don't give any flyboys out there—theirs or even ours—any ideas. Maintain our transit speed. We'll surface tonight as usual, charge up, and then give chase." Jake went below and headed for his bunk to get what sleep he could. It promised to be a long night.

On surfacing after dark, on Jake's orders, *Orca* was put on propulsion charge and set on course to close with the estimated position of the convoy. At 1110, *Orca* sighted two contacts that did not appear to be moving. Approaching closer, Clem identified them as two Japanese destroyers apparently rescuing survivors. "The flyboys must have had a field day," Jake opined.

Jake decided to leave that scene and to instead continue westward to intercept whatever remained of the original convoy. His assumption was that whatever was left of the convoy would still be steaming westbound at about ten knots, still heading for a western base.

What Jake could not have yet known was that the combined U.S. Army and the Royal Australian Air Forces had already routed their Japanese airborne counterparts, and had already sunk four of the transports and three destroyers. The two contacts to the west-southwest were two destroyers, which had remained behind to rescue troops still in the water.

Hours later, her batteries almost fully charged, *Orca* closed on a group of contacts on the surface, which Jake had correctly determined were the remaining elements of the convoy. It was 0042 on March 3rd. The attacking and defending aircraft had apparently long ago retired for the night, as the SD radar showed no air contacts. When *Orca* could maneuver close enough to see anything with the search scope, Clem was able to distinguish and confirm multiple contacts. The closest of these were transports, but at least one was an escort. He assumed there were other contacts out there that he could not see.

There was practically no moon, but the night was clear and visibility was fair, sea calm. Jake closed the boat on silent battery power to where the first of the contacts was barely visible from the bridge, but where *Orca*, being quiet and low in the water, was most likely to go undetected. It was clearly a destroyer, but they were not close enough to tell of what class. Jake decided to open out the range again and make a diesel-powered full-speed end run around the convoy, and then close for a submerged attack. Two and a half hours later, *Orca*, submerged, was in position to attack.

As their targets came into view, Clem, on the search periscope, could see two of the escorting destroyers, one *Fubuki*, a *Mutsuki*, and two of the transports, all bearing south-southwest. The transports, he reported, were much smaller than their earlier kill, only about 1,500 tons, not much larger, really, than their escorts. Their higher freeboard, however, made them only appear larger.

"Line up for a shot at one of the transports," ordered Jake. "If a destroyer gets in the way, so much the better."

They were almost in position for a shot when all hell broke loose. Sonar reported, "Multiple contacts closing fast! Fast screws bearing two-four-seven!"

"We're getting company, Skipper," Clem grunted, as he raised the search periscope and searched on the reported bearing. "Nothing visible, Captain," he said, as he lowered the scope. "Want to try for a sonar fix?"

"No," Jake replied. "We're too close to the destroyers, and even if we only single ping they'll know we're here and stalking them. Damn! I hate to lose a kill! But the last thing we need is to have a possible incoming friendly dropping depth charges on us. We'd best back off and see who our visitors are."

The visitors proved to be a squadron of PT boats, come to wreak havoc among the destroyers and their charges. Jake, not wishing *Orca* to become a target for an errant PT boat, opened to 10,000 yards and listened. He decided to stay submerged until the PT boats were clear, because at this point in the war practically all the PT boats had been equipped with radar, and he preferred that *Orca* remain undetected, even by "friendly" craft.

When the PT boats finally cleared the area, it was almost dawn. The convoy was stopped dead, but all the Japanese contacts still appeared to be afloat. *Orca's* batteries were nowhere near as full as Jake would have liked, but they still had plenty of juice to make it through the day, just so long as they moved very slowly and remained undisturbed.

Orca surfaced again at dusk. Its surface sweeps with both the periscope and, after surfacing, the SD radar had revealed no contacts. Conditions on the surface were pretty much as they had been the night earlier, with visibility only fair. Jake ordered *Orca* to close the scene of the previous night's melee. When they arrived, there were now only four visible contacts; just one appeared to be a transport, and only its bow was above the surface. The other contacts were escorts fishing men out of the water. The Allied air forces, had, apparently, been successfully at work during the day. And now the SD radar (assuming it was still operating properly) indicated that all aircraft had retired for the night. "Let's get a full charge," Jake directed, "and then we can close what's left of the convoy and see what we can see."

The charge had not yet started when sonar reported, "Surface contact approaching, bearing zero-zero-six, range seven thousand yards." Hal Chapman, standing OOD watch, quickly informed the Captain.

Jake made his way to the conning tower, Clem right behind him, and quizzed the sonar operator, an EM3 (SS) from Boulder, Colorado, named James Orsi. "Orsi, how could a contact just suddenly appear, out of nowhere, at seven thousand yards? Is it a really faint sound?"

"No, Captain, it's loud and clear, sounds like diesel and slow screws. And I swear, I had just searched that sector a couple minutes earlier, and there was nothing there."

"You mean a contact just appeared out of nowhere?"

"Well, I *swear* it wasn't there before!"

"Okay. I believe you. What's it doing now?

"Not much of anything, apparently, Captain. Range and bearing are about the same, but maybe it's closing some — not much."

Clem had observed all that had happened. "You thinkin' what I'm thinkin'?"

"Probably. A submarine just surfacing. Charging up, just like we were getting ready to do."

"*Seasprite*, maybe?"

"I doubt it. *Seasprite* is supposed to be on patrol to the north. Her area is miles and miles away.

"Could it be a friendly?"

"Possible — but again not likely. My guess would be a Jap boat, sent out maybe to pick up survivors. Watch and see if she doesn't go on propulsion charge and head south."

Soon thereafter, the contact was tracked heading 187 at nine knots.

"Okay," Jake said, "we keep tracking her by sound. Now that she's making noise herself she won't hear us. Let's us stay on the surface and go on charge as long as possible. If we sit still, she'll be at CPA in about twenty-five minutes. So we don't sit still. We go on propulsion charge ourselves, parallel her course and speed, and give us as much time, and as much in the can, as possible before we begin a submerged attack."

"Sounds about right," Clem agreed. "Are they close enough to smell our diesels?"

"Not likely," Jake responded. "They're pretty far away — *and*, if it *is* a sub, they're probably running their own diesels. Won't hurt to check on the wind direction anyway." He called up to the bridge, "Hal, What's the wind like?"

Hal Chapman, the OOD on the bridge, checked the direction of the diesel smoke. "We're practically standing still, Skipper, and it looks like it's from the north-northwest."

"Great! Thanks, Hal." Jake smiled at Clem, "See, worrywart, not a chance. And even if he gets close, we'll know it's not our smell that will give us away!"

"Just checkin', Skipper."

"Just teasing you, Clem. Your concern was valid enough. I'll bet boats have been lost before by someone not paying attention to the details."

As they ran parallel to the contact's course and speed, they were also approaching the spot where the remnants of the convoy lay. Here and there, objects floating in the inky water passed alongside: sections of wooden grating, some clothing, and a life jacket — the battle's flotsam.

They were also approaching the point where, Jake knew, they would have to line up for an attack on their contact, and they had to do it before they were too close to what was left of the convoy and might invite the inquiry of an enemy destroyer. Here Clem's concern about the diesel fumes was very valid, and, should they get too close, the wind was perfect for carrying the fumes down onto the enemy. He pushed Clem for a firing solution.

"Contact's still on course one-eight-seven, and making nine knots. If we dive now and come right, slow to three knots, she should pass us to starboard at seven hundred yards in about twenty minutes, Captain."

"Good. Make it so."

Clem shouted up to the bridge, "Hal, dive the boat!"

A split second later, the Claxon sounded *Ah-oo-gah, ah-oo-gah,* and "Dive! Dive!" was passed through the boat over the 1MC. The lookouts scrambled down the conning tower hatch, followed closely by the OOD, who pulled the hatch lanyard behind him, holding the hatch closed while the quartermaster of the watch scrambled up the ladder, and twirled the wheel, operating the dogs that engaged to lock the hatch shut. The lookouts, meanwhile, had dropped down the next ladder to the control room, where two of them stopped to man the diving planes. The bow diving planes, tucked up into the hull when the boat was on the surface, were rigged out with the turn of a hydraulic valve handle, positioning them like outspread wings on the bow, control surfaces set to a "down" angle to drive the bow beneath the waves. The after diving planes, clustered with the boat's rudder, were moved to an "up" angle to lift the stern of the boat and help angle the entire boat downward for the dive. Hal Chapman meanwhile had followed the lookouts down the control room ladder where he took control of the dive.

His Chief of the watch, EMC Bob Lione, reported "Green board, Sir!" as he hit the control room deck—advising that the indicator board above the hydraulic manifold showed all green lights, meaning that all the hull openings (such as the hatches and the 36-inch main induction valve, through which the boat gulped air) were shut and all the ballast tank vents were open.

"Very well," Hal responded, verifying for himself that the board was green, and that the planesmen had the bow and stern planes on full dive. "Shut the vents," he ordered. Lione shut the ballast tank vents.

From the conning tower, Dwyer ordered, "Make your depth six-zero feet." (Periscope depth.)

"Six-zero feet, aye, Sir," Hal responded. Then to the planesmen, "Ten degrees down bubble. Make your depth six-zero feet." Once it was clear the boat was headed down, Hal ordered, "Blow negative to the mark." Lione opened the valve that let compressed air into negative tank. He adroitly shut it just as the tank level indicator showed the tank level was approaching the "mark," the set level that was actually marked with a black line on the tank level indicator gauge.

"Negative blown to the mark," he reported. As the boat came to ordered depth, the planesmen eased off on their planes, manipulating them so as to settle the boat at sixty feet.

"At six-zero feet, Sir," Chapman called up to the conning tower, and then "Cycle the vents," to Lione, who operated each of the ballast tank vents in turn, opening and shutting them again, making sure that no air bubbles were trapped in the tanks. A trapped air bubble would squeeze with the pressure if the boat dived deeper, allowing an unplanned slug of water into the tanks, throwing the boat off trim.

"Vents cycled, Sir."

General quarters was sounded, and the word passed, "Battle stations, submerged." Since Hal's GQ station was as diving officer, he simply stayed put, while Bucky Buckner relieved Lione at the hydraulic manifold. Throughout the boat, others scrambled to their GQ stations.

In the conning tower, Clem manned the search periscope. First he swept the horizon, and, finding no surprises, concentrated on the sector in which the target was expected to appear. "See anything yet, Clem?" Jake questioned.

"No, Captain, nothing yet."

Seaman Robert Olds sang out, "Sonar reports twin screws closing, bearing zero-zero-one."

"Very well. Can you give a sonar bearing and estimated range?"

Again Olds sang out, "Sonar reports contact bearing three-five-nine, estimated range six thousand yards."

"Very well. Clem, keep looking." Jake called down to the plotting table. "What do you figure, Lou?" he asked.

"Based on sonar's estimate, target course now one-eight-eight, speed nine knots." Lou Carillo said. Early Sender, at the TDC, used the information to update his firing solution.

"Very well," Jake responded, and then settled down to wait for a periscope observation. "Give me a course to intercept the target if our speed is three knots."

"Recommend course two-two-three, Captain." Carillo responded, calling up from the control room, having already anticipated Jake's request. Clem, who had been working on a maneuvering board solution, nodded in agreement.

"Steer course two-two-three, make turns for three knots," Jake ordered.

From the helm in the conning tower, Henry Coons responded, "Coming right to course two-two-three," as Robert Olds relayed the ordered speed to maneuvering over the sound-powered phones.

Soon, Olds, the phone talker, announced, "Maneuvering room reports making turns for three knots, Captain."

"Very well," Jake acknowledged.

Coons followed quickly with "Steering two-two-three, Captain."

"Very well. Let's see what we can see, Clem."

Again Clem raised the search scope. Another sweep around, and then, concentrating on the place where the target should appear, "I think this is him, Captain, but I can barely see him. Bearing, mark!"

"Squid" Phillips read the number from the scope's bezel, "Three-four-eight."

"No range, yet." Clem reported, as he lowered the scope.

Carillo, on the chart table, updated his plot, as Early Sender did the same in the TDC. Carillo quickly reported, "No change in target course and speed — still one-eight-eight, nine knots. Range should be forty-eight hundred yards."

Jake addressed the phone talker in the conning tower, "Olds, tell sonar to single-ping this guy and get a range. He's on the surface, and with his diesels running, he'll never hear it."

Seconds later, an audible ping was heard, and then, "Sonar reports single-ping range to contact, forty-seven hundred yards, Captain, bearing three-four-eight."

"At nine knots, he advances three hundred yards along his track every minute," Jake mused. "You should be able to make something out pretty quick, Clem." Dwyer nodded in agreement.

A minute later. "Up scope." Clem, still on the search periscope. Squid raised the scope, and Clem rode it up to the surface. "Here he comes, Captain. Definitely a sub. Pouring out diesel smoke. Looks like he's really moving. AOB left ten. Bearing, mark!"

"Three-four-five."

"He's sped up, Captain, can't say for sure without another fix, but if he's held course, it looks like around sixteen knots," Carillo yelled out from below.

"Crap," Jake and Clem muttered in unison. "Single-ping range," Jake again ordered.

"Up scope." The attack scope this time. "See him good, Captain, AOB left one-five. Looks like a B-One or a B-Two. Can't miss that seaplane hangar forward of the bridge. Bearing, Mark!"

"Three-four-four"

"Sonar reports range forty-five hundred yards, bearing three-four-four, Captain."

"Bastard's doing seventeen knots," Carillo volunteered.

"He's finished charging his batteries, and making max turns to get to the convoy. I need a firing solution, people!" Jake lamented, as Clem dialed in the mast height for a B-1 submarine on the attack scope stadimeter.

Use of the stadimeter required first estimating (or *knowing*, if the class of the ship was known) the height of the target's superstructure. Then, by twisting the periscope handle, the operator could optically bring the top of the target's superstructure down to the waterline of the target, and a range could be read from an indicator on the periscope.

Seconds passed quickly. "Up scope. AOB left two-five. Bearing, mark! Range, mark!"

"Bearing three-three-eight, range thirty-four hundred."

"Down scope."

More seconds. Carillo: "Target course one-eight-eight, speed one-seven. Recommend coming left to two-two-zero. Make turns for five knots." Jake made it so.

"How does the TDC look, Early?"

"Good, Captain. Current torpedo track one thousand yards for a straight shot, or seven hundred yards on torpedo course two-four-two. Two point three minutes to go." Squid set the stopwatch.

"Open outer doors forward. I'm taking no chances. All three Mark-Fourteens at this target. Spread three degrees left, center, three degrees right." Early repeated the order.

I hate having to use almost all my Mark-Fourteens on this SOB, Jake thought. *But his sudden burst of speed leaves me little choice. Well, from now on until we're back in port, I guess every shot will just have to be a straight shot.*

"Forward outer doors open, Captain."

"Up scope," Clem ordered. He did a quick sweep around, saw nothing, and then sat on the target. "AOB left five-zero. Bearing, mark! Range, mark!"

"Bearing three-three-one, range nineteen hundred."

Clem left the scope up. "AOB is opening fast, Captain, now left six-zero."

"Coming up on time, Captain." Squid announced, and then, "Time"

"Fire one," Jake ordered. The boat lurched as the torpedo was pulsed from the tube.

"One away," Early responded.

"Fire two."

"Two away, spread left three degrees."

"Fire three."

"Three away, spread right three degrees."

Almost thirty seconds on the dot from the launch of the first torpedo, Clem, glued to the attack scope, let out a whoop. "Bingo!" he shouted, just as the shock wave from the explosion hit *Orca*. Seconds later, Clem whooped again, and another shock wave followed. Then nothing. The final torpedo either missed, which was probable, or it struck but failed to detonate. Not that it mattered. The target sank in a matter of minutes.

"Sonar reports breaking up noises, and fast screws approaching from bearing one-eight-eight!" Olds reported.

Clem swung the scope around to his left. "Holy Crap! We're in for it now! There's a destroyer coming on fast! Down scope!"

"Shut the outer doors forward." Jake ordered. *First things first.*

In this situation, a submarine commander would instinctively turn in whatever direction would let him clear the area fastest. In *this* situation, that would mean coming hard right. In his mind, Jake had put himself in this position many times. Now he was going to see if the strategy he had devised would work. "Left full rudder. All ahead full, make your depth one-zero-zero-feet."

"Maneuvering reports 'all ahead full,' Captain." Olds sang out.

"Sonar reports at least two torpedoes in the water, Captain, bearings one-eight-five and one-eight-eight," Olds then reported. Jake gave a sigh of relief; *Orca* was turning away from the torpedo tracks, and they should pass well astern.

"Passing two-four-zero," Henry Coons on the helm reported.

"Passing eight-zero feet, Captain, on way to one–zero-zero feet," Hal Chapman reported from the control room.

To each of these reports Jake responded, "Very well." Then he ordered, "Make your course two-two-five." Jake planned to pass almost on top of the kill.

"Steady at one-zero-zero feet, Captain."

"Very well."

"Sonar reports torpedoes passed well astern. Fast screws still approaching, and much closer now."

"Single-ping the destroyer. I want a range."

Coons: "Passing two-three-five."

A sonar ping resounded throughout the boat. Seconds later: "Sonar reports contact bearing one-nine-zero, range fifteen hundred yards."

"Passing three-three-zero, coming to course two-two-five."

"Pass the word, 'Rig for depth charge.'"

Watertight doors were shut between compartments, and all ventilation secured. The cooks had already secured the crockery as best they could. "Make your depth two-zero-zero feet," Jake ordered.

"Two-zero-zero feet, aye," Hal Chapman acknowledged, and then ordered his planesmen, "Fifteen degrees down bubble, make your depth two-zero-zero feet."

"Steady on course two-two-five."

"Passing one-four-zero feet, Sir"

The first two depth charge blasts went off on the boat's starboard quarter, a good two hundred yards behind the boat, perhaps, but still jarring everyone's teeth. The shock waves from them and two successive blasts lifted *Orca*'s stern. The boat was still at full-submerged speed, and the boat drove itself down. In no time the boat was passing two hundred feet and was still heading down.

Depth charges by themselves do not have enough explosive force to blast open the pressure hull of a submarine. Only by exploding close enough to the boat do they create enough of a shock wave in the water to crack and breach the pressure hull, causing the surrounding sea to enter the boat at whatever pressure there is at a particular depth.

At 200 feet, for example, the pressure is 104 pounds per square inch (psi), or almost 90 psi over the pressure inside the boat. Water entering a breached pressure hull under that much of a pressure differential can quickly fill the boat. The only defense would be to quickly seal off the breach, or, *in extremis*, the compartment could be sealed off and pressurized, staunching, even reversing the flow at shallow depths. In such an instance, however, any personnel inside the compartment would be sealed inside the compartment. They could be rescued only if circumstances (such as surfacing the boat, or effectively sealing the breach) allowed the pressure inside the sealed compartment to be relieved.

An unstoppable breach at two hundred feet would almost certainly eventually be fatal to any personnel inside a sealed compartment, and, of course, any seawater leaking into the battery compartments would create chlorine gas, and then the only way to save the crew would be to surface.

"Passing two-zero-zero feet and still going down, Captain," Chapman shouted out, the unflappable Chapman's tone calm and matter-of-fact.

Taking a cue from Chapman, Jake forced himself to remain calm. "All stop. All back full."

Another depth charge went off, and then another. These, thankfully, were further astern and to port, but they were still very much felt. The boat slowly pulled out of its dive, but not until it had passed 280 feet.

"Boat settling out, Captain," Chapman reported with the air of a disinterested observer. "Our depth is two-eight-five feet."

"Very well. Tell me when we've stopped going down." Jake had the word passed, "Were there any damage reports?" No damage was reported beyond a few shattered light bulbs and a cracked gauge glass.

"We've stopped now, Captain," Chapman called up to the conning tower, just as another depth charge went off—still astern, but this time to starboard. Jake felt that this time the blast was much closer, but convinced himself that it may have only felt that way. "We're at two-eight-zero feet, Captain!"

Jake maintained an outward calm, belying what he felt inside. "Very well. All stop. All ahead slow. Steady out at two-eight-zero feet, if you can, Hal."

"Aye, Captain, two-eight-zero feet." The planesmen fought the planes to maintain depth.

Another two depth charges, this time decidedly further away, but still jarring *Orca* with their blasts.

After three hours, the destroyer finally gave up the chase, but by that time *Orca* was nowhere near its search area. The crew had counted a total of eighteen depth charges. When it was well into the morning hours of March 5th, Jake brought the boat slowly up to 150 feet and ordered a sonar sweep. Sonar could hear no contacts. Jake brought the boat up to 100 feet, and ordered another sonar sweep. Again, nothing. Finally, he ordered the boat to periscope depth and had Clem do a sweep with the search scope. Still nothing. No contacts.

Finally, satisfied they were alone, Jake ordered the crew to secure "Rig for depth charge," and stand down from general quarters. A very damp, hot, and stinky crew was overjoyed to have ventilation restored throughout the boat. The batteries had been severely depleted, but Jake elected to still remain submerged at dead slow, with all unnecessary machinery secured, until nightfall. He didn't have to tell any crewmembers not on duty to stay in their bunks.

Jake had read somewhere that the German subs, now being successfully countered by the radars and the sonars of the Allied antisubmarine forces in the Atlantic, were being fitted with breathing devices called *schnörchels*, which allowed submerged boats to suck in air from the surface for their diesels while still submerged. Jake wished he had a *schnörchel* now, so that he could safely charge his batteries during the day.

Orca now had seven torpedoes left: four forward and three aft. The one remaining Mark-14 forward was loaded into tube one. Tubes two and three were empty, as was number nine tube aft. The remaining six tubes carried Mark-10s and there were no torpedoes left in any of the racks.

Orca's COB had joined the submarine force originally on the word that submarines were known throughout the fleet as the best feeders afloat. The Navy Department apparently decided that the deprivations suffered by submarine crews, especially submarine crews at sea, should be offset by providing submariners with the best fare possible. Even after the fresh milk and eggs, and the fresh fruit and vegetables ran out, there was still a full larder of canned goods, and a freezer well stocked with steaks and roasts, butter, and plenty of ice cream. Only at the end of patrol, with provisions running low, did the quality of the food served aboard suffer. The boats' tiny galleys and excellent cooks baked fresh bread, pies, and cakes daily, turned out fine meals three times a day, and prepared a "midrats" (midnight rations) spread of cold cuts, cheese, fresh rolls, and other goodies for the midnight watch that would do a five-star hotel proud.

And there was also an "open galley" aboard. This meant that any crewman, whenever he was off-duty and felt like it, could browse through the larder and help himself. It was not unusual to see a shipmate in the galley frying himself a steak for a between-meal snack.

Beverages consisted of gallons of coffee; milk when it was available; fresh lemonade; and "bug" juice, a sweet, fruit-flavored drink made by mixing packets of powder with water. But even in submarines, the U.S. Navy was a prohibition navy, and no alcoholic beverages were served. The only booze aboard (officially) was medicinal brandy, locked tightly up in the pharmacist mate's locker, and inventoried monthly by the XO, every drop accounted for.

It was during the wee hours of March 5th, and *Orca* approached the site where the remnants of the convoy were last observed. The SD radar showed no contacts, and neither did passive sonar. There was debris everywhere in the still black water, and floating bodies. At least a hundred corpses were visible from the bridge, and the night was dark, with only a sliver of light from the moon. Apparently the flyboys had been very successful. A pall of sick depression fell over *Orca* and her crew as they cleared the scene. This may have been victory, but her face was terrible to behold.

The Battle of the Bismarck Sea had indeed been an Allied victory. The Japanese convoy headed to reinforce their western outpost at Lae had been completely routed by Allied land-based air forces. Of the eight transports and eight escorts that had departed from Rabaul, all eight of the transports and four of the destroyers had been sunk. Of the 6,900 troops being transported, only about 1,200 ever eventually made it to Lae. Another 2,700 were rescued and returned to Rabaul.

At dawn, *Orca* was heading west; Lou Carillo had just finished taking morning stars for a fix, and he and his quartermaster, Squid Phillips, had just left the bridge. The SD radar was operating. The boat was scheduled to dive for the day in just a few minutes, when a lone Republic P-47 Thunderbolt fighter approached the boat from due south. The plane was approaching the boat end-on and almost invisible until it was on top of *Orca,* and the port lookout screamed out its presence. Bill Salton had the bridge, and was reaching for the diving alarm in a panic when the plane passed directly overhead, wagging its wings in salute. Luckily its pilot was able to distinguish between American and Japanese submarines.

Relieved, Salton first berated the radar operator, James Orsi, for his gross inadequacy in the most unkind terms, and then immediately reported the incident to Jake, noting that the intruder was now well clear of the boat and headed north.

"Is he on the SD now?" Jake asked.

"Wait one, Skipper, I'll check." Salton relayed Jake's question to Orsi, who responded that the SD radar screen was completely blank, and has been for the entire watch. Salton relayed the information to Jake.

"Okay. The SD must be on the blink again. Have the XO get Joe Bob on it. Meanwhile, take her down for the day." Jake muttered under his breath that the SD wasn't good for much, and hadn't been for the entire patrol. Then Orsi passed the word up that the SD had suddenly come back on line again and clearly showed the retreating P-47.

* * * * *

Hiriake Ito stood on the bridge of his command and looked out on the waters of the Bismarck Sea, just north of Kimbe, on the Island of New Britain. The sea was choppy, and the sky overcast, with only occasional glimpses of a half moon, and a swift tropical breeze blowing from the northeast. His ship, *IJN Atsukaze*, a *Fubuki* class destroyer, was commissioned in 1931, and was modified and upgraded in 1938. *Atsukaze* was armed with six, 127mm, 50 caliber guns; eight torpedo tubes; and thirty-six depth charges. *Atsukaze* could make thirty-eight knots, but on this evening of March 10, 1943, she was cruising alone at a mere eight.

Just a week earlier, *Atsukaze* had been one of eight destroyers escorting a convoy of eight transports out of Rabaul on their way to reinforce the Japanese garrison at Lae, on New Guinea. They had just cleared the headland on the northeast tip of New Britain and were steaming west when the convoy was attacked by American and Australian aircraft. Their own air cover fought bravely, but they were vastly outnumbered, and, ultimately, defense of the squadron was left up to the guns of the escorts. By the end of that first day, March 2nd, the enemy had sunk four of the transports and three of the escorting destroyers. Worse, there were at least 1,500 troops from the sunken transports in the water. The convoy commander ordered *Atsukaze* and another escort, *IJN Harukazi*, to remain behind to rescue survivors while the remainder of the convoy continued west. By the end of the next day, the two destroyers had plucked 1,642 men from the sea, many of whom were badly burned, and returned them to Rabaul.

Hiriake Ito was a *Kaigun Chusa,* or a Commander, in the Imperial Japanese Navy, and had served as Captain of *Atsukaze* since September 1940. He stood 165 cm, or five feet, five inches, tall, and was slightly built. His face was lean and pockmarked, evidence of childhood smallpox. He had piercing eyes, brown, almost black, and he had only to purse his thin lips and glare at an underling to strike terror deep within him. But, if he was strict and demanding, he was also fair, and had earned absolute obedience and respect from every man aboard.

Ito was a graduate of the fifty-third class of the Imperial Japanese Naval Academy at Etajima in 1925, and had served as a surface warfare instructor, and as second in command of the destroyer *IJN Sigure.* Ito was married, a devoted husband and a loving, if stern, father of four children, two sons and two daughters. His sons, at 13 and 9, were too young as yet to serve the Emperor in the military, a career for which Ito had been indoctrinating them since birth. His wife and family lived in the naval port city of Yokosuka.

Apparently, in the wee hours of March 4th, an American submarine had sunk a Japanese boat, *IJN I-36,* which had been en route to rescue survivors.

Earlier that day, enemy aircraft had again intercepted the convoy as it headed west and had sunk the remaining transports and another destroyer, and there were more men in the water. The two remaining destroyers were conducting rescue operations. One of the destroyers, *IJN Kagero,* had been in contact with *I-36* and was on the lookout for her when her captain witnessed the explosions that sank the boat and gave chase to the attacking submarine. *Kagero* expended all but seven of her thirty-six depth charges, but failed to destroy her submerged prey. Her stock of depth charges depleted, and the enemy sub apparently having escaped, *Kagero* returned to the rescue operation.

Now Ito and *Atsukaze* were searching for that submarine, and he had a weapon that might just give him the edge.

At this point in the war, Japanese destroyers had no radar or active sonar. But they did have radio direction finding equipment, as did Japanese submarines. An enterprising RDF operator had discovered that American submarines cruising on the surface emitted a continuous radio signal—probably from their radar set—that RDF could intercept. And, Ito knew, enemy submarines, indeed all subs, typically surfaced at night to charge batteries, and typically stayed on the surface until dawn, when they submerged, and remained submerged, during the day.

Ito found it ironic, and very amusing, that the very equipment that the submarine was depending upon to keep her safe from discovery while surfaced was the very equipment that would betray her. He also knew how radar worked. It depended upon on the signal being sent out from a ship, and then a portion of the signal bouncing off its target and *returning* to its sender at sufficient strength for the contact to be detected. If the return signal is too weak, the contact goes undetected, and an unreflected signal merely continues on its course until it dissipates. Radar, therefore, had an effective range.

Ito reasoned that the radar signal emitted from a radar set aboard the submarine that was capable of detecting his own vessel would be useless if he kept his ship outside its effective range. But, using his RDF, he could detect the radar signal without himself being detected. Continued observations could be analyzed to enable him to determine the submarine's range, course and speed. And if he knew where the boat was, it could be attacked. (He could not know that the radar aboard American submarines at that time had only air search, and no surface search capability, but that actually made no difference—using his RDF he could still use the SD radar signal to pinpoint the boat's location.)

But there was, he incorrectly reasoned, another problem. If *Atsukaze* closed for the attack, the submarine's radar would detect her before she came near enough to do any damage, and submerge. Then, if *Atsukaze* remained in the area, she might herself become the target. But he had a solution around that problem.

Ito's solution was the submarine *IJN I-29*. With his ship in radio contact with *I-29*, Ito could vector the boat on the surface outside the target's radar range to a location where the submarine could submerge and lie in wait to intercept, and destroy, the enemy.

* * * * *

By March 10th, *Orca* had been at sea for fifty-eight days. She had spent the day, as usual, submerged, and perhaps unconsciously, Jake had set the boat's course north-northwest. *Orca* had racked up four kills: two destroyers, a transport, and one submarine, and had damaged a heavy cruiser. Food supplies were running low, and *Orca* had just switched suction to her last two fuel tanks. If they remained on this course, they had only to run another 300 miles from their current position, clear Latangai and New Hanover Islands, turn right between Hanover and tiny Emriau Island, and Pearl would be a straight shot to the east-northeast. If they left as soon as they surfaced the boat that evening, *Orca* could be back at Pearl comfortably, starting from their current position in the South Bismarck Sea, in another sixteen days. Jake decided that seventy-four days on patrol was plenty, and it was time to head for the barn.

* * * * *

Of course, Ito also understood that everything had to be in his favor. He, first, had to detect the enemy submarine on the surface, far enough away so that *Atsukaze* would not herself be detected. So, too, would *I-29* have to be close enough to be able to close the target, attain intercept position, and still be outside her target's radar range when she submerged.

As it turns out, that Wednesday, March 10th evening, and through the early morning hours of Thursday, March 11th, his ancestors were smiling upon Hiriake Ito.

* * * * *

Orca surfaced at dusk. Sonar had heard nothing all day. The searches prior to surfacing with the search periscope and sonar had revealed no contacts. The sea was choppy, and the sky overcast, with only occasional glimpses of a half moon, and a stiff tropical breeze blowing from the northeast. It was a good night for running north-northeast on propulsion charge, and, once the charge was complete, running flat out on the diesels. That way, even with spending the daylight hours of March 11th submerged, by this time tomorrow night they would be in position to turn the boat east-northeast for her run to Pearl. Her SD radar set was turned on. No contacts. *Seasprite* was probably on the surface somewhere in the area as well, but outside of a visual contact, there was no way of knowing for sure without breaking radio silence

* * * * *

At 2213 on March 10th, the RDF operator aboard *Atsukaze* reported a contact 23 km away to the northwest. As fortune would have it, Ito was in contact with *I-29's* commander, *Kaigun Shosa*, or Lieutenant Commander, Emi Hideo, whose boat was 32 km away to the northeast, and 40 km from the contact. Hideo also fixed the contact with his boat's RDF gear, and between his and *Atsukaze's* initial and subsequent fixes exactly determined the contact's course 290 and speed at seven knots. It only remained for *I-29* to do an end-around at speed on the surface and outside the target's radar range, submerge in position, and lie in wait. Running flat out, *I-29's* two-shaft diesel could propel her at 23

84

knots. At that speed, she could advance 43 km every hour, and she could be in position to attack by midnight.

* * * * *

The oncoming OOD had just relieved the watch, as was the custom throughout the Navy, fifteen minutes prior to the actual beginning of his watch. Before coming on watch, he had stopped in the crew's mess for midrats, and had his fill of fresh-baked rolls, cold cuts and cheese. The boat was still headed 290, on propulsion charge, and making seven knots. The sea was choppy, but the overcast sky was starting to clear, and a half moon was now bright, even with the wispy clouds. The wind had shifted, and was blowing from the north, but it was still stiff. The oncoming radar watch had just reported no contacts on either sonar or the SD radar.

Everything appeared to be in order, and the OOD was settling in for a quiet midwatch, when both starboard lookouts screamed and pointed at the torpedo wakes headed straight for the boat. But by then it was too late.

Chapter 6

Pearl Harbor: 25 March 1943 to 7 May 1943

After passing Midway en route to Pearl, Jake tried several times to raise Chet Adams on HF radio. No luck. He hoped that it only meant *Seasprite* was out of radio range.

Orca received a hero's welcome at Pearl Harbor on March 25th, 1943, having successfully completed her first war patrol. The squadron commander, Captain Clarence Macdonough, and his staff were in the crowd greeting the submarine, and Macdonough was the first person to come aboard to greet captain and crew as soon as the boat was tied up and a brow put over by the shore-side line handlers.

"One hell of a first patrol, Jake," Macdonough beamed as he pumped Jake's hand. "The admiral would have met your boat himself, but he's in this big meeting with Spruance. I'm sure you'll be summoned to the presence soon!"

"Thank you, Commodore," Jake said. "We were pretty fortunate — right place at the right time. We were also very lucky, a couple of times, to escape with our tails intact."

Jake, Clem, Macdonough and two of his staff then went down into the wardroom, where the commodore debriefed *Orca's* commander and his XO. Jake was quick to unload onto his squadron commander the problems he had experienced, especially concerning unreliable torpedoes.

"You appear, Jake, to have joined a large club of submarine skippers where the torpedoes are concerned. When you make your official patrol report to the admiral I'm sure he'll want to hear your comments," Macdonough assured Jake.

When a submarine comes back from a war patrol, a relief crew takes over the boat while the regular crew enjoys rest and recreation—R & R. In reality, the boat's regular officers, while entitled to enjoy accommodations at the Royal Hawaiian along with the boat's enlisted personnel, usually preferred to stay at the BOQ and oversee the boat's refit. The boat's chief petty officers and other petty officers frequently shared the same sense of duty, and preferred barrack's accommodations. That is not to say that these officers and petty officers didn't party at the Royal Hawaiian on a regular basis while their boats were in port.

Orca moved the next day to her permanent (for this stay) berth. As soon as the boat had tied up she went into refit. The Navy had upgrades to equipment that had to be installed, and *Orca* would also be getting an improved sonar fathometer, and some other new gear—like an SJ surface radar.

The base offloaded all the remaining six, Mark-10 torpedoes. There was an S-Boat scheduled to leave for patrol shortly, and they were to be transferred to her. It seems, as ridiculous as that sounds, the Navy was short of torpedoes.

Jake had to fight hard to keep his remaining Mark-14. It had been unofficially modified, and he was understandably reluctant to return it to the torpedo stockpile. Jake ordered the inner door to number one torpedo tube padlocked, and kept the only key.

Later in the day Jake received word that he was expected in Rear Admiral Lockwood's office. The "invitation" was for 1400 the following day.

Jake arrived at the admiral's office at 1400 sharp, dressed in his best work khakis and his shoes spit-shined. He was escorted into the admiral's presence two minutes later by the admiral's aide, his old skipper from *S-49*, Harry Loveless. Jake had had only enough time to smile broadly, give Loveless a quick greeting, and shake his hand before Loveless turned him over to the admiral and retreated from his office.

"Uncle Charlie" was a man of medium height, medium build, and with a completely unremarkable appearance. His close-cropped hair was a white-flecked dark brown, and he had a receding hairline. He had a long, straight nose and an oval face that was neither handsome nor ugly. He was not yet 53 years old, but Jake would have guessed he was a few years younger. In appearance, then, Rear Adm. Charles Lockwood was an entirely unimpressive man—*until* he opened his mouth. And then it became obvious why he completely deserved his two stars, and was destined for even greater things.

"Commander Lawlor!" Lockwood sidled up to Jake, put his arm around his shoulder, and took his hand. "Your old skipper has been telling me great things about you, not that he had to. Four kills on your first patrol! And one of them a Jap sub! Very impressive. I'm putting you in for a Navy Cross."

Jake fought off the urge to grin. It took a real effort to keep a serious face. "Thank you, Admiral."

"Sit down, Jake, and tell me all about it."

Lockwood listened intently as Jake narrated the highlights of *Orca's* patrol. He pointed out the unreliability of his SD radar. He also made sure to include his disappointment with the Mark-14 torpedo, and describe how the fish that failed to detonate had endangered his boat. He kept to himself the unofficial modifications to the torpedo his torpedomen had made.

When he had finished, Lockwood stroked his chin in thought. "First I've heard about the air search radar being unreliable. You may just have gotten a crappy unit. But, it turns out your cloud may well have a silver lining. Naval Intelligence has just picked up some Jap traffic bragging about how they can intercept our radar signals with their Radio Direction Finders, and how they already sunk one of our boats. And apparently the radio frequency they were picking up was the SD radar's frequency. A warning signal went out to the fleet this morning, but if the Japs aren't just bragging, then the warning is already too late for one of our guys. But then, if they've sunk as many boats as they say they have, I'd just be running just a two-boat fleet!"

Jake smiled, and the admiral continued.

"In any case, you'll get some extensive modifications to both your radars during *Orca's* refit, and needless to say the SD will be operating at a different frequency when you go back to sea.

"And you're sure enough not alone in your complaint about the torpedoes, as you probably already well know. I'm getting the same rumbles from just about every boat and every squadron commander.

"I've raised hell with BUORD, but even a rear admiral can only do so much with that bunch. I've even tried to get Nimitz' ear, he's an ex-submariner ya' know, but has his hands full running this whole damn war, and even he can only do so much. Hell, BUORD can't even supply us with the *number* of fish we need, let alone fish that work . . .

"But why am I telling you my troubles?" Lockwood chuckled. "It may take a while, but I *will* get this torpedo mess sorted out. Meanwhile, there's a reception at the 'O' Club tomorrow night for a bunch of congressmen from the States. I'll expect you and your officers to be there, give these birds a look-see at some real warriors, and maybe they'll realize that we've got an actual real-live war on our hands right here in the Pacific, and quit spending every last dime in Europe."

"Yes Sir, Admiral, we'll be there," Jake assured Lockwood somewhat unenthusiastically, as the admiral showed him out of his office, turning him back over to Loveless.

"He's quite a guy, Skipper," Jake said to his old boss.

"He is that, Jake, but he's also a tough guy to work for. Sure keeps me hoppin'," Loveless said.

"I can't really say I'm surprised," Jake answered. "Seriously, Harry, you doin' all right?"

"Fine, Jake, fine, really. But you know me. I'm just a worrywart. I can't help but think that Uncle Charlie threw me a bone by putting me on his staff after I lost my boat."

"No such thing. What happened to us could have happened to anybody, and the Board said as much. Don't ever think otherwise, Skipper!"

Loveless smiled. "You're good for my morale, Jake. How about we meet at the 'O' Club for a beer later, and you can give 'em all the gory details about *Orca* and your first patrol. Say about seventeen hundred, when I get off work here?"

"Sounds good, Harry. See you then."

That afternoon at 1700, Jake learned from Harry Loveless that *Seasprite* was overdue from patrol and presumed lost. *Seasprite*, he knew, had also been operating in the Bismarck Sea.

Jake hated these affairs, as did, almost to a man, each of his officers. Bill Salton, the lone exception, had not yet had enough time in the Navy to become jaded.

Crisp and proper in his dress whites, Jake was paraded by Lockwood in front of the congressional delegation and the Allied brass, and *Orca's* accomplishments described as if Jake had accomplished them singlehandedly. The congressmen, at least, appeared to be suitably impressed. But Jake had to believe that the brass knew better.

He was sulking at the bar by himself, nursing a beer, and listening as the small dance band struck up *String of Pearls*. The band was not quite on par with Glenn Miller's, but they did a creditable job.

Jake received a tap on the shoulder. He turned to see a pair of startling emerald eyes, on a level just below his own, set in a lovely freckled face, and staring straight into his. She wore what Jake would call a party dress cut in the style of the day, straight cut and tailored, with padded shoulders that this lady obviously did not need. She wore her long auburn hair swept back and up in the style of the day, but none of that had really registered; Jake was still hung up on the twin emeralds.

90

"Hey, sailor," she said with a mischievous smile, "wanna dance?"

Jake took a second to gather himself, then answered, "Are you sure you want to? I'm a pretty pathetic dancer . . ."

"Oh, I'll take my chances," she said, and not taking "no" for an answer, and flashing another impish smile, she took his arm. There was nothing for him to do but let her lead him out onto the dance floor. They had finished *String of Pearls* and began *I Had the Craziest Dream*, and, while Jake was really not a very good dancer, it seemed as if his abilities rose to the occasion—either that, or she just made him look good. Still, when the band followed with *There are Such Things*, the young lady didn't object when Jake suggested they sit one out. They sat that one out and the rest of the dances that evening as well. Instead, they sat at one of the side tables by the bar, talking the balance of the evening away.

Her name was Kate Shegrue, and she was a Navy nurse from Decatur, Illinois. Jake surprised himself. Aside from his mother and his sisters, he had never been able to sit down and just talk to a woman. Suddenly, here was a lady who had deliberately sought out his company and he found himself opening up to her, telling her things about himself and the way that he felt about things that he never really told anyone else. And more than that, here was a lady who was opening up to him in return. By the end of the evening, he felt as if he had known Kate Shegrue for his entire life.

He learned that Kate was an only child, and that her dad had always wanted a son, and when her mom and dad were unable to have any more children, her Dad did his best to turn her into the son he never had—not that she had minded that one bit. She reveled in all that attention, becoming the ultimate tomboy. What she didn't tell Jake was that little Kate beat out all the boys in her neighborhood at baseball and basketball. That was, at least, until all the boys in her neighborhood got old enough to know that they weren't supposed to play ball with girls, and especially not with girls that were better at it than they were. So, when Kate got to high school, she took up sports that *were* open to girls, and she told Jake that she had excelled in swimming and track. Jake noticed approvingly that she had maintained her athletic build, and that she had the broad shoulders that were the mark of a competitive swimmer.

Kate then studied nursing, and joined the Navy ad an RN when Hitler invaded Poland. She figured her country would get into the fray sooner or later, and that her talents would soon be needed in Europe. But then the Japanese invaded Pearl Harbor, and now here she was, in the Pacific. At 28, she was a full lieutenant and a nursing supervisor.

"And no, I've never been married," she said. "You?"

"No. Not even close. I've never even dated all that much. I'm afraid I'm not much of a social animal."

"Really?" Kate feigned surprise. "You seem to socialize just fine!" She was no fool, and instinctively noted that the attractive submariner she had singled out, standing by himself at the bar, was anything *but* a social animal.

"What I mean is, that I'm a not very good at affairs like this, and except for my mom and my sisters, I'm pretty awkward around women—don't know why, just always have been." Jake looked down and away from Kate, surprised that he had opened up to her this way—after all, he had just met her.

Kate smiled. "Can't understand that. I mean, you're a good-looking guy and you seem really nice, so you think you would be a natural when it comes to . . ." Kate, smiled and batted her eyes ". . . the fairer sex."

Jake smiled back and shrugged. "You think?"

"And your parents are still together, right?"

"Oh yeah. You'd never get those two apart," Jake said proudly. "They're forever."

"Mine too," she said emphatically. "Forever. And if I ever marry, it will be forever too—no matter what happens."

Out of nowhere, she asked, "Jake, are you religious at all?"

"I believe in God, if that's what you mean. I go to Sunday service when I can. I was raised Presbyterian."

Well, Kate thought to herself, *I really couldn't have expected him to be completely perfect . . .*

"I'm Catholic," she said, as if that was the end of the subject.

"That's okay," Jake conceded, not exactly thrilled. "About half my crew is Catholic, I think." He fought for something positive to say. "They *seem* to be the ones who go to services most often."

"You mean attend Mass," Kate corrected.

"Yeah, Mass," Jake agreed. "When they can. Of course they can't when we're at sea. My XO, Clem Dwyer, he's Catholic, and he conducts a Sunday prayer service using rosary beads while we're at sea. My chief engineer, Hal Chapman, does the Protestant service."

"Oh." She paused, as if processing the information, and then changed the subject. She produced a cigarette and a lighter. Jake lighted the cigarette for her. "You don't smoke?" she inquired.

"Nope. Never did."

"I wish I didn't. Cigarettes can't be any good for you. I keep wanting to quit, but everyone around me smokes—all the doctors and most of the other nurses—you would think that *we*, most of all, would know better. Maybe one day I'll stop."

"Most of my crew smokes," Jake admitted. "The boat stinks of stale cigarette smoke and diesel fumes, but you get kind of used to it. After a while, you never even notice it."

"Don't you ever get claustrophobic in your submarine?" she asked.

"Never. I'd be in big trouble if I did. So would anyone else on board. To me it's no different than riding in an elevator. The boats aren't made for people who get spooked by tight quarters."

"I guess. Why do you call subs boats? Aren't they big enough to be called ships?"

"They probably are, at that. *Orca* displaces eighteen hundred tons on the surface. Technically, the Navy says a boat is anything small enough to be hoisted up onto a ship. I think it might be because the very first submarines met that criterion, but I really don't know for sure. Anyway, they've just always been called boats, and I suppose they always will be. The Navy is big on traditions."

"So I've come to appreciate," laughed Kate.

They remained locked in conversation, Kate drawing Jake out of his shell, until the reception broke up and people started to leave. Jake wondered if he had any obligation to take formal leave of the brass and the congressmen, but they all seemed to be quite content to go off without any formality. It was still fairly early, only about 2100 (9:00 PM), but by now Jake wasn't at all anxious to part company with Kate—at least not just yet.

"Walk you home?" he asked.

"Sure. Give me a minute." She walked off in the general direction of the ladies room. Looking after her, Jake decided he definitely liked the way she walked.

The part of the base set aside for staff housing had been untouched by the raid. But the base, as with all military installations, was laid out for efficiency, not beauty. The streets, sidewalks, and pathways were laid out in straight lines.

Any trees or bushes that had been in the way of asphalt had been removed or mowed down, and plantings were later installed where God would have put them in the first place, if only he had known better. But this was, after all, Hawaii, and the foliage that the construction battalions had eventually planted grew lush and beautiful. There were the dracaena and snowbush, and the bright colors of the ginger and the red pineapple. The fragrances of the night-blooming jasmine, the ti, the juniper, and the coconut palm all blended together to allow the casual observer to realize that, after all, this base was set in paradise.

The night was also perfect, with the air cool and clear, and the sea breeze at once salty and fragrant. The stars shone brightly, and a three-quarter moon was rising in the western sky.

"Nice night," Kate said as they strolled, a bit of an understatement.

"Yes," he agreed. "Couldn't be more beautiful." He smiled, as he realized that the comment also extended to his company.

And that was the extent of their conversation as they strolled, properly, arm in arm, as if further conversation was unnecessary, content with just being in each other's presence. They made their way to the section of base housing set aside for nurses' quarters. It wasn't too far from the base hospital, which sat on a high bluff overlooking the entrance to the harbor. All too quickly, Jake thought, they reached Kate's quarters. She had led him to a cottage built in the island style, one in a row of identical, separate units, indistinguishable from one another except for the numbers "123" above the door and the surrounding foliage. All had the same graying, wood siding, with sitting porches along the front of each unit. The huge screened windows had their blackout curtains open, allowing the sea breezes in, acceptable since the cottage interiors remained dark.

"This is it," Kate noted, indicating her particular cottage with a sweep of the hand. The surrounding cottages were also dark— not surprising, with blackout conditions enforced—and quiet, as if none of them had anybody home. Jake suddenly felt as if there was nobody else in the world aside from Kate and him, and it felt good. He knew the idea was stupid, but, still, it felt good.

"Come, sit a while on the porch with me," Kate said. She led him up three stairs to a rickety, wicker settee on the porch. If the cushions were a bit damp from the night air, neither of them seemed to mind.

"Nice place," Jake opined. "All of it for you?"

She laughed lightly, a tinkling bell. "Not hardly. I have three roommates. We share two bedrooms and a single bath. Mornings are bedlam, despite the fact that we're all in uniform and don't even have to worry about what we're going to wear. Still, it's a step or two above the Women's BOQ."

Just then their idyll abruptly ended when a car pulled up in front, a typical motor pool vehicle, nondescript, dull gray, four-door, Plymouth coupe with "U.S. NAVY" stenciled on the side in black letters, and "4023" below. The headlights were hooded, only barely illuminating the road in front. A pretty dark-haired girl stepped out, dressed in a nurse's working uniform. She said something to whoever was still in the car, and then looked after it as it pulled away.

She turned and flounced up the three stairs in front of the cottage and onto the porch.

"Hi, Pam," Kate called out from the dark of the porch, hoping not to startle the new arrival. Pam jumped anyway. "Oh! You startled me," she said.

Kate chortled. "Exactly what I was trying to avoid. Pam, this is Jake. Jake, this is my roommate, Pam Schultz. She's just coming off her shift."

Jake registered a tousled nurse's working uniform, the single silver bar of a lieutenant, junior grade. "Hello, Pam." Jake felt on display as Pam took her time checking him over. Then came an approving smile.

"Hi, Jake. Or should I say 'Commander?' "

Jake, embarrassed and suddenly shy again, said, "Jake will do just fine."

"That's just Jake, then," she said, obviously amused by her pun, as Kate groaned audibly.

"That," Kate offered, "was just terrible. How is Corporal Anderson doing?"

"Oh, Katie . . ." Pam's face registered a sudden sadness. "The doctors did their best. Corporal Anderson expired this afternoon."

Kate was visibly saddened.

"Expired?" Jake, a quizzical look on his face, asked no one in particular. "You mean he's dead?"

"Yes, Jake, he died." Kate elaborated. "The corporal was pretty badly shot up. Guadalcanal was supposed to have been secured months ago, but apparently there were still bands of Japanese soldiers there who had not surrendered. Anderson and his patrol were ambushed by one of them—"

"We honestly thought he was going to pull through," Pam interrupted. "Then a massive infection set in two days ago, and the sulfides wouldn't touch it." She paused, swallowing a breath. "He just didn't make it."

"Right," Jake said, a little cowed. "It's just that when you said 'expired,' it floored me. It just . . . well, it sounded so . . . so . . . *clinical*."

"And it is . . ." Kate allowed, "Clinical. Sometimes you use a clinical term like 'expired' to suppress what you really feel, so you can move on to the next case, start over fresh, and just do your job."

"Right," he said. "I understand. Sorry I said anything."

"No, that's okay. No way could you know." An awkward silence followed. Pam finally broke it.

"Okay, now, why don't I just go inside and leave you two alone?" Not waiting for an answer, she gave a mock salute and retreated inside. Jake could hear her pull the blackout curtains closed. Then a radio came on, tuned to a station playing Hawaiian music, just loud enough to break the earlier mood.

"So much for our tropical paradise," mused Kate. She sighed. "It's getting late anyway, and I have to go to work very early in the morning—0400."

"Ouch," Jake replied. He paused, trying to think of a way to broach the subject. Finally, screwing up his courage, he got it out. "But can I see you again . . . maybe tomorrow evening?"

Kate smiled. "That would be lovely. But my social calendar is very busy. Let's see, Sunday evening, hmmm," she paused, looking for a moment as if deep in thought, "I seem to be free tomorrow evening and just about every evening into the foreseeable future, restricted only by my job's crazy schedule." Then she saw that he was taking her very seriously—he really was, as she had already surmised, very, very awkward around women. "Oh, Jake, I was just teasing. I'm sorry! I would honestly love to see you again."

"I . . . we . . . won't be in port all that long, and I understand the nurses work crazy hours, but . . . but tomorrow evening . . . is that too soon?"

"Not at all, Commander. About when might you be coming by?"

"Around eighteen hundred. Say, dinner, and maybe a movie afterward?"

"Six PM tomorrow, then. But you'll have to get me back at a reasonable hour. I have the 0400-to-noon shift through Wednesday."

Jake stood up to leave, and Kate stood as well. Taking his hand, she leaned up and kissed him lightly on the lips. Jake was startled, and the kiss was over before he had a chance to react. She gave him a self-satisfied smile. "Until tomorrow, then," she said, and shooed him off the porch.

Kate watched Jake walk off. Long strides, determined, erect. *Very military*, she thought, *and very eligible*. When he was out of sight, she went inside. Pam, changed into a dressing gown and ready for bed, peeked conspiratorially around the door to her room.

"He's dreamy," she opined, smiling her approval.

"Yes he is," Kate agreed, "And I think I might just marry him."

It was Sunday, and Jake slept in, skipping services at the Base Chapel. He thought about Kate, musing on how it might be nice to spend the day on the beach with her. He thought about maybe calling her, and then remembered that she said that today was a workday for her, and that she had been at work since 0400, while he had been still lazing in the sack.

After brunch at the "O" Club, he wandered down to the boat. He was not surprised to find Clem there, deep in conference with Bucky Buckner, and Hal Chapman.

Despite it being Sunday, the boat was a hubbub of activity, with base personnel going and coming, electrical cords and hoses strung from the dock and down through the hatches, making such passage difficult at best.

Jake left Clem in the wardroom shuffling work orders, and wandered though his boat. In the conning tower, Early Sender watched as a technician tore into the guts of the TDC, the disassembly required for the installation of an upgrade. Similarly, in another cramped space, another yard tech tore into the SD radar under Chief Leone's watchful eyes. The SD, Jake new, was being replaced entirely with a new unit that operated on a different frequency from the old one, and which was also capable of reaching out six miles, about a half-mile further than the older unit. And *Orca* was being also being fitted out with surface search radar, the SJ, said to be able to pick up surface contacts out to about seven miles.

The radar presentation for the SJ was two separate scopes. The first was an "A" scope. A flat line of light scanned across the screen, and a contact showed up as a triangular spike on that line, called a "blip." The position of the blip, measured from left to right, gave the range to the contact on a horizontal scale. In general, the closer the contact, the higher the blip. But, the higher blip, at a specific range, gave the operator a good idea as to the size of a contact.

A second CRT, the "B" scope, showed the bearing to the contact on a horizontal scale. Somehow, they planned to shoehorn both the scopes alongside the SD scope at the operator's station in the conning tower.

The SJ radar antenna was a parabolic metal affair fixed to the periscope mast, rotated by hand from the conning tower. The antenna was below the surface when the boat was submerged at periscope depth, so the new SJ radar, like the SD, could only be used on the surface. Alternatively, the boat could be broached to the point where the antenna was exposed, but that, of course, would compromise the boat's advantage of invisibility.

Below the control room, the tiny space that contained the sonar consoles was also crowded with three people. Bill Salton's bright red hair made him stand out from the two technicians with him, and he was just leaving to give the techs room to work. He looked like some sort of bug, a praying mantis perhaps, stretching his lanky frame as he unwound himself from the tight space. At six feet, four inches, Salton was the tallest man on *Orca*.

"They're telling me that we'll have to go into drydock, Captain," Salton informed Jake. "It seems we're getting new transducers for our sonars, and another new one for the fathometer."

Back in the forward engine room, number one diesel was being overhauled by ship's relief crew, but with Chief Clements in charge of the crew of enginemen working down below the walkway grating, covered in grease. Jake was surprised—and not a little proud—that the workers included two of his regular crew, Richards and Harding, and that they had actually given up their liberty at the Royal Hawaiian to work on their boat alongside the relief crew.

Now, Jake felt guilty for having slept in. There are no sleepy Sundays when there's a war on.

Friday, Kate was working days, and Jake could take her out for an evening date and not have to get her back home early.

Being the skipper of a submarine in wartime had its privileges. Jake had no problem checking out a vehicle from the motor pool that evening. It was another nondescript dull gray four-door coupe, of course, this one a Ford.

There was a new film that had been out a couple of months and had just reached Hawaii. According to the *Honolulu Advertiser* it had opened to rave reviews on the mainland. The film was called *Casablanca*, and starred Humphrey Bogart. Jake remembered Bogart as the tough-guy hoodlum in a couple of gangster films, and had enjoyed his performances. He didn't know too much about the female lead, a Swedish import named Ingrid Bergman, but noted that Peter Lorre and Sydney Greenstreet were also in it, and he had always liked them. He checked for starting times, and figured he and Kate could have dinner, get into town, and still make the 1900 screening.

Jake wore his one civilian suit. He had been with Kate continually since they met, sometimes on a formal date, sometimes just for a quick quiet walk on the base This particular Friday evening, they had dinner at the "O" Club, mostly because Jake knew next to nothing about eateries in Honolulu, and then they drove off base to the movie theatre. They stopped for ice cream afterwards at a place Kate knew about, discussed the movie that they had both thoroughly enjoyed, and then returned to the base to sit on Kate's porch and look at the stars.

It had rained while they were in the theatre, and now the air was crisp and cool, and a brilliant display of stars filled the night sky. They kissed — a proper kiss — but still had to end the evening at a reasonable hour because Kate had to be at work at 0800. They parted reluctantly shortly after one in the morning.

Jake, who had never before in his lifetime ever dated much, and who had never before in his lifetime *ever* been in love, was hopelessly in love with Kate Shegrue.

By mid-April, *Orca* had been in and out of dry dock.

Besides having her sonar transducers upgraded, *Orca* had her hull blasted clean of the marine growth that had affixed itself to her while sailing in warm southern waters. It was really a bit early for that, because her hull was not that badly fouled, but the shipyard did the job anyway, since she was already in the dry dock. The yard also repainted the hull with a new experimental paint that was formulated to discourage marine growth. Nobody seemed to mind, least of all the yard crew applying the paint, that the main anti-fouling ingredient was a toxic pigment called emerald green, or copper arsenide.

By early May, *Orca* was back at dockside, and ready for sea trials.

It was one of those rare occasions when Kate was off work for an entire weekend, and they had planned a Sunday outing at the beach. But Kate had insisted that Jake first accompany her to Mass that morning.

Normally, Jake would have avoided attending Catholic Mass at all costs. He had been several times before, the first time as a teenager, and found the ceremony at once beautiful and strange – *and* long and boring. First of all, everything except the sermon was in Latin, and he had no clue what the priest was saying, and had little idea as to what was going on.

But the sermon had little, if any, relation to the erudite and sometimes deeply moving sermons he had heard in his own church. Catholic priests' sermons, in his opinion, and based on his admittedly limited experience, were short, pointless, and the principal reason why he found the Mass so boring. This one, delivered by the Catholic chaplain, while still short, at least had a point to make and had made some sense.

But, it seemed important to Kate that Jake accompany her to Mass, and at this point in their courtship, he would never pass up an opportunity to be with her, no matter the sacrifice.

After the ceremony, the chaplain, Father Kleinschmidt, greeted the congregation as it left the base chapel. He was still wearing the vestments that priests wore when saying Mass.

"Katie," he exclaimed, smiling widely, when he saw her, "how great to see you!" Kate smiled back, and, to Jake's amazement, the priest and Kate hugged each other.

"Father Jack," Kate said as she untangled herself from the priest, "I want you to meet Jake, Lieutenant Commander Jake Lawlor."

"Jake, is it? Jack Kleinschmidt! Pleased to meet you. How're you doing?"

"Fine, Father," Jake answered, somewhat warily.

"Great. So, you're a submariner. Don't know how you guys do it. I can't imagine going to sea all cooped up like that. It takes a very special individual to serve on submarines, and while I'll never understand how you do it, I, for one, am glad you do."

Jake couldn't think of anything to say in response, so he just smiled and kept silent. Kate filled the void. "You're right, Father. I was aboard one once for a tour, and I couldn't wait to get off." She looked around and said, "But there are folks behind us. So if you'll excuse us, Father. We're off to the beach."

"Sure thing. Hope to see you both again soon." And, with that, he turned to greet another couple waiting to greet the priest behind them.

Jake wondered how "Father Jack" knew he was a submariner. But then it occurred to him, and that she had obviously said nice things about him . . .

"He seems like a nice enough guy," Jake volunteered as they made their way, arm in arm, to the car.

"Father Jack? He's super! I absolutely love him."

"Really? Well then, maybe it's a good thing that priests are celibate."

"Silly. Don't tell me you're jealous of Father Jack?!"

"I could *never* be jealous of a man who has such great regard for submariners," Jake said with a smile, "but I definitely will keep my eye on him."

Kate pondered the fact that the exchange she just had with Jake would never have happened only a few short weeks ago. He seemed to have grown so much more socially at ease, not just with her, but with everyone. Kate smiled, grasped Jake's arm just a little tighter, and leaned into him.

That night, before turning in, Jake wrote a letter to his parents, telling them about this wonderful girl he had met. Only after describing her, and what she did, and how they met, did he mention that she was Catholic.

* * * * *

Lanikai Beach is on the lower northeast edge of Oahu across the island from the base. Of all the beaches on the island, it has the whitest sand and the calmest surf—perfect for an afternoon in the sun.

Kate wore a blue, one-piece suit in the modest style of the day, with a skirt halfway down her thighs, which still flattered her figure, and Jake couldn't help but desire, as well as admire, the lean, athletic body beneath it.

Jake wore only swim trunks (men had only recently shed the upper part of the male swim suit, which had looked much like an underwear shirt). Kate, for her part, admired Jake's muscular physique, and enjoyed snuggling next to him on the blanket. There were plenty of other people on the beach, and some blankets were only a short distance away. A good thing, she thought. There was no telling what liberties she would allow Jake otherwise.

Following their first date, Kate never again smoked around Jake. He never mentioned it, but somehow she knew he appreciated the fact. She wondered, if he were around her all the time, whether she could quit altogether—not that that could ever be the case anytime soon. *Orca,* she knew, would be going out on sea trials the next morning. He'd be going back out to sea for two days, and then he'd be back—but not for long. Next, there would be a shakedown cruise for the crew (Jake said they'd be at sea a week at a time for three weeks) and then, after that, back out on patrol. But for how long? Who knew? Some boats stayed out on patrol for seventy days. And some boats never came back at all. She didn't want to think about that. This man had come to mean too much to her. She hugged him hard, burying her face against his side.

"Hey," he said gently, "What's that all about?"

"You know what it's about. What you do is dangerous, and you may just leave port and then I'll never see you again. You and that stupid boat you're so damned proud of."

"Oh, Katie," he said, running his hand through her hair, "it's that damn boat that's gonna make sure I come back to you. And besides, you can't be rid of me *that* easily. I'm always gonna be coming home to you." What he said next surprised even Jake. "Get used to it."

She picked her head up. "Why Jake Lawlor! That sounded almost like a proposal!"

"Damned if it didn't," he laughed. He paused a bit, thinking. "You mind?"

"No. Not at all. Not one little bit. And if the offer's still on the table, Commander, I'll take it."

Notwithstanding the people surrounding them, Jake and Kate then shared several long and passionate kisses.

Orca went out for sea trials the next morning, Monday, May 10th. The trim dive was tricky; without a full torpedo load, the boat was light, and the trim tanks had to be almost completely flooded before the boat could hold depth without power to the screws.

There were also some minor leaks, including one at test depth around the newly installed fathometer transducer. To fix it, a yard technician riding the boat went down into the bilge below the control room. There he tightened down on the gland sealing the hull penetration, and that took care of it. All of the other leaks were chalked up to seals drying out from disuse, since they eventually cleared up by themselves.

The rest of that day, and all the following day, Jake put *Orca* through her paces: diving, surfacing, full power runs, and tests of all the installed equipment, especially the equipment that had been updated or modified in port. Everything appeared to be working well. Jake was especially impressed with the SJ radar. It extended *Orca's* eyes well beyond the lenses of the periscope, and Jake was quick to seize on the possibilities of his boat's increased effectiveness in combat.

Jake was concerned that the crew was rusty after six weeks of refit and R & R, but there were three weeks of ISE—Individual Ship Exercises—scheduled before *Orca* would be returned to patrol duty. These particular exercises were absolutely critical, because the modified TDS and the other newly installed equipment could not really be tested without some mock torpedo runs against an actual target vessel. It wouldn't do for his fire control team to be unfamiliar with their tools on a war patrol. It wouldn't do at all.

When the boat reentered port the following evening, Jake was satisfied that the boat itself was ready for action. Now he and Clem formulated their plan to get the crew back into fighting fettle The crew would be deserting the Royal Hawaiian and returning to living aboard during the remainder of the week. ISE was scheduled to begin on May 17th, followed close aboard with *Orca's* second war patrol.

God help me, Jake thought, despite the painful fact that it meant a separation from Kate, *I can't wait!* The idea that he might never return from that patrol never occurred to him.

When the boat was tied up to her berth, and Jake set foot ashore, his first instinct was to call Kate. Then he remembered that she had only just reported for duty and wouldn't be off until 0400 the next morning. He also recalled how proud he was that Kate was a skilled nurse, and how much he hated her miserable schedule. He decided he would wait until noon tomorrow to call, and then maybe they could meet for a late lunch.

The next few days flew by. *Orca* was loaded up with twenty more torpedoes, all Mark-14s. Two of them practice torpedoes with bright yellow, dummy warheads. Chief Walakurski and his team began quietly modifying the other eighteen.

The three weeks of ISE were exactly what *Orca's* officers and crew needed. Inevitably, personnel turnover was a reality, and boats typically turned over at least ten percent of their crew while in port. Orca had suffered a twenty percent turnover due to her unusually long layover in Pearl, and the personnel demands of the other boats going to sea took priority. Some of the new crewmembers were seasoned submariners off other boats, but many were fresh out of Sub School. They all had to be integrated with *Orca's* veterans, learning to work together as if their life depended on it—because it did.

Clem and Bucky ran emergency drills; there were practice torpedo runs in company with *USS Runner*, emergency drills, and gun-firing practice against targets towed both at sea and in the air. When *Orca* and *Runner* returned to port each Friday, Jake felt that his crew was that much sharper, that much readier to face the enemy.

He was glad that *Orca's* crew, with the integration of the new replacements, was now beginning to operate as a team. Intensive training enabled each man to react instinctively in any conceivable emergency. And it gave *Orca* just that much more of an edge in actual combat.

Weekends were busy; there was a great deal to do to get ready to go on patrol, and there wasn't much time to get it all done. Still, Jake managed to make time for Kate. She came off nights, and went on days. They squeezed in time together whenever they could, but it seemed never to be enough. Partings became harder and harder.

As the beginning of June approached, and "it"—*Orca's* second war patrol—became imminent, Kate grew more and more anxious. Unbeknownst to the busy Jake, she cried a lot when they were apart, and the sad events that were part and parcel of her duties as a nurse in a military hospital, seemed all the more sad. She had begun to see Jake in every patient, to imagine him hurt the way she saw the soldiers, marines, and sailors that were in her care hurt. And worse, she knew that the idiot she had fallen in love with couldn't wait to take his damn stupid submarine back out and into harm's way.

June also brought the reply to Jake's letter to his parents in Des Moines — the letter, that is, in which he had written to them about Kate. Letters from Jake's parents came frequently, far more frequently, truth be told, then the ones they received from him. But they never scolded him about that. There had been a stack of them awaiting him when *Orca* returned to port, and there had been several since.

Letters from Jake's parents were mostly letters from his mom. They almost always included a few lines from his dad, but it was Mom that was the letter-writer. The letter he read now included this paragraph:

"Father and I are so glad you've finally met someone that sparks your interest. Your Kate sounds like such a lovely girl! But please be careful, and don't rush into anything. We love you and want you to be happy always – but you know that. You must also know that we'll always trust you to do the right thing."

That was it. There wasn't any word from his mother about Kate's being Catholic – *and* the few lines his Dad normally would have appended were conspicuously missing from *this* letter.

Orders.

Jake was ordered to report to Lockwood's office. It was Monday, May 7th. Provisioned for war patrol, *Orca* was ready for sea.

Jake expected to get a packet of orders from the squadron commander's aide, and open his orders only after the boat had cleared the hundred-fathom curve. Instead, Harry Loveless ushered Jake into a meeting room, where he was met by RADM Lockwood, Commodore Macdonough, and four Marines: a major, a first lieutenant and two sergeants.

The Admiral made the introductions. "You've already met Captain Macdonough. This is Lieutenant Commander Jake

Lawlor, gentlemen, and he is skipper of the submarine *USS Orca*. Captain Lawlor, meet Major Forrest Dilling, First Lieutenant Calvin Jennings, and Gunnery Sergeants Thomas Fallon and James Kelsey."

Jake shook hands all around

"These Marines, Jake, are a recon team that you are going to transport to Tarawa Atoll, and offload for a recon of Betio Island. The Japs have a garrison there and an airfield we want. You wait for the Major and his men to do their job, recover them, and bring them back to Pearl in one piece. During this patrol, Jake, no matter how juicy the target, you are *not* to engage the enemy except in self-defense. Your job is to land these marines and bring them back safely, period. Understood?"

"Yes Sir, Admiral. Understood."

"Very well. As we speak, these Marines' gear is being loaded aboard *Orca*. Berthing arrangements are up to you and the Major, here. It's twenty-four hundred miles from here to Tarawa Atoll, give or take. You need to remain undetected for the whole trip, including during the recon of the atoll. That won't be easy.

"There are shore batteries. There's a submerged, shallow reef that surrounds Betio Island, and a protected deepwater anchorage, a lagoon, outside the reef, just north of the Jap base on the island. On that protected north shore there's a long pier that extends out into the anchorage over the reef. The Japs built it so they wouldn't have to bring in supplies from the anchorage in small boats to get them over the reef.

"We're pretty sure the south side of Betio is deep water, too, but they can't use it for docks because, other than that reef, there's no protection from the open sea. We need to know if an amphibious landing is even possible, and where. And that's where you and these Marines come in."

At noontime, May 7, 1943, *Orca* sailed out of the harbor at Pearl and headed for the open sea and her second war patrol, a recon mission. Once clear of the harbor, she set sail southwest for Tarawa Atoll.

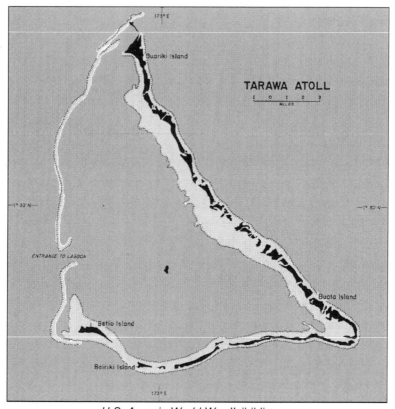

U.S. Army in World War II, ibiblio.org

Chapter 7

Orca: *Second Patrol – 12 May 1943 to 13 June 1943*

The storm hit on their fifth day out of Pearl. Normally, it would have taken just over ten days to reach Tarawa, but nobody figured on a major Pacific storm.

It arrived during the morning watch, just before the boat was planning to dive for the day and follow the usual practice of proceeding submerged during daylight. Hal Chapman had the deck, and spotted an ominous gray-black squall line that filled the horizon, approaching in the early dawn. They were headed straight for it—black and foreboding—promising to turn the burgeoning day back into the deepest night. Chapman called Jake to the bridge.

Jake was working on a long letter to Kate—a letter that he had begun when *Orca* left port, which he would contribute to on an almost-daily basis until either an opportunity came to mail it, or *Orca* returned to Pearl—when he received Chapman's call to come to the bridge.

"Looks like we're headed right for it, Captain, and it looks nasty," Chapman said, when Jake appeared beside him on the bridge.

"Looks like it." Jake gazed into the approaching darkness. "Be on us in less than a half hour is my guess." He really had only one course of action. "Okay, guess there's nothing to do for it. We stay on the surface. Get some rain gear up here for you and the lookouts, and strap yourselves in. If it gets too bad, we'll secure the bridge and man the watch from the periscope in the conning tower."

"Aye, Captain." Chapman checked his watch. Over two more hours to go, and it was about to get very wet on the bridge.

An hour later, *Orca* was in the thick of it. The boat was pitching violently, along with a kind of rolling motion, as she bit through the oncoming sea. Well over half of the crew had suddenly become violently ill.

With each lurch forward, the propellers were coming out of the water, spinning, churning air, and the boat's forward progress abruptly halted. Then the props were submerged again, suddenly biting into the water and straining, then lurching forward again, the props free, wind milling, repeating the process. The diesels were winding up and slowing down in turn, not a good thing for shafts and cylinder liners. Jake ordered the boat to go on propulsion charge. That way the diesels and the generators would run at a set speed, charging the batteries, and the batteries would directly power the motors that turned the screws. The batteries, with no moving parts, wouldn't wear out or break apart if they were called upon to power the boat in surges.

The engine air intake valve had been shifted to take suction from the air in the boat, instead of being routed directly from main induction — the thirty-six-inch wide valve just aft of the bridge — and outside air. Air for the engines still came by way of the main induction valve, but now the boat's interior served as a kind of air plenum, and any seawater that washed over the main induction would be dumped into the bilges, rather than being sucked into the engines. (Air is compressed in the diesel's cylinders as part of the combustion process, but water is an incompressible fluid, so a slug of water sucked into an engine cylinder meant broken or bent cylinder rods and cracked cylinder liners, if not a bent crankshaft or two.

An hour into the storm, Jake made a trip up to the bridge, saw that green water was flooding up through the well deck and down the conning tower hatch, and secured the deck watch. The OOD would stand his watch at the periscope, with the conning tower upper hatch secured, until the weather cleared.

Since 1892, Tarawa had been part of a British protectorate that included all of the Gilbert Islands, and was part of that colony of the British Empire since 1915. The Gilberts had remained British until the Japanese occupied the Islands early in the war.

Major Forrest Dilling, USMC, was unaffected by the boat's rolling, lurching, motion. His team, on the other hand, was in absolute misery, and could not be pried from their bunks. While Dilling's Christian name was Forrest, he preferred to go by "Cracker." Jake had not inquired why, but it did not obviously refer to any deep southern origin, since Dilling was a "Yooper," hailing from Michigan's Upper Peninsula.

Upon coming aboard, Dilling had insisted that he and his team bunk together. Jake assigned them to four bunks in the forward torpedo room, and that had suited Dilling just fine. Except for their inflatable boat, which was secured topside in a locker under the cigarette deck, their gear was stored in the forward torpedo room as well, and that compartment's hatch was to be the team's preferred point of egress and ingress for the mission. The four enlisted sailors who had to vacate their bunks to make room were, on the other hand, less happy, since it meant they had to hot-bunk with four of their equally unhappy shipmates.

When Jake came back down from securing the bridge watch, he found Dilling in the wardroom poring over, for the hundredth time, an old Admiralty chart of the Tarawa Atoll, and a Navy-generated tide table. Dilling was concentrating on Betio Island, the site of the Japanese base at Tarawa.

"How are your guys doing?" Jake inquired.

Dilling chortled. "Not good. Couldn't even roust those ladies from their cribs this morning. They looked so pathetic I took pity on them and just left them lying there.

Jake smiled. "Can't understand that. Thought you 'Gyrenes' had iron stomachs. Though I can't exactly brag on my submariners. About half of my crew can barely make it to their watch stations."

"Tell me something, Captain Jake, if this boat submerged, we'd be below the weather, wouldn't we? I mean, it would be really peaceful about two hundred feet down, wouldn't it?"

"That it would. And if I knew for sure that the storm would pass over us in twenty-four hours, that's exactly what I would have done when I saw it coming. But I have no idea how long this blow will last, so the boat has to stay on the surface and ride it out."

"Why's that?"

"Not to get too technical, but when a boat submerges or surfaces, the center of buoyancy changes, and there is always an instant when the center of gravity and the center of buoyancy actually pass through one another, and at that point the boat can't right itself. If a wave happens to hit at that instant and with enough force, then it's bottoms up, and the boat capsizes. And so, in really rough seas, we stay on the surface and bounce around on the surface all day until the storm passes."

"Right. Okay then. Bouncing around on the surface it is." He laughed. "Still and all, I guess my guys would prefer a nice steady foxhole about now."

"Then they should have joined the Army."

"Bite your tongue!"

Since the Admiralty chart for Tarawa was the only chart they had for the waters surrounding Betio Island and the Japanese base on Tarawa, Jake had to rely on it for planning his approach to the Island. It was an Admiralty chart, and given his experience with an Admiralty chart on *S-49*, he was understandably reluctant to place absolute faith in it. Still, he allowed, since the Gilberts were British waters, the chart should be more accurate than the one *S-49* had of the Dutch waters in the Myakka Straight. The Brits, after all, had been sailing the Gilberts since the mid-eighteenth century.

114

Cracker Dilling was more concerned with what his team might run into on Betio Island itself. The chart had only explicit details of the Island's shoreline. Air recon flights had been few and far between, and other than a general outline of the airfield, and the location of some "visible shore batteries," he had little to go by. Betio was only two miles long and eight hundred yards wide at its widest point. Aside from the open areas that had been developed by the Japanese, it looked to be heavily vegetated, so there had to be places for his recon team to hide. Still, if the Japanese suspected they were there, there would never be enough places to hide. There were about four thousand Japanese on that island, and if their presence was suspected, his team would be flushed out in a heartbeat. His job was to map the enemy facilities on the island in detail, check out those "visible shore batteries," evaluate possible landing beaches, and remain undetected—a piece of cake.

Jake pointed out the submerged reef that the chart showed surrounding the island. "I'm no expert on amphibious operations," he said, "but it looks as if this reef could really screw up any attempt to land Marines on these beaches."

"Not necessarily," said Dilling. "Your guys at Naval Intelligence—there's an oxymoron for you—drew up this tide table. According to it, and the recorded depths of the reef on this chart, we should be okay—a good nine feet over the reef at high tide. The Mike boats [LCMs, or landing craft, mechanized] don't draw much, and the Higgins boats draw only four feet. Then there are the LVTs [Landing Vehicle, Tracked]—the 'alligators'— they can get over anything. If we can get, say even just five feet over the top of the reef, we should be okay. Depends on the range of tide, and whatever and whenever low water is for when we go in. But that's for you swabbies to figure out. They want me to get some depth readings and record the times is all. "

Dilling continued, "Intel says that when the Jap supply ships come in, they anchor here, to the north of the island, and they use this here long dock on the north side of Betio that they built out over the lagoon and the reef to bring in cargo. So it would be my educated guess that the Japs don't want to depend on the tides and small boats to bring in supplies. So, yeah, the tides will be a big factor as to when and *if* we can clear that reef for a landing."

Jake absorbed the features on the chart. It showed the atoll with strings of land as two sides of a right triangle, the lower side running more or less west to east, with the longest side, from the eastern apex to the northwest, and then the side without any land at all running north to south. Betio Island took up most of the bottom side of the triangle, and the interior of the triangle was a maze of shallows and reefs that formed a protected lagoon. Outside of the reefs, especially to the south, the chart showed deep water.

"Okay, then," Jake said, "when we get there, I intend to do a submerged recon of the whole atoll. The chart shows reefs and shallow water all over, so we'll have to stand pretty far off and see what we can see through the periscope. Notice how the islands more or less form a triangle?"

Dilling nodded.

"Well," Jake continued, "we can probably get a really good look on the outside of the triangle, the shorelines where we have some deep water to work in. These interior shorelines are more of a problem. These reefs (he pointed to them) here, here, and here, for example, and these shallows (more pointing) mean we won't get very close to these interior shorelines. The anchorage in the lagoon is fine for relatively shallow draft surface ships like destroyers and minesweepers, but there's not enough water for me to safely submerge in there, so *Orca* going into that lagoon is out of the question. We need to figure out our best shot. We'll have to figure out the best place to land your team."

"I think," Dilling said, "Depending on sea conditions, maybe somewhere on the south side of the island, where we have more jungle cover, or maybe even on this adjoining island, to the east. If the sea kicks up on us, though, we'll have to go in anywhere where we can get some protection from the open sea. But I don't want to go in where we'll be right out in the open for a long time, as we make our way into the beach. One worry is that the south side is where the Japs figure is the most likely invasion route, and that's where most of the gun emplacements are supposed to be."

"Well," Jake said, "If the anchorage is empty, this promontory at the northwest corner of the island might be our best bet—no, on second thought, that's no good either. No telling when a supply ship might come in, and then we're screwed.

"Coming in from the south is still far and away your best bet. We can always wait for the sea to be calm enough if we have to, and insert you from the south at night. But when it's time for extraction, we can't be certain that sea conditions will be cooperative. If they are, we can extract from the south on schedule, and we're done. But if there are heavy seas . . ."

Dilling looked up from the chart at Jake.

"If there are heavy seas," Jake said, "it will be your call. If you can make it to the boat, we can pick you up. Or you can wave us off and we'll come back the next night, and keep coming back until you don't wave us off, and signal you're coming in. But then we definitely use the south side, okay?"

Dilling nodded agreement.

"Now, what about aircraft?"

"What about 'em?"

"Well," Jake said, "in my experience, where there's an airfield, there's liable to be some aircraft."

"Sounds about right," Dilling agreed, chuckling, "Don't know as they have any fighters. Transports are more likely. Possibly even bombers. But until we get on the island, there's no way to know for sure. But we'll be going in and coming out at night. I didn't think the Japs flew at night."

"They don't normally, but they will when they have to," Jake said. "They will definitely scramble whatever aircraft they've got, night or no night, if we're spotted. It will be very unhealthy for *Orca* to be caught on the surface, trying to get you and your guys off that island, with a fighter or two or three taking turns trying to blow us out of the water. "

"Then we'll just have to figure out a way to let you know what to expect," Dilling said. "I'd hate to have to use the radio, but I will if I have to. But I certainly won't know until after my team and I do some recon."

"Fine. But no radio. We'll work out some Aldus lamp signals to do just that. Your signaling to us shouldn't be a problem, since they can only be seen from sea. But our answering signals with lights can be dangerous, because they can be seen from land, and your team wouldn't be the only ones who could see 'em."

"Then you could answer us on the radio. That way there would be no way to trace us from our emitted signals, and no way they could see your signal light."

"That works."

With the details of the expedition worked out, the two men settled back in their seats. Dilling lighted a cigarette.

"How'd you become a Marine officer, Cracker?" Jake asked.

"How'd you mean?"

"I mean, you're a major, so you were commissioned about the same time I was, and you're *not* Academy, or I'd have recognized you. Most of the Marine officers my age are Academy."

Cracker smiled as he replied, "The Military College of South Carolina, Captain. The Citadel, Class of '32. When my buddies in Marine Officer Orientation found out that I was Citadel *and* educated south of the Mason-Dixon line, they started calling me 'Cracker.' It's been 'Cracker' ever since, even though, technically speaking, 'crackers' only hail from Georgia or Florida. But never let it be said that any Marine stood on formality."

"No," Jake chuckled, "Never let it be said."

The storm finally subsided after *Orca* spent five days of tossing and rolling on the surface. On the morning of May 17th, Louis Carillo, *Orca's* navigator, took his first star sights since the storm hit and then the boat submerged for the day. His navigational fix showed that since leaving Pearl, *Orca* had only traversed 1,450 miles. She had 950 more to go until she reached Tarawa. Jake figured they would be there in three-and-a-half days, give or take. They sighted Tarawa through the boat's periscope just after noon on Friday, May 21st.

Jake took most of their first week in the waters around Tarawa doing a recon of the shoreline, recording the comings and goings of the Japanese garrison on the atoll. One byproduct of the recon was Jake's growing confidence in the Admiralty chart. *Orca's* fathometer readings matched the soundings shown on the chart almost exactly. As the boat's recon progressed, Cracker Dilling and his team skulked, obviously anxious for the start of their own in-country recon of Tarawa. They were, however, under Jake's overall command, and, if cornered, would have had to reluctantly admit that careful preparation prior to their insertion might eventually reap dividends. And so it would be proved.

Betio appeared to be the only island that contained any of the enemy. It was by far the largest island in the atoll—long, narrow and flat. Just as it was shown on the Admiralty chart, it was at the southernmost reach of the lagoon, wedge-shaped, the widest part of the wedge to the west, and gradually ending in a point at its eastern end.

The south side of the island was heavily vegetated and not much other than jungle was visible through the periscope, save the meatball flag flying high toward the western end of the island. As the boat rounded the western end of the island, there was a clear view up a runway that ran from west to east along the length of the island.

Peering into the lagoon, the long dock extending north from the island was barely visible. Clearly observed, however, was an armed patrol boat that proceeded from the lagoon and made what appeared to be regular rounds around the entire atoll just outside the reef throughout the night. Jake carefully recorded the patrol boat's schedule, knowing that the insertion and extraction of Dilling's team had to be timed around it. Clem surveyed the boat itself from the periscope, and using radar ranges for perspective, gauged the gunboat to be about seventy feet long. It was armed with a single, forward mounted gun, four-inch or better, and two smaller, side-mounted anti-aircraft guns, probably around twenty-millimeter. In short, the boat's guns were easily a match for *Orca's* own.

The boat also had a large searchlight mounted on its bridge. This it used to light up the shoreline, investigating anything they might find suspicious. Clem had seen it used only once, and it was powerful, bathing the shoreline in its swath with daylight.

Jake, with Clem's assistance, counted fourteen permanent gun emplacements on the Island. These were big guns in at least four of the emplacements, all on the island's south shore. Jake estimated these four were possibly as large as ten-inch. The big guns appeared to be aimed to forestall any attempt at landing from the south, directly from the sea. Apparently the island defenders thought no one would be likely to attempt a landing across the lagoon to the north, although there were at least five smaller-caliber gun emplacements on that shore as well. What other gun emplacements or pillboxes the island might hide would be left for Dilling and his crew to determine.

It was during the month of May 1943, the U.S. Forces attacked and defeated the Japanese forces occupying the islands of Attu and Kiska in the Aleutians. It was also during May that the Japanese submarine I-177 attacked and sank the 3,200-ton, Australian hospital ship AHS Centaur, killing 299.

They timed team insertion around the patrol boat's schedule and the tide table. Not that the tide had to be very high for the team's inflatable boat to clear the reef, because the chart showed at least three feet of water above the reef at mean lower low water, which is the average of the lowest tides recorded for a particular location on the chart.

The final insertion/extraction plan was simple. Insertion would be to the south of the island, with *Orca* surfacing just outside the reef, but in deep water. Sea conditions permitting, Major Dilling and his team would exit the boat through the forward torpedo room hatch, bringing up their gear. The alternative exit point would be the conning tower hatch.

A team of three crewman led by Chief Buckner would assist. Buckner and his men would recover the inflatable from under the cigarette deck, inflate it using ship's air, leaving the inflatable's onboard compressed air cylinder to inflate it for the return trip.

The Marine recon team would get into the inflatable and row ashore, while the COB and his team would return below. *Orca* would submerge to decks awash immediately, and wait for the "all clear," Aldus lamp signal from shore indicating that Dilling and his team had been safely inserted. *Orca* would then clear the area. All this would be done between 0130 and 0230 when the patrol boat would be clear of the area and on its way to the other side of the atoll, and when the half moon would be below the northern horizon.

Orca would then return to the same point, four days later, at 0130, surface with decks awash, and wait until 0200 for a signal light from ashore. If there was no signal, she would return the next night, and so on, for as long as was reasonable, but for at least another four days. If, for any reason, *Orca* missed a day, she would return as soon as possible, and continue to monitor the shoreline for Dilling's signal. If there was still no signal forthcoming after a reasonable period, then Jake would assume the worst, and return to Pearl.

If Dilling's team sent the extraction signal during the original four-day period, and received no radioed acknowledgement from *Orca*, then they would send it again the next night and continue to send it every night following. If they still received no acknowledgement after a reasonable time, they would assume the worst, that *Orca* was lost and would not be returning for them, and that they had to fend for themselves as best they could.

But once the extraction signal was received and returned, Dilling's team would reinflate their boat and row out to the waiting submarine. Then everyone would make the return trip to Pearl aboard *Orca*.

There was a grouping of tiny islands south of Betio, just inside the reef. These were no more than unprotected spits of sand with meager vegetation, and only two were of any size: about fifty feet across. Jake and Cracker had discussed using these for extraction, since it would cut *Orca's* exposure time by half, but decided against it. The plan was rejected because it would require the Marines to inflate their boat on Betio and then paddle out to these outer islands, to wait for *Orca* there. If, for some reason, *Orca* did not show, then the Marines, unable to risk exposure in daylight, would have to return to the Betio shore, and wait until the next night, but this time with a fully inflated boat, one very difficult to conceal from a passing Jap patrol.

It was 0133 on May 27th—Insertion.

Clem, on the periscope, reported to Jake that the patrol boat had cleared the area and had disappeared to the east. Jake ordered the boat to the surface. *Orca* was just outside the reef to the south of Betio, just over two miles from the island's southern shoreline. The SJ and SD radars showed no surface or air contacts, the patrol boat's return signal was hidden in the island's ground return. The fathometer showed 215 feet of water below the boat's keel.

The sea was like a sheet of glass, the night air was clear, and the waning half-moon had already set behind the island. Jake had ordered a full blow, using compressed air, but did not use the low-pressure blowers normally used to completely empty the ballast tanks, because they made too much noise. The boat's decks were still very high and, more important to the Marines, dry. With that much freeboard, *Orca* was an obvious target for anyone on the island with decent night vision. As a precaution, the gun crews were on alert immediately below decks, ready to man their mounts should the situation require. As it turned out, Dilling and his Marines were soon safely in the water, paddling toward the shoreline, and all of *Orca's* gun crew remained below decks. *Orca* silently submerged in place to decks awash, following the insertion from the bridge and by periscope insofar as this was possible.

At 0217, a single, two-second light was observed coming from the shore. The Marine recon team had been safely inserted, and *Orca* submerged completely and cleared the area.

Four days had passed since the Marine recon team had been inserted. At 0130 on May 31st, the patrol boat having cleared the area to the east, *Orca* was on station, watching for a signal from shore. The extraction crew and the gun crews were on standby below decks. No signal came. At 0210 *Orca* cleared the area.

June 1st. *Orca* once again on station offshore of Betio. No extraction signal from shore.

June 2nd. The night was clear, the moon new. Still no sign of the Marines.

June 3rd. Another clear night, but there was a stiff offshore breeze, and the water was choppy. Unlike the other nights, there had been no sign of the patrol boat. This worried Jake, but he decided to surface the boat anyway and search for any signal from the marines. At 0157 a signal was seen. It was the two, two-second light flashes that was the extraction signal, but it was not coming from Betio. The source was much closer, not more than two hundred yards away. Jake remembered the tiny islands just inside the reef. From the bridge, Jake had *Orca* acknowledge with the prearranged radio signal. Jake had just ordered the boat blown high and dry when everything went south.

Suddenly the night was illuminated by a distant, powerful spotlight; the source, Jake knew, had to be the Jap patrol boat that should have cleared the area only an hour earlier. The light was coming from the west, the patrol boat coming out around the end of Betio, and outside the reef. Only about a hundred yards away, to the north, the Marines huddled in their inflatable were easily seen in the suddenly illuminated night, paddling madly for *Orca*. There was a splash well astern, followed by the audible boom of a gun, the patrol boat firing on them, but wildly and just out of range. There were also flashes of small arms fire and popping heard from the beach, but whoever was firing at them was well out of range. Then a big field gun started firing sporadically from the shore to the west, the shells falling thankfully wide and well off target.

Jake ordered the extraction crew and the gun crews up on deck, and then ran back to the cigarette deck to observe the action aft, leaving Clem in charge on the bridge forward. Radar belatedly reported a contact, just on the other side of the island, range 4,000, heading south. The information was relayed aft to Jake by Squid Phillips, whose GQ station for surface action was on the bridge pelorus.

The patrol boat heading south, rounding the reef, Jake thought.

Then Jake heard "I have a man wounded!" The cry came from the inflatable, now only about fifty yards out from the boat. This just as another shore battery opened fire from the east, their aim, thankfully, no better than their compatriots to the west.

Clem also heard the cry from the incoming Marines, and from the bridge, he called down on the 1MC, "Tell the doc we have a wounded man coming aboard." (The "doc" being Pharmacist Mate First Class — PhM1 (SS) — Corey Shields.)

"Contact thirty-five hundred yards and closing." The report from radar again relayed to Jake by Phillips. But now the Marines were alongside, and the wounded man was being lifted aboard by the extraction team, and the boat's guns were manned, ammunition being passed up from below. The patrol boat was still firing on them, but while the shells were coming closer, they were still splashing astern. The small arms fire from the shore had stopped, apparently its futility having become obvious. The big gun to the west fell silent, possibly afraid of hitting the patrol boat. The eastern gun fired again, its shell still wide of the target. Jake's bigger worry was the screaming of aircraft propellers as a plane or planes were preparing to take off from the Betio airstrip.

Chief Walakurski was in charge of the crew on the 4-inch, 50-caliber deck gun. Three men were engaged in passing shells up through the after torpedo room hatch: Seaman James Williams; Gunner's Mate Striker—GMSN (SS)—Joseph Fleming; and Steward's Mate third Class—SM(SS)—Hernando Delacruz. There was one loader, TM2(SS) Austin Rhodes, and another man actually aiming and firing the gun, TM1(SS) Clive Arnold. The maximum range of the four-inch, 50 caliber gun was nine miles, but the gun could only be fired with any kind of accuracy at half that, or about 7,000 yards—and the patrol boat was well inside that effective range.

Unlike *Orca*, a low silhouette on a dark night, at this distance the patrol boat's searchlight presented a clear target. The Chief already had his orders. "Commence firing!" he shouted. The gun barked loudly and hurled the first of many thirty-three-pound projectiles toward the approaching enemy.

Jake, now back on the bridge, observed the chaos forward as the wounded Marine was being passed none too gently down through the forward torpedo room hatch—between shells being passed up—followed quickly by the rest of the recon team. The aircraft could now be heard, rather than seen, as it cleared the end of the airfield and became airborne. The shore batteries had ceased firing, perhaps afraid they might hit the oncoming patrol boat.

The extraction team pushed the inflatable off from the boat, abandoning it to the tide. The three-man *Orca* extraction team then returned below, working around the ammunition being passed up from below, leaving the forward torpedo room hatch open behind them for the gun crew. Once the Marines and the extraction team were safely beneath, Jake's only thought was to secure the guns, submerge the boat and clear the area. He was about to have Clem clear the decks and do just that, or, at a minimum, get the boat moving so at least it wouldn't be a sitting duck target for the oncoming patrol boat.

But before Jake could get the order out, he saw that the plane from Betio was proceeding on a long, lumbering turn as it rounded the east end of the island, and would quickly be lining up for its approach on *Orca*.

That's no fighter, Jake thought. *It's too big and too slow.*

With a clear threat now forward, as well as the other closing quickly aft, he realized that he could never clear the decks fast enough, and that *Orca* was already in the best position to do the only thing she could do under the circumstances — stand and fight.

The 20mm antiaircraft gun mounted forward of the bridge was being manned by TMSN Harvey Stone, a torpedoman striker. "What the hell is that?" he asked as, he took aim at the two-engine monster lumbering toward the boat.

"That," Clem said, "is, I think, a Betty, a small Jap bomber. You may fire at will, Stone."

"Yes sir," Stone said, and began firing. He could see his tracers in the night sky, and, moving the gun, brought his pattern of fire down on and into the approaching bomber. As soon as the shells began tearing into the bomber's wing, it burst into flame. The Betty veered right, toward Betio, and, as it passed down *Orca's* port side, released a bomb. The bomb landed some 150 yards off the port bow, directly hitting the reef, sending shards of rock and shrapnel into the air, and lifting the bow of the boat out of the water a good five feet. Most of the rock and shrapnel landed harmlessly, but some shards dented the boat's saddle tanks and superstructure. One large piece of rock flew over the bridge coaming and struck QM2(SS) Squid Phillips in the head, taking off the top of his skull. Blood and pieces of skull, brains, and clumps of hair spattered the bridge and everyone close by. Mercifully, he was killed instantly. The Betty, meanwhile, veered into the Island and managed to stay airborne long enough to crash there in a massive fireball.

Aft of the bridge, the gun crew was taken unawares by the sudden lifting of the boat from the water. One of the men handling the shells, Seaman James Williams, dropped one, it hit the deck with a clunk, and rolled harmlessly overboard to port, followed closely right under the port lifeline by Williams himself. The other two, Fleming and Delacruz, managed to steady themselves, although Fleming almost fell down the open hatch.

Chief Walakurski fell into the gun, cutting his shoulder, but managed to hang on to the gun and eventually steady himself. Arnold and Rhodes also clung to the gun, and were unhurt.

"Man overboard!" Walakurski shouted, and made his way down the port lifeline to the spot where Williams went overboard. "Keep firing!" he shouted back to Austin and Rhodes.

By now, Jake was back on the cigarette deck. The exploding bomb had affected his hearing, but not badly enough to miss the shout of "Man overboard." He had seen Phillips get hit, but the seriousness of his injury had not registered.

Damn! No way we can leave now, Jake thought. *Can't just take off and leave a man in the water. And now we have another wounded to get below.*

Williams had already swum back alongside when Walakurski reached him, and, holding onto the lower cable of the lifeline. The Chief reached out with his free arm and hauled Williams back aboard.

The patrol boat meanwhile had been coming steadily closer, and was now only a thousand yards away. And whoever was firing the patrol's boat's gun was getting better—the last shell splash was only yards off the starboard quarter. He had an advantage over *Orca's* gun crew: The sub, a steady target, was now clearly illuminated by the boat's spotlight, and he could see his shell splashes and gauge the accuracy of his shooting. Rhodes, on the other hand, firing *Orca's* gun, was being blinded by the oncoming spotlight, and could not see his shell splashes and thus judge his accuracy.

Aiming the four-inch, .50 caliber carefully, Rhodes again took a bead on the patrol boat's spotlight and fired. Seconds later, there was a satisfying explosion, and the light went out. *At last,* thought Rhodes, glad to finally be free of the blinding light, though he still saw circles of light, retinal memory. He continued firing but he need not have bothered. The patrol boat was dead in the water, and was brilliantly aflame. The shell that took the spotlight out had apparently been far more effective than Rhodes had imagined. Soon explosions could be heard as shells aboard the patrol boat cooked off. Jake immediately ordered all guns secured and the gun crews below. In less than a minute, fore and aft, the men had buttoned up their guns and scrambled down below.

Earlier, two of the lookouts, Catinella and Rogers, had drawn the grisly task of bringing Phillip's body down below. Jake could hear propellers screaming on Betio again, and wanted to submerge and clear the area as quickly as possible. Word came up from the conning tower that the after gun was secured, the gun crew was below, and the after torpedo room hatch was secured. "Take 'er down, Clem," Jake ordered as he scrambled down the conning tower hatch.

"Clear the bridge," Clem shouted needlessly, as everyone was already below.

Ah-oo-gah! Ah-oo-gah! the claxon sounded. "Dive, Dive!"

Orca disappeared below the chop just as the second Betty took off from the airfield at Betio.

Walakurski's cut wasn't too long, but was pretty deep and bled a lot. "Doc" Shields closed it with eight stitches, as the COB looked on. The Chief wondered aloud if it would qualify him for a Purple Heart. His hopes were quickly quashed by Bucky's laughter.

First Lieutenant Jennings had taken a round in the leg on Betio, and his femur was broken. Apparently during the early morning hours of June 2nd, a Japanese patrol stumbled upon Dilling's team as they were finishing up mapping gun emplacements on Betio's northeast beach. There had been a gunfight, and, while the Japanese left two dead behind, Jennings had been wounded, their presence on the island had been discovered, and their mission compromised.

They managed to make their way to the south side of the island undetected, but Dilling knew that the team, if it were to survive with one man wounded, would now have to be extracted as quickly as possible. He also realized that the Japanese were not stupid, and that they would be looking for a submarine.

"It would have been obvious," Dilling told Jake, "We might possibly have parachuted onto the island or something, but the only way to get off the island was by sea. And the only way to do that was by submarine. I figured that the Japs, if they couldn't find us, would have figured out that we'd be signaling to a submarine to come get us, and that the sub would have to signal back. I thought that if it was me, I'd station men around the island and look for the sub's signal back, and then I'd go after the sub. I'd sink the sub, and then get the recon team in the water paddling out to the sub."

Jake listened intently, as Dilling continued.

"There was no way I could get to you and tell you what went down, so I figured I could even up the odds a little bit by not signaling to you from the shore, two miles away. Instead I'd get out to that little group of islands just inside the reef, and then we'd be only about two hundred yards away. That way you could still get us off the Island, we would complete our mission, and, if you couldn't skedaddle quick enough, you would at least have had enough time to react to the threat."

"Good thinking. But what if we weren't there waiting? You guys would have been screwed, and the mission a failure."

"Call it a calculated risk, maybe, but I never considered for one second that you wouldn't be there."

"But, Cracker, *anything* could have happened. Any one of a hundred things could have kept us from our rendezvous last night."

Dilling grinned. "Yeah, but they didn't. Now how about we get our info back to Pearl? The High Command's awaitin' on Cracker an' his boys!"

"Doc" Shields had cleaned 1st Lt. Jenning's wound and set and splinted his broken leg with some slats off a vegetable crate. Then he pumped him full of sulfa to ward off infection, and confined him to his bunk.

Jake had Phillip's body cleaned up, but there wasn't much anyone could do to make Phillips' corpse presentable with the top of his head missing. He considered burying him at sea, and he would have done that had they not been on their way back to Pearl. Instead, the body was zippered up into a mattress cover (just as it would have been for burial at sea). Normally, the body would have been transported in an empty torpedo tube, but all the tubes were still loaded. Instead, Jake had space made for it in the cooler. If the cooks were squeamish about retrieving stores from the cooler on the trip back to Pearl, they never mentioned the fact.

The morning watch noted that the boat was trailing a thin stream of fuel oil down the port side. Apparently the Betty's bomb had put more than a dent in one of the fuel oil tanks, either puncturing it, or possibly dislodging a valve seat. From the location of the leak, Jake guessed that it was number one fuel oil tank that had been compromised. As leaks went, it wasn't a very big one, and even should the tank empty itself, there was more than enough fuel in the other tanks to make it back to Pearl. Still, the idea that the boat when submerged would be trailing a telltale oil slick was discomforting.

At 1030 on Sunday, June 13, 1943, *Orca* tied up to a berth at the submarine docks in Pearl Harbor Navy Base, having completed her second war patrol. Her score for the trip was the successful insertion and extraction of a Marine recon team into and from enemy territory; one Japanese patrol boat, damaged, probably sunk; and one Japanese Mitsubishi G4M "Betty" bomber splashed, both by naval gunfire. This at the cost of one crewmember lost to enemy action (QM2(SS) Arnold "Squid" Phillips) and the wounding of Marine 1st. Lt. Calvin Jennings of the Marine recon team. Jake didn't count Chief Walakurski among the wounded.

There was a huge bag of mail awaiting *Orca* when she tied up at the dock, but mail call was put off while 1st Lt. Jennings, strapped securely into a wire basket stretcher, was passed up from below through the forward torpedo room hatch and then waved off to the base hospital in an ambulance.

The next order of business was the transfer of the body of Phillips to the base morgue. The crew lined the rails at attention, as the mattress-cover-enclosed corpse, strapped to a second wire basket stretcher, was passed up through the forward torpedo room hatch and then ceremoniously taken ashore and placed inside a waiting Navy hearse.

Only *then* did the men get their mail. This was the first mail call in over a month, and the men couldn't wait to get their mail. Distribution took only fifteen minutes, the distribution of mail being probably the most orderly and efficient evolution conducted in the armed forces. Jake was rewarded with letters from his parents and his sisters, and with a handful of letters from Kate.

As soon as Jake could detach himself from the brass that had met the boat (which included Rear Adm. Lockwood), and even before his patrol debriefing by the admiral and SUBPAC staff, Jake phoned the base hospital from the telephone at the end of the dock. Yes, nurse Lt. Katherine Shegrue was on duty today, and yes, she would be getting off her shift at 1600, and, yes, she would be more than happy to meet him for dinner at 1800.

Then Jake sat down on the edge of the dock and read every one of Kate's letters.

Chapter 8

Kate: 13 June 1943 to 29 July 1943

After he had digested each and every one of Kate's letters, Jake checked a Chevrolet sedan out of the motor pool and drove to the BOQ for a badly needed long hot shower and a change of clothes.

He stripped naked, and piled his grimy, wash khakis, socks, and underwear in the corner of the room by the closet. He grabbed soap, shampoo, and his shaving gear, and, wrapping a towel around his waist, walked barefoot to the gang bathroom. There he took a long, hot shower, shaving under the decadent stream of glorious, hot, fresh water. Drying off, he padded back to his room. Only then did he notice the stink in the corner of the room, emanating from the pile of dirty clothes.

He dressed in a pair of gray, dress slacks and an open-collared, blue, short-sleeved shirt. He only owned uniform shoes, but he selected his least-used black ones. He was glad that the Officer's Club — the "O" Club — on the base allowed casual dress for dinner. The stodgy "O" club in New London had insisted on either uniform of the day or coat and tie.

Jake drove to Kate's cottage and arrived a few minutes before six o'clock. She was sitting on the front porch, waiting, as he pulled up. He was still getting out of the car, when she threw her arms around him, giving him a long, hard, hello-I-couldn't-wait-to-see-you kiss. When she finally stepped back, smiling, Jake drank her in. She was wearing a simple, yellow, gingham print, sleeveless dress. It had a full skirt that reached just below her knees. Her auburn hair was pulled back away from her face, and her green eyes were leaking tears.

Tears came to Jake's own eyes as he pulled her back into him again, putting his arms around her, just holding her close. "Hi, sailor," she said, whispering into his ear. "You come here often?"

Unable to hold back a chuckle, Jake couldn't think of a single thing to say in reply—so he said nothing and just held her. He wouldn't have been able to get the words out anyway. Finally, he stood back and extracted the twenty-seven-page letter he had written to her in installments while *Orca* was at sea.

"It's not much," he said, "but I wrote whenever I could. No post offices at sea, so no way could I have ever mailed it. But I wanted you to know I was thinking of you."

Taking the letter, Kate again kissed him tearfully—a long, lingering kiss. "I'll read it later," she choked out, and put the letter in her purse.

If pressed, Jake couldn't have told you what he or Kate had for dinner that evening. Kate made most of the conversation, while he mostly smiled, gazing at her like a love-struck puppy. After dinner, they returned to Kate's front porch, sat in the glider, and engaged in some serious necking. Kate read the letter he had written while on patrol, all twenty-seven pages of it. His letter was very much like her own letters to him: newsy, wandering a bit, and, while only occasionally specific, conveying a deep love and burgeoning affection. When she finished Jake's letter, Kate was crying again.

"What's wrong?" he asked. "What did I write in the letter that upset you so?"

"Jake, my true love, sometimes you really are an idiot. I'm crying because you make me so very happy!"

Jake couldn't pretend to understand that. His mother and sisters cried only when they were hurt or sad. Once more, he couldn't think of a single thing to say, so he said nothing and just held her hand.

"Tomorrow," Kate said at last, "you are going to take me to the commissary and buy me a proper engagement ring. And after that, I'm making an appointment with Father Jack so we can find out what we need to do to get him to marry us."

Jake froze. He loved this woman, and definitely wanted her to marry him, but she was moving the process along a lot faster than he had anticipated. He thought they would surely be engaged for a while *before* they talked seriously about marriage. And then there was this war — what if he sailed away and never came back?

Kate caught his reaction immediately, and was apparently prepared for it. "What?!" she said, with just the right tinge of anger in her voice. "I am *not* going to wait for this war to be over, Jake. I want to be your wife, and I want to have our children, but I will *not* wait for you forever. Do you understand? We either do this, or we don't."

"But Katie, think for a minute. What I do is dangerous. Boats go out and never come back all the time. What if —"

"What if nothing," she interrupted, her Irish up now, green eyes ablaze. "If that happens, then it happens, and I'll mourn for you. I surely will. But at least I will have whatever time God allows us to have together, and maybe then I'll even have our child to comfort me." She paused, forcibly calming herself, as tears welled up in her eyes. "You really are *such* an idiot."

"You're right," he said finally. "And I really don't want to wait either."

It was Thursday, June 17th, and Jake had been summoned to a meeting to be held by the Commander of the Pacific Fleet, Admiral Raymond Spruance. It was Spruance, nicknamed "Electric Brain" for his calmness under fire, who had taken command of the Fleet Carrier Force at Midway when its regular commander, Adm. "Bull" Halsey had been sidelined with shingles. And it was Spruance who had orchestrated the American victory at Midway, despite the fact that he had never had a previous carrier command.

Seated at the head of the conference table, Spruance, a tall, gaunt, figure, pointed to an empty chair, obviously inviting Jake to take that seat. Sitting across the table was Major Forrest "Cracker" Dilling, USMC, and a Marine major general unknown to Jake. Alongside the general, and sitting around the table were three members of the general's staff, and an Army lieutenant colonel, who wore the badge of the Army's 27th Infantry. Jake recognized Rear Admiral Harry Hill, who had been battalion officer in the executive staff at the Naval Academy when Jake was still a midshipman. Hill was, Jake learned, currently the commander of Amphibious Group 2. Alongside Hill, Jake recognized two members of Adm. Spruance's staff.

"Uncle Charlie" Lockwood was the last to join the meeting. Once Lockwood was seated, Spruance made introductions all around. The unknown two-star Marine general proved to be Major General Julian Smith. And while Harry Hill would be commander of naval forces for the operation, Gen. Smith was tasked to lead the 2nd Marines, and a part of the Army's 27th Infantry Division for the invasion of Tarawa Atoll.

Major General Julian C. Smith, USMC, the newly appointed Commander of the 2nd Marine Division, was 57 years old and the 2nd Marines was his first combat command. As a colonel, he had commanded a Marine brigade in Quantico, but that was before the war, and his brigade never saw action. His only actual combat experience was limited: as a first lieutenant in the occupation of Vera Cruz in 1914, and as a major in the occupation of Nicaragua in 1930.

General Smith was rankled that he had to fly up from New Zealand for the meeting; he would have preferred that Dilling and the others fly down to meet him. But Ray Spruance had pulled rank, and now Smith and his staff were in Pearl.

Dilling laid out the map he had drawn of Betio Island, along with the Admiralty map of Tarawa Atoll. He pointed out the salient features of the Island, especially the surrounding reef, the airfield, the protected lagoon, and deep-water anchorage north of the Island—and the long dock on the north side, which spanned the reef and the shallows, connecting the anchorage to the shore. He indicated the positions of the fourteen permanent gun emplacements, the forty firing pits scattered around the island, each containing a field artillery piece, and the general locations of pillboxes too numerous to count—"Four hundred, easily, maybe even five hundred," Dilling said. "The island's tiny, two miles long and only eight hundred yards wide at the widest point, but I would estimate that there were more than four thousand Japs on it."

"What about that reef?" Spruance asked. "What were you able to find out about it?"

"Not much, Admiral. We were supposed to take a sounding and record the time when we passed over it. Would have, too, except that it's submerged all the time. We were passing over it in the dark, and we couldn't even see it."

"Guess we have to rely on the Admiralty map, then. Maybe even get some input from the locals," Spruance said. "We need enough clearance to get our Higgins boats over it, if we're going to land the general's Marines on the beaches. How 'bout you, Captain Lawlor? *Orca* did a seaside recon. That map any good?"

"Yes, Sir, Admiral, near as I could tell. My fathometer soundings matched the map soundings almost exactly, and all the land features were right, too, so, I would say the map is good. Of course, we never went nearer to the reef than we had to."

"Right. Major, Betio Island the only place on Tarawa that's got Japs on it?"

"Only place they sat still. We ran into patrols all over the atoll, but the only permanent facilities are on Betio."

"And the airfield?" Smith asked. "What did you see there?"

"Bombers, mostly. Bettys. Counted a dozen of them. Four light recon aircraft. No fighters. At least none while we were there. An unarmed, two-engine transport landed our second day in country, took off the next day. That was about it."

Spruance studied the maps. "Looks like the Japs figure that when we invade, we're gonna invade from the south. Look, their gun emplacements, especially the big ones, they're all sited to enfilade an attacking force from the south."

"That makes the lagoon side the only logical place to land," Smith opined. "The lagoon's protected. The ends of the island, the west side, here, the east end, here," Smith pointed. "And the south side, here and here," he pointed again, "all come from open sea. Imagine trying to cross that reef with any kind of sea running. Nope, the Japs have placed most of their defenses on the wrong side of the Island."

"You, Major," Spruance said, "you were there. Would you try and land on the northern beaches?"

"Due respect, Sir, but I landed my team from the south because that approach was from open sea, and the best place for the submarine if it had to skedaddle quick. If I had known for sure that it was the most heavily defended shoreline, I might have chosen another infiltration point. But then, my recon team wasn't exactly an invasion force, so it worked out for us anyway. In the end, I'd say the Marines are gonna land wherever the general tells 'em to."

At that, the general and his staff smiled grimly; the Army lieutenant colonel looked genuinely uncomfortable, as if he thought that the Marines might actually be certifiably nuts.

"How about it, Admiral," Smith finally asked, addressing Rear Adm. Hill, "can the Navy take those guns out?"

"The big ones, the eight-inchers, most assuredly," Hill replied, "especially if we have a ground spotter on the island. Maybe even most of the field pieces. And the pillboxes? Hell, they're just holes in the sand that the Japs hide in. Won't give them much protection from naval guns. Go in and take Tarawa any way you want, General, and the Navy will pave the way in for you."

"Then we will take Tarawa, Admiral," Smith said, addressing Spruance. "If MacArthur wants that atoll, then the Marines are going to give it to him."

"As you say, General," Spruance said. "As you say."

* * * * *

Kate had picked out a simple ring, a single small diamond set in yellow gold. It cost four hundred and fifty dollars, over a month's pay for Jake, and a good chunk of his savings — more than double Kate's monthly salary. Afterward, Jake caught her looking at it, spreading the fingers on her left hand, smiling proudly. He knew the novelty would eventually wear off, but was happy to share the newness of it all with her — this visible symbol of their engagement — for as long as the novelty lasted.

Father Jack Kleinschmidt was good about it, but pretty much laid it on the line: the Roman Catholic Church did not look kindly on a Catholic marrying a Protestant, and it did everything in its power to discourage such "mixed" marriages. Jake realized, of course, that his Presbyterian Pastor, the Reverend Jacob Roundhead, back in Des Moines, wouldn't be too happy about him marrying Kate, either.

"Father, we're doing this, and we're doing it sooner rather than later," Kate replied testily. "If the Church won't marry us, then we'll just go ahead and live in sin."

"Now, Katie," Father Jack replied, smiling, "just relax. It's not going to come to that, and you know it. Calm down and let Jake and I talk a bit." He turned to Jake. "Jake, while I did say the Church frowns on mixed marriages, I *didn't* say it doesn't permit them. It's just that if you and Kate want to get married in the Church, there are some conditions." (Kate had prepared him for this, and Jake knew what was coming.)

"Now," Father Jack asked, "do you want children?"

"Of course."

"Well, that's the first one, no problem there. You're Presbyterian?"

"Yes, more or less. Since I joined the Navy, I would say I'm more of a 'non-denominational' Protestant."

"Do you have any objection to your children being baptized as infants?"

"Not at all," Jake replied.

"But can you agree to baptize the children in the Catholic Church," Kleinschmidt asked, "and allow them to be raised as Catholics?"

Jake had already discussed this point at length with Kate. He knew his parents would probably be furious, but Kate had sensibly argued that since Jake intended to stay in the Navy, and would frequently be away at sea, the burden of their children's religious upbringing would fall mainly on her. Since she was Catholic, it only made sense that their kids be Catholic. She *did* make the salient point that Catholics were, after all, Christians, just like Presbyterians. Again, even if *he* acceded to her train of thought, Jake was not at all sure that his parents would agree with Kate's logic. It was a sure bet that his pastor would *certainly* never agree with it.

His boyhood pastor had referred to the Catholic Church as "the whore of Babylon," and the Pope as "the Antichrist," and he was sure his current pastor would probably share that opinion.

In the end, however, Jake had a more informed opinion of Catholics and the Catholic Church, and agreed with Kate that it was only logical that they bring their children up Catholic, and that was that.

"Yes, Father, I do agree."

"Second hurdle cleared. If the base chapel were a Catholic Church, I couldn't marry you on the altar. But it's not, so I will. Have the two of you discussed the Catholic Church's position on birth control?" As they had never even touched on the subject, Jake looked quizzically at Kate, who chimed in, "That won't be a problem, Father."

Jake wondered what that meant, exactly, but prudently decided not to pursue the matter there in front of the priest.

"Okay then," Kleinschmidt continued, "the banns. You're both in the military and on active duty, so they can be waived."

Jake had no idea what the "banns" were, and so was glad they were going to be waived—whatever *that* meant.

"Finally, your baptismal certificate, Kate, I'll need to see that."

Jake wondered if he even had one of those, and, if he did, how long it would take to get it to Hawaii. But Father Jack wasn't interested in *his* baptismal certificate, only Kate's.

"Not a problem, Father," Kate said. "I have a copy of it *and* my birth certificate with me."

"Excellent. And your witnesses, they will have to be Catholic."

No problem there, Jake thought. His XO, Clem Dwyer was Catholic, and he'd want Clem to be his Best Man, anyway. He knew Kate had a Catholic friend in mind (her roommate, Pam) who would be her Maid of Honor.

"That's it," Kleinschmidt said. "Sign some papers, Jake, schedule the chapel, and I'll marry you and Kate."

* * * * *

Orca had a burst seam on the port side of number one fuel oil tank, a six-inch tear well below the waterline that looked fine when the boat was standing still, but apparently opened whenever the metal was flexed, as it would in the open sea. It could have been welded up underwater by a diver, but the yard birds decided the boat had to go into dry dock to fix it.

Once in dry dock, the tank was emptied, steam cleaned to remove all traces of fuel oil, and the bottom—normally open to sea—welded shut, so the tank could be pressurized. Five pounds per square inch of air pressure in the tank, and some soap solution, revealed the exact location of the breach in a welded seam. The breach was then gouged out and rewelded shut, and the tank again air tested. The entire operation took four days, including a day to enter the dry dock, and a day to leave. Other than a few dents in her outer skin, *Orca* was now no worse for wear from her encounter with a Japanese bomb.

The boat had only been out on her second patrol for thirty-seven days. The Squadron wanted to turn it around as quickly as possible and get her back out on patrol. But Jake had pleaded for some R & R for his crew and then some ISE to hone their skills. The squadron commander, Capt. Macdonough, had brought the matter up with Uncle Charlie, who eventually reluctantly agreed. *Orca* would have a total of thirty-three days more in Pearl, provided that included two weeks of ISE. That didn't leave much time for a wedding.

Kate made arrangements for use of the base chapel for an hour on Saturday, June 26th. She was lucky to find an open time slot, because June was a very busy month for weddings, even in wartime. Jake checked into the availability of married officers' housing on the base, and found out that there was a long waiting list. Adding his name to the list, he took out a six-month lease on a small, one-bedroom, one-bath cottage just off Lanikai Beach. The rent was expensive, ninety-five dollars a month, but the cottage was immaculate – *and* it had an ocean view. He also paid cash for a 1941 Oldsmobile coupe, with 41,000 miles on it. Automobiles went for a premium in Hawaii; another three hundred and fifty dollars gone.

Trained from childhood to be frugal, Jake had been virtuously setting aside a small portion of his paycheck every month since he was commissioned, and he had built up a nice nest egg. But this whole marriage adventure had used up practically all of it.

Jake and Kate also needed their respective commanding officer's permission to marry, a detail Father Jack had neglected to mention. Macdonough gave his permission readily, provided that he and his wife would be invited to the wedding. Of course, Jake readily agreed, having planned to invite the captain and Lois, his wife, anyway, as well as Adm. Lockwood and his spouse, Phyllis.

Kate's CO, Captain Henry Fernandez, M.D, USN (Medical Corps), also quickly gave his permission.

"You know, Kate," he said, when they met, "while Navy regulations allow Navy nurses to get married, they also say that you *will* be discharged, if you become pregnant. The Navy is a jealous mistress, and doesn't want nurses that can't be relied on around the clock."

Kate smiled. "I know the regs, Captain. I assure you that *that* will not be a problem."

Fernandez returned Kate's smile, thinking that he knew exactly what she meant, and that children were not in the couple's plan for the immediate future. (Apparently, he didn't know Lt. Katherine Shegrue very well.)

Radiotelephone traffic from Hawaii to the mainland was restricted, and civilian phone calls discouraged. They were also expensive — three minutes cost thirty-three dollars. Jake and Kate, as military personnel, managed to place phone calls to their respective families, with each call limited to three minutes. Thus their respective pairs of parents heard the news of their children's upcoming wedding just two weeks before the fact. How well each family received the news was almost impossible for Jake and Kate to gauge, given the poor quality of the transmission and the limited time for each call. Nonetheless, at least both sets of parents now knew that a wedding was in the offing.

* * * * *

The announcement in the *Honolulu Advertiser* was short and to the point:

"Lt. Cmdr. Jacob Lawlor, USN, and nurse Lt. Katherine Shegrue, USNR, were married on June 26, 1943. They were married at 4:00 PM in the Pearl Harbor Base Chapel, Chap. Lt. John Kleinschmidt, USN, officiating. After the ceremony, the happy couple departed the chapel under an archway of crossed swords, provided by the officers of the submarine *USS Orca*, which the groom commands."

Kate was radiant in an off-the-rack, lace-trimmed, white bridal gown and white, tulle veil, and Jake wore officers' dress whites, with sword.

* * * * *

Jake and Kate spent their wedding night, and the following week, honeymooning in the rented cottage off Lanikai Beach. Both had been "saving themselves for marriage," but of the two, Jake was far and away the more inexperienced. Kate may have been a virgin, but she, at least, had been in several romantic relationships before setting her cap for Jacob Julius Lawlor, and had come close to actually having sex at least twice that she could vividly recall. She had suspected all along that Jake was sexually innocent, and she felt some smugness in the knowledge that she, as a nurse, had at least a clinical knowledge of the mechanics of human sexuality.

Even so, Jake's initial ineptitude for marital sex at once surprised, amused, and delighted her. At first, she had to continually reassure him that the intensity of his ardor was absolutely fine with her.

"I love that you're so eager, my love, but I am too, and honestly, I won't break."

For his part, Jake was completely surprised by the sheer force of his own passion, and even more surprised at the power with which Kate returned it. But by the end of their honeymoon, each would have delightedly agreed that both had pretty much gotten the hang of the sex thing.

Each had requested, and been granted, a week's leave. July 5th was an official holiday, and on Tuesday morning, July 6th, both reported back to duty—Jake to *Orca,* and Kate to the day shift at the Base Hospital. With their honeymoon behind them, at

144

each day's end, they met for the drive home, the drive to their home together. Together, at least, until *Orca* redeployed.

The time for beginning the two weeks of ISE for *Orca* came around all too quickly. That meant that for the last two weeks before her deployment, Jake's boat would be at sea for each entire week, coming into port only on the weekends. Jake quickly became accustomed to the routines of married life, of seeing and being with his new wife each and every day, and, even with Kate's crazy nursing schedule, having "regular" sex. It was all so new, so joyful, so exciting, so wonderful. And now it was going to be snatched away. And the Navy was rubbing salt in the wound, because Kate would even have duty over the two weekends.

Once at sea, though, Jake realized that as much as he would miss Kate, he really did love his job. What he did was important, he knew, and, silly as that might sound, he honestly felt that his country was depending on him. He was certain that what he was doing was just as much for Kate — and the family they would have one day — as it was for his Country. And so he got on with it.

Orca had been teamed with a destroyer escort this time, the *USS Daniel White*. The *White* was a brand-new vessel, equipped with the latest in sonar. For its part, *Orca's* two SJ radarscopes had been replaced with a Plan Position Indicator, or PPI scope, which mimicked the chart plot. The boat's position was always in the center of the screen, and any contacts showed as blips of light, which persisted in the screen as the antenna swept past the contact. Further, larger contacts showed up as larger blips in the screen. Their relative position from the center of the screen provided an accurate true bearing and range. An added feature was that the antenna no longer had to be turned by hand, but was rotated by an electric motor attached to the radar mast. As before, however, the boat had to be broached to expose the radar antenna.

While the *White* dutifully acted as target for *Orca* on torpedo runs, readily absorbing strikes from the two practice torpedoes assigned to the boat, *Orca* also had the experience of being detected and cornered with active sonar, and being subjected to mock depth-charging with grenades dropped overboard from the *White*. While the cornering and depth charging were only drills, the terror generated by the experience was very real for Jake and his crew. Jake thanked a beneficent God that the Japanese had not as yet deployed active sonar on most of their ships.

On July 24th, word came down from CINCPAC, Adm. Chester W. Nimitz, that the influence feature on all Mark-14 torpedo detonators was to be deactivated. Henceforward, only the contact pistol would be used to detonate all Mark-14s in the fleet. For some reason, SUBSOWESPAC continued using the magnetic influence feature.

Jake chuckled when he saw the order. All twenty-one of the combat torpedoes loaded aboard *Orca* had already been so modified.

Jake insisted that he and Kate say goodbye at the cottage, and that she not come to the base to see him off. She, too, apparently saw the wisdom in this—it would not do for the crew to see their skipper's wife in tears—so she agreed. The skipper, however, was actually more concerned about his own tears.

On the misty Thursday morning of July 29, 1943, *Orca* departed Pearl Harbor under sealed orders, beginning her third war patrol.

Chapter 9

Orca: *Third War Patrol – 29 July 1943 to 22 August 1943*

As soon as the boat cleared the 100-fathom curve, Jake opened
Orca's sealed orders, which read:

> "Orca *will proceed to the Solomon Islands, there to act in concert*
> *with Allied surface and air forces in the interdiction and destruction*
> *of enemy combatants and supply vessels at sea.* Orca *will operate*
> *under COMSOWESPAC tactical directives in support of Allied*
> *ground action on and around New Georgia and Vella Lavella*
> *Islands.* "

Orca was headed to "The Slot," as New Georgia Sound had
come to be known from its shape and the amount of warships that
traversed it. It was bordered on the northeast by Choiseul, Santa
Isabel, and Florida Islands, and on the southwest by Vella Lavella,
Kolombangara, New Georgia, and Russell Islands. On the south
end of the slot was Savo Island and Guadalcanal, already in allied
hands, and to the north, Bougainville, still very much enemy
territory, as were New Georgia and Vella Lavella.

Jake set course to the southwest. Weather permitting, *Orca*
would cross the thirty-seven hundred miles and be on station in
thirteen days. Jake pushed *Orca*, making the transit at best speed
and, since the weather cooperated (stormy and overcast), mostly
on the surface. *Orca* arrived in the Solomons on the morning of
Wednesday, August 8th.

In a sense, *Orca* had already missed much of the action on
New Georgia. The 4th Marine Raider Battalion had made its first
incursion onto New Georgia in late June, 1943, on Segi Point at the

southeastern tip of the Island. They had met little resistance, and began construction of Segi Point Airfield.

By mid-July planes from the airfield were flying in support of ground action. When *Orca* was departing Pearl, the Marines had already assaulted and secured Munda Point, the Japanese airbase on the southwestern tip of New Georgia. The Marines and the Army were now poised to attack Bairoko Harbor. The Japanese, meanwhile, were fighting a vicious rearguard action around Bairoko, as they scrambled to facilitate the reinforcement of the 10,500 troops on the Island by sea.

The Marines had made their first incursion onto northern New Georgia on July 10th, attacking Japanese coastal guns at Enogai Point, but were beaten back. So also was a subsequent coordinated attack on July 20th, conducted by Marines and Army troops on Dragons Peninsula, which separated Enogai Point and Bairoko.

For *Orca*, hunting enemy shipping in the slot would be dangerous. Protocols had been established for allied submarines to identify themselves to friendly surface vessels, whether surfaced — with Aldus lamp signals or radio signals on a set frequency — or submerged, with identifying flares. But from the air, friendly aircraft were almost as likely to attack an allied submarine as any enemy craft. Bad weather and nighttime, unfriendly to air traffic, these were the submariner's friends.

On August 2nd, 1943, at western end of the Blackett Strait, a narrow channel between the volcanic island of Kolombangara to the north and Kohinggo Island at the northwestern tip of New Georgia to the south, the motor torpedo boat PT-109, under the command of Lt. j.g. John F. Kennedy, USNR, was cut in half by the IJN destroyer Amagiri.

On August 15th, Commander Hiriake Ito brought his destroyer, the *IJN Atsukaze,* to a point just off the northwestern shores of New Georgia Island. Two other ships were keeping station behind him: the 1,500 ton troop transport *MV Kinisaki,* and a 1,200-ton food supply ship, *MV Junyo Maru.*

Atsukaze had left refit in Yokosuka three weeks earlier and stopped briefly at Rabaul to embark 300 troops and to join up with *Kinisaki* with 2,100 troops aboard, and a fully loaded *Junyo Maru.* *Atsukaze* then proceeded en route to Bairoko escorting *Junyo Maru* and *Kinisaki,* and under orders to disembark the 2,400 reinforcements there and to deliver badly needed food supplies. Once safely in port, Ito was to assist in the defense of the base there with his six, 127mm, 50 caliber guns, and, "should it become necessary," to assist in any eventual troop withdrawal to Bougainville.

While in Yokosuka, Ito had taken the precaution of moving his wife and two daughters away from the increasingly frequent air raids from American, carrier-based aircraft on the city, to the relative inland safety of his wife's family home, in the industrial city of Nagasaki.

Ito was fully aware that the war was going badly for the Empire, but was convinced that if winning the war could be made sufficiently costly for the Allies, they would come to the bargaining table, and a negotiated and honorable peace could be obtained. He had vowed, therefore, to do his part to make the war as costly as possible for the enemy.

Rather than approach Bairoko Harbor down the Slot, which was awash in both enemy and imperial shipping and heavily patrolled by enemy aircraft, Ito had elected to approach Bairoko in an end-around from the west via the Blackett Strait.

But Blackett Strait was not without its dangers. The passage was made treacherous by day, by patrolling enemy aircraft, and, by night, by American motor torpedo boats. Then there was the coral reef that lined the strait along the northern shore of Kohinggo Island, and the fact that the Strait was heavily mined. But Ito was confident that he and his two charges would be able to safely navigate the narrow safe channel passage. He had an excellent chart of the channel, and the turning points were fixed by shoreline features. These features may not be visible at night, when he planned his transit, but Ito felt confident he could negotiate the channel by "dead reckoning" alone, that is, negotiate the safe route through the channel, and determining the turning points, by knowing *Atsukaze's* course and speed and the passage of time alone.

Blackett Strait separates Kolombangara from Arundel to the south and Gizo to the west.

Whatever risk was involved, Ito calculated it would be well worth it. First of all, the maneuver would be unexpected. Second, once through the Strait, passage into Bairoko Harbor along the northern shore of New Georgia Island was far safer than the alternative: running the gauntlet down the Slot, and then paralleling the east-to-west route into Bairoko, the very same route that the attacking U.S. Marines and Army Infantry were sure to take.

Bairoko itself was heavily defended by a network of anti-aircraft guns, coastal gun emplacements, machine gun nests, and hidden defensive lines. Taking the port would be no easy task for the Allied forces, and Ito was determined to make the task impossible, or, at the very least, as difficult and as costly to the enemy as possible. *Atsukaze's* guns and the reinforcements and supplies he and his escorted ships carried could, he knew, be vital to the defense of Bairoko.

* * * * *

Thus far, *Orca's* main task had been to avoid Allied shipping. She had been able to operate on the surface on the nights of August 15th and 16th, but remained submerged during daylight. On the night of the 16th, *Orca* was operating on the surface in the waters of the Kula Gulf, northwest of Bairoko and southeast of the Island of Kolombangara, just off the eastern entrance to the Blackett Strait. Off to the southeast, at Bairoko, furious fighting was in progress, as the assaulting Marines and Army units once more struggled to dislodge the Japanese from their last foothold on New Georgia.

* * * * *

Atsukaze could make thirty-eight knots, but on this night of August 16, 1943, she was cruising at a mere eight, a mother hen leading a brood of two chicks through the Blackett Strait.

There had been a full moon on the 11th, and while the overcast sky obscured the moonlight, the weather was otherwise clear, and the visibility, much to Cmdr. Hiriake Ito's dismay, was very good. There was no breeze whatsoever, and the surface of the water was like shimmering glass. He and his convoy would be sitting ducks for any enemy aircraft that braved the night sky or for more motor torpedo boats then he would be able to fend off with *Atsukaze's* guns.

There were the flashes of big guns firing to the southeast, and Ito concluded that this was no time to hold back. And, besides, he was already determined to risk the night passage. The troops and supplies he and his "chicks" carried to Bairoko were, after all, vital to the Imperial cause. There was still the possible presence of PT boats in the Strait, but, by proceeding at night, he at least minimized the risk of being discovered by enemy aircraft. It was bad enough that the waters beyond the Blackett Strait were awash with enemy warships, and worse, enemy submarines.

He had cautioned *Atsukaze's* lookouts to be especially vigilant for enemy aircraft and PT boats. It was on nights such as this that Ito fervently wished the Imperial Naval Command had seen its way clear to outfit its destroyers with radar *instead* of his newly-installed active sound gear—on which his crew had been only minimally trained. And Ito was sure that the bulbous sound head now mounted below the ship's bow would do nothing more than slow *Atsukaze* down.

The passage through the Strait was arduous, but thanks to the excellent visibility, it was possible to establish the channel's turning points by sighting objects on land. If *Atsukaze* had to rely on dead reckoning alone, traversing the Strait could possibly have ended in disaster. The two charges in line behind *Atsukaze* had to been instructed to follow her course precisely—a directive that Ito had drummed into their Masters' heads in Rabaul. And, in the Blackett Strait, at least, fortune smiled on *Atsukaze* and her charges. Not a single aircraft or motor patrol boat had discovered their presence.

Atsukaze had just cleared the channel when a report came to the bridge that one of its lookouts had reported a possible submarine sighting just off the starboard bow. Ito brought his binoculars to bear on the area of the "possible" sighting to the southeast, but could see nothing. Still, he would take no chances. He ordered the word radioed back to his charges that *Atsukaze* was investigating a possible enemy submarine contact, and that they were to hug the southern shoreline and proceed into port at Bairoko at best speed, once they were clear of the Strait. His charges, at least, had cleared the last turn in the channel, and were now on a straight course into the Kula Gulf.

Increasing speed to twenty knots, Ito ordered his ship on a course due southeast. *Atsukaze* was fully armed with eighteen torpedoes (fired from nine torpedo tubes) and thirty-six depth charges. If there *was* a submarine in the area, he would make certain that it would never harm either of his chicks.

* * * * *

Jake could hardly believe his luck. Radar had reported three contacts traversing Blackett Strait to the northwest, but these could very well have been friendlies. He was delighted when the contacts were finally spotted by his lookouts: an enemy destroyer and two marus, clearing the Strait. Despite an overcast sky that night, it was almost like broad daylight out there, and Jake worried that he had been seen by the enemy. As a precaution, he quickly dived the boat, reasoning that if that destroyer had spotted them on the surface, he would have had to dive to avoid him in any case.

With *Orca* submerged at periscope depth, Jake had had Clem raise the scope for a look-see. It was soon obvious that the destroyer had either detected them on the surface, or had seen the scope, because it was making its way toward them at speed. Jake ordered *Orca* to a hundred and fifty feet (a deep dive in these waters) and waited until fast screws passed close aboard to port. He then came back to periscope depth. It was the marus that he wanted.

* * * * *

Ito was in the approximate location where the sub had to be — *if* there even was a sub. He came to dead stop, and waited, his lookouts on full alert. His men, on the passive sound gear, heard nothing but the ships now clearing the channel. He then ordered an active sound gear search. The pings reverberated throughout the ship. The operator reported that he had an echo return, but he was unsure that it came from a submarine. In these shallow waters, he reported that the returned echo might just be a signal bounced off the bottom.

So much, Ito thought, *for this new sound capability.*

If there *was* a submarine out there, had it sighted him? How could it not? Any submarine would have dived by now, and would be biding its time, waiting for *Atsukaze* to clear the area. He knew that the sub would concentrate on destroying his chicks, and that if he kept it down, and kept it deep, his charges would then have their best chance of making port. He ordered two depth charges rolled off the stern, encouraging the enemy, if there, to stay deep.

The active pinging of the enemy's sound gear had sent a shudder through *Orca's* crew. This was a new dimension from the enemy, and a feared one. To a man, they recalled their last ISE in Pearl, and how easily the *Daniel White* had been able to locate them with active sound gear.

Boom! Boom! Two depth charge explosions were heard well off the port quarter. They were at least a thousand yards away, possibly more.

"Have sonar give me a single ping bearing and range to nearest contact," Jake ordered.

Seconds later, the pinging of its own active sonar resounded through the boat.

"Sonar reports range to nearest contact fifteen hundred, Captain, bearing zero-nine-three. Active pinging, but no screw noise, appears to be dead in the water."

"Ask sonar if there are any other contacts."

"Sonar reports two other contacts, Captain, slow turning screws, bearing three-zero-five, range seven thousand, and three-one-one, range eight thousand."

"Another single-ping bearing and range to all contacts."

Seconds later, another single ping was heard.

"Sonar reports first contact still bearing zero-nine-three, range fifteen hundred fifty, still pinging, no screw noise. Contacts two and three bearing three-zero-three, range seven thousand, and three-zero-nine, range eight thousand."

Lou Carillo called up from chart plot, "Contacts two and three seem to be traveling in line, speed nine, on approximate course one-three-five."

"Keep the scope down, Clem, until we're ready to fire," Jake ordered. "That Jap destroyer is making so much noise with his own sound gear that he's not hearing ours. We'll track 'em by sonar, single-pinging every minute or so, and get into firing position on the lead transport that way. We'll fire at the leading maru, and then, when the destroyer comes after us with the bit in its teeth, we'll get a snap shot off at her with the rear tubes."

And then Jake ordered, "Rig for depth charge, but leave the control room hatch open." He knew full well that unless he got a lucky hit, the Jap destroyer would be after *Orca* with a vengeance, and the boat would be due for a pounding.

"Aye, Captain," Clem replied, and set his best guess at the transport's masthead height into the attack periscope stadimeter.

"Make your depth six-zero feet. Ahead slow, course one-seven-zero. Prepare tubes one, two, and three forward, seven and eight aft. Open outer doors."

"Maneuvering reports all ahead slow, making minimum turns."

"Outer doors open. All stations report rigged for depth charge."

"On course one-seven-zero."

"Very well"

By now, a full minute had passed.

"Sonar, single-ping bearings and ranges to contacts?"

"Forward torpedo room reports tubes one, two, and three ready."

"Sonar reports nearest contact zero-eight-four and drifting slowly left, fifteen hundred fifty yards; two others bearing three-zero-three, range sixty-five hundred and three-zero-eight, range seventy-five hundred, both moving left."

"After torpedo room reports tubes seven and eight ready."

"At six-zero feet, Sir."

To Hal Chapman, the diving officer, and to sonar, Jake replied, "Very well," and then said to Early Sender on the TDC, "Set up on the lead transport, Early, bearing three-zero-three, range sixty-five hundred, course one-three-five, speed nine."

"Aye, Captain," Early replied, repeating the order. And, seconds later, "I have it set up, Captain."

Lou Carillo called up from chart plot, "Projected CPA is five thousand yards, bearing two-three-five. Target at CPA in six minutes."

Three minutes later, Jake ordered another single ping range. The target bearing was 279, range 4,500 yards.

"How's it look, Early?"

"Good, Captain, target still on course one-three-five, speed nine. I have a firing solution."

"CPA is forty-three hundred yards, bearing two-three-three, in three minutes," Carillo added.

"Very well. I want a spread of three, Early. Two degrees left and right."

"Aye, Captain, spread two degrees left and right."

Three minutes flew by, and Jake nodded to Clem. "Go!" was unspoken.

Clem, "Up scope." He swung around to the expected bearing of the lead transport, found it, and shouted, "Bearing, mark!"

The former port lookout and newly-promoted QM3(SS), John Catinella, sang out, "two-three-three!"

On the attack scope, Clem manually brought the top of the masthead optically in line with the waterline.

Range, Mark!"

Leaving the scope up, Clem was already swinging it around to the destroyer, and cranking in its estimated masthead height.

"Forty-two hundred yards"

"Sonar reports fast screws closing, bearing zero-nine-six."

Early cranked in the TDC corrections. "I have a firing solution!" he announced.

"Fire one," Jake ordered, and the boat shuddered.

"One away."

"Two degrees left, fire two."

"Two degrees left, two fired."

"Two away."

"Two degrees right, fire three."

"Two degrees right, three fired."

156

"Three away."

Early quickly shifted the TDC to a solution for the destroyer, putting it on a reciprocal course from its last reported bearing, 276, and closing at 20 knots.

"Sonar reports three torpedoes running hot, straight, and normal."

"Bearing, Mark!"

"Zero-seven-six."

"Range, Mark!"

"Nine hundred yards."

"I have a firing solution."

"Down, scope."

"Fire seven."

"Seven fired."

Again the boat shuddered, this time kicking it forward.

"Seven away."

"Spread one degree right, fire eight."

"One degree right, eight fired." Another push felt.

"Eight away."

"All ahead full, left full rudder, make your depth one-five-zero feet."

"Rudder is left full."

"Maneuvering reports making maximum turns."

"Very well."

"Sonar reports torpedo noise disappearing into destroyer screw noise, Captain."

"Very well."

"Sonar reports fast screws, closing."

The destroyer had obviously avoided the oncoming torpedoes, and swung left to port, anticipating *Orca's* move in the same direction.

Two depth charges went off almost immediately, but they were well off to port.

"Sonar reports contact one stopped. No longer active pinging."

"He's stopped to see if he can hear us, Captain," Clem said.

Four minutes after the first torpedo was fired, there was a muffled explosion.

"Well, we hit something, Captain," Clem observed.

"Has to be the transport." Jake observed. "But I suspect that we'll regret having missed that destroyer very soon, now."

* * * * *

Ito was furious. His lookouts had spotted the enemy periscope almost as soon as it had broken the surface, but the submarine had still managed to get its torpedoes fired off. Now, one of his chicks, *Junyo Maru*, had suffered a direct hit forward, and was in flames.

It had been all he could do to escape a similar fate, but he had saved *Atsukaze* and its precious cargo of troops with a quick turn at speed to port, avoiding the ominous oncoming wakes of two enemy torpedoes as they passed by close aboard to starboard. His over-anxious crew had panicked at seeing their wakes, and wasted two depth charges by ejecting them without orders. The ensign in charge of that crew would hear about that later.

Ito had ordered the boat stopped and the active sonar secured to listen for the sub when the *Junyo Maru* was hit. Now, passive sonar had heard the sub, just off *Atsukaze's* starboard bow. The sub had to be just to the left of a slight disturbance in the glassy surface — the knuckle where the sub had turned and gone deep at full speed.

Now he would get that *ujimushi* (maggot). Once over the spot, *Atsukaze* let loose two more depth charges.

Then Ito again brought *Atsukaze* to a dead stop. Perhaps with the sub close by, his new sound gear might yet prove useful.

The charges rocked *Orca* hard, lifting her violently up from behind. Fortunately, *Orca* was already deep enough so that her stern did not broach. And the destroyer's sonar was again pinging away, a frightening probe searching, searching. And now close.

A frightened helmsman reported "Passing a hundred and eighty, Sir."

"We were at a hundred and ten feet, Captain, but we've been blown back up to ninety," Hal Chapman called up from the control room.

"Get her down to a hundred and fifty feet, Hal."

"Aye Captain, a hundred and fifty feet."

"All stations, damage report," Jake ordered, and the talker conveyed throughout the boat."

"After torpedo room reports inner door seal on number eight tube leaking badly. Outer door appears to be locked open."

"Passing a hundred and ten feet again, Captain."

"Passing course one-six-zero, Sir."

Boom! Wham! Two more depth charges went off, this time forward and to port, not as close as the first two, but close enough, this time, to drive down *Orca's* bow and produce a dangerous down angle. There was noise throughout the boat as anything not tightly secured — men included — fell forward. Again the pinging resumed, close aboard, unrelenting.

"Forward torpedo room reports, pit sword well leaking badly." The pitometer log, a device that indicates the boat's speed through the water, is housed in a fairwater called a "sword" because of its shape. The sword extends into the water though a gland in the pressure hull, and is able to be retracted in shallow water or for servicing.

"They're tightening down on the gland, Sir."

"Passing course one-three-zero, Sir."

"All stop." Then, after that order was conveyed to the maneuvering room, "How are they doing forward?" Jake asked.

Hal Chapman called up from the diving station, "Bow and stern planes on full rise, but we're heading down fast, Captain. Passing a hundred and sixty feet. Bubble at two-zero down and not moving."

Despite the seriousness of their situation, Chapman reported it in a steady voice, with no hint whatever of panic. The rest of the crew in the control room drew courage from his even-tempered demeanor, confident that whatever happened, Mr. Chapman, and, by extension, their other officers, would be able to handle it. Still, the pinging from the destroyer's sonar continued, the source still very close.

"What's the fathometer reading?" Jake asked. These waters were shallow, and it wouldn't bode well if *Orca* hit bottom.

"We have fifty feet under the keel, Captain," Lou Carillo, reading the fathometer mounted over the chart table, called up from the chart plot.

"Passing course zero-nine-zero, Sir."

Jake continued to leave the rudder on left full, knowing that now it would help slow the boat's descent.

"Passing a hundred and ninety feet, Captain, bubble now on fifteen degrees down. Request all back full."

The talker manning the sound-powered phones in the conning tower reporting: "Forward torpedo room still taking on water from the pit sword well. Chief says they're gaining on it."

"All Back full," Jake ordered.

* * * * *

Junyo Maru had managed to bring the fire under control and the ship's Master had grounded his ship on the shoals of Kohinggo Island, miraculously avoiding hitting a mine on the way in.

160

This time Ito's active sonar operator was sure he had made contact with a submarine. The operator reported his contact 200 meters further to the south-southwest. Ito secured the active sonar once *Atsukaze* was over the indicated spot and sent two more depth charges over the side.

* * * * *

The pinging stopped and two more depth charges went off, *Boom! Boom!* this time off the starboard stern quarter, and further away. The pinging resumed, not as close aboard as before perhaps, but still very close. Jake realized that if and when the boat recovered depth control, they would be backing in that direction, but right now their survival rested in first controlling the dive.

"You still have bow buoyancy, Jake," Clem interjected, his voice as steady as Chapman's had been moments before.

"Not yet, Clem, not unless it's my only hope." Jake had known he still had the option of putting air into the bow buoyancy tank, thus lifting up the bow, but was leaving that option off the table for the time being. Too much air would release air bubbles to the surface and reveal their position, and air with sufficient pressure to move water at this depth would be likely to then expand and bubble out at any shallower depths, again, giving away their position.

Jake also had the option to blow negative dry, with the same telltale bubble problem, and blowing negative would not lift up the bow the way blowing bow buoyancy would. A third option was putting a bubble in safety tank, another hardened interior tank amidships (ominously, with a capacity equal to the volume of the conning tower), which posed the identical telltale bubble problem.

The best option for the time being, Jake knew, was to see if he could power the boat out of its nosedive.

The fool operating the new sound gear had lost contact again. Ito, unaware of the turmoil going on beneath him as his prey struggled to recover depth control, once more projected himself into the mind of the submarine's commander. If he were in charge of his adversary's boat, he would not easily give up on attacking the second of his chicks.

He resolved to move *Atsukaze* in the direction of the retreating *Kinisaki* and remain between that ship and his last point of contact with the sub, attacking from that direction. As badly as he wanted to destroy the enemy submarine, protecting the troops aboard *Atsukaze* and *Kinisaki* was far more important.

* * * * *

"Passing course zero-seven-zero, Sir."

"Passing two hundred feet, Captain, bubble has eased to ten degrees down."

Better news this time, but delivered in the same steady voice.

Ping, ping, ping, the source further in the distance, now.

"Very well. What's the fathometer reading?" Jake asked.

"We have twenty-six feet under the keel, Captain," Lou Carillo called up from the chart plot.

That wasn't good.

"Depth, Hal?"

"Two hundred and four feet, Captain, bubble easing to seven down."

"Forward torpedo room reports pit sword well leak secured, Sir."

"Excellent!" Jake allowed. "Find out how they're doing aft."

"After torpedo room, report."

"Steadying out at two hundred and five feet, Captain. Bubble now at zero."

"What's the fathometer reading?" Jake asked.

"We still have twenty-six feet under the keel, Captain," Lou Carillo called up from the chart plot.

"Very well. All stop! See if you can hold her there, Hal. All ahead slow. What's your course?"

"Zero-five-three, Captain."

"After torpedo room reports still taking on water. Pumping bilge to sea, but not keeping up. Chief says he's working on a fix for the inner door."

"Very well. Helm, come to course zero-four-five."

"Zero-four-five, aye, Sir."

"Barely holding at two hundred and five feet, Captain," Chapman reported, "but both sets of planes are still on full rise, and we have a zero degree bubble. Boat's *very* heavy, Sir."

"Heavy, aye. See what I can do to help out," Jake replied. Then, to the talker, "Parra, ask maneuvering how much we have left in the can."

* * * * *

The sound gear operator was sure he had a contact. Two hundred fifty meters, bearing two-four-zero. Ito brought *Atsukaze* to that spot, stopped, and waited, his sound gear still searching.

* * * * *

The pinging louder, closer, now.

"Maneuvering, how much is left in the can?" the conning tower talker, Seaman George Parra, who had just joined the boat in Pearl, asked.

Seconds later. "Maneuvering reports about forty-five percent battery capacity, Captain."

"Not great," Jake said.

Boom! Wham! Another two explosions, this time very close to their position, but apparently well above the boat as their net effect was to drive *Orca* suddenly deeper.

163

"Captain," Hal called up to the control room, "we're at two hundred and ten feet and still going deeper. We're having a real hard time staying up." (No panic, just reporting the facts.)

"All ahead two-thirds!"

"Maneuvering answers 'all ahead two-thirds', Captain."

And then, seconds later, "Forward torpedo room reporting, Sir, pit sword's sprung a leak again."

"On course zero-four-five, Sir."

"Very well."

Boom! Another depth charge explosion is heard, still above, but further above than the last two, and this time almost dead astern, the pinging still loud.

"Still unable to keep depth, Captain, passing two hundred and fifteen feet."

"Very well, Hal. I'll do what I can. Keep your planes on full rise. Maneuvering, all ahead full."

"Maneuvering, all ahead full . . . making turns for 'all ahead full', Sir, and forward torpedo room reports pit sword's leak stopped again, but that they may have damaged it, tightening up on the seal again."

"Very well. A damaged pit sword is better than a leaky one."

"Two hundred and twenty feet, Captain."

"Fathometer reading, Lou?" Jake asked.

"We have twelve feet under the keel, Captain," Carillo called up from the chart plot.

There was nothing else for it now.

"Put a bubble in safety tank," Jake ordered. "Three-second blow."

On the hydraulic manifold, Bucky responded, "Three-second blow on safety tank." He opened the valve allowing compressed air to enter the tank for three seconds. "Three-second blow to safety tank complete, Captain," he reported, as he shut the air valve.

"Very well."

"After torpedo room reporting, Sir. Chief says they've jury-rigged a clamp on the inner door of number eight, but the leak hasn't slowed much. And the bilge pump can't keep up."

"We're still too deep," Jake said to no one in particular. Then, to Hal Chapman, "How we doing at holding depth, Hal?"

"Better, Captain," Chapman reported in his same, steady voice. "The speed and the bubble in safety helped. Actually using the planes to get her up, now. We're passing two hundred feet now and rising slowly. But we did get down to two hundred and twenty-five feet before she started to come back up."

Pinging, still loud.

"Good. See if you can bring her back up to a hundred and fifty feet. That would sure help with that leak aft."

"Aye, Captain. I've a five-degree up bubble with the planes at full rise. Plainsmen, make your depth one-five-zero feet."

"One-five-zero, aye," both planesmen sang out. The bow planesman, Rogers, had his planes on full rise to drive up the bow, while the stern planesman had his planes on full dive, pushing down the stern. This was done so as to achieve the desired "up" bubble, that is, putting the boat into an upward attitude so as to achieve the desired shallower depth. The boat was easing up to the desired depth, but painfully slowly.

"Passing a hundred and ninety-five feet, Captain."

"Very well."

* * * * *

Kinisaki was well out of range of the sub now. Ito's job now was to preserve *Junyo Maru* from any further damage.

The sound operator was sure he had contact with the enemy, almost directly below *Atsukaze.* Once more Ito secured the sound gear and rolled off two more depth charges.

Ping! Ping! Ping! Then silence.

Two more depth charges went off, closer this time, still above *Orca*. *Boom! Wham!* Once again, *Orca* was driven deeper, and once more the destroyer's sonar began probing.

"Passing two hundred and ten feet, Sir!" Hall called up to control, as the large shallow-depth, gauge glass shattered, sending shards of glass across the compartment. Seaman Harold Rogers, on the bow planes, was cut over his left eye, and the cut was bleeding badly. Hal Chapman sang out "Medic!" and PhM1C(SS) Corey Shields ran aft from his GQ station in the forward battery to attend to Rogers. He soon had the blood flow staunched, and Rogers never had to leave his station.

Once more, the pinging stopped. By now everyone aboard *Orca* knew what that meant and braced for another pounding.

Yet another depth charge went off, this time astern off the port quarter, about the same depth as the last one. *Boom! Wham!* The boat lurched violently, but this time it was driven up.

"Passing two hundred and five feet, Captain. Boat is rising."

"Very well, Hal, let's try for that hundred and fifty feet again, shall we?"

"Aye, Sir, one hundred and fifty feet." Chapman actually betrayed some amusement in his voice.

Another depth charge, shallower, well to port. *Boom!* The pinging resumed. Was it softer?

"There's only one destroyer up there. How many of those bloody things does he have?" Clem asked, addressing no one in particular.

"Enough, apparently," Jake answered, "to keep us down and deep. Doesn't want us getting a shot off at that other maru. Can't say I blame him—that's what I'd do in his shoes. With all this infernal pinging, our listening gear's probably useless. But then, so is his."

"Back to a hundred and ninety-five feet, Captain, heading for a hundred and fifty feet."

"Sonar, single ping ranges. Can you still see those contacts?"

Soon afterward sonar reported back. "Sonar report two contacts, Captain, one bearing two-four-eight at eighty-five hundred yards, with his bearing drifting east-southeast, and a second, apparently dead in the water, bearing two-five-eight at sixty-five hundred yards."

"Sounds about right. Looks like we crippled the one transport, but didn't sink her. The second one's long gone. The destroyer is doing its best to keep itself between us and the cripple, and to keep us deep – *and* he's doing a good job at it."

"At a hundred and fifty feet, Captain."

"Very well."

"After torpedo room reports they're still taking on water, but the chief has rigged a second clamp on the inner door, and the leak has slowed. Water in the bilge is above the deck plates, but isn't rising anymore."

"Excellent. How's she holding depth, Hal? Can I slow the boat down yet?"

"A hundred and fifty feet, Skipper. I think I can hold it if you just slowly ease down on the speed, Captain."

"Good. All ahead two-thirds."

"Maneuvering answers 'all ahead two-thirds', Captain."

"Very well."

* * * * *

The sound operator had lost contact again. Frustrating. Ito secured the sound gear and dropped another depth charge at the point of last contact, then resumed the sound search. Short of an actual kill, the important thing was to keep the sub away from *Junyo Maru*.

Another depth charge. *Boom!* But this time it was well off the starboard quarter, and barely a ripple went through the boat. The pinging continued, but definitely not as loud as before.

"Make your course zero-two-zero. He's hunting now. We may well have lost 'em."

"That would be nice," Clem offered. Jake chuckled.

"Zero-two-zero, Aye, Sir."

"On course zero-two-zero, Sir."

"Very well. Bring her up to one hundred feet. Hal"

"Aye, Captain, one hundred feet." Then, to the planesmen, "Ten degree up bubble, one hundred feet."

Soon, "One hundred feet, Sir."

The boat now appeared to be under control.

"Very well. I'm slowing the boat again, Hal. Let me know if you have trouble holding her on depth."

"Aye, Captain,"

"Ahead one-third."

And later, "How we doing, Hal?"

"Good, Captain, seems to be holding depth good, now." (And the infernal pinging was no longer audible.)

"Excellent!" Then to no one in particular, "Gentlemen, we're done for tonight. How about we slink off and live to fight another day."

"Sounds good to me," Clem opined.

"Chapman's amazing," Jake said. Clem and Jake were alone in the wardroom.

"Cool under fire," Clem agreed. "Hal will make an excellent skipper, someday."

"Agreed."

A picture of Chapman, balding, lean, a good six inches taller than him (wasn't everybody?) formed in Jake's head. He had handled himself well today. But then, in the end, so had they all.

An hour before dawn *Orca* surfaced into a dense fog and a sea free of any sonar or radar contacts. Her tormentor was last seen on sonar hours ago, retiring to the south. Jake had counted sixteen depth charges, still less than half of a *Fubuki*-class's full complement of thirty-six, but enough to put the fear of God into him and his crew.

The blessed fog, if it lasted, would allow *Orca* to fill her badly depleted batteries, but the outer door on number eight tube was permanently stuck open, at least for the rest of this patrol, and a series of clamps on the inner door was all there was between the boat and the deep blue sea. At least, Jake consoled himself, they had crippled, maybe even sunk, the one transport for their trouble.

On sending a damage report to SUBPAC, *Orca* was ordered to the repair facilities in Brisbane, Australia, just over 1,300 miles away. They could be there in under a week.

Orca arrived at Brisbane on Sunday, August 22, 1943 — Winter down south — and it was freezing. The boat arrived at Moreton Bay in the wee hours of the morning, and the sun was well up before the boat penetrated the harbor. Jake spent the time putting the finishing touches on his continuous letter to Kate, now that he would have a chance to actually mail it to her.

Swathed in foul weather gear, Jake viewed the port from the quarterdeck, as *Orca* actually entered the harbor. Brisbane's harbor was a vast network of maritime facilities spread out over an island that jutted out into Moreton Bay. There were all sorts of submarine repair facilities upriver at Teneriffe: the sub tender *Griffin*; repair and replenishment docks; barracks; and even drydock facilities available — and all that just up the Brisbane River.

Jake hoped for a quick turnaround for the repair of number eight torpedo tube and refueling and replenishing of stores and torpedoes. He had last seen Brisbane during the *S-49* inquiry, which, though it ended well, was not what Jake considered to be one of his most satisfying memories. This visit wouldn't change that impression all that much.

Chapter 10

Brisbane: 22 August 1943 to 26 August

The only problem encountered with "rig for port" was difficulty in retrieving the pit sword. Among other things attended to before entering any port, was retracting the pit sword, cranking the device up into the boat so that it no longer protruded beneath the keel. Apparently, tightening down on the seals that kept seawater out had somehow damaged the assembly, and now it again leaked.

That Sunday morning in August, the boat's mooring lines were made fast to dockside in the Port of Brisbane, Australia, at the sub base well up the Brisbane River in the inner city suburb of Teneriffe. Jake Lawlor, standing beside his XO and exposed to the weather on *Orca's* bridge, felt a damp chill run through his body. It was the dead of winter in the Southern Hemisphere, and Brisbane was far enough south for the weather that morning to be cold and miserable.

Teneriffe was a busy place. Brisbane had been one of the destination ports for the S-boats stationed in Cavite after Pearl Harbor, and while there were four S-boats tied up alongside the sub tender, *USS Griffin,* there were also now three fleet boats there as well. The port had a single dry dock at the beginning of the war, but since it was just the right size to service submarines, and since it was well out of the range of Japanese aircraft in New Guinea, the choice of Brisbane as a submarine service facility for the U.S. Navy was a natural.

By the spring of '42, the *Griffin* had arrived in Teneriffe along with a dozen or so sugar boats. In no time, the port facilities expanded to service fleet boats as well as S-boats, and Brisbane became a homeport for both generations of American submarines and the occasional British boat. Jake had expected to join the brood tied up alongside *Griffin*, but was instead directed to a berth directly alongside the repair dock.

First aboard the boat was an Aussie lieutenant commander in a rumpled uniform, who introduced himself with an outstretched hand and wide smile.

"Trevor Quigby, Mate, Captain of the Port."

Quigby's breath left a vapor trail. In contrast to Jake's buttoned-up, foul weather jacket, Quigby was without an overcoat, and seemed oblivious to the chill. He was short, wiry, and *very* blond. His face was somewhat pinched and craggy, his complexion ruddy, and he had prominent cheekbones, ice-blue eyes, and a continuous smile.

"Commander Quigby, I'm Jake Lawlor," Jake replied, as he shook Quigby's hand, "and this is my Executive Officer, Clem Dwyer. Welcome aboard *Orca*."

Below, in the wardroom, with Clem, and now Bucky, present, Quigby and the Americans first exchanged pleasantries over coffee.

"Coffee. *Oi!* Never understood how you fellas became so straight-laced. Now when you come aboard an Aussie ship," he announced with a broad smile, "we'll be sure and treat you proper . . . offer you a *real* libation."

"So I've heard," Jake acknowledged with a grin.

"Now then," Quigby continued, "understand you fellas have a problem with one of your torpedo tubes. Aft array, wasn't it?"

"Yep, number eight," Clem interjected. "Outer door's jammed open, and inner door's sprung—held shut right now with clamps—a little present from a Jap depth charge . . ."

"Unfriendly fellows, these Japanese. Understand they took offense to your attacking one of their transports. Sensitive fellas, *oi?*"

"Very!" Clem replied with a laugh.

"Any other problems?"

"Pit sword," Bucky volunteered.

"Yeah," Clem chimed in, "pitometer log assembly sprung a leak during the depth charging, and we had to tighten down on the seals so much that we may have messed it up badly. Need to look at it, too."

"Right, then," Quigby acknowledged, "torpedo tube and the pit sword. Reason you're tied up here is 'cause we've instructions to turn you around ASAP. Apparently, your command has special plans for you. We have you scheduled to go straight to dry dock tomorrow morning, and the yard'll put that torpedo tube right in a jiffy. Meanwhile, I understand your own lot will be topping off your provisions, and you'll be refueled when you get out of dry dock. All goes well, and we'll have you back at sea in a week."

"A week," Jake repeated, gazing off into space.

Considering that *Orca* was to go into dry dock, such a fast turn-around was surprising. And this was also the first he had heard of COMSUBPAC having special plans for *Orca*. He wouldn't say anything to Quigby, or question what he had heard, simply because he doubted that Quigby would know any more than he had just told them. He was also sure he would hear about those "special plans" soon enough.

"Sure, if all goes well." Quigby's reassuring response brought Jake abruptly out of his reverie.

That afternoon, a bag of mail caught up with the boat. Jake had already mailed his own long letter off to Kate, and mused that maybe he should have waited until he read the fistful of letters from his wife *before* he had mailed off his own—just in case there was something in her letters which bore comment. But then, of course, he could always write her another.

Leaving the port and provisioning arrangements up to Clem and Bucky, Jake retired to his cabin to read his mail. Saving

Kate's letters for last, he read the three he received from his mother. They bore the usual news about the people in their particular suburb in Des Moines, many of whom were now strangers to him. His father had apparently forgiven him for marrying a Catholic, because he had resumed adding his own comments at the bottom of Jake's mom's letters. Finally, Jake began opening Kate's letters, carefully following the order of their postmarks.

Her letters were newsy, as usual, and filled him in on all the goings and comings at the base hospital, mostly about people he knew only casually or not at all. He avoided the temptation to skip to the good parts of the letters — the places near the end, where she told him how much she loved him and missed him, and exactly what pleasures she might have in store for him when he saw her again. She wrote things that he wouldn't have the nerve to write to her, no matter how much he contemplated them in the depths of his heart. And he treasured her every word.

Something in her fifth letter got his attention:

"I hadn't been feeling too well for a day or two, and consulted one of the doctors at the hospital. He ran some tests and I found out a couple of days later, that it had been nothing serious. Indeed it was all perfectly normal. I'm just pregnant it seems, my darling, and we're going to have a baby. The doctor says that he or she should arrive sometime around the beginning of April."

Still grasping the letter, Jake threw his arms up in the air and let out a joyful "Whoo-hoo!" and ran topside to share the good news with Clem and whomever else he might find.

Later that same Sunday afternoon, Jake led Clem to the wardroom, and both sat down with a cup of coffee.

"What's up, Daddy?" Clem inquired, with a smirk.

Jake acknowledged the reference to his impending fatherhood with a grin. "Been thinkin'.   Remember our last attack, the one on the transport?"

"Do I! I hope we never get another ass-pounding like the one that Jap destroyer handed us."

"Not that," Jake replied. "Before. The approach. Remember?"

"Yeah, okay."

"I wouldn't let you raise the scope until we were ready to fire, remember?"

"Yeah, you didn't want to give the Japs any heads-up as to where we were until we were ready to shoot."

"Exactly. And we relied on sonar information to get us lined up first, then used the scope at the last minute to get the final firing solution."

"Yep. One of your better moments, I would say."

"Okay," Jake continued, ignoring the complement, "we kind of had to keep the sonar information in our heads, compare it with the chart plot in the conning tower, and with the TDC output . . ."

"Okay. Where are you going with this?"

"Okay. We're doing a submerged approach, just like last time. We're using the chart plot in the conning tower, just like always. What if we had another plot going on at the same time, one that processed *just* the sonar information? Then we wouldn't have to stick out anything above the surface until we were good and ready, just like last time. We could use the sonar plot to set up our initial track every time and then, only when we were good and ready, stick up the attack scope, refine our firing solution, and attack."

"You mean do what we did last time during every submerged approach, but get the sonar info down on paper, and be able to make more sense of it."   Clem mulled over the idea. "And where, exactly, will we find room for this plot? The conning tower and control room are *already* jam packed."

"I was thinking right here, in the wardroom. Spread a huge sheet of paper on the table, have a talker relaying the information out of sonar, and plot the situation just as the sonar operator sees it. The talker then relays the plot solution to the conn."

"Okay. And who runs this show? Everybody already has a GQ station for a submerged attack."

"I was hoping you would have some suggestions, Clem."

"Yeah, well . . ." Clem stroked his jaw for a minute or two. "I should be the one to do it, but you have me on the scope."

"And that's not going to change. We make too good an attack team. Who next?"

Clem pondered a bit, then said, "Well, Louie—our navigator—but then who would run the chart plot? I suppose John Catinella could do that, but he's a third class, pretty junior. And he *just* made third class. Besides, he's already on the scope with me. No, Louie needs to stay where he is."

Jake nodded in agreement.

"What about Bill Salton?" Clem suggested. "Right now he's in the sonar room for GQ, but we could easily shift Chief Lione out of the maneuvering room and into sonar—Chief Clements could easily handle maneuvering by himself, without Bobby. And poor Bobby's already in the sonar room most of the time anyway—he's the only guy aboard who can keep that equipment running."

"Right," Jake said. "Having Bobby Lione in sonar at GQ actually makes more sense than having Bill down there. If the equipment goes on the fritz, Bill would just have to get Bobby there to fix it anyway. But can our young ensign do the job on this new plot? You think Salton is up to it?"

"Bill's young, all right," Clem answered, "and he's got a lot to learn, but he's also very smart. He's actually a bit ahead of Joe Bob on getting his dolphins, may even qualify yet, this trip. But he can't run the plot all by himself. Needs somebody to help. John Catinella's the logical choice to help Bill. I hate to lose him on the scope—just got him trained—but I suppose I could always train somebody else on the scope. We could take Henry Coons off the helm and put *him* on the scope. He's a quartermaster striker, and it would be good training for him, anyway."

"Right. Okay. Salton and Catinella it is, and Coons goes to the scope. Now guess who's got the job of setting all of this up and getting these guys trained?"

Clem groaned. Just what he needed, another job. "Can Bucky help?"

"Of course. What's a COB for? You guys can start right after we leave port."

Despite the fact that *Orca* was due to enter drydock at 0800 the very next morning, Trevor Quigby volunteered to take the wardroom into town that night and show them the treasure-trove of pleasures that Brisbane had to offer. Both Jake and Clem declined, and Hal Chapman and Bill Salton had the duty, but Louie Carillo, Early Sender, and Joe Bob Clanton jumped at the chance.

Enlisted men were required to pull liberty in their uniforms, but officers were allowed to go into town in civvies. In fact, it was preferred by the brass that officers not wear their uniform to town unless on Shore Patrol or other official business. If they misbehaved, the theory went, they would be less conspicuous. It actually seemed to the officers that it made them all *more* conspicuous. Any strange carousing men in town in civilian clothes were most likely officers.

Quigby picked up Louie, Early, and Joe Bob, all wearing civvies, in a battered old Chevrolet just after 2000 that evening. "With rationing, petrol's a bit scarce, but you fellas seem to have all you need and even give the Captain of the Port pump privileges. So tonight you get a tour of the city without having to ride the bus into town."

In what seemed like no time at all, they were in the heart of the city. Brisbane looked just like any other small town, exactly as one might find in rural America, but from the early 1930s — mostly wood buildings, with few streets paved, but the dirt streets were currently dry. Automobiles had to be imported to Australia, and they were expensive. There were as many horse-drawn conveyances as there were cars—and there were servicemen everywhere. They seemingly consisted of equal numbers of Aussies and Americans, with a smattering of New Zealanders and Brits thrown in. There were also, surprisingly for the submariners, who came from an overwhelmingly white branch of a largely white Navy, a fairly large number of "colored" American soldiers.

Even on a Sunday night, the town seemed to be bustling with activity. Servicemen seemed to travel in packs, or groups between ten and forty-five persons, almost always dominated by one national service or the other—although there were some groups mixed nationally, inevitably Aussies with Americans. And every group always included females. (The "Negro" troops seemed to travel in groups by themselves, but still with a significant number of white females included. Australian girls, apparently, paid no heed whatsoever to the American practice of strict racial segregation. The Australian girls also apparently preferred American troops to their own—there were far fewer of them attached to the Aussie packs than to the American ones.)

"It's the American PXs, you see," Quigby explained, "they're scattered all about the city, and all loaded with goodies that your fellas can buy, but rationed to our lads. And your boys are better paid as well. Our Sheilas aren't stupid. Hang with the American lads and you share in the benefits. Reasonable enough, you see—but it galls our lads. But enough of that. We're here to have a good time! And here we are."

Quigby pulled up in front of what looked like a saloon from some Wild West movie: wooden porch in front and all, with a big wooden sign over the porch advertising "Mom's Place." All that was lacking were the swinging doors in front.

Inside, Mom's Place on a Sunday night was bustling, filled with a smoky haze and crowded with servicemen of every stripe:

officers and men; Aussies; Americans; New Zealanders; Brits. And women—all young, all about the room, and all apparently available. Everyone, men and women alike, appeared to be very inebriated, or well on their way to that condition.

"Guess there are no blue laws in Australia," Louie quipped.

"At least there are apparently none in Brisbane," Early retorted.

Quigby found them a place at a table in the far reaches of the saloon and went to fetch the first round. He returned with their drinks and four of the local lovelies in tow.

"These ladies are Alice, Janet, Daisy, and Margaret. Alice is with me. Ladies, these here Yanks are me new best mates— practically won Coral Sea single-handed. You need to be especially nice to them."

Chairs for the women appeared from somewhere, and, smiling broadly, the ladies all sat down. Apparently Quigby had planned the event, since he returned to the table with not only the ladies, but also with eight bottles of beer, four clutched in each hand. Other than Alice, each "Sheila" immediately selected a partner, and sat down beside her claim.

Louie and Early were married, but not wanting to make Quigby appear foolish, they didn't shoo their "dates" away. But neither did they have any intention of doing any more than engaging in innocent conversation, or just being a dancing partner.

It was soon very obvious, however, that Joe Bob was very seriously engaged with the Sheila who had attached herself to him, a brown-eyed, 18-year-old blonde named Daisy. And Daisy Norton was a very lovely young lady indeed. Dressed in a simple blue dress that clung to her attractive curves, she drank her beer in delicate sips from the bottle (Mom's Place apparently did not provide glasses to the clientele). She seemed to, in turn, have eyes only for Joe Bob. She was *very* blonde, with a sweet, symmetrical face, and a long, straight nose. Her best features, though, were her doe eyes—large, limpid brown pools. And Joe Bob Clanton dove into those pools head first.

Everyone pretended not to notice when Joe Bob and Daisy got up without a word and left Mom's Place right after the third or fourth round. Louie and Early only hoped Joe Bob had enough sense to make it back to the boat by 0400, when liberty expired. *Orca* was scheduled to go into drydock at 0800 whether Joe Bob was AWOL at morning muster, or not.

Joe Bob Clanton was graduated with a major in Electrical Engineering from the University of Alabama, in Tuscaloosa. That was in 1940, and the Alabama native knew for sure that war was coming, and he wanted in, but he didn't want to get into the fray as an Army grunt. He had never seen an ocean, nor taken the two hundred-mile trip from Tuscaloosa to the Gulf of Mexico, but he was sure the Navy was the service for him.

In appearance, Joe Bob was the epitome of "average." At five feet ten, with brown hair and a medium build, Joe Bob was certainly not ugly, but neither were his even features anything beyond pleasantly handsome. But when he smiled, his smile was bright and prepossessing, and when he spoke, the Southern lilt in his voice was pleasant and soothing. Ask anyone, Joe Bob Clanton was a charmer.

The Navy had just set up an Officer's training program, called the V-7 program. They were accepting applicants for the first classes at *Prairie State*, a school in New York City, set up aboard a converted battleship, the *USS Illinois*. To his surprise, Joe Bob was accepted into the second class to go through *Prairie State*. That very summer, he had an initial training cruise aboard the battleship *USS New York,* and, in February of 1941, he was commissioned an ensign in the United States Naval Reserve along with 479 other classmates.

Joe Bob applied for immediate active duty, and, that March, reported aboard the destroyer *USS Benson* out of Brooklyn, New York. A year later, with the war now declared, he applied for

Officer's Submarine School in New London. Normally, a Naval Reserve Officer wouldn't have a shot at getting into Sub School, but his fitness reports had all been outstanding, and, somehow, Joe Bob was accepted.

He graduated Sub School near the top of his class, and, as a newly promoted Lt. j.g., was assigned to *USS Argonaut* out of Pearl. en route to Pearl, he came down with a serious attack of peritonitis, and was eventually hospitalized in San Diego. When, *sans* appendix, he finally recovered, *Argonaut* had been reported lost at sea, and he was reassigned to *Orca*. Joe Bob, at 25, was the second youngest officer aboard *Orca*, just two years older than Ensign Bill Salton.

Joe Bob made it back to the boat before 0400, but with only minutes to spare. He was not drunk, but he also obviously had not slept. He saluted the quarterdeck watch with "Permission to come aboard," and then went straight to his bunk to get whatever sleep he could before reveille at 0600. He mustered on the dock alongside with the rest of the officers and crew at 0610. Luckily he didn't have much to do to get the boat into dry dock.

By 0820, *Orca* was positioned in the dry dock, and the pumping of water from the dock's tanks had begun. By noon that Monday, the boat was high and dry.

With *Orca* safely buttressed in the drydock, Lt. Cmdr. Quigby's job was done for the time being; it was now up to the American repair forces to assess and repair the damages suffered by *Orca* from her encounter with the enemy destroyer.

Submarine repair in Port Brisbane was headquartered in the submarine tender, *USS Griffin*. The port was originally equipped to service and repair only the sugar boats, and the *Griffin* had a complete supply of spare parts for them aboard. But as the fleet boats arrived, room aboard *Griffin* for spares became scarce, so facilities ashore were expanded to handle stores for these newer boats as well.

There could be found not only a supply of the newer Mark-14 torpedoes, but also parts for the 21-inch torpedo tubes on the fleet boats. And, among all the men in the entire U.S. Navy, there was only one man who knew where each and every spare part for each and every class of boat in Brisbane was, whether it was aboard *Griffin*, or stored ashore, and his name was Chief Machinist's Mate—MMC(SS)—Grady Caruthers.

Late that afternoon, a wizened Grady Caruthers, chewing on the stub of a cigar, conferred with Jake, Bucky, and Clem in temporary office space the port had provided dockside. Chief Caruthers acknowledged Jake and Clem respectfully, but then addressed his remarks directly to Bucky.

"Both doors on that torpedo tube are sprung pretty bad, the outer one worst of all. We'll have to replace that one entirely. But I think we can straighten the inner one, and it'll be okay. Ingenious how you managed to clamp it down shut, by the way. Problem's liable to be on the tube itself. The outer door seal looks good, but the inner one's scored badly. Have to machine it in place. May take some time. Depends on how deep the score marks are. Try to get you out of the dock in a day or two, if we can.

"Rest of the boat looks good, far as I can see, but we haven't looked all that hard yet. And, oh yes, we plan to change out your pit sword assembly entirely. Put a new one in, and then fix yours, if we can, for the next boat that needs one."

"Excellent!" Bucky replied.

With the boat in dry dock, there was only a fire watch posted that night, Chief O'Grady in charge. The rest of the boat was granted liberty.

Clem insisted that Jake join him for dinner in town that evening to celebrate his upcoming fatherhood. They were joined by the rest of the wardroom, and they found the relatively quiet restaurant in town that Quigby had recommended. Just before dessert was served, Joe Bob excused himself from their company claiming "a prior commitment." Clem signaled his displeasure to Joe Bob at this abrupt departure, but Joe Bob, looking sheepish, was not to be deterred, and left. Jake waved him goodbye, not noticing the exchange between the two. Clem then commented under his breath to Jake, "I wonder what was so much more important to Joe Bob than his shipmates?"

"Don't be so suspicious, Clem," Jake chided. "Joe Bob's young and he's single. It's more than likely all perfectly innocent."

"Or not," was Clem's response.

The next morning, Tuesday, Joe Bob was almost an hour late reporting back from liberty. When he was told about it, Jake put the matter into his XO's hands.

"Missed reporting time by almost an hour!" Clem practically yelled in Joe Bob's face. "What if we'd been getting underway this morning to go back on patrol? What the blazes were you thinking?"

Clem had called Joe Bob to the dockside office. They were alone, and, to insure their privacy, Clem locked the door. *Orca* was still in dry dock, and Chief Caruthers was less optimistic than the day before. His crew had run into trouble machining the sealing surface of the inner door of torpedo tube number eight, and the boat might not be out of the dock as soon as he hoped.

"I'm sorry, Clem, honest. I fell asleep, and by the time I woke up, there was no way I could make it back on time, not the way the busses from town run at that hour."

"You fell asleep. From the look of you, though, you didn't get much rest! Well, you will tonight. I'm confining you to quarters during off-duty hours for the duration."

"Please, Clem, no, don't do that! We aren't going to be here that long, and if you do that I won't be able to see Daisy."

"Daisy is it? And who is this Daisy person?"

"Daisy Norton. She's the girl I met first night in. Trevor introduced us," he said, stretching the truth just a bit. "We love each other, Clem, and we're gonna get married."

"Married? Are you nuts? You just met this Daisy Norton, Joe Bob. How could you possibly already want to marry her?"

"I just do is all. Doesn't it just sometimes happen like that? Well, it did with us. I loved her from the moment I first saw her."

"Oh, boy. Love at first sight. No, it doesn't happen like that, Joe Bob, not in real life. You can't possibly know this girl well enough to want to marry her—not in this short a time."

"So you say. But I only know what I know. Daisy's the one for me."

"Okay. I'm done trying to talk sense into you. But Daisy or no Daisy, you can't just overstay liberty and not have consequences. My orders stand. Off-duty, you're confined to quarters until we leave port."

"Yes, Sir." Joe Bob said and left, dejected and seemingly on the verge of tears.

Soon afterward, Clem told Jake what had happened. Jake mulled the situation over. "I kind of feel sorry for Joe Bob. "He's confused and he did a stupid thing. But you're absolutely right, he can't get away without some sort of punishment, and his being confined to quarters is the least he could have expected. You handled the situation just right, and the only way you could have. Let's just hope Joe Bob doesn't do anything else stupid—like jumping ship."

"He's *not* stupid, Jake. He'd never do anything that dumb."

"You mean *you* wouldn't, Clem, and *I* wouldn't. But stupider things than that have been done in the name of love."

That afternoon, *Orca* came out of dry dock. The pitometer log had been changed out the previous day, but the machining on the inner door-sealing surface of number eight was incomplete. The dry dock was needed for another vessel, however, and with the tube's outer door secured, the yard crew was sure they could complete the in-place machining alongside.

With *Orca* tied to the dock, Bucky saw to the topping off of fuel and provisions and the replacement of the fired torpedoes. One of the replacement torpedoes had to be stored in the damaged number eight tube aft, and it could be quickly replaced as soon as the machining was completed, but not until then. Senior Chief Caruthers promised Bucky that the yard machinists in the after torpedo room vowed to work nonstop until the job was done.

Clem made sure that Joe Bob was kept busy. He had to liaise with base communications in any case; documents and code books had to be updated before the boat could get underway. Sea trials might now happen as early as the following day, Wednesday, and if all went well, the boat could possibly leave to go back on patrol the day after that.

Clem gave Joe Bob the duty that night. As Duty Officer, he was expected to be on call all during the night. The watch reported to him in person every time it was relieved, that is, at 1000, midnight, 0400, and 0800. At 0400, he would also normally be on the quarterdeck as the liberty party returned. Clem figured that Joe Bob, no matter how lovesick, would never jump ship when he had the duty. Even if he was dumb enough to consider "going over the side," he would never be foolish enough to do it with the duty section continually checking in with him throughout the night.

Job Bob called Brisbane Information on the dockside phone before going on watch, and got Daisy's number. The number listed for her was a common line, shared with at least two other parties, he was told, and the appended letter "J." He called, and Daisy answered. He quickly explained that he had drawn the duty that night, and would be unable to meet her as originally planned, but would "do whatever it takes" to meet her the following night. She told him how disappointed she was that she wasn't going to see him that night, but that she understood, and

185

that his absence that evening would make her all the more appreciative the following night.

"Tomorrow night may be our last in a while," he said. "There's a good chance we'll be leaving for patrol on Thursday, so tomorrow might be our last chance to be together until *Orca's* back in port, wherever that will be—probably Pearl. I promise, no matter where that is, I'll get you there so we can get married. I love you so much, Daisy."

"I know, my darling, I know, and you know I love you. And if tomorrow is going to be our last night together for a while, I promise I will make it a night you'll never forget."

Joe Bob's gut was in knots as he walked the length of the dock back to the boat. He had just promised Daisy that he would go AWOL so they could be together the next night. Going AWOL, he reasoned, was nowhere near as bad as jumping ship. That was something he could *never* do, and he would make sure he was back on board Thursday morning or whenever *Orca* was heading back to sea. But he had to see Daisy again, even if it was just for one night, and he would suffer whatever the consequences came his way for ignoring the XO's orders and going AWOL.

Meanwhile, Daisy went out that night with her friends, Janet and Margaret. The three women soon found male company to entertain them for the evening. After drinking and dancing into the wee hours, Janet and Margaret went home with their newfound friends. But, to her credit, Daisy went home alone.

The machinists were satisfied that the inner door fit properly at 0150 that Wednesday morning.

Under the watchful eye of Chief Caruthers, Chief Walakurski immediately exercised the inner and outer doors of number eight tube, flooding the tube, and blowing out water slugs alongside, until he was satisfied that the tube was working as it should. Then, beginning at 0300, he pressurized the tube at intervals up to a simulated depth of 300 feet, the test depth for the boat. At each simulated depth, the doors held. Finally, the pressure in the tube held at the simulated test depth for two hours. Caruthers then left, satisfied that his crew had done their job well.

"Now," Wally told Bucky, "we need to take it to sea and be sure the seals hold under actual operating conditions. Then we can load her up and get back on patrol."

"No way we can load a fish *now*, and be ready to go when you've finished your testing?"

"Where would we put it? The only spot I have open aft is in the tube itself. I can't test the tube with a fish in it!"

"What about we secure it to the deck temporarily?"

"Bucky, it would really be in the way," said Wally.

"Makes sense. Let's go bring the Old Man and the XO up to speed."

"So," Jake asked, "if the tube checks out, all we need to come back to port for is to load a fish aft, and then we can take off again?"

"Near as I can figure," Bucky replied. "Of course we'll have to run the measured course to calibrate the pit log. We'd have had to come back into port to offload the technician that did that anyway."

"Very well," Jake said. "Clem, notify SUBPAC that if repairs check out in sea trials to be conducted tomorrow, we expect to be completely ready for sea by tomorrow evening, and await further orders."

"Aye, Captain," Clem said. "Will do."

Encrypted orders came within an hour after Clem had reported to SUBPAC that the boat had completed all repairs, and would be conducting sea trials the next day. Barring unforeseen complications, *Orca* would be ready for sea the following evening. The orders decrypted as follows:

"Orca *is to proceed earliest and at best speed and to arrive at rendezvous point 20 degrees, 36 minutes, 60.0 seconds N, by 148 degrees, 5 minutes, 19.0 seconds E, a point in the Philippine Sea with no nearby landfall. On arrival* Orca *is to join forces with submarines* Seahorse, Conch, *and* Devilray, *forming task group 51.2. Once joined, this force is to conduct coordinated attack group operations under LCDR Warren Blaylock, USN, task force commander, in* Devilray. *Force mission is to attack enemy shipping, disrupting insofar as is possible fuel shipments from enemy-held oil fields and refineries in the Netherlands East Indies to the Japanese homeland."*

Now Jake knew what the "special plans" for *Orca* were that Trevor Quigby had alluded to their first day in Brisbane. What the U.S. Navy termed "coordinated attack groups," the German U-Boat Command called *"rudeltaktic,"* and the Allied convoys in the Atlantic called "wolf packs."

Orca left dockside at 0800 that Wednesday morning, just after the technician from the base came aboard. By noon, they were in water deep enough to dive and test number eight tube. Wally and his crew exercised the tube at fifty feet, one hundred feet, two hundred feet, and two hundred and fifty feet. Both the outer door and the inner door held at each depth.

"Request test depth, Captain," Wally passed the word up to the conn.

Warily, Jake took *Orca* to her three-hundred-foot test depth. When the gauge indicated they were at three hundred feet, Jake had the word passed aft, and also had every man on the boat watching for any leaks of any kind. They stayed at three hundred feet for fifteen minutes. Only minor leaks were reported anywhere aboard the boat. Not only had Chief Caruthers' crew done their job well, so also had the men at Electric Boat who had built *Orca.*

Wally passed the word up that he was satisfied with the yard's work, and Jake, breathing a sigh of relief, brought the boat up to periscope depth. On the way back into port, they ran the measured course, and the base technician calibrated the pitometer log. In the interim, Wally had the after torpedo room crew load one of the torpedoes off its rack into number eight tube. By 1800, they were tied up alongside again. The replacement fish was already waiting alongside, and an hour later it was secure in the newly empty rack aft. By 1930, Wednesday, August 25, 1943, Lt. Cmdr. Trevor Quigby, RAN, was waving goodbye to *Orca* from dockside as she headed back out on patrol.

Belowdecks, at his station in the radio room, the Communications Officer, Lt. j.g. Joe Bob Stanton, was seriously contemplating making his way topside, jumping over the side of the boat, and swimming back to Brisbane. In the end, in absolute misery, he prudently decided to remain aboard.

Louie Carillo laid out a track of some 3,100 nautical miles to the rendezvous point. Averaging thirteen knots, *Orca* should transit to the rendezvous in just under ten days. Arrival on station should then be about 2130 on Saturday, September 4th.

Once at the rendezvous point, *Orca* had to be able to communicate with her sister boats. Boats on patrol were under orders to maintain strict radio silence, and all incoming information was broadcast at regular intervals on very low frequency (VLF) transmissions from their headquarters, in *Orca's* case, SUBPAC. A boat would broadcast on VLF only if routinely reporting in or if a special situation—such as a damage report to headquarters—called for it. The only other exception was the high frequency (HF) ship-to-ship, tactical radio that transmitted line-of-sight, and could only be intercepted and understood by the enemy if they were close aboard *and* just happened to be on the proper transmission frequency. The mere existence of these transmissions, however, and the direction of their source, could be detected by RDF—Radio Direction Finders—with which most, but not all, Japanese fighting ships were equipped. RDF could usually be defeated by limiting transmissions to short bursts, well under thirty seconds, and by limiting HF transmissions to only those absolutely necessary.

The Navy's preferred method of communication ship-to-ship, and the most secure, was still directional light using Aldus lamps and Morse code.

Chapter 11

Orca: *Fourth Patrol — 4 September 1943 to 19 September*

Orca arrived at the rendezvous point at 2300 on Saturday, September 4, 1943, an hour and a half later than Louie Carillo had originally projected. There was a half moon, the air was clear, with a fresh breeze, and the sea was relatively calm, with gentle, two-foot swells—and, in stark contrast to Brisbane, this close to the Equator, it was hot.

And *Orca* was alone.

The SJ surface search radar showed no contacts, nor did the SD air search radar.

Jake called down into the conning tower from the bridge, "Clem, is Louie sure we're at the right place?"

"He says he is. His evening celestial fix was right on where our dead reckoning track showed we should be, and that was just before sunset, just three hours or so ago. So we should be at the rendezvous point, Captain, or at least damned close to it."

"Very well. Guess the other boats just haven't made it here yet. Let's steam at dead slow in a square, say two thousand yards on a side, and keep the can full until we get some company." Then Jake cautioned the four lookouts, "Lookouts, keep a sharp eye out."

"Aye, aye, Sir," the men standing lookout answered in almost perfect unison.

The first contact showed up on the surface search radar the next day, Sunday, just before noon. Both radars had been clear of contacts until then, so *Orca* had remained on the surface. The contact was almost due east, at ten thousand yards. A boat from

Pearl would be approaching from exactly that direction, if indeed the contact were at least one of their compatriots coming from Midway or Pearl.

As soon as he was notified of the contact, Jake made his way to the bridge. Hal Chapman had just relieved the deck, and had the OOD watch.

Seconds later, Clem called up and notified the bridge that he was in the conning tower. "Nothing in the scope yet, Captain," he reported. "And radar reports the contact holding steady at zero-eight-seven, so he's headed straight for us, course one-seven-eight, speed fifteen."

"Very well," Jake acknowledged.

A minute later, "Contact still bearing zero-eight-seven and closing, now at ninety-five hundred yards."

"Very well."

Two minutes later, "Radar reports second contact, Skipper, same bearing, looks to be in line, a thousand yards behind the first which is now at nine thousand yards, second contact at same course and speed, one-seven-eight degrees, fifteen knots."

"Very well," Jake mused, "I hope these are at least two of our guys, sailing in company, and in line."

Another minute passed. "First contact now at zero-eight-seven and eighty-five hundred yards, second contact at zero-eight-eight and ninety-five hundred yards. Both on course one-seven-eight, speed fifteen."

"Very well."

Another minute and, "Third contact, bearing zero-eight-nine, ten thousand yards. Also on course one-seven-eight, speed fifteen. Lead contact now at eight thousand yards, Captain," Clem called up. And then, seconds later, yelled up again "Got 'em on the periscope, Captain! Damn! Sub heading straight on, so low in the water it's almost impossible to spot. Can't swear to it yet, but it looks like one of ours."

"Very well, get Simpson up here, see if we can raise her with the light."

"Aye, aye."

The forward port lookout sang out, "Submarine, one point off the port bow."

"Got 'er, Skipper," Chapman said, "but just barely. Can just make out the top of the bridge and the masts."

As Chapman said this, Jake also spied the contact.

Less than a minute later, RM3(SS) Rodney Simpson was on the bridge, plugging in the Aldus lamp. Aiming the lamp at the oncoming contact, he flashed the letters "AD" in Morse code, meaning "What ship?"

Four letters were flashed back in return "QVXY." Hal Chapman sang out the letters as they flashed, "Queen, Victor, X-Ray, Yoke."

Before Jake could get a word out, Clem called up from the conning tower, "Queen, Victor, X-Ray, Yoke, Captain. That's *Devilray's* call sign." He had read the signal through the periscope.

"Great!" Jake finally yelled. "Acknowledge with our call sign."

Simpson flashed back *Orca's* call sign: "QLDP."

Orca had successfully rendezvoused with the rest of the wolf pack.

Devilray was about 100 yards off to port; *Stinger* and *Conch* were further off, also to port. All four boats were making bare steerageway, staying more or less parallel to one another. The three boats looked identical to the casual observer, but were actually of two different classes, and all three were of a different, older, class of boat from *Orca*.

Devilray was the oldest boat of the four, commissioned in 1940. It was a *Tambor*-class boat, and if one looked closely, it had only one, three-inch, 50-caliber gun forward for both surface attack and anti-aircraft defense. Sonar and radar capabilities identical to *Orca's* were only added hurriedly after the war started.

Stinger and *Conch* were both *Gar*-class boats, which also had only the single deck gun forward. Both were commissioned in 1941, and both were originally equipped with SD radar, but without active sonar. Both boats had since been fitted with SJ radars, and *Conch* had active sonar installed in 1942, but *Stinger* had only passive sonar capability.

Stinger was commanded by Lt. Cmdr. Woodrow Wilson Berghoff, USN. Of all four submarine skippers in the task group (TG), Woody Berghoff was the oldest in years, having joined the Navy out of high school and rising up through the ranks. He was promoted to lieutenant commander the same time as Warren Blaylock, but since he was not an Academy graduate, the Navy gave him a date of rank four days later than Blaylock's and the other Academy graduates promoted at that time.

Conch's skipper was Lt. Cmdr. Calvin Jennings, USN. Jennings was in the same class at the Academy as Blaylock, but had made lieutenant commander in the group promoted just before Jake. That made him junior to both Blaylock and Berghoff, but senior to Jake. And seniority mattered in the Navy.

Lieutenant Commander Warren Blaylock was on the bridge of *Devilray*, and was using the loudhailer to talk to Jake on *Orca's* bridge. Jake also had a loudhailer.

"Ahoy, *Orca*," Blaylock yelled over. "How's it goin', Jake?"

"Good, Warren, you?"

"Great! Mean to get us a few Jap oilers! Get that tube problem straightened out okay in Brisbane?"

"Most definitely. *Orca's* ready any time you are!"

"Outstanding! Can you come alongside and rig a transfer line? We've got a mailbag for you, and it's got your op order inside."

A half hour later, the mailbag was aboard, and the four boats were steaming on the surface due west at six knots, in line abreast, five hundred yards apart. In the mailbag were another handful of letters from Kate, but Jake had to regretfully set them aside for the moment, as he and Clem poured over the operations order in the wardroom.

"Rudeltaktic," or wolf pack operations were more or less invented by the German submarine force in World War I in response to the British use of convoys. By 1942, in the Atlantic, the tactic had been raised to high art, and it was not uncommon for escorting vessels to find themselves up against as few as three, or up to as many as thirty-four boats attacking at once.

German U-boats, operating independently, were prepositioned by central command along a line where they were likely to intercept an oncoming convoy. The first boat to locate the convoy became the "shadower," maintaining contact and reporting the convoy's position, course, and speed back to central U-boat command. Other U-boats would then be notified and directed to join forces in front of the convoy for an organized, mass attack orchestrated from central command. In 1942 alone, U-boats sank over 1,000 Allied ships. By early 1943, however, the tide had turned, as antisubmarine technology and tactics evolved to successfully counter the German submarine threat.

In the Pacific, American submarines adapted wolf pack tactics to suit the different conditions they faced there. The Pacific is over twice the size of the Atlantic, and the Germans had as many as three times the boats that America had. Beyond that, the Japanese did not adopt the convoy system as quickly as the Allies did; they preferred to let merchant ships operate independently at first. Only when their merchant ship losses began to mount, did they, too, early in 1943, adopt the convoy system. Their convoys, however, were very small compared to the Allied convoys in the Atlantic.

Japanese convoys were less well organized than Allied convoys in the Atlantic, with individual vessels joining or leaving the convoy, to or from ports, along the route. Convoys varied from as few as five to as many as twenty merchant vessels, with as few as three to five escorts. Escorting vessels were infrequently older destroyers and frigates, but usually included minelayers, minesweepers, subchasers, and gunboats.

Unlike Allied escort vessels, the Japanese escorts had no radar or sonar until late in the war.

Also late in the war, a special class of kaibokan *escort vessels was employed. A type of frigate, these ships were 220 feet long, heavily gunned, equipped with a dozen depth-charge throwers, and carried 300 depth charges. They were also fast, capable of up to 20 knots, and were equipped with excellent sonar gear.* Kaibokan *were not to be underestimated, but fortunately for the American submarine force, they were employed too late in the war to make much of a difference.*

Convoy air escorts were only rarely provided. Air fleet escort planes were few in number, equipped with very short-range magnetic detection devices and airborne radar, and were typically armed with only a single bomb. The air crews were poorly trained, and usually unable to communicate with surface escorts.

Unlike the German wolf packs, American wolf packs operated under general orders, with attacks not centrally coordinated.

The "op order" was short and straightforward. The task group TG 51.2 was assigned a simple mission, a repeat of the orders *Orca* had received as it left Brisbane: *"Force mission is to attack enemy shipping . . ."* The idea was for the four boats to string out along a line across a convoy route. The first boat to locate the convoy would break radio silence and notify the others. The Group Commander was then to position the boats by radio to regroup and then to intercept the convoy for a coordinated attack. After that, the tactical details were left entirely up to the Group Commander. (Unlike the central command approach of the German submarine command, American submariners were expected to bring the attack to the enemy on their own initiative.)

The op order detailed the radio frequencies that were to be used to coordinate the attack, and noted that any information SUBPAC received regarding suspected or confirmed convoy routes would be broadcast to the force upon receipt. Call signs were assigned to each boat. *Devilray* was "Railroad One"; while *Stinger* was "Railroad Two"; *Conch* "Railroad Three"; and *Orca,*

"Railroad Four"—in the order of their respective skipper's seniority, Jake noted. Of course.

Until otherwise notified, the task group's first line of battle was to be a west-northwest line in the East China Sea, just north of the Formosa Strait. Jake called Clem to the wardroom and passed the op order to him to read. He then retired to his stateroom, pulled the curtain, and settled down to read his mail.

Setting aside letters from his mother and sisters for the moment, Jake sorted the four letters from Kate in the order of their postmarks, and then opened and read each in turn. The first two were newsy letters about nothing much in particular, much like his daily additions to the one lengthy letter he began after he mailed his last to her from Brisbane. They closed with her assurance that she was doing well, that his son or daughter was doing just fine, and that she loved him and missed him. The third letter, dated August 16, 1943, however, was decidedly different and a little disconcerting:

> "I'm about two months along and just starting to show. The morning sickness, thank heaven, is apparently over with, and that is 'a blessing beyond silver and gold!'
>
> I took it for granted that my first visit last month to the base hospital ob/gyn clinic, when my pregnancy was confirmed, would have come to my C.O.'s attention. Apparently not. Henry's look when I alluded to my being an expectant mother took me back a bit. He asked 'When did that happen?' and I just gave him a look back, and he realized how silly the question was. Then he went into this lecture on how we should have been more careful, and I stopped him short and reminded him that I was Catholic, and that 'careful' wasn't part of our vocabulary where married couples having babies was concerned.
>
> He reminded me that my being pregnant was cause for me to be separated from the service. I told him I knew that. Then he got all teary and told me what a great nurse I was and that he needed

me to stay as long as possible, and that he would sit on my separation papers as long as he could. I told him that would be fine.

Well, as it turns out, 'as long as he could' apparently ended yesterday, because as of today I am a civilian again. It's a good thing we decided to hang on to our cottage-by-the-sea, or I would be out looking for housing today. The Navy tells me that while I'll no longer be getting a paycheck, that now you get some sort of allotment to keep me in the manner which I have become accustomed (which I hope means other than homeless and starving!). Father Jack says he'll walk me through the paperwork at this end, but he thinks you may have to sign something, and I might not get on that particular gravy train until you're back in port. Meanwhile, don't worry, my darling, I have quite a bit put away for just such a rainy day, and the baby and I will be just fine until I'm in your arms again.

But do take care of yourself, my love, because when you come home to me there are some papers you have to sign! Love and kisses, darling. Love you! Miss you!

Your loving wife,

Katie"

Warren Blaylock already had pointed the TG in the direction of the line of battle specified in the op order. It would probably mean passing under the Ryukyus Islands somewhere south of Okinawa and then heading due west. And Blaylock was in a hurry, because it was daylight, these were Japanese waters, and they were transiting on the surface at full throttle. Blaylock must have known something Jake didn't, because that evening's broadcast said that there was a MATA convoy (Manila to Takao, and thence to the home islands) forming in Manila and probably leaving that port sometime in the next week.

When they were still well east of the Ryukyus, Blaylock turned the formation west until nightfall. He then turned the group northwest again, and crossed the island chain on the surface equidistant from landfall on Okinawa in the north and Miyakojima to the south.

Dawn found TG 51.2 in the East China Sea, north-northeast of Miyakojima. Blaylock turned the boats due west again in the direction of their intercept station. For the first time since their rendezvous, he ordered that all boats dive and do this leg of their transit submerged until nightfall, a precaution against likely air traffic in the area.

By noon the next day, Thursday, September 9th, TG 51.2 was on station, and settled down to await their prey.

That evening, SUBPAC broadcast that the convoy designated MATA-4, seventeen ships under four-ship escort, now making about eight knots in open sea, had departed Manila at 1000 local time, on September 8th, en route to the home islands via Taipei, Formosa.

Jake wondered how SUBPAC knew that there were seventeen ships in the convoy and four escorts, and that the convoy's speed was eight knots, but he didn't question the quality of the information. Too frequently in the past, SUBPAC had been right on in its predictions. He did know, however, that Japanese convoy procedures were far looser than they were for Allied Atlantic convoys, and that ships frequently split off for intermediate ports, and that other ships from intermediate ports were just as liable to form up with the convoy. He wondered how large the convoy would be after its scheduled stopover in Formosa.

The convoy had to travel about 1,100 nautical miles to where TG 51.2 lay in ambush. SUBPAC reported on the next evening's broadcast that the convoy's average speed was still about eight knots. That meant that the task group had to mark time for at least another four days, probably longer, depending on how long the convoy would stay in Taipei. Blaylock had assigned specific patrol areas stretching across the expected convoy route to each boat.

Each patrol sector was four miles wide, and *Orca's* sector was between *Devilray* and *Stinger*, with *Conch* next to *Stinger*. The boats would follow the standard practice of staying submerged during daylight hours, and surfacing only at night. The four boats were to remain at periscope depth when submerged, however, with their high frequency (HF) radio whip antennae raised.

Conch was the first boat to make contact with the convoy. It was 0006 local time, Monday, September 13th.

"Railroad One, this is Railroad Three," the high frequency radio squawked in the clear. "Multiple radar contacts, bearing one-eight-two."

Minutes later, all four boats had them on their radar screens—at first, an agglomeration of points of light, bleeding one into another, impossible to determine exactly how many contacts there actually were. Soon the pattern became clear. Sixteen contacts, almost uniform in the size of their radar return, forming a ragged rectangle, four across and four deep. Stationed around the rectangle were four smaller contacts, the escorts. The convoy was steaming straight ahead, without zigzagging, on base course 097, speed eight knots.

"Must have lost one of the transports," Jake reasoned. "Probably left the convoy at Taipei."

Then another radar contact appeared, a lone point of light following the convoy, a straggler.

That's seventeen, Jake thought. *No one stayed in Taipei.*

When the initial contact was made, the night was clear, with a full moon, low on the southern horizon. With the TG to the north of the convoy, their targets would be silhouetted against the moon, while the four boats, at least initially, would be attacking from relative darkness.

"Railroad Group, this is Railroad One. Railroad one will submerge and penetrate the convoy from the front. Once inside, we'll pick off as many marus in the center of the convoy as we can. That should draw off the escorts while Railroad Two and Four conduct surface attacks on the flanks. Railroad Three, you make an end-around on the surface and pick off stragglers. After that, improvise! Good hunting, gentlemen. Tally-ho!"

"Railroad Two, roger, out."

"Railroad Three, roger, out."

"Railroad Four, roger, out."

Reason would dictate that the TG Commander take on the least dangerous task and perform the end-around for straggler duty — or, at the very least, conduct one of the flank attacks. That way, the command and control structure of the TG would be best preserved. But that was not the way submariners thought, Jake knew, and of course Blaylock picked the most dangerous approach for his own boat.

Orca was sitting still off the right flank of the convoy formation. Jake knew that *Stinger* was in similar position on the other flank, and that *Conch* was hightailing it at best speed around and out of sight to get behind the convoy. *Devilray* had submerged a while ago, and as hard as he tried, Jake never saw her periscope pierce the surface as he stood on *Orca's* bridge.

It was 0155. The convoy was now in sight, or at least it was from *Orca's* periscope, extended into the air, well above the bridge.

Clem reported up to Jake from below, "Still no zigzagging. Must have a lot of confidence in those escorts. Leading escorts are two gun boats, patrol boats really, little buggers. The right flank, in front of us, is escorted by a destroyer. Old one, a *Kamikaze* class, I think, but still has all her guns, torpedoes, and depth charges, I'd bet. Best we give the old girl due respect and allow her a wide berth, if we can."

"Roger that," Jake responded. "Let her pass by. Then, if she hasn't spotted us, we'll come up behind her and take a shot at a maru or two."

Just then, there was an explosion from inside the convoy, and flames lit up the night sky. *Devilray* had penetrated the convoy and scored a kill.

"Tanker, by the looks of it," Clem called up from the conning tower.

The *Kamikaze* took off and turned sharply to port at speed in front of the convoy, just as the convoy itself began to spread apart in panic. Individual vessels slowed, while others speeded up. There was another explosion from inside the convoy, less spectacular this time, but spectacular nonetheless.

Score another for Devilray, Jake thought.

Jake closed with the convoy, and picked a target, a tanker. The surface approach was textbook, and a spread of three torpedoes, two hits, blew two huge holes in the tanker's side. Immediately, *Orca's* prey was consumed in flames and broke in two. But there was no time to gloat. As the burning tanker's fuel lit up the waters, the boat was framed in perfect silhouette, and the *Kamikaze*, now returning at full speed to her abandoned station, was bearing down on *Orca*.

Jake reacted by turning the boat at speed perpendicular to the destroyer's track, quickly clearing the bridge. *Ah-oo-gah! Ah-oo-gah!* "Dive! Dive!" He sounded the alarm, and drove the boat hard beneath the surface.

No sooner had the boat passed through ninety feet than the first depth charges went off astern and close aboard. *WHAM!* It felt as if the concussion lifted up the stern and stood *Orca* on her nose, and every loose object on the boat crashed forward, including those among the crew who didn't find a solid handhold. (Afterward, Hal Chapman, who was at his GQ post on the diving station, said that the down bubble gauge jumped to its maximum twenty-degree reading and stuck there. He estimated that the boat had actually gone to about a twenty-five or thirty degree down angle.)

Two other depth charges went off. *Boom! Boom!* But the explosions were well overhead, apparently the triggers set at too shallow a depth to do any damage to the boat. But the boat was then diving out of control and passing two hundred feet.

"All stop! All back full!" Jake ordered, then, "right full rudder," all in effort to pull the boat out of its dive.

During all of this, the stern planesman had not been able to get the stern planes off full dive. Emergency drills had trained him for just such an event, and he shifted the hydraulics that operated the stern planes to hand control. (This turns the stern plane control wheel into kind of a hand-powered hydraulic pump, but it takes many turns of the wheel and a great deal of effort on the part of the planesman to slowly move the stern planes.) But this time, even in hand control, the wheel couldn't be budged, and the stern planes remained locked in full dive.

"The stern planes are jammed at full dive, Captain," Chapman reported up to the conning tower, unflappable as always.

"Shift to hand control!" the order was fired back.

"Already did that, Captain—the planes won't move!" Chapman reported matter-of-factly. "And we're passing two-five-zero feet, Sir. Recommend putting a bubble in bow buoyancy."

"Put a bubble in bow buoyancy," said Jake. With the stern planes locked in full dive, Jake ordered what might normally be a desperation measure, given the possibility of air being necessarily vented from the tank at some point in the dive—the air bubble ripping the surface and revealing not only the boat's presence, but its exact location. But it was nighttime and they were in the heat of battle, and one surface disturbance more or less would most likely pass unnoticed.

"Bubble bow buoyancy, three second blow" Chapman ordered. At the hydraulic manifold, Bucky Buckner cycled the valve lever that released air into the bow buoyancy tank, holding the valve open for the specified three seconds.

"Two-seven-zero feet, Sir." The planesman's voice more controlled now, because the boat's descent had visibly slowed. *Orca* was at two hundred and ninety feet before the boat was eventually brought under control. And the stern planes were still jammed on full dive — that is, at an up angle, acting to lift the stern so the angle of the boat itself causes an overall down bubble.

Remarkably, no other mechanical damage had been reported, and, aside from a few bumps and scrapes, there were no injuries among the crew.

Then another muffled explosion was heard, which sonar reported as sounding like a torpedo hitting its mark. It was far off and well astern. Sonar then reported that it sounded as if the destroyer had turned tail and was clearing the area. "Fast screws, fading."

Soon thereafter, sonar reported the unmistakable sound of other depth charges going off in the distance, at least five or six of them. After another ten minutes, when all had been quiet, Jake ordered the boat brought slowly back up to periscope depth to find out what was going on.

"Be prepared to take her deep, Hal," Jake called down to Chapman, as the boat made its way toward the surface. "There may be some bubbles coming out of bow buoyancy announcing our arrival."

If any air bubbles exited from the forward-most tank, however, they apparently went unnoticed. "At six--zero feet, Sir," Chapman sang out.

For once, Jake manned the periscope himself. Following standard procedure, he first did a 360-degree sweep. There were contacts, but none that threatened *Orca*. All he could see were three burning hulks on the surface, at various distances, one of which slipped under the waves as he watched. The rest of the convoy, or its escorts, was nowhere in sight. He ordered the boat broached so that her radar antenna was above the surface, and radar reported contacts to the northwest, apparently heading north.

Orca surfaced. Amazingly, it was only 0405. Jake ordered the radio operator to listen for any contact from the TG, and after ten minutes, decided to try and make contact on his own.

"Any station this net, any station this net, this is Railroad Four, over."

"Railroad Four, this is Railroad Three, over." *Conch.*

"Railroad Two." *Stinger.*

But no Railroad One. Jake worried that something had happened to *Devilray*. If it had, TF Command then fell to Lt. Cmdr. Woodrow "Woody" Berghoff in *Stinger*, who was senior officer present afloat (SOPA) after Warren Blaylock.

Berghoff did what he knew Blaylock would do: ordered the remainder of TG 51.2 to make best speed on the surface, to do an end around what was left of the convoy. Radar now counted twelve ships and four escorts in what was a very ragged formation, now making seven knots and heading 097. Every twenty minutes, the radio squawked "Railroad One, this is Railroad Two. Come in Railroad One, over."

But there was no answer.

Jake got the damage report for the stern planes. Bucky and Hal Chapman had crawled back into the after torpedo room bilge to inspect the hydraulic ram that operated the stern planes, and found the extended cylinder shaft was visibly bent. They were able to loosen the cylinder shaft packing and return the planes to their neutral position, but only by having a chain falls rigged to pull the extended shaft back into the cylinder, spilling about a gallon of hydraulic oil in the process. Deciding that there was no hope for an at-sea repair, they then retightened the packing so there would be no further release of oil. But that hydraulic cylinder shaft would never move again, and if hydraulic pressure was again applied to it, a hydraulic line could very well burst, so they rigged a bypass around the cylinder, taking it off-line completely.

"It'll have to be replaced, entirely, Captain," a discouraged COB and Engineer Officer reported to Jake. "That cylinder shaft is bent so bad that there's no way it will ever move under hydraulic power."

"No way to straighten the shaft?" Jake asked.

"That's case-hardened steel, Captain, polished to a mirror finish," replied Chapman. "I doubt that anyone could straighten it now, not without doing worse damage."

"Well, I guess we'll just have to finish out this patrol with the stern planes locked in neutral," replied Jake. "Could be worse. See to it, Gentlemen, that the whole crew understands the situation. I'll let the XO know that the stern planes are OOC for the duration."

Jake let Berghoff know that *Orca's* stern planes were out of commission and could not be repaired at sea. *Stinger's* skipper asked if *Orca* could still stay in the fight. Jake answered in the affirmative.

Woody Berghoff directed TG 51.2 to proceed northeast on propulsion charge on the surface. When the convoy was well over the horizon, he then ordered a turn to course 097 to parallel that of the convoy. He knew it was well within reach of Japanese air cover from Formosa, and kept the TF on the surface for only so long as he dared.

At 0530, he ordered the three boats to submerge and to maintain the same course at five knots until a half-hour after sunset, at 1830, when the TG would surface. By then, the convoy, assuming it maintained course and speed (and it still hadn't zigzagged), would be only about thirty-six miles ahead of them, just over the horizon and to the northwest. If they made seventeen knots on the surface after that, using the auxiliary diesel to recharge their batteries, they could be abreast of the convoy by 2200, and in position well ahead of the convoy — about twenty miles ahead — by midnight.

The three boats surfaced on schedule at 1840. It was nighttime, the full moon obscured by a cloudy overcast, and the night air smelled like oncoming rain. *Orca's* radar quickly found the other two boats, both off to port, one about six hundred yards, the other about thirteen hundred yards, not too far different from the separation they had had when they submerged.

As planned, they proceeded on the surface in line abreast, course 095, seventeen knots. The convoy could be seen clearly on all three submarine radar screens by 2140. Radar still tracked the convoy of twelve ships and four escorts on course 197, speed seven knots, but now there was another contact, a small one, about five thousand yards behind the convoy, trailing it. Had the convoy picked up a new escort vessel during the night? Berghoff ordered the *Orca* to maintain station five hundred yards off *Stinger*, course 095 to continue to slowly close the convoy. He ordered *Conch* to slow and close with the new contact enough to identify it. If it was a new escort, and *Conch* remained undetected, he was to remain behind the convoy and attack from the rear as he had the previous night. The three boats would begin their attack at 0100.

Later course changes brought the convoy in sight of *Orca's* raised periscope. The convoy looked much as it had the night before, but with five fewer marus. *Orca's* nemesis, the *Kamikaze*, still guarded the convoy's right flank. Given tonight's relatively tight four-by-three grouping of the marus, Jake assumed that *Conch* had picked off the previous night's straggler. This new straggler could not be the same vessel, because, given the size of the blip on the radar screen, this guy had to be much smaller than a maru.

Stinger and *Orca* were pulling well ahead of the convoy when Calvin Jennings' excited voice came over the tactical radio. "The straggler! It's Railroad One! No radio. Railroad One directs Railroad Two to continue to direct traffic."

A much cooler voice answered in return. "This is Railroad Two. Very well. Proceed as planned, except that Railroad One to proceed alongside Railroad Three. Over."

"Roger, Railroad Two. Railroad Three, out."

Orca and *Stinger* had worked their way in front of the convoy and were matching its course and speed. Both boats were still on the surface, far enough in front of the convoy so that they could see it only through their raised periscope. It was twenty minutes past midnight, and a gentle rain had begun.

"Railroad Two, this is Railroad Four, over"

"Go ahead, Railroad Four."

"Railroad Four requests permission to proceed with submerged frontal attack at H-hour, over."

"You sure, Railroad Four? Without stern planes? Over."

"Railroad Four is sure, over."

Clem Dwyer looked at Jake. He wasn't anywhere near as sure as his boss was, and hoped that Jake understood how big a chance they were taking.   He prayed that Jake's show of bravado wasn't going to turn out very badly.

"Very well, Railroad Four, if you're sure. Railroad Two will attack left flank. Smaller escort! Railroad Two, out." Unlike Blaylock, Berghoff wouldn't perform the submerged frontal attack maneuver himself, because, unlike *Devilray* and *Orca*, *Stinger* had no active sonar.

Well, Jake, Clem thought, *I sure hope you know what you're doing.*

At 1252, the gentle rain became a driving downpour, the moon obscured, visibility became nil, and *Orca* was at General Quarters.

Then, at 0100, "All Railroad Engineers, this is Railroad Two. Man your locomotives and watch your cabooses! Good Hunting, Gentlemen. Railroad Two, out."

Jake had turned *Orca* toward the convoy, aimed the boat between the two AKs (cargo ships) on the left, and submerged the boat to periscope depth. He knew the convoy would be on top of them in a matter of minutes, even as he slowed the boat to three knots, course 277.

Clem was on the attack scope. "Can't see crap, Skipper, this rain is murder!"

"Sonar, go active," Jake ordered. "Sonar plot, keep a close eye on all contacts." The conning tower talker, Seaman George Parra, relayed the orders over the sound-powered phones.

"Sonar reports four contacts, Captain, bearings two-seven-five and two-seven-nine, and two contacts at two-eight-two," Parra sang out.

"Very well. See anything yet, Clem?"

"Barely. Looks like we're headed between two of those contacts, Captain."

"Good. Open all outer doors, fore and aft."

"Outer doors open on all tubes, fore and aft."

"Clem, I want to pick these guys off as we go past." Then, to Early Sender on the TDC: "Early, I want a firing solution on the first maru we pass on the right, then, after we fire, pick the next one in line on the left. Right now, everybody in the convoy is on course zero-nine-seven, speed seven, but that will most likely change as they panic."

Clem on the attack scope: "Not much room, Skipper, like threading the needle. These guys are maybe five hundred yards apart. We're almost on top of them!"

The sound of slow turning screws echoed through the boat as *Orca* closed the gap, that sound fighting the pinging of the active sonar as it went into short-ping mode, the contacts now very close.

"What do you see Clem?" Jake asked.

"Rivets!"

"Sonar reports two contacts close; two hundred yards to port and three hundred yards to starboard. Sonar plot shows them passing down either side of us."

"Very well," Jake replied.

Then the turning screws were close aboard on either side; very, very loud, and then less so, passing. Another, new set of screws, approaching.

"Sonar reports two new contacts, bearings two-seven-six and two-seven-eight, seven hundred yards and closing. If they stay on course, they'll pass by on either side."

Sonar still in short pings.

Clem: "The rains let up. Vision's good! First target, bearing mark!"

QMSN(SS) Henry Coons on the scope: "Zero-nine-six."

"Range, mark!"

"Three hundred yards"

Early Sender cranked in corrections to the TDC, and nodded to Jake.

Jake: "Fire seven"

"Seven fired."

"Fire eight"

"Eight fired"

"Second target, bearing mark!"

"Zero-nine-eight."

"Range, Mark"

"Three hundred and sixty yards"

Again, Sender nodded to Jake.

"Fire nine."

"Nine Fired."

"Fire ten."

"Ten Fired"

Orca was just approaching the next two ships in line when the first torpedo struck, blowing a hole in the starboard side of the target. The explosion was deafening. The stricken maru, a freighter, though mortally wounded, did not slow, its intact power plant pushing it relentlessly ahead when the second torpedo struck, but did not detonate.

Seconds later, the second target was struck, further aft than the first, but on the port side. This second explosion *did* disable the ship's propulsion, and *this* target, another freighter, quickly slowed. The last torpedo *Orca* fired missed. Almost simultaneously, there were two other explosions, one well off to *Orca's* starboard, another ahead on her starboard quarter. The other boats at work.

But *Orca's* immediate problems were the two marus dead ahead. In panic, one or both might turn toward her and hit her. Jake was prepared to go deep, but if one of those marus was of a mind to hit its tormentor, he probably couldn't dive the boat fast enough — not without a working set of stern planes. Clem was just as worried as Jake and turned the scope to the two approaching ships, first one, and then the other. "They're turning away, Captain," he shouted, the relief in his voice palpable.

"Sonar plot shows contacts ahead turning away."

And then there was another explosion. *Boom!* This one ahead and to starboard, the fourth ship in the line; it exploded a second time and burned brightly, a tanker. Clem, still at the scope: "This next guy is headed straight for us. Take her down, Skipper."

"Sonar reports contact to starboard closing, Captain."

"All ahead full! Crash dive, Hal! Make your depth one-five-zero feet!"

Hal Chapman: "Full dive on the bow planes! Twenty degrees down bubble! Make your depth one-five-zero feet."

But Chapman thought, and left unsaid, *Great. Crash dive and no stern planes. God help us.*

"Maneuvering reports all ahead full, Captain."

They could hear her screws turning close aboard as the fleeing ship passed directly overhead. Jake felt the boat lurch, first to port, then to starboard, as the ship above carried away the wire safety rails aft, but he couldn't know that the ship's keel just brushed the boat's after deck. It only occurred to him afterward that if the stern planes had been operable and doing their job, lifting the stern up to angle the boat downward, that *Orca's* pressure hull aft could well have been hit during the collision and possibly cracked open.

"Think we just lost our safety railing aft," Clem opined.

"If that's all we lost," Jake answered, "we're bloody lucky."

They were passing one hundred feet when Jake thought to secure the active sonar and close the outer doors fore and aft. At 110 feet, there was another explosion heard, probably another torpedo finding its mark, although it may have been a distant depth charge. When the boat settled out at 150 feet, more explosions were heard; this time they were definitely depth charges. Only, this time, at least, *Orca* was not their target. There were other sounds, too: vessels breaking up as they sank.

At 0215, all had been quiet for about fifteen minutes, and Jake crept *Orca* up to periscope depth. Settling at sixty feet, Clem raised the search scope, did a three-hundred-sixty-degree sweep, and reported what he saw. He described one stricken ship still on the surface: a tanker, surrounded by a burning oil slick. There was some floating wreckage, and men in the water. One of the escorts, a minesweeper, was picking them up.

"Let's finish off that tanker, Clem," Jake said. He had thought about the men in the water, what would happen to them if the tanker were hit again. But he could not risk the tanker surviving the action, bringing fuel home to feed the Imperial war machine.

"Aye, Captain," answered Clem, leaving the scope up, fixed the tanker's position.

Minutes later, two torpedoes sent the tanker to the bottom, their explosions almost blowing the minesweeper out of the water as well. Miraculously, the minesweeper remained afloat. Sadly, there were also now fewer men left in the water to rescue.

"You didn't have much choice, Skipper. I'd have done the same."

"I know," Jake said, "I know."

Clem lowered the scope, and Jake had the boat steer clear of the area. When *Orca* was well out of sight of the minesweeper, he had Clem do another sweep, and this time there were no contacts in sight. Broaching the boat to expose the radar antennae, the search radar revealed three small surface contacts, bearing northeast east, at 5,500 yards. Jake surfaced *Orca* completely and headed in that direction. As *Orca* was closing, one of the three contacts challenged him with a signal lamp: "AD." *Orca* replied "QLDP." The return sign came: "QVXY."

TG 51.2 had reassembled.

Warren Blaylock, in *Devilray*, had been using light signals to *Conch*, the boat closest to him, to relay reports to SUBPAC.

"This is Railroad Three, over."

The other two radio-capable boats responded in turn to *Conch's* HF radio signal with their call signs.

"Gentlemen, Railroad One and Railroad Three are heading to the house, Doctor's orders. I've been instructed by Radio One to release Railroad Two and Four. Railroad Four, the Doctor is aware of your ailment, says you can come home with us, your call, over."

"This is Railroad Four, if all the same with the Doctor, will stay here, over."

This is Railroad Three, wait one." Apparently *Conch* put the question to SUBPAC via VLF.

"Railroad Four, Doctor says 'affirmative,' you're welcome to stay. Very well."

This by light from Railroad One: "There are still seven ships left in that covey of ducks, gentlemen, if you are up for it. But One and Three are heading out. Good hunting, gentlemen. Out."

Orca and *Stinger* watched as *Devilray* and *Conch* headed east on the surface at speed, aiming for Midway and repairs. Jake didn't know it at the time, but *Devilray*, during their initial attack on the convoy on Monday, September 13th, had been struck by one of the ships in the convoy as he was at periscope depth in their midst—in essentially the same position *Orca* would be in the following night—but *Orca* had been far luckier and escaped serious damage.

Devilray had just put torpedoes into the two ships in front of her when the following ship's master panicked, broke ranks, and hit *Devilray's* submerged mast, wiping out her antennae, and bending over her radar mast and both periscopes. The scopes were inoperable, and the boat was unable to use her radios or her radars. Worse, the scope seals leaked so badly that the periscope wells overflowed, flooding the control room bilges so quickly that the pump room was in danger of being compromised. Keeping the pumps in service was absolutely critical; the boat had to surface and stay on the surface. She was only able to escape the melee that night because of the confusion the three other boats had caused with their attacks.

Conch had similar bad luck on Tuesday night. She had been forced under by the *Kamikaze* just as *Orca* had been on Monday, but did not escape damage from the *Kamikaze's* depth charges. Her port shaft seal was now leaking badly, and while her pumps could keep up with the leak while the boat was surfaced, they could *not* with her submerged. *Conch* had to pressurize the after torpedo room, and managed to creep away from her tormentor before the situation got out of control and she absolutely had to surface. By that time, the *Kamikaze* had left to shepherd her remaining lambs, leaving a single escort behind to pick up survivors.

Jake now knew for certain that SUBPAC was aware that *Orca* had no stern planes. Apparently command agreed with him that she was still fit for service.

Stinger and *Orca* then headed north-northwest to seek out what was left of MATA-4.

Not that there was any observed air traffic in the areas easily patrolled by the enemy from the air to begin with, but there was always the possibility that there were enemy patrol planes actively searching for American submarines. Perhaps the TF had just been lucky. There was, however, an area along the Manila-to-Takeo convoy route just north of Formosa, that was too far east of the Japanese airfields outside of occupied China, too far west of Okinawa, and too far south of the Home Islands, for aircraft to overfly an en route convoy and stay overhead for any length of time.

It was in that "sweet spot" that *Stinger* and *Orca* finally found what was left of MATA-4, just before dawn on Saturday, September 18th. Both boats had spent the entire night on the surface, and both had full batteries.

The remaining seven ships and their four escorts were now on base course 022, and the convoy, apparently in deference to their lack of air cover, was now zigzagging, that is, altering course off the base course at irregular intervals in order to confuse an attacking submarine trying to obtain a firing solution. Apparently, TG 51.2 had already eliminated the slower marus, because the convoy was now making nine knots along the base course, despite the zigzagging.

With daylight coming, Berghoff elected to submerge both boats and run a parallel course to the convoy base course, making five knots. As prearranged, the two boats surfaced at dusk, and did an end-around run, positioning themselves so they would be dead ahead of the convoy well after dark. Unfortunately, the night proved to be clear and cloudless, with a bright half moon high in the sky.

"Railroad Four, this is Railroad Two, over"

"Four."

"Railroad Two will attack from the convoy's right, Four from the left. Let's put these guys away and then head for the barn."

"Roger that, Two."

Visibility was so good that when the convoy came into sight at 0145, the marus and their escorts could be seen clearly, but so, also, could the attacking submarines. Neither boat had an opportunity to line up a shot before the lead escort, a gunboat, spotted them and headed for them at speed, firing a small-caliber gun as it approached. The boats were forced to break off their attack and proceed in opposite directions at maximum speed. Fortunately for *Orca*, the gunboat chose to chase after *Stinger*, which crash-dived and quickly disappeared beneath the surface. *Orca*, without stern planes, made a slower dive, but still managed to elude a second escort, the minesweeper, approaching from the left side of the convoy.

Orca's sonar could hear the gunboat dropping depth charges on *Stinger*, four in all. *Boom! Boom! Boom! Boom!* Jake guessed that the four might have been the gunboats full complement of depth charges, because no further explosions were heard. *Orca's* pursuer, apparently content to have forced her prey to submerge, never bothered to drop a depth charge.

Jake fumed as the convoy slipped away, but wisely stood off long enough until the listening sonar confirmed it was safe to come to periscope depth. Clem reported no contacts on the scope, and Jake then ordered the boat broached to expose the radar antennae. The convoy was 9,000 yards to the northeast. If *Stinger* was on the surface, she didn't show up on the radar.

"Railroad Two, this is Railroad Four, over."

No response.

"*Stinger* may just be submerged, or her radio might just be out," Jake said, hopefully.

Jake surfaced the boat, and again approached the convoy at speed and out of sight. This time he positioned *Orca* well ahead of the convoy's base course and to the west of it. He then ordered the boat submerged (hating that the boat, absent useful stern planes, was so sluggish in its response) and closed with the convoy.

At 0300, Jake ordered active sonar to single ping, get ranges and bearings, and then cautioned sonar plot to be alert. At 0320, careful to only expose the periscope for a few seconds, Clem reported the convoy approaching from the south, the escorting minesweeper clearly in view. But the convoy appeared to be heading away from them.

Jake ordered another single ping range and bearing. Sonar plot confirmed that the convoy appeared to be on course 030, speed eight knots.

"Zigging away," Jake thought aloud.

"Probably," Clem agreed.

Just then, there was a loud explosion that came from the other side of the convoy. Clem risked a quick look, and saw that a pillar of flame had erupted from the right side of the convoy. Quickly lowering the scope, he said "Berghoff, you clever bastard, you!"

Jake smiled in agreement. "What's going on now?"

Clem raised the scope again. "They're turning toward!"

"Quick," Jake said, "pick a target and let's get off a shot."

Then: "Open outer doors forward, tubes one and two"

A second later: "Bearing, mark."

"Zero-nine-four."

"Range, mark."

"Twelve hundred yards."

Early Sender, on the TDC, set up the target for a firing solution.

"Forward torpedo room reports outer doors open, tubes one and two."

"I need a target course and speed!" Jake complained. "Sonar, another single ping." And then, "Sonar plot, what've ya got?"

"Sonar reports convoy has zigged to course one-one-five, speed still eight knots," Parra sang out.

"Crank that into the TDC, Early."

"Aye, Captain, one-one-five, speed eight."

"Observation, Clem," Jake ordered. But Clem already had the periscope on the way up.

"Bearing, mark!"

"Zero-nine-three."

"Range, mark."

"Eleven hundred yards!"

Early Sender twiddled the knobs on the TDC. "I have a firing solution, Captain."

"Fire one."

"One away."

"Get me another one, Clem." Again, Clem had the scope up already.

"Bearing, mark!"

"Zero-nine-four."

"Sonar reports torpedo running hot straight, and normal."

"Range, mark!"

"Eleven hundred fifty yards."

"I have a firing solution, Captain." Sender had already set up for the second target on the TDC.

"Minesweeper headed this way, Captain," Clem shouted.

"Fire two."

"Two away."

"Close the outer doors forward! All ahead full! Take her down, Hal, one-five-zero feet. Right twenty degrees rudder"

Before these reports could be acknowledged, there was a loud explosion heard through the water. *Orca* had hit at least one of its targets. The next explosion followed almost immediately thereafter, only this time it was a depth charge. *Boom!* Off the port quarter. Close enough to rock the sluggishly responding boat, but not close enough to cause any real damage. Two more depth charges went off, again off the port quarter, further away this time, as *Orca* made her way deep. *Boom! Boom!*

And then another, more violent, explosion, dead astern.

"Sounds like we hit another one, Captain," Clem announced jubilantly.

"Rudder amidships. Either us or *Stinger*, Clem."

"Has to be ours, Skipper. That was too close for it to be Berghoff's kill."

Another depth charge went off, followed by yet another, both much further astern. *Boom! Boom!*

And then another, louder explosion, further away than the last big one.

"Now that one I'll give Berghoff," Clem said with a grin.

More depth charges, far off this time. "Sounds like he might be paying for it, though."

"One-five-zero feet, Sir."

"Sonar, single ping ranges and bearings, report contacts."

Seconds later: "Sonar reports convoy, three contacts, maybe four, bearing zero-nine-zero, now heading zero-two-two, speed eight. Four, maybe five others, bearing from zero-nine-five to one-zero-zero, appear stopped. Three others, moving erratically. Closest contact now twenty-two hundred yards. It's a mess up there."

More depth charges went off in the distance.

"There's more, Captain—breaking-up noises. Something's sinking close by."

"Bring us back to periscope depth, Hal—six zero feet."

"Six-zero feet, aye."

Minutes later, Clem reported what he saw on the scope. "Three AKs dead in the water, burning. One's well down by the stern and looks like it's ready to sink. Burning oil slick. Two escorts, the two small boys, picking up survivors. No other ships in sight."

Jake directed the submerged boat around the dead and dying and set a course to Pearl.

Once out of sight of the escorts, he ordered the boat broached and the radar antennae exposed. Dead astern, the radarscope showed two large contacts dead in the water, along with two smaller ones. There was also a group of three large contacts and one smaller, 8,800 yards to the north, heading 022 at eight knots.

No zigs or zags.

Jake surmised that these were three marus and one *Kamikaze*-class destroyer, beating a path home. It would soon be light, and both Jake and *Orca* were tired. *Orca* might just have enough fuel left to make it all the way home.

Once well clear, he sent out a message on the tactical frequency: "Railroad Two, this is Railroad Four, over."

He had the message repeated every twenty minutes throughout the remainder of the day and into the night, but there was never any answer.

Chapter 12

Return to Pearl: 21 September 1943 to 8 November 1943

It was Tuesday morning, September 21, 1943. *Orca,* running submerged and having cleared the northernmost Ryukyus Island of Amami, was now running flat out on the surface, heading due east. The boat would not make a turn to east southeast and head for Pearl until she had passed north of the tiny unoccupied Japanese islands of Katano and Nakanoshima, the northernmost cluster of volcanic islands that stretched across the Pacific directly in their path.

"Well, Hal," Jake asked Lt. Harold Chapman, his Engineer Officer, "have we got enough diesel to make it to Pearl, or should we be heading to Midway to top off?"

"Well Skipper, if we restrict our surface running to three engines, we can still make about fourteen knots on the surface and make it all the way to Pearl. That fourth engine just sucks down the fuel, and doesn't really give us all that much added speed."

"Sounds good," Jake replied. "We can't lose *too* much time if our day running is restricted, certainly no more than we would lose if we stopped at Midway. Let's go for it."

Orca approached her berth at the submarine pier at SUBASE Pearl Harbor on Monday morning, October 9th. Jake figured that running on just three engines on the surface had cost *Orca* almost a day in transit, but it had been worth it to avoid a stopover in Midway — and a greater delay for *Orca's* homecoming.

From the bridge, Jake searched among the people lining the pier as they arrived. COMSUBPAC, Rear Admiral Lockwood, and the Squadron Commander, Cpt. Clarence Macdonough were conspicuous at the front of the awaiting crowd. But it wasn't them Jake was looking for.

When he finally spotted Kate, not thirty feet away, he almost didn't recognize her. But it was definitely Kate. She was smiling widely and waving, along with everyone else on the pier, wearing a shapeless yellow print dress that was designed to conceal her almost-three-months-pregnant belly—not that there was that much belly yet to be concealed.

Jake had *expected* her to look pregnant, and it wasn't the presence or absence of a belly that made her look somehow different. She looked somehow softer, somehow more lush, than the Kate he had left behind at their cottage that Thursday, last.

And she never looked more beautiful.

Her eyes were locked on his, and he figured she had probably spotted him before he had spotted her. He was musing on how grimy he probably looked, and how badly he must stink—despite the Navy shower he had taken three hours earlier.

Jake was still lost in his own reverie when Clem, standing beside him on the bridge, rudely elbowed him and shouted, "Jake, look! Oh my God! It can't be, but it is! Look! On the pier! It's Miriam!"

Kate was at least a head taller than the pretty woman with the reddish-brown hair and the broad smile standing next to her. Jake had been so absorbed with seeing Kate that he had overlooked Miriam entirely. He had last seen Miriam in Groton, on that blustery morning—was it really only ten months ago?—when *Orca* set off for the Panama Canal on her way to Pearl. Miriam Dwyer had looked miserable that December morning on the pier, teary-eyed and inconsolable, standing beside and being supported by a solid and stoic Louise Buckner. Jake remembered how miserable Clem had looked as well, as he half-heartedly waved goodbye to his wife. That memory, he knew, was the reason he insisted that he and Kate part at their cottage two months earlier, rather than see him off from the pier.

So much had happened in those two months that the passage of time had seemed that much longer. He took a mental inventory: two war patrols; "The Slot"; Brisbane; depth charges and jammed stern planes; men struggling in the water; *Stinger* maybe lost . . .

But now was not the time for depressing memories! He was home. And as happy as he was for Clem, he was every bit as happy for himself—no, *more* so—because he had come home to Kate!

Also on the pier that morning, greeting her man aboard the arriving boat, was a pretty, brown-eyed blonde named Daisy Norton, standing next to a suitcase that contained all her worldly belongings. And Joe Bob Clanton could not have been more surprised—nor happier—to see her.

"Look at you, Jake Lawlor, you're all rumpled and you stink to high heavens!" exclaimed Kate.

Jake could only grin back at her, ecstatic that his appearance and his aroma had not stopped his wife from hugging him and kissing him with vigor and passion, the memory of which had sustained him over some very difficult moments.

The admiral and Cpt. Macdonough were the first people over the gangway. Jake and Clem were there to meet them, saluting Lockwood and the commodore aboard.

"Hell of a job, men! Hell of a job!" the admiral said with a broad grin. "But there's time enough for an official debriefing with me and my staff in the morning. Let the relief crew take over, you men go home with your lovely wives, and that's an order. See you both in the morning, 0900. And Clem, your Miriam is lovely, just lovely! Now get out of here!"

Neither man argued, although Jake did stop to ask "*Stinger?*"

Lockwood frowned. "No word."

Macdonough added, "Nothing. Probably lost."

If the probable loss of *Stinger* cast a pallor over Jake's joy at homecoming, it was quickly overcome as an exuberant Kate bundled him into their '41 Olds and drove them off the base. They left behind an equally ecstatic Clem and Miriam; Clem not knowing why or how his wife was there in Pearl, but not, at least for the moment, questioning his good fortune.

"Will they be okay?" Jake asked. "Do they have a place to stay? Clem can't take Miriam to the BO—"

"Don't worry about them, silly. Miriam's no dummy. She's been planning this for months. There's a cab waiting to take them to a rental in town, and his stuff from the BOQ is already there."

"And how do you know all of this?"

"Because Miriam has been staying with me at the cottage for the past month. She's on a year's sabbatical from the college, and she doesn't have to be back to work until classes resume next Fall. Isn't that wonderful?"

"Yes, I guess it is. Wonderful."

* * * * *

The last person Joe Bob Clanton expected to see in Pearl was Daisy. He had reconciled himself to the idea that she would never forgive him for promising to meet her that last night in Brisbane— and then never showing up. Of course he never reckoned on the grapevine that existed in the port of Brisbane, and foolishly assumed that the secret comings and goings of the Allied fleet remained well-kept secrets.

"I knew you'd of come to me if you could," Daisy acknowledged, after their feverish embrace on the pier. "So," she said with an impish smile, "I decided to come to you."

"Where are you staying? Where can we go?" he asked.

"I'm not staying anywhere. I just got here two days ago, and it took everything I had to get here. I had to fib my way onto the base," she explained. "Told them I was your wife. I've been sleeping in the park. At least the weather here is nice. And I do so need a bath, Love."

Joe Bob, overcome with joy, grinned. "Well," he said, "We'll just have to find us a place." He led her to a bus waiting to carry the crew to the Royal Hawaiian.

Once there, no one at the hotel questioned Joe Bob's right to a room. The crew of the submarine *Orca* had just arrived in port, and everyone aboard her was entitled to R&R and a place to stay at the Royal Hawaiian, courtesy of the U.S. Navy. Of course it was unusual for anyone to show up with a woman and a suitcase in tow, but women came and went from the hotel at all hours, all the time, and nobody asked any questions.

* * * * *

Miriam Dwyer hadn't seen her husband in months, ten months to be exact—not since he sailed away from her in Groton. She had given him a proper kiss and embrace, despite the man sweat and the diesel stink, and was still amazed, even after almost four years of marriage, at her physical reaction to his touch.

"What is this place?" Clem asked, as he surveyed the apartment on Keeaumoku Street in the Ala Moana district of Honolulu.

"Ours, for the next year or so," she said. "I leased it until next Fall, when I have to be back in Connecticut, or until either your home port is changed, or you get transferred. The lease reads like a wish list."

"How much is this costing us? Can we afford it?"

"What?" she said, her Irish up. "You haven't seen me in ten months, and you have time for stupid questions?"

"You're absolutely right," he said, cowed, and reached for her. "Now's *not* the time for stupid questions."

* * * * *

Back at the cottage, Jake stripped naked and headed for the shower. No "Navy shower" was necessary here. There was plenty of hot water, and he could run it for a long as he liked. He had just gotten the temperature of the water to his liking and was soaping down, when the curtain parted and Kate slipped in beside him. "Move over, sailor," she said with an impish grin. It was a tight fit, but that didn't seem to bother either of them.

Later, in bed, he said "You're sure we didn't hurt the baby?"

"Yes, you idiot, I'm sure."

* * * * *

"This is nice," Daisy said, as she looked about their room at the Royal Hawaiian.

"It'll do for now," said Joe Bob. "We can look for something more permanent tomorrow. Meanwhile, it'll do just fine."

She saw that look in his eyes, and felt her body tingle just as it had whenever he looked at her that way in Brisbane.

He came close to her and folded her in his arms.

"I do *so* need a bath," she said.

"Later."

* * * * *

At 0900 the following morning, crisp in their work khakis, Jake and Clem reported to squadron headquarters and Rear Adm. Lockwood for their debriefing. Clem had brought *Orca's* logbook with him, and he and Jake referred to it as they gave their report.

When they were done, Lockwood commented:

"Jap reports say you disabled a nine-hundred-ton cargo transport at New Georgia. They were able to beach her, but were unable to unload any of her cargo before the Marines finally forced the Japs to abandon Bairoko. So, while technically you didn't sink her, you might as well have, because she's now rusting away on the beach off Bairoko, her cargo probably still rotted inside her.

"The wolf pack was far more successful. *Orca* and the three other boats claim fourteen ships, five of them tankers. The Japs admit to only five sunk ships, with seven damaged."

If Jake wondered how the Admiral could be so sure about exactly what the Japanese claimed their losses were, he was smart enough not to inquire.

"By the way," added Lockwood, "the Jap destroyer that screwed up your after torpedo tube off Bairoko thinks he sank you."

"The other boats in the wolf pack?" Clem inquired. "How'd they make out?"

"You already know that *Stinger* is overdue," Lockwood replied. "*Devilray* and *Conch* made it just fine to Midway. Tender there patched *Devilray* up as well as it could, but they couldn't very well replace her periscopes. She's due back here in Pearl tomorrow. Blaylock's being relieved. Her new skipper, Joe Morgan, will take *Devilray* to Mare Island for a complete overhaul. They'll replace her scopes there."

"Warren Blaylock's being relieved?" Jake was surprised.

"Made full commander. Has a new duty assignment, being sent to the Pentagon, that new headquarters building the War Department just opened. Maybe he can loosen a few screws there for us. By the way, he personally credited *Orca* with three of those MATA-4 kills, and you may well have gotten two more out of the last four kills. That's damn good work."

"Thank you, Sir, but that's great news about Warren Blaylock," Jake replied. "He's a good man. And so's Joe Morgan. He was in the class behind me at the Academy."

"Right. Just made lieutenant commander early. He did such a great job as XO in *Barbel*, that the powers-that-be decided he deserved a promotion and a command right away—all on my recommendation of course. And, incidentally, I've also recommended you for a second Navy Cross," he added with a smirk.

"Thank you, Sir!" Jake replied. "But I missed Harry Loveless. He on leave?" Jake asked.

"Nope, kicked him upstairs. He's in Washington, reporting to Admiral King and the Joint Chiefs. King's an old submariner, and they can swap sea stories."

"And *Conch*?" Clem asked.

"Tender at Midway was able to replace her shaft seal, and *Conch* is back out on patrol. As for *Stinger*, as I told Jake, she's officially missing, presumed lost. Jap destroyer escorting MARU-4 claims to have sunk her. Japs have been dead wrong about such things before, but maybe not this time."

"Woody Berghoff was a hell of a good man," Clem said. "He'll be missed. *Stinger* will be missed."

"Yes," Lockwood said, "he will, she will, they *all* will."

Jake nodded in silent agreement.

"Now tell me about this sonar plot idea of yours . . ."

The next day, a crew from the yard came aboard *Orca* and inspected her damaged stern planes. Bucky followed them aft.

"Bitch of a place to get to," said the lead petty officer, a submarine-qualified machinist's mate first class—MM1(SS). "This'll take us a while. All goes well, should be good in about a week, even with all the crawling in and out."

"Good," Bucky allowed.

Later the same day, *Devilray* came into port and subsequently tied up to her "permanent" berth just forward of *Orca.* Jake was among the first to welcome her, going aboard right after the admiral and the commodore, congratulating Warren Blaylock on his promotion and new assignment.

* * * * *

"So can we agree," Kate asked, "after you, if it's a boy, and Elizabeth Ann, after my mother, if it's a girl?"

"I'm fine with Elizabeth Ann. And Jacob is okay if it's a boy. But *not* a Junior. I wouldn't wish 'Julius' as a middle name, on anybody."

"Okay," Kate laughed. They were lying together naked on the bed, and her newly outsized breasts jiggled when she laughed. "I forgot about the 'Julius' part. How about Jacob Joseph, then?"

"Yeah. Jacob Joseph is fine."

"Jacob Joseph it is then," she said, running her hand over her baby bump.

Jake reached out with his left hand and did the same. "When will he start to move?" he asked.

"First baby, not for about twenty-five weeks. So, *she* probably won't move for another month or so." Then, "Will you be very disappointed if it's not a boy?"

"No, not at all. A girl would be just fine." Jake leaned over and kissed Kate's breast, nuzzling her, his hand moving down her belly.

"Again?" she asked. "So soon? You're insatiable."

"You have to admit," he said, "it *has* been a while."

"Yes it has," she agreed, gasping as his fingers touched her core.

* * * * *

"And you're *sure* you want to marry her? You know, we weren't in Brisbane for even a week. You hardly know this woman," Clem said. "And she looks *really* young. How old is she, anyway?"

"She's eighteen," said Joe Bob, defiantly. "I know all I need to know, Clem. I know we want to get married."

Joe Bob had to have his CO's permission to get married. It was usually only a formality, a permission given almost automatically—but this was different. He knew that Jake might well deny his permission, and Joe Bob knew that, from the world's point of view, Jake would have every good reason to withhold it.

But he also knew, deep in his heart, that the world was all wrong about Daisy and him.

Joe Bob knew better than go directly to Jake. If his skipper turned him down and they went ahead with the marriage anyway, his Navy career would be over, and he might well begin his married life in the brig. He figured that if he could convince the XO to let him marry Daisy, then his skipper would be sure to follow his XO's advice. And if the XO turned him down, he still had the option of appealing to Jake.

"Why not wait?" Clem asked. "If you're sleeping with her anyway, why not just wait until you're absolutely sure, and *then* marry her?"

Joe Bob seethed. His XO, a man he thought was his friend, had just implied that his relationship with Daisy was something he should take lightly, something that he could be flippant about, even, perhaps, that it was something sordid.

Clem registered the look on Joe Bob's face. "I'm sorry, Joe Bob, that was way out of line." Then, "Look, I'll see what I can do. Talk to the Captain. But I can't promise you anything."

Mollified, Joe Bob said "Thanks, Clem. I really appreciate this. You won't regret it."

Clem thought, *I really hope I won't*, but kept the thought to himself.

Clem had approved his qualification notebook, and now Bill Salton was doing his in-port qualification. That meant a grueling half-day spent with the skipper of another boat, answering his questions, demonstrating his competence. He had drawn Lt. Cmdr. David Brandenburg, USN, skipper of the USS *Moray*, a man who had a reputation, among all the junior officers who had qualified under him, as a hardass. He reported to Brandenburg at 1300.

"So, Ensign, you think you should be wearing dolphins, eh?" Brandenburg said, as soon as Salton reported to him aboard *Moray*.

"Yes, Sir, I do."

Confident, Brandenburg thought. *I like that.* Then aloud, he said, "Very well, Mr. Salton, we'll see. Tell me about the batteries aboard this boat."

Salton went about describing the batteries in detail: type (lead-acid); number of cells (126 each); voltage for each cell (1.06 to 2.75 volts depending on the state of charge); approximate weight of each cell (1,650 pounds).

"Very well, Mr. Salton. can you tell me the dimensions of each cell?"

"Yes, Sir. Each cell is fifty-four by fifteen by twenty-four inches."

"Very good, Mr. Salton, but somebody probably told you I'd ask that. Tell me about hydrogen gas generation. At what point does it become dangerous?"

Bill recited the textbook from memory: "All submarine batteries produce hydrogen by electrically breaking down water into its gaseous components. Hydrogen is flammable in air at mixtures above four percent hydrogen, and will explode at mixtures over eighteen percent. Any spark can set off a flammable or explosive mixture of hydrogen in air."

Brandenburg scowled. "Text book. Okay. Let's go aft." He led Bill to an evaporator. "Show me how to operate an evaporator, Mr. Salton."

Bill walked him through the process, pointing out each switch and each valve in the process. This time, at least, Bill noted, Brandenburg didn't scowl. "Very good, Mr. Salton."

And so it went on like that for the day.

At 1800, after five grueling hours, Brandenburg had finally run out of questions and exercises for his examinee. They had covered just about every system aboard *Moray*, from the ventilation system to the hydraulic plant, to mock-manipulating the electrical manifold. With few exceptions, Bill had correctly answered just about every question thrown at him, and had been able to operate every piece of equipment on which he was tested.

Finally, Brandenburg shook his hand. And he was actually smiling. "My compliments to Mr. Dwyer. He has prepared you well. You're a credit to him, your captain, and to your boat. You may tell Clem Dwyer that I'm satisfied, and that you've passed your in-port exam. Congratulations, Bill."

"Yessir, Captain! Thank you, Sir." Salton beamed. Now there was only the underway exam to pass.

* * * * *

"Joe Bob is nuts," Jake fumed. "There is no way he could be ready to marry this woman after — what? — knowing her for all of a *week*?"

"I know, Jake, and I concur completely. But be honest. How long did it take you to be sure about Kate?"

"That's different. I'm a grown man. Joe Bob's still a kid."

"Is he? He's twenty-five, and that makes him older than most of the crew. He's *beyond* old enough to vote and to drink hard liquor. Hell, he's a Lieutenant jay-gee in the Navy, for heaven's sake."

"Maybe so. But it's a matter of maturity. Joe Bob still acts like a kid. Look at Bill Salton, he's only an ensign, but he's *way* more mature than Joe Bob."

"I'll give you that," Clem admitted, then smiled, "but Bill's also more mature than a lot of lieutenant commanders I know!"

Jake laughed aloud. "And I'll give *you* that. But really, Clem, I think Joe Bob's making a big mistake."

"Probably. But I think we'll be making a bigger one if we stand in his way. He's a good officer. Very smart. Does his job well. Bit lazy, maybe, but then I'd be comparing him to Salton, and that's not exactly fair. I think we should let him do what he's made up his mind to do anyway."

"Okay. I hope we're doing the right thing. Get the paperwork started."

* * * * *

"She's done, Chief. New cylinder's in, the hydraulics have been bled, and the system tested out. Time to check 'er out on your own," announced the MM1(SS) in charge.

First Bucky crawled into the after torpedo room bilge and checked out the installation. The hydraulic system had been turned on, and was pressurized. Everything looked shipshape, there were no hydraulic oil leaks, and the crew had done a good job cleaning up after themselves. There had, he knew, been a good deal of hydraulic oil spilled in the course of the repair, but none of that was in evidence.

"Nice clean job," he said to the MM1(SS), and the man beamed. "Now let's check 'er out."

He stationed a man on the stern with sound-powered phones plugged into the boat's communications system, with a long lead through the open after torpedo room hatch. In the control room, he operated the stern planes control, and the talker on the stern verified that the planes were moving from full dive to full rise and back again. Then Bucky crawled back into the bilge again to insure that there had been no hydraulic oil leaks in the interim. There were none.

"Good job. Outstanding. Where do I sign off on it?" The MM1(SS) smiled broadly and handed Bucky the sign-off sheet.

Only when he was satisfied that *Orca* was once again shipshape could Bucky relax, and there were still lots of minor maintenance issues that needed to be addressed. He had considered boarding a military flight to the mainland, en route to Groton and his Louise — but there just wasn't enough time. It was already October 13th, and he knew he and the rest of the crew needed to be back aboard *Orca* on November 2nd. By the time he got to the mainland and took the train across the continent to Groton, he would only have time to kiss Louise and turn around for the trip back. Maybe after the next patrol. *Or more than likely,* he thought, *not until the boat goes in for major overhaul. Or maybe not 'til this damn war ends.*

* * * * *

As weddings go, it wasn't much—a Justice of the Peace at the government building in downtown Honolulu. Clem and Miriam were there as witnesses, as Joe Bob and Daisy exchanged vows. Hal Chapman, Louie Carillo, and Early Sender were on leave, and on the mainland in San Diego with their wives. Bill Salton was at sea aboard *Bullshark,* having spent the night before readying a practice torpedo for a mock attack on a cooperative destroyer in Mamala Bay, and then getting *Bullshark* underway at 0600. The only others attending the wedding were Jake, Kate, and four enlisted men from Joe Bob's crew in *Orca's* radio shack.

Joe Bob had asked for a week's leave for a honeymoon, and it had been granted. The couple planned to spend it seeing the sights on the Big Island, where Joe Bob had booked a room at the Hilo Hawaiian. After that, they planned to return to Oahu and find a place for Daisy to stay near the base.

* * * * *

Of course the commissary was bereft of gold dolphins. Jake found his spare pin and personally pinned it on Bill Salton's uniform. Bill was roundly congratulated by the few people who were still aboard *Orca.* Jake and Clem took him to the "O" Club at 1800, where Clarence Macdonough, Dave Brandenburg, and Foster Dwight, the CO of *Bullshark,* tipped a few brews with the newly qualified ensign in celebration. The drinks were on Bill, of course.

Now, Joe Bob Clanton was the only officer aboard *Orca* who hadn't qualified. Clem resolved to get on his case as soon as that boy returned from his honeymoon.

* * * * *

"Uncle Charlie wants to see you," Commodore Macdonough said over the shoreline hookup to *Orca*.

"The admiral wants to see me? Am I in trouble?" Jake asked.

The commodore chuckled over the phone line. "Not hardly. Wants to talk to you about the sonar plot thing. After I told him about it, he thinks it might be something worth exploring. Any reason you can't be in his office at ten?"

"No, Sir, Commodore, I'll be there!"

At 1000 sharp, Jake was outside of the office of Rear Adm. Charles Lockwood, the Commander of the Pacific Submarine Fleet. Jake was ushered into the admiral's office by the khaki-clad lieutenant who was the admiral's aide. Seated on a wing chair next to the admiral's desk was Commodore Macdonough; he was smoking a huge cigar. The admiral rose to greet him, an equally huge stogie smoldering away in an ashtray on his desk.

"Come in Jake. Good to see you! You know Captain Macdonough, of course." The two men nodded politely to each other as the Admiral asked, "Have a cigar? They're Cuban."

"No, thank you, Admiral, I don't smoke."

"Oh, right. Says in your dossier that you have *no* bad habits."

Jake smiled. "Where does it say that, Admiral? Somebody's been passing along some bad dope."

Lockwood chuckled. "Now sit down and tell me about this new idea of yours. Tell me about sonar plot." He indicated an overstuffed chair on the other side of the desk.

Jake sat down and told the Admiral of his attempt to collate and make sense of the information coming from sonar by plotting it on paper. He described the inconsistencies between sonar, passive sonar in particular, and the more reliable information coming from visual observations and radar.

"But visual observations and radar require you to expose yourself on the surface," Lockwood observed.

"Exactly, Admiral. The information from sonar, especially passive sonar, is squirrely, though, and not entirely reliable. There are salinity layers and thermoclines that change how sound propagates underwater."

The Admiral frowned, processing the information. "Active sonar is much better," he said. "I used the sonar plot information almost exclusively with my last shots at the convoy, and while I wasn't on the surface to observe the kill through the periscope, I'm pretty sure we hit our targets. In any case, the convoy started out that night with seven ships, and afterward there were only three. Of course, it's entirely possible that *Stinger* got all four kills."

"But not highly likely," Macdonough volunteered. "Sounds more to me like Woody Berghoff made two kills before the escorts got to him, and the other two are *Orca's*. But, of course, we'll probably never know for sure."

"Maybe not," Lockwood agreed, "but the sonar plot idea has definite merit. Write it up, Jake, and get it to our bosses ASAP. You should be in port for a few more days yet. Should be enough time."

Jake, figuring he was dismissed, got up to leave.

"One minute more, Jake, we have something else to discuss."

"Sir?"

Macdonough scowled, but the admiral kept on. "You know we have new boats coming on line, more every day . . ." He paused for comment, but Jake kept his silence. He guessed what was coming. ". . . I need skippers, Jake, good men, trained submarine leaders."

Jake raised his right hand, as if to stop the admiral. "I think Clem Dwyer would make an excellent CO, Admiral."

Lockwood beamed. "And so do we, Jake, both the commodore and I. But keep it under your hat for the time being, until we talk to Dwyer."

"Yessir," Jake replied, and left. Somehow, he noted, he felt strangely saddened and elated at the same time.

The following day, Jake got the word that *Orca* was to be ready to leave for her next patrol on November 8th. Now he knew why he was told that everyone who took leave had to report back by November 2nd.

* * * * *

Clem wondered why he had been summoned to the commodore's office. He couldn't think of anything he had screwed up. Maybe the commodore just wanted his opinion of Jake's sonar plot idea. He hoped that was all it was.

"Clem," the commodore began, "why the hell are you out of uniform?"

"Sir?" Clem asked, taken aback.

Macdonough smiled and handed Clem a little box, opened to display a set of gold oak leaves. "Congratulations, Lieutenant Commander Dwyer."

"Oh my God, Commodore! But it's too soon. I'm not even in the zone for another six months—"

"Perhaps you haven't heard, Mr. Dwyer. There's a war on!"

"Yessir! Believe me, Sir, I'm not complaining. I'm just so surprised!"

Macdonough beamed. "And that's not even the half of it. I'm detaching you from *Orca*. Much as I hate to break up the team of Lawlor and Dwyer, we've another assignment for you."

Now Clem was really stunned. First the promotion, now this. What was going on? He hoped they weren't going to give him shore duty like they gave Warren Blaylock.

"*Moray* is leaving to go on patrol on November tenth, two days after *Orca* leaves port. You'll be aboard her, reporting to Dave Brandenburg for your PCO cruise."

"Yes, Sir," Clem said, repeating his new orders aloud, assuring himself that he had heard it all correctly: "*Moray*, November tenth, PCO cruise."

Macdonough reached out and handed Clem a sealed packet. "Good luck, Clem, and again, congratulations. The official notice of your promotion, and your new orders are all in here. It's all official, and your promotion and your orders are dated today, so you can tell anyone with the need to know, including your lovely wife. Jake knew about your orders, but not the promotion, so you'll be able to tell him something he doesn't already know!"

"Yes, Sir. Thank you, Sir!" A still overwhelmed Clem shook the commodore's proffered hand and navigated his way out of his office. He found the men's room and removed the railroad tracks from his shirt collar and replaced them with his new oak leaves. Preening, he smiled broadly at himself in the mirror.

* * * * *

Jake had spoken at length with the commodore about who was to replace Clem as *Orca's* XO. The commodore had suggested several men, well-qualified submariners from other boats, but Jake said he would prefer to promote from within; he wanted someone who had trained under Clem and him and was already familiar with *Orca*. He wanted to make Hal Chapman his new XO.

What he didn't tell the commodore was that he had already floated the idea to Clem and Bucky, and both had agreed that Chapman would be an excellent XO.

"Well," the commodore finally agreed, "Chapman's certainly senior enough, and he's definitely XO material. Okay, Jake, I won't argue with your judgment. Chapman it is. I'll see to it that the orders are cut. But say nothing to anyone until it's official. The admiral still has to sign off on it, and while he's unlikely to have any objections, it's still not official until he does."

"Yes, Sir. Not a word to anyone until it's official."

Joe Bob hiked up his pants and fastened his belt. "Well Doc, what's going on? What's wrong with me?"

Joe Bob and Pharmacist Mate First Class Corey "Doc" Clanton had, in Jake's absence, appropriated the captain's cabin where Doc could examine Joe Bob in some privacy.

"Sorry, Mr. Clanton, but you have gonorrhea."

"I . . . what? I've got the clap? Are you sure?"

"Positive. But you're welcome to get my diagnosis confirmed at the base hospital."

"No, no, I believe you. It's just . . ." It was just that Joe Bob hadn't been with anyone but Daisy since *Orca* had left for her third patrol last Summer. "How long have I had it, Doc, can you tell?"

"Not really. But it can't be that long. Sometimes, men are asymptomatic for several weeks, but it usually shows up anywhere from a couple of days to a week or so."

"Can you do anything for it? Can you cure me?"

"Sulfonamide is the standard treatment, a daily dose for three weeks."

"What can you do for me? Can you get me some?"

"Oh, I can get the drug all right, but I have to tell the dispensary who and what I'm getting it for. There *was* a disciplinary punishment attached to catching clap, loss of pay, I think, but I'm pretty sure that's been rescinded. Too many guys weren't reporting it, and cases were going untreated until they got really bad. But—"

"No, I don't want this to get out. Can a civilian doctor get the drug?"

"Probably. You would have to check that out for yourself."

"Okay. Thanks, Doc. Unless you hear otherwise from me, forget about this, will you?"

"Sure, Mr. Clanton. I never saw you."

Dr. Donald Fong, M.D., practiced medicine out of an office attached to his residence on Ahana Street, not too far from Joe Bob and Daisy's apartment. Fong was a short, round man with a moon face, who wore rimless pince-nez glasses. The idea of a Chinese doctor wasn't half as disconcerting to Joe Bob as was a Chinese doctor who spoke flawless English.

Joe Bob was in civvies: blue linen slacks, and a light gray short-sleeved shirt.

"No doubt about it, Mr. and Mrs. Clanton. I've examined the cultures I took from each of you under the microscope. You both definitely have gonorrhea. I recommend we start treatment immediately."

"Great, Doctor, what treatment are you recommending?" asked Joe Bob. Daisy sat silently next to him with her hands folded in her lap, her eyes downcast. She wore a gaily colored, print dress, one of the ones Joe Bob had bought for her to wear on their honeymoon.

"Prontosil," said the doctor. "Used to be made by the Germans, but it's now manufactured . . ."

Joe Bob tuned out Doctor Fong, as he churned over in his mind his confrontation with his wife the prior day.

He had just returned home from his meeting with "Doc" Shields:

"I've got the clap, Daisy. How about that?"

"What? You've got what?!"

"Gonorrhea, Daisy, the clap, venereal disease, for God's sake!"

"How did you get that?" she had asked. (She obviously had no indication whatsoever that she was sick.)

"How do you think?" (he remembered asking her). "I haven't been with anybody but you for months. I caught it from you, Daisy." (He was angry then, he remembered, and almost in tears.) "I caught it from you."

Daisy's face, he saw, went from registering genuine surprise and concern to absolute horror and fear. "No," she said. "Please, no!"

"What have you done?" he asked. (He remembered that by then he was really angry.) "What the hell have you done?"

"I did it for you!" she cried. "I did it so I could be with you!"

"What?" (He didn't believe her.) Her eyes – those eyes he loved so – then welled up with tears. "What did you do? Why?"

"How do you think I got the money to get here?" she shouted back at him, tears streaming down her face. "I had no money! I have no skills! How else was I going to get money?"

(He remembered telling her) "You could have written me and asked for it. I'd have sent it! You didn't have to sell yourself for money!"

"Didn't I? Would you really have sent for me?" she replied. "Would you have really, with that precious captain of yours doing his best to keep us apart? Would you have sent me money, Joe Bob? Would you? If I hadn't been here waiting for you, would you really have sent for me? Would you have, really?"

"I would have. I would have," he said (remembering how the anger had suddenly drained out of him). (He surely knew that he might very well not have, not with the skipper and the XO and just about everyone else doing their best to talk him out of it.) "I would have," he said again, (not even believing it himself by then). "But God in heaven, Daisy, how could you whore yourself out? How could you even do that?"

"Oh Joe Bob," she said, "I sold everything I owned, furniture, dishes, most of my clothes, everything, and I still didn't have near enough money to get here. I begged and borrowed from everyone I knew, and I still didn't have enough – I couldn't think of anything else. I just knew I had to get here and see you again, so I just did what I had to do."

"Daisy, I . . ." (He realized then, that he had nothing left to say.)

"No, Joe Bob," she said, "God help me, I was willing to do anything – anything – just to be with you and now I've lost you. Now I'm with you, you don't want me. Why would you? Your precious wife is nothing but a whore. I've made such a royal bloody mess of everything." (And she had cried.)

(Joe Bob was calm then. He remembered being calm, all of a sudden.) "No, Daisy, we'll figure this out. I've made an appointment

for us to see a doctor in the morning. Get us both well again. You'll see, we'll figure this out."

(He also remembered that when they went to bed that night that they didn't touch each other. First time that whenever they were together that had happened.)

". . . and of course," Dr. Fong continued, "You mustn't have sex until you're both cured. Can't have you reinfecting one another."

* * * * *

It had taken Harold Chapman two days to get from Pearl to San Diego, where he and his wife Jill made their home. Jill was not well, and the doctors couldn't seem to figure out what was wrong. Hal pulled every string in the book to get this leave. She looked tired and pale when he first arrived, but seemed to perk up after his first two days home. But maybe that was only wishful thinking. He certainly hoped not.

Hal looked more like an accountant than a naval officer: balding, gaunt, a shade under six feet, he was the person you knew whose clothes always seemed too big for him. He had graduated in 1937 from the Merchant Marine Academy in Kings Point, N.Y., and had immediately applied for a commission in the Navy. Kings Point graduates were much in demand in the Navy; their training made them superb seamen and expert marine engineers, well versed in every aspect of steam boilers and diesel engines.

His first duty station as an ensign was aboard the heavy cruiser *USS St. Augustine*, home-ported in San Diego. It was while serving aboard the *St. Augustine* that he became interested in submarines and in the submarine service. He applied for Officer's Submarine School, was accepted, and graduated near the top of his class in May, 1939. While he was still in Sub School, he was promoted to Lt. j.g.

He returned to San Diego for his first boat, *USS S-28*. It was during this tour that he met a petite brunette named Jill Jeanerette. They were married in 1940.

In May, 1942, *S-28* left San Diego for her first war patrol, off the Aleutian Islands. Hal made another four war patrols, developing a reputation for maintaining a cool head under pressure. It was during his fourth war patrol, when now Lt. Hal Chapman received orders to new construction, the *USS Orca*, in Groton, Connecticut.

Hal felt that he and his wife were just getting really reacquainted when it was time to leave her again, and return to Pearl. He was certain then that she definitely looked much better than when he arrived, and she assured him that she indeed felt much better. His orders said he had to report back aboard on November 2nd. Jill was unhappy to have to say goodbye to her husband once again; it seemed that they were always saying goodbye. But she was the wife of a naval officer, and saying goodbye came with the job. And, if asked, Jill Chapman would say that the only regret her marriage to Hal had brought her was that, so far, they had been unable to have children.

American forces landed on Bougainville Island in New Guinea on November 1, 1943, and had established a firm beachhead by the next day. The island was declared secured the end of the month, but isolated pockets of resistance from ragged and starving die-hard Japanese troops actually lasted until the end of the war.

It was at 0800 on the morning of November 2, 1943, and the officers and crew of *USS Orca* were assembled on deck. Bucky shouted "To!" and everyone on deck dropped their salute. But then, instead of the "Dismissed!" that everyone expected, Bucky shouted "Attention to Orders!"

Except for Jake, Clem, Hal Chapman, and Bucky, everyone aboard *Orca* that morning, including many back from leave or extended R & R at the Royal Hawaiian, wondered exactly what was up.

No one had missed the fact that Clem was now sporting oak leaves on his collar, but there was real surprise when Clem read his orders detaching him from *Orca* and directing him to report aboard *Moray* for his PCO cruise.

Hal Chapman was still in shock, having only found out about his new assignment when he returned from leave the day before. Still, he read his orders in the same calm, controlled voice that everyone had come to associate with him. Mr. Chapman was to be their new XO. For many in the crew, this, at least, made up for *Orca* losing Mr. Dwyer.

Finally, Jake informed the crew that they had five days to get *Orca* ready for deployment, and that they would be leaving for patrol the following Monday morning, November 8th.

"Cracker!" Jake exclaimed, when he recognized an old friend sitting at the table along with several other Marine officers and two Naval officers, both Lt. j.g.s whom he didn't recognize.

Major Forrest "Cracker" Dilling, USMC, rose, smiling broadly, to grasp Jake's extended hand.

With Jake that morning was Hal Chapman, who Dilling recognized, and while he nodded to Hal by way of greeting, he asked Jake, "Where's Dwyer?"

"Later," Jake said, in deference to the parade of brass that was just entering the room. Jake recognized Marine Corps Gen. Julian Smith, Adm. Raymond Spruance, and the same Army lieutenant colonel (what was his name?) who had attended the meeting last June in this same room, just after *Orca's* second patrol. That had been the patrol that had been responsible for *Orca's* only casualty to date, QM2(SS) Arnold "Squid" Phillips.

Also in the group this time were Cpt. Macdonough, Adm. Lockwood, and a Marine colonel Jake didn't recognize, but who wore the gold-braided aiguillette on his shoulder that identified him as the general's aide. The colonel promptly moved to the board set up at one end of the room and unrolled a map of a place Jake recognized immediately: Tarawa.

Chapter 13

Fifth Patrol, Tarawa: 17 November 1943 to 19 December 1943

Orca arrived just south of the Tarawa Atoll's principal island of Betio on Wednesday morning, November 17th.

The lone submarine was an advance force for the armada that had sailed behind them, a flotilla—the largest yet assembled—consisting of seventeen aircraft carriers (six CVs, or full-sized carriers; five CLVs, or light carriers; and six CVEs, or escort carriers); twelve battleships; twelve cruisers (eight CAs, or heavy cruisers; and four CLs, or light cruisers); 66 destroyers; and 36 transport ships, along with numerous other support and smaller vessels, including gunboats and minesweepers.

Aboard the transports were 35,000 men (the Second Marine Division and a part of the 27th Army Infantry Division). The overall code name for the operation was Operation Galvanic: a coordinated assault on the Japanese-occupied Gilbert Islands (Tarawa Atoll, Makin Island to the north of Tarawa, and Abamama Island to the south).

The force invading Tarawa wasn't due to arrive until the dawn of Friday, November 19th. *Orca's* job was to land the Navy and Marine recon team that would set the scene for their arrival.

Aboard *Orca*, under the command of Cracker Dilling, was a diverse group of Navy and Marine marauders whose task was to set up two artillery spotter positions, destroy whatever aircraft they found on the ground, and to generally disrupt enemy operations in advance of, and during the course of, the troop landings.

The enemy had been preparing for an American assault ever since August of 1942. That was when the submarines *Argonaut* and *Nautilus* disembarked Carlson's Raiders, a force of 121 Marine Corps Raiders, for a commando attack on the Japanese garrison on Makin Island. The objective of the raid had been to draw Japanese attention and reinforcements away from the Allied landings on Guadalcanal and Tulagi in the Solomons. The Japanese, however, rather than reinforce in large numbers their troops based in the Gilberts, developed a plan to instead fortify their positions there with "impregnable" defenses.

The fortification efforts on Tarawa were concentrated on Betio Island. In charge of those efforts was Rear Adm. Keiji Shibasaki. Shibasaki commanded a force of 2,619 Japanese Marines and 2,217 construction workers, of which, 1,200 were Korean forced laborers.

The earlier reconnaissance of the island fortifications, confirmed by Cracker Dilling and his recon party on *Orca's* second patrol the previous May and June, established that Betio had an elaborate system of fourteen, field gun emplacements, four of which were of major caliber, and hundreds of pillboxes and firing pits. Shibasaki had boasted to his troops that the island "could not be taken by a force of a million men in a hundred years."

Jake waited until nightfall on the 17th before surfacing *Orca* and disembarking his charges. A waning, three-quarter moon had not yet risen when three rubber boats, five men to a boat, set off to cross the shallow reef that surrounded the entire Tarawa Atoll, their immediate objective being the infiltration of Betio Island from its eastern tip.

Betio was a flattened, east-west triangle of an island, a scant three miles long that made up the southernmost part of Tarawa Atoll. Dilling had chosen this point of entry based on the results of his earlier reconnaissance: no close gun emplacements and better jungle cover. The raiders' first order of business was to set up their four Navy gun spotters in secure locations, two each on either end of the island.

The eastern spotters were set up first. There was no way either spotter team could be placed in a hardened bunker, but they could be placed under cover as far away from the action as possible—yet still close enough to do their jobs. This was an easier task with the eastern team, because, aside from the gun emplacements, most of the enemy's facilities were off to the west, and there was simply more jungle cover on the eastern end of Betio.

Leaving the eastern spotting team in place, the remaining two Navy spotters and the Marines made their stealthy way west along the full length of the island, the Marines reconnoitering as they went. Dilling set up the western spotter team as well as possible. There was simply less cover there, and a heavier Japanese presence than to the east. As he left the Navy team in place to return east, he genuinely feared for the west spotter team's ultimate survival.

By 0100 on the 18th, Dilling and his Marines had returned to the eastern end of the island to a secure rabbit hole all their own. The men were well versed in their responsibilities and were well aware that their being discovered by the enemy negated their very reason for being there. They were, however, trained experts at camouflage, and skilled in blending in with their surroundings.

Recon had shown Cracker that the Japanese had been busy bees since last June. There were no apparent additions to the airfield's defenses, or to other interior island defenses, but there was now a log breastwork at the water's edge all along the shoreline—and more pillboxes had been added, along with more bunkers, and even more machine gun nests. Also added were infantry trenches and rifle pits, many of which were encased in concrete. The enemy had obviously planned to stop any invasion force at the shoreline. None of these features were, however, currently manned, their occupants sleeping soundly in their barracks. Only the four large gun emplacements were under guard. Indeed, aside from some meager active patrols, every Japanese soldier on the island appeared to be asleep.

The raiders' recon also revealed that more star-fished wire had been strung in multiple ranks along the shoreline. Tank traps had also been constructed—both obstacles and ditches. Dilling *did* note with satisfaction that it was along the southern shoreline that most of the defenses had been concentrated. Gen. Smith's decision to land his Marines on the north side of the island thus appeared to have been validated.

Cracker wondered why the Japanese had even bothered to build the airfield. There were no fighters there, just three light reconnaissance aircraft, and seven light "Betty" bombers. After dispatching the guards, Dilling's men quickly attached satchel charges to each aircraft; in a few hours those planes would be unable to fly anywhere. At first light, they melted back into the jungle.

They had just settled into their hideaway for the day when the satchel charges they set blew. Cracker chuckled. *Wake up, you bastards*, he thought with satisfaction. *The Marines have landed!* And the invading task force, with another 18,000 Marines from the Second Marine Division embarked, was due to be offshore and ready for action by dawn the next day.

But they weren't. Instead, several flights of carrier-based aircraft, Wildcat fighters and Dauntless bombers, strafed and bombed the airfield, rendering it useless, and blew up whatever buildings were visible from the air. Cracker wondered why blowing up aircraft had been part of the recon mission. Nothing on the airfield tarmac could have survived the air attack. His greatest fear was that the western spotter team would be wiped out by friendly fire before the first invading Marine disembarked from their transports.

The planes did their damage and left. Still, other than the carrier-based aircraft, no part of the invading fleet itself was in evidence. The Japanese came out of their hidey-holes none the worse for wear. They knew an invasion was imminent. Patrols scoured the atoll looking for infiltrators all day long on the 18th, and into the night, and came up empty. Cracker hadn't been worried about his Marines; they were trained for this. They dug in, established a perimeter, camouflaged well, and an alert guard had been posted. It was the Navy spotters he was still worried about—but he needn't have been. He had placed them well, they had been well trained for their jobs, and they were as careful to stay hidden as were his Marines.

When the fleet was, in fact, nowhere to be seen offshore on the 19th, Dilling began to wonder what had gone wrong. There were no plans for *Orca* to extract his team. He knew the sub's orders after disembarking the raid team were to join several other boats and form a reconnaissance arc to the west of the Gilberts, pickets positioned to detect any effort on the part of the Japanese Navy to relieve their embattled garrisons.

The food and water the raiders had brought with them would run out soon; again, he was not too concerned about his men, they could live off the land indefinitely. But with limited food and water, the Navy spotters could only shelter in place for so long. He remembered that the Japanese had beheaded the eight Carlson's Raiders they captured during the raid on Makin in '42, and he couldn't bear the thought of any member of his insertion team, swab jockey or jarhead, being discovered, captured by the enemy, and suffering such a fate. Still, there was nothing to do but wait, pray, and let the mosquitoes feast away.

Picket duty was truly boring. Stay in your assigned area; remain submerged in daylight, periscopes manned and with the radio antennae raised; surface during darkness, and watch the radarscopes. There were seven boats in the screen, stretched across an arc well west of the Gilberts; and to the north, a defensive line between the Gilberts and the Japanese bases on Palau and Guam. The seven boats in the screen, from north to south, were *Harder, Sculpin, Corvina, Tautog, Moray, Orca, and Starfish.* For one of the seven, *Corvina,* this was her first war patrol.

Another arc to the south, between the Gilberts and the remaining Japanese bases on the Solomons, was being patrolled by land-based aircraft out of Guadalcanal. That any source of succor to the Gilberts would come up from the Solomons was very unlikely. The remaining enemy bases in the Solomons, on Bougainville and Buka, were themselves badly in need of reinforcement in response to Allied pressure from the south.

The final, and least likely, source of aid to the embattled IJN forces in the Gilberts was from the Marshall Islands to the north, and the Japanese bases on Kwajalein and Roi-Namur. Spruance left dealing with any possible rescue expedition from the Marshalls up to the armada sent to overwhelm the Gilberts. The message here was clear: the Marshall Islands were his obvious next target.

Of course, if the Imperial Japanese Navy did show up, then all hell would break loose. But as time wore on, it became increasingly evident that the Japanese had decided not to reinforce their perimeter garrisons. Their troops on Makin, Tarawa, and Abamama were to be abandoned to their fate—as sacrificial lambs to the Bushido code.

The invasion force finally arrived on the scene during the wee hours of November 20th. The fleet was spotted almost immediately by the Japanese garrison, and the four big guns ashore, eight-inch Vickers guns the Japanese had purchased from the British in 1905, opened up almost as immediately. A gun duel between the shore battery and the battleships *USS Maryland* and *USS Colorado* began, and with the aid of the Navy artillery spotters ashore, three of the four large guns were dispatched by Naval gunfire before first light. The fourth Vickers gun was also damaged, fell silent, and was fired only intermittently thereafter, and never with any accuracy.

When the battlewagon guns fell silent, just after 0600, aircraft from the carriers *Essex, Bunker Hill,* and *Independence* returned to the island and again unloaded on the Japanese defenses. More

Wildcats strafed the beaches while Dauntless dive-bombers dropped their loads on any remaining man-made structure they saw on the island, giving special attention to the remaining gun emplacements. Strafing the beaches had little effect; the pillboxes, firing pits, and trenches were unmanned, their occupants waiting under cover until the actual troop landings had begun.

Once the planes were done, the naval guns opened up again, battleships, cruisers, and destroyers, pounding the Island. Meanwhile, the minesweepers *Pursuit* and *Requisite*, escorted by the destroyers *Ringgold* and *Dashiell*, swept the entrance to the northern lagoon clear of mines. Only when the naval gun barrage had lifted did the Island's defenders leave their hidey-holes and man the defenses.

The Marine command had divided Betio up into six invasion beaches. The three red beaches were strung out along the northern island shore that faced the length of the airfield — two of these to the west of a long pier that jutted out across the shallow lagoon, the third to the east of the pier.

Green beach was on the west end of the island. The two black beaches stretched across the south side of the island, facing the airfield opposite the red beaches. True to his battle plan, Gen. Julian Smith did not use the black beaches, and concentrated his attack from the red beach, lagoon side of the island.

The naval barrage was lifted at 0900, and the first waves of marines attacked at red and green beaches. It was supposed to have been high tide, with plenty of clearance over the reef for the Higgins boats, which drew four feet. Instead, it was not a normal high tide, but a neap tide. (Neap tides occur when the sun and the moon are perpendicular to each other relative to the earth, and their gravitational pulls tend to cancel each other out. These occur twice a month, and when they happen, high tides are not very high, and low tides not very low. In this case, at high tide on November 20, 1943, at Betio Island, there was only a foot of water over the reef.)

Only the amphibious, tracked vehicles, known as amtracs or "alligators," were able to climb over the reef and bring their Marines to the shore. The Higgins boats and their larger cousins, the LCMs (landing craft, mechanized), got stuck on the reef and were unable to cross it. They could only drop their ramps at the reef line; their Marines had to wade ashore in chest-deep water in the face of withering enemy machine gun fire.

Contrary to Adm. Spruance's predictions, the naval gun barrage had done little to silence the pillboxes and the firing pits. Backpacked field radios, soaked in seawater by troops wading ashore, became useless. Battlefield communications became practically impossible.

Marine snipers who had disembarked at the end of the long pier and made their way ashore along the pier, helped to silence some of the Japanese defenders, as did, by now, Cracker Dilling's raiders from behind enemy lines. Still, the Marines took hundreds of casualties as they fought their way ashore.

Attempts to land armor were equally foiled by the reef. Some of the lighter Stuart tanks managed to gain the shore, as did some of the heftier Sherman tanks. This they did by driving off the LCMs at the reef line, diving into the lagoon, and then driving ashore. Some of these wading tanks sank into craters left in the lagoon from the Naval bombardment and simply disappeared.

Late in the afternoon of the 20th, the spotters ashore identified a group of Japanese officers conferring together out in the open, and called down fire from the destroyers *Ringgold* and *Dashiell*. The group proved to be the Japanese command staff, including Adm. Shibasaki, who were in the open because they had vacated their headquarters to allow it be used as a field hospital. A salvo of five-inch shells wiped out Shibasaki and his entire command staff.

As night fell, the Marines maintained a precarious foothold on Betio. The Japanese defenses fell quiet, no doubt in response to losing their command. Cracker Dilling's raiders made the most of the darkness by silencing two of the still-active enemy gun emplacements.

With daylight on the 21st came stifling heat and humidity. Loss of their command may have been a serious strategic setback for the Japanese defense, but it did not diminish the ferocity of the defenders. Another wave of Higgins boats was sent into red beach two, and, predictably, met the same fate as those sent in the day before. Again, the embarked Marines were forced to wade in to the beach in the face of unrelenting ground fire. This time, the enemy was able to provide another deadly embellishment to their defense: snipers had swum out to grounded and abandoned Higgins boats and LCMs on the reef and fired on the invading Marines from the rear. Others occupied a wrecked cargo ship lying west of the pier, and were using it as a firing platform. This venue, at least, was quickly silenced when naval gunfire turned the wreck into a mass of twisted steel.

Also, with the help of shore-directed naval gunfire, and two Sherman tanks, the Marines were able to roll up the enemy defenses on the western end of the island and gain a firm foothold on green beach. Elsewhere, along red beach, the Marines were able, by the end of the day, to claim some positions as far inland as the northern edge of the airfield. There still existed, however, a stubborn pocket of enemy resistance at the junction of red and green beaches.

The 22nd dawned, as had the day before, hot and humid, but coupled now with the rising stench of the dead. Unlike the night of the previous day, the island defenders had been active throughout the night, with pockets of enemy troops working their way around the invaders. Firefights had broken out all through the night, with Marines unexpectedly defending themselves by firing back into terrain they thought they had already captured.

But the tide of battle had turned. The invasion force along green beach, reinforced by freshly landed troops and armor, quickly eliminated the resistance that had been so intractable the day before. The green beach landing force then rolled up enemy along the southern shore of Betio and fought their way eastward. Marines on the red beaches, also reinforced with fresh troops, did the same in the north.

By nightfall, the bulk of the enemy resistance had been pushed onto the spit of land to the east of the airfield, the very strip that Cracker Dilling and his team had landed on five days earlier.

The 23rd of November saw the inevitable final destruction of the Japanese garrison on Betio. Sheer numbers, naval firepower, and the power and maneuverability of armor, proved to be an irresistible force, even for an enemy determined to fight to the death.

And fight to the death they did. By the time Cracker Dilling's grimy Marines and their Navy brethren had all linked up with their opposite numbers in the invasion force, the Japanese had suffered 4,690 dead. One officer and sixteen enemy soldiers were captured, along with 129 Korean laborers. On the American side, the Marines suffered 1,009 dead and 2,101 wounded. The Navy suffered 687 dead when, on the morning of the final day of the battle, a Japanese submarine torpedoed and sank the escort carrier *Liscome Bay*.

Three days later, on the 26th of November, word was sent to the seven boats looking for a Japanese invasion fleet that the Pacific Command had determined that no such enemy naval presence would be forthcoming. The seven patrolling boats were to proceed in two groups and conduct coordinated attacks against Japanese convoys. The first group, Task Group 57.5, consisting of *Harder, Sculpin, Corvina,* and *Tautog,* were to proceed to the waters north of Palau in the Philippine Sea, there to intercept convoys proceeding north from Palau Atoll to Taipei, Formosa and to the home islands. *Moray, Orca,* and *Starfish* were to form Task Group

57.6, proceed to the waters to the northeast of Palau in the Philippine Sea, between Palau and Truk, and intercept convoys between Palau and the Marshalls.

And so, beginning on the 26th, *Orca*—call sign, Rider Three—in company with *Moray* and *Starfish*, headed northeast. SOPA was Lt. Cmdr. David Brandenburg, USN, skipper of the *Moray*, with Lt. Cmdr. John Waters, USN, in *Starfish*, second in command. As usual, Jake was junior. The trip to their station would take just over four days.

And riding in *Moray* on his PCO cruise, Jake knew, was Clem Dwyer, his former XO. He would miss Clem. He was an exceptional XO and they were a good team.

But now, he had a new XO, Hal Chapman. Jake had seen Hal in action, and knew him as a man able to maintain a cool head when everything seemed to be falling to pieces around him. Like Clem Dwyer, Hal Chapman should prove to be an exceptional XO.

Moving Chapman to the XO position left open the slot of Engineer Officer. Capt. Clarence Macdonough, *Orca's* Squadron Commander, had made it very clear that submarine officers were in short supply, and since Jake wanted to promote from within, there would be no numerical replacement for Clem for the time being. So Jake had to make do with the officers he already had. He considered a variety of combinations, but decided finally that moving Joe Bob Clanton to the engineering position would cause the least disruption to the ship's fighting capabilities. Clanton was, after all, a graduate engineer. And so, Joe Bob Clanton became Engineer Officer, and his new GQ station would be as diving officer.

Bill Salton replaced Joe Bob as Communications Officer, but also retained his responsibilities for sonar. Instead of standing GQ in the radio shack, as Clanton did, Salton would continue to man sonar plot with John Catinella. The GQ post in the radio shack could be covered quite well by Chief O'Grady, who had always stood GQ there with Joe Bob anyway.

Salton's old post as assistant engineer went unfilled. It was pretty much a training post in any case, and Joe Bob still had two experienced chiefs in Bill Clements and Bob Lione to back him up.

Lou Carillo remained Navigator and Early Sender continued on as Weapons Officer.

Task Group 57.6 arrived on station on the last day of November. Rider One, Dave Brandenburg in *Moray,* fanned the three boats out across the convoy route between Palau and Truk and the three boats waited, just as they had on picket duty, manning their periscopes and their radars.

Palau Atoll consists of a group of 250 islands, and forms the western chain of the Caroline Islands. By November, 1943, the Japanese had created a military stronghold in Palau, the most heavily fortified island in the group being Peleliu, at the southern end of the atoll. Protecting the small airfield there were 11,000 crack Japanese troops, along with 2,600 Korean and Okinawan laborers.

Palau was also the assembly point for all Japanese convoys to and from the Marshalls (through Truk), Saipan, New Guinea, the Netherlands East Indies, Manila, Formosa, and the home islands.

SUBPAC alerted the Task Group that a convoy was leaving Palau on December 12th with reinforcements and supplies destined for the garrison at Kwajalein. The encrypted message directed TG 57.6 to *"...expend every effort to detect, intercept, and destroy as many elements of the convoy as possible."* The convoy was reported to consist of five vessels with a two-vessel escort.

Orca was the first boat to pick up the convoy while it was still five miles away. It was late in the afternoon of December 12th and all three boats were submerged, their periscopes extended. Jake reported the contact as masts low on the horizon to both Brandenburg and Waters, and within a half hour, all three boats had the contacts on radar, having surfaced despite the possibility of detection from the air this close to Palau, and were running for assigned positions. *Orca* was to run toward the convoy and get in position to submerge and visually reconnoiter the convoy while there was still daylight. *Moray* and *Starfish* would move to intercept the convoy on the surface after nightfall, to be joined by *Orca* after she completed her recon.

From the size of the radar returns, the convoy itself consisted of three larger vessels and two smaller ones in a two-by-three formation. The escorts were apparently the same size as the two smaller marus, distinguishable only because they were not part of the formation, but were roaming about it. The convoy was zigzagging on a base course due east, making just in excess of seven knots over the water.

Jake submerged the boat, positioning *Orca* at periscope depth so that the convoy would pass close aboard to the south. They should have plenty of daylight left for the recon. From radar, it had been determined that the zigzag pattern being used was ludicrously simple, half-hour legs run ten degrees either side of base course. The two smaller marus in the convoy were running abreast in the lead, followed by the three large ones, also running line abreast. Jake's main worry was the escorts. They were obviously faster than the convoy elements, and were keeping no predictable station on the convoy, changing course and speed constantly. Jake's plan was to track the convoy using sonar and wait until the escorts were past before exposing and using the periscope for visual identification.

Sonar showed that the convoy was moving just as radar had predicted, with a zig minutes before that would leave *Orca* just where Jake wanted her relative to the convoy. Even the escort on the left side of the convoy was cooperating, and appeared to be speeding up, leaving the convoy's entire flank exposed.

When the escort was past, Jake said, "Okay, Hal, here's your chance to shine. Use the search scope and tell me what you see."

Without a return comment, Hal Chapman said, "Up, periscope," and Henry Coons flipped the lever that raised the search periscope. Following protocol, Hal first did a 360-degree search, then settled on one spot.

"Escort, an older destroyer, *Wakatake*-class, I think, stern first, moving away." Then, swinging the scope right, "Port lead ship in convoy, troop carrier, looks like a converted *Mutsuki*-class destroyer. Next in line, tanker. Down scope."

"Sonar, what do you hear?" Jake asked, and the talker conveyed to sonar.

"Sonar reports no change in convoy ships' noise. Fast screws to port, moving away," the conning tower talker, Seaman George Parra, reported.

Jake nodded to Hal.

"Up, scope," Hal said. Another 360. "*Wakatake* still moving away." Swinging the scope to the right, "Make that two troop carriers in the lead. Second maru over in following group is a cargo ship. Can't see too much of the third one in — possibly another cargo ship. Down scope."

Wonderful! Jake thought. *Old calm, cool, and collected himself. Hal Chapman, you'll do just fine!* Then, aloud, "Sonar, can you hear that other escort?" Again, Parra conveyed the question to sonar.

"Sonar reports negative, Captain, convoy making too much masking noise," Parra said.

"Okay, let's see what else we can see," Jake announced to nobody in particular. "Left twenty degrees rudder, all ahead full."

"Rudder is left twenty."

"Maneuvering reports all ahead full."

"Very well," said Jake. Waiting until Orca was in position behind the convoy, he asked, "Sonar, hear that second escort yet?"

"Sonar says negative, Captain."

When he was satisfied with the boat's position relative to the convoy, he ordered, "All ahead slow, make your course zero-nine-zero."

"Maneuvering reports all ahead slow."

"Coming to course zero-nine-zero."

"Hal?"

"Up, scope." Then, "Third ship in second tier definitely a cargo ship. No sign of starboard escort."

Jake wanted to know what the second escort was. He let the convoy disappear over the horizon, surfaced the boat, and did an end run around the right side of the convoy. Meanwhile, he radioed to Brandenburg the information he did have. When *Orca* positioned itself in front of the convoy again, this time to the right of it, it was again zigging toward her, but sonar reported that the escort on this side was lagging the convoy. And now there wasn't much daylight left.

"Take another look, Hal, and keep a weather eye on that escort."

This time, Hal raised the attack scope. Its field of vision was smaller, but it also left a smaller wake than the regular periscope, and was more difficult to spot. He did a 360, then stopped at the escort. "Escort is a *Kamikaze*-class destroyer." Swinging the scope right, "Second tier maru this side definitely a cargo ship. Lead maru this side is another converted *Mutsuki*." Then swinging left again, "And the *Kamikaze* is headed this way. Down scope."

Jake shouted, "All ahead full. Take 'er down fast, Joe Bob. Make your depth two hundred feet."

"Maneuvering reports all ahead full, Captain."

"Two hundred feet, aye," Joe Bob repeated the order. And then to the planesmen, "Full dive on the bow and stern planes, twenty degrees down bubble!"

"Sonar?"

"Sonar reports fast screws approaching from port, Captain, but starting to fade left. Also, slow screws ahead are getting louder."

"Good. I mean to dive under the convoy."

"Passing one hundred feet, Captain," Joe Bob called up to the conning tower from the control room.

"Very well."

"Sonar reports slow screws getting very close, Captain," Parra repeated, conveying the worry he had heard on the sonar operator's voice.

"Very well."

"Passing one hundred seventy feet, Captain."

"Sonar reports slow screws dead ahead and to the right and another set approaching from the left. Fast screws now dead astern."

"Steadying out at two hundred feet, Captain."

"Very well."

"Sonar reports slow screws overhead, Captain"

"Good. Right full rudder, come to course two-zero-zero."

"Rudder is right full, coming to course two-zero-zero, Captain."

"Very well." And a depth charge went off, somewhere off the starboard quarter. *Boom!* "I think," Jake said, "that we'll stay under the convoy for as long as we can. Maybe that *Kamikaze* will run out of depth charges."

Hal smiled. "If he left with a full load, that's one down and thirty-five to go."

Minutes passed, and no further depth charging was heard. *Orca* couldn't keep up with the convoy at full submerged speed, and was quickly slipping astern of the lead tier. Not long afterward, the second tier passed overhead. Soon all sounds of screws had faded away into the distance ahead of them, and Jake ordered the boat to slow.

It was pitch dark, the new crescent moon not yet arisen, when *Orca* surfaced for an end run around the convoy at speed. Jake had radioed the latest recon information to Brandenburg, and hoped that there would be some targets left by the time *Orca* joined *Moray* and *Starfish*.

The crescent moon had risen, and the night was clear. It was not quite yet December 3rd, and *Orca* was running flat out on the surface, when her lookouts reported flashes ahead, just over the horizon, and just to port in the night sky. About ten seconds later, the sound of a distant rumbling reached the boat, well loud enough to be heard over the thunder of *Orca's* four diesels running flat out. Then came another, brighter flash, and, again, in somewhat less time, the roar of a distant explosion.

Orca stood far off from a scene right out of a bad war movie. One of the escorts, the *Wakatake,* was running dead slow in a heavy, crude oil slick picking up survivors. In places, the oil slick was burning, and the screams of men caught in the flames were horrifying and sickening, But the *Wakatake,* working under searchlights (obviously having assumed that all of their submarine tormentors had followed the remnants of the convoy east), was being selective in which of the men in the water it was rescuing. It was pulling aboard some of the men in the water and pushing others off, even shooting at a few with small arms. It took a few minutes for Jake to realize why. The men who were being pushed away were pleading and shouting in English.

Quickly, Jake surmised the earlier events of the night: *Moray* and *Starfish* had ambushed the convoy, and had sunk one or both of the two transports and the tanker. The men in the water were survivors from the two transports, hanging onto debris in the oil-laden water or doing their best to swim in it. Among the survivors were Allied prisoners, men who had been aboard the transport or transports. And the crew of the *Wakatake* was being selective as to which of the survivors would be saved.

And *Orca* could do nothing except stand off and watch and wait until the *Wakatake* cleared the area. Jake thought briefly about torpedoing the destroyer, but that might only set the oil slick further afire, immolating alike the enemy *and* Allied survivors in the water. And that he could not do.

There was another flash over the horizon and off to the east, followed by yet another, and again, seconds later, the rumbling of loud explosions, this time unmasked by pounding diesels. Jake radioed to Brandenburg, describing the scene before him. Four minutes later, the reply came: "Stand fast. We're on our way."

A half-hour later, the *Wakatake*, apparently having rescued as many of its countrymen as it could, left the scene heading west. Pleas and curses shouted in hoarse English sent it on its way. Jake let the *Wakatake* clear the area unmolested, as *Orca* had more important work to do. Jake ordered a single diesel to be fired up, and, slowly, *Orca*, rigging up its own searchlights, and manning the deck gun in case of air attack, made its way into the oil-covered morass.

Put in charge by Jake, PhM1(SS) Corey "Doc" Shields organized *Orca's* crew, setting up an assembly line of sorts to deal with the men being pulled from the water. Most had enough energy left to make it to the side of the boat by themselves and be pulled aboard by crewmembers, but others hung desperately to floating debris, unable to so much as lift an arm.

The Japanese had been efficient; the only Japanese still in the water were dead. To their credit, and on their own initiative, four crewmembers, Coons, Arnold, Rogers, and Olds, let themselves down into the oil slick and swam out to the weakest of the survivors, towing life preservers, and getting them to the side of the boat, where men on deck could haul them aboard.

Once aboard, the survivors were stripped of their clothes—rags, really—and the worst of the crude wiped from their bodies with diesel oil. Some of the men hauled aboard were visible only as bloodshot eyes and white teeth in the oncoming dawn air. Those still able to speak could only thank their saviors as they were led down below decks to the forward torpedo room, where space was made for them on bunks, atop torpedoes in racks, and, finally, on the metal deck.

Only then were they given the water they had been begging for, small amounts at first, larger amounts as they were able to stand it. This was followed by a thin broth, then a sort of gruel. Only when their emaciated bodies could tolerate it, would they be given solid food. Doc Shields moved among the rescued, treating those most in need first, the worst being the burn victims.

Within the hour, *Moray* and *Starfish* arrived and joined in the rescue effort. Brokenhearted, the rescuers watched helplessly when almost as many as they were able to save slipped silently below the oil slick before anyone could reach them.

It had been broad daylight for a full hour when the three boats backed free of the scum. They had pulled 217 men out of the water, none of them Japanese. *Orca* rescued the fewest, 64 men, only because the boat still had all its torpedoes still aboard, and, of the three boats, had the least room belowdecks for passengers.

Moray had taken 81 of the men aboard. But *Moray* was the boat that sank the tanker and one of the transports in the first place, as well as another cargo ship ten miles to the east, and had the fewest torpedoes left. *Starfish*, which accounted for the other transport, and the *Kamikaze* ten miles to the east, had 72 men aboard. By the time the boats reached Midway, eight days later and just under 3,000 nautical miles away, nine of the men aboard the three boats had died.

The rescued Allied troops were among 400 English and Australian prisoners of war who were being transported as slave labor to work on enhanced fortifications on Kwajalein in the face of an inevitable American invasion. Along with 900 IJN Marines, who did not have much better accommodations, the prisoners had been crammed into airless holds, on half rations, aboard the tiny transports. The rescued men said that, before being torpedoed, some thirty men had already died and their bodies tossed overboard. To a man, none condemned the submarines that had sunk their transports. On the contrary, since most had considered themselves dead men already, they regarded the submariners as heroes who had saved far more Allied lives than they had taken.

On December 19th, the three boats of Task Group 57.6 departed Midway and began their trip back to Pearl. For most, it was to be homeport, if not actual home, for Christmas. Jake was among the fortunate few actually headed home.

Chapter 14

Christmas 1943: 23 December 1943 to 6 January 1944

In company with *Moray* and *Starfish*, *Orca* headed into the pier at SUBASE Pearl. It was 0917 on the 23rd of December, when the last of *Orca*'s lines was made fast to the pier. *Orca*, ever the junior boat, had been last in line to tie up, and Adm. Lockwood and Commodore Macdonough were already aboard *Moray* being debriefed on Task Group 57.6's successes and failures, when *Orca* was still putting her first line over to the sailors waiting on the pier.

From *Orca*'s bridge, Jake scanned the crowd for Kate, first catching Clem Dwyer, already on the pier, bear-hugging the diminutive Miriam. Then, there she was, her smile beaming, her bright, emerald eyes flashing. Kate's belly was bigger now, her stylish blue dress doing nothing to conceal a distended abdomen. How far along was she now? Four months? Five? Whatever. She was still the most desirable woman in the world.

"Where's Daisy? I don't see Daisy!" Joe Bob Clanton was OOD, on the bridge, beside Jake.

"That's a pretty big crowd, Joe Bob. She's got to be down there somewhere. But for now, mind the mooring lines," Jake advised, his eyes still fixed on Kate.

"Yes, Sir," Joe Bob said, returning his attention to tying up alongside. Then Jake scanned the crowd for the petite blonde, but he couldn't find her either.

"Maybe she's just late getting here. I'm sure there's a logical explanation," Jake volunteered.

"Yeah, maybe," a crestfallen Joe Bob replied. Once *Orca* was made fast to the pier, Joe Bob scanned the crowd alongside again. Daisy wasn't there. He just knew something awful had happened to his new wife.

* * * * *

"Oh, our baby's active all right. It's got to be a boy," said Kate. "No young lady would kick the living daylights out of her mother like this guy does." She took Jake's hand, and placed it on her belly. "Feel that?"

"Oh my God, yes!" Jake beamed. His smile, Kate reflected, could light up a room. "That's so amazing! But doesn't it hurt?"

"Sometimes, when he kicks something sensitive, but not always. I've become quite used to it. Doesn't even wake me up anymore. And of course, it's not like this all the time. Little bugger sleeps a lot, thank God!"

Jake had been surprised when, instead of heading for the gate for the trip across the island to their beachside bungalow, Kate drove them up to a crisp white cottage in base housing. The low sign on the front lawn in front proclaimed "LCDR J. J. Lawlor."

"What's this?" Jake asked, incredulous.

"Base housing, Silly," Kate answered. "Commander Warren Blaylock's old place. It came open when he was transferred to the Pentagon."

"And our old place?"

"Landlord was very gracious about letting us out of the lease. I soon found out why — it seems he had somebody waiting in the wings willing to pay ten dollars more a month for it. So I guess everybody made out all the way around."

"And once again, heaven smiles down on the Lawlors."

"Or it will, once you get inside and wash that stink off you. And you'd damn well better hurry," she said, grinning lasciviously. "I have plans for your lily white body — but only once it's sparkling clean."

"Yes, Ma'am," he said, grinning back.

* * * * *

Joe Bob took a cab to the furnished apartment he and Daisy had leased in the Ala Moana section of Honolulu. It wasn't very fancy, or very big, but it was all Joe Bob could afford until their housing allowance came through, or a spot opened up in base housing.

On the way over, he thought about how he would get into the place if Daisy weren't there. He hadn't thought it necessary to keep a key (why would he need one?). Well, if his wife weren't there, he would break in if he had to. But why wasn't she at the pier? Hadn't she gotten the word that the boat was due in that morning? He knew he had left the word with the squadron on how to get in touch with her . . .

Outside the apartment, Joe Bob paid the cabbie and then went up and tried the door. To his surprise, it was unlocked.

"Daisy?" he called out as he went inside. No answer. He called out again, louder, "Daisy?" Still no answer.

He went into all three rooms and the bathroom. The place felt empty, as if nobody lived there. All the furniture was in place, and his stuff was still there, but there was nothing of hers in the closet or in any of the bureau drawers. In the cupboard were only an open box of Cheerios and a container of Morton Salt—"When it rains it pours." He opened the refrigerator. Empty, but obviously scrubbed clean. Only his toothbrush and shaving gear in the bathroom, and his stuff in the closet. The place was deserted, and Daisy was gone.

He looked around for a note, something, *anything*. Nothing. She was just gone.

* * * * *

Jake's interview with the admiral was brief. Lockwood had already spoken to Brandenburg and Waters.

268

"So, Jake," Lockwood began, "never got to fire a shot in anger this go 'round, eh?"

"That's correct, Admiral," Jake admitted, somewhat crestfallen, although he really had no reason to be. The admiral, after all, didn't seem to be, in the least, upset.

"Never mind. Some patrols go like that. But *Orca* and your men did yeoman duty in any case. Brandenburg couldn't praise your boat enough—Waters either. Your scouting of that convoy set up their attack and put a hell of a dent in Hirohito's war machine. And then there are those couple hundred Aussie and Brit troops that owe their lives to you. Well done. *Orca* has earned the holidays in Hawaii. Make the most of it. I have plans for the Emperor in 1944, and *Orca* will play a big part in them.

"We'll be looking forward to it, Admiral." Jake replied in all earnestness.

* * * * *

Harder and *Tautog* came into Pearl a week behind TG 57.6. Both boats had lost contact, first with *Corvina,* then with *Sculpin,* during operations in the Philippine Sea against a Japanese convoy en route to the home islands. The convoy had been well escorted, and the attacking boats had a thorough going over as a reward for their successful efforts, but neither *Corvina* nor *Sculpin* was ever heard from again.

* * * * *

Miriam had obviously been to the Lawlors' new digs before. She seemed to know where everything was—knowledge that Jake didn't yet have. Navy wives are like that; they gang up together while their men are at sea.

Dinner was wonderful. Kate outdid herself, prepared something Jake had never had before, an Italian dish called "lasagna." It was absolutely delicious. Miriam brought the salad, and there was fresh bread — and even a fruity red wine.

After dinner, on what passed for the veranda, Jake and Clem sat, nursing full glasses of wine. Clem picked up his wine glass and looked at it disapprovingly. "Not awful, mind you, but I prefer a good glass of beer."

"You'll take what you're given," Jake mock-scolded him.

"You're right."

"Orders?" Jake changed the subject.

"Yep, just got 'em. Must've gotten a good review from Brandenburg. These are prime! New *Balao* class boat — being built in Mare Island — *USS Viper*. Ever see a picture of a viperfish? Nasty looking. Huge teeth and lower jaw. Lures its prey with a fluorescent 'thingamabob'."

"Sounds absolutely vicious! But a new deep-diving boat! I'm a little jealous — but not much! So, when do you leave?"

"In a week or so. Need to wrap up here, pack, and find transportation east. I may have to go on ahead of Miriam, but I hope not. Can't say I'm not looking forward to some time in the yards getting the boat ready. Be like when I reported aboard *Orca*. Get to go home to my wife every night. I could get used to that, you know."

"I hear you. At least I'm home-ported in Pearl, so I get to see Kate whenever the boat's in. Not everybody's that lucky. Look at Bucky."

"Right. Did he get to go on leave, finally?"

"Yep. Even with his leave papers in hand, it was like pulling teeth to get him off the boat. Gave Walakurski a 'to do' list a couple of pages long of stuff he wanted done before he gets back."

"And Wally will do 'em, too. Make a fine Chief of the Boat himself."

"Don't get any ideas!" said Jake. "Bad enough I had to lose my XO."

"True," Clem laughed. "You did have the best XO in the fleet."

Jake smiled. "I did at that. But I suspect the new one's not going to be too long in catching up."

"Me neither, "Clem agreed, seriously. "Me neither."

"Jake, about Wally —"

"You're kidding, right?"

"No, I'm not kidding. Especially not when I said he'd be a great COB. Please, just think about it. He'd be perfect for *Viper.*"

"Crap, Clem. First you, then Wally? Give me a break!"

"Please, just think about it, okay?"

"Okay, I'll think about it, but I'm not *promising* anything."

Clem seemed satisfied with that, and didn't push the issue further. But he knew he had planted the seed, and he was confident that eventually Jake would come around. It would, after all, be a great opportunity for Walakurski.

* * * * *

Joe Bob's first week back in Pearl proved a busy one.

He found out that Daisy had left a Brisbane address with base personnel for forwarding her allotment.

It cost him more than he could afford, but Joe Bob bought out the rest of the six months' lease they had on the Honolulu apartment, and moved back into the BOQ.

He checked into getting a divorce. The Navy lawyer he consulted told him getting married in Hawaii was really easy, but *not* getting a divorce. Luckily for Joe Bob, it was easier for a man to get a divorce than it was for a woman, and one of the grounds for which the territory granted a divorce was abandonment.

And so Joe Bob sued for divorce from Daisy Norton on the grounds that his wife had abandoned him. It could take years, he learned, before the divorce became final.

After that he placed a notice in the personals in the *Honolulu Advertiser*:

"I, Joe Bob Clanton, am no longer responsible for the debts of Daisy Clanton, nee Norton, she having left my bed and board."

But Daisy would continue to receive her Navy allotment as long as they were legally married and he was on active duty. There was nothing he could do about that. And Daisy, not his mother, would receive the $10,000 government life insurance payout in the event he was killed in action. Strange how those things worked out.

Joe Bob spent every day thereafter crawling through *Orca's* bowels, completing his qualification notebook. He had been working on that notebook since he had reported aboard in Groton, and it was barely ten percent complete when *Orca* was made fast to the pier and Daisy was nowhere to be seen. He presented the completed notebook to Hal Chapman for his evaluation just before Christmas.

* * * * *

It wasn't much of a tree. The Lawlor household's spruce was short and scrawny. Christmas trees were imported from the mainland – *and* expensive. Most of the needles had fallen off by the time Christmas arrived. Still, it *was* Christmas and they did have a Christmas tree. Kate decorated it with strings of popcorn dyed with food coloring, bright ribbons, and Christmas cards. She topped it with a cardboard star she covered with foil from a Camels cigarette pack. (Since she had quit smoking, this last item had to be obtained from a neighbor.)

Kate insisted they attend midnight Mass. Jake made it very clear that he was going only because she insisted, but once there, he was glad he had come. While, despite Kate's informative narrative, he didn't understand most of what was going on, he had to admit that the ceremony itself was beautiful, and he had no trouble joining in with the singing of the Christmas carols — before, during, and after the ceremony. He left uplifted and joyful, full of the spirit of Christmas.

* * * * *

Hal Chapman managed to call Jill in San Diego the day after Christmas. He tried to call earlier, but the phone lines to the mainland were so overloaded that getting a call through was impossible. Her letters had pointedly omitted any mention of her health, and Hal took that as a bad sign.

"Jill, honey, it's Hal."

"Oh, Hal darling, how wonderful to hear from you! What a nice surprise! Did you have a good Christmas?"

"As good a Christmas as I could without you, hon. I miss you."

"Oh, and I miss you too, darling."

"Jill, Sweetie, level with me. How are you doing? How are you feeling?"

"Oh, Hal, I'm okay. You shouldn't be worrying about me. You have far more important things to worry about."

"Never mind that. I do worry about you, you know that. What do the doctors have to say?"

"Same as always. More and more tests. Whenever I'm feeling crappy, they have no idea why. But I'm still surviving, and right now I'm doing just fine. You really mustn't worry."

"Easy for you to say. I wish I could be there with you. We're due to go into overhaul rotation pretty soon. I should be able to come home again then. God! How I miss you!"

Their allotted three minutes flew by. When the operator broke into their conversation to tell them their time was up, they had only been able to exchange an "I love you" before the line went dead.

When Hal hung up the phone he realized he really didn't know any more about the state of Jill's health than he did before the call.

Chief Boatswain's Mate Wendell Buckner hadn't seen his home in Groton since *Orca* set out for the Panama Canal, over a year earlier. It was a sturdy little house, the main part of which dated back to 1792. Bucky had always meant to add a garage, but, when the war started, he sold their car. Louise didn't drive, and he was never home, so there didn't seem to be much point in hanging on to it.

When the cab pulled up to the house just the day before, he recalled that somehow the place seemed so much smaller than he remembered.

Bucky paid the cabbie, went up to the house, and rang his own front doorbell. Louise had answered the door. She was just 18 when they had married; that was 26 years and four kids ago. She had been a plump, pretty teenager then. The woman who greeted Bucky at the door was still on the plump side, and, at 44, there were traces of gray in her brunette hair. But the sparkling brown eyes were the same, and the genuine delight in seeing her husband after a year's separation, made her, for Bucky, still the prettiest woman on the face of the Earth. They embraced with all the passion he remembered, and Louise wept tears of joy just the way she always did whenever he came home from the sea.

Christmas had come and gone well before Bucky had exited the train from New York in New London, but on December 29th, the Buckner family gathered around the table for a belated Christmas dinner. John, Bucky and Louise's eldest, was there with his wife, Mildred, and their only child, Wendell.

Also at the table were the Buckners' two grown daughters: Emma and Eloise.

Finally, there was their youngest, Charles, 16, in his junior year at Groton High School. Charles wanted to drop out of school and join the Marines. Louise was having none of it. He had hoped he could convince his Father to change her mind, but was still working up the courage to ask him.

There may have been a war going on, but at least for Christmas 1943 his whole family was together, everyone was healthy, and Bucky couldn't have been happier.

* * * * *

"Are you sure you're ready?" Hal asked Joe Bob.

"Ready as I'll ever be. I'd like to leave on our next patrol sporting dolphins, if it's at all possible."

"Oh, it's possible all right. I have to admit you did a really good job on your notebook. I'll have to clear it with the skipper, but I seriously doubt if he'll object to setting you up for your orals. If he says okay, then I'll set them up for you."

"Thanks, Hal, I really appreciate that."

* * * * *

"But Dad, you weren't any older when you joined up!"

"I was seventeen. You're *six*teen. And I really didn't have much choice. It was either join up or spend another year in reform school. You can thank God you don't have to make a choice like that, and I for one am certainly thankful that you don't. No, Son, your Mother is right. Your first priority is graduating from high school. You can think about joining up after that."

"But Dad, they need men now. I can always finish school later. My recruiter says—"

"I don't give a *damn* what your recruiter says!" Bucky shouted back. Charles was taken aback. He knew his Father had a temper, but he rarely raised his voice inside the house, especially within earshot of his Mother.

Back in control, Bucky took a softer tone with his son. "Charlie, there's a war on, and your recruiter has only one job to do—sign up as many kids as he can. His problem with you is that you're underage, and you can't go unless your Mom and me agree to let you. And we are both in agreement. You're not going anywhere until you graduate."

"But Dad, the war will be over by then!"

"I only hope to God you're right. But I'm afraid there will still be plenty of war left when you're ready for it. And think about this. With that high school diploma in your pocket you'll have a hell of a lot better choice of training schools you can apply to—and of duty assignments. You go into the Marines now, at sixteen, they'll push you right through boot camp and send you straight onto the firing line as a grunt.

"And another thing, with a high school diploma, you'd be eligible for an appointment to Annapolis or West Point. You could go in as a second looie. How about that?"

"I don't want to be no officer! I just want to go in and kill Japs! I just want to do my duty!"

Bucky sighed. "Want to kill Japs, do you? You think that's all there is to it? You go join the Marines and you get to kill Japs?" Then he angrily raised his voice. "Let me tell you, boy, I've killed my fair number of Japs in this lousy war, and it's not this glamorous, patriotic thing you think it is. They're people, Son, same as you and me, and they bleed, and they die, and they've got families that love them every bit as much as we love you. Now you stay in school and you graduate, and *then* you can join up with our blessing if you still want to, but not until then. Got it?"

"Yes, Sir, I've got it!" Charles replied just as angrily, turning and leaving the room.

"No, I don't think you do," Bucky whispered to himself. "I just thank God they can't touch you before you're eighteen without our permission. And I hope and pray you'll come to understand why someday."

* * * * *

Back in Pearl, Joe Bob did his in-port in *Harder* and her skipper, Cmdr. Sam Dealey, took him through his paces, questioning him about every piece of equipment aboard, and running him through in-port emergency drills. Joe Bob sweated his way through it, and, by the end of the day, Dealey gave him a passing grade.

For his at-sea exam, Joe Bob drew Dave Brandenburg in *Moray*. Brandenburg had given Bill Salton his underway exam, and Joe Bob felt that he was in no way as squared away as Salton. *Moray* was due to leave for patrol on January 5, and Brandenburg agreed to let him get the boat underway on the morning of the 3rd, run a submerged torpedo approach, fire the dummy torpedo he prepared the evening before, and return to port that evening.

Joe Bob was sure he made no major mistakes during his at-sea, and his dummy torpedo scored a solid hit on the target, a destroyer escort that predictably maintained a steady course and speed—hardly a realistic battle situation. Brandenburg grilled him on approach tactics, and put him into theoretical situations for which there was no "right" answer. Joe Bob answered as well as he could, but then later thought of other ways he could have better handled several of the theoretical situations. He was sure he had screwed up royally, but by then there was nothing for it. He managed to bring the boat back into port well, navigating the channel without any errors, and bringing the boat alongside her berth expertly. That, he hoped, would make up for any earlier mistakes.

The following day, Joe Bob got the word to meet Hal Chapman aboard *Moray* where "Captain Brandenburg would give him an evaluation of his at-sea performance." He was to report aboard at 1130 sharp. Joe Bob was terrified.

Joe Bob reported aboard *Moray* at 1130 sharp on January 4th. The OOD at the gangplank told him that Lt. Cmdr. Brandenburg and Lt. Chapman were waiting for him down below in the wardroom. Joe Bob went down into the boat and made his way to the wardroom. Waiting for him there were Brandenburg, Hal Chapman, and, to his complete surprise, Jake. Without a word,

Jake took out a pair of gold dolphins and pinned them on his shirt.

"And now, young man," Dave Brandenburg informed him, "You will join us at the 'O' Club and properly wet down those new dolphins of yours. Drinks are on you, of course."

"Of course, Captain," a much relieved and exuberant Joe Bob replied. "It will be my pleasure."

The yard birds in Pearl and her relief crew had been busy over the holidays. *Orca* had been fitted out to fire the Mark-18 electric torpedo. The Mark-18 was not as fast as the Mark-14 — 29 knots versus 46 — nor did it have quite the explosive power, but it could swim almost as far, and it was wakeless; there was no bubble trail to follow for the escorts to locate the firing submarine, and no telltale wake to warn the target of impending disaster.

Modeled after the British-captured German G7e electric torpedo, the Mark-18 was powered by a battery-driven electric motor, but just as did a steam-driven torpedo, it had its unique problems. The batteries gave off hydrogen gas, and they had to be recharged regularly. Ventilation in the torpedo compartments was critical if hydrogen concentrations were to be kept below explosive levels, especially when any torpedoes were on charge. Fires and hydrogen explosions aboard boats outfitted with the torpedo were not uncommon. Like the Mark-14, it was gyroscopically controlled, but unlike its steam-powered cousin, both its influence and contact exploders were generally considered to be reliable.

It didn't seem right, getting underway for a war patrol on a Saturday, but it wasn't up to the officers and crew of *Orca* to reason why. Not that they had any reason to complain. They were one of two boats in Pearl that got to spend the holidays in port, and the other one, *Eel*, was in extended refit. And so it was that they were underway, fully loaded with twenty-four Mark-18 torpedoes.

Ensign Harry Hastings, USN, had reported aboard just two days earlier. Hastings was Academy '43 and fresh out of Officer's Basic Submarine School. It had previously been the Navy's practice that officers first spent some time in the surface fleet before sub school, but Hastings was part of a new program designed to get young officers aboard the boats earlier in their careers.

Bucky had barely made it back. His military transport had just arrived at Hickam Field in the wee hours, and he had only enough time to get his duffel bag aboard and tour the boat before duty stations were called away. He also had barely enough time to bid farewell to his old and valued shipmate, TMC(SS) Clyde Walakurski. It seems he was headed to Mare Island to become the new COB on *Viper*, Mr. Dwyer's new command. His numerical replacement had come from the relief crew, a First Class Gunner's Mate—GM1(SS)—named Roland Eifel. Eifel was from Baton Rouge, Louisiana. Bucky met "Frenchie" briefly on his tour through the boat.

And *Orca* also had a very special passenger aboard, his two-star, blue pennant flying from the conning tower. Not that the Navy Department was happy about it, but *Orca* was ferrying Rear Admiral Lockwood to Midway. Apparently Uncle Charlie said that if the powers that be wanted him in Midway, then the only way he was going there was by submarine.

And on that bright, sunshiny January 6, 1944 morning in Pearl Harbor, Kate Lawlor was absent from the pier as her husband's boat let go all lines en route to Midway. As usual, Jake and Kate had said their goodbyes at home hours earlier.

Chapter 15

Sixth War Patrol: 6 January 1944 to 23 February 1944

Midway is 1,140 nautical miles west-northwest from Pearl. *Orca* was making the trip almost entirely on the surface, but Jake was concerned that about one-fifth of his crew were replacements, and fully intended to see to it that his new people were up to speed with his regulars. That meant drills. Admiral Lockwood's presence aboard would not affect that, even if it meant extending the time it took *Orca* to reach Midway. Indeed, "Uncle Charlie" would not have it any other way. If it were entirely up to him, he would skip Midway, stay aboard, and ride *Orca* as she embarked on her sixth war patrol.

Admiral Lockwood bunked in the XO's cabin, and insisted on taking the hitherto unused upper bunk, although Hal Chapman had offered him the lower one he normally used. It was obvious from the very first that the admiral was thoroughly enjoying himself. He would roam the boat at all hours, engaging officers and crew in lengthy conversations. He had the knack of making other people feel that what they had to say was important to him. Perhaps because it was.

It was *Orca's* fourth day out of Pearl, Bill Salton had the eight-to-twelve, morning watch as OOD, and Harry Hastings was his JOD, or Junior Officer of the Deck. JOD watches were the Navy's way of training junior officers to qualify to stand OOD watches as soon as possible. The typical JOD rotated four-on and eight-off; in other words, he stood every third watch until he qualified. The remaining four officer watch standers rotated OOD duties and thus stood every fourth watch. They were, therefore, anxious to get the junior man qualified and added to the rotation so they could then have the deck only every fifth watch.

It was a beautiful day, and visibility was at least ten miles; the ocean was a brilliant sapphire, with a fresh breeze and gentle swells, and the sky was entirely cloudless. *Orca* was zigzagging on the surface on a west-northwest base course, and the XO had said he wouldn't be in the conning tower to direct emergency drills for another hour or so. Salton had let the off-watch crew up on the cigarette deck to get some sun, but no more than six at a time. As was his prerogative, Salton delegated the duty of keeping track as to who and how many were on deck to Hastings, his JOD.

With every "permission to come up?" Harry would scan the deck and insure that there were less than six up before granting permission. There were already six up on deck when the Admiral stuck his head up through the hatch.

"Permission to come up?"

In utter confusion, Hastings looked to Salton for guidance. After all, there were already six visitors on deck, and the admiral would make it seven. Salton never hesitated. "Permission granted," he said. "Good morning, Admiral!"

"Good morning, Mr. Salton, Mr. Hastings," the admiral said as he climbed up onto the bridge. "What an absolutely beautiful day! Smell that air!" He then retired to the cigarette deck and was soon deep in conversation with those already up on deck and enjoying the sun.

A half-hour later, Hal Chapman called up from the conning tower, "This is a drill, Mr. Salton, SD radar reports an enemy plane contact. Dive the boat."

"Dive the boat, aye, aye, Sir. Clear the bridge! Clear the bridge!" Salton watched as six bodies careened down the bridge hatch, followed by the four lookouts and his JOD. On glancing aft, he saw no one. He quickly pulled the diving alarm lever twice, sounding the Claxon, yelled "Dive! Dive!" into the 1MC, and scrambled below himself, pulling the hatch shut after him, the boat already on its way down.

When he arrived at the diving officer's station in control, Hastings was already there waiting for him. After following the diving protocol, and settling the boat out at one hundred feet, Salton casually asked Hastings, "When we dived, the admiral had already gone below, right?"

"What?" Hastings hesitated.

"The admiral. He'd already gone below before we dived, right?" Salton was clearly agitated.

"Yeah, sure, I think so."

"You *think* so! Good God, man, you only *think* so?"

Hastings' only answer was a look of sheer terror. Without hesitation, Salton reached up and pulled the lever above his head, sounding the Claxon three times, yelling, "Surface, surface, surface. Man overboard!" into the 1MC.

"What the hell?" Hal Chapman asked, as Salton hurriedly made his way back up to the bridge, closely followed by a chastened Harry Hastings and four lookouts.

"The admiral!" he responded loudly in passing. "I'm not sure we didn't leave him up there!"

Later, everyone in the conning tower would say that it was the only time anyone has ever seen Hal Chapman look rattled.

Jake was suddenly in the conning tower beside him. "What's going on?" he asked, as Chapman gave the orders for a Wentworth turn, a broad turn maneuver designed to turn a ship around so it ends up going exactly back down its former track. "I don't remember your having said anything about 'man overboard' drills."

"Salton thinks he may have left the admiral on the bridge when we dove the boat." As he said that, the information that the man overboard party was manned and ready in the forward torpedo room was passed up to the conn. They would wait beneath the forward torpedo room hatch until ordered to open it and come up on deck.

Now Jake was rattled. "Chief of the Boat to the conn," he shouted down to the control room. In less than twenty seconds, Bucky was in the conning tower. "Bucky, there's a possibility we might have left the admiral topside on that last dive. Go quietly through the boat from stem to stern and report to me as soon as you find him, *if* you find him."

"Yessir," Bucky replied evenly, and quit the conning tower.

Meanwhile, *Orca* was back on the surface retracing her steps. Eight sets of eyes: four lookouts, the OOD, the JOD, the XO, and the captain, were scanning the surface, looking through their binoculars for any sign of a man in the water.

"There, Sir, something floating there," the forward port lookout shouted, "just off the port bow." He pointed to what looked like the head of a man, just above the surface. When approached, however, it proved to be just a floating coconut.

Several minutes passed. Then Bucky called up from the conning tower, "Captain?" Jake looked down at his COB's grinning face. Quickly Jake put his forefinger to his lips, giving the "Shhh" sign to his COB.

"Keep searching," he said to the men on the deck, as he went below into the conning tower.

"I found the admiral in the forward engine room," Bucky reported. "He was sitting on an inverted bucket, deep in conversation with Rich Richards, the engineman on watch. They were practically shouting at each other over the noise of the diesels. Seems the Admiral thinks that Fairbanks-Morse makes a better diesel than General Motors, and Richards was giving him an argument, saying he'd take a Jimmy over an F-M anytime. You gonna tell them topside?"

"Not quite yet," Jake countered. "Do them good to sweat it out a bit longer. It will serve them right for scaring the crap out of me. And Bucky . . ."

"Yes, Captain?"

"Thanks."

"Anytime, Skipper," he said, still grinning.

Orca took six days to reach Midway. The boat tied up alongside several other submarines in port: *Spearfish* (Lt. Cmdr. Thomas Clanton, USN); *Tarpon* (Lt. Cmdr. Chester Pearson, USN); *Searaven* (Cmdr. Hanson Voss, USNR); *Cray* (Lt. Cmdr. James Fortnoy, USN); *Perro* (Lt. Cmdr. John "Jack" Petrosky, USN); and *Hermit* (Lt. Cmdr. Carter Vaughn, USNR). Once there, a reluctant-looking Admiral Lockwood disembarked. He had looked happier and more content on the trip than Jake had ever seen him. Once his feet touched shore, however, the customary grave demeanor Jake normally associated with the admiral reappeared instantly.

"Meet me up in headquarters for your orders at fourteen hundred," he said. "The base will top off your fuel tanks and provisions, and you should be back at sea by nightfall."

"Yes, Sir, Admiral," Jake replied.

Jake arrived at headquarters early, only to discover that Tom Clanton, skipper of *Spearfish*, Chet Pearson of *Tarpon*, and Jim Fortnoy of *Cray* were already there. They were soon joined by Hanson Voss of *Searaven*, Jack Petrosky of *Perro*, and Carter Vaughn of *Hermit*. At 1400 on the dot, the admiral's new aide greeted them and ushered the COs into a large conference room. All took seats around a large, highly polished mahogany conference table. The table, Jake mused, seemed out of place in the otherwise drab, windowless room, its plywood walls painted a flat light green, and its only decoration two maps. The larger of the two maps was of the entire Pacific theater, and covered one wall completely. The smaller featured a string of islands that looked somewhat like a necklace tossed haphazardly across the sea; its pendant, and the southernmost island, was the largest. Jake recognized the atoll, and its largest island: Kwajalein.

"Gentlemen," Admiral Lockwood began, after convening the meeting and making introductions all around, "this meeting is for the benefit of the submarine commanders in the room. The Army, Navy, and Marines are about to commence Operation Flintlock."

Flintlock is Admiral Spruance's and the Joint Command's plan for the capture of the Marshall Islands from the enemy. It will begin with the invasion of Kwajalein and Roi-Namur nineteen days from today.

"Any enemy forces coming to the aid of the enemy in the Marshalls will most likely come from Truk. Another, less likely, but possible, source of succor would be Palau.

"Your job, submariners, will be to place your boats in position to first detect and report any Japanese reinforcements coming by sea to the aid of the enemy from these places, and then to attack."

He pointed to the larger map on the wall, and put his finger on a tiny spot of land in the middle of nowhere, "Oroluk Island, just east of Truk," he said. "I want *Spearfish* to the North, *Searaven* to the south. SOWESPAC already has three boats patrolling off Truk—*Thresher, Apogon,* and *Angler.* In this area . . ." He swept his hand well to the west of the Marshalls and Truk and around another tiny spot, again seemingly in the middle of nowhere. ". . . around Palau, I want *Orca, Cray, Perro,* and *Hermit.* Jake, this is pretty much the same thing as *Orca* did west of Tarawa last November, so it will be nothing new to you. But for you other skippers, this is how I need you to do this . . ."

Lockwood went on to describe how picket duty was conducted, and assigned each boat a more specific patrol grid.

"You leave for your stations tonight, gentlemen. I expect *Spearfish* and *Searaven* to be on station and on guard within the week—*Orca, Cray, Perro,* and *Hermit* in about ten days. Once Kwajalein is secured, you will be given new assignments. Good luck, gentlemen!"

Orca arrived on station on the morning of January 22nd, nine days before the planned assaults on Kwajalein and Roi-Namur.

The Palau Islands were a string of islands some nine hundred nautical miles east-southeast of Manila. The greater Palau Islands consisted some two hundred islands surrounded by coral reefs, but the three principal islands were strung out to the north. Palau, Koror, and Ngeruktabel were only about ninety miles from end to end. Palau was important to the Imperial war effort because of its strategic position just a thousand miles north of New Guinea, five hundred miles east of the southern tip the Philippines, seven hundred miles west-southwest of Guam, and another thousand miles east-northeast of the NEI. Palau was the assembly point for ships supplying the Empire; anchorages protected by coral reefs were available off Palau and Koror (the principal port), and an active airstrip had been built at Peleliu on heavily fortified Ngeruktabel Island to the south.

Orca had drawn the northernmost patrol area, a fifty-mile square off the north end of Palau. The other three boats had similar square operating areas to the south of *Orca*: first *Cray*, then *Perro*, then *Hermit*. Air patrols were active out of Peleliu, and Japanese antisubmarine patrol aircraft were reportedly now radar-equipped. While the presence of these particular aircraft was uncertain, air traffic was nonetheless fairly heavy, so surface operations were limited regardless. And it was only on the surface (or with the boat broached) that a fleet boat's radar was operable.

Thankfully, the Japanese rarely sent convoys out of Palau at night, so there was little incentive for night air patrols to be conducted. At least, then, the four boats could surface at night in relative safety and charge batteries. Their instructions were to watch and report. They were not to initiate action against any target, no matter how tempting, until the contact or contacts were first reported and permission to attack given.

* * * * *

Hiriake Ito observed Sub-Lieutenant Saburo Takashi as he maneuvered his command, *IJN Atsukaze*, a *Fubuki* class destroyer, into the anchorage at Koror Bay at the southern end of Palau. Ito liked Takashi. The man was, in his judgment, more intelligent than his peers and an excellent ship handler. He would go far in the Imperial Navy — or, at least he would go far had not Japan, in Ito's opinion, been losing the war.

Takashi dropped anchor in the exactly correct spot, and Ito felt the destroyer strain into the anchor chain as the flukes bit into rocky bottom. Satisfied that *Atsukaze* was held fast, Ito surveyed the other ships in the anchorage. Two tankers, up from Sulawesi, were anchored off to the west, and there was a small cargo vessel, Ito judged it to be about 1,900 tons, off to the east, toward the port. These, he judged, were to be among his "chicks," the convoy being assembled for him to escort north to Manila. In the port, he knew, snugly tied up alongside at Koror, were three of the new *kaibokan: Mikura, Kibuki*, and the older *Iki*.

These *kaibokan*, or "sea defense ships" were specifically fitted for escort duty. They were, Ito knew, lightly gunned, capable of just 19.5 knots flat out, and only 60 meters long. But each was fitted with more advanced sonar than his own ship, and even radar — which the Imperial Japanese Navy had yet to install on its destroyers! Moreover, the back third of each of these vessels was equipped with six depth charge throwers, and each *kaibokan* carried up to one hundred twenty depth charges — this compared to the mere thirty-six *Atsukaze* carried. Ito was, he freely admitted to himself, envious of these tiny ships' antisubmarine capabilities. No matter. He was to be in charge of the convoy, the senior commander of this escort force, and *Mikura, Kibuki*, and *Iki* would be his to fight in battle should it come to that. And, of course, Ito sincerely hoped it would come to that.

Picket duty; nothing more boring than operating submerged at five knots all day with the search periscopes and passive sonar manned. The worst of it was, during daylight hours, with an op area fifty miles wide and fifty miles long, half of the IJN could slip by *Orca* or any of the other three boats undetected. At night, at least, unless an aircraft stumbled close by, they could operate on the surface with both radars blasting away, and have an even chance of detecting an enemy relief force headed east. The good news was that none of the patrol aircraft appeared to have radar — or, if they did, their pilots didn't know how to use it.

The last of his chicks had arrived, and Ito had his orders. The convoy would consist of seven marus: two tankers and five cargo ships. Ito would command the escort force in *Atsukaze*, and *Mikura*, *Kibuki*, and *Iki* would take station on his command. The convoy was to proceed northwest to Manila, but was *not* to leave Palau by first steaming west out of Koror Bay.

Submarines had been detected in the past lurking in the deep waters directly off Koror Port, so, to avoid detection, the convoy elements would first steam northward out of the Bay, entering the waters immediately off the western coast of Palau. There the relatively shallow water and a seaward outer reef protected them from submarine observation and interference. Only when they had cleared the north end of the Island and the protective reef would they assemble in deep water and proceed onward.

And so it was that Hiriake Ito assembled his brood north of Palau and proceeded en route to Manila. It was later on that same day that the first wave of Army and Marines landed on the northern ends of Kwajalein Atoll. As Ito and his flock made their way to the northwest, *Orca* was in the southern end of her op area, and their passage thus went undetected.

Having learned the lesson of the futility of direct frontal assault on dug-in enemy in Tarawa, the Army's 7th Infantry Division landed on the westernmost, while the 4th Marine Division landed on the easternmost, of the two northern ends of the Kwajalein Atoll. Both forces moved south, using mobile gun emplacements and island-hopping their way down toward the flanks of the enemy force defending Kwajalein. The Marines overran Roi-Namur on February 1st and 2nd, while the Army, under bombardment from the assembled Naval fleet, which included the USS Tennessee *and B-24 bombers from Apamama, took two days longer to wipe out the enemy forces on Kwajalein Island. By February 4th, then, the entire Atoll was in American hands.*

* * * * *

It was soon obvious to Pacific Fleet Command that the Japanese had abandoned the garrisons in the Gilbert and Marshall Islands to their fate, and that there was never any plan in place to reinforce them.

On February 6th, *Orca*, *Cray*, *Perro*, and *Hermit* were released from picket duty and instructed to form a task group, TG 510.1, and conduct combined operations (heaven forbid that the Navy would use a term like "wolf pack") against enemy shipping around Palau. Jim Fortnoy in *Cray* had been in Jake's class at the Academy, but had received his lieutenant commander rank several months behind Jake. *Perro* and *Hermit* were new boats, *Perro* on its first, *Hermit* on its second war patrol. They were Jack Petrosky's and Carter Vaughn's first commands, and both had just received their half-stripes in the last half of '43. Miracle of miracles, Jake was SOPA — senior officer present afloat — *and* TG Commander!

Jake's first order of business was to assign op areas around Palau. The easiest way to do this was to simply flip the op areas assigned for picket duty to the other, western, side of the atoll, with *Orca* patrolling to the north, and *Cray*, *Perro*, and *Hermit* strung out to the south, just as before. Standard protocol was to be followed: first boat to make contact with a convoy leaving port was to become the shadow, maintaining contact until as many of the other boats as possible could assemble for a coordinated attack. Call signs were: *Orca*, Cowboy One; *Perro*, Cowboy Two; and *Cray* and *Hermit*, Cowboy Three and Cowboy Four. Following standard protocol, radio transmissions were to be kept to a minimum, and to be as short as possible.

In the past, boats patrolling off Koror Port missed intercepting convoys even when SUBPAC had broadcasted dates, destinations, composition, and approximate times that convoys were leaving Palau. Jake figured that short of a SUBPAC transmission notifying the task group of a convoy forming in, or departing from, Palau (how did they do that?), their best bet of intercepting a convoy would still be with *Cray* and *Perro*, which were patrolling off Koror. *Orca* and *Hermit* he positioned on the hunch that the enemy might just be using some other, unknown sallying point. In any case, if either *Cray* or *Perro* did spot a convoy, the other boats could join up with them soon enough.

* * * * *

Hiriake Ito and the escorts under his command had successfully delivered all of their chicks to Manila without incident. Or, at least, without incident to the tankers and cargo vessels. *Kibuki*, the newest of the *kaibokan*, had blown her port diesel about a hundred miles south of Manila, and would possibly he laid up in the Manila repair facility for some time. Her captain, a young lieutenant, had been immediately called on the carpet for the incident by a hastily convened review board.

"The engine was defective from the first," he told the board. "It never ran satisfactorily, and could never make the same number of revolutions as the starboard diesel. The engine has underperformed from the start and must have been delivered defective from the factory." The lieutenant's explanation was deemed unsatisfactory by the board, and he was reduced in rank and reassigned to the Manila repair facility staff.

The repair facility examined the engine and found that water had somehow entered one of the five, 300mm cylinders. Further examination showed that the cooling water channels, cast into the cylinder block and around the blown cylinder, had been badly cast, and had probably leaked slightly from the start. What started as a pinhole leak gradually increased over time until it finally leaked enough water into the cylinder to cause its failure. The ship's former captain had been correct; the engine had been delivered defective from the factory. But, of course, the members of the review board could admit no such mistake. Fixing the engine would be a major operation, and would require its removal from the vessel. Even then, welding and re-machining the casting would be difficult—perhaps impossible. Best to replace the engine altogether—except that they didn't have one to replace it with.

Ito's orders were to return to Palau with his escorts and shepherd another convoy, this time to Guam. That would be a dangerous trip, over 1,300 kilometers or 710 nautical miles, all of it in enemy submarine-infested waters. He loathed the loss of the use of one of his *kaibokan*, and requested from Perimeter Command that *Kibuki* be allowed to rejoin his escort group operating on her single engine. He argued that while her maximum speed would be reduced to fifteen knots, that was still well in excess of speed of the average escorted vessel. Even with one drive train gone so that she would lose some of her ability to maneuver, *Kibuki* would nonetheless be invaluable to the escort group in her role as a sonar and radar platform, and for her ability to engage the enemy with her guns and her one hundred and twenty depth charges.

Despite the fact that the slower *Kibuki* would add the better part of a day to the return trip to Palau, IJN Perimeter Command saw the wisdom of Ito's request. Also at Ito's urging, Sub-Lieutenant Saburo Takashi, hastily made a brevet Lieutenant, assumed command of the *kaibokan*. On February 6th, *Kibuki*, in company with *Atsukaze*, *Mikura*, and *Iki*, and running with a constant slight right rudder and her one diesel running flat out, set sail for Palau.

* * * * *

It was early morning, February 14th, Valentine's Day. Jake thought about Kate, how he would like to be giving her a bouquet of roses and a box of chocolates to celebrate the occasion. Resolving to put that in his, by now, twenty-three-page letter

291

later, he redirected his thoughts to the tactical situation. The patrolling submarines had just submerged in their respective op areas. There had been no SUBPAC notifications of any convoys forming in Palau. Several vessels had been detected entering Koror Port, but none of the boats had been in position to attack.

"This is Cowboy Four," Carter Vaughn in *Hermit* transmitted. "Unescorted AK, traversing my op area and heading for Koror. Am maneuvering to attack. "

"This is Cowboy One," Jake responded from *Orca*. "Proceed. Out."

An hour later, *Orca* received this transmission: "This is Cowboy Four, no joy." This meant that *Hermit* was unable to attain firing position.

"Roger Cowboy Four, One, out."

A bird in hand, Jake thought, upon receiving Vaughn's report, meaning that he felt perfectly justified in letting *Hermit* proceed with her attack despite the fact that it would have alerted the enemy of at least one submarine's presence.

Perhaps it's just as well that Hermit *was unsuccessful. They still don't know for sure that we're out here, and chances are we'll get another shot at that AK when she leaves port as part of a convoy.*

At midmorning the same day, *Orca* was submerged in the northern end of her op area. Early Sender had the watch and called Hal Chapman to the conning tower

"I think that's a mast on the horizon, bearing zero-one-three," he said, "How about you take a look-see."

"Roger that," Chapman said, as he manned the search scope. "Definitely a mast, or cluster of masts, rather. Possible warship, and heading our way. Get the skipper up here."

"What's up," Jake inquired, as he ascended the conning tower ladder.

"Contact, Captain," Hal said, offering Jake his position at the periscope. "Here, take a look."

"Definitely a warship of some sort, but not a big one. Probably a destroyer. We should alert the others. Early, go below and have radio let the other three boats know we have an unknown contact. I have the conn."

"Ay, aye, Sir," Sender replied, and scurried below.

"Looks like this guy might just fall into our lap, Hal. But wait on sounding GQ for now. Let's see how this pans out. Does sonar have anything at all?"

"I'll check." A few minutes later, he informed Jake, "I pointed them in the right direction, Captain, but sonar doesn't hear a thing."

When the superstructure was visible over the horizon, and the contact was definitely identified as a destroyer, sonar finally reported: "Multiple contacts, bearing zero-one-five, right bearing drift."

"That's not right, Skipper," Chapman observed. "If they're going to clear the outer reefs and head south to Koror, then they have to come our way. That bearing drift should be left."

"So you would think," Jake replied, abandoning the scope to Chapman. Checking with sonar, sonar confirmed that the contact's bearing drift was definitely right.

Jake went below to the control room. He moved to the chart table and examined the Palau chart. *Unless they're going to go to Koror via the other side of the northern reefs*, he thought.

Then, calling up to Chapman in the conning tower, he said, "Hal, the chart definitely shows a wide opening on the north end between the reefs. First, there's a leg to the southeast, then south all the way along Palau Island's west coast. If they hug the coast, there's a more or less straight shot into Koror, with only the last little bit unprotected by reefs to the west. Could be that's where these birds are headed."

Jake climbed the ladder back into the conning tower, where he wouldn't have to converse with his XO at the top of his lungs. "If so," he continued, "the convoys could have been leaving from the northern end of the Island all along, and that would explain why so little traffic, individual ships or convoys, have been detected leaving port, sailing straight to sea, west out of Koror. My guess is that the Japs *always* use this northern passage, and we're just now discovering it."

Hal began singing out bearings and ranges to the destroyer. Soon afterward, John Catinella, the watch quartermaster, reported "Contact course one-seven-six, speed fifteen."

Now a second contact, another, smaller, warship became visible. "You nailed it, Skipper. They're heading for that breach in the reefs. But the bad news is that we'll never get into firing position submerged."

"No, Hal, but we'll all four be waiting for them when they come back out. For now, signal 'No joy,' to the other boats."

Hal watched helplessly as four warships, a *Fubuki*-class destroyer, and three smaller destroyer escorts, steamed steadily south down the other side of the reef.

* * * * *

The tropical depression formed on February 20th just northeast of Yap, an island roughly halfway between Palau and Guam. Conditions were perfect: an unusually warm ocean, an updraft of warm humid air hitting high cooler air, forming cumulo nimbus clouds, and a low pressure area below. Surrounding air then rushed to the low-pressure area, the clouds above forming into long, spiraling bands. A rotating, inertial force, first described in the mid-nineteenth century by French scientist Gustav-Garspard Coriolis, caused the incoming winds to swirl counter-clockwise around the low pressure area as the humid air below was drawn upward and dispelled by high altitude winds. Slowly, drier high altitude air was drawn down through the center of the system, forming an "eye." Finally, cyclonic force winds began swirling around the eye, the storm building, as the prevailing winds pushed the system southwestward.

By the evening of the twentieth, the outer bands of the storm pelted Yap with driving rain and high winds, and the path of the storm began a slow curve to the southwest, on a direct path toward Palau.

* * * * *

Jake stationed the four boats in a fan pattern well outside the entrance to Palau's north sallying point. He put the less experienced skippers Petrosky and Vaughn, in *Perro* and *Hermit* respectively, on the flanks, while he in *Orca* and Fortnoy in *Cray* were stationed just west and north from where Jake was betting the next convoy out of Palau would emerge into the open sea.

And they waited.

SUBPAC broadcast that convoy PAMA-32 was forming in Palau, six ships and four escorts, bound for Manila, and scheduled to leave on or about February 20th.

After a week of waiting at the north end of Palau Island, Jake began to think he had made a bad bet, and that the convoy was either leaving or had left directly out of Koror and into the open sea. But in the wee hours of the eighth day, February 22nd, when all four boats were operating on the surface in pea soup fog, *Orca's* radar watch reported multiple vessels in line, emerging from the Palau Island ground return close by the west side of the northern tip of Palau Island, and heading northwest out to sea.

Jake, called out of his bunk to the conning tower, pictured the escorts coming out first, followed by the convoyed ships, and the convoy forming up at sea only after all the vessels had cleared the reef. His boats could then attack during the confusion as the convoy was forming up. But his plan was to be thwarted, and the boats of TG 510.1 were in for a surprise.

Chapter 16

Commander Hiriake Ito stood on the bridge of *Atsukaze*, first in a line of ten vessels that had been hugging the western coast of Palau Island, northbound at five knots. The visibility was terrible: the night dark, with a heavy ground mist, the shoreline of Palau a brooding blackness to the east. His navigator, a tall, gaunt, cerebral lieutenant from Sasebo, reported the barometer falling precipitously. A large storm system was on its way; best for the convoy to clear the harbor and be well underway before it arrived.

Ito's ship and the others in the column were showing bright stern lights to keep the vessels in line. Once the radars aboard the *kaibokan* showed them clear of Palau and two tiny islands north of the tip of Palau, the line of ships could then turn northwest to clear the last reefs and make for open sea. Once in open sea, and once the visibility was good enough, the six "chicks," two tankers and four cargo vessels, were to form ranks two abreast and three deep. Ito then planned to set the *kaibokan* in position in front of the convoy and on both flanks, placing his own ship to the rear of the convoy. Normally, he would have his ship, the largest escort, at the head of the pack, but his *kaibokan* had radar, and *Atsukaze* did not. At least, that was the plan.

But for the time being, *Atsukaze* was headed northwest for the channel between the reefs to open sea, and was being followed by Lt. Saburo Takashi in *Kibuki*, then *Mikura*, the four cargo ships, the two tankers, and finally *Iki*. Every ship in the convoy had been warned of the oncoming storm, to literally batten down the hatches, and to secure any loose gear topside.

"Captain, *Kibuki* is reporting four radar contacts to the northwest more or less evenly spread along an arc from three-zero-two to zero-one-four degrees, each out about forty-five hundred meters," the bridge talker reported excitedly.

"Ask him if these contacts are large." As Ito awaited Takashi's reply, *Mikura* reported identical radar contacts.

"Captain, *Kibuki* reports that the contacts are small. Possible enemy submarines. *Iki* now also reports the contacts."

Acting quickly, Ito ordered *Mikura* and *Iki* to break ranks and proceed at flank speed to close the two closest contacts, the two immediately outside the passage through the reefs. If they were submarines, the *kaibokan* were to attack. Once *Mikura* and *Iki* were safely clear of the formation and headed for the reef passage, he ordered Takashi in *Kibuki* to stay behind and shepherd the chicks to safe anchorage inside the reefs. Then Ito took *Atsukaze* out to engage the enemy, *if*, in fact, it was the enemy. This could, after all, be much ado over a bunch of sampans.

* * * * *

"Radar shows that two of those bastards have broken ranks and are headed straight for us," Hal Chapman calmly informed Jake. "Looks like they're doing about nineteen knots. Other three boats are reporting the same thing. I don't know how they know it, but these guys know exactly where we are."

"One thing for sure," Jake countered, "they know we're out here even though they couldn't possibly see us with this visibility. For now, how about we all do a quick one-eighty and skedaddle on the surface while we still can stay ahead of 'em. If they get too close, we can submerge and evade. Pass the word to the other boats."

* * * * *

"Captain, both *Mikura* and *Iki* report that they were unable to close with the contacts, and that all four are now headed out to sea at twenty knots."

"Very well," replied Ito. "Tell *Mikura* and *Iki* to disengage and return to the formation." Then, thinking aloud, he explained to no one in particular: "So we know now that they are enemy submarines, that there are four of them, and that they will no doubt be waiting for us. So we will bide our time here until daylight, and possibly some better visibility, before we venture out to meet them? Their teeth are formidable, perhaps, but this time I am hardly toothless."

* * * * *

"What was *that* about? Those bastards knew exactly where we were — they were headed straight for us," Hal Chapman mused.

"Only one explanation," Jake said. "Those pint-size escorts we saw the other day either have radar *or* something very much like it. How else could they know exactly where we are in this soup? And if they have radar, what *else* do they have? Perhaps the Japs have finally gotten serious about countering our submarines. My guess is that these little buggers are also armed to the teeth. Probably got about fifty depth charges aboard."

"Okay, so let's say they have radar," observed Hal. "That means that surface attacks are out. We're limited to submerged attacks. *But* we could still take advantage of our surface speed to maneuver on the surface, just stay out of their radar range. I'm betting those escorts that were headed for us were going flat out."

"Exactly," said Jake. "It means we position ourselves in advance of the enemy's track so as to engage the enemy submerged," practically quoting the submarine tactics textbook. "Now they had to be getting ready to form up that convoy — what did SUBPAC call it?"

"PAMA-32."

"Yeah. And so we also know they're en route to Manila. So we'll fan out our four boats on the route to Manila and use our SJ radars. The first boat to make contact would report convoy course and speed and then run out of radar range. Then we could all maneuver at speed, on the surface, and out of radar range, to intercept."

"Sounds good, Captain," Chapman agreed. "I'll see to it that the other boats are notified and set up their positions. But here's a complication—Louie says the bottom is dropping out of the barometer and we've got a biggie on the way."

"Then we'll just have to deal with that if and when it happens. Make sure the other guys know about it. Meanwhile, we go ahead and set up that intercept."

On February 17th and 18th, 1944, carrier-based aircraft destroyed the Japanese naval base at Truk in the Caroline Islands. On February 20th, U.S. land and carrier-based planes attacked and destroyed the enemy's base at Rabaul on the island of New Britain in the Australian territory of New Guinea.

Palau was hit with 69 mile-per-hour winds on the evening of February 23rd, as what had started as a tropical depression off Yap, became a full-fledged typhoon. The storm pelted the atoll throughout the night, causing extensive damage to Japanese port facilities. One cargo vessel, riding on a mooring buoy off Koror, slipped its mooring line and was swept out to sea. Torrential rains caused extensive flooding, and the airfield at Peleliu was unusable for several days.

Before striking Palau, however, the typhoon's path had veered sharply north, so the island had only experienced a glancing blow. By the morning of the 24th, the wind on the Island had subsided and the rain fell only intermittently as the outer bands of the storm passed over the atoll. By that evening, the storm was gone.

Thursday, February 24th, 1400, the boats of TG 510.1 were operating on the surface, their SJ and SD radars active. There was a slight sea return on the SJ radarscope, because the sea was choppy, with four-foot swells, and white-capped waves. Cowboy Two was the first to make contact with the advancing convoy.

Actually, *Cray* didn't have a radar contact on its PPI, rather the scope showed a slight flicker, evidence to an alert operator that another radar was operating downrange. Of course, their own radar might do the same on the intruder's receiver, but that operator would have to be as skilled as *Cray's* to first, notice, and, second, to interpret the anomaly. As soon as the scope flicker was reported to a hastily awakened Jim Fortnoy, he ordered the *Cray's* radar shut down. He was gratified to learn that his OOD had already done so.

"Cowboy One, this is Cowboy Two," Fortnoy reported to Jake on the tactical radio. "PPI flicker indicates approaching radar. Recommend Cowboy Two immediately submerge, close, and track contact visually and with passive sonar, over."

"This is Cowboy One. Excellent plan, Cowboy Two. Submerge, close, and track passively."

"Two. Roger that, Cowboy One. Wilco. Out."

"This is Cowboy One. Targets possibly closing. Cowboys Three and Four are to cease all emissions and submerge to periscope depth in present location. Leave your radio antennae up. Use optics and passive sonar only. Acknowledge. Over."

"Cowboy Three. Roger. Submerge, radio whip up, and use passive detection only. Wilco."

"Cowboy Four. Acknowledge submerge, leave whip up, and use passive only. Wilco, One."

"Very well, Three and Four. One, out."

* * * * *

Lieutenant Saburo Takashi in *Kibuki* led the convoy designated PAMA-32. His ship was stationed five hundred meters out in front of the convoy of six vessels, two abreast by three deep, four cargo ships in front of two tankers. The weather was unusually warm for that time of the year, with a hot sun burning its way through band of fast-moving, wispy clouds overhead.

Visibility was excellent. A stiff, warm and humid breeze from the east whipped up little whitecaps in the surrounding, heaving sea.

PAMA-32 was heading for the northern tip of the Philippine Island of Samar, on a base course of 306 degrees. There would be plenty of air cover available once the convoy reached Samar, but until then, PAMA-32 would zigzag on its base course of 306. The pattern was a simple one: ten minutes on 291, then right to 321 for another ten minutes. And progress was slow. The slowest ship in the convoy, a 1,650-ton cargo ship, could only make 9 knots; that meant that their actual speed on the base course was just over 8.5 knots.

Kibuki's radar was activated, as was *Mikura's* and *Iki's*. The other two *kaibokan* were stationed on the left and right flanks, respectively, of the convoy. All three ships, and *Atsukaze,* stationed at the rear of the convoy, were operating their active sonar. And, since leaving Palau, there had been no contacts whatever.

Ito had risen early, and was standing on the bridge of *Atsukaze,* scanning the dawn horizon through his binoculars, enjoying the stiff, hot breeze. The men who operated the American submarines, he knew, were not fools. They now knew the capabilities of the *kaibokan* and would not expose themselves to their radar without good reason. He also knew that that the American submariners he had surprised at Palau would never give up and would eventually attack his convoy by any means available to them. The *kaibokan* radars merely limited the enemy's surface operations. He had warned all captains and masters that it was vital that the lookouts on every vessel in the convoy stay alert for submarine periscopes. He prayed that if that storm were coming it would arrive quickly, for it would provide excellent cover for the convoy.

* * * * *

At the very moment that Hiriake Ito stood on his bridge, Jim Fortnoy had his eye fixed to *Cray's* search periscope observing the progress of the escort on the convoy's left flank. He had had to bring the boat up to fifty-eight feet so that the periscope lens was clear of the heaving sea. During an earlier observation, he had gotten a visual bearing, single-pinged the ship, and gotten a good range reading. The escort was so busy pinging away with its own sonar that it never noticed *Cray's* ping. He worked the problem backwards and calculated the escort's masthead height at eighteen feet, so he could use the periscope's stadimeter to get a range if he so chose. The boat had been riding up and down with the sea, so he did his best to time his observations to when the boat was riding the top of a swell.

"Bearing, mark," he called out.

"Zero-eight-five," his quartermaster sang out.

"Range, mark."

"Four thousand, three hundred and twenty yards."

"Down scope. Quick, get a single ping range."

Moments later: "Four thousand, three hundred yards."

"Excellent. Preliminary course and speed?"

From the chart table, where his XO, Lt. Dakota Bloom quickly drew lines on a maneuvering board, "Course three-two-one, speed nine."

"Come right to three-two-one," Fortnoy ordered, paralleling the convoy, seeking to maintain contact as long as possible, even at his best sustainable submerged speed of five knots.

He waited.

Seven minutes later, he ordered, "Up Scope." Then, "Bearing, mark."

"Zero-eight-three."

"Range, mark"

"four thousand, six hundred."

"Sonar single-ping?"

"Four thousand, six fifty."

From the chart table: "Course three-two-one, speed nine."

Seven minutes later: "Up scope." Then: "He's zigged toward. Angle-on-the-bow port one-zero-zero. Bearing, mark."

"Zero-eight-zero."

"Range, mark."

"Four thousand, five hundred thirty."

"Down scope." This time, confident his stadimeter ranges were accurate, Fortnoy did not ask for a confirming sonar range. "What kind of course have you got on him?" he asked his TDC operator.

"With that AOB, Skipper, two-nine-five."

"Very well. Helm, come left to two-nine-five."

"Two-nine-five, aye."

After thirty minutes, Jim Fortnoy was fairly confident he had the convoy's base course, speed, and zigzag pattern figured out. He hated to let it slip past *Cray* without taking a shot at it, but that was just what he did, as he assumed shadow position. As he slipped his boat astern of the destroyer at the tail end of the convoy, he radioed, "Cowboy One, this is Cowboy Two. Convoy base course three-zero-six, speed eight-point-five. Ten minute zigs. Left course two-nine-one, right course three-two-one. Over."

"Roger that, Cowboy Two. Base course three-zero-six, speed eight-point-five. Ten minute zigs. Left two-nine-one, right three-two-one. Cowboy One, over."

"That is correct, Cowboy One. Two moving to shadow. Out."

"Cowboy Three and Four, this is Cowboy One, did you copy? Over."

"Cowboy Three copied, convoy base course three-zero-six, speed eight-point-five. Ten minute zigs. Left two-nine-one, right three-two-one, over."

"Cowboy Four copied, convoy base course three-zero-six, speed eight-point-five. Ten minute zigs. Left two-nine-one, right three-two-one, over."

"Very well, Three and Four, Cowboy One, out."

That night, under the light of a waning moon, the dogs of war were unleashed.

* * * * *

It was just before midnight on the 25th, and Ito had just settled into his bunk, when he heard the first explosion. He threw on a kimono, and rushed to the bridge. His XO, Lt. Cmdr. Shoici Koroki, a short, thick, and oily sycophant whom Ito couldn't stand, reported in an excited voice, "There's been an explosion on one of the cargo vessels, the *Shinryu Maru*. The master reports a torpedo strike, but it couldn't be. *Mikura* was right there beside her when it happened, and reported that no torpedo wake was sighted."

"So a torpedo without a wake was used!" Ito barked. "Have *Mikura* immediately do an active sonar sweep to port. Find that Submarine!"

As Koroki rushed off to convey Ito's orders, there was another explosion, this time on the tanker *Jakarta Maru*, immediately in front of *Atsukaze* and to starboard. It was followed perhaps a half-minute later by a second explosion on the same vessel. The tanker burst into flames, as her cargo of fuel oil ignited. Despite the deteriorating sea conditions, Ito could just make out two distinct torpedo wakes leading to the stricken ship, with a third wake having passed her astern. But a fourth torpedo wake was far more frightening. This wake was pointed at a spot in the ocean that the bow of *Atsukaze* would occupy in a matter of seconds.

"Back emergency!" Ito shouted into the voice tube to the engine room. "Full right rudder," he called to the helm. He held his breath as the torpedo wake disappeared under the bow of his ship, which was shuddering, slowing, and turning. Then he gratefully let that breath out as the wake continued past.

The torpedo must have missed, he thought, *but by only a hair's width.*

"Full ahead," he ordered, setting a course down that last torpedo wake. En route to his submerged prey, he ordered the remaining convoy vessels to make best speed on course 306 with *Kibuki* to remain with them as escort. He then ordered *Iki* to join him in hunting the tanker's tormentor. Behind him, as the cargo ship *Shinryu Maru* stood burning, down by the stern and dead in the water, the stricken tanker *Jakarta Maru* exploded and blew apart in two pieces; both halves sank like stones in a matter of minutes. *Jakarta Maru* left behind nothing but a burning oil slick on the roiling sea, which, along with *Shinryu Maru's* smoky blaze, at once brightened and blackened the night sky.

* * * * *

Jack Petrosky, in *Perro*, knew he was in trouble. Two of the three torpedoes he had aimed at that tanker, had erased it, all right, but his fourth had missed the destroyer. *Perro* was now in for it, as the destroyer bore down on her.

"All ahead full, right full rudder, take her down! Make your depth one hundred feet, and make it quick."

"Full dive on the bow and stern planes, fifteen degrees down bubble, make your depth one hundred feet," *Perro's* engineer officer Lt. Joel Himmelfarb shouted, acknowledging and executing the order with the same command. As the boat was driven downward, the pinging above grew ever louder as the destroyer bore down on *Perro*.

"He's after us and he's pissed," Petrosky muttered under his breath to no one in particular. Then, aloud, he said, "Rig for depth charge." The boat was passing eighty feet, and leveling off to a five-degree down bubble, when the first depth charge went off well astern and to starboard. *Boom!* "He's not on to us yet," Petrosky observed to his XO, Lt. Frank Witherspoon.

"Sonar reports a second set of screws above, Captain," the conning tower talker, Seaman Bob Hooker, announced. "And he's pinging on us."

"Steady at one hundred feet, Captain," Himmelfarb reported.

"All ahead one-third," Petrosky ordered. "Rudder amidships. What's our heading?"

"Zero-two-seven, Captain," the helmsman announced.

"Very well, come right to zero-three-six." That would point *Perro* in a direction ninety degrees off the convoy's base course. If Petrosky wasn't able to shake his pursuers, he could at least draw them away from the convoy and give the other boats better odds at sinking a few more marus. Then, almost as an afterthought, he ordered, "Rig for silent running."

Now only one source of pinging could be heard. One of the ships above *Perro* had stopped using their active sonar.

"Steady on zero-three-six."

"Sonar reports one contact, screws stopped, dead in the water, echo locating. Second contact coming on fast," Hooker announced.

Then came a string of depth charges, close aboard and directly overhead. *Boom! Wham! Wham! WHAM! Boom! Wham! WHAM!*

"What in hell?" was all Petrosky could think to say as the boat whipsawed beneath his feet. Directly overhead in the conning tower, the bridge hatch lifted off its seat and reseated, admitting a shower of water under pressure, soaking the personnel below.

"Take her down to two hundred feet. All compartments, damage report!" shouted Petrosky. As the boat headed down to 200 feet, the damage reports came in. The forward torpedo room reported two sea valves had lifted off their seats. The forward engine room reported that sections of gasket had blown out of the engine air induction valve and the main induction valve. The after torpedo room reported the most damage: a four foot by two foot dent in the pressure hull just forward of tube eight—no evidence of a crack in the hull, though. A sea valve casting had cracked, and water was spurting from it, producing a flat stream of water the size of a knife blade. The stern planes were also making noise whenever they were moved. Other compartments reported minor damage, and bits of cork insulation and splinters of glass were everywhere.

"Steady at two hundred feet," the report came up from Himmelfarb.

"Sonar reports that second ship now stopped and echo locating" Hooker announced. "First vessel now coming on fast."

Two more depth charges went off, still overhead, but now set too shallow to do much damage. And so it went. Each of the two vessels overhead taking turns, one apparently having enough depth charges aboard to release a half-dozen at a time.

"We're being double-teamed," Petrosky noted to no one in particular, "and they don't appear to be ready to give up on us any time soon."

Perro had suffered the worst damage from the second vessel's initial attack. Subsequent attacks by both ships were on the mark, but the depth charges were still set too shallow, and the physical damage they caused was minor: more glass shards and chunks of cork insulation. Psychological damage to the crew—from the ominous pinging and incessant pounding—was something else again.

Jake had tried to reach *Cray* on the tactical radio before he fired two Mark-18s at the cargo ship. He wanted to invite Jim Fortnoy up to join in the fray, but *Cray*, as shadower, had obviously slipped so far behind the convoy that she was out of range of tactical radio.

And now *Orca*, having drawn first blood by torpedoing the cargo ship, was also getting a going over from one of the "pint-sized escorts." Jake had taken the boat deep to 200 feet from the first, however, and the *kaibokan* had difficulty locating the submarine. Going slow enough to echo locate the boat, the pint-sized escort would establish contact, only to lose it as it sped up to unleash a flurry of depth charges. Invariably, *Orca* was elsewhere when the charges went off — *and* the charges were set too shallow anyway. The worst effects *Orca* suffered from the explosions were some violent jolts that threw crewmembers off balance and broke a few dishes.

Jake maneuvered *Orca* so as to slowly draw the escort west, and away from the convoy. "If I can keep this guy busy," he reasoned with his XO, "and away from the convoy, then the other boats will have one less escort to worry about."

Jake was completely amazed at the number of depth charges the little escort carried. At each pass, there were up to a half-dozen explosions, and there were multiple passes. He eventually lost count. And the little bugger was persistent, if not — thank God — terribly accurate.

After two hours had passed, and *Orca* and had drawn her pursuer several miles west of the convoy's track, Jake decided he had had enough of the two vessels' little dance. Despite any evidence of success, the escort showed no signs of giving up and abandoning the chase. Evidently an occasional positive active sonar contact was sufficient to assure the escort of ultimately succeeding: either sinking its adversary or forcing the sub to surface. In desperation, Jake decided to try a tactic that had been widely written about before the war, but had never actually become doctrine. If it worked, *Orca* would turn the tables and become the escort's stalker.

Using reports on the escort's approximate location from passive sonar, Jake slowly maneuvered the boat into a position where he could pinpoint the escort's exact location using active sonar. When he had done so, he found that the escort was still actively searching over the last spot he had found *Orca*. Trusting that the escort's active sonar would mask *Orca's*, Jake ordered sonar to single-ping the escort. But sonar reported that it could get no return from the escort.

"No return, " Jake mused aloud to his XO. "Why can't we get an echo return off this guy? He's practically overhead!"

Chapman thought a bit. "The sonar dome's mounted under the bow. The active sonar is designed to acquire targets ahead of and below us. Maybe our bow superstructure is in the way?"

"Maybe. Let's see."

Jake had Joe Bob slowly change *Orca's* attitude to a fifteen-degree up bubble. This time sonar reported a single-ping bearing and range to the contact. Then, with Early Sender operating the TDC, and Lou Carillo on the chart plot, Jake ordered sonar to single-ping the escort enough times to get bearings and ranges so a course and speed could be calculated. The chart plot soon reported course 096 at five knots.

The torpedomen in the forward torpedo room were astonished when Jake ordered the outer doors opened on tubes three and four.

"I have a firing solution, Captain," Sender said.

"Very well, fire three."

One Mark-18 was sent on its way.

At 29 knots, Jake knew, a Mark-18 traveled about 980 yards per minute. The escort was twenty-three hundred yards away, and a hundred and ninety feet above, so he figured travel time was just over two minutes and twenty seconds, doing the math in his head. But it had to climb to its running depth of ten feet without wavering, and without broaching in a very busy sea. A broach might throw off the torpedo's gyroscope and take it off course. All sorts of things could go wrong. *Maybe I should risk coming up to periscope depth, and attack the usual way.*

Exactly two minutes and twenty-two seconds later, *Mikura* was hit just forward of her starboard screw. When *Orca* did come up to periscope depth, the escort was seen to be afire and dead in the water. The outer doors on tube four were still open, and Jake was thinking about putting a second torpedo into her, when, apparently, an armed depth charge went off astern, blowing off the entire aft end of the ship. She sank minutes later. Jake ordered the outer doors closed on tube four.

After sweeping the horizon at a shallow periscope depth of fifty-seven feet and seeing nothing, Jake ordered the boat broached so the SJ radar could be activated. The sea action was so violent, however, that attempting to broach was an exercise in futility. Jake finally had to order *Orca* surfaced. But grappling with the escort for almost three hours had taken *Orca* miles away from the convoy's track. There were no contacts within the range of the radar, no "flickering" on the PPI, and none of the other TG units answered the tactical radio.

Jake ordered *Orca* to proceed on course 306 at maximum speed for the sea conditions, which proved to be ten knots, hoping to reconnect with the elements of TG 510.1 and intercept—*and* destroy—the remnants of the convoy.

And then the rain began.

* * * * *

LT Saburo Takashi led his charges north in heavy seas, the convoy now making a steady ten knots, *Kibuki's* radar showing no contacts whatsoever, aside from the four ships following two by two. The winds had picked up markedly since morning, and now rain pelted the bridge windshield, with the sky darkening noticeably. The remnants of PAMA-32 were still executing the same zigzag pattern as before, fifteen degrees on either side of the base course of 306. At ten knots, and in such heavy seas, *Kibuki's* active sonar was effectively useless, so Takashi would occasionally take his ship up to its maximum speed (in these conditions) of twelve knots, open up a good lead on the convoy, then slow to five knots and use his active sonar to search for submarines ahead. They had left the other escorts and the two torpedoed vessels behind, four hours earlier, and had not had any additional trouble so far.

But Takashi's luck was about to run out.

* * * * *

Cray had been shadowing the convoy on the surface just out of the escort's radar range, when the action began without them. Fortnoy ordered flank speed along the convoy's track as soon as he saw the flashes on the horizon. Out of range of the tactical radio, he could only imagine what was going on up ahead.

After ten minutes, radar reported three contacts up ahead. One appeared to be dead in the water, while the other two appeared to be milling about with no apparent purpose. It took *Cray* another half-hour to reach the battle scene. One contact off to port was a cargo ship ablaze, down by the stern, listing to port, and dead in the water, pitching and yawing in time with the heaving sea. Boats filled with men had been somehow put over the port side, despite sea conditions, and were clearing the ship. The blazing ship let off sufficient light to illuminate the rest of the battle scene.

Off *Cray's* starboard quarter was one of the radar-equipped escorts running hard and firing into the air what looked like a dozen depth charges (well, maybe not that many, but a lot). In company with the escort, the destroyer was off to one side and making bare steerageway, dancing ungracefully to the tune of the heaving sea around her.

Somebody below is getting a thorough going-over, Fortnoy thought, *and a huge hole is being blown in the ocean. And if we're on that escort's radarscope, she's ignoring us. That will be her mistake.* Fortnoy had decided to make his boat's presence known.

It's firing run completed, the escort was sitting in place, moving up and down with the increasingly violent ocean swells, its angle on the bow, Fortnoy estimated, starboard 80. Then the destroyer started a run. Fortnoy quickly decided to get a snap shot off at the bouncing, sitting duck. In a matter of seconds, two Mark-14s were on their way, half-a-degree spread, aimed directly at the escort, still heaving up and down in one spot with the motion of the sea, and about two thousand yards away.

Sit there, you sucker. You only have to stay put for about one and a quarter minutes, Fortnoy prayed. *And the sea gods have to cooperate!*

Not quite one and a quarter minutes passed, and *Iki* was hit, a flash of fire and a column of water rising from her hull amidships. Perhaps three seconds later, the second fish passed beneath her harmlessly as the upwelling ocean lifted the stricken ship from the torpedo's path. At almost the same moment, the *Shinryu Maru* capsized and the battle scene's source of illumination disappeared. The night was suddenly dark. Still, as an infuriated Hiriake Ito searched the scene for this new player, the dark looming presence of *Cray*, low in the water, heaving up and down, could not be missed.

* * * * *

By first light on February 26th, Takashi had begun to feel confident that the remaining four vessels of PAMA-32, under *Kibuki's* watchful eye, would make their way to Manila without further incident. After all, *Atsukaze* and his two sister ships had immediately counterattacked the enemy, and there was every possibility that they had prevailed. His only worry now was the weather, which was growing steadily worse. The sky was dark, the sea confused, with waves up to three meters high moving in all directions, and heavy wind gusts coming from the east.

Then there was a bright flash off *Kibuki's* starboard quarter followed by a loud explosion, and the lead cargo ship in that position, *Sanaye Maru*, burst into flame. Only then did his starboard lookouts report what could be three torpedo wakes in the heavy chop off their bow. As the stricken ship slowed and veered off to the right, Takashi maneuvered his ship down the barely visible trace of the nearest wake, and dropped a pattern of a half-dozen depth charges over the spot where the three wakes appeared to converge. Doubling back, he ordered a sonar search over the same area, but came up empty.

Hermit, a hundred and fifty feet below and five hundred yards to the north, had heard the explosions going off dead astern, and felt their now gentle push in the water as the shock waves dissipated past the pressure hull. *Hermit's* novice skipper had ordered his boat to clear the escort's search area as quickly as possible, and was soon planning just how to reposition his boat for another attack. Carter Vaughn mulled over just how two of his torpedoes could have possibly missed, even given sea conditions.

* * * * *

As *Iki* sank slowly, bobbing up and down, Ito ordered *Atsukaze* to be steered directly at *Cray*, picking up speed as the gap between them closed, intending to ram. But Jim Fortnoy had already ordered flank speed, and first ordering rudder full left, and then, when *Cray* was pointed almost directly at the oncoming destroyer, ordering rudder amidships, he maneuvered his boat so that it sped past the destroyer close aboard and along that vessel's port side. *Cray* crash-dived just after it passed the destroyer's stern. By the time Ito had *Atsukaze* turned and the course reversed to search for this second submarine, *Cray* was passing a hundred and fifty feet, on her way to two hundred.

Atsukaze then spent two hours echo locating, attempting to locate either of the two submarines Ito knew to be below. Finally, as the rains began and the wind increased to gale speed, Ito gave up the search and turned his ship north to rejoin the convoy.

* * * * *

At two hundred feet, more or less, Jack Petrosky in *Perro* had his hands full. He had to direct the efforts to save his boat, and also try to make sense of what was going on in the ocean above him.

Petrosky worried that possible slow venting of the main induction and air supply trunk as they flooded past the blown gaskets may have been leaving a trail of air bubbles. Or, another possibility, the initial pounding *Perro* received may have ruptured a fuel oil tank or a fuel line and there might be a telltale oil leak. In any case, he had been unable to shake the two ships above tenaciously attempting to either sink his boat or force it to the surface.

Depth control had been almost impossible; only the skill of *Perro's* diving officer, Joel Himmelfarb, had kept the boat within plus-or-minus ten feet of ordered depth. The DC (damage control) crew in the after torpedo room had been unable to staunch the leak in the sea valve casting. Any material stuffed into the crack quickly blew back out at them, but the DC crew was reluctant to forcibly pound anything into the crack, for fear of widening the crack and only making a bad situation much worse. Thus the after torpedo room bilge was flooding up past the deck plates, making the stern heavier and heavier, and the trim pump was continually losing suction to that bilge.

Isolating the compartment and pressurizing it would slow down the leak, but there was that dent in the hull to consider: What if pressurizing the compartment caused that weak spot in the pressure hull to give way completely?

Perro's stern planes were still noisy, but were working. The air conditioning had been secured when "Rig for Silent Running" was ordered, and the air in the boat was hot, rank, and wet. But battery capacity was already alarmingly low, so turning the air conditioning back on was out of the question. With the boat's trim giving problems, "Rig for Depth Charge" had to be breached to enable a bucket brigade to transfer water forward, keep ahead of the rising bilge water aft, and avoid grounding out the electrical motors. The dent in the pressure hull was scary alright, but appeared not to have affected the boat's watertight integrity — for now. Through it all, the sweating, the terrifying pounding, and the sheer anxiety, *Perro's* crew did everything Petrosky asked of them. *Perro's* drain pump, however, was not keeping up with the challenge, and the water level in all the bilges was still slowly rising no matter what he or his crew did.

Above, for the first three hours, the two ships taking turns making depth charge runs on *Perro* had managed to maintain contact, keeping the boat deep. After the first few runs, the second ship made only dry runs, dropping no depth charges. *Has it run out?* Petrosky wondered. But the second ship seemed to have an inexhaustible supply of the infernal devices, dropping patterns of anywhere from four to six over on top of *Perro* with each pass. And together with the depth charge explosions, the incessant pinging of their sonars, first from one, then the other, back and forth, was quickly driving everyone aboard the boat nuts. Then sonar reported the arrival of a third set of fast screws, and things above *really* got muddled. A torpedo — no, *two* torpedoes — in the water, an explosion, then, later, sinking and breaking-up noises. More fast screws reported, two sets, and then a submarine diving.

Two more hours of echolocating passed. Make that two more hours of incessant pinging, but — thank God! — no more depth charging. The boat was getting heavier and heavier. With the battery getting lower and lower, and, unable to maintain sufficient speed, despite Joel Himmelfarb's best efforts (and a bubble in the safety tank), the boat began to sink deeper and deeper — 250, 300, 325, 350, 380 feet. The boat's pressure hull was audibly straining with every foot of depth passed, and that dent in the after torpedo room hull was very much on everyone's mind. Finally — fast screws above fading.

Another half hour passed. *Perro* was now far below test depth, the deep depth gauge reading four hundred and fifteen feet.

Blowing noises, the other boat surfacing.

The other boat has *to be one of ours*, Petrosky reasoned. Confident that *Perro* was well clear of the other boat, he ordered his own boat to the surface, blowing all ballast tanks. The boat surfaced in a heavy storm, *Perro* bobbing in the water, and Petrosky almost slipped on the ladder while scrambling up to the bridge. A quick glace aft revealed a surfaced submarine also bouncing in the rough sea, silhouetted against a hazy early morning glare. Further east, the tossing underside of the capsized cargo ship was still visible. But Petrosky's only concern was the submarine.

It *is* one of ours!" Petrosky shouted. He ordered "This is Cowboy Three" sent out on tactical radio.

The response, "This is Cowboy Two, welcome topside, Three, the coast is clear," drew tears of grateful relief to *Perro's* skipper's eyes.

Jake had just arrived on the scene when *Hermit's* target, on the other side of the convoy from *Orca*, went up in flames. *Orca* had performed much the same maneuver that *Hermit* had, but from the west of the convoy rather than the east, and had submerged along the convoy's projected track, waiting to pounce. The sea was in such a state, with white-capped waves, and ten-foot swells, that periscope depth became fifty-six feet before enough of the scope could be exposed to see anything. Jake ordered *Orca* headed into the oncoming sea to minimize the boat's motion, and Hal Chapman, manning the periscope with difficulty because of the pitching deck under his feet, reported that the radar-capable escort had veered off to the east in search of whichever one of TG 510.1's boats had scored the hit. But now the convoy had scattered, the remaining three vessels taking off in different directions, and there was no way that *Orca* could get into position to dispatch any one of them.

"What about the cripple?" Jake asked Hal.

"Wait one." He adjusted the scope, slewing the handles right. "Okay. It's on fire, there's a good blaze aft of the wheelhouse, but it's got way on. Bearing, mark."

The QM of the watch, QMSN(SS) Henry Coons read "One-zero-three."

"That wasn't a very good bearing. The boat's bouncing around too much. Down scope," Hal ordered.

"Can we get into position to finish it off?" Jake asked.

"Possibly. How about we get a single-ping range on it?"

Jake ordered a single-ping range on the contact at 103. Sonar reported back that the boat was pitching too much to get a range

"Steer one-zero-three to close the target," Jake ordered (*Orca* had been making three knots). "Make turns for five knots," he ordered, bumping up her submerged speed to better close the target.

Seven minutes later, Hal raised the periscope again. He first did a three hundred and sixty-degree sweep. Besides the target, and in the early morning light, he couldn't see anything but waves washing over the scope lens. Jake ordered to boat up to fifty-five feet. "Can't find the escort at all," he volunteered. "Wait one. I think I have her."

With the boat at fifty-five feet, Chapman could barely make out the escort off in the distance. He couldn't see the other three ships in the convoy at all. "Bearing to escort."

"One-one-zero."

"Escort's pretty far away, Skipper, barely visible. My guess is about eight thousand yards, max. Probably still working over whoever's down there." Swinging the scope left, he put the crosshairs as best he could on the target. "Bearing."

"One-zero-one," Coons sang out.

"Down scope. Another lousy bearing, I'm afraid. Guessing range to be about six thousand yards. And it looks like they're putting the fire out, Skipper," Hal reported.

Another seven minutes passed. "Up scope." Hal had to swing the scope further left to observe the target. Bearing!"

"Zero-nine-nine."

"Fire's out, left bearing drift, and she's definitely farther away. My guess is seven thousand yards. Looks like she's gotten underway and we're losing her, Captain," Hal said.

"Yeah, and the weather's getting crappier and crappier, and if we surface to go after the AK, we'll have that escort on our back. Some days you just can't make a buck."

Perro had to wait until the engine intake and ventilation induction piping was drained before the boat's engines could be started and a much-needed battery charge begun. Once the diesels were on line, Petrosky raised Jim Fortnoy over the tactical radio.

"Cowboy Three, this is Cowboy Two, over."

"Go ahead, Two."

"Two has a dented pressure hull and blown gaskets on the engine intake and main induction valves. There is a cracked and badly leaking sea valve casting in the after torpedo room, and the bilges are flooded. And those are the problems we *know* about, over."

"Roger, Two. Sounds like you had a pretty good going over. Nothing for it but for you to head for the barn. Do you need us to escort? Can you dive? Are all electronics working? Over."

"Two can dive, once the can is full and the bilges dry, but not very deep, and most likely cannot stay down for long. All electronics are working. Thanks anyway, but negative on the escort. Over."

"Roger Two. We'll stick around for a bit anyway."

An hour later, the weather had deteriorated to the point where Petrosky was anxious about *Perro's* chances of making it to Midway. The swells were getting higher and the wind was blowing harder and gusting from the southwest. *At least the wind will be at the boat's back as we head to Midway, no aircraft will be flying in this muck, and in these seas diving the boat is out of the question anyway*, Petrosky thought.

So, on the morning on February 26th, *Perro* limped off in the direction of Midway, and *Cray* headed north to attempt a hook-up with the remainder of the Task Group.

Jake, waiting until the *kaibokan* had disappeared over the horizon, and with the cargo ship now long gone, surfaced *Orca*. An SJ radar sweep showed only one contact in the sea return, and it was headed away from *Orca*, steaming north-northwest at ten knots. It had to be the escort in search of the remaining convoy elements. Jake knew the escort had radar, and might now know *Orca's* location. But chances were, with the boat's low profile, and with the sea conditions, that *Orca* was lost to the escort's radarscope in the sea return. He ordered radar to keep watch on the contact just in case, and to notify him immediately if the contact changed course toward *Orca*. Fifteen minutes later *Hermit* surfaced, bobbing in the rolling waves.

The typhoon had changed course again, and was now headed due west, straight for a landfall on the southern end of the Philippine Island of Mindanao. As the eye of the typhoon passed over the warmer waters of the Kuroshio Current, just east of the Philippines, the typhoon gained in strength. The storm was now seven hundred miles wide, packed a hundred and eighty mile per hour winds around its eye, and was ambling along to the west at an uneven eight knots.

Perro was caught up in the outer bands of the storm, headed northeast, and on a propulsion charge. The boat was making turns for ten knots, but with the following seas was actually making more like thirteen over the ground. But following seas were also termed "pooping seas" for the danger of waves crashing down on the boat's stern, and pushing it violently forward. Pushed violently forward, the boat might very well then meet the next wave ahead straight on, and slew around broadside to the oncoming sea. Waves hitting broadside could then heel the boat over. Heel any vessel over far enough, and it *will* capsize. The safest course of action would be turning the boat into the wind and riding out the storm. Petrosky was well aware of the danger, but was also aware that by carefully paying attention to sea conditions and the boat's speed, *Perro* could "run before the sea," and actually gain time on her trip home.

Only once was control of the boat lost. An unusually high wave broke over the after deck, and before any corrective action could be taken, the boat was sitting in the depth of a trough, broadside to the oncoming waves to port. She heeled over a full twenty-five degrees to starboard before righting herself. Luckily enough, the next wave had far less power, and the quick reaction on the part of the OOD (the intrepid Lt. Himmelfarb), ordering a hard left rudder and a short burst of speed, turned the boat into the oncoming waves. *Perro* was then able to confront the angry sea more safely, if not more comfortably. Petrosky looked on the incident as a warning from the Almighty, and resolved to wait out the rest of the storm headed *into* the sea.

* * * * *

Kibuki was not so lucky. The *kaibokan* were not well designed to begin with, with her superstructure really being too high for the hull. Now, with the majority of her remaining depth charges secured topside, *Kibuki* was even more top-heavy. Lieutenant Saburo Takashi was well aware of the problem, but was then heading into the teeth of the typhoon, and it would have been outright murder to order any men on deck to stow depth charges below. Compounding the problem was the availability of only the starboard engine and the requirement to keep constant right rudder on to compensate. There was nothing for it but to keep *Kibuki* headed into the sea and try to ride out the storm.

As it rode the surging sea, the ship suddenly veered sharply to port. Too late, Takashi saw the rogue wave—it had to be forty meters high—tower over the starboard beam. *Kibuki* was lifted up high out of the water as if it was no more than a cork float on a fishing line, and then slammed down on her port side into the trough below. The rogue wave curled over the ship, rolling the vessel over as it advanced, its energy finally dissipated as it crashed onto the sea below, all foam and white water.

And when the wave was gone, so was *Kibuki*.

The *Sanaye Maru*, having unknowingly escaped *Orca's* murderous intentions, was making its way northwest, with the intention of escaping the worst of the storm by rounding the southern tip of Mindanao, placing the island's mountains between it and the oncoming storm, running west under Zamboanga, and then north to Manila. *Hermit's* torpedo, had it struck the ship below the water line, would have surely sunk her, but sea action had disturbed the torpedo's depth control mechanism, and it had broached, hitting the ship and exploding above *Sanaye Maru's* water line. Putting out the subsequent fire, and shifting ballast so as to list the ship to port and minimize flooding, her crew managed to get the ship back underway, and escape *Orca*.

But *Sanaye Maru* could not escape the oncoming typhoon. The driven sea began to pour more and more water into the hole in her side as the wave height increased, until the ship floundered, and the inevitable could no longer be denied. Too late, the order to abandon ship was passed. Men died trying to launch lifeboats in the height of the storm; others were washed over the side; still others went down with the ship.

The three other ships in the convoy, two cargo ships and the tanker, had the same, more or less obvious, plan: seek shelter from the storm by rounding the leeward, southern, tip of Mindanao, and then running west, making their way through the Zamboanga Straight north to Manila. It was there, two days later, that Ito found them, running north along the Mindanao coast.

* * * * *

Orca, in company with *Hermit*, had ridden out the storm more or less in the same spot where *Hermit* had torpedoed the *Sanaye Maru*.

Jake had reported to SUBPAC that "TG 510.1 attacked and sank one cargo vessel, one tanker, and two destroyer escorts. A third cargo vessel was damaged. A violent storm caused the TG to break off action, and caused TG leader *Orca* to lose contact with *Cray* and *Perro*."

SUBPAC responded with an encrypted message saying that ". . . both *Cray* and *Perro* have reported in. *Cray* was battle ready. *Perro* has been damaged and is returning to Midway." A rendezvous point was designated for TG 510.1 to reform and await further orders.

When they arrived at the rendezvous point the morning of March 1st, *Orca* and *Hermit* found *Cray* waiting for them. On reporting in, SUBPAC ordered TG 510.1 ". . . to proceed at best speed to intercept convoy designated GUPA-17 leaving Guam this date en route Palau and engage. Convoy consists of two merchants, one escort." The three boats took off due west at full speed to intercept the enemy.

TG 510.1 arrived at the intercept point just after midnight on March 2nd. Jake had selected a point halfway along the main shipping route between Guam and Palau, just northeast of Yap. Any point along the route was easily accessible to Japanese patrolling aircraft out of either Guam or Palau, and Jake warned the other Captains that their boats were very vulnerable to discovery from the air. He ordered the three boats to fan out along the probable route, and await the enemy — *Cray* to the west, *Orca* in the center, and *Hermit* to the east. TG 510.1 then settled in to wait.

The three boats did not have long to wait. Four hours after they arrived at the intercept point, *Orca's* SJ radar operator reported a line of three contacts, closest one at ten thousand yards, and heading toward the boat from the north-northeast. Jake sent a message to the other boats reporting the contacts. Within minutes all three boats had them on their PPIs.

Jake ordered "General Quarters, Torpedo Action Surface." He was on the bridge, and Hal Chapman was in the conning tower. There was a waxing half-moon biting through the haze high in the northern sky, and visibility was about six thousand yards. There may have been contacts out there, but nobody on the bridge could see them, no matter how hard they stared through their binoculars.

"Convoy course two-three-seven, speed nine knots," Louie Carillo reported up to the bridge from the chart plot, and Early Sender cranked the information into the TDC. The convoy, radar reported, appeared to be holding on a straight course, without zigzagging.

Jake grew suspicious. "I'll bet they have air cover. Make sure the SD radar operator stays alert. And warn the other boats," he called down to the conning tower.

Hal Chapman passed the word.

Let's assign target," Jake called down again. "There's one for each of us. We'll take the lead contact, *Hermit* the second in line, and *Cray*, the last in line."

Again, Hal passed the word to the other boats.

"Radar reports air contact, bearing zero-five-five, range six thousand," the conning tower talker shouted up to the bridge.

"Quick, Hal," Jake ordered, "Alert the other boats. Have 'em dive."

"Cowboy Two and Cowboy Four, this is One. Air contact bearing zero-five-five, range six thousand. Dive your boats, out," Hal sang into the tac radio.

"Cowboy Two, aye, out."

"Cowboy Four, aye, out."

Jake pressed the diving alarm. *Ah-ooh-gah! Ah-ooh-gah!* "Dive, dive," he spoke into the 1-MC. Four lookouts, a quartermaster, and Jake, in that order, scrambled down the conning tower hatch. Jake pulled the hatch lanyard taut as he hit the deck of the conning tower, waiting while the quartermaster dogged down the hatch. "Make your depth six-zero feet."

At periscope depth, with radar blind, all three submarines had to now rely on their periscopes and their sonars.

On the search periscope, Hal first did a three hundred and sixty degree sweep of the horizon and then concentrated on the reported bearing of the oncoming targets. "Nothing visible, Skipper."

"Aircraft?" Jake asked.

Hal adjusted the periscope lens to look upward, and did another sweep. "Nothing, Captain. Down scope."

"Very well."

And they waited.

Every seven minutes, Hal raised the scope for another observation. The third time he raised the scope, he reported, "I have something, Captain, a hull low in the water, looks like maybe a minesweeper, probably the escort, angle on the bow starboard two-zero."

"Have sonar get a single ping range to the lead target," Jake ordered. Sonar quickly reported back that the target range was 4,900 yards.

Early Sender cranked the new information into the TDC. "Course two-three-five, speed nine," he reported.

Jake changed *Orca's* course to starboard, so as to decrease the torpedo's gyro angle and to close the target. "CPA?" Jake asked Early.

"Five hundred yards in just under three minutes," he replied.

"Open outer doors forward, tubes one and two," Jake ordered, knowing he now had to act quickly. He let a minute pass and ordered another single-ping range, as Hal raised the scope for a final target bearing.

"Bearing."

"Zero-five-zero."

"Range, forty-seven hundred."

"I have a firing solution, Captain," Early Sender sang out.

"Fire one."

"One fired," the talker reported.

To Early Sender: "Spread the second torpedo two degrees right."

Early adjusted a knob on the TDC. "Two degrees right entered, Sir."

"Fire two!"

"Two fired."

"Sonar reports two fish in the water, hot, straight, and normal."

Less than thirty seconds had passed when the first explosion was heard. *Boom!* Hal was watching the action through the periscope. "We got her, Captain. Direct hit aft. Definitely a minesweeper. " Everyone waited for a second explosion, but there was none.

"One fish missed," Jake announced to no one in particular. Then another explosion was heard, followed closely by another.

Chapman swung the periscope left. "Can't see too much, Skipper. Hazy. Looks like a cargo ship. She's been hit on the side away from us. Chalk one up for Carter Vaughn."

Less than a minute later, another explosion was heard. *Boom!* Chapman swung the periscope further left. "Can't see anything, Captain. But I'll bet that that was Jimmy Fortnoy's work."

Another five minutes passed. Another explosion. Then again, several minutes afterward, another very loud explosion was heard. "What was all that, I wonder?" Hal said.

"Absolutely no idea," Jake said.

Ten minutes later, sonar reported breaking-up noises. Raising the scope, Chapman could see only *Orca's* target, still afloat, afire, dead in the water. "Minesweeper," he observed. "Wood hull. Hard to sink."

"Have the other boats surface and report in," Jake said, as he ordered *Orca* to the surface.

"This is Cowboy One. Two and Four surface and report, over," Hal spoke into the tac radio. The other two boats acknowledged the order and surfaced. It was first light, and the visibility was fair, about seventy-five hundred yards. Except for the minesweeper's burning, floating, hulk, and pieces of flotsam everywhere, they were alone. All three boats immediately lit off their diesels and began charging their batteries. From *Orca's* bridge, Jake used his binoculars to scan the surface, looking for men in the water. There were none. The other boats reported in:

"This is Cowboy Two. Three torpedoes expended, two hits. One AK sunk, over."

"This is Cowboy Four. Three torpedoes expended, two hits. One AK sunk, over."

"This is Cowboy One. Good shooting! One fired two fish, one hit. Target minesweeper still afloat. But that's only five explosions. We counted six. What gives? Over."

"This is Cowboy Two. Sixth bang was a bomb from that patrol plane. Dropped it about five hundred yards astern. No damage, but scared the crap out of Cowboy Two, over."

Laughing, Hal replied over the tac radio, "This is Cowboy One. Very well. Out."

It was obvious that TG 510.1 had made a clean sweep of convoy GUPA-17, and Jake so reported to SUBPAC.

SUBPAC responded with a congratulatory signal, and ordered the task group back to Midway.

Chapter 17

Back to Pearl: 8 March 1944 to 1 April 1944

The remnants of TG 501.1 arrived at Midway on March 8th.
Perro had arrived three days earlier, and the base repair crew took
one look at her, delivered her mail, filled her fuel tanks, loaded
provisions, and sent her on to Pearl. She left Midway the previous
day.

As senior boat, *Orca* was first in, followed by *Cray* and
Hermit.

Later, in a sweltering Quonset hut that served as, among
other things, SUBPAC Headquarters Midway, Jake, Jim Fortnoy,
and Carter Vaughn received their orders. *Cray* and *Hermit* were to
"relax and take a week's R and R on the island—it has some
excellent baseball fields—while the boats are topped off—fuel and
provisions—and then go right back out." Jake had expected *Orca*
to receive the exact same orders, instead, he heard, "*Orca* will top
off—fuel and provisions—and head for Pearl."

There was also a huge sack of mail awaiting the *Orca* on her
arrival at Midway. Jake had to leave the boat before mail call, but
when he got back there was a stack of mail awaiting him in his
cabin. Most were letters from Kate. He arranged them in
chronological order and began to read each, opening the letter
with the oldest date first. He devoured all thirty-four at one
sitting. They had been newsy letters, about the happenings on the
base, meetings with other Navy wives, how much she missed
him, and the wonder of the growing child in her womb. He
thought briefly about mailing his own forty-two page opus to

Kate before leaving Midway, but decided that *Orca* would arrive in Pearl before the letter got there, and he might just as well deliver it in person.

There was a knock on the bulkhead. When Jake looked up, he saw Hal Chapman standing there with a very worried look on his face and a letter in his hand.

"Hey Hal," Jake said, "what's up?"

"It's this letter. It's from Jill's sister. It says what Jill would never tell me. She's sick, Jake — sick bad. Her sister says that Jill is dying. Jake, Jill is all I have." Hal, the most composed person Jake had ever met, was on the verge of tears.

"Oh Hal, I'm so sorry. Let me see what I can do about getting you leave to see her when we get to Pearl."

"Can you do that?"

"I can try."

"Thanks Jake. I'd appreciate anything you can do."

During the entirety of *Orca's* sixth war patrol, new crewmember GM1(SS) Frenchie Eifel had slowly integrated himself into the rest of the crew aboard *Orca*, learning the boat's peculiarities, and earning the respect of the GQ team in the forward torpedo room. With Weapons Officer Early Sender's blessing, he had taken charge of the small arms locker and assumed all responsibility for the boat's guns.

After leaving Midway, and on the way back to Pearl Harbor, Early, with Hal Chapman's approval, had Eifel conduct gun drills and officer and petty officer training on all hand-fired weapons aboard: the M1 carbine, the .45 caliber pistol, and the Thompson submachine gun. By their second day out of Pearl, the gun crews were able to man and limber the guns in under a minute after being called away, and every officer and petty officer (Captain included) had fired each type of small arm from the cigarette deck.

It was during one of the last gun drills just before reaching Pearl that Early Sender had his accident.

After observing the gun drill, he was going down the ladder at the forward torpedo room hatch, when he slipped. Losing his footing completely, he fell hard onto the metal deck below, cleanly breaking the femur in his left leg. Doc Shields set the leg as best he could by feel, using wooden slats from a vegetable crate and adhesive tape to immobilize it. But he was also very happy that the doctors at the Pearl Harbor base hospital would soon be able to X-ray the leg and correct whatever mistakes he might have made in setting it.

At 0900 on a sunny and already hot Monday, March 13, 1944, *Orca* tied up to the pier at SUBASE Pearl. Jake spotted Kate on the pier. She was wearing the same yellow outfit that she had worn the last time *Orca* had returned from patrol. But all he could do was wave to her and see her wave back when his attention was diverted to the gangway that had just been set down between the boat and the pier. There, Adm. Lockwood and Capt. Macdonough had started to board the boat, but had graciously stepped aside and made way for Early Sender, who was being carried off the boat in a stretcher. Everyone watched with rapt attention as Early was loaded into the ambulance that was going to take him to the Base Hospital.

With *Orca* secured to the dock, Jake rounded up Hal and they went below to the wardroom to greet the commodore and the admiral.

In the wardroom, the admiral said, "Look, I won't keep you. I know Kate's waiting for you, Jake, so we'll make this short and sweet. You can give us a detailed debriefing tomorrow, 0900.

"But just let me say that this was a great patrol, Jake, Hal. You and the other three boats did one hell of a job. And I know you expected me to turn *Orca* around at Midway and let you get right back to it, but I called you back to Pearl for a couple of reasons. First of all, I've got a special job I need you to do, and second, there's the little matter of the presidential unit citation that we are awarding your boat and its crew."

"A PUC?" Jake asked, surprised. "For what?"

"For that little matter of rescuing those British and Aussie POWs last December. *Moray* and *Starfish* got PUCs too. Already awarded theirs. Aussies are also awarding all three boats their government's Meritorious Unit Citation. Four of your men — Coons, Arnold, Rogers, and Olds — will be awarded the gold Navy Lifesaving Medal, and the Pharmacist's Mate, Shields, will get a silver one. Dave Brandenburg in *Moray*, and John Waters in *Starfish* have been awarded the Navy and Marine Corps Medal for their boats' part in the rescue, and the Brits have awarded each of them their Distinguished Service Cross. And, oh by the way," Lockwood beamed, "you'll be getting both of those too. And I'm also recommending Navy Crosses for all three of you skippers for the jobs you did on *this* patrol."

"I'm flabbergasted," Jake said. "Really, I don't know what to say."

The Admiral chuckled. "You don't have to say anything. Just make sure you and your crew show up at the ceremony. Oh, and that will be Friday morning at 1000. Everybody in dress whites."

"Yes, Sir," was all Jake could think of to say.

After Hal and Capt. Macdonough had left the wardroom, Jake held the admiral back and asked about emergency leave for Hal. When he heard why Hal was requesting leave, Lockwood scowled. "That's tough," he said, "really tough, and since you're in port anyway I'm inclined to grant him leave. But with Sender out of commission, you're already down one officer, and with the mission I have in mind for *Orca*, you're going to *need* an XO. Any of your other officers ready to step up to that plate, even temporarily?"

"Not really. Louie Carillo is almost there, but not quite."

Lockwood scowled and stroked his chin, thinking. "Okay. Here's what I can do," he said. "*Perro's* gonna be down and out for a while, and Jack Petrosky's got an officer on board he's pretty high on. Name's Joel Himmelfarb. Made lieutenant last year. I was about ready to tap him for XO of one of the new boats being commissioned anyway. How about he rides with you for a while? He could be your acting XO and you could check him out. And that way Chapman gets to go on leave."

"Thank you, Admiral," Jake said. "Really, I can't thank you enough."

"Least I can do. Now you better get your butt topside and go find that pretty lady of yours."

"Yes Sir, Admiral, I'll do just that."

"And what was so damned important you left me standing here in the hot sun while you and Hal kibitzed with the brass? In case you hadn't noticed, there was this pregnant lady waiting out here."

Without a word, Jake took his wife into his arms and kissed her hello. He wasn't quite prepared, however, for the ardor with which she returned his kiss. When he finally stepped back to gaze into her face, he could see that she had that look in her eyes—a look he had seen before, a look that electrified and excited, a look that stirred him physically.

He stepped away, still holding her, but at arm's length. His eyes scanned downward, stopping at where she carried their unborn child. Kate watched his eyes as they moved, saw where his gaze had stopped, saw where they were fixated. When last Jake saw Kate, she had just started to show, but now she was swollen, her belly prominent. The baby was due, he recalled, the end of next month, late April, or maybe early May.

"Not exactly the sexpot you married, right?" she said, abruptly ending his reverie.

"Oh, God no, Kate, you look fine," he said, attempting to repair any hurt his staring at her belly may have caused. "You look uncomfortable is all, and it's my fault. I made you wait out here in the sun. I'm really sorry, honey, honest, but it couldn't be helped. It really *was* important."

Good recovery, she thought, but said instead, "Never mind that, you jerk. I'm hot and tired, and right now I'm so randy I can hardly stand it. Get me home!"

As Kate hustled Jake off the pier toward their Olds, he explained to her "what was so damned important." After taking it all in, and, as she lifted herself into the passenger seat, she said, "Oh, that's so awful about Hal's wife. I've never met her, of course, but Hal is so sweet that she must be a wonderful woman. It's all so sad. I'll pray for both of them, of course, and so should you."

Jake thought about that for a minute. He hadn't prayed for anything in a long time, not since he was a teenager. "Yeah," he said, finally, "perhaps I should."

"Oh, honey, I'm so sorry!" Kate said. "I got so wrapped up in poor Hal and Jill Chapman's troubles that I forgot to congratulate you on all those awards. And they're giving you a medal! *Two* medals! I *am* so proud of you!"

"No, you had your priorities in exactly the right order. Jill's being so sick is far more important than any medals . . ."

She gave him that look again. "Now get me home," she said, "so I can tear your clothes off."

Kate hadn't been joking about the immediacy of her physical needs. No sooner had Jake parked the car in the driveway, then she was out the passenger side door and on her way to the front door of the cottage. She opened the door wide and waited there impatiently for him, pulling him inside when he got there. Then she slammed the door shut and pulled him toward the bedroom. Never mind that despite an early morning shipboard shower he still exuded *Orca's* distinctive aroma of diesel fuel, cigarettes, and unwashed bodies.

Jake had always been the one to pace their lovemaking. But here was a new Kate, a Kate he had never met before. *What's gotten into her?* he wondered silently (yet thankfully). Though a bit astonished, he was cooperative. Kate pounced with an ardor that demanded he match it, with a seemingly bottomless need that promised to drain him and leave him wasted and breathless. It may have taken him a few seconds to match that demand, but match it he did, responding with very much the same passion.

Afterward, as they lay, for the time being sated and gasping beside each other, Jake looked again at his wife. He had seen her naked before, of course, but never like *this*. To anyone else, this bloated, distended woman was hardly an object of desire. For Jake, she was, more than ever, the most desirable woman on earth.

"What the devil was *that* all about?" he finally asked her.

"I haven't the slightest," she said. "But, for days now, since they told me you were on your way here from Midway, our making love was all I could think about—how much I wanted you, how badly I *needed* you.

"This war stinks, Jake, I hate that it keeps us apart. And I hate how I'm forced to live like a nun for days and weeks and months at a time, and how I suddenly feel like a nymphomaniac when you're finally home.

"And at the same time I feel so ugly, Jake, like a bloated, beached whale. I couldn't imagine you ever wanting me again, and I do so need you to need me and want me." She sniffled. "My God. I'm *so* screwed up!"

"No you're not," Jake said. "But war definitely does screw things up, so it makes us feel like we're all screwed up too. But we're not. We're only holding on tight to what keeps us sane. You, Kate, you keep me sane. You must know that no matter what, no matter what happens, I'll *always* love you, I'll always need you, and I'll always want you." Again, he gathered her into his arms, pressing his body against hers, passion reawakening. Slower now, less urgent. Different perhaps, but somehow with the same intensity.

＊ ＊ ＊ ＊ ＊

Joe Bob Clanton had settled into his room at the B.O.Q. He showered, and was getting ready to catch the bus into town to meet some of his engineering gang at the Royal Hawaiian, when there was a knock at the door. He opened the door to two somber-looking officers in dress blues: a lieutenant and a lieutenant commander. The lieutenant, he saw, wore a cross on his collar—a chaplain. He held an envelope in his hand and a small package.

"Lieutenant j.g. Joe Bob Clanton?" the lieutenant commander asked.

"Yessir," he said, "I'm Clanton."

The lieutenant commander identified himself as Lt. Cmdr. Painter, from the Base Administrative Staff, and introduced the lieutenant as "Chaplain Ryder." After that, he fell silent.

"I'm afraid," the chaplain, began, "we have some bad news for you. The last allotment check to your wife in Brisbane, Mister Clanton, was returned by the Australian authorities uncashed. When we inquired as to the reason," he handed Joe Bob the envelope, "we received this notification from the Queensland Territorial Government. I'm sorry to have to tell you this, but it appears that your wife has died."

Joe Bob stared back at the two men, uncomprehending. "Died?" he repeated. "Daisy *dead? How?*"

"The details are sketchy," the Chaplain continued. "The death certificate in that envelope simply lists 'death by misadventure.' But it appears that she was shot to death. The Navy is still making inquiries as to the details."

"Shot to death?" Joe Bob whispered.

"So it seems," Ryder answered. "As I said, the Navy is still getting the details. Is there anything I can do to help you?"

"No . . . no, that's okay. We were estranged. I've filed for divorce. Still . . . that's pretty awful. *Shot*, you said?"

"So it appears. When no one claimed the body, the Queensland Government ordered it cremated. These," he held out the package, "are her remains."

After the two men left, Joe Bob went back into the room, set the package on the bureau, and opened the envelope. Inside were a letter and a death certificate. The letter, to the Navy Department from the Territorial Government of Queensland, said pretty much what Chaplain Ryder had just told him. Terse and to the point. He looked at the death certificate. *"Name: Daisy Clanton, nee Norton. Date of Birth, 4 February 1924. Date of Death, 18 December 1943. Cause of Death: Misadventure."*

He tried to remember where he was on December 18th. *Oh, yeah*, he thought, *on the way back to Pearl from Midway. We had just dropped off those Aussie and Brit troops we fished out of the drink.* And when he came back to Pearl, he remembered, Daisy was gone. Now he was back in Pearl again, and Daisy was back too—all that was left of her. Ashes in a tiny box. Now she was really gone. Forever. Then Joe Bob laid down on the narrow bed and wept.

The next morning, March 14th, as Jake walked into Admiral Lockwood's office at 0900, Hal Chapman was already aboard a military transport plane en route to San Diego.

After Jake made his official report as Task Group 501.1 Commander, and once again received the admiral's commendations on a job well done, Lockwood described *Orca's* next mission.

"We got them on the run, Jake, and we're going to keep it that way." He unrolled a map, using various objects on his desk to stop it from curling back up: an inkwell, a paperweight, and the telephone. "This," he said, "is Biak Island. Just off the northern coast of the Dutch part of New Guinea. And this," he said, pointing at another spot on the map, a bit further to the east, "is Wakde Island. The Japs got 'em, and MacArthur wants both of 'em. Steppingstones to the Philippines. And the Navy is gonna help him get 'em. I want you and *Orca* to do a photo recon of these islands, and we need it yesterday.

"The technical aspects of the mission will be handled by PRISEC—the Photographic Reconnaissance and Interpretation Section, Intelligence Center. There's an officer from PRISEC assigned to the base, he'll be working with the shop, installing a bracket on your attack scope for the special camera we use. Damn thing is German—a Primarflex it's called. Apparently we can't make one near as good. Nothing we have today is even close. The Navy had to put ads in photographic journals and newspapers all over the country to find whoever owned one of these particular models and buy them up. They found a total of ten. You'll get to take one of them on this trip and a couple of enlisted guys from PRISEC who'll ride with you and show your people how to use it—*and* also to show you how to develop the pictures it takes. Oh yeah, the base will be setting up a darkroom and photo lab in your lower sound room.

"And, while you may have to scrape your crew back off the walls at the Royal Hawaiian, they'll only be getting a week's R and R. I want you back at sea next week, the latest, so that the PRISEC guy—lieutenant, name of James—so he can train your officers and crew on the equipment. You'll get a week of ISE to get ready, then it's off to the Solomon Sea."

Jake suddenly thought about Kate's probable reaction to the news that he'd only be in port for two weeks, and almost missed the admiral's next comment.

"And . . . oh yeah . . . Himmelfarb will be riding with you."

"Yessir," Jake said, recovering. "Himmelfarb. Right."

Hal Clanton stepped off the plane at North Island Naval Air Station on Thursday morning, March 16th. The weather was more or less perfect: bright sun in a cloudless sky, seventy-one degrees, with a light breeze. The air base was on the north end of Coronado Island, just outside of San Diego; and San Diego boasted year round near perfect weather. A bus transported Hal to the base visitors center, where he used a pay phone to telephone his sister-in-law, who lived on the island. Fifteen minutes later, she picked him up in her pre-war Plymouth coupe.

Christine Parker was Jill's pretty younger sister. Like Jill, she was a blue-eyed brunette. She wore a blue, print sundress and a concerned expression.

"How is she?" was Hal's first question, after they exchanged greetings.

"Not good. She perked up a bit when she heard you were on your way home, but Mom says she's just been hanging on 'til you got here. She's so weak, Hal, so thin, and no color. I'm afraid you'll barely recognize her."

"And the doctors *still* have no idea what's wrong with her?"

"No, they don't. Every theory they come up with eventually gets shot down. Last one was that it might be a brain tumor. But if there is one, they can't seem to find it. I think that now they're just whistling in the dark."

To replace the ferry that had served its purpose before, the Navy built a pontoon bridge between the island and the California mainland. Chris drove them across it. "We going to Balboa?" Hal asked, meaning Balboa Naval Hospital.

"No. To your house. They sent her home two days ago. Mom moved into the guest room. She's been taking care of her, keeping her comfortable."

"You mean the doctors have given up on her," Hal said, dejected.

Chris sighed. "I'm afraid so."

Friday, March 24th, dawned hot and foggy. By 0900, the fog still persisted, the sun trying hard to bite through it, a bright yellow orb still clothed in a gray shroud.

The admiral preferred to hold such assemblies at dockside rather than on the ostentatious parade ground on the upper base. After all, *Orca* herself, a gray eminence in the background, was in every sense just as much a recipient of the Presidential Unit Citation as was her crew.

Dressed in his crisp, dress white uniform, Jake stood alone in front of his officers in line behind him. Behind them, in three neat rows, *Orca's* enlisted stood, also in fresh, dress whites. For Jake, aside from the choke collar, the bright, white, cotton uniform was not all that uncomfortable, even with the ceremonial sword, a dead weight hanging by his side.

Facing *Orca's* assembled crew was Admiral Lockwood and his staff, dressed in the same uniform as Jake and his officers, but with a greater preponderance of gold braid. Behind them was a more or less ragtag audience of wives, girlfriends, just plain friends, neighbors, and other onlookers. Jake was happy to see that some thoughtful person had provided Kate and another expectant mother in the crowd with chairs.

The ceremony was also thankfully brief, taking a little more than half an hour. Besides awarding the PUC and the medals, the admiral had also announced some promotions: Ens. William Salton to Lieutenant, Junior Grade, EN1(SS) Richard Richards to Chief Engineman, and GM1(SS) Roland Eifel to Chief Gunner's Mate. Salton had already known about his promotion, but the new chief petty officers did not. Once again, all the bunks in *Orca's* goat locker — the chief's quarters — would be filled.

Twenty-six hundred miles to the east, Jill Jeanerette Chapman slipped quietly and peacefully away into endless sleep while her husband held her hand.

The enlisted camera experts from PRISEC who would ride *Orca* on the mission turned out to be two photographer's mates: PhoM1 Robert Allessi and PhoM1 Stanley Huff. Neither sported white dolphin patches on the right forearms of their dress blues, Jake noted, so neither one was a qualified submariner. They did prove, however, to be well qualified in periscope photography.

Orca was back at sea for ISE at first light on Monday the 27th. Since photographs had to be taken in daylight, that meant the boat would be returning to port as soon as it got too dark to photograph. Kate's ire was abated somewhat by the fact that her husband would at least be sharing her bed during *Orca's* week of ISE. Jake was pleasantly surprised by the stoicism Kate displayed when he told her that *Orca* would be going back out on patrol on the following Saturday, April 1st. It never occurred to him that she might be putting on a show for him, and that she cried frequently when he wasn't around.

"You need a bracket to hold the camera steady," Lt. Philo James explained to Joel Himmelfarb and the conning tower watch. "Try and hold the camera up to the scope with just your hands, and your exposures will be so fuzzy they'll be useless." He would be repeating the same message to each of the three groups of watch standers that rotated through the conning tower during the day.

"This camera is a Bentzin Primarflex," James continued. "It's a kraut camera with a single-lens, reflex viewfinder and a focal-plane shutter. You really don't need to know what that means, but trust me, this baby is ideal for periscope photography. The beautiful thing about this camera is that what you see in the viewfinder is just what you would see if you were looking through the periscope. You see exactly what the camera sees.

"You need to get in as close as possible to the coastline you'll be photographing, but, of course, there are practical limitations. You'll be at periscope depth, of course, that's sixty feet, and your skipper probably won't tolerate anything less than another twenty feet under the keel. So you're limited by the coastal water depth. Then again, most of these Pacific islands have coral reefs—something else to worry about. Five hundred yards from the coast is ideal, but sometimes you'll have to settle for a mile. Just get in as close as you can.

"You'll need to have six feet of scope out of the water. More would be better, of course, but the scope will be up for what you guys would probably consider a long time—long enough to shoot a whole roll of film, twelve exposures — and it would probably be a good thing if it didn't stick up so high and for enough time that anyone on the beach could spot the scope.

"This week we'll be practicing along the local coastline, so you'll have good depth charts, and no worries about mines — because here we know exactly where those babies have been sowed. I don't know exactly where you guys are going, but wherever that is, I know the Navy will give you the best information they have available on conditions there.

"Like I said, you'll shoot a whole roll of twelve pictures for each periscope exposure. The field will be eight degrees in high power, and you'll rotate the periscope about four degrees after each camera shot to get a picture overlap of three or four degrees. Before you expose each roll of film, you have to fix the position of the submarine accurately based on landmarks. You note this position on the chart, writing on the chart the number of the film roll that you expose in that position. Vectors are also drawn on the chart to show the included angle covered by that roll of film. After you expose that roll, the boat moves down the coast and repeats the whole process all over again. You want an overlap of about fifty percent on each successive film roll to make sure you don't miss anything.

"Allessi or Huff will then take the exposed film rolls below and develop them, mounting each photo so as to match with the one next to it. That way you'll generate a continuous panorama of the coastline. If, for any reason, any of the pictures aren't any good, you'll have to take them over again. Always easier to get 'em right the first time.

"Okay, that's the process. I know it sounds complicated, but trust me, once we do this a couple times you guys will get the hang of it easy. So let's get to it!"

And so it went for the next five days.

On Friday night, March 31st, the last day of scheduled ISE, a crew from the base was awaiting *Orca's* arrival dockside. That night, while the rest of her officers and crew slept ashore, Bucky Buckner oversaw *Orca's* replenishment and readiness for sea. Room was found for several cases of unexposed film.

On Saturday morning, April 1st, on an otherwise bright, sunny, cheerful day, a packet of orders from JICPOA, the Joint Intelligence Center, Pacific Ocean Area, awaited Jake when he arrived at the boat. He and Kate had already said their goodbyes, and he accepted the packet with a heavy heart.

Chapter 18

Seventh Patrol: 1 April 1944 to 29 June 1944

Lieutenant j.g. Joe Bob Clanton stood on *Orca's* cigarette deck gazing out to sea. The night was crystal clear, the moon was waxing full and high, and the sea, a sheet of smoked purple glass, was disturbed only by *Orca's* bow wake and her efflorescent trail. *Orca* was three days out of Pearl headed west-southwest in a hurry, generating a gentle wind as she cut through the otherwise still air, four engines coughing diesel smoke into the night.

It was 0200, but Joe Bob didn't have the midwatch. Harry Hastings had it, and he was up front, on the bridge. The four lookouts, stationed above him in the shears, searched the horizon through their binoculars. Joe Bob was not alone, but he might as well have been. Nobody there was paying much attention to him, leaving him alone to think his thoughts. In his hands, he held the little box that the chaplain, Lt. Ryder had given him — the box that held all that was left of his wife Daisy.

He thought that maybe, given what he was about to do, he should perhaps say a prayer. He thought he probably could remember the Lord's Prayer if he put his mind to it, but it had been a long time. Joe Bob believed in God, all right, but he didn't think that God was all that much concerned about Joe Bob Clanton, or any other individual for that matter.

He stumbled through the Lord's Prayer as he opened the box, stopping and starting the phrases over again twice, so that forgotten words might come back automatically. When he finished the prayer, he turned the box over, dumping its contents slowly over the side. The ashes, almost white in the moonlight, were caught up in the breeze and scattered, carried away and swirling out of sight. When the box was empty, Joe Bob tossed it over the side as well, and hoped that God had heard his prayer and was at least a *little bit* concerned about Daisy.

Ten days after departing from Pearl, on Tuesday, April 11th, 1944 *Orca* arrived off the northern coast of Dutch New Guinea, in the Solomon Sea.

The packet of orders from the Joint Intelligence Center, Pacific Ocean Area, or JICPOA, were very clear. JICPOA specified the exact photographic coverage it wanted, and provided all the charts, tidal data, list of navigational aids and landmarks, and aerial recon photographs that would be needed.

Orca was to first proceed to the north coast of Dutch New Guinea, southwest of Wakde Island, and photograph the mainland coastline around the village of Arare. From there, they were to proceed further down the coast to a point due south of the Island, a village called Toem. Not mentioned in *Orca's* orders, one or both of these coasts was to be selected for the initial landings, a staging point for the actual invasion of Wakde. No minefields were expected along this section of coastline, as the enemy had no known installations there.

Next, the tiny island immediately south of Wakde, Insoemanai Island, was to be reconnoitered. It would be captured to serve as an artillery platform for the actual invasion of Wakde Island — again, a fact not revealed in the JICPOA directive — and, finally, the entire southern coastline of Wakde Island, from its westernmost tip to the easternmost tip, a distance of about five miles. There were no known minefields around Insoemanai or on this side of Wakde Island. There were, however, known minefields on either side of the channel approaching the harbor on the northern side of the Island.

With Wakde reconnoitered, *Orca* was to proceed up the coast northwest to Biak Island. The Bosnek-Sorido coast of Biak was to be photographed, a distance of about fifteen miles. Here, Jake correctly assumed, would be the site of the actual amphibious assault on the island. Again, JICPOA noted no known minefields along this coast of Biak Island. There were known minefields, however, on the north shore of the island along the approaches to Korim Bay. But who could say that the Japanese had not sowed other mines off the Biak Island coastline?

Jake's biggest concern, however, was operating in the shallow waters of the littoral shelf off New Guinea. Although the waters off New Guinea (the Solomon Sea) contained some of the deepest water in the pacific (the New Britain Trench, for example, was some 30,000 feet deep), *Orca* would be operating close to the mainland, where the water was nowhere near as deep. While the Dutch Admiralty charts JICPOA provided showed soundings of 60 meters (197 feet) 500 meters (547 yards) off the Arare coastline, some of the recorded depths off Insoemanai Island were much shallower: 25 meters (82 feet). A submarine's lease on life depended on being able to disappear into the deep — the operative word being "deep."

The charted depths off the Bosnek-Sorido coast of Biak Island were not much better, with some readings as shallow as 32 meters (105 feet).

Nonetheless, *Orca* was there to do a job, and the photographing began during the midmorning of April 11th, with the boat in starting position two miles west of Arare and five hundred yards off the coast. The coastline there consisted of about two hundred yards of beach that ran up into a tangle of palm trees and jungle, with no sign of life.

As the boat proceeded more or less westward along the coast, Jake was gratified to find that the Dutch charts matched *Orca's* fathometer readings. As it was along the Hawaiian coast where they had practiced for this mission, the biggest challenge was maneuvering the boat and maintaining a straight course between the selected landmarks. The next biggest challenge proved to be establishing the landmarks themselves.

344

While all of *Orca's* officers had received the training, somehow the job of periscope photographer devolved onto the new acting XO, Lt. Joel Himmelfarb. Jake had to admit that he was impressed by Himmelfarb's performance in that role, and so gave his passive acquiescence to the arrangement. He had observed the young man carefully, and had to admit that the handsome, likeable, black-haired, and dark-eyed Jewish boy from Brooklyn, New York, appeared to be competent and intelligent.

Himmelfarb also worked well with Lt. Lou Carillo, his navigator, who, when required, manned the search periscope and helped pinpoint the more obscure landmarks. Carillo was actually senior to Himmelfarb, but didn't seem to mind that he was now reporting to his junior. Otherwise, the search scope was used by whatever OOD had the watch to make regular three hundred and sixty-degree sweeps in search of intruders. Aside from an occasional fishing canoe out to sea and off in the distance, however, there had not been any close-in contacts sighted.

But progress was slow, and by the end of good daylight on the first day, they had only produced photographs of the first two miles of the coastline, and had made it only as far as Arare itself. It wasn't until they reached Arare that they observed any signs of human habitation along the shoreline. There they saw huts built up on stilts with walls of bamboo woven with palm, and palm-thatched roofs. The nearest were about a hundred yards from the shoreline and reached back into cleared jungle. Brightly painted canoes fitted with log outriggers were pulled up on the beach, and bronze-skinned native Papuans, oblivious to their offshore observers, went about their business: old men mending nets, bare-breasted women arranging fish on drying racks, children playing.

At dusk, *Orca* retired from the shoreline to head back out to sea where, after dark, the boat would surface and recharge batteries. On the way out, Bill Salton, standing OOD watch on the periscope, observed the fishing canoes, which had stood out to sea during the day, heading back inshore. He was careful to keep the scope down while they passed overhead to return to their village.

Jake was concerned with their lack of progress on the first day.

"Not to worry," PhoM1 (Photographer's Mate, 1st Class) Allessi, assured Jake, as he and PhoM1 Huff showed Jake the photographic panoramas they had produced in the tiny darkroom set up in the depths of the lower sound room. "These are some really good shots, and everybody starts slow. You'll see, Captain, we'll do much better tomorrow." Jake hoped he was right.

At dawn on Wednesday, once again, *Orca,* heading inbound for the Arare shore, silently passing under the outbound canoes on their way to the fishing grounds.

The crew did indeed do much better that day, completing the run down the coast line to two miles past Toem with daylight to spare. Toem proved to be a twin to Arare, although perhaps a little smaller. It was when *Orca* was at periscope depth and outbound back to deep water that what came to be termed "the incident with the canoe" occurred.

Bill Salton was once again the OOD, and had just raised the scope to do a routine look around when he found himself staring directly at a fishing canoe. Aboard the canoe, two Papuan natives were staring right back at him. He hurriedly lowered the scope and called Jake to the conning tower. Joel Himmelfarb was right behind him.

"What's up, Bill?" Jake asked. Salton described what had just happened. "Okay," Jake said. "And how long ago was that?"

Salton quickly checked the ship's log and his watch. "Eight minutes ago, Captain."

"All right. Let's take a look . . . up scope." When the scope was up Jake began a slow sweep, and then stopped dead. "Holy smokes!" he exclaimed. He stepped back from the scope and motioned to Himmelfarb. "Take a look at this Joel. You won't believe it. These guys are tailing us."

Himmelfarb manned the scope. "Holy . . . you're right, Skipper. I don't believe it. Okay if I get a picture of this?"

"Go for it. We can show it to Pacific Command and see if they think it compromises our mission or not."

* * * * *

"That Lieutenant Himmelfarb, Captain," Huff opined, "he's a natural with the camera."

Jake examined the pictures that Joel Himmelfarb had taken just an hour earlier, the paper still damp from the developing tray. They showed two wiry Papuan natives, standing in an outrigger canoe, in various poses, smiling and waving at the periscope camera, almost as if they knew they were being photographed.

"Mr. Himmelfarb shot the whole roll, and some of the other shots were pretty good, too, but these were the best. Like I said, Captain, he's a natural with the camera."

So it would seem, Jake thought. *And these two seem friendly enough.*

After Huff left, Jake reviewed the incident in his mind, evaluating its importance. *Even if those two guys in the canoe say something to the Japs, they didn't meet us close enough to the shore for the Japs to figure out what we were doing. And that's if these guys even talk to Japs. And, nowhere near those two villages did we see any sign of Japs – nobody in uniform, no Jap patrol boats, not even a building that looked like it might have a Jap inside it. Nothing. Well, we've reported what happened. Let's see what Pacific Command thinks.*

Pacific Command's response was brief and clear: *"Incident noted. Proceed as previously ordered."*

"So be it," Jake mused. "Proceed as ordered. Tomorrow, off Insoemanai, we won't have near as much water to work in, and I'm betting it will be a lot busier."

Joel Aaron Himmelfarb was born in Pforzheim, Germany, December 29, 1919, the son of Isaac Himmelfarb, a Jewish diamond cutter, and his wife Leah. Their ancestors had lived in Germany for at least two hundred and fifty years, and the

Himmelfarbs, while they were devout Orthodox Jews, were also *thoroughly* German. Their second son, Joel, was one of four children born in Germany.

In 1930, when Joel was not yet 11, the Himmelfarb family boarded a steamer bound for New York City. Such was the demand for skilled diamond cutters on New York City's international diamond exchange, that the Diamond Dealer's Club had extended an invitation from that organization to skilled diamond cutters in both Germany and Belgium to come to America.

The Himmelfarbs made their home in the Bedford-Stuyvesant section of Brooklyn, in a rambling two-story house

From the first, Joel strained against the confines of a strict upbringing. The attractions of the wider outside world beyond "Bed-Sty" called to him.

In his teenage years, Joel came to the realization that he was not like other boys. Girls were not sexually attractive to *him*, or he to *them*. Instead, he was attracted to other boys. Being raised in an Orthodox Jewish family, however, Joel was well aware of the Torah's condemnation of any man who acted on such inclinations.

Joel was expected to follow his father into the diamond business, but he had other aspirations. He wanted to leave home and attend college. When his father flatly refused to indulge his second son's ambitions, Joel researched various institutions of higher learning that would give him his coveted college education for free. He sought, and obtained, admission to the Naval Academy.

Annapolis was the farthest away he had ever been from Brooklyn. In June, 1940, Joel graduated near the top of his class, and after a year in the surface fleet, he applied for submarine school. His first duty station in submarines was in the newly re-commissioned *S-48* out of New London. After just seven months aboard *S-48*, he pinned on his dolphins. In August, 1943, Lt. j.g. Himmelfarb was reassigned to *Perro* out of Pearl Harbor, where he served as Engineer Officer under Jack Petrosky.

348

Circling the coastline of Insoemanai Island on Thursday proved no more eventful than the previous two days. If a sudden rainsquall had not interrupted the picture taking, they would have finished with Insoemanai that day and begun on the Wakde coastline. But as it was, they were lucky to have the Insoemanai coast completed by the end of the day.

On Friday, Himmelfarb started photographing the west end of the southern shoreline of Wakde Island, moving east. The aerial photographs JICPOA had provided showed an airstrip along the length of the island, running east and west, but nothing associated with it was visible from the sea — no outbuildings, not even some sort of a control tower.

There was a brief moment of concern when a truck sped by along the beach, but it never stopped, and never gave any sign of spotting *Orca's* scope.

The soundings dropped off quickly as the boat approached the narrow strait separating Wakde and Insoemanai, and Jake had to give permission to continue photographing when the soundings were approaching eighty feet. As it turned out, the shallowest fathometer depth encountered was eighty-one feet. Once through the Wakde-Insoemanai strait, it was time to call it a day and head back out to sea.

On Saturday, *Orca* completed its photo recon of the Wakde Island coastline. Beginning where they left off the day before, just east of Insoemanai Island, the boat worked further eastward. The shoreline with much like that photographed the day before, until the boat worked its way around the promontory that jutted out toward the New Guinea coast. Once the boat was clear of the promontory and working eastward, signs of human activity began to appear — a building along the beach, then a short dock. People moved about the dock, a dozen or more half-naked Japanese soldiers, oblivious to the periscope offshore. Once the boat was past these landmarks, the shoreline returned to its previous dullness.

Strangely enough, for an island with a landing strip as its major topographical feature, there appeared to be no planes flying. The information provided by JICPOA did say that the allies had maintained control of the air now that Army and Navy aircraft had reduced the Japanese base at Rabaul to rubble.

With this leg of the operation complete, *Orca* made her way back out to sea.

Sunday morning found *Orca* off the southern coast of Biak island. In contrast to Wakde, Biak was a busy place; a roadway that ran along the entire coastline that *Orca* was to recon saw continuous and regular vehicular traffic.

There were also coral reefs along the entire coast, and most of these were close into the shoreline.

Orca worked her way east. Sorido was a village of stilt-mounted huts, a dozen or so built in the shallow waters just beyond the reef. Each hut had what appeared to be a small dock, and native islanders in canoes were moving between the huts. Up past the village of Sorido, the beach stretched out flat for about a mile, where it gave way to what appeared to be vegetated cliffs.

The boat was able to move closer and closer to the shoreline as it approached the village of Borokoe, another dozen or so houses of bamboo and plaited palm built up on stilts, this time on the beach itself. More native islanders, no Japanese soldiers.

As the boat moved east, it was able to move closer inshore and take some good photos of the next village, Menoebaboe. It looked very much like the villages on the mainland, no Japanese soldiers, and far more natives.

Beyond Menoebaboe, and before the next village, Sboeria, was an airstrip, shown on the air recon photo as Mokmer Airfield. No aerial activity whatsoever was seen. At Sboeria, daylight failed, and *Orca* stealthily made her way back out to sea. Either everybody ashore was blind, or simply uninterested. Nobody noticed the periscope sticking up high out of the water not a half-mile offshore.

And so it went, from April 17th through Thursday the 20th. Orca continued her shore reconnaissance moving from one village to another: Sboeria to Mokmer, Mokmer to Parai, to Ibdi, on to Mondom, and then to Bosnek. Aside from several gun emplacements, the only feature worthy of note on this entire stretch of beach was the continuous vegetated cliffs inland.

On Friday, *Orca* completed its mission at Biak Island, moving from Bosnek to Soriari, yet another busy village of native huts built on stilts. Here the entire shoreline consisted of very little beach and fairly high coral cliffs. By midafternoon, *Orca* was back in the Solomon Sea proceeding east southeast along the northern coast of New Guinea, headed for the "U.S. Advanced Base in New Guinea" at Port Moresby. General MacArthur was there, and he wanted to see those recon photos.

"I'm glad that's over, Captain," Joel Himmelfarb confided to Jake. "It was nerve-wracking. I was sure any minute some guy on the beach would start jumping up and down, pointing at me looking at him through the periscope."

Jake laughed. "Yeah, well, isn't that pretty much what happened off Arare?"

"True that. But Skipper, we were well off the coast at the time, and they never actually caught us in the act of photographing the coastline."

"Right. Probably why the powers that be decided we should finish the job."

Himmelfarb looked pensive for a bit, then said, "One thing, Captain . . ."

"Yes?"

"That coastline we just finished photographing, off Biak . . ."

"What about it?"

"Those cliffs just off the beach. Why land there? Wouldn't the Japs just sit on top of those cliffs and pick our guys off as they tried to land?"

Now Jake grew pensive. "That would be my guess," he said. "I sure hope MacArthur knows what he's doing. It's possible — just possible — that he knows more about Biak Island and the Japs than we do."

Orca rounded Paga Point and entered the protected harbor at Port Moresby Sunday afternoon, April 23rd. Jake stood on the bridge and surveyed the harbor. It was hot, very hot, the sun was shining brightly, and yet it was raining: a soaking deluge that had started without warning. *Orca* had been directed to the pier off Granville East, a makeshift city of ten huge pyramid tents that housed the Army and served as headquarters for the U.S. Advanced Base in New Guinea.

Just as *Orca's* line handlers were securing the lines passed over from the dock, the rain stopped as suddenly as it had begun. Jake as well as everyone else topside was soaked to the skin. Through it all, the sun had been very much in evidence, and now it was raising steam from wet clothing. The dockside line handlers had less of a problem in that regard; they were dressed only in shorts, and showed off magnificently bronzed bodies. They also seemed immune to the cloud of mosquitoes that descended on *Orca* as soon as the rain had stopped.

Looking out from dockside, Jake saw gun emplacements, tanks, trucks, jeeps, motorboats, and a whole fleet of amphibious "alligators." Anchored off in the distance were four LSTs (Landing Ship, Tank) and a squadron of PBY Catalina flying boats. But aside from the machine products of the 20th Century, the "U.S. Advanced Base" looked as if it had not advanced very far at all. Port Moresby appeared to be simply a temporarily inhabited clearing in the jungle — one that the jungle would certainly reclaim one day soon. There were only one or two "permanent" structures: small Quonset huts. Otherwise, there were only those neatly arranged huge pyramid tents, bordered by native villages: more bamboo and plaited-palm huts on stilts. Everything else visible was mountainous jungle. It was hard to believe that, for two long years, the Japanese had fought bitterly to dislodge the Allies from this little bit of paradise. And now, lucky for us, it was firmly and forever in Allied hands — the fortunes of war.

What Jake could not see from *Orca's* bridge was Port Moresby's real purpose for existence: the seven airfields that had been carved out of the jungle, radiating out from the port that supported them like spokes on a wheel. Each one was named for its distance from the port: Three-Mile Air Drome, Five-Mile Air Drome, Seven-Mile Air Drome, and so on, Twelve, Fourteen, Seventeen, Thirty. Manned mostly by U.S. Army Air, but also by Royal Australian Air, these bases housed light and heavy bombers, fighters, reconnaissance, and support aircraft.

By far the best thing about Port Moresby was the bag of mail that awaited *Orca* there. Jake found a stack of letters delivered to his stateroom. There were two letters from his mother, but most of them were from Kate. As was his practice, he arranged these in reverse chronological order, and began reading the oldest one first. They were very much like those he had received before — newsy, narrating stories of the people and events on the base, and comments on what was going on in the national news: The Democrats were expected to nominate FDR to run for an unprecedented fourth term at their convention in Chicago this Summer, and the Republicans were expected to rally around New York Governor Tom Dewey as their candidate.

Kate had always been vocal about her support for Roosevelt and his New Deal, and Jake had voted for FDR the first time he was old enough to vote, in 1932, and then again in 1936. But when he ran for an unprecedented consecutive third term in 1940, Jake had to ignore the sour feeling in the pit of his stomach in order to vote for him again. This time, if he really did run again, Jake had already decided that four terms were two too many, and he was going to vote for whoever the Republicans ran against him. But he would share that bit of information with Kate only if pressed.

Kate's letters also expressed her exasperation with her size, and lack of any ability to be comfortable whenever and however she lay down to sleep. She really couldn't wait for this baby to put in *his* appearance (she was still certain it was going to be a boy).

There was also a sensual undercurrent in these letters not present before. They were not pornographic in any sense of the word, of course, but they expressed a longing for him, a need for his physical presence, his touch, that she had never before verbalized. Jake thought about this, and realized that while he had always felt exactly the same way about Kate, he had never been able to express the depth of his feelings for her, not with the spoken word, and *certainly* not in writing. Now he envied that ability in Kate.

He thought about his own multi-page letter to his wife, the one he would be posting to her later that day. It was boring and bland in comparison to these. Still, it said all he was capable of saying, and he hoped with all his heart that it would be enough for her.

MacArthur insisted that the officer in charge of *Orca's* photoreconnaissance remain available to answer questions regarding the boat's handiwork. So it was that Joel Himmelfarb had to report to General Headquarters, Southwest Pacific Area, for the week of April 23rd, nominally reporting to Rear Adm. William M. Fechteler. It was Fechteler who was in overall command of the Wakde-Biak operation, codenamed Operation Hurricane. Joel was introduced to the Admiral briefly, and was commended on what a fine job *Orca* and her crew had done. After that, he was sequestered for the remainder of the week in a sweltering remote corner of one of the pyramid tents, surrounded by maps, paperwork, recon photos, and Army and Navy intelligence gurus.

As *Orca's* commander, Jake was required to put in an appearance at a Tuesday evening reception, there to meet the brass, including Admiral Fechteler and General MacArthur. The uniform for the reception was undress whites, open-collared, white, cotton shirt and trousers, a uniform designed for the tropics. But Port Moresby's heat and humidity were such that Jake was soaked through to his skivvies by the time he reached the air-conditioned Quonset hut where the reception was held.

Fechteler was Jake's height, broad-shouldered, with a meaty face and a ready smile. He held Jake in brief conversation, commenting on the great job the submarine force had done in taking the war to the enemy until the rest of the fleet could catch up with them. He impressed Jake as a competent, no-nonsense commander — most likely an officer who led from the front. His résumé, to date, Jake knew, had been impressive: Academy; Class of '16; the battleship *Pennsylvania* in WWI; and, more recently, commander of the destroyer, *Perry,* and the battleship *Indiana.* Fechteler had just been promoted to Rear Admiral, and was now in command of Amphibious Group Eight, which would provide Naval support for the Army for Operation Hurricane. *(Fechteler was eventually promoted to Admiral and appointed Chief of Naval Operations.)*

General Douglas MacArthur was taller than Jake, unsmiling and grave — *and* a bit paunchy. Jake's first impression of the man was that he was a bit vain — he wore his dyed hair in a comb-over to cover his bald pate. Jake was only able to shake hands with the general, receive a brief greeting, and to be thanked for the role *Orca* played in the upcoming operation. What Jake took away from their meeting was a lasting impression of the General's voice: sonorous, impressive, commanding. MacArthur had a voice that reminded Jake of his boyhood and the then minister of his church, a name now forgotten.

General MacArthur, the Supreme Commander for the Allied Powers, Southwest Pacific Area, had graduated first in his '03 class at West Point, served honorably and gallantly in WWI, and had twice been recommended for the Congressional Medal of Honor (which was twice refused him). Between the wars, MacArthur had served as Superintendent of the U.S. Military Academy at West Point, and later became the Army's youngest Major General.

Yet here was the same man now disparagingly nicknamed "Dugout Doug" for having left his command in the Philippines while the Japanese were advancing on Bataan and Corregidor—even though he had left only when specifically ordered to do so by President Roosevelt.

In April, 1942, MacArthur was eventually awarded the Medal of Honor—for leading the valiant though unsuccessful defense of the Philippines. (The Medal of Honor had also been awarded to his father before him, the first time in history that both a father and son had been so honored.)

Not much for sipping cocktails and making small talk, Jake stayed off by himself. His mind drifted back to Pearl—and Kate. She was due any day now. At his wife's urging he had prayed for Jill Chapman. That, Jake thought, had not gone well. Now he prayed for his wife and the baby she carried. *This time, Lord, please hear me.*

Jake had to wait until the General and the Admiral retired, signaling to their juniors that they could leave the reception as well. He swatted at dive-bombing mosquitoes all during the short walk back to the pier and his command.

When *Orca* let go of her mooring lines on Monday, May 1st, both the boat and her crew were more than ready for sea—ready to leave the heat, humidity, and the mosquitoes behind. Also left behind were Photographer's Mates Allessi and Huff and the Primarflex camera; they would all three be flown back to Pearl.

Orders had come from SUBPAC to return to the West Pacific waters north of Palau and "conduct independent action against enemy shipping." It would take *Orca* six days to reach her assigned patrol area. En route, Jake became a father.

A smiling Bill Salton presented Jake with the message from SUBPAC:

"Personal to LCDR Jacob J. Lawlor, USS Orca, commanding: Congratulations. You are the father of 7 lb. 6 oz. baby girl Elizabeth Ann Lawlor, born 0935 Honolulu time, 4 May 1944. Mother and child are resting comfortably."

Thank you, God, Jake prayed, and meant it.

On Wednesday, May 17,1944, elements of the U.S. Army made an unopposed amphibious landing on the mainland of Dutch New Guinea at the village of Arare. From that staging area, assaults were made on Insoemanai Island, which served as a platform for field artillery, and then on Wakde Island. The airfield on Wakde Island was securely in American hands by the evening of the 18th.

At 2000, local time, Thursday, May 18th, Elizabeth Ann Lawlor was just two weeks old, and *Orca* had been on station for eleven days without a single contact. The report came down to Jake in the wardroom from the conning tower: "Sonar reports small contact closing, Captain, bearing 082, estimated range 10,000 yards. Estimated course 076, speed five."

In these climes, and at this season, the sun was just beginning to set at 2000. *Orca* had been submerged during the daylight hours, and was preparing to surface for the night and charge batteries.

"Coming up," Jake announced, as he mounted the ladder into the conning tower. Once there, he saw that Joel Himmelfarb was already there, and Lou Carillo had the watch. "What've we got?" Jake asked.

Carillo answered, "Small contact, Captain. Nothing in the scope yet, but sonar has picked him up. Says it's twin screws, diesels making such a racket he could barely make out the screws. Could be a sub on the surface."

"Okay. Joel, you get on the scope. Louie, sound General Quarters."

"Sir!" both men answered simultaneously, and the GQ alarm rang throughout the boat. In just under two minutes, all stations reported manned and ready. Carillo had turned the conn over to Himmelfarb, and moved to the control room and the chart plot. Harry Hastings now manned Early Sender's former GQ post on the TDC. Bill Salton was in the wardroom on sonar plot, and Joe Bob Clanton was the diving officer.

"Time since last observation?" Himmelfarb asked.

"Eight minutes," replied Henry Coons, standing quartermaster watch.

"Sonar bearing and estimated range?" Himmelfarb asked. SN(SS) George Parra, the conning tower talker, relayed the question down to sonar. A few seconds later, he said: "Sonar reports contact bearing zero-eight-two, range ninety-five hundred yards."

"Up scope," Himmelfarb ordered. He first did a 360-degree sweep of the horizon, and then settled out on bearing 082. "Nothing there yet, Captain," he said. Then: "Wait one, I've got something. Just a mast on the horizon. Down scope. Don't think that's a sub, Captain. Mast like that, it's some sort of surface ship."

"Very well," Jake answered, "let's see what develops. What's the contact's estimated course and speed now, Lou?"

"Same as before, Captain, zero-seven-six, speed five," Carillo called up from the control room.

"CPA?" Jake asked Carillo for the closest point of approach.

"On our present course and speed, Sir, three hundred yards, in forty-three minutes."

"Okay. For now, let's assume this guy's estimated course and speed are good. What's a good course and speed for us to get a CPA of no less than a thousand yards?"

"We come to two-five-six, Captain, and maintain three knots, CPA will be eleven hundred yards, in twenty-eight minutes," Carillo answered.

"Very well, come right to course two-five-six, make turns for three knots."

Jake's orders were acknowledged, and the boat slowly came around to course 256 degrees. Word then came up from Maneuvering, that the boat was making turns for three knots.

"Contact bearing and estimated range, sonar?" Himmelfarb asked.

The talker, Parra, relayed the question and sang out the answer: "Zero-seven-four, estimated range eighty-five hundred."

"Up scope." Per protocol, Himmelfarb made a sweep then settled on bearing 074. "Got 'em, Captain. Little guy. Can just make out his bow. Angle on the bow port, twenty."

"Very well," Jake answered. "If he's a little guy, what in blazes is he doing out here?" No one volunteered an answer.

Eight minutes passed. Himmelfarb made another observation. "Definitely a small boy, Captain. Some sort of patrol boat, or gunboat. Bristling with antennae. Intelligence gathering, maybe?"

"Out here?" Jake asked, addressing no one in particular. "What kind of intelligence is there to gather out here? We're in the middle of nowhere!"

"Got me, Captain," Himmelfarb answered. "But a boat that size, maybe thirty-five, forty feet long, it's not worth a torpedo. Almost time to surface anyway, how about we blow him out of the water with our deck gun?"

"Not yet, Joel, not yet. Something very fishy here. Twin diesels, and the boat you describe, should be able to make twenty-five, maybe even *thirty* knots. Yet he's diddling along at just five. Gathering intelligence where there isn't anything to gather? Something stinks," Jake said.

The contact continued to maintain course and speed. Jake turned *Orca* to port, and slowed to bare steerageway, keeping the boat's bow pointed at the contact. "Watch your depth, Joe Bob," he yelled down to the control room. "You may have to just hover for a while."

"Roger that, Captain. I'm on it," Clanton hollered back up from the control room.

"Sonar's got something else, Captain," the conning tower talker reported. "Another contact, twin screws, bearing zero-seven-zero. Says the racket the first contact's diesel was making masked the second contact's signature."

"Ask sonar if they can give me any estimate on range to the second contact, but sonar is not, I repeat, is *not* to go active." The conning tower talker repeated Jake's order.

"Sonar reports maybe six or seven thousand yards, Captain."

"Very well," Jake acknowledged.

Himmelfarb ordered the scope up and searched on bearing 070. "Nothing there, Captain, nothing I can see."

"Well, Joel, what do you think now?" Jake asked.

"I think, Captain, that we should just sit tight, and see what develops. If you're thinking what I'm thinking, then that little boy, our sitting duck, is really a decoy, and that second contact might just be a submerged Jap sub. We surface, and start to blow that little boy out of the water with our gun, and we become the sitting duck for that Jap sub."

"My thoughts exactly. It's getting dark. If there is a sub out there, and he doesn't know we're here, then he'll be surfacing soon to recharge his batteries. So if he's there, and when he *does* surface, we'll be waiting for him." Jake ordered, "Open outer doors on tubes one, two, and three." He nodded to Himmelfarb, "Just in case we're right."

Minutes later, the patrol boat passed CPA, and continued off westward holding its course and speed.

Ten more minutes passed.

"Sonar, bearing to second contact?" Jake asked. The answer came back: 310. Almost dead ahead. Himmelfarb put the scope up, and swung to bearing 310.

"Holy crap!" Himmelfarb yelled. "A sub, Captain, not one of ours, a Jap sub—I make it a type B3!"

Like a Leviathan rising from the sea to catch a breath of air, a Japanese submarine had suddenly broached the surface dead ahead of *Orca*.

"Joel, you're sure this is a Jap sub?" asked Jake.

"Positive, Captain. Definitely a B3." Joel moved aside to give Jake a quick look.

Moving quickly in place, Jake peered through the scope. "Definitely not one of ours," he agreed. "Down scope. Make ready tubes one, two, and three," he ordered.

Seconds later, Joel ordered the scope raised again. "Getting a range," he said, and Himmelfarb quickly set the mast height on the stadimeter to twelve feet, and optically brought the top of the target's mast down to the waterline.

"Thirteen hundred and fifty yards," the quartermaster read on the periscope's bezel.

"He'll be practically dead in the water, Harry, just starting up his diesels," Jake said to Harry Hastings on the TDC.

Hastings adjusted the machine with a slight movement of his left hand. "Then I have a firing solution, Captain," Harry Hastings replied.

"Fire one," Jake ordered.

"One fired." One wakeless, electric, Mark 18 torpedo sped toward its target.

"Spread half degree left, fire two."

"Half degree left, two fired," Hastings came back, and the second Mark 18 was on its way.

"Now we wait," Jake said. Himmelfarb had lowered the scope; now he raised it again, eyes on the target.

"Time since first torpedo was fired?" Jake asked.

Coons looked at his stopwatch, which he had set when the first torpedo was fired. "One minute, twenty—"

Before he could finish, a shock wave was felt through the water, followed by a loud explosion dead ahead. Everyone had just let out a lungful of air, when the first explosion was followed by a second, seven seconds later.

"Damn," was all Himmelfarb could say, "I wish I had that camera."

"And you're sure it was a type B3?" Jake questioned.

"Positive, Captain," Himmelfarb responded. "Popgun just forward of a long bridge, long vertical masts fore and aft, and a wire antenna strung from stem to stern."

"Mister Himmelfarb, have you been studying your enemy ship profiles?"

Himmelfarb grinned. "It's a curse, Captain. Memorizing enemy profiles is just a way to pass the long and lonely nights!"

Fifteen minutes later, *Orca* was on the surface, charging batteries. Radar reported surface contact bearing 258, range 9,000 yards and opening. Estimated course, 256, speed 32 knots. The "little boy" was clearing the area at speed. Now, even if *Orca* *could* catch him, he still wasn't worth a torpedo.

The message from SUBPAC was short and to the point:

"19 May 1943 1210 IJN force consisting of transports, cruisers, destroyers and auxiliary vessels departing Palau with air support this date for relief of garrison, Biak Island, NNG. All units in area are directed proceed at speed and engage."

Jake ordered a quick response. His dispatch to SUBPAC reported their position north northwest of Palau, and said "Orca proceeding at best speed to comply."

"We've got to go about six hundred miles to intercept that relief column, Captain," Lou Carillo told Jake. "If we proceed on the surface at twenty knots, we can make that in twenty-eight hours."

"Make it happen, Lou," Jake replied.

Orca arrived on the relief column's track during the wee hours of May 21st, after only an hour's delay caused by a quick dive to avoid a patrolling aircraft. The radar screens were empty, and there were no other vessels or aircraft in sight.

"What now, Skipper," Joel Himmelfarb asked. "Sit and wait? Go back up the track? Down the track?"

"What would *you* have us do, Joel?"

"Well, here's my thinking. SUBPAC's message just gave us departure date, and not the time. With those transports and auxiliaries, they couldn't be making more than ten knots. If they hadn't left yet, then we are here early, and we should sit and wait for 'em. But if they'd already left, then they've probably already passed us, and we should chase 'em down the track. Either way, going back up their track doesn't gain us much."

"Good thinking," Jake replied. "Let's go down the track, then. Worst case, we run into our own people getting ready to hit Biak, and, if that happens, then we turn back to intercept."

It was early morning on May 22nd.

"Those all look like *our* guys, Captain," Joel said, peering through the periscope. "I make out one heavy and one light cruiser, and a bunch of destroyers."

"Okay, that means that the Jap relief column is still behind us. Let's reverse course and go back quietly. Last thing I want is to get clobbered by our own people," Jake said.

Unknown to the men in *Orca*, however, two squadrons of B-24 Liberator bombers were taking off from Durant Airfield (17 Mile Drome) at that very moment. As they passed Rogers Airfield (30 Mile Drome) overhead, three fighter squadrons — P-39 Airacobras and P-40 Warhawks — took off and joined them. These were, in turn, joined by six more B-24s from the now refurbished airfield on Wakde Island. These flights flew undetected over the submerged submarine churning northward on the same course.

But *Orca* was still hours away when the bombers and fighters met the enemy relief column.

The fighters made short work of the enemy air support, clearing both Mitsubishi G4M "Betty" bombers and Nakajima Ki-43 "Oscar" fighters from the sky. Those aircraft that were not destroyed were forced to limp back to Peleliu. The bombers, meanwhile, attacked and sank one light cruiser and a troop transport. They heavily damaged a second light cruiser, another transport, two destroyers, and an auxiliary cargo ship. In the end, the entire relief column turned back for Palau. American losses consisted of one aircraft: a P-39.

That evening, *Orca* surfaced in a debris-laden sea. SJ radar showed two contacts close together, 10,000 yards to the north northwest, course 350, speed 5 knots. Jake was about to order a course and speed to close with the contacts, when a message arrived from SUBPAC to search for the downed P-39 pilot, and giving the approximate position where his P-39 had gone down. As *Orca* moved at speed to that position, Jake ordered a searchlight to be rigged on the bridge. From that point, and working outward, the boat began to sail a grid pattern, searching for the downed airman.

The search continued through the moonless night and into the morning watch. At 0450, when there was just a glimmer of light appearing on the horizon, the boat hit pay dirt. Army 1st. Lt. James Hudson, of the 40th Fighter Squadron out of Rogers Airfield was hauled aboard — wet, hungry, and grateful.

While Hudson was being outfitted with dry clothes, fed, and bunked down in the XO's quarters, *Orca* proceeded at speed on course 350 in an effort to intercept the radar contacts of the night before.

Just under two hours later, the two contacts reappeared on the radar at 10,000 yards, still on course 350 at 5 knots. Jake ordered General Quarters, and put *Orca* on a course to intercept.

With the boat still on the surface at twenty knots, both contacts were clearly visible inside of four minutes.

The two contacts were a destroyer and a light cruiser in tow. Himmelfarb described the cruiser as a *Nagara*-class light cruiser. Her two forward stacks were gone, as was most of her superstructure forward. The B-24s had obviously scored at least two devastating hits, but had not sunk her. Jake considered his options and quickly decided on a course of action. The cruiser was the obviously disabled vessel, while the towing *Asashio*-class destroyer most likely still had all her teeth. He decided that the unusual situation called for unusual tactics: he would conduct the attack, in daylight, on the surface. Jake would hit the destroyer first, and, once that ship was destroyed or disabled, only then would he attack the cruiser. He cleared the bridge, except for Henry Coons, who was the GQ quartermaster, and himself. Joel Himmelfarb was below on the periscope, and Harry Hastings was on the TDC.

"Give me a firing solution on the lead vessel, the destroyer!" he shouted down the conning tower hatch. "And keep calling off the range to it." Then he ordered rudder changes to point *Orca's* bow at the destroyer. He did so with two things in mind: to minimize the boat's silhouette in relation to the target and to simplify the firing solution. "Open all outer doors forward," he ordered.

"All outer doors forward open, Captain, target range fifty-two hundred yards."

"Very well. Joel, I want you to keep adjusting our course so we stay pointed at that destroyer."

"Aye, Captain," Himmelfarb yelled up in reply.

Directly ahead, the destroyer, apparently having finally sighted her attacker, let out belches of black smoke from her stacks as she struggled to increase speed.

"Not yet, baby, not yet," Jake mumbled. "Don't snap that towline just yet." As he said that, the towline was lifted out of the water, and was pulled taut. Miraculously, it held; the cruiser was jolted suddenly forward, and the towline fell back into the water.

"Thirty-four hundred yards, Captain."

"Very well, make ready tubes one and two."

Once again, the towline was lifted out of the water. Once again it held. But this time it stayed out of the water. Jake expected the line to part any second, and wondered why the destroyer captain hadn't simply ordered the line cut so that his ship would be free to fight.

"Sixteen hundred yards, Captain. One and two ready. Target speed now six knots, and we have a firing solution," Joel called up to the bridge

"Very well. Fire one."

"One fired."

"Seven hundred yards."

"All stop. Spread second torpedo two degrees left."

"Two degrees left." This time it was Harry Hastings who acknowledged Jake's order.

"Fire two."

"Two fired."

Jake watched, expecting the towline to part at any instant, expecting the then-freed destroyer to surge forward, and the two torpedoes to pass the destroyer harmlessly astern. "Just a minute more," he said aloud. "Hold for just another minute," he prayed.

The towline snapped and the first torpedo struck the destroyer aft of its superstructure almost simultaneously. Ten seconds later, the second torpedo struck, blowing off the ship's bow. With the strain of the towline suddenly gone, the ship surged ahead only to plow a furrow in the water in which to sink itself. It was given a push from behind to send it on its way, as the crippled cruiser, unable to stop itself, crashed into her stern.

"All back full! Make ready tubes three and four. Shift target to the cruiser."

Jake had to back *Orca* away in order to give the boat enough room to torpedo the cruiser. The destroyer's commander was not quick enough in responding to the submarine's presence to limber the ship's guns and fire on *Orca*, but such was not the case with the cruiser. While it could not bring its big guns to bear, 25 and 13mm shells from its smaller guns began whistling by *Orca's* bridge, some bouncing off her deck, and some piercing sheet metal. Remembering the loss of "Squid" Phillips off Betio, Jake ordered Coons below, but stayed on the bridge himself.

"Range to the cruiser?" he yelled down the bridge hatch. Jake was pleased to see that without being told, Himmelfarb was now keeping *Orca's* bow pointed at the cruiser.

"Six hundred yards."

From Hastings: "I have a firing solution, Captain."

"Spread one degree right and one degree, left. Fire three."

"Three fired."

A 25mm shell struck a glancing blow off fuel ballast tank 3A on the port side, tearing a long gash in the tank. Fuel oil immediately began leaking from the tank, spreading out from the boat as an iridescent sheen on the water.

"Fire four."

"Four fired."

Forty-three seconds after the first torpedo was fired, the Mark-18 struck the cruiser just aft of her seaplane-launching crane. Twenty seconds later, the second torpedo struck just under what the B-24s had left of her forward superstructure. Despite the two hits, the determined enemy sailors aboard the cruiser kept the small caliber shells coming.

"Twelve hundred yards."

"All stop. All ahead full."

Once the boat had forward way on: "Dive, Dive!"

Jake rang the claxon twice and scrambled down the hatch. Firing from the cruiser stopped only after *Orca* had long since disappeared beneath the surface, followed by a telltale oil slick.

The boat initially dove deep, but soon afterward came back to periscope depth. Joel Himmelfarb observed the stricken cruiser through the periscope.

"What do you think, Joel, do we expend another torpedo to finish her off?" Jake asked.

"Not necessary, Captain. She's going down, and her crew knows it. They're abandoning ship. They're putting boats over the side, but most are just jumping into the water."

"Okay. We'll stand by until she goes down."

Two and a half hours later, just as Jake was about to expend a third torpedo on her, the cruiser lifted her bow out of the water and slipped backward below the surface.

"What's up, Captain?" Himmelfarb asked, as he joined Jake in the wardroom. He had just settled into his bunk when the steward, Delacruz, told him the Captain wanted to see him in the wardroom.

"We have orders to ferry First Lieutenant Hudson to Port Moresby. Apparently the powers that be in Southwest Pacific Area headquarters are pissed that we took time out to sink ships, and endangered the Lieutenant's life."

"And the lieutenant couldn't care less, Sir," Jim Hudson said. The tall, fair-haired, lanky, Oklahoma farm boy, wearing someone's borrowed khakis, had suddenly appeared behind Himmelfarb. Hudson had slept through his first twelve hours aboard the boat, awakened refreshed, and then availed himself of some of the best food in the Navy. He was taking a self-guided tour though the boat, and had just decided that a fresh cup of coffee in the wardroom was in order.

"Didn't mean to eavesdrop, Captain," he said, "but I couldn't help but hear what you said. You and your men and this ship have a job to do, just like me, and you needed to go ahead and do it. I'm just grateful as all get out that you could take time out to fish me out of the drink."

"You're welcome," Jake said, meaning it.

In the twilight hours of Wednesday, May 24th, *Orca* surfaced and set out once again for Port Moresby. On Thursday morning the OOD noticed that the boat was trailing oil, and notified Jake. Jake brought the Engineer Officer, Joe Bob Clanton to the bridge with him and asked, "Are we doing anything to stop the bleeding, Joe Bob?"

"We are, Captain. We've been taking suction from Four A and B, and they're pretty much down. Then we'll valve off Three B, take a suction on Three A, and transfer its fuel to them. Once Four A and B are full up, if there's anything left in Three A, and there shouldn't be, we'll have to dump it. The only problem is that Three A will be filled with seawater then, and Three B with fuel, so we may just list a little bit to port because of the weight difference. We may look a bit strange, but at least we won't be leaking oil. We'll have to get to a repair facility to get that tank fixed, though. If it was a clean bullet hole, we could probably have plugged it with a neoprene plug 'til we got back in. But that gash will need a welded patch."

"Okay, Joe Bob! Sounds like you've thought it all out. Good job, and proceed as planned. I doubt whether they can do anything to repair the tank in Port Moresby, but we can ask."

While en route to Port Moresby to disembark their passenger, Jake sent off a message to SUBPAC describing the damage to tank 3A. In the dispatch, he said that while the damages could not be repaired in house, they had compensated for the damaged tank, and that *Orca* was still ready for action.

Chapter 19

Orca pulled into Port Moresby on Saturday, May 27th, just as the Army was hitting the beaches on Biak Island.

The 41st Infantry Division landed 12,000 men on Biak Island, all along the coastline reconnoitered by Orca. *The initial May 27th landings were unopposed aside from some light small arms fire from the cliffs overlooking the beach. The Japanese command had decided to abandon the beaches and instead put up stiff defenses inland. Some 10,800 troops defended the island, and put up withering ground fire in defense of the Island's airstrips. The Japanese managed to hold firm until mid-June, when reinforcements from the 24th Infantry Division were deployed, and the last of the airfields finally captured. The Island continued to be defended by a stubborn enemy from caves inland, and was not completely secured until mid-August.*

Jake never had the opportunity to ask the authorities at Port Moresby if they had the capability to repair the leaking tank. No sooner had the boat arrived and 1st. Lt. Hudson had disembarked, orders came from SUBPAC to join Pacific Command Task Force 58, assembling under Admiral Spruance's orders off the Marianas Islands. *Orca* departed Port Moresby the next morning with fresh provisions, all fuel tanks except 3A topped off, listing slightly to port, and followed by a cloud of mosquitoes.

Once again, the only fond memory of Port Moresby was the satchel of mail that was delivered to *Orca* there.

It had been less than a month since *Orca* last received mail, so the stack of letters from Kate was smaller this time. And now, instead of reading the oldest letter first, Jake went directly to the first letter Kate wrote after their daughter was born. That letter was postmarked May 7th. It read:

"Darling, I can't tell you just how beautiful she is. She's perfect. Ten tiny little fingers and ten tiny toes (of course I counted them!) and the sweetest little face. At first I was so worried that she wasn't nursing, and then when she finally started, worried that maybe I wasn't making enough milk, or that maybe something was wrong because my nipples hurt so. Never mind that the pediatric nurse kept assuring me that all that was normal, and that she was just fine, and that I had plenty of milk.

Now that we're out of the hospital, and home, I can say I didn't realize just how good I had it in the base hospital. When Elizabeth was hungry, a nurse brought her to me, and I could just lie there comfortably and watch her as she nursed. (You can't believe how much suction such a tiny thing can produce!) When she was finished, she would fall asleep in my arms and then a nurse would take her and put her in the bassinette next to the bed and we'd both get a nice rest until it was time for one of us to eat again. Here at home, though, there's only her, and me and everything revolves around her schedule. I can't seem to get enough sleep!

I need to make arrangements to get our baby baptized. I was thinking that Pam could be Godmother and Clem her Godfather. Of course Clem is nowhere near Pearl, but he could still be her Godfather by proxy. I need to write and see if he's willing. So much to do!

I could really use some help here, Darling, and can't wait for you to come home! I do miss you so! And now so does our little Elizabeth!"

Jake set the letter down, unable to finish reading it for the moment. He had never before felt so robbed by this war, had never felt so deprived by it. Thousands of miles away he had a baby daughter he had never seen, might never see. And there also was a wife who needed him. The evil in the world had prevailed, and it had deprived him of all that was good. He had never seriously questioned his role in this war before, but he was questioning it now. How much could he and this tiny boat he rode in do against such evil?

And then Jake Lawlor prayed. He prayed to a God he had almost forgotten. He prayed that the evil in his world would just go away.

Admiral Nimitz, from Pacific Fleet HQ in Hawaii, was preparing to invade these islands, and starting with tiny Saipan, would work his way south and west, pulling the noose tighter and tighter around the enemy's neck, until they were left dangling with nowhere to go.

For its part, the Imperial Japanese Navy was preparing for *Kantai Kessen* (decisive battle), one that could no longer be delayed, since capture of the Marianas by the Americans would put the home islands within range of the new B-29 Superfortress strategic bomber.

The last day in May, *Orca* reported to Commander, TF 58, off the Marianas. TF 58, assembled by Fifth Fleet Commander, Admiral Spruance, and under the command of Vice Adm. Marc Mitscher, was to see to it that the IJN did not interfere with Nimitz's plans. An invasion force was preparing to hit Saipan, and it would be protected by the naval forces under his command. On arrival, *Orca* was given orders to patrol off the San Bernardino Strait, off the Philippine Island of Samar. Her orders were to report enemy sightings first, before any attack.

Orca was on station on June 5th, when, 1,500 miles away, a flight of 77 B-29s hit the Japanese railway system in Bangkok, Thailand.

The noose was being drawn tight.

Orca had been on station ten days. It was 1835, and the visibility was good: ten thousand yards. The boat was submerged, and had been all day. Joe Bob Clanton was OOD. He had just raised the scope for a sweep of the horizon, when mast after mast appeared on the western horizon. Without hesitation, he sounded General Quarters.

"What's up?" Himmelfarb asked, as he climbed into the conning tower, Jake close behind.

"Masts on the horizon, Joel, lots of 'em."

"Very well, I relieve you." Then, to the men coming on station in the control tower, "I have the conn." Joe Bob scrambled below to take over the diving officer's station.

"What do you see, Joel?" Jake asked, as Himmelfarb raised the scope and peered through it.

"Just as Joe Bob said, Captain, masts hull down on the horizon, lots of 'em. Carriers and battleships, looks like."

"Okay. Much as I'd like to set up an approach and sink a couple of these babies, our orders are to notify the Force Commander first, before any attack. We have to surface to use fleet radio to do that, but we can't surface until after dark, or we'd be an easy target. I'll go below and start drafting a message to Force Command. With all these enemy ships topside, we'd better stay at GQ. Keep an eye on 'em, Joel. And start counting."

"Aye, Aye, Sir."

Daylight stays late in June. It wasn't until 2017 that *Orca* could safely surface and begin a charge. But the first order of business was to send an encoded message to the Force Command:

"15 Jun 1217Z. Enemy fleet sighted 13 deg 4 min 50 sec N, 124 deg 28 min 39 sec E at 1035Z course 067 speed 16.5. At least two large carriers, two light carriers, three battleships, twelve destroyers, and three oilers. Orca."

Unknown to the men in *Orca*, two hours after having sighted the enemy fleet, another sighting was made by *Seahorse*: carriers and cruisers, coming up from the south, two hundred miles east of Mindanao. A battle was brewing, one between the IJN forces converging on the Marianas, and Mitscher's TF 58, which, under Spruance's orders, had been split off from the force assembled to support a Marine force landing on the island of Saipan earlier that same day. TF 58 was tasked with turning away the Japanese fleet.

Also on June 15, 1944, and through the next day, the first land-based attack on the Japanese home islands was conducted by forty-seven B-29s based in India.

Jake had intended to keep the boat on a propulsion charge and shadow the Japanese fleet that had been sighted earlier. That way, even if he could not maneuver the boat into an attack position, he could at least alert command on the fleet's location and progress. That was his intention, at least, until Number 2 engine blew a cylinder liner.

Assuming the enemy fleet maintained its course and speed, given the need to charge *Orca's* batteries, and with Number 2 engine out of commission, it would take most of the night to eat up the 30-mile lead the enemy already had on the boat.

It was thus almost 0500 before the stragglers of the enemy fleet showed up on *Orca's* radar. Jake ordered this latest position radioed to fleet command, but realized it would again be daylight before the boat could be maneuvered into anything like attack position on a straggler. And that assumed that any of the capital ships, equipped with radar, did not detect *Orca*, and order one or two of the twelve destroyers in their company to hunt *Orca* down.

Orca trailed the Japanese fleet until dawn, sent out one last position report, and submerged for the day. Frustrated perhaps, but at least with a fully charged battery.

Orca's enginemen set about replacing the cracked cylinder liner.

When *Orca* surfaced after dark on the 17th of June, all engines were back in commission. Jake ordered the boat on propulsion charge and set out in search of the enemy. What he did not know was that sometime during the day the two elements of the Japanese fleet had joined up, and now numbered five large carriers, four light carriers, five battleships, thirteen heavy cruisers, six light cruisers, twenty-seven destroyers, six oilers, and twenty submarines.

TF 58 was made up of five task groups. TG 58.1, 58.2, and 58.3 each contained two fleet carriers and two light carriers. TG 58.4 consisted of one fleet carrier and two light carriers. TG 58.7 was made up of seven battleships and eight heavy cruisers (which included Spruance's flagship, *Indianapolis*). These capital ships were supported by thirteen light cruisers, fifty-eight destroyers, and twenty-nine submarines (among which was *Orca*).

Left behind to support the amphibious forces at Saipan were eight battleships and eleven cruisers.

Orca sailed the waters of the Philippine Sea the entire night searching for the enemy, but came up empty. Once again, her frustrated commander ordered her to submerge for the day at sunup on Sunday, the 18th.

Sundown on that Sunday found *Orca* back on the surface, the Marines on Saipan in control of the island's airfield, and TF 58 well to the north of the Marianas, maneuvering to stay out of range of the enemy's land-based fighters on Guam. The conjoined enemy fleet was maneuvering well to the west of Guam, searching for the American fleet.

Orca was finally able to once more locate the outer fringe of the enemy force during the night and report its location. But this time, either located by enemy radar or its transmission detected and triangulated, it also found itself diving to avoid a destroyer that had apparently been vectored to its position. The destroyer dropped depth charges on the spot where *Orca* had dived, but, by that time, the boat was deep and well away from any danger.

An hour later, Jake ordered *Orca* to periscope depth, and, with no enemy in sight, once again surfaced the boat. But the enemy had disappeared from the radar screen. Forty-five minutes later, at dawn on the morning of the 19th, he ordered the boat submerged again.

Early that same morning, a Japanese Zero had located the American fleet, reported its position, and attacked a destroyer, which promptly shot it down. An airstrike by enemy planes based on Guam was ordered, and it was met by a flight of F6F Hellcats from *Belleau Wood*. The event established a pattern that would repeat itself continually over that day and the day following: thirty-five enemy aircraft were shot down with the loss of just a single Hellcat.

Enemy carrier-based aircraft then joined the fray and met the same fate. Fifty-two enemy aircraft were splashed, with the loss of one more Hellcat, and some damage to the battleship *South Dakota*.

In the early afternoon of the 19th, *Orca* was at periscope depth, more or less treading water at three knots and with an easterly heading, when OOD Bill Salton called Joel Himmelfarb and Jake to the conning tower.

"What's up?" Jake asked.

"*Something's* up. I see some masts on the horizon, about bearing zero-seven-zero. They don't seem to be coming our way, but they're not going away, either. I think we may have located our Japanese friends again."

Himmelfarb raised the scope, did a sweep of the horizon, and settled at bearing 070. "Got 'em," he said. "They're still hull down, but the masts are clearly visible. And there are lots of 'em. Take a look, Bill. They look closer to you than when you first spotted them?"

Salton manned the scope. "Definitely closer. They're headed our way," he said, and lowered the scope.

"Captain?" Joel asked, anticipating Jake's orders.

Jake grinned. "Make your course zero-seven-zero, make turns for seven knots. Let's see what mischief we can get into."

Seven minutes later, another observation, and it was obvious that the contacts were closing. Jake ordered General Quarters.

The first contacts were destroyers, spread across the horizon; at least five were visible, and closing fast. Jake slowed the boat back to three knots, and set course 066, aiming to pass equidistant between the closest two destroyers.

Joel waited until he estimated that the two destroyers were each abeam. He raised the scope and quickly swept the scene. "Starboard contact, bearing, mark!"

"Zero-five-zero," Henry Coons shouted out.

"Range, mark!"

"Five hundred and sixty yards."

"Port contact, bearing, mark!"

"Three-three-six!"

"Range, mark."

"Four hundred and eighty yards."

"Down scope."

"Contacts on course two-four-five, Captain, speed twenty-four knots," Lou Carillo called up from the chart plot. Harry Hastings silently entered the data into the TDC.

"These destroyers are pickets. We're bound to have a big one headed our way, Joel, and I want to hit him and hit him *hard*. Look again, and tell me what you see coming our way."

"Aye, aye, Captain. Up scope." It hadn't been the recommended seven minutes between observations, but Himmelfarb knew better than to question Jake's order.

"I see a cruiser. Bearing, mark!"

"Zero-six-zero."

"And a carrier, a big one. Bearing, mark."

"Zero-seven-seven."

Joel swung the scope left. "And another cruiser, bearing, mark. Down scope."

"Three-five-nine."

"Set your stadimeter height for the carrier, Joel. Come left to zero-four-zero."

"Zero-four-zero, aye," the helmsman repeated. "Coming left to zero-four-zero."

"I need a range and a firing solution," Jake said. "Get me a range, Joel."

"Steering course zero-four-zero," the helmsman reported.

Himmelfarb ordered the scope up again. "Carrier's recovering aircraft," he observed. "Angle on the bow starboard six-zero. Bearing, mark!"

"Zero-seven-nine."

"Range, mark. Down scope."

"Twenty-eight hundred yards."

"Open all outer doors forward, make ready all forward tubes," Jake ordered, and the order was relayed to the forward torpedo room.

A tense five minutes passed. "Again, Joel," Jake ordered.

The attack periscope was raised again. "Bearing, mark," Himmelfarb sung out.

"Zero-nine-two."

"Range, mark. Down scope."

"Nineteen hundred."

"Target course two-four-five, speed twenty-five, Captain," Carillo volunteered. "CPA will be nine hundred yards in four minutes."

"I have a firing solution, Captain," Hastings said.

"Very well," Jake acknowledged. "Harry, I want to fire all six fish, one degree spread between each fish. Final observation, Joel."

Again the scope was raised.

"Angle on the bow, starboard eighty five, bearing, mark."

"One-zero-seven."

Joel twisted the stadimeter handle. "Range, mark. Down scope."

"One thousand yards"

"Fire one." Jake ordered.

"One fired," Hastings replied.

And so it went, until all six torpedoes had left the forward tubes. The first explosion was heard forty-seven seconds after the final torpedo left the tube. Then two other explosions were heard.

"Take a quick look, Joel, then we get the blazes out of here," Jake said.

Joel rode the scope up. "Carrier's dead in the water, Captain. Big fire forward—must have hit a fuel tank. Flashes from explosions on the flight deck, and she's down by the bow. Down scope."

"Joe Bob," Jake yelled down to the control room," take 'er down, one-five-zero feet."

"One-five-zero feet, aye, Captain!"

And *Orca* got the blazes out of there.

Subsequent air action on June 19th, between carrier-based American naval air forces and land and carrier-based Japanese air forces had the same results as earlier: lopsided victories for the American side. The fight continued into the next day, with the Japanese fleet finally retreating from the field. In the end, the Battle of the Philippine Sea cost the Japanese three carriers (two to submarines), two oilers, and over six hundred aircraft. The United States suffered the loss of a hundred and twenty three aircraft, eighty of which simply ran out of fuel and had to be ditched by their pilots. To American Navy fliers, the battle became known as "The Marianas Turkey Shoot."

On June 29th, *Orca* returned to home base at Pearl Harbor, listing slightly to port, her seventh war patrol now in the logbook.

Chapter 20

Joel: 29 June 1944 to 17 July 1944

The usual cheering crowd waiting behind Admiral Lockwood and Commodore Macdonough greeted *Orca* **as the boat** approached the pier at Submarine Base Pearl.

Jake scanned the crowd from the bridge and quickly singled out Kate. His wife stood to one side, holding up a squirming bundle that she spoke inaudibly to and cuddled cheek-to-cheek — Jake's first glimpse of his infant daughter. Kate looked amazing. She wore a blue print sundress that clung to her in the morning breeze. Jake sincerely hoped that the admiral and the commodore would make their greetings brief.

"Great patrol, Jake," was "Uncle Charley's" handshake greeting. The commodore stood behind him, silent, smiling. "Debrief tomorrow at Oh Nine Hundred. Now get off this boat and meet the new woman in your life!"

It took a split second for Jake to realize that Lockwood was referring to Elizabeth Ann. "Yes, Sir, Admiral," Jake said, with a grin, and the three men left the boat together, Jake splitting off and hurrying to his waiting wife.

As the officers and crew left the boat, the relief crew boarded and began the refit that would once again make *Orca* ready for sea.

Jake gathered both Kate and the baby in an open-armed embrace, kissing Kate soundly.

When he finally stepped back, a grinning Kate held Elizabeth Ann out to her father and said, "Welcome home, Sailor! Funny thing happened while you were gone."

Jake, holding his daughter for the first time, said, "She's beautiful. Just beautiful. And *you* . . . you, too. You're *both* just so beautiful!" And with that, his daughter broke into a howl to wake the dead. "What? What did I do?"

Kate giggled, taking back her daughter, "Nothing, nothing at all. She's been cranky all morning, and now she's probably hungry. Let's get her to the car. You drive and I'll feed her."

Elizabeth quieted in her mother's arms, but still fussed. She nuzzled Kate, her head turned to the side, looking to nurse.

Their Olds was parked at the end of the pier. When he got in on the driver's side, Jake noticed what looked like one of their bureau drawers wedged into the back seat, blankets neatly arranged inside it. "What's that for?" he asked.

"Well, I couldn't very well hold her while I was driving, now, could I?" Kate answered. "That's a baby bed for Elizabeth, for when I'm driving and there's no one to hold her."

Kate pulled a large white cloth from a bag on the floorboard and, settling into the car seat, draped it across her shoulder. Jake watched, fascinated. She fiddled with her clothing, and, finally, brought their baby to her exposed breast. Elizabeth immediately stopped fussing, her mouth desperately searching for and finally finding her mother's nipple. She began nursing noisily. Kate draped the cloth over both her breast and the baby's head for modesty. Then she smiled at her enthralled husband. "You can take us home any time now, Commander," she said.

* * * * *

Joel Himmelfarb was in no-man's land. He didn't know whether his assignment as acting XO on *Orca* was still in effect, or whether he should report back to *Perro*. When he went up to squadron headquarters, they were unable to tell him anything, other than that his old boat was already at sea, had been for a week. All anyone would say otherwise was "Come back tomorrow and maybe we can tell you more."

He then asked after Hal Chapman, who was, as far as he knew, still *Orca's* XO, inquiring if he had returned back to the base. Still, no one could tell him anything other than the same theme: "Come back tomorrow, and maybe we can tell you more." He went back to his room at the BOQ disheartened and confused.

After a long shower and a change of clothes, he sat back and thought long and hard about his situation. Finally, he realized that, regardless of which boat he was attached to, he still wanted to pursue his newly discovered passion for periscope photography.

Later that afternoon, he sought out and found Lt. Philo James, the man who had instructed all of *Orca's* officers in periscope photography before the boat's last patrol.

"Okay, so if I can't get a Primarflex, what kind of camera would be almost good enough?" Joel asked James.

"Well," Jones replied, "the Eastman Medalist is pretty much what most of the boats use, but it's *hardly* up to the job. Some boats have had better success using the National Graflex, Series II, and the Eastman 35, which, by the way, was specially designed for periscope photography. Both of these cameras have reflex viewfinders, which make them way better than the Medalist. Neither one is nearly as good as a Primarflex, of course, but they're probably the best available otherwise."

"Okay. National Graflex Series II or Eastman 35. And where might I locate one of these cameras?"

"I'm really not sure," Jones answered. "But there are a couple of photographic supply stores in Honolulu, on Kinau Street, catty-cornered from the art museum. You might try there."

* * * * *

The next morning, the last day of June, 1944, Jake reported to the admiral's office for debriefing. Using *Orca's* log for reference, he went over *Orca's* seventh patrol exploits in detail for both Admiral Lockwood and Commodore Macdonough.

"Great patrol, Jake," the admiral said, reiterating his dockside greeting of the day before, the commodore nodding in agreement. "Even General MacArthur sent his personal thanks and compliments. And you bagged a carrier. That's got to be worth another PUC for the boat, and another Navy Cross for your collection."

"Thank you, Admiral," Jake replied. "I have a great team on a great boat."

"Well said. Now the commodore has an update for you. Some modifications to *Orca* that are being done over the next three weeks while you're in port."

Jake made a mental note that *Orca* would be back on patrol in three weeks, then asked, "Modifications?"

"I think you'll like these, Jake," Macdonough said. "To begin with, a modification is being made to your SJ radar antenna. The antenna will be mounted on a retractable mast. That way, you'll be able to raise the antenna when you're at periscope depth, and you'll no longer have to be surfaced to use the radar."

"That's great!" Jake responded. "I wonder why somebody didn't think of that sooner?"

The commodore chortled. "Somebody *did*. The skipper on the *Permit* jury-rigged a retractable antenna on his boat. We're just copying a good idea.

"Next thing," Macdonough continued, "the electronics boys have come up with a new LF antenna for fleet transmissions. Looks kinda like a football. It's also being fitted on a second retractable mast so that you can send and receive fleet transmissions at periscope depth from now on. You'll no longer have to surface to send a transmission like you did when you sighted that Jap fleet off the San Bernardino Strait."

"Excellent!" Jake said. "But now, if I may, I have a couple of questions. I need to know about Hal Chapman and Early Sender. When will they be coming back to *Orca*?"

The Admiral chuckled. "I thought you'd be asking that. Well, here's the scoop. You know we're short of submarine officers—*especially* experienced, qualified submarine officers. Some months, we've got as many as four new boats being commissioned. Most months, there are at least two new ones. They need crews, and they need officers."

Jake knew instinctively that he wouldn't like hearing what was coming next.

"Hal Chapman is an experienced XO, and, with some credit to you, a darn good one. I've assigned him as XO on the *Mollusk*, which will be commissioned in Mare Island less than a month from now."

Jake was crestfallen. Good for *Mollusk*, bad for *Orca*.

"Sender's story is a bit different. When his leg healed, he was assigned to a relief crew, and then was immediately sucked up by Henry Faulk for *Lemonshark*. Faulk's no dummy. He recognizes talent when he sees it. Right now, Sender's on patrol in *Lemonshark*."

Jake unsuccessfully did his best to hide his disappointment. "Okay, Admiral, but what do I do for an XO? I'm still down one officer."

"Understood," Lockwood replied. "But you still have Himmelfarb. How did he work out as XO?"

"Great. But I understood that Himmelfarb was on temporary assignment. Won't he be needed when *Perro* goes back to sea? Besides, he's junior to Lou Carillo. Temporary assignment is one thing, and Lou accepted Joel as acting XO on that basis without any problem, but *permanent* assignment as XO might well be another thing altogether. I know that Lou is a professional, but we're all human, after all."

"*Perro's* already back at sea. Now level with me, Jake," the Admiral replied, as if he hadn't even heard Jake's concerns, "how did Himmelfarb really work out as XO?"

"Actually," Jake replied, "he was excellent. I would retain him as XO in a heartbeat if it weren't for the fact that I might also ruin the best navigator in the fleet in the process."

"You really think Carillo might react that badly?"

"Admiral, I honestly don't know. I would hope that he would take it like the professional he is, but I know he has aspirations to be an XO himself, and might not be able to overcome his disappointment. Like I said, we're all only human."

"Well, the last time we spoke, you said that you thought Carillo wasn't up to being an XO yet. How do you feel about that now?"

It finally dawned on Jake where this conversation was going. He thought for a minute before answering, realizing that he had just been manipulated by a master. Nothing for it but to give in gracefully. After all, what he was about to say was at least the truth. "Judging from the way that Lou took the initiative and worked alongside Himmelfarb," Jake said, "I think that now he might just be ready."

"I was hoping you'd say that," the admiral answered, triumphant. "But I also know you're not going to like my solution to your little problem." He dropped his eyes and stifled a grin. Macdonough, who had been silent during this exchange between Lockwood and Jake, now allowed himself the hint of a smile.

The admiral continued, "I want to transfer Carillo to *Hermit* as XO—add some more experience to that wardroom."

"And then I'm down three officers!" Jake said. He could hardly hide his dismay.

"Not if you keep Himmelfarb," Lockwood wryly answered. "Then you'd only be down two."

"All right, down two then," Jake replied, accepting the inevitable. "So who's being assigned to *Orca*?"

"Two men, Jake, one with submarine experience, another who's new to subs, but with surface fleet experience. Lieutenant j.g. Gary Clark will be a transfer from *Anemone*. He's got his dolphins, and Jim Clancy in *Anemone* fought like hell to keep him. But he's been in *Anemone* since May of Forty-Two and it's time for him to move on."

"Okay," Jake thought, "Clark sounds good, especially if Clancy wanted to keep him."

"The other man is Lt. j.g. William Kinkaid the Third."

"Admiral Kinkaid's son?" Jake interrupted.

"The very same," Lockwood answered. "Third generation Navy. But I don't want you to hold that against him. He's actually made quite a name for himself in destroyers."

"I didn't mean it that way, Admiral," Jake said with some embarrassment. "Not at all . . . just surprised I guess."

"I didn't think you did. But I want you to know, Jake, both of these men are two of the best that we have. And I want them to learn from the best. And I *mean* that."

"Thank you, Admiral. And I'll do my best," Jake replied, accepting the compliment. "You know I will."

"I *do* know you will. Now do you want to tell Himmelfarb that he's your permanent XO, or do you want the commodore here to tell him?"

"With all due respect to the commodore," Jake said with a smile, "*I'd* like to tell him."

"Then do it," Lockwood grinned. "I hear the poor man's been in limbo worrying about what was to become of him."

Jake smiled. He knew the feeling.

"That went well," Clarence Macdonough said.

"You think so, Mac?" Charles Lockwood replied. "Make no mistake. Jake Lawlor knew he was being played. It's just that we've got all the face cards, and he knows that too."

"Perhaps, Admiral. But I do believe he understands why we make the decisions we make. And I know that he wants to win this war and get it over with just as badly as we do. Lawlor is one of the best sub drivers we have, and the people he trains are some of our best. Look at Clem Dwyer in *Viper*. Dwyer learned from Jake Lawlor in *Orca*, and now *Viper* is tearing up the Japs in the Northern Pacific. That's not so much different from Mush Morton training Dick O'Kane in *Wahoo*, and now O'Kane in *Tang* is one of our best sub commanders."

"True," Lockwood agreed, "but I also don't want to leave Lawlor facing the enemy buck naked. I truly believe Himmelfarb will be an asset, but is he as good an XO as Chapman was? We'd already pulled Early off *Orca*, and now Carillo besides? Jake's good, but he can't run his boat without good help. Look at Morton. He was the best sub driver there was. Then we take his XO and give O'Kane *Tang*. Now Morton and *Wahoo* are gone."

"Come on, Admiral. You can't possibly blame losing *Wahoo* on O'Kane's absence. It's a war, Admiral. We're going to keep losing some boats just as long as we keep sending them in harm's way. You know that, I know that, and *they* know that. You certainly can't beat yourself up about it."

"Can't I?" Lockwood replied. "If I'm entitled to gloat over every victory, and I do, then I'm also going to take every loss personally. I'm afraid it goes with the job."

Macdonough could think of nothing to say to answer that.

* * * * *

Joel Himmelfarb, dressed in civilian clothes, wandered along Kinau Street in downtown Honolulu. He had already been inside one store, and the man behind the counter had no idea how to locate either a National Graflex, Series II, or an Eastman 35 camera—much less a Primarflex. He had better luck in the second store.

A clean-cut, dark-haired, young man behind the counter seemed delighted to see Joel.

"Yes, sir, may I help you?"

"I hope you can. I'm looking for a special camera. I need either a National Graflex Series Two, or an Eastman Thirty-Five camera, or, even better, if you have one, a Bentzin Primarflex."

"I can't help you with two of those, but I do happen to have an Eastman Thirty-Five available."

"You *do*? May I see it?"

"Certainly." The clerk disappeared into a back room behind the store.

Minutes later, he reappeared with a box in his hand. He opened it, took out the camera, and began to describe its features to Joel.

"How much?" Joel asked, interrupting his spiel.

"It's not cheap. This camera runs seventy-five dollars."

"Wow, you're right. It's *not* cheap." He thought for a few seconds. "But it's what I want. I'll take it."

The clerk carefully put the camera back into its box, as Joel counted out the seventy-five dollars from his wallet. He put the money on the counter and pushed it toward the clerk, who, in turn, pushed the box across the counter to Joel. In the process, he put his hand over Joel's and the money. Joel let go of the money and began to withdraw his hand, but the clerk held it fast. Joel looked up at the clerk, and saw that he was smiling at him, knowingly, as if they shared a secret. Rattled, Joel jerked his hand away, grabbed the box, turned, and made to leave the store.

"Wait!" the clerk called after him. "Don't you want a receipt?"

"Never mind," Joel called back over his shoulder, and quickly left the store.

When Joel got back to the BOQ, there was a note waiting for him from Jake, asking Joel to meet him at the Officer's Club at four o'clock that afternoon. *Now what?* he wondered. He had thoroughly enjoyed his time in *Orca*, but was very cognizant of the "acting" label before the coveted designation of "XO." He was also well aware of his junior status to the boat's navigator, Lou Carillo, although Carillo had never been anything but gracious to him.

Hal Chapman was referred to in hushed tones by the rest of the wardroom as the best of the best, and surely he would be returning to reclaim his job as XO. No, the cards were stacked against Joel ever getting that billet permanently.

Still, he mused, working with Jake Lawlor had been quite an experience. Only rarely did one come across a skipper that employed his people so effectively. The very idea of having the XO on the scope during an attack was revolutionary.

So what could he expect next? *Perro* was at sea, having just left a week ago, and might not be back in port for some time. Perhaps it would be stopping at Midway, and he could catch up with it there? Or maybe he would be assigned to a relief crew to wait for his old boat's return? Assignment to another boat? Shore duty? (God forbid!)

And why would Jake Lawlor have to *meet* him? Just to tell him — *what*? Maybe just to thank him for acting as his XO over the past couple months? Another loose end just hanging out there.

And what was that incident at the camera shop all about? he asked himself, as he looked in the mirror mounted over the lavatory. *How did he know about me? Do I have some big "Q" for "queer" stamped on my forehead that only he could see?*

The worst part of the experience was that for a split second — before he tore his hand away — Joel had been tempted. And it was a temptation to which he could never afford to surrender. Just a hint of his hidden proclivity, and his career in the Navy was over. Never mind returning to *Perro*, or getting the billet as XO on *Orca*. There would never be another billet of any kind, anywhere in the Navy, if it ever came to light that Joel Himmelfarb was a "homo." The only thing he'd get then was the brig. No, he had come too far and worked too hard to throw it all away now.

Joel arrived at the "O" Club ten minutes early, only to find Jake already at the bar, waiting for him. Like Joel, Jake was dressed casually in civvies, tan slacks, and an open-collared, Hawaiian shirt. Compared to some Joel had seen, Jake's shirt was understated: frangipani and palm fronds.

"You did say sixteen hundred, didn't you, Captain?" Joel asked. "Am I late?"

Jake glanced at his watch, "No, you're actually early. Come," he said, pointing to the bar stool next to him, "sit down. Can I order you anything?"

"Sure," Joel said, as he sat down and relaxed. "A Bud would be great."

Jake signaled to the bartender. "Another Budweiser here, please."

After Joel had been served, the two men sat and drank quietly for a minute or two, before Jake broke the silence. "Well, Joel, how did you like riding in *Orca*?"

"To be completely honest, Captain, I can't say I've ever enjoyed anything more. You have a great wardroom, a great crew, and a happy boat. It was an absolute pleasure."

"I'm glad you feel that way. Because, from now on, you're my new XO."

Joel could not hide, first, his surprise and then his absolute delight at the news. "Skipper! What can I say? I'm flabbergasted! You're *sure* about this?"

Jake chuckled. "I'm sure. Welcome aboard, Mister Himmelfarb." Jake extended his hand to his new XO, who took it in his own, and shook it vigorously.

They spent the rest of their visit discussing the other changes to *Orca's* wardroom and the boat's new antennae modifications. Before they parted, Jake extended the invitation to dinner that Kate had insisted he extend, for the following Tuesday afternoon, Independence Day.

July 4th dawned bright and sunny, and by noon it was very hot, and the humidity was stifling. It hadn't cooled off much by evening, but what cooling there was could be attributed to a steady breeze coming off the ocean. When Joel knocked on his captain's front door at 1800, Jake greeted him with a sleeping baby cradled on his left arm and a cold Budweiser in his right hand.

"These are both mine," Jake said, "And while you can't have the baby, you can come in and get your own Bud."

"I'll take you up on the beer, Skipper, but that baby is awfully cute."

Jake just smiled back and ushered Joel inside.

Equipped with a cold beer from the kitchen fridge, Jake brought Joel into the dining room, where Kate was setting the table. "Kate, honey, I'd like you to meet my new XO. This handsome fellow here is Joel Himmelfarb."

Joel had seen Kate from a distance when *Orca* entered port, but was unprepared for seeing her up close. Smiling, hand extended in greeting, Kate Lawlor was, he thought, a formidable presence. While he may not have been sexually attracted to women, he was nonetheless fully capable of appreciating their beauty.

Although Kate was dressed simply in one of the print sundresses she preferred, here was a lady who looked to be the perfect match for the skipper Joel had come to admire. Kate wore her auburn hair down that evening, framing her freckled face, and her emerald eyes simply sparkled. "I'm so pleased to meet you, Joel," she said. "Jake has told me so much about you."

"None of it is true, Kate, honestly. I'm nowhere near as much of a scoundrel as he says."

Kate laughed. "Really?" she said, taking him up on the joke. "You're not as bad a rapscallion as he says you are?"

Joel frowned. "Hmmm," he said, "I'm sure I would have a snappy comeback to that if I knew what a rapscallion was."

And Kate broke up laughing. Joel knew that, from that moment on, he and his skipper's wife would get along famously.

The days flew by.

By Wednesday, July 12th, *Orca* was alongside an active mooring dock, ready for sea trials.

Since dining at the Lawlors on the 4th, it had been a busy week for *Orca's* new XO. Joel arranged for Harry Hastings to take his in-port exam with Lt. Cmdr. Wilton Fischer in *Halibut*, which Hastings passed. Now Harry would be missing *Orca's* sea trials.

He would instead be getting an underway exam from Jim Fortnoy in *Cray.*

Joel had, along with Jake, also welcomed aboard first Lt. j.g. Gary Morton Clark, USN, who would be relieving Bill Salton as communications officer. Salton, in turn, was to become the boat's new navigator. Clark was, Joel noted, already submarine qualified, and could most likely be quickly added to the OOD watch list. He was a tall and lanky good-looking Montanan, and the crew immediately nicknamed him "Coop," after Gary Cooper, because he somewhat resembled the film actor and shared his first name.

A day later, Lt. j.g. William Foster Kinkaid, III, USN, reported aboard. Kinkaid was short, lean, and blond, and he looked like he was no more than 16 or 17 years old — this, despite the fact that he had served with distinction aboard a destroyer in the Atlantic for over a year before sub school, and was 24 years old. Kinkaid would work with Joe Bob Clanton as assistant engineering officer. One of his first orders of business, Joel knew, was to get Kinkaid on the watch list and then submarine qualified. The crew, playing off his youthful appearance, instantly dubbed Kinkaid "Billy the Kid."

Joel had also enlisted Bucky Buckner's help in crawling through *Orca's* guts and learning everything he could about his new home. He discovered, with Bucky's help, that while *Orca* was not all that different than *Perro,* she did have her peculiarities.

And he raised the attack scope and checked out the old camera mounting brackets. The Eastman 35 required some minor bracket modifications, which were quickly made with MMC(SS) Clements help.

Orca returned from her sea trials with a few problems.

The retractable masts for the radar and radio antennae worked just fine as far as their being able to move up and down went. For the first time the boat was able to do a radar search and to receive and transmit on the fleet LF radio while at periscope depth. And tank 3A, which had tested tight at the base, showed no sign whatever of a leak.

However, both new retractable masts leaked at the gland seals. Each produced a steady, pencil-thick stream at periscope depth, and a definite spray at *Orca's* three hundred-foot test depth.

And, for some unknown reason, the forward torpedo room hatch had also leaked at test depth.

The repair yard worked though the night to repair the leaks, but at sea the next day, the 13th, only the forward torpedo room hatch had sealed properly.

That evening, the wardroom met at the "O" Club to wet down Harry Hastings' new Dolphins. The wetting down party, of course, was, by tradition, paid for by the qualifier. Also by tradition, the boat's skipper left the party early. This was at least one Navy tradition that Jake was thankful for.

The following day two technicians from the repair yard rode the boat and attempted to repair the leaks with the boat underway. They managed to reduce the leaks, but not to reduce them to tolerable levels. The yard then spent another night working on the mast seals. The next day, the 15th, the leaks were judged to be at tolerable levels.

On Sunday, July 16th, the boat was provisioned for sea, all her fuel tanks were topped off, and twenty-one Mark-14 torpedoes were loaded under Bucky Buckner's watchful eye. Jake had lobbied hard to continue carrying Mark-18s, but they were in short supply and Jake was overruled at the Squadron level. Jake was sorry to see the Mark-18s go, but the boat's torpedomen were just as happy they were gone. To their way of thinking, the Mark-18s were a maintenance nightmare, and the very real danger of a torpedo catching fire would not be missed.

Jake kissed his wife and child goodbye and was driven to the boat, arriving at 0600 the morning of July 17th. A packet of sealed orders awaited him by dockside messenger. The packet was not to be opened until *Orca* had passed the one hundred fathom curve. At 0800, *Orca* let go all lines and headed out to sea on her eighth war patrol.

Chapter 21

Eighth Patrol: 17 July 1944 to 12 September 1944

It was July 17, 1944, and *Orca* had 3,400 nautical miles to cross en route to her assigned lifeguard station off the coast of Yap Island, in the Carolines. Once on station, the boat would again join the Fifth Fleet under the overall command of Admiral Raymond Spruance, and become a unit of TF 53.

On July 19th and 20th, P-47 Thunderbolt fighters of the US 7th Army Air Force, based on Saipan, attacked Tinian Island. Also on the 20th, US Naval Forces (TF 53) bombarded Guam. The noose around the Japanese home islands continued to tighten.

To arrive on station in time, by July 25th, the boat had to average almost eighteen knots over eight days, and the weather would have to be close to perfect. While the days were getting shorter, there were still, every day, almost twelve hours of sunlight. It was relatively safe to run entirely on the surface as far as Wake Island, the first two thousand nautical miles. These were supposedly "friendly" waters, and although Wake was still officially in Japanese hands, the garrison there had been effectively isolated and was literally starving. *Orca* passed by Wake on July 21st, and the weather was indeed perfect: calm seas and overcast skies.

On July 21st, the 3rd Marine Division and the 1st Provisional Marine Brigade, supported by elements of Navy TF 53, launched a two-pronged amphibious assault on Guam.

It was July 21, 1944, and with 1,400 nautical miles to go, *Orca* was now in not-so-friendly waters. Jake decided to stretch the concept of "daylight," and run flat out on the surface for fourteen hours a day, and then run submerged at five knots for the remaining nine hours of daylight. Once again, the weather had to cooperate. The sea gods did indeed favor *Orca*: the water remained calm, and the skies stayed overcast.

On July 24th, the 4th Marine Division invaded Tinian.

Orca arrived on station off Yap in the wee hours of the 25th, and reported to the TF Commander in the "new" carrier *Yorktown* (the first ship of that name was sunk at the battle of Midway). *Orca* was, along with *Plunger* and *Pollack*, one of three boats on lifeguard duty.

Over the following three days, the carriers *Yorktown*, *Franklin*, and *Wasp* launched air raids on the Japanese garrisons on Yap, Ulithi, and the Palaus. By the time the operation was concluded, *Orca* had rescued two Navy fliers who had ditched their aircraft in her lifeguard area. The operation was considered a complete success, in that enemy aircraft out of Peleliu were kept fully occupied and were unable to provide support to their embattled Japanese forces on Tinian and Guam.

Both *Orca* and *Pollack* were then ordered to take up lifeguard station off the Island of Woleai in the Carolines, in support of land-based air strikes against the enemy garrison there.

Enroute to Woleai, Jake took advantage of the transit to gain some training for his new GQ team. Using *Pollack* as a target, he had his new navigator, Bill Salton, train Billy Kinkaid to take over his old position in sonar plot.

Kinkaid immediately grasped the problems and capabilities of sonar plot, which was a graphic plot of *Orca* and a target vessel (or vessels) using information from passive sonar (*and* active sonar target bearing or range information, if available).

At first glance, without range information, bearings-only information from passive sonar alone appeared useless. But Kinkaid quickly grasped the concept of calculating the rate of change from one observation of target bearing to the next. It would give the observer an idea of relative speed, and whether or not *Orca* was closing with, or losing her target (or, how a sudden change in the bearing rate of change could indicate a target zig).

Kinkaid learned to trust, and work with, *Orca's* sonar operators. Their range estimates, for example, based on sound volume alone, Kincaid discovered were frequently accurate to within a hundred yards.

Jake also delayed surfacing in the evening until after *Pollack* surfaced. He would then set GQ, and practice a submerged approach using the recently installed ability to raise the radar antenna and get an accurate target range to *Pollack*. That information was then incorporated with past practice so as to speed up the process of arriving at a firing solution.

When the Woleai operation was concluded on August 1st, both *Orca* and *Pollack* had each rescued a downed Navy flier. Both boats were then ordered to return to stations off Yap, when land-based aircraft from Saipan and Guam again pounded the enemy airfield at Peleliu. That operation was concluded by August 8th. While *Orca* had no ditched aircraft in her area, *Pollack* rescued two more fliers, one Navy and one Marine.

On August 10th, both Tinian and Guam were declared secured. (Actually, some enemy holdouts from both islands did not surrender until after the war was over. On Guam, a Japanese Army Sergeant, Shoichi Yokoi, finally surrendered on January 24, 1972.)

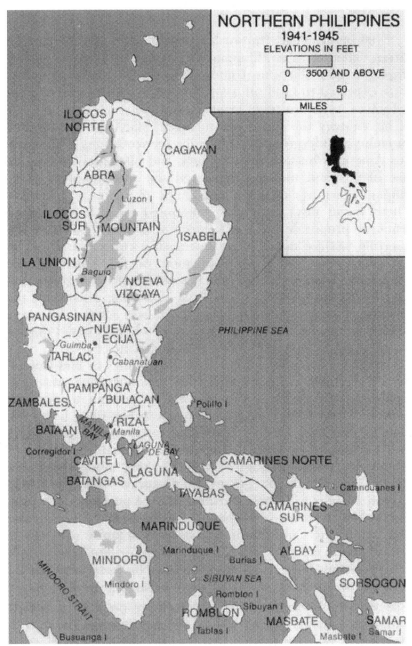

U.S. Army Special Operations in World War II, by David W. Hogan, Jr. Center for Military History Publication 70-42 Department of the Army Washington, D.C., 1992

* * * * *

A flight of twelve Liberator B-24J "flying boxcar" bombers of the 7th AAF took off from Saipan at 1830 on the evening of August 12th.   Their mission was to bomb the IJN facilities in Cavite, the Philippines. The base was located on the southern shores of Manila Bay on the Island of Luzon. Cavite had been the site of the U.S. Naval facility where Jake's old boat, *S-49,* had been stationed, and now it was being used by the Imperial Japanese Navy. The base had been relatively invulnerable to American air power, and while it was now well within the range of a B-29 Superfortress operating out of Saipan, there were not, as yet, any B-29s operating from there.   And General MacArthur was in no mood to wait for them in order to prove a point.

The flight was provided with fighter air cover for the first leg of the trip: P-47s also flying out of Saipan. The P-47 fighter-bomber had an eight hundred-mile range, extendable to a thousand miles, with drop tanks instead of a bomb load. Still, the B-24s could only be escorted for the first 500 miles of the 1,650-mile trip to Cavite. And the first leg was by no means the most dangerous part of the trip.

The B-24J had an operating range of three thousand miles fully loaded: with an eight thousand-pound bomb load, and a crew of ten. The round trip from Saipan to Cavite was 3,300 miles. To extend their range, then, each of the twelve planes taking off that evening carried a reduced bomb load, jury-rigged drop tanks, and a crew of seven. Even at that, fuel would be tight, and the planes returning to Saipan would be landing on fumes.

In anticipation of the flight, *Orca* and five other boats had been assigned lifeguard stations along the "feet wet" (over water) portion of the route, in the event that one or more of the bombers might have to ditch on the return trip. *Orca's* station was the closest to Luzon, in the Philippine Sea, three hundred miles offshore.

On station at 0700 on August 12th, *Orca* submerged for the day in a choppy sea, under clear skies. After dark on the 12th, she was on the surface charging batteries, when the outbound flight passed overhead at 30,500 feet. The SD radar screen remained blank, and no one aboard *Orca* saw or heard a thing.

The first pair of bombers was over the target at 0012 on Sunday, August 13th. The enemy was taken by complete surprise, and the first four aircraft made their runs and turned for home unscathed. By the time the fifth and sixth bombers made their runs, Japanese anti-aircraft guns had been manned and were filling the sky with flak. Meanwhile, twenty-seven IJN Mitsubishi A6M Zero fighters, land based at Clark Air Base, forty miles to the northwest, were being scrambled.

The remaining three pairs of bombers made their runs through increasingly heavy flak, as two more guns joined the fray, now aided by searchlights. Amazingly, though four of the aircraft received minor flak damage, all twelve B-24s were on their way home by 0036, their bomb bays empty. By 0118, however, the Zeros out of Clark were all over them. With the reduced crews on the Liberators, not all of the aircrafts' guns were manned, so radio operators and flight engineers left their stations to man the waist guns. As long as the Liberators maintained a tight formation, they were able to hold their own against the Zeros, downing three of them by 0137.

However, one of the twelve, the *Laura Mae*, took a direct hit to its outboard port engine at 0139, and a large section of the port wing was blown off. The pilot fought hard to regain control, and managed to keep the plane flying, but the aircraft veered off course to the south, leaving the formation. Smelling blood, five of the Zeros broke off action against the main formation and swarmed the stricken aircraft.

For the next hour, the *Laura Mae* fought off her attackers, the pilot exhibiting remarkable skill in flying a four-engine airplane with only three engines and part of a wing missing. Remarkably, he was able to keep the enemy fighters at bay with frequent changes in course, speed, and altitude. At 0146, the tail gunner mortally hit one of the zeros, and it disintegrated in midair. By 0157, however, the tail gunner and the flight engineer had both been hit, and the bomber was now so badly damaged that the pilot ordered the radio operator back to his post to issue a "Mayday" call. At 0200, he ordered the crew to their parachutes, but, to a man, they preferred to take their chances and ride the aircraft down. At 0216 the *Laura Mae* crash-landed on a jungle-clad mountain on Mindoro Island.

The navigator suffered a broken leg in the crash, but lived, and the pilot and the radio operator both survived unscathed. The rest of the crew was killed. The four Zeros overhead called in the crash location and returned to base.

The remaining eleven bombers had continued westward in tight formation, fending off the remaining nineteen zeros. Just before the formation flew over the Luzon coast, two more zeros were hit and spun from the sky. The remaining zeros then broke off the fight and returned to base. Seven of the Liberators were severely damaged, but their pilots managed to keep them airborne.

At 0153, *Orca* was on station on the surface when the flight passed overhead. Again, no one on board heard or saw anything, and the SD radar screen remained blank.

All eleven B-24s were glad to see the squadron of P-47s that greeted them at 0416 and escorted them the remaining five hundred miles to Saipan. By 0612 that Sunday morning, all the eleven surviving B-24s were safely on the ground. The seven crewmembers of the *Laura Mae* were counted as "missing in action."

At sea, meanwhile, the five submarines, which had stood lifeguard duty for the flight, were riding out a sudden violent midsummer storm.

The *Laura Mae* had come to rest in a bamboo and palm thicket, mowing down vegetation and plowing a short, curved, pathway through dense jungle. The starboard wing had sheared off when the propellers on that side dug into the ground on impact, and the plane had spun around to the right. Fuel from the ruptured wing tank had spilled out and soaked the soil, but, miraculously, the plane did not catch fire.

The pilot and the radio operator splinted and wrapped the navigator's broken leg as best they could while he was still inside the aircraft, and then slowly and carefully extracted him from the wreckage. As careful as they were, however, it seemed that their every movement caused him to wince and groan with pain.

Once outside, they propped him up against the closest palm tree, where he promptly passed out. They returned to the aircraft to retrieve the four bodies still inside. While in the process of dragging the first corpse from the plane, they felt themselves being watched. Four men had silently emerged from the jungle, Filipinos in ragged clothes, all wearing wide-brimmed hats of woven palm, armed with rifles and machetes.

"You American?" the nearest one asked in heavily accented English.

"Yes," the pilot answered. "U.S. Army."

The man grinned, a wide brown grin with gapped teeth. "MacArthur!" he said.

"Yes," the pilot answered, smiling back. "MacArthur. He's my boss."

Now all four Filipinos were grinning. Their spokesman said, "Quick. We must go. Pretty soon Japanese come take you prisoner. We take you where you be safe." As the man spoke, five other similarly clad men emerged from the jungle. They had been only a few feet away, but had been completely invisible.

The pilot pointed to the navigator. "He has a broken leg. We can't move him. And there are bodies in the plane. Besides this one," he pointed, "there are three more bodies inside."

One of the men who had just come on the scene knelt next to the unconscious navigator and inspected the jury-rigged splint. "Lousy job," he said, and proceeded to remove it as another man went into the jungle, machete in hand.

In a few minutes the second man reemerged carrying four smooth, straight branches. The navigator awoke in pain, alarmed, saying "What the hell?" as the man kneeling beside him cut away his trousers, tearing the cloth into strips, and set his leg.

"Relax, Charlie," the pilot advised. "I think they're here to help." He tried to calm the navigator, who then screamed in pain, as the kneeling man manipulated his leg to set the bone. The man then began splinting the broken leg, using the cut branches, binding them in place around the leg with the torn strips of cloth. As he was doing this, two other men rigged a stretcher using their shirts and long poles.

"We go now," the spokesman said.

"We can't," the pilot replied. "The bodies. My crew. We have to bury them."

"Why?" the spokesman asked. "They dead. We bury them, the Japs only come, dig them up. No point. We go now."

The others had already moved the navigator onto the makeshift stretcher, and two men were lifting him off the ground. The pilot still hesitated, and looked to the radio operator for some support.

"They're right," the radio operator admitted. "We *should* go." Overruled, the pilot shrugged his shoulders and followed the stretcher-bearers into the jungle.

They were well into the underbrush when the pilot noticed that their party now totaled only seven men: the three survivors from the *Laura May*, and the four Filipinos they had originally encountered, two of whom were now bearing the stretcher. The five others, including the man who had set the navigator's leg, had apparently remained behind. *Or had they?* thought the pilot. They could be anywhere in this jungle, he realized, and he would never know it, just as he had never known they were there in the first place.

In December 1941, Japanese forces invaded Mindoro, and in January 1942 entered the tiny village of Papylan in the mountainous interior of the Island. The town's population was rounded up in the village center and segregated. Able-bodied men and older boys were separated from the young women and older girls, and the remaining elderly men and women and the very young children placed in a separate group with the village priest, an American Franciscan missionary.

The able-bodied men and older boys were bound together to be marched off to the coast and into forced labor. Three of the men resisted, among them Bartolomeo Bacatplan, the 21-year-old husband of Delvina Bacatplan, and father of their baby son. The Japanese officer leading the raiding party, as an example to the others, had the three resistors beaten and bound, then summarily drew his katana, *the long razor-sharp, single-edged sword he wore as a symbol of his rank, and beheaded all three in front of the whole village. When the priest protested, he was clubbed senseless.*

As the young men and boys were marched off, the elderly men and women and the very young children, including Delvina's baby son, were locked inside the church with the priest.

The young women and girls were then systematically beaten, repeatedly raped, and left for dead. The village, including the occupied church, was then burned to the ground. The men and boys were never heard from again. Delvina Bacatplan was among the women who survived.

Just over four hours after the *Laura Mae* crashed, a Japanese scouting party armed with rifles and a light machine gun warily approached the wreck of the downed aircraft. The soldiers were dressed in jungle fatigues, and wore short-billed pointy caps with neck cloths. There were fifteen soldiers and one officer, a *Rikugun-Shoi*, the IJA (Imperial Japanese Army) equivalent of a second lieutenant.

The five Filipino irregulars approached the party silently from behind, noiselessly dispatching their equivalent number in the rear guard, which included the soldier carrying the machine gun. They then moved noiselessly to pre-assigned ambush positions. When the remaining eleven soldiers and their officer broke from the jungle cover to surround the downed B-24, the Filipinos opened fire from positions in the jungle. Each man carefully and accurately targeted only the nearest enemy, and as one target fell to the ground, he moved to the next one standing.

The Filipinos emerged from the jungle, rifles at the ready. The Japanese had been incapacitated to a man, and were unable to offer any resistance as the Filipinos moved from man to man, the quick and the dead, and, wielding machetes, decapitated them. The five bodies of the rear guard were dragged into the clearing and also relieved of their heads.

The sixteen headless bodies were then stacked on the ground that had been soaked with fuel spilled from the downed aircraft. Taking all the ammunition, weapons, food, and anything else of value that the soldiers carried, along with a bag of sixteen heads, the Filipinos set fire to the wreck and moved off into the jungle.

The Japanese had used Filipino slave labor to construct a number of "corduroy" roads on the island. These roads used logs from felled trees in two perpendicular layers to hold back the jungle growth and provide a relatively smooth and dry path for motor vehicles. These "paved" roads permitted access to previously inaccessible parts of the Island, allowing the Japanese to reach and harvest ancient stands of Philippine mahogany. Whenever any of these enslaved workers became rebellious, they would be summarily decapitated and their heads mounted on poles along the roadside as an example to anyone else similarly inclined.

That evening, an IJA truck was lugging logs from the interior to the coast on one of these roads, when its Japanese driver was horrified to see sixteen heads mounted on poles along the roadside. On each head was a short-billed pointy cap with a neck cloth.

In response to submarine activity in the South China Sea, Japanese shipping from the NEI in the south to Manila was being rerouted from the vulnerable South China Sea passage between the Spratly Islands and Palawan Island. The new route was the more protected passage to the east, through the Celebes Sea and the connecting Sulu Sea. Once in the Sulu Sea, Japanese ships traversed north to Manila past the western shore of Mindoro Island for the dash to Manila Bay. Shipments from Palau east to Manila had long employed this route, and diversion of NEI-sourced shipments to this same route had the advantage of maximizing the effectiveness of escorting air and sea cover.

The Allies had infiltrated coast spotters, watchers who holed up on Islands all along this route: two on Mindanao, and one each on Negros, Visayas, and Mindoro. Each was equipped with a suitcase-size mobile LF radio to report Japanese ship movements.

The coast spotter on Mindoro was Liam Wallace, a New Zealander who had been on post for almost two years. He had survived by being constantly on the move and by staying in constant touch with the irregulars of the Filipino Resistance, who continually harassed the Japanese occupation forces and called the Mindoro jungle home. It was one of these guerrilla bands, led by the woman, Delvina Bacatplan, which now contacted Wallace. It appeared that Bacatplan's irregulars had rescued three American airmen, one of whom had a broken leg.

That evening Wallace radioed the news to the listening station in Port Moresby.

It was August 18, 1944, and a midsummer storm had finally blown itself out. *Orca* had been on the surface all day, and remained there as night fell. At 2100 a message came through from SUBPAC.

"Give me a route to Dongon Bay off the west coast of the Island of Mindoro in the Philippines, Bill," Jake said to his new navigator, Lt. j.g. Bill Salton. "It seems that we've been ordered to pick up three airmen there."

"Where, Skipper?" Salton asked.

"Dongon Bay. Mindoro. These are the coordinates." He handed a transcribed copy of their orders to Salton. "There's a coast spotter there who's going to guide a landing party ashore. Seems the Island's crawling with Jap patrols looking for these three guys, one of whom has a broken leg, and there's a bunch of Filipino irregulars keeping them on the move and out of enemy hands."

"Sounds like a good plot for a Ronald Reagan movie," Salton said. "But I volunteer to lead the shore party."

"No you don't. *My* navigator doesn't go anywhere. And I have to think long and hard before I send *anybody* ashore."

Two nights later, on August 20th, *Orca* surfaced off the southwest coast of Mindoro Island, and headed into Dongon Bay. Earlier, there had been a lively discussion in the wardroom as to who, exactly, was to lead the landing party. To a man, every officer except Jake (who may have wanted to but really could not) had volunteered.

Afterward, Jake consulted with Bucky and Joel Himmelfarb in the wardroom. They discussed possible scenarios the landing party might encounter ashore. What if the spotter had been captured, forced to talk, and the Japanese were lying in wait for them? What if the airmen weren't at the landing area and had to be fetched from the interior? What if . . . ?

Together they decided a team of five men — one officer and four enlisted — could probably deal with whatever they ran into ashore. They would certainly have to be well-armed and capable of defending themselves, in the event that the rescue plan had been compromised, and there really was a Japanese ambush awaiting them.

It was Bucky who argued that the men they sent better know how to handle whatever firearms they carried. He reminded Jake that it was Frenchie Eifel who had trained the officers and crew on small arms. He recommended that Frenchie be brought into the conversation. Chief Eifel was summoned to the wardroom and asked who on board, officer or enlisted, might best acquit themselves with small arms.

"No question," Eifel said, "among the officers, it's Mister Clanton. He can hit a fly on the wall with an M1 from two hundred feet. Regular deadeye. Among the enlisted, that would be me."

"Oh no you don't, Frenchie," Jake said. "No sneaking in the back door to volunteer for this mission."

"Not sneakin', Captain, just statin' fact," Eifel replied. "I'm the only man jack aboard that could begin to outshoot Mister Clanton. If you want to send your best team of sharpshooters ashore, that would be us."

"All right. Say I send you two, who else?" Jake threw the question out for general discussion.

"Need somebody good on an Aldus lamp," Joel said."

"Olds or Rogers, maybe," Eifel said. "But not Simpson, the regular signalman, 'cause he's a lousy shot."

"Olds, then," Joel said. "He's bigger and stronger."

"Then for just flat-out smarts, along with some shooting ability, maybe Orsi, LaGrange, or Rubidot—take your pick," Eifel added.

In the end, Jake went over the list of possible candidates with Bucky, Frenchie, and Joel Himmelfarb, and decided to send the team of five that embarked in the rubber boat launched that night from *Orca's* awash afterdeck: Lt. j.g. Joe Bob Clanton, GMC Roland Eifel, EM3 James Orsi, and Seamen Robert Olds and Jack Rubidot. Jake gave each man an opportunity to respectfully decline the assignment. None would.

The inflatable rubber boat filled with five men, their weapons, equipment, and supplies, left *Orca* astern and headed for shore on Mindoro Island, and, in a perfect world, a rendezvous with Liam Wallace. The waters of Dongon Bay were calm, but the quarter-moon had already set, and it was pitch black.

A two-second-long light shined from the shore every thirty seconds, guiding in *Orca's* shore party. Just before bumping onto the beach, the men aboard the boat heard a friendly voice calling out in down-under English: "Over here! Liam Wallace at your service, Yanks!" The men jumped out of the boat, and Wallace helped them drag it ashore. In the dark, Wallace was just a moving shadow with a voice.

"Hello. I'm Joe Bob Clanton, and this here is Chief Frenchie Eifel, Petty Officer Jim Orsi, and Seamen Robert Olds and Jack Rubidot."

"Happy to meet you gentlemen," responded Wallace. "But the quicker we unload, stow this boat, and clear the beach, the better. I much prefer to have nice protective jungle cover around me."

"I take it the airmen are not here, and we can't just load them in the boat and turn back around?" Joe Bob ventured.

"No," Wallace allowed, "they're not here. They're still up country."

"Okay," said Jo Bob. He then addressed Olds. "Send a signal back to the boat. 'All clear, no airmen present.' "

Soon the deflated boat was hidden off the beach in the underbrush, and the party of six, lead by the New Zealander, made its way to what was his base camp for the night.

Once the "all clear, no airmen present" signal was received from the shore, *Orca* slipped quietly back out to sea. The boat was to return every day at 2300 for the next ten days to look for a signal from the shore of Dongon Bay

At the base camp, Orsi asked Wallace, "You Australian? You *sound* Australian."

"Bite your tongue!" Wallace hastily replied. "I'm a Kiwi! New Zealander, born and bred!"

"No offense, Man," Orsi said, and quickly backed away. Wallace just chuckled.

"So, Mister Wallace, tell me about these Filipino irregulars who are hiding our three fliers," Joe Bob said.

"Delvina's boys?" Wallace replied, and briefly told Delvina Bacatplan's story. "Filipino Resistance. Now, Delvina and her boys have become the number one pain in the ass for the Japs on this Island. She ambushes them, disrupts their operations, kills their troops. But what she does mostly is liberate her fellow Filipinos—the ones that the Japs have enslaved and use to do their dirty work. Most of her boys are former slaves. She gets them healthy, and then she and her cadre train 'em and turn 'em into Jap killers."

"And when are we going to hear from this Delvina person?" Joe Bob asked. "Does she even know we're here? How do we contact her?"

Wallace chuckled, and answered Joe Bob. "She knows you're here all right, Lieutenant. And we don't contact *her*—she contacts *us*. I 'spect we'll hear from her 'fore long."

Then he addressed all five of them. "Sleep while you can, Mates. No tellin' when next you'll have the chance." With that, he stretched out on the jungle floor and made himself comfortable.

Joe Bob posted Frenchie and Olds as the first watch, giving them instructions to awaken Orsi and him in three hours to relieve them.

By first light, only Wallace and Rubidot had slept through the night.

They didn't know he was there until suddenly he was—a Filipino in ragged clothes, wearing a wide-brimmed hat of woven palm. He was short, with smooth skin the color of light coffee, and didn't look much over twelve. He had a rifle slung over his shoulder and a machete hanging at his side.

"Hello, Phillip," Wallace said. "I see you found us."

In the dawning light the Americans got their first good look at Wallace, a short, thin and wiry man with long white hair and beard, sparking blue eyes, and a bulbous nose.

"Not hard," Philip replied. "You all very noisy."

Wallace chuckled. "Join us for breakfast?" he offered.

"Ate breakfast," replied Philip. Then, he addressed the Americans. "You eat quick, please. Delvina waiting. You come get American fliers."

"Why didn't you just bring them with you?" Joe Bob asked the boy. "We could have had them long gone by tonight."

Philip shrugged his shoulders. "You come. One man, leg broke. Delvina says you come."

Joe Bob thought something was very fishy about the whole situation. The guerrillas obviously already knew that *Orca's* shore party had landed, and probably didn't need the Americans' help to get the three fliers, including the one with the broken leg, to Wallace's temporary base camp. What was the point of their traveling inland to the guerrilla camp? Just to make nice with this Delvina person? It made no sense. He cast a questioning look at Frenchie, and the chief raised one eyebrow and shook his head; he didn't like the situation either.

Joe Bob turned to Wallace for some support. "Any of this make any sense to you?" he asked.

Wallace just shrugged. "Delvina wants to see you, and you want to get those fliers back, then you'd best go see her, Lieutenant."

Joe Bob didn't like it, but after a quick breakfast, he and the rest of the shore party left Wallace behind and followed the boy, Philip, into the jungle.

It was two hard days' march to the guerrilla camp. The first day's march was to the northwest along the Dongon River, relatively easy terrain, but Philip set a grueling pace. They did not stop to eat until the dusk, when, exhausted, the Americans fell asleep on the ground where they sat.

That night they kept no watch.

Philip woke the shore party at first light. It was Wednesday, the 23rd. Joe Bob immediately castigated himself mentally for the laxity of not setting a night watch, but realized that none of the Americans, himself included, would have been able to keep their eyes open.

After a quick, cold breakfast, Philip led them away from the river and entered the jungle. The going was much harder than the day before. Philip skillfully led them through the bush, moving swiftly and silently, and Joe Bob and the shore party had all they could do to keep up. When they finally reached the jungle clearing where Delvina Bacatplan's irregulars made their camp, it was, according to Joe Bob's wristwatch, already 1700.

He and his men were thirsty and hungry. Sensing their thirst, Philip took them to a spring inside the camp to fill their canteens. Once at the spring, the boy dropped to his knees and stooped to drink.

Inside the camp, and en route to the spring, they had passed people engaged in various tasks along the way, mostly men, but some women. All were dressed like Philip, in what looked like baggy rags. They also all wore the same style of broad-brimmed plaited palm hat that Philip wore. And each person stopped what they were doing, and, with a bright smile, said *"Mabuhay!"* and seemed to be entirely comfortable with their presence. It was as if everyone there knew they were coming, and they were quite welcome. They spoke with each other in a language nothing like any the Americans had ever heard before.

"What language is that?" Joe Bob asked Philip.

"Filipino language," he answered. "Tagalog."

"And where did you learn to speak English so well?"

"American school, Manila," he answered.

Still beside the spring, Philip said, "Drink. Fill your canteens. Wait here. I go now."

Before Joe Bob could protest, the boy was gone

After the other four slaked their thirst and filled their canteens at the spring, Joe Bob drank his fill and filled his own canteen. When he looked up, there was, he thought, one of the most beautiful women he had ever seen. Not that he could see much other than her face, because she was dressed in the same rag-bag uniform as everyone else. Even the raven-wing black hair that framed her face was mostly hidden under that ubiquitous broad-brimmed plaited-palm hat. The woman shared with the boy, Philip, that same smooth, coffee-with-cream, clear complexion. She had an oval face with a small, somewhat flattened nose, and large, bright eyes, liquid black. And she was tiny, not even five feet tall. She greeted him with a broad, full-lipped smile. "Hello, Lieutenant," she said, extending her hand, "I am Delvina Bacatplan."

Joe Bob took her extended hand. Unlike her face, her small hand was rough and calloused, her nails broken and short. "Joe Bob Clanton," he replied.

* * * * *

Only a scant forty miles up the coast from Dongon Bay is Mindoro's principal city, Sablayan. When *Orca's* shore party was just arriving at the guerrilla camp, a convoy of trucks carrying forty-two elite IJA commandos entered the confines of the Japanese garrison at Sablayan. Their leader was *Rikugun-Shosa* — Major — Takeshi Shizuka, a veteran of the jungles of Burma. The troops he led were jungle fighters, especially trained to move quickly and silently through jungle terrain. Each man had mastered the use of the West Java *karambit,* a short-bladed, curved knife, for silent, up-close work, and each was an expert marksman.

Shizuka was an American citizen, born in Bakersfield, California, to Japanese immigrants. He and his family had moved back to Japan when young Takeshi was still in the fifth grade, and settled in Nagoya. His education was resumed in the local army military cadet school, and he was eventually accepted into *Rikugun Shikan Gakko,* the Imperial Japanese Army Academy. Shizuka was tall, slender, and athletic—a handsome man. He never married, and dedicated himself instead to Bushido and to the Army.

Rikugun Chusa—Lieutenant Colonel—Gaku Chiba was garrison commander at Sablayan. Unlike the ascetic Shizuka, Chiba was a short, fat, lazy man, who had achieved rank through family and political connections. He commanded 240 regulars, some of whom supervised work gangs of slave workers: mainly 1,150 Filipinos, but also 350 Koreans. He had pleaded with the authorities in Manila for aid in putting an end to the Mindoran insurgent forces, and perhaps his description of their latest audacity, the sixteen heads mounted along the roadside, had been the catalyst that brought Shizuka and his commandos to Sablayan. *Whatever the reason, it was,* Chiba thought, *about time.*

"Welcome, Major," Chiba said, bowing. Shizuka said nothing, acknowledging the base commander's welcome with a slightly deeper bow. "It's high time Manila sent me someone capable of dealing with these infernal insurgents," Chiba groused. "How am I to provide the home islands with needed lumber if I am continually harassed by these devils?"

"How indeed," Shizuka allowed. "You say you have a man who can guide me to their camp?"

"Yes, I do. One of their number, a boy really. Thinks by helping us we will release his father from the Santo Tomas prison. The boy's father was an official in the puppet Quezon government."

"And will we?"

"Will we what?"

"Release his father from prison."

Chiba guffawed. "We will not!" When he regained his composure, he said, "Actually we cannot. The boy's father was executed two months ago," Chiba chuckled, "but the boy doesn't know that."

He continued, "The boy speaks no Japanese—only that native Filipino jabber and the English the Americans taught him. I use one of my staff, Captain Shigamitsu, as an interpreter to translate his English to Japanese. He can do the same for you. Feel free to take Shigamitsu along with you."

"No need," Shizuka said. "I speak English. He would only get in the way. And I doubt that your Captain could move as quickly and silently as my men. Where is this boy?"

"He should be along any time now. Said he had to return to the insurgent camp, or their leader—a woman, mind you!—would become suspicious. Meanwhile, please join me for dinner and tea."

* * * * *

"And these are the men you have come to rescue," Delvina said.

Three men in bedraggled USAAF flight suits looked up at Joe Bob and the *Orca* crewmen from beneath a lean-to of bamboo poles and palm fronds. One of them emerged from under the lean-to and introduced himself, hand extended. "Boy, am I happy to see the Navy! I'm Roger Plunkett, formerly commander and pilot of the *Laura Lee*."

Job Bob shook the man's extended hand, saying, "Joe Bob Clanton. And these guys are Chief Frenchie Eifel, Petty Officer Jim Orsi, and Seamen Robert Olds and Jack Rubidot."

"Glad to see you!" Plunkett said, and he introduced the other two men with him. "And this guy with the broken landing gear," Plunkett explained, "is my navigator, First Lieutenant Charlie Warren. And this is my radio operator, First Sergeant Norman Zane."

"Gentlemen," Joe Bob acknowledged. "We're all off the submarine *Orca*, and we're here to take you back to base at Saipan."

"Roger that!" they responded, and began asking Joe Bob about the logistics of the journey.

"Whoa!" Joe Bob said, holding up his hands in self-defense. "Getting you to the shoreline is pretty much up to our Filipino friends. Once we get back to Dongon Bay, I can get you out to our boat. And we better get there quick, 'cause we've only got a ten-day window when *Orca* will be coming into the Bay looking for us, and the better part of three of those days is already gone."

The four of them looked to Delvina, who, until then, smiling, had only listened to their conversation.

"Not to worry," she said. "We will get all of you to Dongon with time to spare. But, if you gentlemen," she indicated the B-24 crewmen and the four enlisted sailors, "will excuse us, I have something I wish to show Joe Bob."

"Certainly," they agreed. Delvina led Joe Bob away from the lean-to.

"No way!" an irate Joe Bob said. "Absolutely not! If I showed up with thirty-seven extra civilians, my Skipper would toss me overboard. And I wouldn't blame him." Now he understood why Delvina had insisted that he and his men come to the guerrlla camp.

"Please, Joe Bob, you must!" implored Delvina. "If you don't take them with you . . ." a sweep of Delvina's hand indicating a group of old men, women, and children occupying a compound in the center and most-protected part of the camp, ". . . they will die. We cannot protect them from the Japanese forever. We must stay continually on the move, and with them here, our movements are restricted. Wherever we are, we must always leave fighters behind to protect them, and we may one day not move them quickly enough if a particular camp is threatened. All that goes away if you take them with you, if you take them to safety on your submarine!"

"But Delvina, It's not *my* submarine. It's Uncle Sam's. And it's not all that big. Rescuing three airmen is one thing. Rescuing half of the population of Mindoro is something else again!" Then Joe Bob pictured the sixty-four, diesel-covered Aussies and Brits *Orca* had fished out of the waters off Palau.

Delvina smiled, sensing Joe Bob's resolve was wavering. "Thirty-seven people is *not* half the population of Mindoro. And Mindoro is *United States* territory. You may have stolen this country forty years ago, but you have been good to us, educated us, let us elect our own government, and even promised us independence. So, these people, we Filipinos, we are *your* people. You *must* take them with you."

"Let me talk to my men," Joe Bob said, wavering. Delvina sensed victory.

That night, at 2300, August 23rd, for the fourth time, *Orca* entered Dongon Bay, surfaced with decks awash, and looked for a signal from the shore. An hour later, *Orca* submerged and retired to deep water.

Joe Bob slept fitfully on a bed of thatched-palm mats and under a blanket. He awoke, startled, as the blanket shifted, and a warm body moved under the blanket beside him. "Shhh," it hissed. "It's me."

"Delvina?" Joe Bob whispered.

"Yes. Shhh," she said.

Joe Bob reached out for her, his fingers touching bare flesh . . .

* * * * *

Major Takeshi Shizuka awoke at 0542 on the morning of Thursday, August 24th, after a comfortable night in the garrison at Sablayan. He knew the exact time and date because he wore a Swiss-made, Omega watch—a "chronograph"—that his father had given him when he graduated from the *Rikugun Shikan Gakko.* It would be, he hoped, his last comfortable night until he had killed all of the insurgents and razed their camp. He rose, washed, and then dressed in the same jungle fatigues he had worn into the camp. He strapped on his *ketana*, the sword he wore in country as the only symbol of his rank.

In the spare officer's mess, Shizuka ate a light breakfast of rice, preserved fish, and tea. He ate and left quickly, lest he run into the camp commandant, Lt. Col. Chiba, to whom Shizuka had taken an intense dislike.

In the garrison courtyard, Shizuka was pleased to find his *Socho* — Sergeant Major — Akito Genda leading the troops in calisthenics. How proud he was of his men! While each one would gladly and without hesitation lay down his life for the emperor, each one also understood that their first duty to the emperor was to take the lives of his enemies! Here were the finest specimens of Japanese manhood, trained both to move quickly and silently in jungle terrain, and to remain hidden and motionless for hours when required. And, to a man, he knew they were as anxious as he was to march into the jungle and find and kill the enemy.

And so it was not at all to Shizuka's liking that he and his men had to wait until noon before Chiba's informer arrived at the garrison gate.

Putting on a show for Shizuka, Chiba berated the boy for keeping the major waiting. The boy took the verbal abuse in silence, not understanding a word of the Japanese, but well aware that he was being berated for something. Shizuka, meanwhile, took the boy's measure. He could not be more than a teenager, he thought, but he had the look of one who had suffered much and had survived. When Chiba had quit his tirade, Shizuka addressed the boy.

"He says that you are late, and that you were expected first thing this morning."

Startled, the boy looked up at the major, surprised that he had addressed him in English. "It could not be helped," he replied. "If I left the camp too early, they would be suspicious."

Now Chiba looked uncomfortable, unhappy to be cut out of the conversation.

"I am Major Shizuka. What is your name?"

"Philip," the boy answered.

* * * * *

Philip led the commandos inland. He had counted them carefully. There were forty-two of them, including the sergeant major and the major. When Shizuka had asked, he had told the major that Delvina commanded about fifty armed men. Actually there were far fewer—only thirty-six. The major had taken in the information without any outward sign of concern. He obviously had supreme confidence in his men. They were, Philip had to admit, very quiet, even making little noise as they marched along the corduroy road that led into the island's interior. They did not, he noted, march, military style, in step. They moved, instead, like Delvina's guerrillas moved, with instinctive precision, silently, and as individuals.

It was dusk, and they were still on the corduroy, when Philip said to Shizuka, "We stop here for the night. Tomorrow we leave road. Head inland."

"We will stop here," Shizuka replied, "but not for the night. We rest, eat. Then we head inland. We will not stop until we reach the guerrilla camp. You can find your way there in the dark, can you not?"

"I can. But maybe your men get lost in the dark," Philip answered.

"Let that be *my* worry."

There was a not quite, three-quarter moon overhead when the commandos left the corduroy road and were led into the jungle.

419

Once under the jungle canopy, however, it made little difference. It was pitch black, except where the infrequent shaft of moonlight could penetrate.

Philip moved quickly through the thick tangle of underbrush, seeming to effortlessly find a trail where none should have existed, even in the almost complete darkness. The luminous dial on Shikuza's Omega chronograph read 0312, August 25th, when the commandos reached the outskirts of a clearing, which Philip said was the guerrilla's camp. Shizuka directed Sgt. Maj. Genda to keep the troops well back from the clearing, while he and Philip made their way to its edge.

Philip had led the commandos, Shizuka saw, to what was obviously a burned-out and deserted village. There was no sign of life whatsoever. Not that he had expected to see anyone other than sentries moving about at that hour, but there were no corralled livestock, no hanging clothes, no sign at all of recent human activity. And, what humans leave behind, the jungle reclaims—the place was overgrown. The most convincing of signs all that the place was deserted was that there was no stink of human waste. What Shizuka did smell, however, was a trap. "It looks like a burned-out village," Shizuka whispered testily to Philip. "And if this is the guerrilla camp, where are the guerrillas? And where are the sentries?"

"It *is* a deserted village," Philip whispered back, uncowed. "Delvina and men sleep in the middle of village—the village square. And what good are sentries if you see them? See those houses there?" Philip pointed out some burned-out huts built off the ground on stilts.

"Huts without a roof, overgrown underneath. Yes, I see them."

"There is sentry post in that one," Philip whispered. He pointed out a nearby hut. "And one in that house. He pointed to another hut, much further away.

"How many sentries are posted?"

"Eight."

"And you know their locations?"

"Yes."

"Good. Wait here."

Shizuka crawled back into the jungle, where Genda waited with the commandos, and where he gave Genda specific instructions. Then Shizuka returned to where Philip waited.

Genda selected eight of his men and passed on to them the orders that Shizuka had given him. He and the boy would guide each of them to their targets. They were then to wait for his, Genda's, signal. On his signal, they were each to approach their assigned sentry station and take out the sentry. But if they found no sentry at their location, then they were to raise the alarm, because then the boy had lied, and all of this was an elaborate trap.

Genda and the eight men then moved up silently to the edge of the clearing where Shizuka and Philip were.

"Philip, you will show Sergeant Major Genda where each of the sentry posts are. He will post a man at each. Just before first light, when the signal is given, they will be the first to move."

Philip led Genda and his men, crawling, around the camp. At each sentry point, a man was dropped off. Finally, Philip and Genda were back where they had started. An hour had passed, and they found Shizuka sitting there cross-legged, apparently in meditation.

"I heard you from twenty meters away, Genda. You are getting old," Shizuka whispered in Japanese.

"Not so, Major. You heard the boy," the Sergeant Major replied in the same language.

"I did, but not until he was much closer."

"No, Sir. That was me," Genda grinned.

* * * * *

In the wee hours of August 24th, when Joe Bob awoke, it was still dark. He reached out for Delvina, but she was not there. He wondered if he might have dreamed the whole incident, her coming to him in the night, but then realized that he was naked under the blanket. And he knew that he had crawled under the blanket the night before wearing his skivvies. He reached around under the blanket until he found them, then put his underwear back on.

At first light, Rodolfo, one of Delvina's lieutenants who spoke fair English, shook Joe Bob and the other Americans awake. "Eat," he said. "Today we head for coast. Must start early. Get to river by nightfall."

Joe Bob and the others had not quite finished breakfast, and he noticed that the civilians were already packed up and were ready to travel. He had wondered whether the stuff they would insist upon bringing with them would even fit on the submarine, but when he saw how painfully little they had, he realized he need not have worried. He also saw that at least three of the women were visibly pregnant, one of whom looked like she was about to give birth any second. It occurred to him that, never mind the Japs finding and killing them, some of the civilians might well not survive the rigors of the journey itself.

Two men came with an improvised stretcher and, mindful of his leg, loaded Charlie Warren onto it. Then everybody followed Rodolfo out of the camp. On the way, Joe Bob realized that the rest of the camp was deserted — no Delvina, no resistance fighters. Other than Rodolfo, the two men carrying the stretchers, and two others, only the walking Americans and a few of the civilians were armed. (Plunkett and Zane carried carbines, obviously provided by the guerrillas.) Delvina and the rest, he reasoned, must have gone ahead to make sure that the way was clear. Of course. That had to be it.

* * * * *

It was 0439, fifteen minutes before first light, when, cupping his mouth, Genda gave a call. It was the shrill, screechy sound of a Macaque. Eight commandos moved silently, almost invisibly forward, their *karambits* at the ready. Using his field glasses, Shizuka could barely spy the two shadowy forms of his men as they approached the only two guard posts in his field of vision. He watched as they melded into the underbrush beneath the huts, and he could no longer see them.

Shizuka had heard nothing, but that was exactly what he would have expected if the boy had been telling the truth.

At 0454, first light, Shizuka nodded to Genda, and Genda again gave the Macaque call. All around the periphery of the village, thirty-five ghostly shapes emerged from the jungle, making their silent way toward the village center and the sleeping insurgents.

As the commandos passed the huts where the guerrilla sentries had been posted, eight shadows joined the thirty-five. Shizuka and Genda, with Philip in tow, led the commandos in their sector toward the center of the insurgents' camp.

Shizuka concentrated then on leading his men forward silently, intent on maintaining the element of surprise. Behind him, the men who had joined his contingent from the sentry posts fell back from the others. As he and his men advanced on the village square, he counted more burned-out huts, two larger scorched buildings, vacant animal pens, silent hen houses, and what appeared to be an incinerated church in the distance. The buildings gave way to an open area in the center of the village.

Philip, pointing, whispered, "There it is. Village square." The village square, where the blanket-wrapped forms of the sleeping guerrillas were clearly visible. Since the commandos had approached the square in groups from all around the periphery of the village, the square was completely surrounded. And now what Shizuka smelled was victory.

* * * * *

August 25th was the second day of their long march to the coast through the wilds of Mindoro. The going was really rough — *and* slow. There were thirty-seven civilians, old people, pregnant women, women carrying babies and toddlers, boys and girls, doing the best they could — the jungle, unyielding, denying passage.

Even given that the third airman had to be carried there on a stretcher, had it been just the *Orca* contingent and the two mobile airmen, they and the five Filipinos with them could have easily made the coast by nightfall the following day.

As it was, Joe Bob figured, they would be lucky to make the coast in another five days. They had landed, he remembered, at Dongon Bay at 2300 on the 20th. If nothing unforeseen happened, they could be on the coast by the 30th. They could still make it within *Orca's* ten-day retrieval window — *if* nothing unforeseen happened.

* * * * *

Despite the spare light — it was not yet dawn — Shizuka could clearly see the forms of men huddled under blankets, sleeping out in the open. Leaving Philip behind, he drew his blade, and pointing it at the village square, he urged his men forward. "Quickly now," he whispered at least loud enough for the men closest to him to hear.

When they were almost on top of the sleeping Filipinos, he raised his *ketana* high, shouted, "Banzai!" and, rushing forward, brought the blade down hard onto the nearest sleeping form.

Genda and the men behind him took up the cry "Banzai!" and with their *karambits,* dispatched the remaining sleepers. But there had been no cries, not even a moan, from the sleeping forms, their blankets now slashed to ribbons. And there were no bodies and no blood.

424

Shizuka took the first bullet. It pierced the back of his skull before the *craaak* of the rifle could reach him. He fell face forward, dead before he hit the ground, still clutching his *ketana*. The commandos, superbly trained, reacted immediately, but not quickly enough for the nine of their number, including their commander, already killed by the guerrilla enfilade. The twenty-nine remaining commandos, twelve of whom had also been hit, fell flat to the ground and squirmed around so that they formed a ragged circle facing the incoming fire.

Sgt. Maj. Genda had survived the first volley unscathed, and, from the center of the circle of his troops, directed the commando response to the enemy. Some of the Japanese were firing indiscriminately into the surrounding village. "Hold your fire!" he shouted. "Do not waste your ammunition. Fire only when you have a clear target."

The guerrillas had the advantage. Firing from the cover of the bypassed buildings, many of them now climbed high enough so that they were firing down on the now supine and surrounded enemy. Delvina had given her men instructions similar to those Genda just had given his: they were not to fire until they could detect distinct movement. No sense shooting a man already down and out of the fight.

As dawn broke, the guerrillas' advantage grew with the rising sun. The irony had not escaped Delvina, who made the burned-out church her headquarters. The rising sun would enable the death of those who fought under the rising sun. God did indeed have a sense of humor — *a bit macabre, perhaps*, she mused, *but a sense of humor nonetheless.*

By sunrise, at 0545, only Genda and two other commandoes remained alive. Three of those wounded in the guerrillas' first volley had bled out, and the others had been picked off where they lay. As the sun rose, Genda had briefly considered surrender, but immediately rejected the idea as dishonorable.

There was, after all, dishonor enough in having been defeated by such inherently inferior beings. His only thought was to take as many of the enemy as possible with him. He whispered loud enough for the other two men still alive to hear, "Remain motionless. They will think we are all dead. Eventually they will come. When they do, be ready."

One of the other two slowly reached around for his *karambit* and received a bullet in the brain for his trouble. Genda cursed him for a fool. Now they were only two.

* * * * *

Delvina walked out of the back of the burned-out church, where she could not be seen from the village square. It was well past sunrise. Early morning, perhaps seven o'clock, she guessed. They would leave the bodies of the Japanese where they fell, including the eight under the "sentry" huts. Her men had cut those eight down as they rose from the underbrush and made to climb up to the platforms of the huts where the Filipino sentries were supposedly posted. As for the others, it was almost sinful how easily they had been cut down. And she had not lost a single one of her own.

She had ordered twenty — the bulk — of her men to leave the village and go quickly to the head of the Dongon River. There, they were to prepare rafts so that the civilians could journey down the river in relative comfort and speed. She would join them soon with rest of her troop, except for the five that had been given "head duty." But first she had to go and visit Bartolomeo and their baby son.

"Can you forgive me for sleeping with the American, Bartolomeo?" she asked, her question addressed to the wooden cross in the churchyard that marked her husband's overgrown grave. "There were no others before him, you know," she said aloud, "and I have missed you so. I don't know what came over me, really. But he is beautiful as you were beautiful, and I have been so lonely. Please forgive me."

Their child, she knew, had been buried with his father, and she thought that maybe she should say something to him as well, but realized, sadly, that she could barely picture him in her mind. She had known her son for only a short time.

Then Delvina cried. She had not cried in a long time, not since the night when she and the other women survivors buried them.

The sun was climbing high in the sky. The jungle canopy provided some shade, but the heat was stifling. Joe Bob's uniform was soaked with sweat, and it seemed that he had emptied his canteen at least five times already—and it was not yet mid-morning. His legs were aching, he was tired, and another three-quarter-day's march lay ahead. He had no idea how the civilians were able to stand it. But aside from a few whining and complaining children, the Filipinos seemed to be doing just fine. Even the three pregnant women, and the two men carrying Charlie Warren's stretcher (and who had yet to be relieved) appeared as if all-day marches in August were an everyday occurrence, one taken completely in stride. He had come, he realized, to admire and respect these amazing people.

Joe Bob remembered how cool it had been during the night, almost cold, and how comfortable it had been under that blanket. Then, he remembered Delvina waking him. The blanket was not for comfort then, but for concealment.

He chased the thought from his mind. She had disappeared in the night, after all, and he might never see her again.

* * * * *

The sun was climbing high in the sky. Genda and his man had remained motionless. But if he was patient, so were the Filipinos. Huge flies were buzzing all around, laying their eggs on the dead. Occasionally one would land on him, on his skin, and he had to concentrate to keep from flinching.

At last! He could hear them now, approaching. They were wary, as well they should be, whispering in their gibberish language, even though there was no clear reason to be whispering. Then he heard the *whish* of their blades as they mutilated the dead around him. He had been patient, and now he must *remain* patient.

They were closer now, five of them, Genda guessed, maybe more. Then, one kicked his foot, and he jumped up, *karambit* slashing out, cutting flesh. He barely felt the machete that came down hard on his neck at the shoulder, neatly severing his carotid artery and biting into his brainstem. Sergeant Major Genda was dead before his body crumpled beneath him.

Another commando, close by, also jumped up when Genda did. Well before he could get close enough to any of the men on "head duty" to do any damage, he was cut down by a bullet fired from a hastily shouldered, but accurately aimed, carbine.

"Damn," one of the "head duty" men, the victim of Genda's blade, said in Tagalog, "he cut me. I'm bleeding!"

"Let me see," another answered, and inspected the wound. "It's deep, Ernesto. I suspect you are going to die."

"You fool," Ernesto answered. "That's not funny. That Jap bastard could easily have killed me."

"But he didn't," the other man answered. He tore a length of cloth from the bottom of his shirt. "Here," he said, "wrap it with this. It will stop the bleeding for now, but that wound will have to eventually be sewn up — and soon."

As Ernesto wrapped the cloth around his wounded arm, the other man, looking down at Genda's corpse, said, "You did a good job on this one, Ernesto. His head is practically off already."

Ernesto smiled. "When he jumped up, I just swung my machete at him without even thinking!"

The "head duty" party also had the responsibility of gathering up the enemy's weapons. Carbines and those unusual knives with the strange blades, were being gathered and stacked in the village square. Ernesto approached the now headless corpse of Maj. Shizuka, attracted by the glint of the sun off his blade, the *katana* still clutched in the major's lifeless hand. Ernesto stooped down, and, prying away dead fingers, claimed the sword as his own. He examined the keen edge, and wielded the weapon as he imagined its original owner might. It made a whistling sound as it cut through the humid air.

"That's a fine weapon," his companion volunteered.

"Not really," Ernesto said. "It's certainly very sharp. But it's too long for close-in work. I prefer my machete. It's shorter and heavier. And *this* blade would be useless for cutting underbrush."

Ernesto added Shizuka's sword to the pile of the other weapons stacked in the village square.

* * * * *

When Joe Bob and his party reached the Dongon River on the evening of August 27th, Delvina and her troops were waiting for them. Lined up along the riverbank were six rafts, constructed of lengths of bamboo, strung together with woven vines.

"They are not very big," Chief Eifel observed. "They will never hold all of us."

"They not meant to," Rodolfo answered. "Those who can will still have to walk along the riverbank. But now old people, pregnant women, and the children float down to the bay. We make better time."

"We should," Eifel agreed.

Joe Bob approached Delvina warily. "You disappeared. I thought I might never see you again."

"You might not have," she said, "if some things had worked out differently. But I had some urgent business to attend to at Papylan, my old village."

"Urgent business?" Joe Bob repeated.

"Yes," she said. "And now our urgent business is to get these people safely to your submarine."

Joe Bob winced. He was almost certain that Captain Lawlor would never refuse to bring the civilians aboard and transport them to safety, but he was nowhere near as certain that the skipper would ever forgive him for putting him in that position to begin with.

* * * * *

At 2300 on August 29th, *Orca* surfaced, decks awash, in Dongon Bay for the tenth time. If the shore party was not there this night, Jake would bring the boat into the bay one last time.

But there it was, the signal from the shore.

A half-hour later, the rubber boat that made for the shore ten nights ago was back alongside. In it were Joe Bob Clanton and three other men, one of whom was lying flat in the boat, his leg bound up in a splint.

Jake was on the bridge when the men came aboard, and watched as Joe Bob introduced the airmen to Joel, who was on deck. He watched as Bucky supervised getting the airman with the broken leg gingerly down into the boat via the forward torpedo room hatch.

One more round trip, get the others back aboard, and we can get out of here, he thought. But, by then, Joe Bob was on the bridge beside him.

Jake didn't know whether to praise his engineer for his compassion or to murder him on the spot. Either way, he thought, the admiral would understand. But then again, maybe not.

Joe Bob was right. The man really didn't have any other choice, and neither did he. He had already sent the rubber boat back to shore with Joe Bob to fetch the first load of civilians. He only hoped he could get all of them and *Orca's* shore party aboard before dawn.

It was Bucky who came up with the idea of stringing a line from the *Orca* to the shore. That way, two men could haul on the line and move the boat back and forth with minimal paddling. And that way, the round trip was cut to less than forty minutes instead of a full hour. Each trip brought six more souls aboard— seven round trips total. The last group came aboard just before dawn. And Joe Bob had made every trip.

The last trip was the hardest for Joe Bob. He had to say goodbye to Delvina, and she had made it very clear on the trip downriver, that her men must never suspect that they had been lovers. If they ever suspected that she had succumbed to the feelings of an ordinary woman, they would never again follow her. To them she must be as the Blessed Virgin reborn, pure and undefiled. They would never hold a man to the same standard, of course, but such things are not subject to reason—they just *were*.

How do you say goodbye to a woman who you long to touch without actually touching her? For Delvina's part, her liquid black eyes spoke volumes: *Goodbye. I may never see you again, but I will never forget you.* Joe Bob might have said as much to her with his own eyes without knowing it, but she knew, nonetheless. What he *did* know was that leaving her there on the shore of Dongon Bay and returning to *Orca* was one of the hardest things he ever had to do.

* * * * *

Doc Shields checked out Charlie Warren's leg as soon as he was aboard and settled in a bunk in the XO's cabin. The leg should have been set, wrapped, and encased in a plaster cast. But Shields guessed correctly that the guerrillas had no more access to plaster than he had aboard *Orca*. So they had done exactly what he had done when Early Sender had broken his leg: they set it and immobilized it with splints, and, as near as he could tell, had done every bit as good a job as he could—better, perhaps. He told Warren as much, and the man seemed relieved.

Back out at sea, Jake sent a lengthy message to SUBPAC and Pacific Command, describing the situation aboard *Orca*. The reply was terse and to the point. The boat was to proceed to Saipan, where all her passengers, civilian and military, would disembark.

The other Army Air Corps officer, Cpt. Plunkett, was bunked in the wardroom. It was an awkward and uncomfortable arrangement, but Jake refused to displace a junior officer from his bunk. First Sergeant Zane was assigned a bunk in the "goat locker," as CPO quarters were known.

The civilians were split between the forward and after torpedo rooms—twenty-two aft and fifteen forward. While actual bunks were found for the three pregnant women, the rest were happy to make space for themselves wherever they could, and for most, that meant a blanket stretched out on a steel deck. Mastering the mysteries of the head proved a challenge, but eventually all except the smallest children were able to use it unaided.

The most pregnant of the pregnant women gave birth on the second day out of Dongon. The child, a boy, was born at 1400 local time on August 31, 1944, in the after torpedo room of the submarine *Orca*. Doc Shields tried to assist with the birth, but was shooed away by women who had ably attended countless other new mothers. So it was that the civilian population of the after torpedo room increased to twenty-three.

Having civilians aboard was a different experience altogether than having the rescued Aussies and Brits aboard during *Orca's* fifth war patrol. Those men, while almost twice in number as the civilians, were near death. In fact, two of the men in *Orca* did die, as did seven more in the other two boats involved in that rescue operation.

These passengers, on the other hand, including the elderly, were mostly in very good health. Confining them to the torpedo rooms proved to be impossible, and disregarding the sternest admonitions of the crew, they wandered the boat freely, the children especially, and were curious about *everything*. Despite repeated warnings, they were fascinated by the gauges, the valves, and the knobs, and could not resist touching and turning and twisting. Joel took to ordering a "rig for dive" check done almost every other hour.

When the boat finally reached port in Saipan, on September 4th, *Orca* was almost out of food and her crew out of patience.

In Saipan, after the passengers were off the boat, orders came for *Orca* to proceed to the newly set up naval base at Majuro, in the Marshall Islands, 1,580 miles to the east-southeast. There, her needs would be attended to by the submarine tender, *Sperry*, and the supply ships and tankers anchored there.

Orca departed Saipan for Majuro on the morning of September 7th, and arrived in Majuro in the afternoon of Tuesday, September 12, 1944. In Majuro, *Orca* tied up alongside *Sperry*.

Jake took stock of the past fifty-five days: three Navy airmen rescued off Yap and Woleai; three Army Air Corps fliers rescued off Mindoro; and thirty-seven—no, thirty-eight—Allied civilians rescued off Mindoro as well.

Thus it was that *Orca* ended her eighth war patrol, returning to port for the third time from patrol, still carrying a full load of torpedoes. Jake consoled himself with the fact that one of those times, her fifth patrol, had earned *Orca* and her crew a Presidential Unit Citation. Some things were every bit as important as sinking enemy shipping—and some more so.

Chapter 22

Majuro: 12 September 1944 to 28 September 1944

Majuro Atoll in the Central Pacific consists of fifty-six separate islands, the largest of which is Majuro Island at the southern tip of the atoll. The Navy base on Majuro Island was built principally to support air operations. The submarine base at Majuro, Jake thought, appeared to be an afterthought.

The airfields on the island, a Loran station, and some medical facilities, appeared to be the products of some deliberation and planning. The sub base not so much. The only submarine service facility ashore was an R & R camp for submariners, Camp Myrna, built by men from the submarine tender *Sperry.* And it was not exactly the Royal Hawaiian.

The minor repairs *Orca* and the three other subs at Majuro required were being done by *Sperry.* To replenish stores, *Orca* had to pull up alongside a supply ship — for fuel, alongside a tanker. Fresh water, at least, was supplied by twenty-one, shore-based distilling units, which cranked out about fifty thousand gallons a day. The boats tied up alongside *Sperry* were thus able to receive fresh water piped into, and from, the lone pier.

The sub base was more a fleet anchorage than anything else. Most of the men in *Orca* stayed on board rather than sleep in the tents on Myrna, and, with water piped aboard from the shore, they could even shower daily, and actually get some of their laundry done.

Now, if only their mail would catch up with them.

* * * * *

On September 15, 1944, U.S. and Australian troops invaded Morotai in the NEI, and the U.S First Marine Division and the Army 81st Infantry Division invaded Peleliu, in the Palaus. The noose tightened still more.

Orca had been in port less than a week when the word came down that the boats tied up alongside *Sperry* had to move out into the anchorage. Riding at anchor meant that the shore-supplied water was no longer available, and movement on and off the boat was strictly by launch. Inconvenient to say the least.

But the reason for the move soon became clear when, on the morning of September 19th, tugs pointed *Sperry* at the harbor entrance, and the tender took off for Pearl. Later that same day, the submarine tender, *Howard W. Gilmore*, entered port and tied up alongside Majuro's only pier, where *Sperry* had been only hours before. Further orders directed *Orca* to be the first boat to leave the anchorage and tie up immediately alongside the *Gilmore*.

Jake was taken completely by surprise when the first person off the gangway from the *Gilmore* to come aboard *Orca* was his Squadron Commander, Cpt. Clarence Macdonough.

"Commodore!" was Jake's surprised greeting to Macdonough when he came aboard.

"Hello, Jake," was Macdonough's smiling greeting. "I'm probably the last person you expected to see in this God-forsaken place!"

"To put it mildly, Sir," Jake said. "What brings you halfway across the Pacific to visit *Orca*?"

Macdonough chuckled. "Uncle Charlie, mostly. Seems the admiral has a special job for you to do. And he sent me to explain it, and to make sure that you understood that you have the option to turn it down without prejudice. I mean, that you *really* understood that you had that option."

"Sounds ominous."

"It is that. But what it is, mostly, is dangerous. *Really* dangerous. How about you get Himmelfarb, and we meet aboard the *Gilmore,* say, in about an hour, and talk about it?"

"Will do, Commodore. Joel and I will see you in an hour."

As Macdonough departed *Orca,* a far more popular visitor was boarding the boat: the mailbag.

* * * * *

Jake barely had time to put the letters from Kate in reverse chronological order and open the top two, when it was time for Joel and him to meet with the commodore. Still, he got to read them quickly, and to admire the black-and-white snapshots Kate had sent of Elizabeth and herself. The baby looked pretty much the same as she did when *Orca* left Pearl in mid-July, not at all surprising since Jake had taken the pictures himself with Kate's Brownie camera. He planned to give the letters and snapshots much more attention later.

With Joel in tow, Jake explained to the OOD on the *Gilmore's* quarterdeck that they had a meeting with Captain Macdonough. After a minute or so on the sound-powered phones, the OOD directed Jake and Joel to the flag quarters on the ship's 04 level, forward.

When Jake knocked, Macdonough opened the door and said, "Well, I see you found me." He nodded to Joel, "Good to see you again, Joel. Come in, gentlemen, come in."

The flag quarters aboard the *Gilmore* were fairly spacious, and there was even an area off to one corner with a small table and some chairs. It was probably meant for the admiral's mess, but Macdonough had set it up as a conference area. He directed Jake and Joel to two of the chairs, and took one himself. There was a chart spread out on the table, which Jake recognized as one used frequently aboard *S-49.* It was a chart of Manila Bay.

"How much do you gentlemen know about mine laying?" the commodore asked.

"Just what I've read in the manual, Commodore," Jake replied.

Joel nodded. "Same here, Sir."

"Okay," Macdonough explained, "it's not something a sub is called upon to do very frequently. Practically all mines are laid from the air these days. But sometimes, and this is one of them, a sub is the best and only way to lay 'em. Here's the deal. No secret that MacArthur is anxious to get back on Philippine soil. The sooner the better, and it may even happen as soon as next month. And Nimitz is sure that when the land invasion is imminent, the Jap Navy is going to throw everything it has left against us.

"Uncle Charlie wants the sub force to do its bit to befuddle the enemy and insure Allied success. So he came up with the idea of maybe mining the channels at Manila Bay."

"But the bay is too shallow," Jake objected. "The average depth is less than sixty feet. When I was stationed there in *S-49*, at Cavite, you had to go in on the surface—and *stay* on the surface."

"And there was very good reason for that," Macdonough agreed. "The bay around Cavite where the sub base was is really shallow—here, see? By Sangley Point? Three-and-a quarter and four-and-a-half meters, that's just ten-point-seven feet and fourteen-point-eight feet. No way you could transit that area submerged. But remember, I said the admiral just wants to mine the channels. They're deep enough so that it could be done submerged."

Joel had been examining the chart. "Barely," he conceded, "and not very safely. Look at these channel depths at those points. South Channel, twenty-seven meters. That's just eighty-eight feet. And here, the North Channel, just twenty meters. That's sixty-five feet. At periscope depth we'd be almost scraping bottom."

"But it could be done," Macdonough said. "And we'll want you to go in on a spring tide. There will be spring tides in mid-October when we do this. Spring tide will give you an additional one-point-two meters — that's just under four feet — added to these chart readings. Of course, the admiral said he would back off if you still thought it was too risky."

Jake had been listening, scratching his chin. "Definitely risky," he said, finally, "but maybe not impossible."

Joel looked at his boss as if he had just lost his mind. "Good God, Skipper," he said, "submerged at these depths we'd be visible from overhead. Remember what it was like off New Guinea? We were at periscope depth and those two natives were able to look down into the water and see us, and actually follow the boat? Even if we managed to navigate the bay at periscope depth, all it would take is a plane passing overhead and seeing us, and we'd be dead meat."

Jake chuckled. "Not highly likely. Manila Bay is so filthy you can't even see your hand in front of your face, six inches underwater. Besides, if we do this, we'll do it at night, get in and get out. No, that's not the deal breaker. *Here's* the deal breaker: Say we manage to get in and out without scraping bottom, what 's to keep us from straying out of the channels? How do we navigate at night? Look, the channels are about two miles wide, and both sides of the channels are heavily mined. Too many feet one side or the other, and it's 'Goodbye, Charlie.' "

"You've got prominent coastal features all around you," the commodore said, "and now you've got radar when you're submerged. You can navigate by radar."

"We *might* be able to do that," Jake said.

Joel fell silent. He thought they were both nuts, but would never say it aloud. Instead, he said, "Not so sure the shoreline could be mapped with radar. Don't know that it's ever been tried. Radar is used to locate ships and airplanes — ground return is usually regarded as just so much clutter. Anyplace we can practice this?" he asked.

The commodore grinned. "Of course there is. The perfect place to practice is right here in Majuro. And, best of all, I get to ride the boat when you do it! Now let's talk about mines . . .'

The commodore took Jake and Joel down into one of the *Gilmore's* cargo holds.

"Here we are, gentlemen, the Mark-Twelve, Model Three, submarine-launched magnetic mine." The neatly stacked mines were shaped like torpedoes, with smooth aluminum outer skins. The diameter looked pretty much the same as that of a Mark-14 torpedo, but the mine appeared to be much shorter. Jake figured maybe eight feet or so long. "Each one carries fifteen hundred and ninety five pounds of Torpex," Macdonough continued. "You can squeeze eight of these babies in the same space as three Mark-Fourteen torpedoes. The Admiral sent you forty of them, along with eight practice models."

"Wait a minute," Joel interjected, "you can only lay mines from the after tubes. *Orca* carries ten torpedoes aft, so no way could we lay all forty you brought. We could only lay twenty-four, twenty-five, maybe twenty-six, max — assuming we go to sea with no torpedoes aft at all."

"Good point," Macdonough allowed. "But what if we could rig your boat so you could lay mines from your forward tubes, as well?"

"You can do that?" Joel asked.

"Pretty sure we can."

"So Admiral Lockwood sends us forty mines," Jake mused. "Does the admiral expect we'd leave fifteen torpedoes behind to make room for forty mines? That would leave *Orca* carrying only nine torpedoes."

"No, explained Macdonough, "the admiral sent forty mines so you wouldn't leave *any more than* fifteen torpedoes behind. He's pretty much left the number of mines you'll take on this trip up to you. And another thing, each of these mines has been modified with a time-delay device, so it won't deploy for several minutes — and then, *still* not go active until ten days after it's been planted. That way, you can even retrace your steps if you have to, and pass over these mines without the danger of setting them off."

"But what about the mine mooring cables?" Joel asked. "I'm guessing you'd have to have some sort of deployment delay on the mines, if we were going to sow them from the forward tubes. Otherwise the cables might get snagged on our bow planes. But what if we really *do* have to retrace our steps, and the mines are already deployed? Maybe they *won't* go off, but with the boat submerged, won't the cables catch on our bow planes? Won't we end up dragging a mine or two — or a dozen — behind us?"

"Not if the cable-shedding device the boys from the *Gilmore* are going to install on *Orca* works as well as we think it will," the commodore replied.

"Seems like the admiral and you thought of everything," Joel said, without much conviction.

Back aboard *Orca*, Jake finally got to reread and enjoy his mail. Almost half of Kate's letters included snapshots of their daughter, and each one made Jake painfully aware of just how much this war was depriving him. He had a daughter growing up thousands of miles away. He was her father, and he should be there with her. Instead, it fell to his wife to be all things to their child, to hold her when she cried, to play with her, to nurse her when she was sick, to read to her, and to rock her to sleep. *She'll say her first word, and I won't be there to hear it. And this damn war could go on forever!*

The Japs were losing — they *would* lose — but they wouldn't give up until every last one of them was beaten. God help both sides when the home islands were at last invaded. Jake could envision the casualties on both sides. They would number in the millions. What a waste.

Lieutenant Joel Himmelfarb, pencil, paper, and weapons manuals in hand, did some calculations. Jake's guess, it turned out, as to the length of the mines, was pretty close: each Mark-12 mine was actually seven feet, ten-and-a-quarter inches long. Eight of them in line would take up sixty-two feet, ten inches. A Mark-14 torpedo is twenty feet, six inches long. Three of them, laid end-to-end, would occupy sixty-one feet, six inches—a difference of one foot, four inches. The commodore had said eight of the mines would squeeze into the same space as three torpedoes. *Well,* thought Joel, *the commodore did say "squeeze."*

That afternoon, as torpedoes were being offloaded and eight practice mines brought aboard, the "boys from the *Gilmore*" were installing the cable-shedding device on *Orca's* bow. While Bucky was overseeing those activities, the commodore was below briefing the wardroom on the purpose of the following day's exercise. Jake was amazed that none of his officers appeared to be the least bit nonplussed by the idea of creeping into Manila Bay and mining the shipping channels.

The next morning *Orca* left the *Gilmore's* side with eight practice mines in the forward torpedo room in place of *four* of her Mark-14 torpedoes. One of the four torpedoes offloaded the day before had been removed from tube one. The other three came off the torpedo racks. The tube would accommodate only two mines, so two torpedoes had to be removed from one rack to "squeeze" four of the mines on that rack, while the other two mines took up the space where the fourth torpedo had been.

The "cable-shedding device" was simply a pair of cables coming out of a mechanism that looked like an oversized arrowhead. The device was attached to the end of a length of steel tubing extending forward off Orca's bow, and attached to the hull below the bull nose. The arm increased the boat's length forward by several feet. The after end of each cable was attached to the forward tip of each bow plane, so that when the bow planes were deployed, the two cables formed a steep angle from the bow. A pulley-and-roller-guide mechanism inside the arrowhead and a spring inside the arm worked to keep the cable taut, while still not interfering with the normal functioning of the bow planes. The crewmembers who observed the installation immediately dubbed the device "The Christmas Tree."

Snagging a mine cable on the stern planes was never mentioned, because it was never an issue. The stern planes were fixed in place by design, and were already equipped with an elaborate guard of steel tubing built to protect them, the rudder, and the boat's propellers from dock pilings. This same guard would perform double duty as a fairwater that would shed any mine cables aft.

"We would have foreseen the problem, if only we'd thought about it," Jake said to Harry Hastings, his Weapons Officer. The day's practice run had gone poorly, and the boat was headed back into port. In the wardroom, *Orca's* officers were holding a *post mortem*, led by Commodore Macdonough, on the day's activities.

"Everything would have been fine, if we planned to fire two mines at once from all the tubes, one tube at a time," the commodore explained. "But we really only want to sow one mine at a time, and use just one tube to sow all the mines. So, this morning, your torpedo men had to remove a mine from number one tube before we could deploy the one left in the tube, deploy that mine, drain the tube, then reload and fire the second mine. Then they had to drain the tube again, load and fire the next mine, and so on, deploying the rest of the mines one at a time. I don't fault your men. They were moving as fast as they could. But the whole operation was just *too* slow. We have to do something different."

"Why is that, Sir?" Hastings asked. "We deployed the rest of them pretty quickly. Considering all the manhandling involved, twenty minutes, eighteen seconds, per mine isn't all that bad. The only glitch was with the first ones that were loaded in the tubes. But we can *surely* figure out a way around that. Besides, we'll be deploying them both fore and aft. If we alternate, that's just over ten minutes per mine.

"Let's see," the commodore said. "To minimize your exposure in the shipping channels, the boat will need to go as fast as possible, which, submerged, is a sustainable five knots. The North Channel is the most heavily traveled, so we'll want to plant the mines closer together there. Every twelve hundred yards or so. The North Channel is eight-point-three miles long, so that's fourteen mines. At five knots, you cover about a hundred and seventy yards per minute, so that's seven minutes you'll get to load and shoot each mine. But your best time this morning, shooting the mines that were loaded into the tubes directly from the racks, was ten minutes, six seconds, or ten-point-one minutes per mine – *three* minutes too long. You'll have a bit more time to deploy each mine on the South Channel. It's eighteen miles long, and, if the spacing there is opened up to fourteen hundred yards, you'll have just over eight minutes to load and shoot each mine. But that's *still* two minutes less than ten-point-one minutes.

"The South Channel's eighteen miles long, thirty-six thousand yards," Jake acknowledged. "So, at fourteen-hundred-yard intervals, that's twenty-six mines. Fourteen on the North Channel, twenty-six on the South — forty mines total. Strange how that works out to *exactly* the number of mines the admiral sent," Jake noted.

"Isn't it," Macdonough said, smiling.

A half-minute of pensive silence passed before Billy Kinkaid spoke up. "I'm sure we can deploy each mine faster if we just organize the work better," he said. "This morning, we worked the two mines in the tubes first—and there's no avoiding that—then the four of the mines on the port side first, then, finally, the two on the starboard. Each mine had to have the chain hoist attached in turn, lift collar secured to the mine first, in order to lift it off the rack. What if we get *another* collar, and install it on the next mine to be loaded in advance? We do the mines in the tubes first. Like I said, no way to avoid that.

"To do that, we have to use one collar to handle the mine we pull from the tube. But while we're doing that, we install the second collar on one in the rack—and so on—installing the spare collar on the next mine in turn, while the mine in front of it is being deployed. And we alternate the side of the boat we're loading from each time, giving us some room to install the spare collar on the next mine. That way we save the time it takes to install the collar. Besides, with some practice, we'll improve on the timing anyway. Heck, we're almost there."

"That's an excellent observation, Lieutenant, and I'm sure we could scare up a couple extra lift collars," the commodore said, pensively.

Kinkaid looked confused, afraid he might have embarrassed the commodore. His look quickly disappeared, however, when Macdonough beamed at him. Jake was smiling too. "Good thinking, Billy," he said.

Another pregnant silence followed.

"Now about the radar," Joel volunteered. "Bill, how'd that work out?" he asked Salton.

"Not great. But that may be the fault of the particular terrain around this atoll. No mountains. But at Manila Bay the Bataan Peninsula is one big mountain to the northwest. And Corregidor is five hundred and ninety feet high, and should be easy to pick out. Then there's Fort Drum on the east. They're all pretty decent landmarks that should show up well on radar. Of course, another option is that we might get lucky, find a ship to follow in."

"No, thank you," Joel replied. "I want as little channel traffic around as possible. Preferably none. Get in and get out unnoticed."

"My sentiments exactly," Jake agreed.

"And we do have a good chart," Salton continued, unfazed, "and a fathometer to check our depth. We could use soundings to help us navigate as well."

"I've got copies of shore spotter reports for the last couple months for the bay, so you'll at least know what kind of ship traffic to expect," the commodore said, "just in case you change your mind about following a ship in."

"That's good information, Commodore," Jake said. "And we'll take it with us. But I still don't think that following a ship in is wise. No place to go except through a minefield if they spot us."

"Okay, gentlemen," the commodore said. "That's your call. Now what say we do it all over again tomorrow. We'll use Mister Kinkaid's plan, and see if we can't get the timing down a little better."

"I hope we don't have to do this *too* many more times, Skipper," Joel confided to Jake after the meeting. "Retrieving those practice mines is a bitch."

A week later, and *Orca's* fore and aft torpedo crews had mine laying technique down to a science, including the "two-in-the-tube shuffle," as her torpedomen dubbed that beginning portion of the exercise.

"I believe you're about ready," Macdonough told Jake. It was Wednesday morning, September 27th. "And I really like young Kinkaid's attitude. He's the admiral's kid, right?"

"Yes, Sir. He is, and I'm observing that he's also a bright young man in his own right, and a welcome addition to *Orca's* wardroom."

"I suspect you're right about that," Macdonough agreed. "But back to the matter at hand. It looks like you and your men might just pull this Manila Bay thing off."

"I'm not so sure," Jake replied. "We still haven't resolved the radar navigation question. What if we travel three thousand miles to Manila Bay, and discover there's really no way to safely navigate the channels?"

"I think you're selling your man Salton short, Jake. If it can be done, he'll be able to do it."

"I agree that Bill's good, Commodore, but can he make the equipment do what it wasn't designed for?"

"Look, Jake. I know that part of it is a bit iffy. But I have a fall-back position for you to use if you absolutely have to."

"And what's that, Commodore?"

"If you get there, and you find that there's no way you can get up those channels and into the Bay safely, then sow as many of those mines as possible as close to the sea-side channel entrances as possible. I mean, get in as close as you can without entering those Jap minefields. Okay?"

"Okay, Commodore. I'll keep that in mind."

"One more thing."

"Commodore?"

"I just found out I need you to plant those mines as close as possible to October Tenth. And that's not just so you can catch the spring tide. I can't really tell you why exactly, although you probably can guess."

Jake could indeed. Once sown, the mines had a ten-day delay built-in before they self-activated. Big doings were obviously planned for the Philippines on or around October 20th.

"So what are our orders, Commodore?"

"Depends. The admiral made it very clear from the beginning, Jake, this evolution was entirely voluntary. Are you up for it?"

Jake chuckled. "If I wasn't, I think I'd have mutiny on my hands. Yes, Sir, we're up for it."

"Outstanding! Okay, then . . . next question . . . how many mines are you taking with you?"

"In for a penny, in for a pound. We'll take all forty with us, Commodore."

"You just cost me a case of Scotch. Take a tip from me, Jake, never bet against the admiral."

"I'll remember that, Sir." Jake wondered that he was so predictable.

"Okay," Macdonough said, "I'll cut your orders while you get *Orca* ready for sea. Let's plan to get you underway tomorrow afternoon, the latest . . . and Jake?"

"Yes, Sir?"

"I sure as blazes wish I were going with you."

"I know that, Commodore. I know that."

Orca got underway from Majuro en route to Manila Bay at 1400 on Thursday, September 28, 1944. The boat departed for her ninth war patrol carrying forty Mark-12, Mod 3, magnetic mines and nine Mark-14 torpedoes. It really was a "squeeze," but twenty mines were carried forward, and twenty aft. Two mines each were in torpedo tubes one forward and eight aft. The remaining tubes were loaded with torpedoes. One more torpedo was on a rack forward, and one mine forward and one mine aft were lashed to the deck. Jake was unhappy about the last bit, but there was no way he wasn't going to sow all forty of the mines the Admiral had sent.

Chapter 23

Ninth Patrol: 7 October 1944 to 29 October 1944

Orca arrived at the mouth of Manila Bay on Saturday evening October 7th.

Bill Salton had checked the Manila tidal charts for Tuesday, October 10th. High tide would be at 0157, 1.04 meters (3.41 feet) above MLLW (mean lower low water, the depth recorded on the charts); low tide was at 0852, 0.22 meters (0.69 feet) above MLLW. So *Orca* would have *at least* as much water to hide in as was shown on the chart. The full range of the spring tide would not occur until the 19th, with the new moon, but their orders were to sow the mines on the 10th, or the 11th at the latest. The new moon would also be best for hiding in the night, but they would have to make do with a waning half moon. Whatever was happening on or around the 20th, would probably be taking advantage of the maximum spring tide or the new moon, or both.

The plan was to mine the North Channel entrance first, since its soundings were the shallowest, and thus take advantage of high tide. *Orca* would enter the North Channel submerged at five knots, laying fourteen mines down the channel's 8.3-mile length. The boat would then proceed approximately ten miles across the Bay to the South Channel, lay twenty-six mines along the channel's eighteen-mile length, and withdraw to deep water. Simple.

At five knots, the whole 36.3-mile evolution should take seven hours and sixteen minutes, not taking the tidal current into account. If everything *did* go according to plan, the tidal current should be nil while *Orca* was negotiating the North Channel, and the tide should be going out, with the current in the boat's favor, as they went down the South Channel. That was, of course, if everything went according to plan.

Orca spent the next two days and nights watching and waiting. The comings and goings of ships, in and out of both channels, were carefully recorded and compared with what was observed by Allied shore spotters over the past two months. As the commodore had said, the traffic was heaviest on the North Channel. It was thankfully noted that almost all of the shipping traffic exiting the Bay did so during the daylight hours, and that this was consistent with the spotter's reports. As for traffic entering the port, while heavier in daylight, inbound traffic also regularly occurred at night. Again, consistent with the spotter's reports.

From this information, it appeared that the best strategy for entering and leaving the channels might be to use only the outbound side of the channels, since no ships should be leaving port at night. Bill Salton, Jake, and Joel discussed this strategy on the evening of October 8th.

"Not good," said Jake. "We would only be laying mines on the exit side of the channel that way."

"And why is that bad, Captain?" Joel countered. "We should be more concerned about keeping ships from exiting the bay then entering it, no? Wouldn't we want to keep their ships bottled up in the bay? Better targets from the air?"

"You're right about that, but once the Japs figured out that only the outbound channels were mined, what would stop a ship from exiting the bay using the inbound channel?" Jake replied.

"Nothing," Joel said, chagrined. "Okay. We need to mine both sides."

"What if we're sowing mines, and a ship shows up?" Salton asked.

"We move over to the other side of the channel," Joel said.

"And if there's already a ship on that side of the channel?" Salton parried.

"Not highly likely," Joel said

"But what if it happens?" Salton asked again.

"Then we're screwed," Jake said. "So we'd better pray that doesn't happen. You pray much, Joel?"

Joel laughed. "I'm Jewish, Skipper. We're always praying."

"Well, keep it up. We're gonna need all the help we can get tomorrow night."

Orca surfaced at dusk, Monday evening, October 9th, and started a four-engine, battery charge. The boat hadn't done much during the daylight hours except traverse the mouth of Manila Bay, out around the one hundred fathom curve, and avoid enemy shipping. *Orca* was, therefore, ready to begin laying mines with batteries fully charged at midnight.

A kind of loose GQ was set. Bill Salton was on the chart plot, and EM3(SS) James Orsi was on radar. Both would remain on station throughout the night, as would the mine-laying teams in the forward and after torpedo rooms. Joe Bob Clanton was the diving officer, and Joel Himmelfarb manned the periscope. Jake had the conn. Sonar plot was manned in the wardroom by Billy Kinkaid and QMSN(SS) Henry Coons.

Any rest obtained by the mine-laying team would be grabbed while the boat traversed from channel to channel in the Bay.

The boat was at fifty-seven feet, three feet above normal periscope depth, with the search scope and radar mast raised, as it approached the entrance of the North Channel. As navigator, Salton's job, besides keeping *Orca* in the channel and out of the minefields on either side of it, was to call out recommended course changes to keep the boat on a zigzag course up the channel so that the mines were laid on alternate sides.

Orsi was singing out radar bearings and ranges, via sound-powered phones, to agreed-on points on the Bataan Peninsula and on Corregidor. Salton had also hoped that Orsi would be able to get a bearing and range on Fort Drum, but the SJ radar was unable to acquire it. It should have been within radar range, but Salton guessed that perhaps the antenna being just above the surface had reduced the unit's normal capabilities.

Using Orsi's two callouts, Salton, with QM3(SS) John Catinella's help, was still able to plot the boat's position on the chart, and to check the charted sounding (adjusted for the tidal influence) at or near that position against the fathometer reading. At each of the first positions he plotted while approaching the channel entrance, Salton was gratified to find that the fathometer readings matched the tide-adjusted sounding on the chart.

At 0030, Salton determined the boat was on the left side of the North Channel seaside entrance, and recommended laying the first mine. *Orca* was on course 073, and was maintaining five knots. There was just over eight feet under the keel, but the boat's keel depth of fifty-seven feet agreed with the tide-adjusted sounding on the chart.

Seconds later, a mine was deployed from torpedo tube one, forward.

"Recommend coming left to course zero-six-three for approximately seven minutes, Captain," Salton called out.

"Very well, come left to course zero-six-three," Jake ordered.

"Left to zero-six-three, aye," the helmsman repeated, turning the wheel left until the boat began to swing around to the new course, then centering the wheel to halt the swing as the boat approached the ordered heading. When *Orca* was on the new course he called out, "On course, zero-six-three, Sir."

"Very well," Jake answered.

Just over seven minutes later, Salton determined the boat was twelve hundred yards into the channel and on the right side of the outbound lane. "Recommend mine deployment, Captain, then coming right to course zero-eight-four."

Very well," Jake replied. "Deploy mine number two aft, come right to zero-eight-four."

"After torpedo room reports mine deployed, tube eight."

"Coming right to course zero-eight-four."

"Having trouble holding depth, Captain," Joe Bob called up to the conning tower. "We're at five-eight feet. The boat is getting heavy. I'm pumping water out of trim tanks." This was not unexpected. Two large rivers and dozens of smaller fresh water streams empty into Manila Bay, so that the bay water is much less salty than the open ocean. (As water salinity decreases, so does buoyancy.)

"Very well," Jake answered. He considered reminding Joe Bob how critical it was to maintain depth control, but Joe Bob, he knew, was already well aware of that fact. Instead, he called down to Salton, "How much water do we have under the keel, Bill?"

"About seven feet, Captain," Salton answered. "Should be closer to eight."

"Very well. Joe Bob, let me know if you need more speed."

"Aye, Captain," Joe Bob replied. "But we should be okay."

Just under eight minutes after the second mine was deployed, the third mine was released forward, this one at about the center of the inbound channel.

For whatever reason, Jake noted, the operation wasn't going as fast as planned. *Maybe it's the zigzagging that's slowing us down.* Perhaps they weren't quite making five knots because the boat's bottom had become fouled. *Orca* was just coming up on high tide in the bay, so there shouldn't have been any current.

Maybe there's a current running against us for some unknown reason, thought Jake. *Whatever. Nothing for it now but to just keep going.*

Salton recommended, and Jake executed, another zig left. And so it was that *Orca* proceeded up the channel, navigating on radar bearings and ranges, and matching fathometer readings with adjusted chart soundings.

The sixth mine had just been sown, and the boat was en route to the launch point for the seventh, when the conning tower talker announced, "Sonar reports contact bearing two-nine-zero."

"Very well," Jake acknowledged. "Do you have him on radar, Orsi?"

Parra, the conning tower talker, relayed the question.

"No, Sir," the radar operator replied. "At that bearing, though, he'd be lost in ground clutter."

"Very well." Then Jake said to the talker, "Call down to sonar plot and tell them to keep an eye on the bugger."

"Yes, Sir," the talker said, and relayed the message down to Billy Kinkaid in the wardroom.

"They're on it, Sir," Parra reported back a few seconds later.

By that time, the seventh mine had been deployed right where it should have been, in the inbound channel.

"Whatever it is, it's moving pretty fast," Kinkaid remarked to Henry Coons in sonar plot in the wardroom. "The bearing rate is left and over a degree a minute. If he's close in and headed to this channel, he's moving along at twelve knots at least. How far away does sonar say he is?"

"Estimated eighty-six hundred yards and closing."

"Well, he's got to skirt this shoal . . ." said Kinkaid, pointing to a spot on the chart marked "Los Cochinos," where the maximum sounding was four meters (thirteen feet), ". . . that is, if he draws any water at all, and he's planning on coming up the channel."

Sure enough, when the bearings showed the contact had cleared the shoal, then the bearing drift slowed, almost approaching zero. The contact had either turned to head for the channel, or was headed back out to sea.

"Get an estimated range," Kinkaid said. But Coons had already asked for one.

"Six thousand yards and closing."

"Report that to the conn," Kinkaid said. "Contact heading for the channel, estimated range, six thousand yards and closing."

Sonar plot's analysis was confirmed by radar, which had finally acquired the approaching vessel. Bill Salton was now facing double duty on chart plot, trying to juggle both the mine-laying navigation, and tracking the contact at the same time.

"Tonight, I'm like tits on a boar hound, Skipper," Himmelfarb volunteered. "I've been searching for that contact, but there's nothing to see. How about I get off the scope and help Salton and Catinella on the plot?"

"Good idea," Jake said. "Go."

At the chart table, Joel said to Bill Salton, "How about you and Catinella concentrate on the mine laying, and I'll pay attention to the contact?"

"Yes, Sir," Salton said, relieved.

On the radar, Orsi was now calling out bearings and ranges over the sound-powered phones to the two land points for navigation, and bearing and range to the contact.

Within minutes, Joel had plotted the contact's course and speed. The vessel was on course 075, and approaching the inbound channel at twelve knots. It would be actually in the channel in two minutes. Harry Hastings was also tracking the contact on the TDC in the conning tower.

As Joel was calling out the contact's course and speed, the eighth mine was just being deployed in the outbound channel.

Salton then recommended a course to sow the next mine, the ninth, in the inbound channel, as Jake had ordered it, and the boat was swinging right.

"Contact now in the channel, inbound lane, slowed to eight knots, course zero-seven-four, range four thousand yards and closing," Joel called out.

"Very well," Jake acknowledged.

Jake thought for an instant how he'd love to send a torpedo down this bird's throat, but knew the idea was wishful thinking.

"Wait a second. At eight knots, this guy will be on top of us in four minutes," he suddenly realized. "We're turning right into the path of that oncoming vessel!"

"Helm, belay my last! Rudder amidships! Come left to course zero-seven-three!" Jake shouted.

Just as Jake was giving those orders, Kinkaid, in sonar plot, noting the contact's bearing was remaining constant, called up, "We're on a collision course with the contact, Captain!"

Joel and Salton were shouting out pretty much the same thing, with Salton recommending coming left to course 065.

With the boat settling out on course 073, Jake asked his Navigator, "Where exactly in the channel are we, Bill?"

"We're on the right side of the outbound channel, Captain. Recommend we come left some more to course zero-six-five, and just go ahead and sow this next mine in the same channel."

"Agreed." Jake said. "Helm, come left to zero-six-five."

"Zero-six-five, aye, Sir."

Suddenly Jake wanted to kick himself for being so stupid. *How is it a ship enters the channel at night and lines itself up perfectly in the inbound lane?* he thought. *Range markers!* There had to have been channel marker lights turned on for the vessel, two lights that when lined up, one over the other, told the incoming vessel that it was in the center of its lane.

"On course zero-six-five, Sir."

"Very well. Up scope."

Jake manned the scope on the way up, and swung it so he could look down the length of the channel. Sure enough, there they were. Range lights. "Joel, Bill," he yelled down to chart plot, "we have some range lights!"

The ninth mine was launched just as the contact, a freighter of about 1,500 tons, passed by *Orca,* 500 yards to starboard, blissfully unaware of the submarine's presence.

Mines nine through fourteen were laid in the North Channel without further incident. Navigating the channel was immeasurably easier, now that there were range lights for guides. And, thankfully, their Japanese hosts were lax about extinguishing them, even after the freighter was well out of the channel and into the bay.

Orca entered the bay itself, and set course for the bayside entrance of the South Channel. The mine laying in the North Channel had taken longer than anticipated, and what should have taken an hour and forty minutes had required an hour and fifty-five. It was 0225. High tide had occurred sixty-eight minutes ago.

"Recommend course zero-eight-zero for bay-side entrance to South Channel, Captain, with turn to course two-zero-five in two hours."

"Very well," Jake said, and ordered the new course. *We won't be there until 0425*, he thought, *and that channel's eighteen miles long. At five knots that's three hours and thirty-six minutes. We won't be back in deep water until 0801. That's broad daylight! And that's if everything goes right. Well, there's no turning back now.*

Soon the North Channel's range lights were no longer visible. Either the boat had passed their visible arc, or they had finally been turned off. Meanwhile, the mine-laying teams were getting what rest they could.

It looked as if everything was going to go right—until it didn't.

They had just made the turn at the head of the bay end of the South Channel, and laid the first mine in the outbound lane from tube eight. The South Channel is made up of two sections. The upper section is the longest: fourteen miles. The lower section is a four-mile-long dogleg, a dogleg fifteen degrees to the left for an outbound vessel.

Himmelfarb had returned to the scope. "Captain," he said, "I have some more range lights."

"Where?"

"Straight ahead. I have the lower one at . . . bearing, mark!"

"Two-two-five."

"At two-two-five, and the higher one at . . . bearing, mark!"

"Two-two-six."

"Two-two-six, which means we're on the left side of the center of the outbound lane," Jake observed.

"Roger that," Salton agreed, when informed that the range lights had been sighted, and what they implied about the boat's position. "That's right where we should be."

"And it also means we have an outbound ship headed this way," Himmelfarb added.

"Any radar contacts?" Jake asked.

"None reported yet, Captain," Salton volunteered. "But we didn't see the last contact on radar until it was almost on top of us. And, Captain, we're ready to lay the next mine. We seem to have picked up speed. I'm plotting us at seven knots and the pit log agrees. Must be an outbound current."

"Forward torpedo room, deploy sixteenth mine," Jake ordered. "Must be an outbound current, indeed. Make turns for three knots. Any contacts on sonar?"

"Mine deployed from number one tube forward."

"Recommend coming right to course two-three-zero, Captain," Salton said.

"Making turns for three knots, Captain."

"Come right to two-three-zero," Jake ordered.

"Two-three-zero, aye,"

"Sonar reports no contacts, Captain."

"Very well. How we doing on speed, Bill?"

"About six knots, Captain," Salton answered.

"Captain, we may have a problem . . . I have inbound channel range lights as well," Joel said. "Must have just come on. They weren't there on my last sweep."

"Very well. Bet we don't have any contacts in that direction either," Jake observed. "Keep sending those bearings to both sets of lights down to Salton, but I don't want to hear about them unless I need to, okay?"

Himmelfarb nodded his understanding. More information than Jake needed right now.

"How far is the dogleg?" Jake asked, yelling down to chart plot.

"Twenty-five thousand, two hundred yards, about twelve and a half miles, Captain," Salton answered, then said "Recommend deploying mine aft."

"After torpedo room, deploy seventeenth mine. New course?"

"Two-zero-zero, Captain. And we're back up to seven knots."

"Come left to course two-zero-zero. All ahead slow."

"After torpedo room reports mine deployed aft, number eight tube. Sonar reports contact bearing zero-four-five and closing."

"Steering course two-zero-zero, Captain."

"Very well. That sonar contact must be our outbound vessel."

There followed, for Jake, at least, three minutes of blessed quiet.

Salton was using the range light bearing information from Joel, and integrating it with the radar information from Orsi. Orsi was thus far able only to get a range and bearing from Corregidor, the Bataan coastline having become ground clutter. Fort Drum was still out of range. Salton might have been able to navigate the channel with the scant radar information (a single bearing and range only), but it would have been a close run thing. From the Navigator's standpoint, then, the pesky contacts that caused the range lights to be lit were a blessing!

"Recommend deploying mine forward, Captain," Salton sang out, ending Jake's quiet time.

"Forward torpedo room, deploy eighteenth mine," Jake ordered.

"Recommend new course two-three-zero, Captain, and we're still at seven knots. Must be quite a current," Salton said.

"Come right to course two-zero-zero. All stop," Jake ordered. *Perhaps we can just ride along on the current.*

"Maneuvering room reports all stop, Captain."

"Coming right to course two-zero-zero."

"Forward torpedo room reports mine deployed forward, number one tube. Sonar reports first contact bearing zero-four-six, closing, and new contact bearing two-zero-zero."

"There's that inbound ship," Jake mused aloud.

"Steering course two-zero-zero."

"How does the fathometer read, Bill?"

"Seventeen feet, Captain—best all night."

"*Something's* going right. And our speed?"

"Still seven knots, Captain. That's one heck of a current."

"Just so long as the torpedo rooms can keep up. Tell Orsi I need a range on those contacts."

"Roger that, Captain. He knows they're out there, and he's looking for them. But he hasn't even picked up Fort Drum yet."

"Very well."

Mines nineteen through twenty-one were deployed, just over five minutes apart. The deployment teams in the torpedo rooms, Jake knew, were scrambling. They had *never* been able to move that fast during practice.

Still no contacts on radar. "What's our speed now, Bill?" Jake asked.

"Just under eight knots, Captain."

"Call the torpedo rooms. Check with Arnold forward and Rhodes aft. Ask if they're doing all right."

A minute later, the talker reported, "Both torpedo rooms say they're doing just fine, Captain."

"Very well."

"Sonar reports first contact bearing zero-three-three and closing slowly, second contact bearing one-nine-five and closing."

"Very well. Anything on radar?"

Salton replied, "No contacts, but we've acquired Fort Drum on the radar, Captain. And recommend deploying mine forward.

"Very well, forward torpedo room, deploy mine number twenty-two."

"Forward torpedo room reports mine deployed, number one tube."

"Recommend coming right to course two-three-zero, Captain."

"Very well. Come right to course two-three-zero."

"Radar reports contact bearing zero-three-four, range nine thousand yards, speed nine knots and closing."

"Coming right to course two-three-zero."

Jake called down to Salton, "Can't spare Joel on the scope, Bill. You're going to have to do double duty — lay mines and track contacts."

"Aye, aye, Captain." Salton replied. "Contact one is coming down outbound lane at nine knots. We're doing eight, so the closing speed is one knot. We're just over five miles into the channel, with thirteen miles to go. It'll take him thirteen hours to catch us."

"Very well. That's good news."

Three minutes later, Salton called out, "Recommend deploying mine aft."

"Very well. After torpedo room deploy mine number twenty-three."

"After torpedo room reports mine deployed, tube eight."

Mines number twenty-four through twenty-nine were deployed without further incident. *Orca* was still moving down the channel at eight knots, moved along by only the swift, outbound, spring tide current. The ship behind them in the outbound lane was 8,900 yards away. The boat had just passed Fort Drum abeam to port, when sonar reported the second contact was bearing 210 and closing.

"Recommend deploying mine forward, Captain," Bill Salton called up from the Chart Plot in the Control Room.

"Very well. Forward torpedo room, deploy mine number thirty," Jake ordered.

"Forward torpedo room reports mine deployed, tube number one."

"Very well."

"Recommend coming right to course two-two-eight, Captain," Salton said.

"Very well. Helmsman, come right to course two-two-eight."

"Come right to two-two-eight, aye, Sir."

"Radar reports second contact, Captain, bearing two-one-two, range eighty-five hundred yards, closing."

"Finally," Jake said under his breath. Then, aloud, "He's got to be in the inbound lane, Bill, in the dogleg, and getting ready to make his turn. Get me a course and speed."

"Aye, Captain." Salton answered.

Two minutes later. "Course zero-one-five, speed seven knots. He *is* in the dogleg approaching the turn."

"Very well. How long 'til he passes us?"

"Wait one, Sir. Recommend deploy mine aft."

"After torpedo room, deploy mine number thirty-one."

"He should pass us in thirteen minutes, Captain."

"After torpedo room reports mine deployed, tube eight."

"Very well." Jake then called down to Salton, "We'll stay in the outbound lane 'til he passes us. Lay the next mine in this lane if we have to."

"Aye, Captain, recommend come left to course two-one-five."

"Helmsman, come left to course two-one-five."

"Coming left to course two-one-five, Captain."

"Radar reports contact two, bearing two-one-two, range fifty-five hundred yards."

"He should be making his turn any second now, Captain," Salton called out.

On the scope, Joel said, "I can see him, Skipper, big tanker. Gotta be nine thousand tons. He's turning toward us."

"Radar reports contact bearing two-one-four, Range four thousand."

"Looks like he's headed up the wrong lane, Captain. You'd think a mile-wide inbound lane would be an easy target, even for a big fella like that," Joel said.

"I don't like this, Joel," Jake said. "All back full."

"Aye, Captain. All back full"

Jake willed the boat to slow, but, even backing full, the best *Orca* could do, battling the outbound current on battery propulsion, was slow to two knots. He realized he had only bought a minute or two, but it might be enough for the tanker to complete its lazy turn.

"Maneuvering reports all back full, Captain."

"Zero angle on the bow. Damn thing looks like he's aiming for us, Captain," Joel said.

"Radar reports contact two bearing two-one-five, range thirty-five hundred, closing."

"Looks like he's turned into our lane, Captain," Salton called up from the chart plot.

Jake contemplated coming left into the inbound lane, and passing the tanker to starboard. But what if the tanker suddenly decided to get into its proper lane? *Collision dance!*

"Radar reports contact two, bearing two-one-five, range three thousand, closing."

"What in blazes is he thinking? He must see that his range lights are not lined up!" Joel said, eyes still glued to the periscope. "Head for the inbound lane, Skipper?"

"Not yet. He's got to come to his senses! Worst possibility is if he changes lanes while we're alongside."

"Roger that," Joel agreed.

Collision dance!

"Radar reports contact two, bearing two-one-five, range twenty-five hundred, closing."

"Sound the collision alarm!" Jake said. The alarm sounded, and immediately all watertight doors were slammed shut and dogged down, all ventilation flappers were shut, each compartment sealed off from the rest of the boat. "Leave the conning tower hatch open," Jake ordered. An exception to Condition Zebra, but Jake wanted to maintain verbal contact with the control room.

"Radar reports contact two, bearing two-one-five, range two thousand, closing."

"Okay," Jake said. "I've waited long enough. Left full rudder. All Stop. All ahead full."

When all the orders were acknowledged, Jake called down to Salton, "Let me know when we're in the middle of the inbound lane, Bill."

The helmsman was calling out the heading of the boat as the course bearings drifted by. "Passing two-zero-five. Passing two-zero-zero."

"Rudder amidships."

"Rudder is amidships, Captain."

"Radar reports contact two, bearing two-four-five, range one thousand, closing."

"We're in the center of the inbound lane, Captain," Salton shouted.

"What's our speed?" Jake asked.

"Twelve knots." For a submerged sub, and thanks to the outbound current, *Orca* was flying.

"Come right to course two-one-five."

"Coming right to two-one-five, Captain."

"Holy crap, Jake, that crazy idiot is turning toward us!" Joel, still on the periscope, shouted out.

Collision dance!

"Radar reports contact two, bearing two-seven-zero, range three hundred, closing."

The tanker was entirely oblivious to the submarine under its bow, but if the tanker's master was determined to hit the submerged boat, he couldn't have picked a better moment to turn toward.

"Left full rudder." Jake was turning *Orca* to the left, the boat was still making maximum turns, and he was still hoping to slip past the tanker. He waited until he felt the boat turn under him. "Rudder amidships." If he could just maneuver the boat to the edge of the inbound channel, maybe he could still slip past . . .

"We're entering the minefield!" Salton shouted out.

"All stop! All back full! Right full rudder!" Jake issued orders in an effort to stop the boat in its tracks, but the unrelenting outbound current continued to move it inexorably forward. A mere two knots, perhaps, but forward, nonetheless.

Orca was in the minefield. The tanker, meanwhile, had finally lined up the inbound lane's range lights, and was heading into safe harbor, still blissfully unaware that it had almost collided with an enemy submarine. The collision dance was done, and the tanker had swung its partner into the minefield.

The Japanese deployed only contact mines. These were buoyant spheres packed with explosive, and moored to the sea bottom. Protruding from the spheres were acid-packed horns, which, when struck, activated a battery that electrically exploded the mine. Everyone knew that no submarine would be foolish enough to enter the bay submerged. The minefields in Manila Bay were therefore designed to discourage enemy warships from entering the bay on the surface. As such, the mines were deployed so that their tethered spheres floated just two meters (6.7 feet) below the surface.

Inside the minefield, at two knots, engines still backing full, with full right rudder, *Orca* was executing a slow right turn that, barring disaster, would eventually bring her back into the inbound lane of the South Channel.

There was, of course, no way for the boat to detect, and deliberately avoid, an underwater mine. Chances are, that if you are in a minefield, you *will* run into one. And the first mine *Orca* ran into *should* have blown her out of the water. But as it was, the boat struck not the mine itself, but the mine's tethering cable. For any other sub, the cable would have caught on a bow plane, and the forward motion of the boat would have dragged the mine itself down to it. Once the mine struck the hull of the boat, it would explode. But *Orca's* "Christmas Tree" caused the mine cable to bypass the port bow plane, and the cable was then dragged along the boat's hull until it was shed astern.

The noise of the cable dragging down the port side of the boat petrified *Orca's* occupants. Thankfully, however, no one aboard the boat actually died from fright, even when the second cable *Orca* struck was likewise shed harmlessly.

And then, the boat emerged from the minefield, still intact.

Bill Salton quickly determined the boat's location. *Orca* was in the inbound lane, at the southern edge, four hundred and fifty yards above the turn into the dogleg. The entire episode, from the time the last mine was deployed to *Orca's* emergence from the minefield, had lasted only twenty-seven minutes.

Mines number thirty-two and thirty-three were already in the tubes, ready to deploy when *Orca* emerged from the minefield. Jake ordered thirty-two launched in the center of the inbound lane where they were, and then launched thirty-three in the outbound lane as the boat turned into the dogleg. Once in the dogleg, Jake again ordered "All Stop" and allowed the current to move the boat downstream.

The remaining seven mines would be sown in the dogleg itself. They would be sown at a 1,200-yard spacing, rather than the 1,400 yards originally planned, and, moving at the speed of the current, the torpedo room crews would really have to scramble.

The boat was heading into the inbound lane, when Jake asked, "Where is contact one?"

"Radar reports contact one is bearing zero-two-five, range fifty-three hundred yards."

"He's still in the outbound lane, Captain, making nine knots. He won't catch us if we keep riding the current. We're making seven-and-a-half knots," Bill Salton volunteered. "Recommend we deploy a mine forward."

"Forward torpedo room, deploy mine number thirty-four."

"Forward torpedo room reports mine deployed, tube one."

"Very well."

Mines number thirty-five through forty were sown without further incident, with number forty sown right at the entrance to the inbound lane.

It was daylight when *Orca* left the South Channel and made for the open sea. But they had managed to sow twenty-six mines in the South Channel in just over three hours. It was 0723 on October 10th.

The plan was to remain submerged for the rest of the day. Everyone was exhausted. The air aboard was rank, but there was still sufficient oxygen, and spending the day submerged making bare steerageway would conserve what little battery capacity remained.

But then there was that ship right behind them, exiting the South Channel. It just so happened that *Orca* should be in a good position for a submerged approach. And there were, after all, nine torpedoes aboard.

"She's a tanker, Captain," Joel said, looking through the attack scope. "Riding high in the water, so she's probably empty. My guess is that she's heading back to the NEI to pick up another load of fuel. Angle on the bow, port twenty-five. Down scope! Lower the radar antenna."

"No," Jake countered. "Belay that. Leave the radar antenna up. Get me a range and bearing to the tanker."

"Radar has her bearing zero-six-zero, range seventy-seven hundred yards," the talker reported. Jake knew he was taking a chance leaving the radar antenna up, but had decided to risk it.

Four minutes later, radar reported the contact still bearing 060, but at range 4,700 yards.

"I have her on course two-seven-zero, speed twelve knots. CPA three thousand yards in just under twelve minutes," Salton said.

"Lower the radar antenna. Come left to three-zero-zero, make turns for five knots," Jake ordered. "Let's see if we can get closer."

Seven minutes passed.

Joel raised the scope and the radar antenna again.

"Radar has contact bearing zero-five-eight, range eight hundred yards," the talker reported.

"Angle on the bow, port thirty. Down scope. Lower the radar antenna," Joel said.

"All stop, come right to three-four-zero, open outer doors forward," Jake ordered.

"I have a firing solution on the TDC, Captain," Harry Hastings said.

"Maneuvering reports all stop. Forward torpedo room reports outer doors opened forward, Captain."

"Coming right to three-four-zero"

"CPA of five hundred yards in one minute, Captain," Salton reported.

"Up scope," Joel ordered. He rode the scope up, then reported, "Angle on the bow, port ninety."

"Firing solution still looks good, Captain. Torpedo run five hundred and sixty yards."

"Very well. Fire two," Jake ordered.

"Tube number two fired, Captain."

"Spread one degree left, Harry," Jake said.

"One degree left, aye. One degree left set," Harry said.

"Sonar reports torpedo running hot, straight, and normal."

"Fire three," Jake ordered.

"Three fired."

"Sonar reports second torpedo running hot, straight, and normal."

There was a shock wave that made the boat tremble, followed by the sound of a loud explosion.

"Got her, Captain," Joel said. "Quick, give me my camera!"

Joel mounted his Graflex 35 to the brackets on the scope. Just as he snapped the first picture, there was a second explosion. Looking through the camera's viewfinder, he snapped a second picture. "She's blown all to pieces, Captain," he said. "With nothing but fumes in her tanks, she was like one big bomb."

Jake was concerned that the tanker might have sent out a Mayday before she blew apart, but Joel opined that she went up so fast that it wasn't very likely. In any event, Jake played it safe and *Orca* spent the rest of the day submerged at dead slow.

At 1940 hours, when the boat surfaced, the air inside was really foul, and the battery was down to twenty percent capacity. After firing forty mines and two torpedoes, there was positive air pressure inside the boat, and the bridge hatch had to be cracked open slowly to let the pressure bleed off.

The enginemen started the engines, then shifted the air intake to the boat itself, and there was a complete air exchange inside the sub in a matter of minutes. Only then was engine air intake shifted back to the engine air induction trunk.

That evening, *Orca* received orders to proceed to the Palawan Passage, and perform picket duty, along with *Darter* and *Dace*.

On October 11, 1944, the first air raid against Okinawa was conducted by carrier-based aircraft from Admiral William "Bull" Halsey's U.S. 3rd Fleet.

Leyte, Center for Military History Brochure, (Pub 72-27)

Palawan Island is the westernmost of the large islands that form the Luzon group. It is a 400-mile long, narrow island extending northwest from Borneo in the south to Mindoro in the north. The south coast of the island is on the Sulu Sea; the north coast is on the South China Sea

The Palawan Passage is the long open channel formed by the north coast of Palawan Island, and the Spratly Islands to the west. It was this channel that most enemy merchant vessels had eschewed for the safer, more protected routes through the Sulu Sea. *Orca's* picket station was the westernmost of the stations assigned to the three submarines in the passage, and the boat arrived on station at 0300 on October 13th.

On October 18th, B-29 Superfortresses flying out of the Marianas attacked the Japanese base at Truk.

On October 20th, the U.S. 6th Army, under General Douglas MacArthur, conducted an amphibious assault on the Island of Leyte in the Philippines, supported by the U.S. 7th Fleet, under the command of Vice Admiral Thomas Kinkaid. By that evening, the beachhead was well enough established so that Gen. MacArthur could come ashore and broadcast "People of the Philippines, I have returned! By the grace of Almighty God, our forces stand again on Philippine Soil."

On the morning of Friday, October 20th, the fully loaded tanker *Mexico Maru*, which had sojourned in Manila for the past ten days, made for the outbound lane of the North Channel. The tanker had been prepositioned at Manila as part of "victory" plan *Sho-Go 1*, the major Japanese naval operation plan for defense of the Philippine Islands. It was now en route to a planned north Sulu Sea rendezvous with the "Center Force," currently assembling in the port of Brunei on the island of Borneo, an element of *Sho-Go 1*.

The *Mexico Maru* had just entered the outbound lane of the North Channel when it struck a mine. The starboard side of the tanker's bow was ripped open, spilling fuel oil into the Channel. The force of the explosion drove the vessel into the inbound lane, and the ship's master was slow to react and get his vessel under control.

The tanker traveled another 1,100 meters before it began to answer the helm, but by then it had struck a second mine. The subsequent explosion obliterated what was left of the bow, and ignited the fuel oil that now spread out over the surface of the channel and beyond. The ship's master eventually managed to back the ship out of the channel and into the bay, with what was left of its bow ablaze.

The second row of tanks was soon compromised and spilling oil into the bay, further fueling the spreading waterborne conflagration. Before firefighting boats managed to reach the stricken tanker, the whole forward half of the vessel was on fire.

The Port of Manila harbormaster then diverted all shipping traffic to the lesser-used South Channel, until the mines could be cleared from the North Channel. That was, until later the same morning, an outbound freighter struck a mine in the South Channel. The Port of Manila was therefore effectively shut down entirely for two weeks, until the mines in both channels could be cleared.

And so it was that shipping in the Port of Manila played no part whatever in what came to be known as the Battle of Leyte Gulf.

Darter's captain was Cmdr. David McClintock, USN, a 1935 graduate of the Naval Academy. *Dace* was commanded by Lt. Cmdr. Bladen Claggett, USN, who was also USNA '35.

At 0016 on October 23rd, *Darter's* radar operator detected a large grouping of ships coming up the Palawan Strait and passing her picket station at a range of 30,000 yards.

As SOPA (senior officer present afloat), McClintock had been made aware of *Orca's* limited torpedo count, and in alerting the other two boats to the enemy's presence, he ordered *Orca* to race ahead to the northern end of the strait before *Darter* and *Dace* closed with the enemy fleet for visual contact.

The Japanese force that had sortied from its base in Brunei, and was traversing the Palawan Strait that night, consisted of: five battleships; ten heavy and two light cruisers; and fifteen destroyers. The "Center Force," one of three Japanese fleets converging on Leyte Gulf to oppose the U.S. landing, was commanded by Admiral Takeo Kurita, from his flagship, the heavy cruiser *Atago*.

Darter was the first to actually sight the enemy. By then, however, the fleet was already well on its way northwest, and well past the two boats. Both *Darter* and *Dace* quickly took off in an end-around pursuit of the enemy fleet, and *Darter* broadcast the first of three contact reports.

Both boats proceeded at full power to get ahead of the Japanese, and, by first light, were submerged in advance of the fleet and positioned for an attack. *Orca*, meanwhile, was well north of their position, submerged and awaiting the Japanese at the northernmost end of the strait, just off Palawan Island.

In *Darter*, McClintock had maneuvered his way past the destroyer screen, and, at 0500, found himself in perfect position for an approach on an enemy heavy cruiser. *Darter* came to course 035, speed three knots, to close the target.

McClintock employed the usual method for a submerged approach, with the captain on the periscope. "I have a heavy cruiser in the crosshairs," he announced. "Angle on the bow starboard twenty-five, bearing, mark . . ."

"Two-nine-three."

"Range, mark . . ."

"Seventy-two hundred."

"Down scope."

Seven minutes passed.

"Up scope . . . target angle on the bow starboard two-zero, bearing, mark . . ."

"Two-nine-five."

"Range, mark . . ."

"Sixty-three hundred."

"Target course zero-three-zero, speed thirteen," came up from Chart Plot.

"Very well," McClintock acknowledged, and waited another seven minutes. "Up scope. Angle on the bow, starboard three-five. Bearing, mark . . ."

"Two-nine-nine."

"Range, mark . . ."

472

"Forty-six hundred."

"I have a firing solution, Captain," the TDC operator reported.

"Very well. We'll fire on the next observation," McClintock replied.

Seven minutes later, at 0524, McClintock fired a spread of six torpedoes at the enemy cruiser, and scored four hits. He was entirely unaware that he had fired the first shots, and drawn first blood, of the Battle of Leyte Gulf. He was also unaware that his target had been the heavy cruiser, *Atago*, the enemy force commander's flagship.

At 0534, *Darter* then fired a second spread at another heavy cruiser and scored two hits, crippling the ship.

At 0556, *Dace* fired and scored four hits on a third heavy cruiser.

Both Atago *and* Dace's *target, the* Maya, *sank.* Atago *sank so rapidly that Admiral Kurita was forced to swim to survive and was picked up by the destroyer* Kishinami.

Takeo, *the cruiser that had been crippled by* Darter's *second torpedo salvo, turned back to Brunei, escorted by two destroyers and shadowed by both* Darter *and* Dace. *On October 24th,* Darter *ran aground on the Bombay Shoal, and had to be abandoned. Her crew was picked up by* Dace. Takeo *managed to limp back to Singapore without further incident. In Singapore, however, there were no repair facilities able to return the vessel to service.* Takeo *languished there, out of the fight, until the end of the war.*

While Kurita's Center Force had been bloodied, it remained formidable. *Orca*, submerged, spotted the fleet on radar as it rounded the tip of Palawan Island, but was out of position to launch an attack. Jake ordered the LF radio antenna raised and sent a contact report.

By 0800, Kurita's force had entered the Sibuyan Sea, where it was attacked by aircraft from Enterprise. *About 1030, additional attacks were launched from the carriers* Intrepid *and* Cabot, *hitting three of Kurita's battleships and badly damaging the heavy cruiser* Myoko. *Later air attacks launched from* Intrepid, Essex, *and* Lexington *further damaged* Mushashi, *one of the battleships that had been struck earlier. As* Mushashi *withdrew, she absorbed additional hits from planes off* Enterprise *and* Franklin.

At 1523, a Japanese aircraft land-based at Luzon, slipped past the U.S. air defense and scored a direct hit on the carrier Princeton.

Kurita finally turned his force around to get out of the range of the aircraft. At 1715 he turned the fleet about again and headed for the San Bernardino Strait.

Princeton *was beyond saving, and had to be scuttled about 1730. At about 1930,* Mushashi *capsized and sank.*

A second Japanese strike force, the "Southern Force," consisting of two battleships, a heavy cruiser, and four destroyers under the command of Admiral Shoji Nishimura, attempted to enter Leyte Gulf from the South by way of the Surigao Strait. It was obliterated by the 7th Fleet Support Force under Rear Admiral Jesse Olendorf. In the end, only the crippled enemy cruiser Mogami *and one destroyer were able to retreat back down the strait. A backup force of one heavy and one light cruiser and four destroyers under Vice Admiral Kiyohide Shima attempted to join the fray, only to later retreat in confusion. In the process, Shima's flagship, the heavy cruiser,* Nachi, *collided with* Mogami *leaving her dead in the water.* Mogami *was sunk the next morning by air attack.*

At 0300, October 25th, the remnants of Kurita's force emerged unopposed from the San Bernardino Strait and steamed southwards off the coast of Samar. Standing in its path was only Rear Admiral Clifton Sprague's force of sixteen, slow, unarmored, escort carriers and its screen of small destroyers and destroyer escorts. The destroyers, outclassed, bravely took the cruisers under fire, as did the escort carriers until they could launch their aircraft. Two destroyers, Hoel *and* Roberts, *were sunk. Without air cover, Kurita's fleet suffered multiple air strikes. One escort carrier,* Gambier Bay, *was sunk by a Japanese battleship. Convinced that he had been engaged and bloodied by a major carrier* strike force, Kurita retreated back through the San Bernardino Strait and escaped.

As the surface action was coming to a close, a land-based "Special Action Force" launched kamikaze attacks against U.S. ships in Leyte Gulf and off Samar. This was the first such attack in the war. The escort carrier, St. Lo, was sunk, the first vessel to be lost to a kamikaze attack.

A third Japanese force to the north, under Vice Admiral Jisaburo Ozawa, consisted of four heavy aircraft carriers and three light carriers, three light cruisers, and nine destroyers. This "Northern Force," could deploy only 108 aircraft, and had been positioned as a decoy so as to lure away from the battle the bulk of Halsey's carrier forces. In that regard, it largely succeeded. On October 25th, airstrikes from carriers under the command of Vice Admiral Marc Mitscher struck Ozawa's fleet, sinking one heavy and two light carriers, and a destroyer. Another light carrier and a light cruiser were crippled. All but a few of Ozawa's 108 aircraft were destroyed.

Orca was on the surface in the northern Sulu Sea during the wee hours of October 26th, as the remnants of Kurita's "Center Force" made their way home. At 0314, a large contact was reported on radar at a range of 13,500 yards to the West, apparently headed for the Linapacan Strait, just north of Palawan Island. The contact was proceeding on course 270 at speed, some twenty-seven knots, and was not zigzagging.

There was, that night, a bright, waxing, three-quarter moon. It was low and to the South in a cloudless sky, and the visibility was good, perhaps eight thousand yards. Jake set GQ and positioned the boat with the target between *Orca* and the moon, submerged to periscope depth, and waited.

At twenty-seven knots, Jake calculated, this target was moving at better than nine hundred yards per minute. If he was going to get a shot off at all, he had best have *Orca* lined up perfectly, and fire without hesitation. There would be no second chance, because once this baby passed by, *Orca* could never catch her. Besides, *Orca* had only four fish forward and three aft.

"Come right to course two-three-five," he ordered. He left the boat's speed at three knots.

Joel Himmelfarb was on the scope, straining to see something on the latest radar bearing, 094. "Nothing to see so far, Captain," he reported.

"Radar has her at eighty-five hundred yards, Joel. Visibility's probably not good enough, but keep looking."

"Eyeballs peeled, Captain," Joel said. Then, a minute later, "Can barely make her out, Skipper. She's like a shadow. Big bastard, though. Bearing, mark . . ."

"Zero-nine-five."

"Down scope."

"Radar reports contact bearing zero-nine-five, range seventy-eight hundred."

"Still haulin', Captain," Salton, on chart plot, called out. "Still on course two-seven-zero, speed two-seven."

"Leave the scope up, Joel, otherwise she'll pass us right by and we'll miss her."

"Aye, Captain. Up scope," Joel ordered. Two minutes had passed since the last observation. "Got her," he said. "She's huge. Has to be a battleship. Angle on the bow, starboard one-zero. Bearing, mark."

"Zero-nine-six."

"Radar reports contact bearing zero-nine-seven, range sixty-three hundred."

"Very well."

"Still on course two-seven-zero, speed two-seven," Salton said. "CPA is eleven hundred yards in six-point-seven minutes."

"Torpedo run?" Jake asked Hastings on the TDC.

"Not bad, Captain—1,800 yards," Hastings answered.

"But not great. Make turns for five knots."

"Maneuvering reports making turns for five knots."

"That helps, Captain," Salton called up. "CPA now at seven hundred yards in six-point-five minutes."

"Torpedo run?"

"Better, Captain—fifteen hundred yards."

"Still not great, but the best we're going to get. Open outer doors forward. Make ready all tubes forward."

"Radar reports contact closing fast, bearing one-one-eight, range thirty-two hundred."

"Outer torpedo doors forward are open, Captain. Torpedo tubes one, four, five, and six, ready."

"Angle on the bow starboard three-zero, Skipper," Joel said. "She's a Jap battle cruiser, *Kongo* class. Thirty-five thousand tons at least."

"CPA in two minutes, Captain," Salton said.

"Tell me when the angle on the bow is starboard seven-zero, Joel," Jake said. "That will be final observation."

"Aye, Captain. Almost there."

Seconds passed.

"Son of a bitch! The bastard's turning away!"

"Fire one," Jake ordered.

"Forward torpedo room reports tube one fired."

"Spread one degree left, fire four," Jake ordered.

"One degree left, four fired."

"Forward torpedo room reports tube four fired."

"Sonar reports two torpedoes running hot, straight and normal."

"Time for first run, two-point-four minutes, Captain. Second run two-point-seven minutes."

Two minutes passed. Then two and-a-half. Then three.

"Two misses," Jake concluded. "I just wasted two torpedoes."

Joel watched as the target moved away, opening up the distance between them.

Jake sent out a contact report, just in case there were any other boats in the battlewagon's path.

Fifteen minutes later *Orca* surfaced. The moon had almost dipped completely below the southern horizon, and the sky was carpeted in starlight.

Three days later, October 29th, *Orca* received orders to return to Pearl for refit. Just 4,600 nautical miles to home.

A week later, as *Orca* was bypassing Midway, the boat received word that FDR had been reelected president for a fourth term, and that Lt. Cmdr. Jacob J. Lawlor had been picked up early for promotion to commander.

Chapter 24

Refit, Pearl: 13 November 1944 to 8 January 1945

Orca reached Pearl, and pulled into the sub base in the early afternoon, Monday, November 13, 1944, just two days after the Navy bombarded the tiny island of Iwo Jima in the Philippine Sea for the first time.

Unlike at Majuro, there was a crowd of families, friends, and well-wishers on the pier to welcome them. Vice Admiral Lockwood stood out alone from the crowd, undress whites, his cover and epaulettes trimmed in gleaming gold. Jake's gaze skipped past him, and he waved to a brightly smiling Kate holding the sleeping Elizabeth. Jake swore that his daughter had doubled in size since June.

The word "SUBPAC, arriving," was passed over the 1MC as the Admiral stepped onto the quarterdeck. Commodore Macdonough was conspicuously absent.

"Good afternoon, Admiral," Jake greeted Lockwood. "Welcome aboard."

"Glad to be aboard. Good to see you, Jake. And allow me to be the first to say you're out of uniform."

Jake grinned. "Very few commissaries at sea, Admiral."

"That's true. That's why I brought you these." He handed Jake a small box containing two silver oak leaves. "Congratulations, Commander, and you'll need a new cover, too."

"Yes, Sir. I guess I will." (Now a field grade officer, Jake would have to have a hat with a visor trimmed in gold "scrambled eggs.") "Thank you, Admiral, getting these new collar pins from you means a lot," Jake said.

"Nonsense. Glad to do it. And you earned them. You and *Orca.*"

"Thank you, Sir."

"Okay, Commander Lawlor, tomorrow be in my office at ten hundred hours. Now go home with your wife and daughter."

"Aye, aye, Sir!" Jake replied.

At 0800 the next morning, before his meeting with Jake, Vice Adm. Lockwood greeted another member of *Orca's* wardroom in his office.

"You wanted to see me, Admiral?" Lt. j.g. Joe Bob Clanton asked, as he entered the admiral's office.

"I do, Lieutenant. Sit down, and I'll tell you why you're here," Lockwood replied, indicating the plain wooden chair facing his desk. Joe Bob sat down stiffly, wondering what terrible thing he had done that had singled him out for the admiral's personal attention.

"Relax, Mr. Clanton," Lockwood said, smiling. "You're not here for an ass-chewing. Quite the opposite, in fact."

"Sir?" Joe Bob replied.

"Seems that the job you did for us on Mindoro Island has brought you to General MacArthur's attention. He has specifically requested that the Navy fly you directly to his field HQ on Leyte for a special assignment."

"General MacArthur?" Joe Bob said, incredulous.

"None other. But understand this. This mission is entirely voluntary on your part. And no one else in the Navy knows about it outside of me and my staff, and now you. You can refuse this assignment without prejudice, and nobody else in the Navy will know. Certainly not your boss, Commander Lawlor. Understood?"

"Yes, Sir. But what is all of this about?"

"Recapturing the Philippines, Clanton, the project most dear to General MacArthur's heart.

"The Army's success on Leyte was due to three things," Lockwood continued. "The troops of the Sixth Army, of course, the Navy, by keeping the Jap fleet off the Army's back in Leyte Gulf, and the Filipino guerrillas by attacking the enemy from the rear. The thing that MacArthur thinks they could have done better was coordinating with the guerrillas. That's where you'd come in."

"Me? What do I know about coordinating the guerrillas and the Army?"

"More than you think, apparently. Now what I'm about to tell you is Top Secret. If you've already made your mind up that you're not interested, we can stop right here and you can be on your way, and there will be no repercussions. None. Hell, you're the engineer officer on a U.S. Navy submarine, and none of this is in your line of duty. Nobody would blame you for not volunteering."

"Thank you, Admiral, but I'd never sleep again if I didn't find out what this is all about. And if the general and you think this is something I can do, then I guess it *is* in my line of duty. Keep going, please, Sir."

"Very well," Lockwood said smiling (of course he had never expected any other reaction). "MacArthur is planning another amphibious operation. His next target is Mindoro."

Clanton's face lit up. *Mindoro! Maybe I'll get a chance to see Delvina again!*

"He wants to do this no later than a month from now," Lockwood continued, "and you know something about the guerrilla forces on the Island. He wants you to go in ahead of the invasion force, establish contact with your friends there, and act as liaison for the campaign. You up for that?"

Joe Bob made a show of deliberating before he responded, but he had already made up his mind. Mindoro. Delvina. "Yes, Sir, I think I am," he said finally.

"Very well, Mr. Clanton, I'll get the ball rolling."

It had been an interesting night at the Lawlors'. At six months, Elizabeth was now sleeping through the night, and as soon as she was put to bed, Kate decided to make up for four months of enforced celibacy. Not that Jake had put up much resistance — or any resistance at all, for that matter.

The next morning, Jake reported to the admiral looking tired, but happy. The uniform of the day was undress khakis, and Jake had his new silver oak leaves pinned to his collar.

Jake had already filed the report for *Orca's* eighth patrol with Commodore Macdonough at Majuro, and he now made the ninth patrol report.

"I knew it could be done, and I knew that if anyone could do it, you could," the Admiral said, elated. "I would have loved to have seen that harbormaster's face when he found out that both channels into his precious harbor had been mined!"

"Do you know if we did much damage, Admiral?"

"No, we don't know. Probably won't know until MacArthur liberates Manila, and maybe not even then. We may even have to wait until the war's over to find out. But, at a minimum, we've kept that port out of the war for at least a couple of weeks, and just at the right time, too. You and your people have done a great job, Jake. I'm putting you in for another Navy Cross, Jake, and *Orca* in for another PUC."

"Thank you, Sir. I know my crew will be delighted . . . now tell me, please, Sir, what's become of Commodore Macdonough?"

"Been kicked upstairs. Gave him command of a light cruiser, the *Fort Lee*. Hated to see him leave, and he hated to leave the submarine force, but submarine billets for senior captains are like turkey's teeth. No place to go but the surface navy. You're a bit junior to take his place, Jake, but I could pull some strings . . ."

"Thank you, Admiral, but no thanks! My place is at sea, at least until this war is over."

"I know how you feel, Jake. Believe me, I do. But face it. You've made nine war patrols in *Orca*. Eleven war patrols, overall, if you count one on *S-49* and your PCO cruise. And you're a commander, now. It's about time in your career for a shore billet — on staff, or a sub base maybe, or at Sub School — there are plenty of jobs in the submarine force that help win the war besides driving a boat."

"I understand that, Admiral, but I'm certain I can contribute the most by staying at sea. Besides, you have quite a few full commanders serving as submarine skippers — and every one of them is senior to me."

Lockwood laughed. "Okay. You'll stay where you are for now. But think about it. You can't stay at sea forever, and still advance your career. Just think about it."

"I will, Sir. I *will* think about it."

"Now, I have something else to tell you that you're not gonna like . . ." Lockwood let Jake in on Joe Bob's mission to the Philippines.

The shipyard put *Orca* straight into dry dock. Over a year sailing in tropical Pacific waters had left an accumulation of marine growth on her hull, all barnacles and hairy moss that had to take at least a knot off her top speed. *Orca's* hull would be sandblasted clean. Then a naval surveyor would inspect the boat's hull for weaknesses, and insure that any necessary structural repairs were made. Finally the hull would be given two coats of gray marine enamel, heavily dosed with copper arsenide, to retard marine growth.

Out of dry dock, the list of unaddressed maintenance projects would finally be addressed under the watchful eye of Chief Wendell Buckner.

Then there would be the upgrades. Among these would be the installation of a Radar Warning Receiver. The RWR is a device designed to detect radar signals and warn the operator that the boat was being "painted" by radar, and provide a bearing to the source. While the RWR would provide the frequency and strength of the signal, it could *not* provide a range to the source. But the RWR *did* detect the first incoming signals, almost always before the signal strength was sufficient to provide a return (echo) signal back to the source. It could thus potentially reveal the presence of an enemy's radar emission before he saw you on his radarscope.

Other improvements included higher-capacity evaporators, and the replacement of the periscope electrical hoists with hydraulic ones. While *Orca* had experienced no problems with her electrical periscope hoists, other boats had, and the hydraulic ones were considered far more reliable, and had become standard equipment on the newer fleet submarines. They operated off the boat's main hydraulic system, and used long hydraulic cylinders to raise the periscopes, relying on gravity to lower them.

Barring any unforeseen difficulties, *Orca's* refit, including sea trials, was scheduled to be completed in eight weeks. This meant that the boat would be in port over Christmas, and not go back on patrol until after the new year. For some of the crew it provided an opportunity to enjoy their accumulated leave, and possibly even enjoy spending the holidays at home. For most crewmembers, however, it meant reassignment to one or another of the relief crews, or permanent assignment to another boat for sea duty. There *was*, after all, a war on.

But Jake had not anticipated losing any of his officers. There was plenty of accumulated leave to take, and plenty of work to do for the boat's refit. But the officer who should have most to do with *Orca's* refit, his engineer, was off playing Marine — or whatever — with the Army. Jake realized that he might never see Joe Bob again, and not just because MacArthur had taken a shine to him. What he had been told about Joe Bob's "temporary assignment" sounded dangerous enough even *without* the details. And the Devil . . . was always in the details.

* * * * *

Three days after he had arrived at Pearl, Joe Bob Clanton was back in the Philippines, the final leg of the journey made on a PBY out of Saipan. Apparently, the plan to build a landing strip on Leyte capable of handling B-24s had to be scrapped because of the thoroughly inhospitable terrain. The airstrips that were built on Leyte were jammed with fighters and fighter-bombers. So it was that air transport to Leyte Field HQ for Joe Bob required a seaplane and a landing in Leyte Gulf.

What Joe Bob did not know (nor did Vice Admiral Lockwood) was that the main purpose for invading Mindoro was to secure terrain suitable for a B-24 landing strip. The original plan had been to bypass Mindoro, just as Wake and Rota had been bypassed.

Field HQ on Leyte was a messy affair. Joe Bob thought it made Port Moresby look like Brisbane in comparison. The hastily constructed Quonset hut that housed Gen. MacArthur and his staff was pointed out as they passed it, but was apparently hallowed ground and off limits to a lowly Navy Lt. j.g. Maybe it was MacArthur himself that had requested him for the job, but apparently the general was too busy to explain the job's details.

Instead, Joe Bob was escorted to one of the larger tents, and introduced to Lieutenant Colonel George Jones, Commander of the 503rd Parachute Regimental Combat Team. Jones was a spare man with a shock of brown hair and a ready grin. He had enlisted in the Army at nineteen and came up through the ranks.

The original assault plan for Mindoro was to use Jones' team to parachute behind enemy lines in advance of the amphibious landing. But, since there was no suitable transport aircraft available, the jump had to be cancelled. Jones and his men were held in such high regard, however, that MacArthur picked them to spearhead the amphibious operation as a ground force.

"George Jones," he said, and stuck out his hand.

Shaking the proffered hand, "Joe Bob Clanton, Colonel."

"So, Lieutenant, HQ tells me you've made first-hand acquaintance with the guerrilla forces on Mindoro. That right?"

"Yes, Sir."

"Tell me about it."

And Joe Bob told Jones the story of his eight days on Mindoro, leaving out the part about his having slept with the guerrilla commander.

"So, their leader, this Delvina Bacatplan, I've heard good things about her. Tell me, Lieutenant, is she really all that capable?"

"Very much so, Sir," Joe Bob nodded in assent.

"Well then, let's make sure nothing bad happens to Mrs. Bacatplan and her troops, shall we?"

"Nothing will, if I can help it, Sir," Joe Bob countered.

"Outstanding . . . well, first off, I want you to meet the combat radioman who's going in with you."

"Radioman, Sir?"

"You ever operate a field radio?"

"No, Sir. But I'm sure I could learn."

"Me too. And so you shall. But if one of you gets taken out, then we're operating blind, with no direct communication with the guerrillas. No, you're taking a radioman. Besides, the damn thing weighs forty-five pounds. *And* he's trained to carry it, and you're not." He called outside the tent. "Send Sergeant Riley, in here, will you?"

"Yessir," the disembodied voice replied.

Soon thereafter: "Sir, you sent for me?"

"Yes, Sergeant. Come in."

A young man entered the tent and saluted. Joe Bob saw that he was a slight, skinny kid, maybe in his mid-twenties. He was wearing Army fatigues, and a ball cap with a lightning bolt insignia.

"Sergeant Riley, I'd like you to meet Navy Lieutenant Clanton. This is the officer who'll be in charge of your little expedition to Mindoro. While we're setting up with the guerrillas to meet you on the Island, I want you to check him out on your equipment. Can you do that?"

"Yes, Sir. Happy to, Sir."

"Excellent," Jones said. Then, he said to Joe Bob, "You're set up for a cot in the junior officer's tent. You'll find your duffel bag next to it. The sergeant here will show you where the tent is when you're ready to crap out. Tomorrow, you'll both be briefed on the operation. You'll be leaving for Mindoro in two days. That's it, men. You're dismissed."

* * * * *

On Friday morning, November 17th, Jake, Kate, and Elizabeth boarded a Pan Am Clipper for the fourteen-hour flight that would take them to Los Angeles. From there they would be taking two trains and a bus to reach Decatur, Illinois, where Kate's parents would meet their new son-in-law and only granddaughter. From Decatur, they would take a bus and a train to Des Moines to visit with Jake's family. Jake had only thirty days leave, so they had to be back in Pearl on December 16th, a week and a day before Christmas. Kate thought that it was probably just as well, because then they wouldn't be able to spend the holidays with either family, and wouldn't be accused of playing favorites — not that either set of parents would ever think of such a thing.

Jake had been uneasy about taking leave while *Orca* was in refit, but Bucky and Joel convinced him that the refit was in good hands, despite Joe Bob's absence, and, anyway, he would be back in plenty of time for the completion of the yard work and for sea trials.

He was even less comfortable about taking little Elizabeth Ann on a 4,000-mile journey across an ocean and half a continent. But Kate had been insistent. She scolded him for thinking that babies were too fragile or inflexible to make such a trip. "She's healthier than either of us," Kate said. "And she'll be perfectly happy just so long as she can eat, sleep, and poop." In the end, Jake, admitting to himself that he knew practically nothing about babies, gave in.

The train left sunny, warm Los Angeles and passed through Phoenix to Santa Fe, where they changed trains and boarded another. The second train went through progressively colder country: Wichita, Kansas, and St. Louis, en route to Springfield, Illinois. The two trains transported them across 1,955 miles in three days. In Springfield, they had to transfer to a Greyhound Bus for the forty-one-mile trip to Decatur. The weather there was overcast, and it was very cold. "It always looks like this just before it snows," Kate said.

"Yeah," Jake agreed, "And it reminds me how glad I was when they home ported *Orca* at Pearl."

Kate's parents met them at the Decatur bus station in their 1939 Chevrolet. After greeting their daughter and meeting Jake, they admired their granddaughter and generally acted like proud and overjoyed grandparents. The drive to the Shegrue home was short, about six miles. All during the drive, Kate's father kept apologizing for not driving to Springfield to meet them. "Everything's rationed," he explained, "especially gas."

The Shegrue home at 423 Williams Street, was a modest, two-story, brick house with a detached garage that backed onto a city park.

* * * * *

The field radio BC-654 really was a beast. Not only was the fool thing heavy, but also it was awkward and boxy, and it never seemed to ride well on your back no matter how you adjusted the straps. Joe Bob was forever grateful that Lieutenant Colonel Jones had decided that Sergeant Jimmy Riley's services would be necessary. Despite his spare frame, Riley hefted and carried the radio effortlessly.

For all its unwieldiness, however, the BC-654 transceiver was simple enough to operate. Riley swore that the set had enough power to transmit and receive from one end of Mindoro to the other on a good day. But Joe Bob was afraid to ask him what would happen on a bad day. He figured he'd find out soon enough.

Jimmy Riley was a pleasant enough young man. He'd joined the Army right after Pearl Harbor on his eighteenth birthday. He had asked for assignment to the Signal Corps, and his request had been granted in the sense that the infantry had trained him as a radio operator. He had lived every one of his first eighteen years in Philadelphia, and until he was sent to Fort Dix, New Jersey, for Basic, Riley had never left Pennsylvania. "And looka me now," he'd say. "I jump outa airplanes, and I'm in the effen Philippines! Who'd a thunk it?" He was full of stories of "stuff we done back in Philly." And Joe Bob liked him.

On Saturday morning, November 18th, Joe Bob and Riley were called to Lieutenant Colonel James' tent and briefed on the details of their transit to Mindoro.

Jones rolled out a map of Mindoro Island. He used strategically placed coffee mugs and a bayonet to stop the map from curling up again.

"There will be no insertion by submarine this trip, men," Jones said. "Instead, the Navy has kindly arranged for transport and insertion by PT boat. The boat will pick up you and your gear tomorrow evening, and you will travel at night and hunker down during the day until you reach the island. The Army has contacted the coast watcher on Mindoro—I believe you know him, Clanton—Liam Wallace?" Joe Bob nodded in the affirmative. "Says he knows *you*, anyway—and Wallace has made contact with the guerrillas on Mindoro. He's arranged for the Filipinos to meet the PT Boat in the wee hours on Wednesday, November twenty-second.   If, for some reason, you're delayed, they'll look for you as well on the twenty-third and the twenty-fourth.   Rendezvous will be at the mouth of the Bongabong River, on Mindoro's southeast coast, here . . ." He pointed to a spot on the map.

"Now the invasion is planned to take place on the opposite side of the Island," Jones continued, "at Mangarin Bay, immediately south of the town of San Jose." Again, Jones pointed to the location on the map.   "D-Day is Tuesday, the fifth of December.   That will give you plenty of time to reacquaint yourself with the Filipinos and maybe do some reconnoitering.

"Problem is, we're not sure exactly how many Nips there are on the Island.   We're pretty sure we can handle just about anything they throw at us, but it would be nice to know for sure just how much that is.   We *do* know there are Nip garrisons at Calapan in the north, Pola in the east, and Sablayan on the west."

Jones' fingers moved across the map, as he continued speaking. "In the south, where we want to hit them, there's already a small airstrip, outside of San Jose." Another touch of a finger to the map. "The objective is to take it, and hold it so the Engineers can enlarge it to handle B-24s.

"We think there are anywhere from four thousand to eight thousand troops on Mindoro in these garrisons and another five hundred or so scattered all over the Island. Air recon shows work camps here and there on the Island, mostly lumbering operations and a couple copper mines, but they use forced labor to work them, and that shouldn't require all that many troops. Still, you never know.

"So it would be good if you and our Filipino friends could fill in the blanks."

"We'll do our best, Colonel," Joe Bob said.

* * * * *

Jake thought Kate's parents, Beth and Brian, couldn't have been more welcoming. They treated Jake like the son they never had, idolized their only daughter, and spent endless hours fawning over, and playing with, Elizabeth. Their grandchild at six months was alert, babbling, smiling, and laughing. She was able to sit up on her own, turn over by herself, and was just beginning to crawl. She was still nursing, but had started eating solid food — rice cereal mostly. Beth Shegrue eagerly took over as much of her daughter's motherly duties as possible. She changed, bathed, dressed, fed, and even read to Elizabeth at bedtime.

The Shegrues had been married for six years before Kate had put in her appearance. They had wanted more children, but, as Beth Shegrue explained, "It wasn't part of God's plan for us."

Brian worked as a comptroller for a local company that manufactured heat exchangers and pressure vessels. He worked weekdays, of course, and that left Jake at the Shegrue home for Kate and Beth to fuss over when they weren't fussing over the baby. Jake had long forgotten what it was like to be the center of attention of the five women he grew up with, and now found that readapting to a similar situation made him somewhat uncomfortable. So when Brian invited him to his workplace for a plant tour, he eagerly accepted.

"We do a bunch of stuff to support the war effort," Brian explained. "Those shell and tube heat exchangers over there — the small ones — they go into Sherman tanks. We turn out ten of those a day, all certified and tested, ship them up to General Motors in Detroit. Do a lot of industrial stuff, too. That big heat exchanger over there, for instance," pointing to a fourteen-foot long, six-foot diameter, shell and tube unit being fitted with tubes, "is going to a fertilizer plant in Florida. And we make boilers, too . . ."

After the plant tour, Brian took Jake to lunch at a local beanery. "Eat lunch here 'most every day," he said.

"I can tell," Jake said. "Everyone here seems to know you."

Brian laughed. A small, balding man with a smiling face, his whole body laughed when he did. "Everybody in Decatur knows everybody else. You're from the Midwest, isn't it that way where you're from?"

"Not exactly. But, to be fair, Des Moines is a little bigger than Decatur."

After lunch, and with the tour over, Jake left Brian, and walked back to Williams Street, perhaps three miles, maybe four. It wasn't a particularly pleasant day, overcast (does the sun *ever* shine in Decatur?), with a cold, blustery wind. Jake was thoroughly chilled when he finally arrived at 423 Williams Street.

* * * * *

The trip from Leyte to Mindoro was different, yet much the same for Joe Bob. As a submariner, he was used to nighttime surface cruising, and hiding out in the daytime, except that in a sub, there were more places to hide.

Still, Joe Bob thought, that *PT-142* was a remarkable craft. The eighty-foot long boat was built almost entirely of plywood, and had very little armor. But *PT-142* made up for being lightly armored by being fast. It was powered by three powerful Packard gasoline engines, and was capable of speeds up to forty-one knots. Its main armament was four torpedoes, launched from tubes on the boat deck. There was also a 40mm gun forward, and two, twin .50 caliber guns aft.

At 0100 on the 22nd, *PT-142* was idling off the mouth of the Bongabong River on the southwestern coast of Mindoro. The boat drew only five feet, but even that was too deep a draught for it to navigate up the Bongabong. Silt deposits at the mouth of the Bongabong allowed only flat-bottomed boats to cross from the sea to the river and vice-versa. Joe Bob and Riley had to wait until 0150 before *PT-142's* light signal to the shore was returned, and they could embark in the inflatable that was to take them and their gear ashore.

Two men from the PT boat were at the oars, and would return the inflatable to *PT-142* once they had unloaded their cargo. The boat approached the shoreline cautiously, four rifles at the ready. It was not until they responded "MacArthur" to the enquiry "Who goes there?" and the cheer went up from the shore that they relaxed a little.

* * * * *

Beth and Brian Shegrue were devoutly religious and staunchly Catholic. Jake came to that conclusion not by anything they said — they were careful to avoid the subject in conversation with their Protestant son-in-law — but by their demeanor and their behavior. They certainly prayed a lot. They said grace before every meal, and Beth prayed over Elizabeth every time she went to bed, even if it was for just a nap.

Sunday morning was reserved for Mass. Jake was accustomed to attending Mass with Kate on the base, but the church in Decatur was something else again. St. James Catholic Church was a tall, imposing, Gothic structure of red brick that stood almost by itself on South Webster Street. Jake figured that the church would be practically empty, judging from the paucity of cars in the parking lot, and so was surprised to find the church packed for ten o'clock Mass. Remembering that gasoline was rationed, it dawned on him that most of the people there had walked to church.

Communion was still in progress, and Beth, Kate, and Brian had returned to their pew where Jake and Elizabeth awaited them, when, suddenly, Elizabeth let out a shriek loud enough to animate the saints' statues that lined the church. Kate relieved Jake of the screaming baby, and both mother and child retired at speed in the direction of the narthex.

The Mass was concluded swiftly after the communicants had returned to their seats, and the Shegrues and Jake found Kate and the still-crying Elizabeth waiting for them outside the church.

"Let's get home," Kate said. "She's wet and hungry."

* * * * *

Delvina had sent Rodolfo and four other armed men to meet the Americans. Rodolfo greeted Joe Bob warmly, and shook Riley's hand vigorously. "Welcome," he said to both.

Joe Bob and Riley nodded in return.

"If Delvina knew MacArthur sending *you*, Joe Bob," said Rodolfo, "she be here to welcome you herself."

He then turned to greet Riley.

"Jimmy, you are most welcome," Rodolfo said. "Did Joe Bob tell you story 'bout how we wore him out on trip down to Dongon Bay?"

"Mr. Clanton ain't been all that talkative, Rodolfo, but I sure would like to hear that story sometime—"

"And I'm sure Rodolfo would be only too happy to tell you all about it, Riley," Joe Bob interrupted, "but I'm betting we have some traveling to do through the jungle tonight. You'll get to see how much fun it is first hand."

"Okay, Mr. Clanton, if you say so," Riley replied. "Then how 'bout we get started before these effen mosquitoes eat me up?"

But Rodolfo had already parceled out the equipment that Joe Bob and Riley had with them to the Filipinos that were with him. Two of them had started off into the jungle carrying the packs of rations, clothing, and blankets that he and Joe Bob had brought.

"Not the radio. That's mine," Riley said, reclaiming the BC-654 from the guerrilla who was about to pick it up.

"As you wish," Rodolfo said. "Leave it, George," he said to the guerrilla in Tagalog, waving him ahead.

Riley hoisted the radio onto his back, picked up his rifle, and followed Joe Bob and the Filipinos into the jungle. Once under the jungle canopy, he noted, the night got suddenly very dark. He soon observed that the four Filipinos up front had either melted into the darkness, or had taken off by themselves. *No problem.* Joe Bob and Rodolfo were still visible.

When he was sure that his eyes had adapted completely to the darkness, Riley realized that the four men up front had indeed disappeared, and that he, Joe Bob, and Rodolfo were by themselves.

"We liable to run into any Japs?" Riley asked.

Rodolfo laughed. "We do, then they in trouble. Not that they have big trouble finding us with all noise you make."

"Waddya mean?" Riley said. "I'm being very quiet. And why 'zactly would the Japs be in trouble? There's only three of us."

Rodolfo laughed again. "They in trouble 'cause they run into Gregorio, David, George, and Daniel before us *first*."

"I get it," Riley replied. "Those are the four guys you came wit'. They're up ahead at point, right?"

"Yes. They *very* good point men."

They kept walking through the darkness and well into the next morning. Riley was surprised how chilly it had gotten during the night, and how quickly it heated up in the morning — *and* how damp it was. His clothes were clammy, whether he was sweating or not. He was used to carrying the radio *and* a pack, but had to admit to himself that the walk through the jungle was wearing him out. Rodolfo was sympathetic, and made frequent water and rest stops, but Riley was still getting *very* tired.

As the sun peeped through the jungle canopy, and rose in the sky overhead, the march inland continued. About noon they stopped to rest. The four other Filipinos joined them, setting down the gear they carried. Hearing Tagalog spoken was old hat to Joe Bob, but was a new experience for Riley.

"What language is that?" Riley whispered to Joe Bob. "I thought the Philippines was *American* territory. Rodolfo speaks pretty good English, so how come these guys don't?"

"The language, Riley, is Tagalog. It's the Filipino language, at least in this part of the Philippines. For Filipinos, English is their second language. And while lotsa Filipinos speak English, not all of them do."

"Oh," Riley answered. "Wish they'd talk English, though. People talking 'foreign' around me gives me the willies. Always think they're talkin' 'bout me."

One of the four Filipinos, the one Rodolfo had identified earlier as George, stretched out on the ground and promptly fell fast asleep. The other three disappeared back into the jungle, probably, Joe Bob thought, for sentry duty.

"We can stand sentry, Rodolfo," Joe Bob offered. "On the boat that got us here, all we did was sleep. Riley and I are well rested. We could easily stand sentry."

Speak for yourself, Lieutenant, Riley thought, *but I'm beat. Hope 'ole Rodolfo doesn't take him up on that offer.*

"That is okay, Joe Bob," Rodolfo answered. "My men familiar with jungle and jungle sounds. Do not be offended, but you not able to stand sentry good as them."

"I understand," Joe Bob agreed, "and I'm not offended."

And I'm *grateful*, thought Riley.

"Good. Eat something. Rest," Rodolfo said. "We start again later, after rains. It is cooler then."

After it rains. Great, Riley thought. *We'll be soaked and our stuff will be soaked. Welcome to Mindoro.*

* * * * *

The rest of their week in Decatur flew by for Kate, who reveled in the attention her parents showered on their visitors. She dreaded the day when they would have to pack up and leave. "All good things," she knew, eventually ended. But, still, when the day finally came for the Lawlors to take their leave, Kate was saddened, almost to the point of tears. She finally did cry, but only after her mother had broken out in tears at their leaving.

"I'm going to miss you so much," Beth said tearfully. "I was just starting to get acquainted with my new son and granddaughter, and now you all have to go!"

"Oh, Mom, please stop crying," Kate said. "You're making *me* cry."

"I can't help it," Beth said, still crying

And then Elizabeth started to cry.

Jake and Brian stood by, not crying, but feeling as if they were about to. Sad and useless.

* * * * *

They reached the guerrilla camp at first light. Joe Bob noted that nothing about the place was familiar. While he had no idea where he was, exactly, he knew it was only sensible that the guerrillas stay continually on the move. He realized that this camp had to be in an entirely different location from the one he had visited last August. And that, he rightly concluded, was why nothing appears familiar.

Still, while it *was* different, it was somewhat the same: The same friendly smiles, the same warm greeting — "*Mabuhay,*" "Welcome" — and those same hats of plated palm leaves.

"Joe Bob!" shouted a teenager, running from the gaggle of onlookers, and suddenly hugging him. A familiar face, smiling from ear to ear.

"Philip," Joe Bob said, genuinely glad to see the youngster. Rodolfo laughed at Philip's exuberance.

And then, there she was.

At first, Philip was upset that Joe Bob unceremoniously detached himself from his encircling arms *until* he saw the reason why: Delvina. There was the same oval face with that small, somewhat flattened nose, and large, bright eyes of liquid onyx — eyes a man could drown in. And she wore a broad, full-lipped smile.

"Wow," Riley said aloud, as Joe Bob and Delvina embraced. The thought that followed was best left unspoken: *What a gorgeous babe!*

Joe Bob and Delvina hugged and laughed, and hugged some more. Delvina's men grinned in approval of their leader's affection for the American. Joe Bob and Delvina, with some difficulty, refrained from kissing each other. They mustn't let the troops know how deeply involved they *really* were, Joe Bob. reminded himself.

"Joe Bob," was all Delvina could say, over and over again, when they finally let go of each other. Joe Bob could only look at her with a silly grin on his face.

* * * * *

Kate endured the bus ride to the train station in silence. She was still visibly saddened. Holding a now sleeping Elizabeth, she stared out through the grimy glass of the bus window at the passing gray landscape that reflected her mood. At first, Jake tried to engage her in conversation, but eventually gave up and stared off into space, locked in his own thoughts, catching her mood and still feeling useless.

The train to Peoria and Des Moines was a half hour late getting into Springfield. It didn't tarry, and was only fourteen minutes behind schedule when it left the station. It was supposed to take just over eight hours to go from Springfield to Des Moines, but it took almost nine, and the train was nearly an hour late getting into Des Moines.

Jake's father and mother and two of his sisters, Rachel and Ester, met them at the train station.

Jake's mother, Sally, and her daughters, bonded and cooed over Elizabeth. Sally immediately claimed possession of her new granddaughter, as Jake and his father shook hands (among the Lawlor men, that passed for a warm and affectionate greeting).

Jake's father's name was Ezekiel, and he hated it. He went by "Zeke," and that's how Jake introduced him to Kate.

Kate took her father-in-law's proffered hand, used it to pull herself close, and hugged him. "Dad," she said, and, claiming her child from Sally, handed her to him, "this is your new granddaughter, Elizabeth."

Jake was surprised to see his father smile broadly and take Elizabeth from Kate.

* * * * *

Joe Bob stretched out his blanket apart from the others, hoping to provide some privacy for a nighttime visitor. He knew he was exhausted from the trek inland, but still fought to stay awake. It was a fight he would quickly lose.

The next morning he awoke refreshed, but quite alone. He shook Riley awake, and they walked over to where they might find some breakfast, which was a porridge of some starchy root vegetable and goat's milk, served with an herb tea. Delvina ate sitting cross-legged under a palm, and Joe Bob, bringing his breakfast, left Riley with the others and took the place beside her.

"I've missed you, Delvina," he said.

"I missed you too," Delvina replied with a smile. "I never expected to see you again."

"I always knew we would see each other again," Joe Bob said. "I just never expected it to be until after the war. When the opportunity came to come back to Mindoro, I jumped at it."

Delvina's smile broadened. "So you did. This was a wonderful surprise. But when you left to return to your submarine, you did not say you would come back to me after the war."

"As I recall, I was so choked up I didn't say much of anything."

"No, you did not. But the sadness in your eyes said much." She looked solemnly down at her plate. "I came to you last night, you know."

"No, I *didn't* know. Why didn't you wake me up?"

"I tried. But you would have none of it. So I gave up and let you sleep."

A shadow was suddenly cast over them. When they looked up, a short, wiry man with long white hair and beard, sparking blue eyes, and a bulbous nose stood over them.

"Do you know this fella?" Delvina asked Joe Bob, indicating a smiling Liam Wallace.

"Wallace!" Joe Bob shouted. Standing, he grabbed the man's hand and shook it. "Sergeant Riley," he called out to the radioman, "Com'ere and meet Liam Wallace. He's the guy who welcomed us ashore last August. And be careful you don't say he's Australian," he added, as Riley joined the group. "Liam Wallace, this is Sergeant Jimmy Riley."

"Hello, Jimmy Riley," Wallace said, offering his hand.

"Pleased to meet ya," Riley said, shaking his hand. "The Lieutenant here tells me you been dodgin' Japs for years."

"That I have. Though from what I hear, my dodging days may be over."

Later, Delvina, Joe Bob, Riley, Wallace, Rodolfo, and another two of Delvina's lieutenants, Geraldo and Jose, sat under a banyan tree in conference.

"I'm here," Wallace explained, "because there's no longer a need for a ship spotter on Mindoro, or anywhere else in the Philippines, for that matter. With air bases on Saipan and now on Leyte, our airmen cannot only spot, but can attack, enemy ships. I'm here because I brought my radio."

"We already got a radio," Riley interrupted. "That's why *I'm* here."

"And a fine radio it is, I'm sure," Wallace said, chuckling. "But it's a *field* radio—HF, high frequency, short range, right?"

"Right," Riley said. "It's all we need to talk to the men hittin' the beach."

"Exactly. But *my* radio is LF—low frequency, long range. I can talk to Port Arthur, or to MacArthur in Leyte, if I want—and I have. Well, maybe not MacArthur himself, but you know what I mean."

500

"Okay," Joe Bob said, "so we have communications with Leyte HQ. Not sure why we need that, but I guess that's good."

"It most certainly is," Liam said. "When did they tell you D-day was, Joe Bob?"

"December fifth. A week-and-a-half from now."

"Well, there's been a delay. New date is December 15th. You'd've had a long wait if you were at the landing zone on the fifth."

"I'll say," Joe Bob agreed.

"And that's why *I'm* here," Wallace said. "My instructions are to sit tight, receive, and acknowledge only. I'm not as secure as your field radio, Riley. The Japs can locate my transmissions easily if I stay on the air long enough. I'm not to transmit *except* to acknowledge HQ's transmissions, or unless there's an emergency—at least not until you have an accurate count of the enemy forces on the Island."

"Well," Delvina said, "if MacArthur wants us to count the Japanese, then the more time we have, the better the count we can give him. It *is* a big island."

* * * * *

Zeke and Sally had remodeled the house that Jake grew up in. They had knocked down the wall between his old bedroom and that of his sisters, Rachel and Ruth, doubling its size. There was now more than enough room for a full-size bed and a crib for Elizabeth. The crib was, apparently, a hand-me-down, used by several of Elizabeth's "Des Moines" cousins, not that the sleeping Elizabeth cared much, one way or the other.

Sally led her visitors upstairs to the room, almost as soon as they got back to the house, saying, "It's late, and well past Dad's and my bedtime. Dad's got to get up and go to work in the morning, so I'll leave you three to settle in for the night. Anything you need, Kate, before I go?"

"Nothing I can think of, thank you, Mom."

"Good. Jake knows where everything is, anyhow. Sorry there's no bathroom on this floor, Kate. You'll have to use the one downstairs. Dad and I have always meant to put one in up here, but never quite got around to it. Maybe after the war is over, when you can buy things again. But listen to me babble on . . ." She smiled at them. "I'm *so* glad you're here! Good night, children."

"Good night, Mom," Jake said.

"I love them," Kate said, after Sally left.

"I'm glad, but kind of surprised," Jake said. "I knew Mom would be no problem, but I'm honestly surprised by my Father. You know he wasn't exactly pleased that I married a Catholic. But," he added with a smile, "you seem to have gotten him past that."

"I don't think you give your Dad enough credit. And I think Elizabeth had something to do with it, too," Kate said, smiling. "But now, I'm exhausted, my baby's sound asleep, and that bed looks awfully inviting."

* * * * *

Delvina had split up her forces four ways, sending each group to reconnoiter a separate part of the island. Rodolfo took his men north, Geraldo east, and Jose south. Delvina took the western part of the island, and made sure to take Joe Bob along with her.

* * * * *

Just weeks before, Tina Salut had been plying her trade in Manila's outskirts, seeing to the baser needs of Japanese officers. She took up her trade when she was just fifteen, the same year the Japanese invaded her homeland. Her father had been an officer in the Philippine Commonwealth Army, and he and her mother died when a shell hit their Manila home and killed them, along with her younger brother. Tina survived the blast untouched. She took up "the trade" to avoid starvation. She was young and pretty, and soon became a favorite of the invading army's officers. Over the past three years, she had even picked up the ability to speak passable Japanese.

Tina would keep her eyes and ears open, and would pass on whatever tidbits of information she gleaned from her clients to the Resistance. When her information proved to be both reliable *and* valuable, the resistance movement came to regard Tina as a valuable asset, overlooking the ways and means involved in gathering the information.

General Tomoyuki Yamashita, Commander of the Philippine Occupation Force, knew that the invasion of Luzon by Allied forces was imminent. Yamashita had requested troop reinforcements from the home islands, and was assured that a support fleet carrying those reinforcements was en route. Nonetheless, he thought it imperative to gather as many men as possible from the surrounding command posts, specifically for the defense of Manila. With that in mind, Yamashita ordered all troop commanders in the northern occupation district to IJA headquarters in Manila. There they would meet to discuss the defense of the city, and the role they and the men they commanded would play in it.

Among these was Lieutenant Colonel Gaku Chiba, garrison commander at Sablayan, Mindoro. Chiba was a short, fat, unattractive man, in charge of some 240 regular troops, 350 Koreans, and 1,150 Filipino forced laborers. He did not consider his command a military operation. It was, as he saw it, clearly a commercial venture. The troops under him were there only to ensure that the flow of raw materials, the lumber and the copper ore, made it from their source on Mindoro to the home islands. Chiba would, naturally, bring his troops north to Luzon if ordered. The Koreans, of course, were forced into the Army, and would probably prove useless, while the Filipinos would seize the opportunity and join the Resistance. The result of the move, as

Chiba saw it, would only be an overall net addition to the forces the IJA would have to face.

"No," he argued to the attractive little Filipina who ably saw to his needs that night in Manila, "it would be far better if Yamashita left me and my garrison alone in Sablayan. The defense of Manila should be left up to those best able to provide it. Besides, when the reinforcements arrive from Japan, there will be no need at all for us. Yamashita is worried over nothing."

So impressed was Chiba with the services the Filipina provided, that he tried to persuade her to return to Mindoro with him. Tina had no intention of doing so, but told him she would think about it anyway.

Tina did pass onto her Filipino contacts the information Chiba provided her, and informed them as well of Chiba's invitation (this last more of a boast as to her prowess in extracting information than anything else). She was surprised when they told her to take him up on it, to go to Mindoro, and that they would pass her contact information on to Delvina Bacatplan.

And so it was that Tina Salut was in the garrison at Sablayan when Delvina and Joe Bob were reconnoitering the western side of Mindoro in advance of the Island's invasion.

* * * * *

"No, Son," said Zeke Lawlor, "I have to admit my daughter-in-law is not bad—for a *Papist*, that is."

"Dad, you can't be serious. And it's *Catholic*, not Papist. How could you possibly think that *anyone*, not just Kate, but anyone, is bad just because they don't share your religious beliefs."

"Well, not too long ago you would have said *our* religious beliefs. That's what worries me, Son. I used to be assured of your salvation. Now I'm not so sure."

"Are you saying that Kate is going to hell?"

"Her? No, probably not. She's never known any different, and she seems to be a good person. It's *you* I'm worried about. You used to know better."

"I'm fine, Dad. I haven't changed what I believe—what I've *always* believed. And I've never believed that God cares all that much about one religion or another, just the content of a person's soul. And I know that Kate has a beautiful soul."

"And then there's my granddaughter," Zeke said, changing the subject. "How could you have agreed to bring her up a Papist?"

"Catholic, Dad, Catholic—and a Christian, just like you and me. And Kate. My wife, Kate, who'll be the one to raise her as a Christian, because I'm at sea all the time and I'm hardly ever around my daughter. And if Elizabeth turns out to be as good a person as her mother, I will thank God for it every day."

Zeke Lawlor had nothing to say in answer to that. But he was still concerned about his son's chances for salvation.

* * * * *

Tina Salut had the run of the Sablayan garrison, allowed to come and go as she pleased per the commander's orders. She had told Chiba that she was a devout Catholic, and had to occasionally go off into the jungle alone to pray to her God, or she would lose her soul. Chiba knew the Filipinos were a superstitious lot, and saw no reason not to indulge her. So he agreed, but insisted that whenever she left the compound she must take along two of his soldiers for her protection. She pouted. What didn't Chiba understand about her requirement to be "alone" for her prayers? she asked. But he would not budge. On the other hand, he also neglected to inform anyone on his staff of the requirement.

When Tina left the compound, unattended the first time, the garrison guard knew better than to stop her, but inquired up the chain of command if she had the commandant's permission to come and go on her own. When politely asked, Chiba waved off the inquiry with "Tina Salut comes and goes as she wishes," and it was left at that.

But so far, Tina had gained no useful information to pass along to her guerrilla contact, Diego Carras, and, truth be told, she was becoming more and more disgusted with Chiba and his demands for her "special talents." She was sorry that she had ever agreed to come to Mindoro, and thought the Resistance had made a big mistake in sending her there.

On what passed for a winter night in Mindoro, Tina left the garrison for her regular meeting with Diego. It was a bright night, with the moon high above, waxing full. As usual, she simply walked off into the jungle until Diego mysteriously appeared alongside, just as he had from the first. This time, she was surprised to find Diego in the company of two others, a man and a woman. The Filipinos began talking together in Tagalog.

"Tina," Diego said, "this is our leader, Delvina Bacatplan, and this man is an American, Lieutenant Joe Bob, who has come to help us." Joe Bob, hearing his name, nodded and smiled.

"Delvina Bacatplan. They talk about you in Manila. You are famous."

Delvina smiled at Tina, pleased. "I am happy to meet you, Tina. It is important that you know why the Resistance sent you here. The Americans are coming soon to Mindoro to free us from the Japanese. They are coming to Mindoro even before they go to free Luzon. They need an enemy troop count. You need to find out how many troops there are here at Sablayan."

Tina smiled broadly. The very first thing she did was count them. At last, she could provide some useful information, and then maybe quit Chiba. "There are two hundred and thirty-eight Japanese regulars, and three hundred and thirty-one Koreans. The Koreans will fight for the Japanese, but *only* because the Japanese will kill them if they don't. There are also eight Japanese officers, the colonel, the *baboy* who runs the place, and a staff of seven. The compound also holds many half-starved Filipino *alipin*. There are so many Filipino slaves that they are difficult to count, but there are at least seven hundred of the them in the camp. There are more, I know, at the workstations, the lumber camps, and the mines, because the colonel says so. Also, I have heard the guards talking."

"Excellent, Tina. That is good work," Delvina said.

"What did she say?" Joe Bob asked, in English.

"I am sorry, Lieutenant," Tina said, in English. "I should have reported in English so you could understand us."

"No way you could know that I can't speak Tagalog," Joe Bob said.

Delvina quickly repeated Tina's report in English. Then, in English, Tina reported what Chiba had told her in Manila, that the Japanese were pulling troops out of Mindoro for the defense of Manila. "My guess is if you told that to the Filipino Resistance in Manila, Tina, then MacArthur already knows about it. But we'll pass it on again, anyway."

"I must get back now," Tina said. "No need to raise suspicions. But you must let me know when MacArthur will come to Mindoro, Lieutenant. You *must* let me know, and then I can deal with the pig, Chiba, and leave this place."

"You'll know when he's coming, Tina. You'll know," Joe Bob said. "You'll be close enough, you'll *hear* him coming."

Tina smiled broadly in anticipation.

* * * * *

Another tearful leave taking. This time, Jake thought, the entourage of well-wishers took up half the Des Moines train station. His mom and dad were there, of course, but so were his four sisters, their husbands, and his fifteen nieces and nephews, two of them still in diapers. It was a Saturday, December 7th. Pearl Harbor Day. This whole mess had started just three years ago—for America, anyway. The rest of the world had started killing each other even earlier.

Then came the endless train ride: 1,810 miles of *clickety-clack, clickety-clack*, Des Moines to Kansas City, on to Wichita, change trains in Santa Fe, on to Phoenix and finally reaching L.A.

Next was the Pan Am Clipper back to Pearl: 2,560 miles in just 14 hours.

On Monday afternoon, December 11th, the taxi left Jake, Kate, and Elizabeth in front of their cottage on the base. Jake noted they had painted over the rank on the sign in front of their house. It now read "CDR. J. J. Lawlor."

The three of them had twice crossed an ocean, traveled around the western half of the United States, and done it all in thirty days. As Kate had predicted, their baby daughter survived the trip none the worse for wear, changing climates without so much as a sniffle.

* * * * *

The American invasion fleet was spotted on December 12th, coming across the Sibuyan Sea and into the Philippine Sea toward the southern tip of Mindoro. Even then, the Japanese High Command was sure that the mass of ships and men would continue on up past Mindoro for an attack on Luzon.

The only forces at the disposal of the Japanese to hurl against the fleet were *kamikaze* suicide fighters. Days before, USAAF and Navy fighters had bombed and strafed the airfields on Luzon to eliminate as many *kamikaze* aircraft as possible, but many survived. One *kamikaze* managed to penetrate air cover and strike the oncoming invasion fleet on December 13th, hitting the light cruiser, *Nashville*, killing 130 men. Other *kamikaze* attacks on the 14th damaged two LSTs (tank landing ships).

On the morning of the 15th, six escort carriers, three battleships, six cruisers, and other supporting warships began pounding the Mangarin Bay shoreline, using naval gunfire and carrier-based aircraft.

508

Tina Salut was lying sweaty and naked on a *futon*. Next to her was an equally naked, sexually sated, sleeping *and* snoring Lt. Col. Gaku Chiba. Then Tina heard the naval guns booming in the distance. Lieutenant Joe Bob had told her that she would first hear the invasion and then know that MacArthur was coming.

Tina got up quietly and found Chiba's straight razor lying beside the washstand. She returned to the *futon*, knelt, and calmly sliced open Chiba's throat from ear to ear. Dark red blood spurted from severed arteries, splashing her. Chiba was awake now, eyes suddenly open wide, but able to make no sound beyond a pathetic gurgle. Tina watched him bleed out as she washed his spattered blood from her body and then dressed. Then she calmly walked out of his quarters and exited the compound.

The guards ogled her as she walked past their post and into the surrounding jungle.

Lieutenant Colonel George Jones had read the intelligence reports coming out of Mindoro, the reports he had sent Lt. j.g. Clanton and Sgt. Riley to get, but he was not sure he believed them. They said that there were no more than one thousand Japanese troops left on the entire Island, that the Japanese had transported thirty-five hundred troops, their entire garrison at Calapan, on barges from Puerto Galera, on the north end of the Island, to Luzon.

So, Jones was pleasantly surprised when he and his paratroopers went in behind the naval gunfire on the 15th of December and actually met little resistance.

His radioman was in contact with Sgt. Jimmy Riley the whole time, directing the small force of fifty or so Filipino guerrillas inland toward the grossly outnumbered and fleeing Japanese. At morning's end, his paratroopers were shaking hands with the grinning guerrillas.

By the afternoon of the 15th, the Army Engineers had already begun construction of the airfield extension, and enlargement southeast of San Jose.

* * * * *

"What happened to the Christmas Tree?" Jake inquired.

Joel Himmelfarb had been going over the maintenance projects that the yard had accomplished while Jake was on leave. "The yard birds removed it," he replied. "Seems the tensioning spring that kept the cables taut was corroded away. The warrant officer in charge of our refit said that spring steel and seawater were incompatible. He said if he replaced it in kind, it would be gone again after a couple of months at sea, and then the cables and the pulleys would just rattle around and make noise. So I had him remove it."

"Probably for the best," Jake said. "Guess we'll just have to stay out of minefields from now on. Still, I'm kinda sorry to see it go. Sure saved our butts back there in Manila."

"It did that," Joel agreed.

Christmas at the Lawlors was a festive affair. The Lawlors had invited the wardroom officers who weren't on leave to their house for a turkey dinner. Joel Himmelfarb was there, as were Bill Salton and Gary Clark. A surprise guest was a sunburned Joe Bob Clanton, who had returned from the Philippines just three days earlier.

Billy Kinkaid returned from leave on the day after New Year's, 1945. While *Orca* was in refit, he had completed his qualification notebook to Joel's satisfaction, and had taken and passed his in-port exam aboard *Cray* under Jim Fortnoy.

On January 3, 1945, General Douglas MacArthur was named Commander of all U.S. Ground Forces in the Pacific Theater, and Admiral Chester Nimitz Commander of all Naval Forces. Preparations were underway for the planned assaults of Iwo Jima, Okinawa, and Japan itself.

On January 3rd, while *Orca* was undergoing sea trials, Billy Kinkaid was taking his underway exam with Carter Vaughn aboard *Hermit.*

The following Friday, after *Orca* had returned to port from successful sea trials, the wardroom put a serious dent in Billy's wallet, as they washed down his shiny new dolphins.

On Monday, January 8, 1945, *Orca* left port in company with *Hermit* on her tenth war patrol.

On January 9th, the U.S. 6th Army invaded Lingayen Gulf on the Philippine Island of Luzon.

Chapter 25

Tenth Patrol: 8 January 1945 to 27 March 1945

Their orders were brief and to the point. *Orca* was to proceed, in company with *Hermit*, to support Fifth Fleet operations under the overall command of Admiral Raymond Spruance.

Land operations were underway in the Philippines, with the U.S. 6th Army under General Walter Krueger in firm control of Lingayen Gulf and ordered by MacArthur to advance south as rapidly as possible to secure Manila. Admiral Spruance was tasked with assuring that Krueger's back was protected from the IJN. The Japanese Navy was, at this point in the war, more or less a "fleet in being," that is, a fleet kept in port for its own safety and for its value as a potential threat to the opposing force. The Japanese had been forced into this position first, by the extensive damage to the fleet suffered in Leyte Gulf, and, second, by the relentless U.S. submarine campaign interdicting fuel shipments to the home islands.

Ray Spruance was by nature calculating and cautious. While not expecting any interference from the IJN in the Philippines, he wanted nonetheless to be prepared for it. To that end, he had established a picket line in the South China Sea, an arc of twelve picket submarines on patrol off northern Luzon and between Luzon and Formosa. The picket boats were to be in addition to land and carrier-based aircraft already tasked with the same mission. Under Fifth Fleet Command, *Orca* and *Hermit* were now en route to relieve *Bugara* and *Ray*, two SOWESPAC boats already on picket station.

Transiting the forty-eight hundred nautical miles to their patrol station at best speed would take *Orca* and *Hermit* sixteen days. Jake was concerned that *Orca* had experienced a forty percent turnover in her crew while the boat was in refit. Although most of the replacements were qualified submariners, men off other boats or relief crews, they were not used to working together, or with *Orca's* officers. That meant constant drills. The crew practiced torpedo attacks, collision drills, fire drills, and gun drills. Frenchie Eifel requalified all the officers and chief petty officers on small arms.

Once again, Jake worked on getting the boat to dive in under thirty seconds. *Orca* and *Hermit* practiced approaches on one another. When the two boats arrived on their respective stations on January 24th, Jake was still not happy with the crew's progress, but he had to admit that they had come a long way since *Orca* left Pearl.

The crews of both *Bugara* and *Ray* were happy to be relieved. Each had been on station for over six weeks, and neither boat had seen anything other than Allied shipping and aircraft. Jake hoped that *Orca* would not have to stand picket duty for any six weeks.

On January 28th, Allied forces reopened the Burma Road, the supply lifeline linking Burma to southwest China.

On February 3rd, the U.S. 6th Army attacked the Japanese forces in Manila.

In 1941, when retreating before an advancing Japanese Army of overwhelming force, MacArthur had declared Manila an "open city." General Tomoyuki Yamashita, Commander-in-Chief of IJA forces in the Philippines, while not declaring Manila an "open city," withdrew his forces to Baguio, just northeast of Manila, where he planned to meet the Allied invasion. He left behind orders only to destroy bridges and vital installations in Manila when an invasion force appeared.

Left in command in Manila, Rear Admiral Iwabuchi Sanji, Commander of the 31st Special Naval Defense Force, now commanding both IJN and IJA forces, was determined to follow the navy plan rather

513

than the army plan of abandoning the city. The navy plan called for defending the city to the last man. On February 6th, MacArthur declared that "Manila has fallen," but in fact the battle for the city had barely begun.

On February 14th, the twelve boats on picket duty were ordered north to support the impending invasion of the island of Iwo Jima.

On February 16th, U.S. forces recaptured the Bataan Peninsula.

On February 19th, the 3rd, 4th, and 5th Marine Divisions invaded the tiny Japanese stronghold of Iwo Jima, a volcanic island only 4.5 miles long and 2.5 miles wide, just 600 miles south of Tokyo. Despite being pounded for days from the sea and from the air, the 23,000 island defenders were hardly touched. Fighting from a network of caves, dugouts, tunnels, and underground installations, the Japanese were determined to hold out to the last man.

On March 2nd, U.S. Paratroopers recaptured Corregidor.

Manila was finally liberated on March 4th. In the interim, the Japanese took out their frustrations on the city's populace – mutilating, raping, and murdering thousands. In the end, 1,010 Americans, 16,665 Japanese, and an estimated 100,000 to 500,000 Filipinos lost their lives in the battle for the now ruined city.

Tokyo was firebombed by Marianas-Islands-based B-29s on March 9th and 10th. Fifteen square miles of the city were turned into cinders. Estimates of civilian casualties ranged from 75,000 to 200,000. The noose around Japan tightened further.

On March 13th, both *Orca* and *Hermit* were detached from the Seventh Fleet and returned to SUBPAC. Both boats had been at sea for sixty-three days, and were ordered to Majuro for refueling and replenishment. Picket duty had been boring and monotonous, and, in any submariner's playbook, a waste of their assets and capabilities. Now, before both boats, lay a 2,900-mile journey to Majuro, with its ball fields, tent city, pebbly beach, and

3.2 beer. And while the IJN was keeping the units of its remaining surface fleet in port, their submarines were still very much a presence to be reckoned with in the Pacific.

As SOPA, Jake was responsible for ensuring that the transit to Majuro was done safely and economically. While there were no unfriendly aircraft to concern him, Jake was very much aware of the enemy submarine threat. And after sixty-three days at sea, both boats were low on fuel. Jake decided that prudence called for submerged daylight operations and a random zigzag pattern on the surface at night. This would reduce their average speed of advance to nine knots. That meant just over another two weeks at sea. Jake transmitted the plan to Carter Vaughn in *Hermit*, who while less than ecstatic about it, agreed that it made perfect sense.

Hermit was not equipped with a radar mast, so *Orca* was always the first boat to surface at night after both periscope and radar search.

On March 21st, in the wee hours of the morning, the weather turned foul, with the two boats locked into what seemed an endless line of thunderstorms coupled with violent seas. Both boats were restricted to the surface, and were operating in propulsion charge mode, battery propulsion with the diesels charging the batteries.

Submarine batteries are the lead-acid type, and charging them generates hydrogen gas. Hydrogen is odorless and colorless, and an extremely high-energy fuel. It burns with incredible speed and is easily ignited in the presence of sufficient oxygen. Both submarine battery compartments are equipped with hydrogen meters that measure hydrogen concentration, which policy dictates must never be allowed to exceed three percent. The meters are continuously monitored during charging to insure that the policy is followed.

Both *Orca's* and *Hermit's* battery compartments used a closed-cell ventilation system. Each battery cell is closed off with tubes connected to it that allow the battery ventilation fan in each compartment to constantly draw a steady stream of air across the top of each cell and evacuate the generated gas.

Electrician's Mates aboard fleet submarines were easily identified: they were the ones whose clothing was always shot full of holes, the result of crawling around in the battery compartment in the presence of battery acid. Aboard *Hermit*, the electrician on watch, whose job it was to monitor and log the hydrogen meter readings on the mid-watch the night of March 22nd was EM3(SS) Larry Bowers.

At 0115, Bowers entered the forward battery compartment to read and record the hydrogen concentration meter. He was alarmed to find that the meter read 5.2 percent. Without notifying anyone, and determining that the reason for the elevated reading was that the battery ventilation fan had stopped, he decided to test the fan power switch. He cycled the switch, turning it first off and then on. When he turned the switch back to the "on" position, it generated an electrical spark. In a split second, the compartment was ablaze.

The first indication aboard *Orca* that *Hermit* was in trouble was when the forward port lookout reported pinpricks of light appearing on *Hermit's* deck. Gary Clark was standing OOD, and, while he could barely make out the outline of *Hermit* off to port, was quick to note that the other boat was rapidly falling behind. He ordered "all ahead slow" in response, and passed the word "Captain to the Bridge." When he determined that *Hermit* was actually dead in the water, he ordered "all stop."

"What's up, Gary," Jake asked, as he came up through the bridge hatch. It was pitch black topside, raining heavily, and the seas were heaving, tossing the stopped boat about like so much flotsam.

"It's *Hermit*, Captain. She's dead in the water, and I think those are men on deck—a lot of them. I'm pretty sure those tiny lights are the flashlights on their life vests. I asked our radio watch to try and raise them, but they're not answering their call sign."

"Very well. Set GQ."

"Aye, Sir," Clark responded. He sounded the GQ alarm, and passed the word "Battle Stations, Surface," on the 1MC. Minutes later Joel Himmelfarb was on the bridge, and, once apprised of the situation, relieved Clark of the conn. Clark was happy to leave the bridge and report to his GQ station in the warm, dry, radio room.

"Send up the loudhailer," Jake ordered, yelling down the bridge hatch. Then, to Himmelfarb, he said, "See if we can get close enough to make voice contact, Joel."

"I'm trying, Skipper. But the weather and the sea aren't cooperating."

After twenty minutes of maneuvering, Himmelfarb had finally brought *Orca* close enough to *Hermit* for Jake to attempt to make voice contact. "Ahoy, *Hermit*," Jake called out using the loudhailer.

"That you, Jake?" came a thin voice in the wind, barely audible. Jake recognized Carter Vaughn's voice.

"Yes. What's happened?"

"Fire below, Jake . . . battery fire . . . lost one man, got the rest up on deck . . . spread so quickly . . . too much smoke," was all Jake could make out over the wind.

"What can I do?"

"Get some of my men off . . . boat's sealed . . . stay with DC crew . . . restart engines."

"COB to the bridge!" Jake yelled down to the conning tower. "Get Bucky up here!"

Within minutes, Bucky was apprised of the situation, and had a crew in inflatable life vests out on *Orca*'s heaving deck. "Get me close enough to get a line over, please, Mr. Himmelfarb," he called up to the bridge, as some of his men broke out the rubber boat and inflated it.

It took a full half-hour before Bucky could get a monkey fist (a knotted ball of hemp attached to the end of a heaving line) over to *Hermit*. The men on *Hermit's* deck pulled the light line aboard, then the heavier line attached to it, and finally the light hawser attached to the inflatable. Just as he had rigged the inflatable to bring the Filipinos aboard in Dongon Bay, Bucky rigged the inflatable to bring the men of *Hermit* across to *Orca*. The difference was, of course, that at Dongon Bay it wasn't during a violent rainstorm and a "State 4" sea — with waves between four and eight feet high.

Nonetheless, slowly the men from *Hermit* were brought aboard *Orca*, eight at a time. The inflatable had made the bouncy transit twice when a sudden swell washed over *Orca's* deck. One of Bucky's crew, a seaman named Stanley Olson, making his first patrol aboard *Orca*, lost his footing and was swept under the cable rail and out to sea.

As the word "Man Overboard" was passed, TM1(SS) Clive Arnold quickly secured a length of line around himself, secured the other end to a stanchion, and jumped in after him. After about five minutes had passed, and neither man had answered repeated shouts, Bucky told his men to pull Arnold back aboard. But there was no one at the line's end.

Now Jake was faced with a decision. He could secure the transfer operation and begin a search for the two *Orca* men overboard, or give them up for lost and continue the rescue of *Hermit's* crew. Jake sadly realized that locating either man in the dark, in the driving rain, and in such sea conditions was practically impossible. There was nothing for it. He ordered the "Man Overboard" detail secured.

The transfer of the men from *Hermit* continued without further incident until just a skeleton crew remained aboard.

Vaughn then requested, and Bucky sent over, two air packs. The idea was to send two men below and aft to restart an engine, and clear the smoke from inside the boat. But when the after battery hatch was opened to let the men go below, flames leapt up through the open hatch. Facing the inevitable, Carter Vaughn reluctantly gave the order to abandon ship.

An hour later, at first light on March 22nd, the only man left aboard *Hermit* was her single casualty, EM3(SS) Larry Bowers.

At 0640, *Orca* sent a single torpedo into the abandoned submarine. It took *Hermit* just ten minutes to roll over and disappear below the waves. Only then did Jake order a search for the two men who were lost at sea during the night. The sea state and the weather were the same as they had been, but at least it was now daylight.

The search continued until dark, when Jake finally ordered that the boat's course set, once again, for Majuro.

Iwo Jima fell on March 26th. Almost the entire Japanese garrison was wiped out at the cost of over 6,800 Marines killed and almost 20,000 wounded.

On Tuesday, March 27th, *Orca* entered the anchorage at Sub Base Majuro. Three days later, on March 30th, a Naval Board of Inquiry was convened to investigate the loss of the submarine *Hermit*.

On April 1st, the U.S. Army invaded Okinawa.

Chapter 26

Eleventh Patrol: 27 March 1945 to 6 July 1945

Operation Ten-Go, was an attempt by a ten-vessel Japanese attack force to relieve the beleaguered forces fighting the Allied advance on Okinawa. *The force was led by the super battleship* Yamato. *The force was ordered to penetrate enemy lines, beach themselves, and then fight from shore using the naval guns as field artillery and the sailors as ground forces. The force was detected by American submarines when it left Japanese waters and was attacked by carrier aircraft while still far from Okinawa. After a two-hour battle, on April 7th, the* Yamato *was sunk, along with a light cruiser and four destroyers. The remainder of the force turned back.*

Not even the two bags of mail that awaited *Orca* at Majuro could disperse the purple miasma brought on by the convening of a Naval Board of Inquiry.

The Board of Inquiry took ten days to conclude its business, interviewing all the officers and most petty officers on *Hermit*, and Jake, Joel, Gary Clark, Bucky, and several crewmembers who were on *Orca's* deck the night of March 22nd.

The only person who really knew what had happened, of course, was EM3(SS) Larry Bowers. But since he had gone to the bottom with *Hermit*, the Board did the best it could to piece together the events that took place that night. The Board correctly concluded that the fire had occurred in the forward battery compartment. Since it spread so rapidly, it was also concluded that it was a hydrogen gas fire. The Board decision read in part as follows:

"The Board determines that Hermit's *officers and crew failed to respond adequately to the emergency caused by a fire in the forward battery compartment, and that such failure ultimately resulted in the loss of the boat . . .*

. . . Condition Zebra was never set. This was evident, since the boat sank so quickly after having been torpedoed.

The forward battery compartment was not isolated in a timely manner. In a fruitless effort to rescue Petty Officer Bowers, the compartment was not isolated until approximately five minutes after the fire started, and the entire ship's ventilation system was not secured until sometime after that. The Board therefore concludes that the fire had already spread throughout the boat through the ventilation system before the forward battery compartment was finally isolated . . .

. . . once the fire had spread throughout the boat, and the smoke became so thick that the decision was made to evacuate the boat, all outside sources for oxygen to feed the fire were properly shut. The engine air intake valve and the main induction valve were secured. All deck hatches were opened as required for the evacuation of ship's personnel and properly shut when the boat was evacuated. There was nonetheless sufficient oxygen remaining in the boat such that the fire continued to burn for some time afterward. There was also evidently sufficient heat remaining in the boat to cause flashback when the after battery hatch was reopened in the effort to reenter the boat and restart the diesels.

The Board concludes that the loss of Hermit *could have been prevented if the boat's officers and crew had been properly trained to respond in just such an emergency. The responsibility for training the boat's personnel to properly react to just such emergency situations lies squarely on the shoulders of her commanding officer . . ."*

The Board stopped short of recommending that Lt. Cmdr. Carter Vaughn be bound over for Court Marshal. But Carter Vaughn's Naval career was finished. As for *Orca's* part in the incident, the decision concluded as follows:

"The Board commends the officers and men of Orca *for their response to the emergency aboard* Hermit, *especially for their safely evacuating the entire crew, save for the one man lost to the fire. It is regrettable that the rescuing boat lost two of her own men overboard as the result of darkness, foul weather, and rough seas. The Board supports* Orca's *commanding officer's difficult decision to continue the rescue operation and to delay the search for the two men lost overboard. Unfortunately, the two men, Petty Officer First Class Clive Arnold, and Seaman Stanley Olson, were never recovered."*

* * * * *

Commander Hiriake Ito had finally received what he had been requesting for over two years: radar. Installed on the ship he commanded, *IJN Atsukaze*, a *Fubuki*-class destroyer, was a Type 22 air and surface search and fire control radar.

What was left of the "invincible" Imperial Japanese Fleet now languished dockside in the various home island ports. Even if the naval command was of a mind to sortie the fleet, it would be impossible to do so in any numbers for lack of sufficient fuel.

Atsukaze herself was in Yokosuka, and had been since, with the rest of the fleet, she had ignominiously retreated from Leyte Gulf. Ito had taken advantage of the layover to visit his family in Nagasaki. Now his ship had been given a task, a task he convinced fleet command that he could accomplish only if his ship was finally equipped with radar. And now he had it. The very latest kind. The Type 22 could detect swarms of aircraft at 35 km (38,300 yards), a single aircraft at 17 km (9,800 yards), and a large surface combatant at 34.5 km (37,700 yards). Even more important, he had been given seven new crewmen, transfers from the cruiser *Tone*. They included a lieutenant who had functioned as radar officer; four ratings trained as radar operators; and two technical ratings skilled at maintaining the equipment.

Ito was to take his ship south down through the Formosa Strait, hug the China coast to Vietnam, and only then cross the

South China Sea to Borneo. On Borneo, *Atsukaze* would meet a convoy of six tankers being assembled in Brunei. Ito was then to refuel in Brunei, and escort the tankers back to Japan along the same route.

Ito requested that at least two *kaibokan* be assigned to accompany *Atsukaze* on the assignment. He was informed that all available *kaibokan* were required for defense of the home waters, but he could have two minesweepers and another destroyer. Refusal of the assignment was, of course, out of the question, and Ito accepted the company of two minesweepers and the destroyer as graciously as he could.

The two minesweepers assigned were *Number-19*-class vessels, *Number 21* and *Number 23*. These were lightly armed vessels that carried thirty-six depth charges and one depth charge thrower. Each was capable of making twenty knots.

The assigned destroyer was *Fuji,* an ancient *Momi*-class ship, which, at 84 meters long (275 feet), was not much bigger than a minesweeper. *Fuji* had been modified for anti-submarine duty, and carried thirty-six depth charges and two depth-charge throwers. Her top speed was thirty knots.

None of these three vessels was equipped with radar, and only *Fuji* had both active and passive sonar capability.

Air cover, courtesy of the IJN 901st Air Flotilla, was also promised to Ito. The 901st had been flying out of Takeo and operating between Formosa and Shanghai since October 1944, using outdated planes that were nonetheless equipped with radar and were capable of attacking with one, or sometimes two, bombs. None of the planes were equipped with guns, however, and they were thus unable to strafe targets. Some of the planes, about a third, were equipped with *jikitanshiki*, magnetic anomaly detectors, capable of detecting the magnetic signature of a submerged submarine to depths of 120 meters (390 feet).

But Ito knew that the pilots of the 901st were poorly trained and their aircraft unreliable. There was also the inconvenient presence of the British closing in on Formosa from the east, which threatened the Formosan airfields used by the 901st. And so, while he was perfectly willing to be pleasantly surprised, Ito had minimal expectations as to the effectiveness of the 901st

Atsukaze and her three companions left Yokosuka for Brunei on the day that it was announced that the American president had died. Ito regarded the event as an auspicious sign for the success of his mission.

* * * * *

On April 13th, *Orca* left Majuro to begin her eleventh war patrol. Her orders were to proceed to a patrol station in the Formosa Strait, about 3,100 miles from Majuro. She arrived on station on April 25th.

With the northern Philippines firmly in Allied hands, the only route left open for the Japanese to ship precious fuel from their captured NEI oil fields to Japan was along the China coast and through the Formosa Strait. Any attempt to ply the seas east of Formosa was suicide, since Allied air cover from Luzon and the carriers supporting the invasion of Okinawa claimed complete air superiority over those waters.

Orca settled in for what promised to be a long and, for lack of targets, fruitless patrol.

* * * * *

The normal route from Yokosuka to Brunei traversed 2,300 nautical miles. The circuitous route *Atsukaze* and her escort group had to take, however, added another 350 miles to the journey. The relative slowness of the minesweepers limited their speed of passage to eighteen knots. The group left Yokosuka at dusk on April 14th, and arrived in Brunei on the morning of the 21st. Not a single aircraft of the 901st Air Flotilla was sighted during the entire passage. The only aircraft detected on *Atsukaze's* radar were well off to the east, and were probably those of the enemy.

The Japanese had occupied all of Borneo since mid 1942. Since then, Brunei, on the upper northern coast of the island, was used as a staging area for shipping and as a fleet refueling depot.

From the first, the Japanese administered all of Borneo with an iron fist. In Brunei and elsewhere on that part of the island, the notorious *Kempeitai* were responsible for policing the local Malay population. The *Kempeitai* were answerable only to the military commander and the War Ministry. They thus had virtually unlimited power. The *Kempeitai* used savagery and torture in the administration of what the native Malays termed "Japanese Justice," whereby the slightest infraction was met with brutal consequences.

Reversal of fortunes for the Japanese in the war had only caused the military command to double down on its oppression of the locals. The Brunei that Ito and his group of escorts sailed into in late April of 1945 was a virtual police state, one run based on fear of an increasingly effective Malay Resistance and the advancing Australians.

But being serviced by a police state had its advantages. The six tankers that *Atsukaze* and the other three escorts were to herd back to Japan, were lined up, fueled, and awaiting their arrival. The fear that pervaded the colony's administrators had also permeated the psyches of the tankers' masters and their crews. It had somehow overshadowed any fear of very real dangers of their upcoming transit, and so all were anxious to leave Brunei as soon as possible. It took less than a day to refuel the escort group and lay on what few provisions were available.

Before the loss of Luzon, a convoy such as this would have been assembled in Manila, and be designated as a MATA convoy — Manila to Takeo, and assigned a number. But now, Manila was in enemy hands. And there had never been a Brunei to Takeo convoy route as such. *Atsukaze* and her brood were therefore simply designated BT-1 for "Brunei to Takeo Number One" by the Admiralty.

Just before departing Brunei, Ito, as convoy commander, assembled the six tankers' masters, along with the other three escorts' captains. They met in the spacious crew's mess aboard *Nisshin Maru,* at 17,600 tons displacement, the largest of the six tankers making the trip. In front of each man was a tiny empty porcelain cup. Ito gave the assembly a quick lesson in the convoy etiquette he had developed personally, the result of sometimes painful experience:

"Your ships are to keep station on one another, maintaining five hundred meters separation at all times. You will be directed to zigzag as a defense against enemy submarine attack. The zigzag pattern will be a random one, with course changes radioed only from *Atsukaze.* There will first be a course change warning. Each vessel shall then acknowledge receipt of the order in turn, using your call signs. After all ships have acknowledged the order, there will follow a command to execute the course change. You are then expected to execute these changes immediately and together.

"Failure to come to the new course on the order to 'execute,' " Ito warned them, "could well result in a collision with one of your neighbors. You *will* function as a unit. Failure to do so could be just as disastrous as an enemy torpedo. Your best protection against submarines is to stay together and maintain order.

"Pay no attention to what *Atsukaze* or the other escorts are doing. While we will maintain station on the convoy most of the time, we might well break off to investigate a possible contact at any time. Pay *no* attention to us. Your first responsibility is to maintain your station.

"The convoy pattern will be two columns in three ranks. These are your assignments. First rank, left column, *Kaijo Maru.* Right column, *Kazahaya.* Second rank, left column, *Tao Maru.* Right column, *Toho Maru.* Third rank, left column, *Erimo.* Right column, *Nisshin Maru.*"

Ito had arranged the ships according to their displacement, and, hence, their relative size.

"Are there any questions, gentlemen?" Ito asked. "If not, then let us discuss radio discipline. You are to maintain radio silence at all times unless acknowledging an order, or unless you are experiencing a genuine emergency. Is that understood?" Ito's gaze passed from master to master.

Each nodded in turn.

"Very well. Steward?"

A steward filled the tiny porcelain cups that had been placed in front of each master with *sake*. Last of all, he filled Ito's and the other captains' cups. Ito lifted his cup in front of him, and the others followed suit. "To the Emperor," he said, draining the cup.

"To the Emperor," the others answered, draining theirs.

BT-1 set sail from Brunei at dusk on April 23rd. Its departure was immediately reported by the Malay Resistance to Allied Command HQ in Port Moresby.

Ito's greatest fear was of enemy submarines. As long as it hugged the coastline, the convoy had a good chance of remaining undiscovered by enemy aircraft. Discovery by enemy aircraft, of course, meant that the convoy was certainly doomed. The anti-aircraft capability of *Atsukaze* and the other escorts was limited, and, while they might be able to repulse one, or possibly even two, attacking aircraft, they would be quickly overcome by any air attack in force. To Ito's reckoning, since there was nothing for it, there was no point in worrying about it.

Submarines were another matter. He had bested enemy submarine attacks many more times than he had been bested by them. And now he had radar.

* * * * *

The message from SUBPAC added some spice to what had been, for *Orca*, another boring week on patrol. It seems that a convoy, designated BT-1, consisting of six tankers and four

527

escorts, had departed Brunei on April 23rd, and was en route to Japan.

The entire fleet had been alerted, and it was *". . . vital to the war effort that none of this cargo reaches Japan. All units are to be on the lookout for the convoy. Any units making contact are to report the fact and their position to Fleet Command before attacking. It is imperative that BT-1 never reach Japan."*

The radar-warning receiver—the RWR—was the first device to detect the oncoming convoy. *Orca* was on station in the Formosa Strait, northwest of the Pescadores. It was 0412 the pre-dawn morning of April 29th, and *Orca* was still on the surface. The sea was choppy, with a stiff wind and frequent whitecaps. It was quite possible that a storm was brewing. The RWR gave the bearing to the detected emission as 253 degrees. Neither the SD nor the SJ radar had indicated any contacts.

Jake stood on the bridge with Harry Hastings, who was beginning the morning watch as OOD. Joel Himmelfarb was in the conning tower, on the search scope. The sky was overcast, black, and the visibility poor. Jake reasoned that the convoy, if this RWR contact was indeed the convoy, would probably be hugging the China coast so as to stay as far away as possible from any patrolling Allied aircraft.

On the other hand, the RWR contact might be an *enemy* anti-submarine patrol aircraft. Whichever it was, since the RWR had just picked up the signal, it was unlikely that the radar that had emitted the signal was close enough as yet to have received a return signal, and so to have located *Orca*.

If the RWR contact is an aircraft, Jake reasoned silently, *it will be on top of us soon enough, and the SD radar will give enough advance warning for us to submerge and avoid any damage.*

Okay, then, let's assume it's the convoy. It'll be headed northeast and hugging the China coast. We can put Orca *in position for a daylight, submerged intercept if we close the target's track So, to close the track, we head northwest to the coast.*

528

"Make your course 315," he told Hastings aloud. "All ahead full." It was 0416.

As the boat closed toward the China coast, the RWR bearing began drifting very slowly to the left. Such would be the case if the contact was on the surface, and heading in *Orca's* general direction. But it would also be the case if the RWR contact was an aircraft headed almost directly toward them. Jake checked his watch: 0425. Ten minutes had passed since the initial RWR report.

Say it's an aircraft and its radar range is thirty-five hundred yards, he thought, *and say we detect it at forty thousand yards. Even if it's a slow plane, like a flying boat, going about a hundred and eighty knots, and that's about six thousand yards per minute. In ten minutes, it would have travelled sixty thousand yards, and would have been on top of us about three minutes ago. No, this is no aircraft. It's a surface contact, and we're closing its track.* "Excellent!" he said aloud.

Orca dived at 0535, submerging to fifty-eight feet, two feet higher than the usual periscope depth, and with the radar mast extended. On diving, the RWR had the contact at bearing 247. The dawn sky was overcast, but visibility was fair, about ten miles. The sea was still choppy with the same frequent whitecaps.

"Good," Joel remarked. "It makes us harder to see, even this close to the surface with all our junk sticking out."

By then, the boat was only about twenty miles off the China coast, roughly opposite the Chinese port of Xiamen.

"Sonar reports multiple contacts closing, bearing two-three-eight."

It was 0542.

"Very well," Jake acknowledged.

"Radar reports large contact bearing two-three-one, range thirteen thousand," the conning tower talker reported ten minutes later.

"Very well."

Orca was still on course 315, but, submerged, was now making only three knots.

By 0602 the "large" radar contact had morphed into multiple contacts, bearing 235, at a range of 10,000 yards.

"The contacts are on course zero-five-four, speed ten, Captain," Bill Salton called up from chart plot. "They could possibly be heading into port at Xiamen."

"Give me a course to intercept, then, Bill," Jake said.

"Wait one, Skipper," Bill answered.

"Radar reports pattern of ten contacts, Captain. Probably a convoy of six with four escorts. The six largest contacts are sailing in a two by three grid. The four smaller ones, largest one on point, two on the flanks, one behind."

"Recommend course two-six-eight, speed five, to intercept in twenty-two minutes, Captain."

"Come left to course two-six-eight. Make turns for five knots. Raise the LF antenna. We need to make a contact report as soon as we get visual confirmation that this is our convoy."

At 1607, radar reported the multiple contacts now on bearing 233, range 8,000.

"The contacts appear to have zigged right Captain!" Salton called out.

Joel, on the periscope, said, "Got them in sight, Captain. Definitely our convoy. Bearing, mark!"

"Two-three-two."

"Destroyer in lead, *Fubuki*-class, angle on the bow port forty," Joel continued. "Damn! They're gonna run right past us."

"Send out that contact report, now!" Jake said. "And let's see if we can still make an approach." Even as he said it, Jake knew that the opportunity to attack had probably passed them by. Still, he slowed the boat back down to three knots, and turned her around to head due east, hoping against the odds for a chance at a kill shot.

Minutes later Gary "Coop" Clark had sent up the text of a contact report from the radio room for Jake's approval. Jake read through it quickly.

"Good, send it," he said, as he initialed the draft and sent it back to Clark.

At 1615, just when Jake had given up all hope of launching an attack, Joel said, "The convoy's zigged again. This time it's a zig left and toward us! Bearing, mark."

"Two-one-eight."

"Get a radar range," Jake ordered.

"Radar reports range to lead contact, sixty-five hundred yards."

"Lead destroyer angle on the bow is port five, Captain," Joel reported. "Headed almost straight for us."

"I have him on course zero-three-eight, Captain," Salton called up from chart plot. "Still at ten knots."

"I say we just sit here, Captain," Joel said. "Let 'em come to us. Looks like he's zigging every ten minutes or so, so we'd best just sit and see what he does next."

"Sounds about right," Jake said. "But I'm gonna show him our butt so we can go either way when he zigs again . . . Come left to zero-four-zero."

"Coming left to zero-four-zero, Captain."

At 0621, Joel took a 360-degree sweep and then another observation through the scope. "Bearing, mark."

"Two-one-zero."

"Destroyer's angle on the bow still port five."

"Get a radar range," Jake ordered.

"Radar reports range to lead ship forty-two hundred yards."

"Still on course zero-three-eight, Captain. Speed ten," Salton called out.

"Time since last zig?" Jake asked.

"Eight minutes."

"Joel, another look-see in two minutes," Jake said.

"Aye, Skipper."

At 0625, Himmelfarb raised the scope again. "Bearing, mark."

"Two-one-five."

"Angle on the bow, port eight. No zig yet, Skipper."

"Keep the scope up . . . Range?"

"Three thousand yards."

"Do you have a firing solution, Harry?" Jake asked Hastings on the TDC.

"I do on the lead destroyer, Captain," Hastings replied.

Jake was about to ask for a bearing and range to the nearest tanker when Joel shouted out, "He's zigging! The S O B is zigging left!"

It was 0626.

"Crap!" was all Jake could think to say. "Okay, let's see where he settles out. This might still work out."

At 0628, Joel did a 360-degree sweep, and then took another observation. "Bearing, mark."

"Two-three-nine."

"Destroyer angle on the bow, starboard forty-five."

"Radar reports range to lead ship, twenty-five hundred yards. Range to nearest ship in convoy, twenty-four hundred yards."

"With that angle on the bow, Captain, I have the lead ship on course three-five-zero, and, using speed ten, I have a firing solution on him," Hastings said.

"Good, Harry, but hang on. I want one of those tankers. What do you see, Joel?"

The time was 0630.

"Okay. Here's the lead destroyer, bearing, mark."

"Two-four-eight."

"The lead tanker, bearing, mark."

"Two-three-nine."

"Here's the escort on the right flank—a minesweeper—bearing, mark."

"Two-one-seven."

"And—Oh boy!—all the way at the end of the line—the last tanker in the right column—it's huge! It must be fifteen thousand tons at least!"

"Then that's our target," Jake said. "This will be a stern shot. Open outer doors aft. Keep the bearings and ranges to this big bugger coming. And make sure radar knows we want the last ship in the right column."

"Bearing, mark."

"Two-one-zero."

"He's still turning the corner, Skipper," Joel observed.

"Range thirty-two hundred."

"Don't forget to watch those escorts, Joel. We've had our scope and antenna exposed for a long time, now."

"Aye, Captain."

Five minutes passed.

0635. Using the continuous ranges and bearings being called out, Bill Salton had the target tanker on course 348 and speed 10 knots. The latest bearing and range had the tanker at bearing 290 and 3,000 yards. But the CPA was 2,800 yards. That was a long torpedo track, even for a Mark-14 with a supposed 4,500-yard range at 46 knots.

"I'd like to get in closer, but it is what it is," Jake said. "You have a firing solution, Harry?"

"I do, Captain."

"Very well. We'll fire all four tubes aft. Fire seven."

"Seven fired."

"Spread one degree right. Fire eight."

"One degree right set, eight fired."

"Spread one degree left. Fire nine,"

"One degree left set, nine fired."

"Spread two degrees right. Fire ten."

"Two degrees right set, ten fired."

"Sonar reports four torpedoes in the water, all running hot straight and normal."

"Left full rudder, all ahead full," Jake ordered, thinking that if he missed, maybe he could bring his bow tubes to bear.

Not quite two minutes later, the first torpedo exploded on target. Joel watched through the scope as the target kind of shuddered, but didn't slow, when the first torpedo struck. The target *did* slow when the second torpedo struck, sixteen seconds later. Joel had his camera on the scope, took two pictures, then quickly resumed scanning to see how the escorts were reacting.

Another twenty seconds passed, and the third torpedo had obviously missed. The minesweeper on the right flank of the column had turned toward *Orca*, as did the trailing destroyer, both perhaps having sighted the periscope and radar antenna, and obviously intending to run down the torpedo wakes.

Joel had the scope and the radar antenna on the way down, when a third and final explosion was heard, and Jake had ordered the boat deep. Everyone in *Orca* assumed there had been a third hit on "the huge tanker," but it had actually been a strike on the trailing ship in the left column, the 6,500-ton *Erimo*.

Never mind bringing the bow tubes to bear, although turning toward the convoy immediately after firing had actually been a fortuitous move. It put *Orca* on a course parallel to that of the convoy, as she dived to 150 feet, and, with a subsequently ordered left turn, eventually underneath it. The two escorts took turns dropping depth charges over the spot where the torpedo wakes converged, but by then their target was long gone.

Orca snuck off to the east-southeast. When well clear of the convoy, the boat came up to periscope depth, raised the LF antenna, and sent out a battle report to SUBPAC. The report stated that *Orca* had engaged BT-1, and had definitely struck and disabled one tanker, giving the latitude and longitude at which the action had occurred. Then Jake turned the boat north and waited for dusk to surface and regain contact with the convoy.

Chapter 27

Ito was furious. Not yet halfway along, and already a third of the convoy was lost. In retrospect, though, he didn't know what he could have done differently. The convoy had been zigzagging with random course changes and at differing intervals. Radar had seen and found nothing, neither before nor after the attack. But now he escorted only four tankers north. *Erimo* was lost, sunk by what could only have been a lucky shot, and *Nisshin Maru* as good as lost, dead in the water, her decks and the waters around her ablaze. In two hours, if she was still afloat, the *Nisshin Maru* would be nothing but a burned-out hulk.

After *Number 23* and *Fuji's* initial depth charge attacks, *Fuji* had searched the area with active sonar, and found nothing. Her captain was sure there had been only one attacking submarine, since only one volley of torpedoes had been fired, and had so reported to *Atsukaze*. The sub had been lucky. One volley fired and two tankers lost. The convoy had been *un*lucky. For Ito, there was nothing for it but to leave *Fuji* behind to search for survivors, and get the rest of his brood back en route to Japan.

Just before noon, *Fuji* rejoined the convoy, taking station at the rear. She had picked up only six survivors, all from *Nisshin Maru,* three of them suffering from third degree burns. Two of these would be dead before nightfall.

BT-1 continued on a base course of 030, with *Atsukaze* at point, the two minesweepers on the flanks, zigzagging with random course changes and at differing intervals. But now, with the slowest tanker, *Erimo*, lost, the convoy could proceed at twelve knots. At 1200, Ito ordered the increase in speed.

At 1215, just south of Nanri Dao Island, Ito changed the convoy's base course to due east. Once Nanri Dao was cleared, he returned the convoy to base course 030, remaining on that course until the island of Haitan Dao, to the west, was cleared. At 2020, Ito turned the convoy to the left on base course 340 until, at 2250, it was roughly opposite the port city of Fuzhou. Now, clear of the Formosa Strait and in the East China Sea, BT-1 returned back to base course 030.

Shortly before 2300, aboard *Atsukaze*, radar reported that a contact had just appeared on its screen, bearing 070, at a range of 25,600 meters (28,000 yards).

The 8,000-ton *Kazahaya,* lead ship in the convoy's right column, was having trouble maintaining BT-1's new 12-knot pace. The ship did well enough maintaining speed when the convoy was running on a straight course, and even during the frequent zigs to the right, when the other ships were required to maintain station on her. It was the just-as-frequent zigs to the left that were the problem. It was then that *Kazahaya* had to lay on extra speed to maintain station—extra speed that her steam plant simply could not deliver.

After falling behind twice on zigs left, and receiving stern admonitions from the Convoy Commander Ito to keep pace with the rest of the convoy, *Kazahaya's* master called his chief engineer to the bridge.

"We are unable to keep up with the rest of the convoy. This ship once had sufficient power to steam at fifteen knots, but somehow now we can barely make twelve. Why can you not deliver that power?" the ship's master asked.

The chief engineer, eyes downcast, delivered the explanation: "You will recall, Sir, that back in Borneo, we had to plug off another five tubes in our main boiler. That brought the total of plugged tubes in that boiler to forty-seven. The boiler needs to be completely re-tubed, Sir,"

"And when or where were we supposed to do that?" the master replied. "The repair yards are in Japan. Time for that when we get back. We need to do something *now*. Otherwise I will have to tell Commander Ito that he must slow the convoy down to accommodate our limitations. And I cannot do that. We will *not* lose face!"

The chief engineer thought for a while. "I will do whatever is possible."

"See to it," the master said.

* * * * *

At 2030, Jake brought *Orca* up to periscope depth. With no contacts in sight, he ordered the radar mast raised. Again no contacts. He then surfaced the boat. The weather had cleared, and the sea had smoothed out since morning, with the moon high in the sky, and almost full.

"Anything on the RWR?" he asked from the bridge.

"Nothing," the word came back.

Leaving the bridge to OOD Billy Kinkaid, he went below for a powwow with Joel Himmelfarb and Bill Salton at the chart plot.

"We're just about forty miles north of where we started out this morning," Salton noted.

"Okay," Jake said, "let's assume that the convoy is still heading for the barn, still hugging the coast. We know where they were at 0700. Where might they be now?"

"They've had a thirteen-and-a-half hour head start, Skipper," Salton noted, "at ten knots they're ninety-five miles away by now."

"Okay, then, how do we catch them?"

"If we parallel their assumed course and could make twenty knots, it would take us nine-and-a-half hours just to come up even with them—and by then it'll be daylight again."

"Then we'd better get started. If we can at least locate them, we can broadcast their position to the rest of the fleet," Jake said. "Give me a course, Bill."

"Yessir. Zero-three-zero should put us on a parallel course, zero-two-seven to close them."

"Very well. Joel, tell Billy to bump us up to full speed, course zero-two-seven."

"Aye, aye, Captain," Joel said, and then disappeared up the conning tower hatch.

Jake could feel the diesels rumble as they opened up to full speed. He made his way into the radio room, a closet-sized space in the after part of the control room. Gary Clark was there with the watch stander. "Coop, I want a sharp watch kept on the RWR. Let me and the XO know the second you get a contact."

"Yes, Sir, Captain," Clark replied. "And Skipper?"

"Yes?"

"Evening dispatch came through from SUBPAC just a few minutes ago. Joe Bob Clanton's been bumped up to full lieutenant. Thought you might like to be the one to tell him, Sir."

"That I would, Coop. That I would." Smiling, Jake left the radio room.

* * * * *

Lieutenant Commander Peter Scrivener, USN, commanding officer of the submarine, *Mullet*, on patrol in the East China Sea, had received the contact report from SUBPAC, and was on the lookout for the convoy, BT-1. It was 2300 on April 29th, and the boat had just surfaced for the night, and was charging batteries. Scrivener was on *Mullet's* bridge, enjoying the fresh air. The sea was calm, and the night clear, with a day-old, full moon lighting up the sky.

Mullet was a Portsmouth *Tench*-class boat commissioned only a year earlier, and Scrivener was her first and, thus far, only, CO.

The boat was on its third patrol, and, aside from shooting up a couple of junks, had yet to draw blood.

Scrivener was of a mind to charge up *Mullet*'s batteries and then go looking for that convoy. BT-1 would be hugging the China coast, he reasoned correctly, so he headed the boat in that general direction: west. *Mullet* was in no hurry, making just over five knots.

* * * * *

Kazahaya's chief engineer had few options. With so many main boiler tubes plugged off, there was insufficient steam being generated to supply the power needed to propel the ship faster than twelve knots. Reluctantly, the chief engineer did the only thing he could to generate more steam: he changed out the oil nozzles to provide more fuel to the boiler, and to increase the operating temperature.

Soon afterward, the boiler was operating above its design temperature. But then there was sufficient steam going to the huge reciprocating steam engine to make turns for fifteen knots— but only briefly.

With increased boiler temperature, the pressure in the steam drum also had been increased. Thus, as soon as the increase in steam volume became significant, the safety valve on the steam chest lifted, and all that was gained was lost. Once again, *Kazahaya* was restricted to less than fifteen knots. After this happened twice, the chief engineer, out of fear of the ship's master and against his better judgment, wired the safety valve shut.

After that, *Kazahaya's* propulsion engine had all the power it needed.

If Ito was alarmed at the appearance of the radar contact now at bearing 073, he did not show it. Radar had said the contact was a small vessel, and it was still 16,500 meters away. Radar observations over the past hour showed the contact had been steady on course 270 at five knots.

Probably just a fishing boat.

It was now past midnight, and BT-1 was working its way northeast along the China coast, inside a string of small islands. The contact had disappeared off the radar a half-hour ago.

Then disaster struck.

Ito was asleep in his cabin, when his XO, Lieutenant Commander Shoici Koroki, a short, thick, and oily sycophant, whom he couldn't stand, reported that there had been an explosion aboard *Kazahaya*, the leading ship in the right column. *Kazahaya* had lost all power and was dropping out of the formation.

Ito ordered the convoy slowed to five knots, and awaited word from *Kazahaya's* master as to the extent of the problem and how long it would take to fix it.

The report came back that *Kazahaya's* main boiler steam chest had exploded, and that the damage was still being assessed. The ship's master could give no estimate as to if or when the ship could regain motive power.

Ito was unwilling to wait around and put the other three tankers at risk. There was nothing for it but to detach *Fuji* to stay with *Kazahaya*. If necessary, the disabled tanker could then be taken in tow by the destroyer. Ito realized that, under the circumstances, *Kazahaya's* chances of ever reaching Japan were slim, but there was always the possibility of *Fuji* towing the tanker to a Japanese-occupied Chinese port. In any case, his first responsibility was to the survival of the rest of the convoy.

The fiasco had already cost him an hour.

Ito formed up the three remaining tankers in line. Then, at twelve knots, with *Atsukaze* in the lead, and the two minesweepers on the flanks, BT-1 resumed its journey up along the China Coast.

At 0041 on the 30th, *Mullet* picked up the remnants of BT-1 on radar bearing 257, range 11,700 yards. *Mullet's* radar operator had described four large contacts and four smaller ones, but they were in two groups. One of the large contacts and one of the smaller ones appeared to be dead in the water, while a second grouping of three large contacts and one smaller one, in line, and two smaller flankers, was heading 030 at five knots. Scrivener sent a contact report to SUBPAC, describing what the radar operator had seen on the scope. SUBPAC came back confirming that the radar contact could well be the remnants of BT-1, which had been successfully engaged by *Orca* the day before.

Scrivener turned *Mullet* north at 0050, and maintained five knots. He still needed a couple of hours or so to fully charge batteries. Shortly afterward, his radar operator reported that the convoy had increased speed to twelve knots. Scrivener ordered the convoy's speed change and latest location radioed to SUBPAC.

SUBPAC alerted Pacific Fleet HQ that a convoy of enemy tankers, designated BT-1, had been located, and gave its last reported position, along with the convoy's base course and speed. Vice Admiral Lockwood did his best to convince Fleet Admiral Nimitz that destruction of the convoy was vital to keeping what was left of the IJN fleet bottled up in Japan. Nimitz agreed to contact Fifth Fleet and see if any aircraft could be spared to attack the convoy.

The battle for Okinawa had been raging for a month, and while the Allied forces were winning, the battle was costly in both lives and equipment. In charge of Fifth Fleet Naval forces in the battle was Admiral Ray Spruance. At 0100 on April 30th, Spruance received a request from Nimitz to, if possible, attack a fuel convoy off the China Coast. Spruance agreed to send a mixed flight of F6F Hellcats and SBD Dauntless bombers off the escort carrier *Cowpens* to attack the convoy.

At 0305, a flight of five Dauntless dive-bombers and three F6F Hellcats took off from the deck of the *USS Cowpens,* and headed for the China coast, and the last known position of BT-1.

* * * * *

The contact's course change to the north was brought to Ito's attention. Its speed had remained at five knots. A fishing boat would easily be expected to make such a course change while actually fishing. He was still not alarmed.

* * * * *

At 0300, batteries fully charged, Scrivener ordered *Mullet's* speed increased to eighteen knots, and began to close with what he was now convinced was the remnants of BT-1.

* * * * *

The contact's change in speed finally alarmed Ito. This was no fishing junk. He dispatched *Number 23* to close with the contact and investigate, using *Atsukaze's* radar and tactical radio to guide the minesweeper to the target.

* * * * *

Mullet's radar showed that one of the convoy's flanking escorts had left the formation and was headed in their direction. The closing escort's speed was twenty knots and its bearing was 273 and constant. It was on a course to intercept, and at 0320 was 8,100 yards away.

"I have him in sight, Captain," *Mullet's* forward port lookout sang out three minutes later. "She's small, like maybe a patrol boat."

Scrivener had been training his binoculars in that direction ever since radar had reported it heading their way. He already had his gun crews standing by below decks, just in case he decided to fight it out on the surface. It took another minute or so before he spotted the intruder. "Radar range to closing contact!" he shouted down to the conning tower.

"Six thousand yards," the answer came back.

"Smaller than we are," Scrivener said to himself, just as he spotted a gun flash aboard the escort and a splash far short of *Mullet*. He held down the switch on the 1MC. "Gun action, port," he said distinctly into the device.

Within seconds, the forward torpedo room hatch swung open. The men coming up had to scramble to keep their footing, as the boat heeled over to port, Scrivener turning toward to minimize the escort's target. In less than a minute, the gun crew had sent the first five-inch shell off toward the escort. It splashed harmlessly on the escort's port side, but it was well within range. There had already been two more shells fired from *Number 23*, and they had bracketed *Mullet*.

Make this next one count, Scrivener mentally pleaded with his gun crew as they fired the next round. It was another miss, splashing off the target's starboard bow. Scrivener could hear the next shell whistling toward *Mullet*. He would swear he felt the rush of air as it passed over the boat just forward of the bridge.

It was *Mullet's* third shell that finally struck home. The round penetrated the minesweeper's hull just forward of the port side of her bridge, and exploded below decks, crippling one of the vessel's two boilers. *Number 23* quickly slowed almost to a dead stop. But she still had teeth. Another 120mm shell had already been fired off in *Mullet's* direction, but, with the sudden change in speed, fell far short of the submarine's bow. *Mullet's* next round was again right on target, and blew the minesweeper's 120mm gun off its mounts, sending its gun crew flying into the air. Two more shells fired at leisure from the submarine left the escort aflame and sinking. Scrivener turned his boat north again and set off in pursuit of the rest of BT-1.

It was 0402.

* * * * *

Ito had left the bridge and stood over the radar console to watch the battle unfold between *Number 23* and the enemy submarine. He found following the action, as two blips in the screen closed and melded together, fascinating. When they broke apart, and one stayed behind unmoving as the other headed in his direction at speed, he called down to radio and asked if *Number 23* had reported in.

When all efforts to raise *Number 23* on the radio failed, Ito left *Number 21* in charge of the convoy, and turned *Atsukaze* south to engage the oncoming enemy.

The Nakajima E2N, "Dave" Type 15 floatplane was flying the route south between Shanghai and Taipei; its destination airfield had just been repaired after being bombed by the British. The plane, a unit of the 901st Air Flotilla, was almost an hour-and-a-half into what was normally a two-hour flight, when the radar operator picked up some surface contacts along the China coast, heading north-northeast. The pilot had been alerted to be on the lookout for a convoy of tankers heading toward the home islands, and if it located the convoy, to stay with it as long as the aircraft's fuel supply allowed.

The Nakajima pilot dipped the plane down to 900 feet above the ocean surface and buzzed the contacts for visual identification. This *had* to be the convoy: one escort leading a column of three tankers.

As the plane regained altitude, the radar operator made a second surface contact heading southwest. When the pilot turned the plane in that direction to investigate the new contact, the radar operator picked up yet another surface contact. The pilot set a course to put both the new contacts in line, and then dived back down to 900 feet for visual identification.

The first contact was a Japanese destroyer. The second was an enemy submarine, cruising on the surface. The pilot regained altitude and began a 360-degree turn to return and attack the submarine. By the time he had completed the turn, the submarine had disappeared below the surface, so the plane dropped a dye marker over the spot where the submarine had dived.

Robbed of its target, the Dave turned back to the convoy. It would fly escort as long as its fuel held out.

It was 0435

Ito cursed the aircraft. The submarine had given every indication that it had intended to remain on the surface and engage *Atsukaze* in a gun battle. It was a gun battle that *Atsukaze* was sure to win. Now all he could do was search for the sub and attack it with depth charges.

Ito headed *Atsukaze* to where the dye marker had been dropped, stopped his ship, and then ordered his passive sonar operator to listen for the submarine. After a few minutes, some noises were reported on bearing 315. At dead slow, Ito turned his ship to course 315. The same noises were heard, drifting to the right. He turned the ship to follow the reported bearings, and, when he thought the time was right, ordered an active sonar search – *and* made positive contact. After dropping two depth charges over the spot, he repeated the process.

* * * * *

Below, *Mullet* had been taken off guard and hurt badly by the initial depth charging. A sea valve in the forward torpedo room was leaking a pencil-width stream, and there was a dent in the pressure hull just forward of the officer's head. Scrivener knew that whoever it was that was after them knew his business, and that *Mullet* may be in for a long day. He was glad now that he had decided to fully charge the boat's batteries before taking off after the convoy. Now he needed to see if he could shake off whomever it was hunting them. His thoughts were interrupted by a second round of depth charges, close and off to port.

It was 0455.

At 0455, the mixed flight of bombers and fighters arrived at the last known position of convoy BT-1, and, finding nothing, turned to the reported base course of the convoy: 030.

Twelve minutes later, the flight leader located the convoy: three fuel tankers in line behind an escort.

The three fighters moved in first, strafing the four vessels below, setting the lead tanker and the escort on fire. The bombers followed, the first three scoring direct hits on the first and third tankers in line. By then, three of the four vessels were ablaze. The next two bombers in line struck the first two tankers in line, the lead tanker being struck with a bomb for the second time. The second tanker in line, *Tao Maru*, exploded when its boiler was struck, broke apart, and sank almost immediately.

One of the Hellcats caught sight of the "Dave" floatplane departing the scene and attacked it, blowing it out of the sky.

At 0503, the flight turned back east and headed for the *Cowpens*.

* * * * *

It was 0530 on April 30th, and *Orca* had been running flat out for over nine hours. For the first four hours, the boat stayed on course 027, until it was southwest of Nanri Dao Island. Leaving Nanri Dao to the east, she crossed the narrow passage between the island and the mainland, and then turned east-northeast, passing under Haitan Dao Island. Once clear of Haitan Dao it returned to course 027. There had been no radar contacts, and the RWR had shown no indication of the presence of anyone else's radar.

"Where are we, Bill?" Jake asked, as he stood by the chart plot in the control room.

Salton pointed to a spot on the chart. "Right about here, Captain, in the East China Sea, right on the hundred and twenty-first meridian, northeast of Fuzhou, and fifty miles, more or less, off the coast. We're gonna have to turn northeast pretty soon, or we'll run aground on the China coast."

"And still no sign of the convoy?"

"No, Sir."

"Well, we'll just have to submerge for the day. I was hoping we'd catch up with them before daylight. Some days it doesn't pay to get up in the morning."

Salton couldn't think of anything to say in reply.

* * * * *

The cat and mouse game between *Atsukaze* and *Mullet* continued throughout the morning of April 30th, with *Mullet* drawing *Atsukaze* farther and farther out into the East China Sea.

Ito was well aware of what had happened at first light. *Atsukaze* had heard the frantic cries for help radioed from *Number 21*, but there was little or nothing that could be done about it. *Atsukaze* was too far away to begin with, and if that were not so, there was undoubtedly little *Atsukaze's* antiaircraft capabilities could have done to alter the inevitable end of the encounter. Indeed, all that would have happened was that *Atsukaze* herself would have joined *Number 21, Tao Maru, Toho Maru,* and *Kaijo Maru* at the bottom of the East China Sea.

And then, finally, the submarine below managed to slip away just before noon. In the next war, Ito vowed, he would command a submarine!

It took most of the morning but *Fuji* finally succeeded in getting a towline over to *Kazahaya* and managed to get the two ships headed back to the west and the port of Fuzhou. By the evening of April 30th, they reached the mouth of the Minjiang River. They proceeded upriver to the anchorage of Caoxiazhou Point, where, at nightfall, *Fuji* dropped the tow, and both ships dropped anchor.

The next morning, May 1st, *Fuji* weighed anchor and proceeded back downriver to the East China Sea in search of BT-1. There were no facilities in Fuzhou capable of affecting the necessary repairs to her boiler, and so *Kazahaya* and her precious cargo remained in Fuzhou for the duration of the war.

* * * * *

Mullet had taken a beating. Whoever it was attacking on the surface had dropped twenty-eight depth charges on her, and about ten of them scored near misses. The pressure hull was dented, and there were pieces of cork insulation and shards of glass everywhere. Maybe two or three gauges had retained their glass, but that was it.

Thankfully, the dozens of leaks suffered were quickly brought under control, and whatever seawater reached the bilges was handled by the drain pump. Worst of all, Scrivener wasn't even sure what it was exactly that he had done to shake the hunter off his tail. All he knew was that he and his crew were glad it was over.

The worst part of it was that *Mullet* had suffered the beating after sinking just one tiny escort, a boat not even as big as herself. A beating like that deserved at least an aircraft carrier!

On the May 1st evening fleet broadcast, the word came to both *Orca* and *Mullet* that the remainder of BT-1, three tankers and an escort, had been destroyed by aircraft flying off the *Cowpens*.

Jake wondered what had happened to the two missing tankers. He would probably never know.

Orca returned to her station in the Formosa Strait.

* * * * *

On May 4th, with her father on duty 4,900 miles away, Elizabeth Ann Lawlor celebrated her first birthday.

On May 8, 1945, Germany surrendered unconditionally to Allied forces in Europe. With victory in Europe now secure, and two of the three axis powers out of the war, there remained one enemy left for the Allies to conquer: the Empire of Japan. Among the Allied powers, however, the Soviet Union had not yet declared war on Japan.

* * * * *

Orca had been on fruitless patrol for three weeks when, on Friday, May 25th, orders came through to relieve *Pisces*, one of the submarines assigned to TF 57, standing picket duty north of Okinawa. *Orca* relieved *Pisces* on May 29th.

Orca's main task was to search for and report enemy activity in its sector. The only enemy activity it saw, however, was the swarms of enemy *kamikaze* aircraft as they passed overhead. Early detection allowed Allied land and carrier-based aircraft sufficient time to scramble and intercept the *kamikazes*. As time passed, the number of these attacks thankfully became fewer and fewer.

Orca remained on picket duty until Okinawa was secured on June 22nd, at which point she was then ordered to:

". . . refuel at Saipan on the way back to Pearl Harbor. On reaching Pearl Harbor, all preparations are to be made for a change of command. Commander Jacob J. Lawlor will be succeeded as Commanding Officer, USS Orca, by Lieutenant Commander Francis X. Witherspoon . . ."

There was nothing in the orders as to Jake's next duty assignment.

Chapter 28

Special Ops: 6 July 1945 to 2 September 1945

Everything was a jumble, Jake thought, with much uncertainty and many unanswered questions. There was the joy of seeing Kate and Elizabeth, and actually watching his daughter walking to him. There was losing custody of the "other woman" in his life — *Orca* — and losing command of her after three years. Would her new commander love and understand her and the men who sailed her? What would his next assignment be, and where in the world would it take him? How would his new job, whatever it was, affect Kate and Elizabeth? Would they have to leave Hawaii?

There were no ready answers.

After he had given his verbal patrol report to Vice Admiral Lockwood, the admiral told Jake he wanted to hold the change of command ceremony as soon as possible.

"Got to give Witherspoon the wind in his sails," Lockwood said, "and you need to move on. It's time, Jake. Actually, it's well past time. There isn't a submarine driver out there who's had command of a boat as long as you have, or made as many war patrols. And I have an important job for you to do right here."

"I was wondering about that. There was nothing in the change of command orders about my next assignment."

"That's because the job I had in mind for you didn't exist until the day before yesterday, when the Navy Department finally approved it. Your title is 'OIC, Special Submarine Operations,' as part of my staff here in SUBPAC."

"Officer in Charge of *what*? What exactly is 'Special Submarine Operations?' "

"Pretty much anything I need someone of your capabilities and experience to do, but all directed at final victory and the invasion of Japan.

"It's no secret that the invasion is imminent. And, given our experience in Okinawa, it's going to be an expensive operation in both blood and treasure. It's never been determined exactly what role the submarine force, if any, will have in 'Operation Downfall,' but you'll have until November to work that out. November First—that's when we're going in."

Lockwood continued, "I want you to be my 'go to' guy on this. You'll be working closely with your counterparts in the surface Navy, the Marine Corps, the Army, and the Army Air Corps. I don't expect you'll get much sleep over the next few months, and you may have to spend some time in airplanes going from place to place. So, there it is. Well, what do you think?"

Jake was silent for a few moments, turning it all over in his head. "Wow," was the first thing out of his mouth. "That's a lot to think about. You said 'Operation Downfall?' "

"Yes, that's what they're calling it."

"November First? That's just three months away."

"Right. But understand the War Department and the Joint Chiefs have already set policy, and the base plan has been in place for well over a year. What's left to work out are the fine details, and that's where you and others like you will come in. But make no mistake. You are right. Three months is still not very much time."

"Well, Sir, it sounds like one hell of a job. There's so much to think about, it makes my head spin. And I'm not even sure where I'd begin."

"You'll figure it out," Lockwood said. "There's no doubt in my mind you can do the job. The question is, do you want the job?'

"Honestly, Admiral, I'd rather keep driving *Orca*. But if I can't do that, then this job sounds about as good as 'next best things' get . . . Yes, Admiral, I want the job."

"Good. I'll have your orders cut and in your hands this afternoon." Lockwood extended his hand. "Welcome aboard, Commander Lawlor."

To celebrate, Jake and Kate enjoyed the luxury of a Saturday night out—an actual date: dinner and a movie. Elizabeth was safe at home, in the care of a responsible teenager, the daughter of a Hellcat pilot, who lived next door.

Free from the everyday concern over *Orca*, and not yet ensconced in his position at SUBPAC staff, Jake was determined to focus on nothing beyond the enjoyment of the company of his wife. Dinner at the Royal Palace Restaurant was just so-so, Jake thought, although Kate remarked that she thoroughly enjoyed her meal because she didn't have to cook it.

Then, there was a double feature at the Honolulu theater. Before the feature films began, the Pathé newsreel featured the capture of Okinawa. After the battle scenes decrying the fanatical enemy resistance (soldiers with flame throwers flushing the enemy out of their caves), Japanese civilians, including women holding babies, were shown jumping off the cliffs to their death rather than be captured. Kate gripped Jake's arm in horror. "How awful," she said. Even the Tom and Jerry cartoon that followed didn't do much to improve the somber mood.

The first feature was a film called *The Man in Half Moon Street*, a potboiler about a mad scientist who had discovered a way to prolong life indefinitely, only to find out that it was a lousy idea. The main feature was a lot better, *A Song to Remember* , starring Paul Muni, Merle Oberon, and Cornel Wilde. It was about the life of the pianist and composer Frederick Chopin (played by Cornel Wilde, of course). Jake thought the story was pretty soppy, but that the music was gorgeous. Kate, on the other hand, loved the entire movie.

During the drive home from the theater, Jake couldn't get the "Fantasy Impromptu" out of his head.

* * * * *

Joel Himmelfarb knew Frank Witherspoon well. Lieutenant Commander Francis X. Witherspoon, USN, had been his XO on *Perro*, where Joel had served as engineer officer. Joel had always liked and respected Frank, and he felt they enjoyed a good relationship. Together, they had experienced the pounding that *Perro* had taken back in February of '44, when *Perro* had her hull dented and was forced down below test depth by a pair of really determined Jap anti-sub ships.

Joel recalled that Frank kept his head about him then—but they *all* had, really, most of all their skipper, Jack Petrosky—and would probably be a great CO in *Orca*. And he was now to be Frank's XO. *Funny how things work out*, he thought.

SUBPAC wasted no time in scheduling the change of command ceremony. The event took place on Sunday, July 8th. There were all sorts of dignitaries, a band, dress whites, Admiral Lockwood, SUBPAC staff, *Orca's* officers and crew, and lots of civilians. But it was all over too quickly. When it ended, Commander Jacob J. Lawlor, USN, was no longer CO of the submarine *Orca*. And when that reality finally hit home, it sent Jake into a purple funk that he couldn't shake completely for days.

Orca was back at sea on July 9th, but *not* to go back on patrol—that wasn't scheduled until later in the month, on the 18th. That was to give Captain Witherspoon a feel for his new command, while out to sea for a week's ISE.

During the week, under the tutelage of his XO and Chief Buckner (his COB), Frank Witherspoon crawled through the bowels of his first command, *Orca*, hoping to get to know her as intimately as his predecessor had.

"I think," Bucky confided to the other chiefs assembled in the goat locker, "that our new skipper's gonna do just fine."

* * * * *

On Monday, July 9th, Jake reported aboard SUBPAC HQ with his orders in hand. Admiral Lockwood welcomed him aboard, and assigned him a desk outside his office.

"This is your new command, Jake," the admiral said, pointing at his desk and grinning. "Although I don't expect you'll spend much time driving it. As I said, you'll probably spend a lot of time *out* of the office. But don't forget you still work directly for me, and I'll want regular briefings, along with a weekly written report—short and to the point, please, just like your patrol reports.

"Meanwhile I have some light reading for you." Lockwood dropped two large volumes labeled "TOP SECRET" on his desk. "First job will be to let me know what you think of these. Lunch is 1205 in the mess. See you later."

Jake sat down and began to absorb what turned out to be the operation plan for Operation Downfall.

Jake quickly determined that Operation Downfall was split into two separate sections—hence the two volumes—Operation Olympic and Operation Coronet.

Operation Olympic was aimed at the capture of the southern third of the Japanese island of Kyushu, using Okinawa as a springboard. It was scheduled to begin the following November and December with the capture of the offshore islands of Tanegashima, Yakushima, and Koshikijima. These islands would provide secure anchorages close to the action for ships not needed near the landing beaches, and for damaged ships. The actual invasion of Kyushu would follow on December 1st. There were thirty-five landing beaches chosen, all named for automobiles: Austin, Buick, Cadillac, through to Stutz, Winton, and Zephyr.

Operation Coronet was concerned with the invasion of the Kanto Plain, near Tokyo, on the island of Honshu. It was planned to begin later, in April of 1946. Olympic would capture airbases on Kyushu to provide land-based air support for Coronet.

Olympic also included a deception plan, Operation Pastel, which would be an attempt to convince the Japanese that instead of an invasion, Allied intentions were to first encircle, then bomb and starve the Japanese into submission. Pastel would require the capture of bases in Formosa, China, and Korea. Jake immediately pounced on the idea that perhaps Operation Pastel should replace Operations Olympic and Coronet altogether.

It also occurred to Jake that the progression of American and Allied victories across the Pacific, culminating in the taking of the Philippines and Okinawa, would make such direct invasion plans obvious to the enemy. He knew that the Japanese would be waiting for the Allies to invade, and were making preparations to resist the invading force even as he sat there. He also knew that they were preparing to fight right down to the last man, woman, and child.

Jake recalled the newsreel showing Japanese civilians committing suicide rather than be captured by the invading Americans. He was sure that what would be the largest amphibious operation of all time, bigger even than the landings at Normandy, would be met with the same fanatical resistance. He envisioned Allied casualties numbering in the millions, with enemy casualties, military and civilian, perhaps ten times that.

The "op" plan for Project Downfall began with an assessment of the forces at the disposal of the Japanese High Command. As Jake read through the enemy troop estimates — six divisions — he thought them rather optimistic.

Countering the estimated opposing enemy force, for Operation Coronet, a corps was assigned to each of the thirty-five beaches. They were projected to outnumber the enemy three to one, with three Japanese divisions stationed in the south, and another three in northern Kyushu. But Jake reasoned that the Japanese had plenty of time between the loss of Okinawa and

November 1st to build up their forces to counter the landings. It was, Jake thought, well within the realm of possibility for the Japanese to have already withdrawn sufficient troops from China, Manchuria, and Korea, and to train and equip new forces, to reach parity with the invasion force.

For Jake, the main question was which of the two anti-invasion strategies might the Japanese employ: resist invasion on the beaches, as they did in Tarawa; or abandon the beaches and take the fight to fortified positions inland as they did in Saipan, Iwo Jima, and Okinawa. Neither strategy proved effective, in that neither ultimately repulsed the landing force, although the latter strategy certainly proved the most costly in terms of casualties inflicted on the invaders.

Certainly, Jake thought, not even the Imperial General Staff thought that Japan could still win the war. The best that the Imperial General Staff could possibly hope for at this point was a negotiated armistice. To achieve that end, they might well incite a war-weary American public to clamor for peace by making total military victory as costly as possible. He thought, therefore, that the Japanese would probably opt for using fortified defensive positions inland again, as they had in Okinawa, and bleed the Allies into coming to the peace table.

The assessment of IJN capital ships available for use by the enemy was more realistic than the troop estimates, Jake thought, and was probably backed up by aerial reconnaissance. Capital ships would be easy to count from the air. They numbered four battleships and five aircraft carriers. And all of them had sustained some, as yet unrepaired, damage. There were also two cruisers, twenty-three destroyers, and forty-six submarines. Jake took some satisfaction knowing that fuel for this fleet was in such short supply, thanks to the U.S. Submarine Service, that they would probably not be much of a factor in the upcoming battle. They might well be used, however, as stationary gun platforms in opposition to Operation Coronet. In Jake's opinion, every one of them should therefore be destroyed from the air as soon as possible.

Jake knew there were also an unknown number of midget submarines (but *at least* several hundred), at least a hundred *Kaiten* human-guided torpedoes, and well over a thousand *shinyo* suicide boats. There was no way of assessing the *actual* number available, but they would be expected to be employed extensively.

Yeah, Jake thought, *especially against troop transports.*

The Joint Chiefs' biggest worry was the "divine wind" *kamikaze* planes. Less than 1,500 *kamikaze* attacks in the Battle of Okinawa resulted in the loss of 30 warships and three merchant vessels. All the warships lost were destroyers or smaller vessels. Some carriers, battleships, and cruisers suffered damage from these attacks, but none were sunk. There were thought to be just over 2,000 aircraft available to the enemy for *kamikaze* attacks, and the Japanese defense planners were expected to be relying heavily on them.

Precisely, Jake thought, *and they'll find anything that can get off the ground, fill it with explosives, and find some poor suicidal bastard willing to fly it, and to crash it against us.*

Again, he thought the op plan's estimate of aircraft available to the enemy optimistically low. Double or triple that number was probably more like it, Jake figured.

After lunch, Lockwood called Jake into his office.

"Well, what do you think so far?" he asked.

"I think, Admiral, that the estimates of enemy strength in the op plan are overly optimistic. The Japs are certainly smart enough to know *if* we're coming, *where* we'll be coming from, and *what* we're prepared to throw at them. I think they'll be mustering everything they have to throw back at us. They have maybe four million men at their disposal, *if* they could ever arm all of them—and I seriously doubt that they can. But they could probably field about a million armed men if they wanted to. And counted within that million are the most capable troops they have left: veterans from China, Manchuria, and Korea."

Lockwood listened attentively.

"I think the invasion plans themselves, Olympic and Coronet, are both pretty logical, Admiral, *if* you're going to attack the enemy head on," Jake continued, "but for the life of me, Sir, I can't figure out why we've decided to do that—hit 'em head on. We have enough ships, submarines, and aircraft to completely and effectively blockade and isolate Japan. Seems to me that the smartest thing to do would be just that, and starve them into submission. Regular bombing raids by General Arnold and his boys might even speed up the process. That way, we'd suffer minimal casualties, and probably the Japs would suffer far fewer casualties in the end than if we'd actually invaded."

Lockwood snickered. "That's *exactly* what Nimitz wanted to do. It was MacArthur who insisted we invade. I suspect that Truman and the War Department sided with MacArthur, thinking that the American public was tired of war and wanted to end this thing as quickly as possible. A siege would take at least a year, maybe even two, before it brought Japan to her knees. That way the damn war could last until maybe '47—or even longer. The public might think we decided to settle for a stalemate. Besides, MacArthur has the politicians convinced that he could have the war wrapped up by the middle of '46."

"Yes, Admiral, but is the American public ready for a million Allied casualties?"

"Perhaps not, Jake—not if they knew in advance. But who's gonna tell 'em? By the time the casualty figures come in, Operation Downfall will be well under way, and the American public will do just what they have done—suck it up, grit their teeth, and carry on."

Jake lowered his eyes and pursed his mouth. Lockwood, meanwhile, looked out the window, thinking. Finally, he said, "Jake, Tell you what I'm gonna do. Seems like you and Chet Nimitz think a lot alike. I'm gonna make you SUBPAC's representative on his planning staff for Operation Downfall. You'll like Nimitz, and he'll like you. He cut his teeth in submarines."

Jake smiled.

"Your Kate's gonna hate me for this, Jake, but pack your bags. You're going to Guam."

* * * * *

Commander Hiriake Ito thought it something of a miracle that he managed to bring *Atsukaze* back into port in Yokosuka in one piece. He thought that he and his ship had had it when a roaming PBY sighted *Atsukaze* off Mishima, south of Kyushu. He pictured a squadron of Corsairs or Dauntless bombers being directed his way and making short work of his ship, when the gods intervened and sent rainsquall after rainsquall, right up until nightfall covered his passage into Tokyo Bay.

On arrival, on July 4th, Ito made ready to pull *Atsukaze* into the fueling docks to replenish his fuel supply, only to be turned away. *Those six tankers that were lost would have helped*, he thought, *but would still have been too little and too late.*

Reluctantly, Ito turned his ship into line, outboard of the destroyers already tied up to the fleet service pier. It dawned on him that without fuel, *Atsukaze* would probably never put out to sea again, and that thought pained him.

The next day Ito received orders that took him by complete surprise. First, he was promoted to the rank of *kaigun-daisa*, or captain. Second, he was to relinquish command of *Atsukaze* to his XO, Lieutenant Commander Shoici Koroki. Finally, he was to leave Yokosuka immediately, and report to Admiral Soemu Toyoda, Chief of the Navy General Staff, at the recently relocated Imperial General Headquarters just outside Nagano. No reason was given for any of these changes.

A month earlier, Admiral Soemu Toyoda had just been named to succeed Admiral Koshiro Oikowa, who had been Chief of the Navy General Staff since the latter part of '44. Unknown to Ito, Admiral Oikowa had resigned the post in protest over Emperor Hirohito's refusal to consider seeking peace with the enemy at a time when it was clear that the war was already lost.

Ito had met Admiral Toyoda back in '43, when the admiral was in command of the Yokosuka Naval District where *Atsukaze* was home-ported. He remembered the Admiral as a short man, somewhat stout, with a round face, close-cropped hair, and a sparse moustache. Toyoda had come to command the Yokosuka Naval District after having been demoted from the Supreme War Council for championing the funding of Naval aircraft over the desires of the Army. The generals dominated the council then, and still did.

Ito had been named by the Destroyer Fleet Commander to a task force formed by Toyoda to advise his staff on ways and means to more effectively assess and repair battle damage to naval vessels. Ito was then chosen by the other members of the task force to present their findings to the admiral and his staff (a job, that, in fact, no one had wanted, and since Ito was junior . . .). The task force's recommendations were actually quite good, and Ito presented them well. The admiral had apparently been favorably impressed by the young commander, and had taken a shine to him.

Now, Toyoda was back, this time as Chief of the Navy General Staff, the Supreme Commander of the Imperial Japanese Navy, and he wanted Ito to work for him.

On July 9th, Ito reported to Toyoda's staff, headquartered in the underground bunker in the mountains outside of Nagano. The IGHQ, the Imperial General Headquarters, had been moved there from the Imperial Palace in Tokyo after that city had been firebombed. It was here that Emperor Hirohito, Head of State and the Generalissimo of the Imperial Japanese Armed Forces, now held court.

It was probably the most uncomfortable plane ride Jake had ever experienced. The B-29 Superfortress had come directly off the Boeing assembly line in Wichita, Kansas, and had flown non-stop to Pearl Harbor. Jake boarded the aircraft at Pearl, and, eleven hours later, the plane landed in Guam. It had been a daytime flight, with the plane racing the sun, and so Jake found himself adjusting his watch in Guam to nearly the same time that he had left Pearl. Of course, he did not sleep on the plane, and now he would not see a bed for at least another twelve hours.

On landing, Jake shouldered his duffel bag, and found transportation to the Pacific Fleet HQ where Fleet Admiral Nimitz held sway.

Chester W. Nimitz, USN, graduated from the Naval Academy in 1905, seventh in a class of 114. After graduation, Nimitz served in a series of surface ships until 1909, when he joined the submarine service. He rose to command the original *Plunger* (A-1), *Snapper* (C-5), and *Narwhal*(D-1). In 1913, he began a tour of staff and surface fleet assignments, returning to submarines from 1917 through 1919.

Over the next thirty-two years he served in progressively more responsible command positions, including command of both cruiser and battleship divisions. In 1939, Nimitz became Chief of the Bureau of Navigation where, under his aegis, techniques were developed for refueling ships at sea, which became crucial to the Navy's success in the upcoming war.

Ten days after the Japanese attack on Pearl Harbor, FDR appointed Nimitz Commander, U.S. Pacific Fleet, with the rank of admiral. He assumed command of the Pacific Fleet aboard the deck of the submarine *Grayling*. Nimitz shifted to the offensive in the Pacific as soon as men, material, and arms became available, and saw the Navy through Coral Sea, Midway, the Solomons, and Leyte Gulf.

On December 19, 1944, five days after Congress established the five-star rank of Fleet Admiral, FDR appointed Nimitz to that rank. Nimitz was one of only four men, besides Halsey, Leahy, and King, ever to hold that honor.

The previous January, with the Philippines secured, Nimitz moved the Pacific Fleet HQ from Pearl Harbor to Guam to be closer to the action.

"So you're the *wunderkind* Charlie sent me, are you?" was Nimitz's greeting to Jake as he was ushered into his sparse office in Guam.

"Sir?" was Jake's surprise response.

"Relax, Commander," Nimitz said, a smile on his face, "if Charlie Lockwood thought enough of you to send you to me here in Guam, then that's good enough for me. Not that I didn't do some checking up on you myself. Quite a bloody swath you've been cutting through the Japs in *Orca*, and I have to hand it to you. I'll even admit to being a little jealous. Mining Manila Bay, that took some balls."

"I had a lot of help, Admiral," Jake said, now a bit more relaxed.

"Sure you did. Some of the best men in the fleet. Submariners."

White-haired and lantern-jawed, Nimitz looked average in every way: average height, average build, next-door-neighbor demeanor. Jake knew enough not to let appearances fool him. Nimitz was anything *but* average.

"So," Nimitz said, "You've read the Operation Downfall op plan. Tell me honestly what you thought of it."

Jake told Nimitz exactly what he had told Lockwood, going over the op plan point for point. He gave Nimitz a critique of the plan's assumptions, tactics, estimates of troop and equipment strength, and why the remnants of the Japanese fleet should be destroyed dockside before initiation of Operation Coronet. Nimitz listened attentively and without expression. When Jake had finished, he seemed lost in thought for a few minutes.

"Now I see why Charlie sent you to me," Nimitz said finally. "You'll be glad to know that, when the time comes, Hap Arnold and I already have a plan in place to destroy their ship-mounted guns from the air. In any event, I want you on the planning group that's going to take Downfall to the next level. You're now officially attached to my staff on TAD—temporary duty—from SUBPAC. Come on, I'll introduce you around. Welcome aboard, Captain."

"Thank you, Admiral, glad to be aboard, but, begging your pardon, Sir, it's commander."

"Not according to the letter of recommendation Charlie Lockwood placed in your jacket a few months back, nor the letter of approval I added to it. As of yesterday, according to the Bureau of Personnel, you've been promoted to captain."

Jake was speechless. Eyes wide in surprise, he finally managed to say, "What? Why? I only just made commander, Admiral. Heck, they just got the sign changed in front of my house on the base. How could it happen?"

Now Nimitz laughed. "It can happen because I'm a bloody fleet admiral, and I can *make* it happen! Of course, if you don't want to accept the promotion—"

"Oh, no, Admiral! I accept all right! Captain! Wow, I can't wait to let Kate know! Wow."

"Here, I believe these are yours." Nimitz took a pair of collar pins out of his pocket—silver eagles. "Now, besides the fact that you've earned this promotion, and that you deserve it, there's another reason why you've been promoted. Now you'll be able to hobnob with those bird colonels on MacArthur's planning staff in Manila on an equal footing. The Army's always been funny about things like that, you know."

Jake smiled.

"Okay, sailor," Nimitz said, "now put those birds on your collar and I really *will* introduce you around. Through that door," he pointed, "is my personal head. You can use the mirror in there, make sure they're on straight."

After Jake left the room, Nimitz chuckled, pleased with himself. "Don't get to do that kind of thing often enough," he said under his breath, "not near often enough." And then he chuckled some more.

* * * * *

Hiriake Ito had not yet seen Admiral Toyoda, but was scheduled to meet with him that afternoon to discuss his assignment. Meanwhile, he was shown around the underground headquarters by Lt. Daisuke Mamoru, a member of the admiral's staff, distinctive aiguillettes marking him as an aide.

Mamoru showed him the officer's mess, his desk in the large chamber that accommodated Toyoda's staff, and his quarters. Ito was delighted that his sea chest had already been placed at the foot of his bed.

They passed by an isolated part of the underground labyrinth, marked by an elaborately carved double doorway, and two armed guards, standing at stiff attention. "That," Mamoru said, "is the Emperor's quarters. His offices are through those doors, and beyond them are the living quarters for the Emperor and his family. The stables you passed by at the entrance to the headquarters are for the Emperor's horses—not all of them, just his favorites."

"Of course," Ito answered, with no trace of irony. The Emperor was, after all, a living god, the Son of Heaven, and every effort rightly should have been made to insure his serenity.

Later in the day, the admiral met with Ito.

"Captain Ito," Toyoda said, "you were once able to impress me with your problem-solving abilities. It is no secret that the war is lost and that our home islands are facing imminent invasion. My predecessor Admiral Oikowa's staff, some of whom I have retained, have formulated, along with representatives of the IJA, a plan to counter the invasion force. The plan is called Operation *Ketsu-Go*. The main thrust of the plan is to inflict such tremendous casualties on the invading force that the will of the American people to continue the war will falter and the Allies will accept a negotiated peace. I believe that the objective of the plan is sound, but I am not at all sure that the plan, as written, is feasible or optimal. I want you to take command of the IJN planning group. I want your group to conduct a thorough review of the plan. You must study, analyze, and revise the plan for Operation *Ketsu-Go* so as to maximize the probability of its success.

"Understand that even if your group's recommendations are sound, I can only see to it that they will be implemented by the ground, sea, and air forces of the IJN. The IJA General Staff must also agree to whatever changes you recommend if they are to be executed by the Army. So, therefore, your logic for implementing these changes must be both sound and persuasive.

"In the end, of course, if the Army is not agreeable, and we feel strongly enough about our case, we can always bring our cause up before the Emperor." (He paused for effect.)

"Now," he asked, "can you do this?"

Ito knew instinctively that when a superior officer posed such a question, there was no room for equivocation. He therefore answered without hesitation, "I can, Admiral."

"Excellent. You will begin immediately. Here is a copy of the plan for Operation *Ketsu-Go*. You have until the morning to study and become completely familiar with it. Tomorrow, first thing, my aide, Lieutenant Mamoru, will introduce you to your planning group. I have anticipated your answer, and they are expecting you. I believe my aide has already shown you to your quarters?"

"Yes, Admiral, he has."

"Then you may go now."

"Thank you, Admiral." Ito bowed deeply. The admiral bowed back, a bow shallower than Ito's, and Ito left the room, the operation plan, marked "Most Secret," tucked under his arm.

Ito spent all evening and most of the night studying Operation *Ketsu-Go*.

Ketsu-Go, or "Decisive," had projected an Allied invasion taking place in July or August of 1945. Ito knew, however, that the resistance on Okinawa had unexpectedly proven so effective that the American advance was slowed, and that now no amphibious operation would likely be mounted before the end of typhoon season. To do otherwise involved too much risk. So, the earliest an invasion could take place would be October, with November more likely.

The Allies had command of the sea and the air. Fortunately, a number of divisions of both Army and Navy troops had already been transferred back to the home islands from China, Manchuria, and Korea. Further transfers from these theaters were probably now impossible. Still, there were at least a million men available for immediate mobilization in the home islands.

The one problem would be supplying them with sufficient arms and ammunition.

Since the Allies had command of the sea and the air, Ito thought, they could be expected to blockade the Islands, and to continue to bombard Japanese cities from the air.

Ketsu-Go contended that the American advance through Okinawa, and the suitability of the terrain for amphibious operations, signaled that the enemy's initial invasion would probably be launched on the beaches off southern Kyushu. Ito agreed with the supposition.

In theory, he knew, the Allies could launch an amphibious attack anywhere in the islands, but the beaches off southern Kyushu and the beaches of the Kanto Plain surrounding the capitol were the most suitable. Of these, the approach through southern Kyushu was, for the enemy, by far the most feasible.

Ketsu-Go placed a great deal of emphasis on the use of Special Attack Units, or air, sea, and undersea *kamikaze* units. Ito agreed that such tactical units promised the most success in delaying the inevitable. The plan also stressed that the main objective of the *kamikaze* attacks should be the troop and equipment transport ships. With that strategy Ito was in wholehearted agreement.

The plan evaluated the success of the *kamikaze* air attacks at Okinawa, noting that one in every nine air attacks was successful in scoring a hit. The plan, citing the home islands' less favorable terrain for U.S. radar, estimated that one in six attacks would be successful.

The plan further estimated that ten thousand aircraft could be pressed into *kamikaze* service. This included all available fighters, bombers, and trainers. In addition, there was an adequate stock of engines to outfit the construction of additional trainer-type aircraft using wooden airframes and fabric airfoils. The plan estimated that the sum total of available aircraft would sink over four hundred ships.

In addition, there were 300 *kairyu* midget submarines, 120 *kaiten* manned torpedoes, and 2,412 *shinyo* suicide boats also available as Special Attack Units.

If successfully employed against the troop transports, Ito thought, *perhaps a third of the enemy landing force could be destroyed before ever reaching land!*

Ito moved to the section of *Ketsu-Go* that dealt with Japanese ground forces. There were two strategies discussed: engage the enemy on the beaches, or engage the enemy from fortified positions inland. Japan had used both in the past. At Tarawa, where the former strategy was used, the defenders proved vulnerable to naval gunfire and air bombardment, and, once the beach defenses were breached, there was nothing left in reserve to engage the enemy.

The latter strategy was used at Peleliu, Iwo Jima, and Okinawa. There, Japanese forces ceded the beaches to the enemy, and had, instead, fortified and held the most defensible inland terrain. In terms of the number of enemy casualties, the ultimate Allied victories on these islands were their most expensive.

Ketsu-Go proposed an intermediate position between the two strategies: first—employing the bulk of defensive ground forces far enough from the shoreline to avoid most exposure to naval gunfire, yet close enough to deny the enemy a secure foothold before being engaged; second—held in reserve and still further back, additional forces would be prepared to move against whichever ground engagement constituted the enemy's main thrust. While he was not an expert in ground offensive strategy, the plans proposed appeared reasonable enough to Ito.

Earlier, in March, there had only been one division in Kyushu. Through June, sufficient forces had been moved from Manchuria, Korea, and northern Japan to build troop strength in Kyushu to almost 800,000 men under arms. That number was expected to be exceeded, reaching almost a million by August. Also by August, the ground forces in the entire homeland were expected to exceed sixty-five divisions.

Perhaps, thought Ito, *but can we supply such a force with sufficient arms and ammunition?*

Ketsu-Go made no mention of provisioning these ground forces, and Ito made a note to have his staff investigate that aspect of the plan.

Finally, the plan described the formation and organization of the Patriotic Citizens Fighting Corps. It would include all healthy men aged 15 to 60 not already under arms, and all women aged 17 to 40. The Corps was to provide combat support, and, ultimately, engage in combat. There were, however, no uniforms, little training, and few real weapons beyond some outdated muskets and longbows. The Corps was mostly armed with bamboo spears, knives, hand tools, and farm implements.

At this juncture, a dismayed Ito organized his notes for his audience with Admiral Toyoda the following day, and retired for the night.

Ito met with Admiral Toyoda the following morning, and, holding nothing back, gave the admiral his critique of Operation *Ketsu-Go*. He was unsure how the admiral might react, but felt that he must provide his honest analysis, come what may. He was pleasantly surprised by Toyoda's reaction.

"Very good, Captain Ito. But I honestly expected nothing less from you."

"Thank you, Admiral."

"Now you and your staff must work on maximizing our strengths and minimizing our weaknesses. What would you say is our greatest strength?"

"That we are fighting to defend our homeland, Admiral. The enemy must bring the fight to us, invade us from the sea. Our men are the most tenacious fighters in the world, and we will fight to the death to defend our own soil, our families, our culture, and our Emperor."

"Well said. And our greatest weakness?"

"Material, Admiral — weapons, ammunition, fuel."

"Again, agreed. So then, what do we do?"

"Put all our available strength, everything we have, up against the enemy's weakness. Exact from the enemy the greatest possible price in blood.

"Unlike *our* military, which is answerable only to the Emperor, the American military is answerable to civilians, who, in turn, answer to the American public. The will of the American people to continue the fight must be broken before a negotiated peace is possible. The only way to break the will of the American people is to inflict so many casualties on their forces that continued pursuit of the war becomes unthinkable.

"First use our Special Attack Forces," Ito continued, "air, sea, and undersea, to hone in on, and attack, the enemy transports. As much enemy manpower as possible must be destroyed before it ever sets foot on sacred Japanese soil.

"Then, use the strategies already in place to meet the invader on land with overwhelming force, using everything we have and can possibly throw at them, every man, weapon, and bullet we can muster. Only the greatest possible measure of spilled enemy blood will bring the Americans to the peace table."

Toyoda smiled at his young protégé. "We must do exactly that," he said. "We *will* do exactly that."

On July 19th, the heavy cruiser Indianapolis *made port at Pearl Harbor to pick up weapon components, and what amounted to one half of the world supply of enriched uranium. These were to be transported to Tinian Island, in the Northern Marianas.*

* * * * *

Over the next three weeks, flying back and forth between Guam and MacArthur's HQ in Manila, Jake conferred with his Army, Army Air Corps, and Marine counterparts. He swore he spent more time in the air than some bomber crews. Each week he filed written reports to Admiral Nimitz (copy to Admiral Lockwood), and whenever he was back in Guam, met with Nimitz. As busy as he was, Nimitz always made time to meet with "Lockwood's *wunderkind.*"

Jake met with Nimitz on July 25th, and discussed some of the improvements and enhancements to Downfall that had made it into the op plan.

"So what about the *kamikaze* planes, Jake? I understand that the Army's finally coming around to the Navy's estimate."

"Not quite, Admiral, but they're getting closer. They've finally come up to the Japs being able to employ six thousand planes. Now remember, that's up from thirty-four hundred in May."

"And our estimate?"

"Naval Intelligence says it'll be more like eighty-eight hundred aircraft."

"Your thoughts?"

"I've seen ONI's assumptions and calculations, Admiral, and, if anything, the Office of Naval Intelligence is being conservative."

"And what can we do to counter the threat?"

"Well, we've already planned to provide secure anchorages for the transports and supply ships, but that won't stop at least some of their aircraft from getting through. Our best defense, and our experience at Okinawa backs it up, is destroying them in the air before they can get to our ships. Army and Navy Air are proposing Big Blue Blanket."

"I love these fancy names. So what in blazes is Big Blue Blanket?"

"Well, Admiral, what it amounts to is replacing some torpedo and dive bombers with additional fighter squadrons on the carriers, and converting some B-17s to airborne radar pickets. The idea is to use the B-17s to vector the fighters onto the *kamikazes*."

"Sounds good to me, Jake. What's your take?"

"Same as yours, Admiral, but while that would be fine for the actual invasion, I'd still like to take it one step further."

"How's that?"

"Well, suppose we go in to the invasion beaches a couple weeks before the actual landings, using ships loaded stem to stern with anti-aircraft guns. We make all the right moves, signaling 'here comes the amphibious invasion' to the enemy, and lure out the *kamikazes* on their one-way flights. They come out looking to find and hit transports, but all they find is a sky full of AA shells and land-based fighters from Okinawa shooting at them, vectored in by those B-17s. Those fighters, by the way, are already in Okinawa—the USAAF Fifth and Seventh Air Forces and our Marine air units."

"Beautiful. Put my personal stamp of approval on that plan. Make it happen."

"Yes, Sir."

"What's next?"

"The Army wants to move everything up a month. Begin Operation Olympic on October First, instead of November First. Give the Japs a month less time to prepare."

"Hmmm," Nimitz replied, "By 'Army,' I trust you mean General MacArthur. Well, if *he* can be ready by then, we certainly can be. What else?"

"Ground force estimates, Admiral."

"Yeah, what about 'em?"

"We're revising them upward. The beginning of the month, we figured between three or four hundred thousand were on Kyushu. Now Army Intelligence has discovered another four divisions, with still more on the way. They know we're coming, Admiral, and have pretty much figured out where. And they're going to throw everything they've got at us."

"Well, it's no secret that I didn't vote for going in and hitting the enemy head-on," Nimitz said. "And if we do, it's going to be costly. But the Navy will still do its very best to make it work."

"Yes, Sir," Jake said. He continued on. "Originally the Army figured a three-to-one advantage in troop strength. Now it looks like it might be approaching one-to-one."

Nimitz was lost in thought for a few moments. Then he said "We're invading them from the sea, and they're defending their homeland. Parity in numbers can only be a recipe for disaster. Looks to me like the Army planners have to do some serious rethinking. But, hell, I'm just some dumb swabbie."

Jake thought it best not to comment on that.

On July 26th, the Indianapolis *reached Tinian and unloaded its cargo. Two days later, the ship arrived in Guam. After some personnel exchanges, it left Guam en route to Leyte. At 0014 on July 30th, the cruiser was attacked by the Japanese submarine* I-58, *and was struck by two torpedoes. Twelve minutes later, the* Indianapolis *rolled over and sank, taking 300 men to the bottom with her. Eight hundred men survived the sinking and were left adrift in the water. The Navy had no knowledge of the incident until the survivors were spotted from the air three days later.   Only 321 men came out of the water alive; of these, four later died from exposure.*

On Monday, August 4th, back on Guam after another whirlwind airplane tour, Jake again met with Nimitz.

"How goes the Downfall planning, Captain?" Nimitz asked.

"Actually, Admiral, it seems to be coming face to face with reality."

"Really? In what way?"

"Well, it seems that Army Air reconnaissance has been mapping troop movements on Kyushu, and has revised upwards the number of troops massing in the south. Now the figure is 900,000 to a million."

"Good Lord! There goes any advantage in manpower."

"Exactly, Admiral. The thinking is that with all that manpower concentrated on Kyushu, the rest of the Islands must be sparsely defended. The Army is looking at alternative invasion sites. But after considering a bunch of places, there really are only two decent landing sites—southern Kyushu and the Kanto plain. They finally came up with the idea of skipping Olympic altogether and proceeding directly to Coronet."

"Whoa," the Admiral said. "That means we'd be out of range of fighter support from Okinawa. Air defense and troop support would be strictly up to the carriers. Our guys are good, but are they good enough to handle nine thousand *kamikazes*? And another thing, our carriers are really vulnerable to *kamikaze* attack. The Brits were smart enough to put steel decks on their carriers, but ours are of wood. Good old traditional teak. One *kamikaze* hit, and up they go in flames."

"True, Admiral," Jake countered, "but if we're right, they'll be skipping the carriers and going after the transports."

"Perhaps, Jake," Nimitz answered. "But if your aircraft's been hit, and you're gonna die anyway, and there's this 'target of opportunity' in front of you . . ."

"I catch your drift, Admiral," Jake said.

On August 6, 1945, at 0815, the Enola Gay, *a B-29 Superfortress out of North Field in the Marianas, dropped the first atomic bomb on the city of Hiroshima, Japan. Parts and fuel for the uranium bomb, nicknamed "Little Boy," had been delivered by the now-sunken cruiser* Indianapolis. *The detonation released the equivalent energy of sixteen kilotons of TNT. Sixteen hours later, President Truman called on Japan to surrender, warning them to otherwise "expect a rain of ruin from the air, the like of which has never been seen before on this earth."*

"Best kept secret in the world," Nimitz told Jake. "I assume the Joint Chiefs knew about it, but they weren't sharing. 'Need to Know,' after all. The Japs will have to capitulate now."

"Don't be so sure, Admiral," Jake replied. "You well know that they don't think at all as we do."

"Well, I guess we'll see. The president has given them an ultimatum. Hopefully, Jake, all your efforts this past month or so will have been a complete waste of time."

"I certainly hope so, Admiral."

* * * * *

"Just one bomb?" Toyoda asked.

"So it seems, Admiral," Ito said. "Hiroshima is in ruins. Twelve hundred hectares have been destroyed. At least seventy thousand dead, perhaps as many as eighty to ninety thousand, including twenty thousand troops. Another seventy thousand wounded. Whatever medical facilities remain are overwhelmed. It is a disaster of historic proportions."

"One bomb. Incredible. And now the American president has issued an ultimatum. 'Surrender,' he says, or more will follow. The Emperor has called a meeting of the Supreme Council for the Direction of the War in one hour. I want you in there with me."

"Yes, Sir, Admiral," Despite the horrific circumstances that caused his inclusion in the meeting, Ito could not help but be elated. He would sit in on a Supreme Council meeting with the Emperor himself!

The Council Chamber was part of the underground complex dedicated to the Emperor's exclusive use. The ornate chair reserved for the Emperor at the head of the Council table was empty when Toyoda and Ito entered the room.

When the chairs around the council table were filled, present were: Prime Minister, Admiral Kantaro Suzuki; Minister of Foreign Affairs, Shigenori Togo; Minister of War, General Korechika Anami; Minister of the Navy, Admiral Mitsumasa Yonai; Chief of the Army General Staff, General Yoshijiro Umezu; and Chief of the Navy General Staff, Admiral Soemu Toyoda.

Admiral Suzuki had succeeded the cadaverous, goggle-spectacled, General Hideki Tojo as Prime Minister the previous July. The Emperor forced Tojo to resign after the fall of Saipan.

Behind the men seated at the conference table, was a second tier of chairs for their advisors. Ito sat behind and immediately to the left of Toyoda.

Five minutes later, everyone stood and bowed low as the Emperor entered the room. He was already seated and had indicated for everyone else to take their seats, when Ito first dared to look at him.

Hirohito was the personal name of Emperor Showa, the 124th Emperor of Japan. Hirohito, the name by which he was known throughout the world, ascended the Chrysanthemum Throne in December 1926, at age 25. Therefore, he was head of state when Japan invaded China in 1931. In 1941, he assented to the plans that called for war with the Allied forces of the United States, Britain, and France, if diplomatic efforts with those countries failed.

Also in 1941, he assented to Japan's joining the Tripartite Pact with Nazi Germany and Fascist Italy. (He had to have been apprised of, and to have consented to, the inhumane treatment of Chinese prisoners of war, and to the use of toxic gas against the Chinese.)

The Hirohito that Ito now examined surreptitiously was a man meticulously dressed in the Western style. He was a man of slight build, with a shock of black hair, rimless glasses, and a wispy moustache. In short, a most ordinary-looking Japanese.

575

When he spoke, calling the meeting to order, he said in a high-pitched voice, "Gentlemen, we are assembled here to consider the travesty perpetrated by the enemy against the people of Japan, and our response to it and to the subsequent ultimatum issued by the President of the United States."

Each of the men around the table was asked for an opinion, and each gave it. The two generals urged the Emperor to stay the course, and to continue with the preparations for the defense of the homeland. In this opinion, they were joined by Admiral Yonai. The sole civilian at the meeting, Minister Togo, urged the Emperor to sue for the immediate opening of peace negotiations with the Americans. It was not until then that the Prime Minister, Admiral Suzuki, spoke up:

"That suggestion, Minister Togo, is a foolish one. You have already been working with America's ally, the Soviet Union, with whom we have a non-aggression pact, to broker such peace negotiations with the United States. Thus far, nothing has come of it. Of course, I believe you should continue with that initiative. As to President Truman's ultimatum, I would choose to ignore it for the time being.

"But, in the end, I still maintain that the only way to bring the Americans to the bargaining table is to make the war so costly for them that the American public will give their military no other choice. Aerial bombing destroys, but does not *occupy* territory. To occupy our homeland, they must invade. And it is when they invade that we will make the war so costly for them that they will have no other choice but to negotiate."

Finally, Toyoda spoke up. "I agree, Your Majesty, with Admiral Suzuki, for the most part. But I also feel that we should do our best to buy time. I recommend that the Foreign Affairs Ministry (here he nodded to Minister Togo) abandon efforts to negotiate through the duplicitous Russians. They are still smarting from their defeat at our hands in 1905. Rather we should open channels of our own, directly with the United States. They might well be looking for such an opening from us, considering that their president has issued this ultimatum."

Ito unconsciously nodded in agreement, thinking Toyoda's proposition was most reasonable.

Hirohito, expressionless thus far, looked around the room. His gaze finally rested on Toyoda. "Thank you, Admiral," he said, still stone-faced, but with fury flashing in his eyes. "But there will be no negotiating with the enemy. We will redouble our efforts to meet the enemy on our beaches and push him back into the sea, once they invade. We will ignore the ultimatum from the United States."

With that, Hirohito stood up, and the rest immediately followed suit. He made a shallow bow and left the room, as everyone else bowed deeply and held their bow until the Emperor had left the chamber.

On August 8th, despite its non-aggression pact with Japan, the Soviet Union declared war on Japan. Shortly after midnight on the 9th, Soviet forces invaded the Japanese puppet state of Manchukuo (Manchuria).

Also on August 9th, absent any response from the Japanese, the B-29 Superfortress Bockscar, *took off from the Marianas. Aboard the aircraft was a plutonium-fueled bomb named "Fat Boy." The primary target had been the city of Kokura, but the target was obscured by clouds and drifting smoke. Abandoning the original target after several passes, the aircraft turned to its secondary target, the city of Nagasaki. "Fat Boy" was released over Nagasaki at 1102. The detonation released the equivalent energy of twenty-two kilotons of TNT.*

After the second bomb was dropped, President Truman issued another statement. It read, in part: "We shall continue to use it [the Atomic Bomb] until we completely destroy Japan's power to make war. Only a Japanese surrender will stop us."

Ito's family, his wife and four children, were living in Nagasaki when the blast occurred. The blast was more powerful than the bomb dropped over Hiroshima, but the surrounding mountains limited the blast area to 673 hectares (2.6 square miles). Estimated deaths were between 40- and 80,000 people.

Admiral Toyoda did his best to comfort his devastated protégé. "There is always the possibility, Captain Ito, that some or all of your family survived," he said.

"I would it were possible, Admiral, but it is impossible. My father-in-law's house, where my wife and children were living, was just a short walk from his factory. The factory was in the middle of the industrial district, right at the center of the blast. The survival of my wife and children, and the survival of my in-laws, is not possible. They are all gone. There is no way it could be otherwise."

Toyoda, relenting from trying to console the inconsolable, said, finally, "The Americans are barbarians. They must be made to pay for this. To release such a weapon against a civilian population is unthinkable We must encourage the Emperor to stand up against such savagery, and to stand up to the American barbarians."

Toyoda's harangue conveniently ignored the raping, mass murders, and gassing of whole civilian populations by Japanese forces in China, and the myriad other war crimes committed against civilians in the other countries conquered in order to form the "Greater East Asia Co-Prosperity Sphere."

On August 10th, the Supreme Council for the Direction of the War was reconvened.

As before, when the Emperor went around the table, again the two Generals expressed their desire to pursue the war to the death, and were once more joined by Admirals Suzuki and Yonai. Finally, and to everyone's surprise, this time Toyoda threw his lot in with them. "The *ban'i*, these American barbarians, have no respect for our people, our culture, or our struggles," he said. "They mean to annihilate us. We must resist them to the death."

The civilian Foreign Affairs Minister, Togo, kept silent, cowed by the now unanimous military.

For the first time any of them could remember, Hirohito showed emotion. He looked around the table, wearily. He said, "Duty is heavier than a mountain; death is lighter than a feather." The military men around the table recognized the statement as a precept from the *Imperial Rescript to Soldiers and Sailors*. It was frequently recited to *kamikaze* pilots prior to takeoff.

"We must, now, do our duty," Hirohito continued. "Our duty is to Japan, our duty is to the Japanese people.

"For our culture, for our way of life, for Japan to continue as a nation, first our people must survive. It is clear now that the enemy has the power to annihilate us, to wipe Japan off the face of the earth without setting foot on the homeland. So if we are to survive as a people, we have no choice but to capitulate."

"But the *ban'i* will execute Your Majesty," Suzuki said, in utter surprise and shock at the Emperor's sudden reversal in position from their last meeting.

"Then so be it," Hirohito replied. "Death is indeed lighter than a feather. If my people are willing to die for me, then I must be willing to die for my people. And so must you all. Minister Togo, inform the Americans of my decision."

"Yes, Your Majesty," Togo answered, staring down at the table. "I will see to it at once."

On August 14, 1945, after intense behind-the-scenes negotiations, a recorded radio address by Hirohito was broadcast to the Japanese people, announcing the surrender of Japan to the Allies.

* * * * *

"So, it's over," Jake said.

"So it would appear, Nimitz acknowledged. "And thank God that now we don't have to invade. Their military would have fought us to the death, and so would have the civilian population.

Any fool can see the irony in that. By dropping the A-bombs, Truman actually did the Japs a favor. What an indictment of the utter folly of modern warfare that we should view the deaths of a hundred and fifty thousand men, women, and children as a favorable outcome. But a hundred and fifty thousand dead pales in comparison to what the numbers would have been, just on their side, if we actually had to invade. At least this way, none of *our* boys died."

"So, no more invasion," Jake said. "Thank God. You are right, Admiral. In the end, war is madness. We would have faced each other on their soil and beat each other's brains out—and for what? The war was essentially over anyway. They were already beaten. Why did it have to take annihilating everyone inside two of their cities to prove the point? It's all sheer madness."

Nimitz said nothing in reply. He just stood there beside Jake's desk in the bullpen outside his office.

"Guess I'll be heading back to Pearl, right Admiral?" Jake said, intoning it more as a statement than a question.

The Admiral chortled, "Not quite yet, Lawlor. There's the little matter of the surrender. According to the terms, the Japs have to be completely demilitarized. That means all war material, ships, planes, guns, bayonets, bullets—all of it—gets inventoried and turned over to the Allies. I've already spoken to Lockwood. Well . . . actually, I pulled rank on him. You're going to stick around a while and help us do that."

Jake found it difficult to hide his disappointment. The war was over. Now all he wanted to do was to be with Kate and Elizabeth.

Nimitz caught his mood. "Only a few more weeks, Captain, then you can go home to your family. But first you'll be going to Japan with me on the 28th, when the occupation begins, to get the turnover started. And then, you'll be attending the surrender ceremony on the 2nd, aboard the *Missouri*. By the way, if I'm not mistaken, your old boat, *Orca*, will be in the bay, too, representing the Submarine Force."

Despite his disappointment at not going back to Pearl immediately, Jake managed a smile and said, "Thank you, Admiral, for taking me along. It will be a chance to be an actual part of history."

"My pleasure, Captain Lawlor, but if I'm not mistaken, you've been part of history since the Japs bombed Pearl Harbor. We all have."

On the 18th of August, the Soviets invaded the Kuril Islands.

The occupation of Japan, by the Supreme Commander of Allied Powers, General Douglas MacArthur, began on August 28th.

The formal ceremonies for the surrender of Japan to the Allies took place on September 2, 1945, on the deck of the battleship, *Missouri*, named after the home state of the U.S. President. The majestic ship was moored in the Bay of Japan when, at 0900 the instrument of unconditional surrender was signed by Japanese Minister of Foreign Affairs Mamoru Shigemitsu, and, for the Japanese armed forces, General Yoshijiro Umezu, Chief of the Army General Staff. Shigemitsu had just relieved Shigenori Togo as Minister of Foreign Affairs a week earlier. General Douglas MacArthur signed for the Allies.

During the ceremony, the United States' submarine *Orca* was anchored in the Bay along with other units of the Allied Pacific Fleet.

Epilogue

Joe Bob Clanton debarked from the Puerto Galera Ferry after the three-hour ride from Batangas. He had landed in Manila three days earlier, and it took that long to make his way from the bombed-out carcass of that once-beautiful city to the northern tip of Mindoro Island. He had planned to try and charter a boat at Batangas to take him to Mindoro, and was pleased to find that the restored Commonwealth of the Philippines had resumed ferry service only a week earlier.

Joe Bob knew he might well be on a fool's errand. Mindoro was a big island, and Delvina could be anywhere on it, even assuming she was still on Mindoro to begin with. Yep, a fool's errand. But he had to at least *try* to find her.

He had a plan, more or less. Ask around, work his way down to the coast to the district capitol, Sablayan, see what he could find out. Okay, it wasn't much of a plan, he conceded, but he didn't have any better ideas.

He had mustered out of the Navy a month earlier, resigning his commission. With the war over, they were pulling boats out of commission left and right, and *Orca* was to be mothballed and put in the reserve fleet. And now, there were too many officers for the number of billets available. He was told he could have stayed in if he wanted to, but he would have had to switch to the surface Navy. The scarce submarine billets were being reserved for Regular Navy officers, USN after their names, and Lt. Joe Bob Clanton was Naval Reserve, USNR. But the truth was he really didn't want to stay in. He wanted to get out and find Delvina.

The trip down the coast to Sablayan took two days. The roads were lousy and, besides sharing the crowded ride with farm animals, the rickety bus kept breaking down.

When Joe Bob finally reached Sablayan, it was already dark and everything was shut down. He carried his duffel from the station to the nearest hotel, a seedy-looking place that made the dump he stayed in in Manila look like the Ritz. He managed to raise a night clerk and rent a room. He had to pay for one night in advance. He was exhausted and, when he reached his room on the second floor, he lay down on the bed in his clothes, and fell fast asleep.

Upon waking, he was amazed that he had made it through the night without being carried off by one of the giant water beetles that crawled the walls. He sat up, and the bed broke beneath him. Undaunted, he stripped, wrapped himself in the thin towel the hotel thoughtfully provided and walked down the hall to the bathroom. The shower dribbled rusty water.

Before he left the hotel, he asked the day clerk if he had ever heard of Delvina Bacatplan. The clerk had not. Joe Bob then went in search of breakfast. He found a little café, an actual hole in the wall on the side of a decrepit old building, which actually served an excellent breakfast of eggs, bread, and ham, but no coffee. They had bottled beer, and he drank that instead. He asked the owner if he had heard of Delvina and, in return, only got a blank stare.

He was just walking down the street after breakfast when he saw her—well, not her exactly, but her picture, on a flyer stuck to the wall on the side of a building. Under her smiling face it read "Delvina Bacatplan, for Representative, Mindoro District, Liberal Party." Once he saw the one poster, he saw others, almost one on every street. He asked around and got directions to Liberal Party Headquarters.

Located in a better part of town, which was still not saying much, Liberal Party headquarters was not much bigger than his hotel room. Joe Bob went in. The brightly dressed young woman at the front desk shuffling papers looked kind of familiar. Joe Bob was certain he had seen her somewhere before, but just couldn't place her. It was unlike him, he knew, to forget such a pretty face.

"Miss?" he said, and she looked up.

"Lieutenant!" she exclaimed. She noted the puzzled look on his face and smiled broadly. "You do not remember me, do you." She said it as a statement of fact, not a question. "It is me, Tina, Tina Ortiz — well, it *was* Tina Salut."

Memories of the war flooded back into Joe Bob's head. The Sablayan Jap garrison, and the woman who had infiltrated it — the woman who . . . "Tina! Of course. How could I have forgotten? Tina . . ."

"Who could blame you for forgetting?" she said, still smiling broadly. "We met only once. It was dark and under very different circumstances." She stood up, proudly displaying her obviously distended belly. "I am married now — to Haraldo Ortiz." She stroked her stomach. "We are having a baby."

"So I see," Joe Bob lamely replied. "Congratulations!"

"Thank you," she said. "But I am guessing you did not come here to see me. You are, of course, looking for Delvina?"

"I am. How can I find her?"

"She is running for District Representative," Tina said. "And the District encompasses the whole Island. It is very large, and Delvina is doing her very best to reach out to all potential voters, and —"

Joe Bob interrupted her. "Have you got her schedule? Where is she supposed to be today? Tomorrow? I have to find her."

Tina smiled. "Why?" she asked coyly. "Does the candidate owe you money?"

"Not hardly," Joe Bob replied, smiling back. "No, the candidate is a very special lady, and I've traveled all this way just to see her again."

Tina, still smiling, raised a knowing eyebrow. "All right . . . tomorrow she's in Rizal, then she goes to San Jose, and so on around the Island. If you like, I can write the dates and places down for you."

"That would be swell. How do I get to Rizal from here?"

"Let me see . . . there's a bus that runs three days a week. I think maybe it runs tomorrow. Or maybe the next day. I'm not sure."

"How did Delvina get to Rizal?"

"Oh, the Party gave her a Jeep to use while she is campaigning. She drives it herself." (When the U.S. Army left, it left a great deal of equipment behind, including lots of jeeps.)

"Where can I get a Jeep? Can I *buy* one, or maybe rent one?"

"I do not know anyone who can sell you one, but my husband's cousin Enrico has one. He might rent it to you."

"Great. Where can I find your husband's cousin . . . Enrico was it?" Tina nodded in the affirmative, and he repeated, "Where can I find Enrico?"

She drew him a map. "Tell him his cousin's wife, Tina, sent you. And if you wait a few minutes while I write it down, I will give you Delvina's itinerary for the next two weeks."

"Excellent, Tina. Thank you."

The ride to Rizal was only marginally more comfortable than the trip to Sablayan.

As it turned out, Enrico not only had a jeep, he was willing to drive him to Rizal and beyond, if necessary, in exchange for food, shelter, and a dollar a day. And of course Joe Bob had to buy the gasoline.

There weren't exactly a lot of gasoline stations on Mindoro, and exactly *none* between Sablayan and Rizal. Enrico had strapped four, twenty-liter jerry cans to the back of the jeep, and had just drained the fourth one into the Jeep's tank, when they reached Rizal around midday. After giving Enrico money enough to buy lunch, Joe Bob when off on foot to try and find Delvina.

Rizal was not exactly a metropolis, and when Joe Bob found Delvina, she was in the midst of an enthusiastic crowd of fifty or so supporters in the city square. Joe Bob figured that there was time enough to surprise her afterward, so he found a spot on the edge of the crowd, where he hoped she wouldn't spot him. He listened to her stump speech, but didn't understand a word of it, because it was delivered in Tagalog. Judging from the response of the crowd, however, he guessed that she was striking all the right notes. It looked to Joe Bob as if Delvina was coming up on her big finish, when their eyes met, and she was suddenly struck dumb. "Joe Bob," she said, finally, "you're here?"

And Joe Bob just grinned.

They were married in a civil ceremony in Mansalay. Delvina agreed to the civil ceremony only because she couldn't find a priest to marry them, and because Joe Bob readily agreed to marry her again whenever they finally did locate a priest, and because it didn't look good for the candidate to be sleeping with him if they weren't married.

In Pinamalayan, they finally *did* locate a priest, a Franciscan missionary, who had successfully eluded the Japanese for the entire war, and made it official before God.

The election was held a month later, and Delvina lost in a landslide to the National Party candidate.

With the election lost, Joe Bob tried to convince Delvina to move back to Alabama with him, but Delvina was intent on staying in the Philippines.

On July 4, 1946, the Republic of the Philippines became a reality. A month previous, Joe Bob had opened an engineering business in Sablayan, designing and building water and sanitation systems. The company did well, and before long had expanded into building and operating telephone systems. In five years Clanton Engineering LLC was doing business all over the country.

In the same five years, Joe Bob and Delvina had three children, all boys.

About the Author

Gene Masters is a retired consulting engineer living in East Tennessee with his wife, Ruth. They have two grown daughters, and two grandchildren. He is the author of several technical treatises, including his doctoral dissertation, but War Patrol is his first serious attempt at fiction.

Masters received a commission in the U.S. Navy on graduation from Notre Dame, and his first tour of duty was aboard a transport in the Western Pacific. His second tour was aboard a re-commissioned and updated diesel-electric submarine, the USS Angler. Angler was originally commissioned in 1943, and made seven war patrols in the Pacific before being decommissioned. Her updating to an SSK-class boat in the 1950's fitted her for operation against cold war submarine adversaries with advanced soundproofing and sonar. Masters left Angler and active duty after a Mediterranean tour. Later Naval Reserve assignments included the diesel-electric submarines *USS Manta* and the *USS Ling*.

After active duty, Masters pursued a career in engineering, and served in various companies until settling into a career as a consulting engineer. He retired in 2009. *Silent Warriors* is his first novel.

The author enjoys hearing from readers and can be reached via email at: 240boat@gmail.com. He welcomes comments from readers, and always replies promptly. Readers interested in learning more about the author can visit his website at: www.genemasters.net.

Made in the USA
Coppell, TX
10 September 2020